A Song For Ireland

Ted Emery

Published by New Generation Publishing in 2013

Copyright © Ted Emery 2013

First Edition

www.newgeneration-publishing.com

timjoemery@gmail.com

New Generation **Publishing**

County Wexford

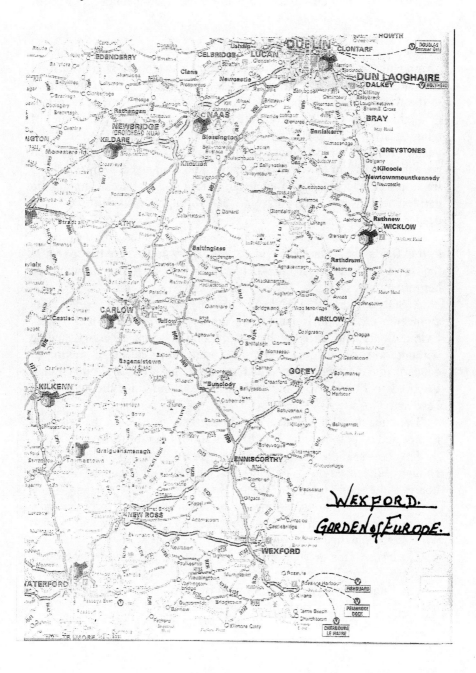

WEXFORD.
GARDEN of EUROPE.

Beware the empire builders. Those who deny freedom to others, deserve it not for themselves and under a just God, cannot retain it for long. A cat, pent up becomes a lion.

Ireland, known as the stepping stone to Europe is just that, and in the geographical context is not much bigger than a stepping stone. Her mild and equable climate is a reflection of the fact that her shores are bathed in the warm ocean waters of the North Atlantic Drift, where extremes of high or low temperatures are virtually unknown, her issue of bounteous harvests, the finest in the world, so that for seven hundred years, ravaging tyrants, many of them garbed in ermine cloaks and crusted tiaras, ambitious aristocracy and maniacal royalty and imperialism, every now and then caused repression to create among the natives, enthusiasts and martyrs that brought forth courage and desperate resolution.

She has had her share of Hitlers, Stalins, Pol Pots and very many killing fields, the difference being, these august louts were the spawn of their own kind and caused mayhem among their own. Ireland imported her tormentors.

A SONG FOR IRELAND is the story of the dying years of the eighteenth century in Ireland when the cat became a lion and roared. Extraordinary and unlikely heroes of simple stock emerged, people without rank or insignia and for a brief time, caused a tremor of concern and admiration in equal measure that echoed from County Wexford to London to Paris to Washington and a hundred places in between.

The endeavors of a young Dublin barrister to harness the might of France and Napoleon himself in his search for help for Ireland.

The boy-soldier whose's rebellion lasted half a day but whose epitaph still echoes down through the centuries and is quoted wherever liberty is the spur.

The country Catholic curate who amassed an army of forty thousand peasants, among them the "running magazines", a thousand women who fought and died with their men

The trials of the ordinary people of Wexford, the young servant girl, her loves, her desires, her fears and her love for "An Englishman".

The English journalist, in love with two women, who told the world of the Terrible Beauty that was Ireland of 1798.

CHAPTER 1

Bridget Rose Tansey had a variety of Gods, all of whom she wooed and worshiped in ways convenient to her needs. It wasn't avarice or greed that brought her from abject poverty to a woman of some substance, but a necessity and nothing has more strength than dire necessity and Bridget Rose's necessities made for her, a good bargain. If there was guilt in it, then her courage abounded in the health of her two sons for whom she said she would kill which she did, and for whom she said she would die, which she did.

She maintained that it was the ultimate misfortune to be born a Catholic in Ireland of the 18th Century, or in any century for that matter, for the pouring of holy water was a branding iron on the forehead of an infant, that gave it calamities all the days of it's life. For that reason, she didn't just name her boys, but nicknamed them with a numbing blow from which they would find it difficult to recover.

The little family had already a fine Protestant surname, the gift of her husband, Matthew Tansey, who must have had some accident of sanity when he forsook his Protestantism to be baptised in the Catholic Faith, this at the age of twenty-five, a year before he met Bridget Rose McGarry, pet named to Bridie by a doting father, a fine Catholic girl named after the pagan patron, Saint Bridget, whose father was converted and christened by Saint Patrick himself.

This all happened in the North of Ireland, a cesspit of religiosity, a den of puritans and puritanism and where to be a Catholic was to be consistently oppressed in popery. Bridie Rose found a reluctant priest somewhere to christen her brood – George Reginald Tansey for her first born. She would instruct him from an early age, "you're named for the King of England". One can't be more Protestant than that. Her second born, Henry came coughing and wheezing into the world, perhaps a consumptive objection to the name, he was in constant need of care.

She schooled Georgie and Hen that they had inherited the blessing of a good breeding, but had momentarily fallen on hard times. So who can say what kind of emotive reactions a woman will resort to, when finding herself in an explosive situation in County Armagh in the mid 1780's. Armagh was the most densely populated rural area in Ireland. The linen industry flourished and competition to rent land became fierce, especially near the market towns where the water-powered washmills, bleach greens and dye works were located. She never told her boys about how a girl named Bridget Rose McGarry found herself embedded in the daily ferocity of sectarian violence, when Catholics, mainly handloom weavers rivalled their Protestant neighbours for tiny bits of farmland and were able to survive and outbid their opponents through a self-imposed frugal existence on a diet of potatoes and buttermilk, plain living in a sort of voluntary poverty, while their Protestant neighbours were more intemperate, oatmeal and pig meat being a necessary part of their diet.

Ridden with envy and fooled by demagogues, the Anglo Scottish Protestant settlers were a menace to ordinary normal living and because of their names and growing up as helpers to their parents, it was assumed they were as them. Bridie schooled the boys that if they wanted to be left in peace, they should go along with them and to her husband's chagrin, she would drag her boys off to service and even enrolled them in that Protestant tradition of a school on Sundays.

The Tanseys lived in the middle floor of a tenement house in the shadow of one of the biggest mills in Armagh. It was named The Blackwater Mill, after the river that was a constant presence, as it provided the power for the mill, and as if to extract her dues and keep all in mind of her bounty, would flood the ground floor of the tenement when she would have a mind to, the odours awakening reminiscences for years to come. The Armagh air was constantly thick with smell, the steam in the drying sheds and beetling mills, the rot that invaded one's senses, the thick mucus bleach and the various effluvia merged into a single pungency that became curiously acceptable, but everyone was aware it was a crucifixion to Henry.

The consumption of his frail body was already shutting him off from the world. The summers gave him fresh impetus when Bridie would wheel him in his perambulator into the countryside, when the towns and villages of the North turned white like snow, when the swats of shining white linen were spread on the bleach greens so the reflection in the sunlight stung your eyes.

Seventy thousand souls, Catholic, Protestant, Anglican, and Presbyterian had little to combine their miserable lives with each other than the production of linens, yet few of them could afford a square foot of the finished product, a requisite to the vanities of the grand tables and boudoirs of the privileged.

Drunken affrays between gangs of weavers became openly sectarian and so were formed an exclusive Anglican association, named The Peep-O-Day Boys, their purpose; to push out economic competition from Catholics for leases and rents in the linen producing business. She would expound to her boys, the madness of the "peepers" when the whole of South Armagh became a cesspit of simpletons and madmen. Hellhounds were let loose on Catholic homes, destroying their weaving

6

equipment and burning cabins with arms supplied by the magistrates. Mr. Tansey would try to reinforce their home against attacks from lunatics who would attack people in their beds with little regard for consequences, so that in desperation, he joined the Catholic movement : The Defenders.

In the year 1789, America celebrated the tenth birthday of Georgie Tansey with the selection of Mr. Washington as its first President and the year the people of that country proclaimed their first festival of Thanksgiving. The boy's birthday on this Earth saw the National Assembly being inaugurated in France to oppose the dominance of the aristocracy and sowed the seeds of the revolution that was to follow.

Matthew Tansey was a good Northern Catholic, forsaking his Assendancy Protestantism and christened into popery before his first son was born. As the boy grew, coming to the age of understanding, he felt that his father had no hold on his mother's affections, that their union was a kind of a convenience to survival in the North. Hard work, often a drain on all emotions, left little room for anything other than habit or duty, everything else untouched for too long. So when Tansey senior was killed in a sectarian skirmish in a place called Loughgall, outside the house of Mr. James Sloane, their mother schooled her boys again, never to forget his name, and be a Protestant when necessary or when convenient.

As Matthew Tansey was drawing his final breath in a cornfield in Loughgall, Mr. Sloane and a dozen "peepers" were inside drawing up a kind of constitution. The five page document, drawn up in a moment of passion, was duly signed by all present, in a cauldron of tobacco smoke and port wine and placed with sanctimonious reverence, in the centre of Mrs. Sloane's mahogany dining table. A constitution should be a document for rulers and people, covering with the shield of its protection, all classes of men at all times and under all circumstances.

The document on Mr. Sloane's table, the constitution for the Peep-O-Day Boys, also known as the Wreckers, had a title from Hell, a universal perversion to abuse instead of elevate. The newly named Orange Order had a purpose; the exclusion of Roman Catholics as members, as citizens, ineligible for the human race.

Bridie never got to bury her husband, his body wouldn't be found for two months, when the reapers found him at harvest. Magistrates, on apprehending a "low fellow", finding him dead or alive, would hunt for his family, specifically if he had sons, who would one day walk in father's footsteps.

On a year when the puppet government of Ireland prayed in session for the safety of the king of France, who tried to flee his country,

7

without success, on a year when the first prison ship sailed from Ireland to a place on the other side of the world, called Botany Bay, Mrs. Tansey gathered her meagre belongings and headed south, leaving behind her the ear-splitting sounds of fife and rod beating drums, an accursed symphony of noisy desperation. Within a month of its foundation, the Orange Order took to the streets in a call to violence, a violence perpetrated by some kind of legitimate authority.

Life was something Bridie Rose learnt to dominate. Her life had been one offensive after another, and now of necessity, new resources came to her surface. There are a few times in life when as long as we live, a remembrance would stay painfully and sharply engraved in our memory. Such a day was to happen soon for Bridget Rose Tansey and the King of England.

Like all great cities, Dublin was callous, both to the happiness and miseries of others, and as a twelve year old, Georgie Tansey soon became aware of both extremes. Ten years before the new century, that city was a new age metropolis. The whole golden boom was in the air. Splendid buildings sprouted up on both sides of the Liffey. Great generosities combined with its outrageous corruptions were in total contradiction to the tortuous death-struggle of the rest of Ireland.

Dung was cleared from the back streets every evening and the mansions of the silver-barred roads and crossroads had toilet rooms inside the palaces and things called faucets, where water, hot and cold was there at the twist of such a thing. The privileged had street lighting and one could ride on coaches from Merrion Square, Phoenix Park or Saint Stephen's Green, all the way to Cork. The capitol was also squalid and sinister, where a man could disappear with suddenness and completeness of a candle flame that is blown out. The upper class had built the city's first workhouse in James's Street.

Necessity never burdened Bridie with convictions. Always comfortable in her own approval, she put her self-respect in her pocket for the time being and sought out the house of alms.

The little family presented themselves at the gates of the workhouse. It was early spring and Hen was able to keep up in the freshness of the light wind that asserted its way from the bay. Over three days they came to stand against the railings of an unsentimental building over which a grey cloud of drudgery seemed to settle, while Dublin seemed to bask in pale sunshine. Over a hundred weary and indignant souls clambered daily for admission, their children barefoot and filthy, played on the cobbled stones, oblivious to their state, oblivious to the futility of their future, their parents, dull eyed with dormant thoughts, dead before they expire. On the first day, the heavy gate never opened, so they came earlier the following day, and the next. The family were constantly inspected by a uniformed man from inside the railings while the rabble outside shouted abuse at him and at each other.

Bridie felt the pain of want. In Dublin at the tail end of the eighteenth century, to be poor was hard, but to be a part of a destitute race in a land of plenty was the very bottom of hardships, and nowhere did she feel that pain but here in this terrible public place. The family of three must have stood out among this rabble, pretty well dressed and orderly, the mother would hold the keeper of the gate in an observation that showed concentration, with a certain doggedness, even precocity, unsettling him each time he passed.

On the third day, five crude boxes were brought through the gates. Men with bent down heads against the task placed the coffins on a flat cart, a tired horse strained against the pull, the dead burying the dead. An hour later, the boxes were brought back empty, their crude lids askew. Here you don't live proudly, she thought, so why should you die proudly.

Mr. Jonas Bundy had steel grey eyes, vital and calculating, a face incapable of any kind of emotion, except that of gain and profit, as Bridie Tansey was soon to learn. The Master of Saint James's simply realised the world as he saw it, and in the little family that stood out among the disinherited as he perceived it, he recognised chance and a wise man turns chance into good fortune. There were scuffles at the gate as the uniformed guard prised the three through and they were instructed to follow him inside.

She was aware of narrow grey corridors stretching into a grey horizon, from the central entrance hall. The sombre dull light, tenebrous and foreboding, almost concealing little knots of destitution huddled in obscure corners, under stairways and in alcoves at the edges of her vision. Henry seized her hand, a nervous spasm seizing him and his breathing became laboured. Master Bundy's quarters were in sharp contrast to the wretchedness all around. Comfortably furnished, with a fire burning in an ornate fireplace, the flames gilded the brasses that adorned the mantle. A huge chandelier hung from the ceiling rose, its candles trimmed and ready.

"We can pay, Sir." Bridie loosened the shawl that protected her from the light spring breezes, allowing her hair to fall about her shoulders, unveiling what was left of her attractiveness, which the hardship of the past weeks had threatened. He turned to meet her and evidently saw no impediment to the beauty hidden beneath, but the hint of mild seduction, a weapon she wielded very well.

"If you can pay, madam, there are plenty boarding houses in

Dublin."

She was quietly insistent, maintaining her assurance. Georgie stood beside her while Henry stood motionless, his eyes, captives of the dancing flames of the fire.

"We've been staying in these places for the past two weeks and I fear for my children, my youngest is puny, sir." Georgie pulled Hen closer and the youngest Tansey coughed on cue.

Bundy's severe face softened. "How can you pay madam?" as if mildly accusing her of something.

Bridie took a soft pouch from her carpet bag and spread its contents on the table, "I'm a lacemaker, Sir, cuffs, necklaces, cravats and collars for gentlemen."

Georgie watched with relief and with a tincture of pleasure, at the older man's obvious appreciation of the ornate merchandise, where the dark wood of the table shone through the intricate lacework, like sunshine through a church window.

She hurried on. "We would be no trouble Sir, the boys help me in my work. It is said you run a good safe house."

Mr. Bundy had delicate hands, ran his fingers over the twists and turns of the threads. "Perhaps we can work something out, Madam. You must know that to maintain a humanitarianism like this costs money and it is my duty and responsibility to realise the world as I see it according to the usage of the day."

He ran on to further verbiage, but Bridie kept her patience, knowing he was making a case for himself, not for her. "Our humanitarianism is the mark of an inhuman time. Here at Saint James's we do our bit for the benefit of mankind. We provide laundry services for the house, but also for our kind patrons, for which they pay, I must emphasise. We manufacture and sell items of furniture, clothing and many other commodities. We find that, even in a place like this, there is an ability to produce. Everyone here has a value so that we not only sell commodities, but we sell ourselves and we feel ourselves to be commodities. We school and provide cooks, parlour maids, stable boys, pantry rabble for those who can purchase their time. Even the dead have their values, infirmaries pay well for items suitable to their experiments in the interest of research. Our shop does not have a smiling face madam, it's all just good housekeeping."

Mr. Bundy instructed her to come back tomorrow, where two small rooms would be made available on the second floor. "We try to segregate the denominations, Catholics maintain themselves on the lower floors, there can be trouble among those Catholics, so we will give you an upper floor, more conducive to your kind of work."

Bridie's gratitude would resemble almost a servitude, but she knew it was a debt which would go on accumulating. He allowed her enough time to satisfy his ego, then held his hands up in mock protest. "As I have said, Madam, we will come to some kind of agreement."

The rooms were sparsely equipped. There was a fireplace with crude cooking utensils . Bridie's cot in the corner of the larger room left space for a table beneath the window on which she could work her trade. A sort of dresser which really consisted of a series of boxes and shelves, took up almost an entire wall. The second room housed a cot each for her two boys, just nails hammered into the wall, for hanging clothes. Just off the big yard to the rear of the complex was a row of latrines to which there was a constant flow, so that Mother insisted they keep their visits to late night or early morning. Here was also located, a huge laundry, the smell of carbolic steam pervaded the corridors day and night.

Nobody knew, right away what kind of "agreement" Bridie made with Captain Bundy, but Georgie was old enough to know that his gain was mildly dishonest, her's a necessary one, as in St. James's, her instinct for self preservation became the strongest and most alert and persistent of her motives.

Though the quarters were cramped, situated to the rear of the huge dark building, shaped for melancholy, totally bereft of promise, there was luxury here, compared with those living down below. As Georgie passed through the corridors, coming and going and becoming bolder in his curiosity, he could see through open doors, rooms full of adults and children, as many as eight or ten eating and sleeping in cramped dirty conditions. The one window looked down onto a great courtyard, where those unable to gain accommodation inside, made for themselves, a village of canvas and rags. At the entrance of each hovel, the unfortunates lit their fires, both for warmth and cooking, but also to deter the rats that ran like house pets around the yard. At night while Mother worked at her thimbles, needles and threads, Georgie would look down on the fires that made a sky of the ground. While he listened to the sounds of depressed poverty, Henry would cough himself to sleep, sleep to Hen was half health, while Bridie would squint through the lamplight, knitting and knitting. She would study her boys through the flame, forever so good at drawing on resources.

"We won't be here for long, G., I promise", she would say. Often, she would turn his name into a kind of signature, when making a point of importance. Her son liked it and she knew it.

She already had a foot in the door to eventually escape the constant dangers that hangs over your head in a place like this, where mendacity

11

and want can exasperate into crime. The only time he remembered his mother crying was when frustration and weariness and the misery of poverty assailed her on a day when her finished crochet pieces were stolen while she turned her back for a minute in the laundry. On the day of their acceptance, when Captain Bundy went to fold her embroideries into their little pouch, Bridie Rose pushed it across the table to him, the beginning of their "little agreement", two months rent in advance. It was evident he was impressed with her boldness in the business of the day and more so, by the individual profit that beckoned.

Her last two shillings was spent in a tiny haberdashery shop in Aungier Street to replenish her thread and needles that came in little bobbins and reels, which the industrious little shopkeeper advised that sixpence would be returned when she brought the bobbins back. But they were hungry for the first time in Dublin. Hope and granite determination in her had as many lives as a cat and that determination dawned from fear for her boys, fear that increased the cares of her life and sweetened her labours.

CHAPTER 2

Humanity and inhumanity mingled in a cauldron of high-toned altruism in St. Stephen's Green in the city centre, every Tuesday, Thursday and Saturday. Alms were given from some sort of pity to Dublin's beggars. So called humanitarians paid a few coppers to watch through a grid of railings. The Society Of Friends feed the poor, often bringing with them, larder leftovers and half unwanted dinners, on days when the philanthropist played God and left very satisfied with himself and his charity. He brings his lady wife, in suitable and well governed modesty to hide her ostentation and affectation behind the halo of her ego, an ill-mannered brat or two at her heels, to be taught the necessity of distinguishing themselves from the lesser classes and what might happen to girls and boys who misbehave. Little boys and girls in velvets and satins and suitable bonnets, who smirked and stuck out their tongues at Bridie and Hen, as she guided him to a quiet corner as far away as possible from the ogling audience. They were each given a bowl of offal and crude bread, Mother, an old cloak about her face, hidden in its folds, portraying the proper countenance of subjective gratitude. Henry needed no tuition in beggary, his coughing and wheezing and his congenital stooped little frame stood him in good stead for a bit of charity. Georgie stayed outside the barrier, she said he looked too healthy. He would watch her move through the hunched, haunted rabble and the terrace of spectators, some pointing out here and there at some poor wretch of interest, some well inebriated, having had their rich man's roast in one of the hostelries across the road and rich enough to be publicly charitable.

"Hey, fella, eat it all now, I paid good money for that. She looks fed enough, there now, give some to your mother."

For a few coppers, the vulgarians expected some entertainment, ribaldry rippling here and there in their afternoon's entertainment. Their miserable donations were necessary so the Quaker workers would endeavour to turn a deaf ear.

The Tansey visits to the arena became a hopeless period of frustration and anger. How suffering makes people petty and vindictive and a thirteen year old boy would sometimes admonish the bullies and shout them down. He would watch her pour some of the stew into a can she had hidden inside her cloak, to bring outside to him, while Hen would stuff a lump of bread into a pocket, the drunks continuing to enjoy the spectacle. As long as he lived, he thought, he would never forget his hatred of them, the hatred of their vileness, the bellied gluttons, the pomposity of the stiffed-backed gentlemen and their ladies, whiling away the useless expenditure of their time. "The beggars are outside here with me."

After their third visit, the supervisor of the Society of Friends became aware of the slender attractive woman and her delicate son, that she was somehow a step or two removed from the general guests. She lacked the outward signs of destitution. He saw the struggle in her, the struggle between a kind of pride and an empty purse. Georgie saw him study her, was he going to question her about her means, what qualifies one in the state of deprivation. Then the man looked at Georgie and came to the barrier. The boy began to move away. The supervisor was a tall blonde haired man of middle age, with a kind and pensive face.

"Come inside son", he said, his voice full and deep, with no strain or tension in its timber, despite the circus. He opened the gate, enough to fit the boy through, giving the rabble a wintery look. Goergie sat by his mother and the tall man returned with a man sized dish of glorious offal and two fine lumps of bread. Her face filled with painful gratitude. "In future, all three of you", he warned with a warm smile.

Soon they didn't have to come to Stephen's Green anymore, except to walk along the gardens and duck ponds and sit on a bench like respectable Dubliners. Bridie approached the tall Quaker and he became aware again of her certain delicate pride, her well mannered self esteem shining out and he wondered again what had brought her to this.

She asked his name, "Your first name, sir?"

Half amused, his eyebrows raised in enquiry . "John, Madam, my name is John."

**

The big grey building wore a sort of scowl on an otherwise bright day in Dublin. Captain Bundy was waiting for her at the door of his quarters on a day when good fortune, up to now hidden in her closet, to-day began her flattery. The Master of the house gave her a quizzical look and for a moment, Georgie thought something was amiss, perhaps they were breaking some kind of house rule in begging at Stephen's Green. Mr. Bundy's countenance had, he thought, softened in the past few weeks, toward them and then suddenly the good, well-rounded face broke into a tinsure of a smile, resting across the palms of his big hands, the eight pieces of embroidery, stolen from the laundry two weeks before. Bridie's breath softened into a sob.

"Not alone have we found them", he said, " but we have a buyer.

Something as prize - worthy as this is easily found in a poorhouse, Madam, before it's sold on, now come inside"

Lord Ponsonby was a heavy bodied wigged aristocrat and member of the House of Parliament, suitably jowled and evidently a man in the prime of his egotism, used to setting value on himself and very little on others. When introduced to Mrs. Tansey, he scarcely looked at her, as if to conduct the business through Bundy."The merchandise is acceptable, " he said to the Master, however, it IS second hand, and due to Captain Bundy's alertness in recovering them, I must say, they are after all, stolen goods in a way." He hesitated grandly," I shall be generous", looking at Henry, who as always coughed when he thought it would be a spur to his mother's negotiations. "Seven shillings, I think would be generous". "Your Lordship is generous, seven shillings is a fair price, perhaps your lordship would have a friend who might purchase the other set".

Mr. Bundy smiled into his fireplace and threw Georgie a delicious look from under his heavy eyebrows. The boy feared for her, knowing what seven shillings would do for them, the poor must be practical.

"However", she continued and the peer looked at her for the first time, "you might like to buy the two sets for say twelve shillings, that would be a considerable discount" She had surprised him before he had time to arrange himself for her manipulation." Twelve shillings, perhaps your Lordship might have a friend in Parliament who would appreciate it as a gift". The silver coins shone bravely on Mr. Bundy's table, while His Lordship gave her the concession of a smile. Before she carefully wrapped the sets in their velvet pouch, she said, her confidence rising a step further. " The motif on the sets is one of my more successful designs, Sir, it's known in Italy as the Della Francesca Motif, it is popular among the nobility of Europe." Bridie's little bit of genius seemed to soften the blow on his injured ego. "Really, Madam......the..." "Della Francesca, your Lordship."

That one minute's success paid for the wheels of past drudgery. Bridie scrounged and saved like a lunatic squirrel. Lord Ponsonby turned out to be an unsuspecting benefactor, as the finding of the lost pieces and the visit of His Lordship, put in motion a spectacular conglomerate, consisting of Captain Bundy and herself where their "little arrangement" made sense for both. He would now be paid 20% commission on all business put in her way. He had brought some commerce to her life, recognizing in her the propensity for frugality as being almost a virtue. He would entertain many of the trustees of the Workhouse to a glass of port wine and biscuits where Bridie would exhibit her needlework and invite orders.

Between them, they created a good little corporation. Her gains were hard worked for, often in candle light into the night, she would often fall asleep, the needle and thimble still in her hand. However, her little purse got heavier and she became a welcome visitor to the little haberdashery shop off Aungier Street. Her work appealed to the vanities embedded in those, desiring to be observed, the narcissist, willing to sacrifice their purse for those vanities. Linen kerchiefs with delicate sprigging crochet borders, cuffs to ornate a gentleman's shirt sleeves and immaculate needlework in a celebration of threads and strands. She had developed a technique of decorative open-cut work embroidery in leafy sprays and scalloped edges, her neck ties and cuffs, finished in button hole stitching for easy removal and laundering. It was Marsh's library that provided the cream to crown her endeavours. With Georgie, she sifted through the books of art and industry in the beautiful new building. From a book named "Crochet, Laces and Needlework of The World," she devised titles for her creations, a vocabulary to flatter that male conceit. Modes were devised: "The Marletto," "The Sausepolero" from Tuscany. Georgie would poise himself to her amusement in the whispering atmosphere,"this mode is ideal for you, my Lord, its delicate entwinement of it's stitching, perfect for evening wear, while the Della Francesca is perfect for public appearances, devised by the famous renaissance painter. Then my Lord, the glorious Biennale International, what better when Your Lordship speaks in the house of Parliament, and for a little extra, your initials or perhaps your family coat of arms, on the cravat and the handkerchiefs". If Bridie needed a shop window, then Mr. Bundy found it there in the most unlikely place; The Irish House of Parliament.

**

Many members of Mr. Grattan's Parliament were also trustees of the Workhouse. Henry Grattan was the puppet Irish Prime Minister. When the dark room next door became vacant, once the home of some poor wretch and his family, Bridie became the new occupant of her very own sprigging room, rent free. On the day when Mr. Bundy's " Times" reported the theft of one of His Majesty's ships, The Bounty, by mutineers led by a Mr. Christian, Bridie took her boys to the House of Parliament, a palace of a building, near College Park, from where the whole of Ireland is governed, she told them. "All the laws are made here," she whispered looking down on the assembly from the visitors' gallery. On visitors day, the first Thursday of the month, a strict rule was enforced, "No Catholics." She had to sign the visitors' book. In her

16

bold Protestant handwriting, she wrote "Rose B. Tansey and her sons George Reginald and Henry Tristan." "If that doesn't sound Protestant enough, then I'm a Catholic," she whispered. "Captain says the king doesn't read very well, so everything is to be written in very simple language, before he'll pass it." Mr. Bundy winked at Georgie when they were leaving for Parliament. "Watch now, it's ladies day when all the members put on a show. My Lord will inspect the gallery, like a grace before meals, then each act is a course, each scene a different dish. Watch them, dear boy," he whispered to him, "and be entertained, for 'tis a place where members play at being serious, but act out the comedies. Many of them, it must be said are in favour of relief of the Catholics, but they belong to the old Whig party. That club is now just an eating and drinking aristocratic society, it has no feeling for the common man and none at all for the common woman."

The good Captain had become landlord, benefactor, imparter of valuable information, business partner and sometimes, over a glass of port wine, a friend, who because of their community of interests, perhaps sought a desire for companionship, even affection. It was obvious to Georgie, his mother was uneasy with these mild affections, so he, as her book keeper, attended all future meetings. The Master of St. James's was a friend who, when wishing her well, also thought of his own well being.

The quiet respectable little family watched the coming and going on the floor of Parliament, while they continued their political education. Bundy was right. How the wiggery played to the gallery, the ladies in their finery, suitably impressed. Men with the fate of Ireland in their hands, some hands and collars and cravats adorned in Bridie Tansey's Marletto or Sansepolero, waived ornate handkerchiefs in extreme emphasis in the making of a point of order. Mr. Keogh, the speaker, a vain immaculate man and leader of the Catholic Committee, though, of course, he was a Protestant, in Bridie's Biennale mode, complete with kerchief, had been pleading for Catholic reform . Mr. Bundy had said that Irish politics was the most complex in the known world. Mr. Connolly, to her delight , was properly attired and suitably vain, spoke in favour of Mr. Keogh's motion. However, Mr. Grattan, the Irish Prime Minister, and the powerful Lord Leinster, agreed with the motion, but their contributions were lost to Bridie. "Not nearly vein enough," she whispered, "dull and plain cuffs and collars." However, the tail end of Mr. Grattan's speech did impress her and the words lived with her.

"I conceive it to be a sacred truth, that the Irish Parliament shall never be free, until the Irish Catholic ceases to be a slave." Georgie

17

whispered, "I like him, Mother."

Mother nudged her boys like a giddy schoolgirl, when Lord Ponsonby stood; her first client. However her illusion became disillusion at his message and that of the grumpy Lord Charlemont in their opposition to any relief of the Catholics. A great cloud of white cabbages, hideously tucked up under his sweating chin, combined with pale powdered headgear, made him look, said Bridie, like a porky looking out through the back end of an un-sheared sheep.

"You have no feelings for the community, Sir," interrupted Connolly. Ponsonby shouted above the din that was erupting in some back benches. "These blasted people, a nation in the palm of a weed that grows in Rome, in the grip of an ageing bachelor. These people would be just as wise, Sir, as if a man had a mortification in his bowls, to be very solicitous about a plaster on his sore finger."

"I've a mind to demand my laces back," Bridie fumed, as the well off ladies behind her applauded in their finery. "And that other one, he pays double, if and when he comes visiting, remember that when you're writing in your little book." She pointed to the chart, remember his name now George." A Mr. Flood began berating Mr. Grattan on some point or other, and Georgie saw his mother frown at that man's accusations that the Irish Parliament was destroying, as he said. "this Protestant nation, that he would strive for a further Renunciation Act from Westminster." Neither Bridie or her boys, or no doubt, the fine ladies around them, knew for sure, what the grump was suggesting, but by the tone of his voice, it was something unpalatable and evil in it's seed. "How can it be a Protestant nation," Mother fumed," when three quarters of us are Catholic." Her thirteen year old son tugged at her sleeve, aware of the social upstarts around them, "lots of them are wearing your laces, Mother, they make you rich," he hissed, "no Catholic has bought yet, that we know of." She whispered through her fingers, "That one too pays double."

**

Georgie got to know the grandeur of Dublin, sometimes as guest of Captain Bundy, when the Captain would take them for drives in his carriage. In his endeavours, after six month's residence at St. James's, he moved the family for an extra 5% commission from the "little enterprise," as he called it, to an upper floor flat on Grafton Street, a spacious four roomed apartment with large bright windows, the ground floor of which was a splendid haberdashery, the tenant; a small Jewish gentleman, who was more than delighted to allocate a special corner of his shop to her creations, for the magic 20%. Grafton Street was where the rich of Dublin did their shopping in their urge to consume. Captain Bundy would call every fortnight and Bridie would have tea with him, in the smaller of the four rooms, her parlour, after which he would take the boys for, as he called it, "a scove," around the city. Sometimes Bridie would take the scove, to his delight and on a few occasions, he persuaded her to allow him treat them to afternoon tea at the sumptuous Shelbourne Hotel. Henry delighted in these scoves, as did his brother, but mother hated the Shelbourne, the imperial attitude of, especially the women, their egotism, an anaesthetic to their stupidity.

The beautiful houses surrounding Stephen's Green, overlooked the Green itself while the twenty acres of common was for the use of the residents, festooned with flower beds, immaculate lawns, ponds full of waterfowl and neat little stone bridges and waterways. Captain Bundy's lively horse, ears pricked to the sound of his own hoofs on the cobbles and the lovely new Carlisle Bridge, would respond to his master's every utterance, as they passed the Custom House, which, he said took ten years to build, and only was completed in the past year, and the magnificent Four Courts, still under construction. The superb works being carried out by the Dublin Streets Commission did nothing to impress Mrs. Tansey. In the Captain's superb carriage, she was unimpressed, almost unattached to the shopping arenas and recreation facilities, though Bundy tried hard to impress.

Hen was enthralled at the wonders of the city, especially viewed from the carriage, but Mother never showed enthusiasm in praise of Dublin.

"Built by peasant rack rents and peasant slavery," she confided later, her voice pinpricked with a bitterness. "Their coppers and their corpses laid the foundations." She brightened , not wanting to spoil their day and Mr. Bundy's kindness. "Just something I read in The Journal, words written by a man named Mr. Wolfe Tone."

"Who is he, Mother?" the younger asked.

"Don't know Son, but funny how I remember his words, so brave and his unusual name. I read that many months ago."

Georgie would slip out to wander the city on bright days and while Hen slept. On pauper days, he would walk by the Green on the far side of the street, still haunted by what seemed now, illusions of their experiences a short while ago. Like all great cities, Dublin had it's dark side. Georgie would find himself wandering through the dirty dark laneways, which If his mother knew of the places he had been frequenting, she would forbid him further freedom. The warren of narrow streets, inhabited in conditions of inadequate services, without sanitation, all hidden away behind the splendid wide carriageways and gracious buildings, seemed to fascinate him. Here lived the labouring poor, the builder's lackeys, mother spoke about, the small tradesmen, the underprivileged, the beggars. They, like the cabin and cottage dwellers of the countryside, outcasts without a penny, without a vote, the pawns of never ending sequences of humiliation and neglect. He could feel the depression shaking itself awake in an early morning as in the freezing cabins and huts of Wexford and Cork and Tipperary and beyond and remembered again his mother's words on Mr. Wolfe Tone.

One such laneway was an artery onto fashionable Kildare Street, right in front of the town house of Lord Edward Fitzgerald and his brother the Duke of the provence of Leinster. He wondered how many poor fellows lay in it's foundations, how many ghosts occupied the one hundred rooms, a lovely lonely looking pile of stones, wondering how it would be, trying to find your way about these rooms, trying to get out and then he thought how these inside felt imprisoned, for it looked more a prison than did Mr. Bundy's workhouse.

Chapter 3

For a year and a half, the Tansys had been guest of the establishment in return for that 20%, six months at St. James's and a full year living and working above the now extremely popular Goldberg haberdashery.

Bridie had been having tea with the captain, who it turned out, showed great understanding in the business of politics and had many friends in high places, who had come to appreciate his expertise in the running of the largest workhouse in the British Isles. His ability to accommodate himself to his staff and to all the inmates, who relied on him for succour and shelter, most of them Catholics, stood him in good stead with the authorities. Riots were few, and Captain's efforts at reform for the poor were beginning to work in a Protestant dominated city.

By now Bridie had two assistants from his "hotel", as she called his establishment, two quiet subdued young women, hand picked by Bundy himself, two women eager to learn and please and give to their narrow lives, some meaning task.

"You're a good man Captain, she said, you should have been baptised."

"I oppose no religion or system, dear lady, except one that condones man's inhumanity to man, I am wisely careful never to set up my own, for I am an apostle of practical atheism."

Georgie watched him look at her and had come to realise, long ago, how he extracted such pleasure in her company, in his eyes, things unsaid, emotions he could never clarify, for the boy had come to the decision that the man was in fact, a shy person, especially in the company of lovely women. As always, her son would be present at such meetings, no matter how they might have touched on any kind of intimacy, no matter how innocent.

"Do you believe in God?" he asked, a dainty cup held in a sizable hand.

"When it suits me, I have a religion, Captain. He's done me no favours in my life, except my children."

"If there is a God, Mrs. Tansey, atheism must surely be less insulting to Him than religion, for there are few good men in religion. Look what religion is doing to this country of ours."

"I met two good men," she replied, her eyes moistening, in the trailing wisps of the nightmare that could have consumed her, had matters turned differently. "Two good men, in two years, Sir, a good man in you and a good man we met one day in St. Stephen's Green."

Again, the man thought of the proposition, festering at the back of his mind, that veiled corner that trembled to win a tinge of her affections. As each visit progressed to the next and the business side of the meeting was dispensed with, Georgie became more aware of how his presence was destroying the man's ambitions and at times, he would notice just a pinprick of intolerance in his voice when he would speak to him, so on more than one occasion, he decided to let his mother to her fate, she was a big girl now, should be able to take care of herself. On leaving the room, he smiled inwardly at the childish acknowledgement lighting on the good face of the captain.

"And now dear lady," Bundy put an assuring hand on her arm, one afternoon,"your next customer is a very important man indeed."

**

Charles Watson-Wentworth, 2nd. Marquess of Rockingham was a tall quietly spoken aristocrat, with a high forehead and vital grey eyes, a man stamped with the brand of class. Mr. Bundy had his carriage bring her and the boys to a suite of palatial rooms in one of the newly built four storey town houses on the edge of the Phoenix Park, a place of extreme comfort, outdoor activities and lazy pastimes for the rich, whose minds are in constant need of relaxations in houses that for evermore would be stamped for the times of the reign of King George111.

Bridie had by now entered fashion, securing three outfits with suitable head dressings, shawls and bonnets. It wasn't vanity or ostentation that possessed her to visit the second hand emporiums of Frances Street, but a commercial necessity, very much applauded by her boys and admired by Mr. Bundy. Georgie and Hen danced around her in her parlour, clutching the soft folds of velvet and brocade, Hen wearing the bonnet, his brother, the shawl. The mother was an amateur in style, but nobody would have known. There was no awkwardness to her gait, totally at ease in the confident sway of her hips as she kicked the hem of the skirts as she paraded for them. Again her eldest could wonder, not just at her beauty, for he was biased in that department, but she seemed to have developed a set of attitudes, designed for appropriate occasions, and occasions such as this came rarely.

And now, His Lordship, the 2nd. Marquess of Rockingham in England, friend of King George, Lord of The Bedchamber, leader of the House of Lords, Viscount Higham, Viscount Malton, Peerage of Ireland and not once, but twice, Prime Minister of Great Britain, awaited her services.

She wanted to leave Hen at home, but Mr. Bundy suggested he should go, "I want him to see the whole package, His Lordship is fond of children, he's a patron of a number of orphanages across the water."

Georgie brought his mother's attaché holdall, with her precious samples and like her, the boys were suitably dressed in neat jacket and britches, hair tied back and ribboned, Georgie with raised heels to add an inch.

"Right Honourable and Most Honourable, such laurels bestowed on an ordinary man, Madam", said Bundy, "can wear him down, each one, a thorn pinned to his lapel. The gentleman you will see is looking all the worse for the wear, like your youngest, he is consumptive."

Little was spoken as she was allowed to run a measuring tape around the anointed wrist and collar areas, in the presence of his butler, who instructed her to speak, only when spoken to and looking at the boys, with a mild disapproval, like "keep the brats in their place." Lord Rockingham did have a pallor, she noticed the tiredness behind his sensitive eyes as he observed her at close quarters. Bridie would call the various measurements to her assistant and carefully Georgie would record them in his journal. She could hear the strain of the old man's breathing and noticed his interest in Henry, as the youngster stood near the massive fireplace, obviously in his own little world, under the stern gaze of the horrid butler. Rockingham seemed amused at the little drama, as she inspected again her sons entries. "He's very good at figures Sir' and writes better than myself."

His voice was full and deep, like an old relic. "Your hands are talented for other things, young lady, it is easy enough to write words and figures."

"Does your Lordship require that I include any emblem, perhaps an initial, a coat of arms...it would be a little extra.....?"

"No, dear lady, I am tired of banners and emblems. Let them be unadorned and your talent shine out. I shall require three sets."

"Your Lordship is very kind."

He smiled, there was a narrow warmth in the effort, his teeth looked stained. "And now, Madam, I wish you to make something very special. I wish you to make a half cape to fit over my shoulders and to come half way down my back, to my waist, and that will tie at the front in a special clasp which I will provide". He pointed at her display which had been spread out on the great dining table, "this mode, as you have said, Della Francesco." He continued, turning his butler about and placing his open palm on the servant's centre back. "This is where you will make the inscription." He took a card from inside his doublet, "it's for somebody about my size." The little card, in gold leaf, showed a

23

crown and lettering which read "George Rex."

Bridie looked at him quizzically, trying to understand

"It's a gift for His Majesty."

She looked again at the little card, running her fingers over the emblem. "It will be the very best, Sir," she whispered.

"See that it is, Madam." He patted Hen on the head as he left the room and left them to the mercy of the butler.

**

She worked frantically until her fingers cramped, her two assistants worked overtime. Captain Bundy was aesthetic . Not to dilute the pleasure, he insisted "we must find you a bigger place, get you more help." He could see it all now, a whole industry of young women and not so young, bending to the beautiful task, "and the clergy, we haven't touched the clergy and if it be known, they're the ones with the money and the vanity, the bishops, lace for the bishops."

Two weeks later, Lord Rockingham stood before Mr. Goldberg in the Grafton Street shop. The little Jew fussed and fretted that His Lordship might take a chair, while he went upstairs to fetch Mrs. Tansey. The knock on her parlour door was a staccato of nervous little tapping and to her surprise, Bridie found the shopkeeper framed in the imposing figure of the peer, the Lord of His Majesty's bedchamber. He seemed to fill the little room. The gold clasp, and brooch in the shape of a coronet sparkled bravely on a piece of velvet. It had little clasps and eyes, so her threads could be buttoned through. She was aware of him, looking through to the large sprigging room. " I thought you might like to have the clasp before you finished the cape, I will ask you to keep it safe until the work is finished," he said, his breath labouring after attacking the stairs.

"There is no need, Sir, your order is finished and ready for you to take with you, I was about to ask Captain Bundy as to delivery to your house." Her emotions were in a tumult as she ached that he might not be satisfied. Hen came from his bedroom, sleep in his eyes. Georgie moved quickly from the sprigging room and herded him back inside.

"My younger son, Sir, he's delicate."

She took Lord Rockingham's order from the cupboard and laid it out on the table for his inspection, all the pieces including the cape, handling it like she would a relic. He turned it for an overall inspection, examining the royal inscription. With cautious hands, she manipulated the threads through the little eyes of the clasp and waited.

" 'Tis a work of art, Madam, a gift, indeed fit for a king."

She folded the merchandise into her special pouches. He asked to see the sprigging room, where the three girls sprang to their feet in half courtesy, knowing right away, he was the important aristocracy that Henry hadn't ceased to talk about in the past fortnight, the "best friend of the king."

The great Englishman had tea with Bridie, quietly taken by the kind of magic she could weave, like an invisible garment around her, colours mixed, shaded and blending, as different silks under different lights. She played mother with the tea pot and the sugar lumps, almost at ease now. He wanted to know of her son's poor health then apologised in a way an aristocrat might do, with an even office stare, that the work again was excellent, but he did not have enough money on his person. She should come to the phoenix Park mansion in two days to make a settlement.

He was again conscious of the industry, working its way through the day in the room next door, the young boy, and his illness and the dark high stairway.

"Captain Bundy suggests you might move to a better accommodation, Mrs. Tansey," he said, "he sees great things for you in the business of couture."

"My Lord," she smiled, "the good captain would have me a conglomerate. Two years ago, I feared for my life in the North and for my sons. We left in the night because of the political aspirations of my husband, who died for his commitment. Almost hungry, we lived under the extraordinary goodness of Captain Bundy."

The peer smiled, a posture of mock suspicion. "Not just to your benefit, Madam, Bundy is charitable indeed, but in him, pure charity can be an expensive article. I am aware of your agreement."

"That agreement works well for us, Sir, and look at us now, in this fine place and here am I, having tea with a Prime Minister of all of Great Britain."

The euphoria of the past hour dispelled, as she looked down on busy Grafton Street. "The truth, Sir, is that I won't be here much longer. I miss the country. If truth be known, I do not like Dublin." She hurried on, "not just Dublin My Lord, it's the city, any city, the hustle, the dangers. I miss the monotony of a quiet life, it stimulates the creative mind for me. The city has just a face, no soul."

She smiled and replenished his cup. "My son is consumptive, he could die here, he needs clean air. I think Wexford, I'm told the climate is good."

Unexpectedly and surely, out of character, he reached for her hand and pressed it gently, then shook Georgie's hand as the boy rushed to open the door for him. "Mid day after tomorrow, Madam, there is a matter I wish to discuss further".

The boy looked searchingly at his mother, "you're leaving Dublin?, couldn't help overhearing."

She made no answer and later they were re-stocking her little corner in the shop below, Mr. Goldberg, hands wringing in his usual neurosis, a little man whose constant anxiety was the normal course of his existence

"Why did he come here, Mrs. Tansey?"

"He came to see me on a matter, Mr. Goldberg, it really is nothing of your business."

"Is he satisfied, pleased with the place, I try to keep it in proper condition, the window, I change every two weeks, the stairway...", he left the sentence hanging, then, "I cannot afford a further increase".

She frowned. "Mr. Goldberg...?"

"Landlord, Madam, do you not know he is our landlord, he owns the building, he owns half of Grafton Street."

Captain Bundy put Bridie straight on His Lordship's acquisitions. Lord Rockingham owned lands in abundance in the counties of Wicklow and Wexford and acreage of roughage on Blackstairs and Mount Leinster, an inheritance, that if it were to be examined, would, no doubt, throw out a fortune, ill-gotten, like that of many a well off Englishman, domiciled in Ireland, if only for a few weeks a year. Men, who by some great material or spiritual bonanza, in a past century, found themselves acquiring and possessing nothing short of a principality, for services to a gluttonous empire.

She believed everyman, the architect of his own fortune or misfortune and the fact that Mr. Charles Watson-Wentworth flourished at the misfortune and expense of the Irish peasant and the good will and gratitude of Mr. Oliver Cromwell, the Rockingham dynasty was something she might think about on another day. His Lordship's stipend for her labours was more than generous, but "that matter" he had mentioned, had opened yet another door, through which she peered with trepidation.

**

To say that Master Bundy was crest-fallen at the prospect of her departure would be the truth. His evident attraction to her would suffer a major disappointment not to mention the impediment to his future earnings and the glorious future. He had such plans and wondered if she might change her mind and inwardly, cursed the grand old man of

26

Rockingham for his interfearing charity. On her last day in Grafton Street, a day, Mr. Goldberg said was a breaking of his heart, Bridie had tea with the Captain in the Shelbourne Hotel and when he left her home, there seemed to be an understanding between them that G. recognised, of some kind of arrangement for future business.

She had sat her boys down, the warmth of her eyes, eager and intense, and told them about her meeting with His Lordship. "His Lordship owns half of Ireland," she said. "If you stand on a mountain, he owns everything you can see around you and most of what you cannot see."

"Who gave it to him, Mother," asked Hen, wide eyed in his asthmatic wonder.

"He stole it," interjected his brother. "Mr. Bundy said as much, he says the country outside of Dublin is in a struggle to even stay alive. Mr. Bundy says..."

"Captain Bundy simply doesn't want us to go, G.," she said sternly. She spoke slowly, breaking up her carefully rehearsed words, laying the background anxiously, pleading for their understanding. "His Lordship has given us a fine cottage in Co. Wexford, with a couple of acres of land, a house big enough for us, for our work. He will write to a fine school for places for you both, it's two years since you were at school, George. He's sending a carriage tomorrow to take us there, the journey will take a few days." Hen, already sensing the euphoria of the adventure ahead, wheezed himself into a fit of coughing.

She cupped his face in her hands, "His Lordship says it will be good for you in the fresh air, my baby."

Georgie had gotten to like Dublin, the grand golden boom in the air, the fine buildings, the wide clean carriageways, the obvious wealth available to those who reach for it, the advantage of being a Protestant in a city where to be Catholic was to be deprived of all privileges, of the basic fundamentals of democracy, where he would wear his Protestant hat and swear an oath to the king on his eighteenth birthday.

Then for only the second time in his life, he saw her dark tired eyes misting over. She hugged him, he was as tall as her now, in his higher heels. She fixed him in that all encompassing passion that was always there behind her eyes. It was her moment of commitment. She felt at this anonymous adventure, a curious, weakening excitement.

"Two years ago, we were paupers, Son, begging on St. Stephen's Green. We laid aside our dignity in the workhouse, though Captain Bundy was kindness itself, but a kindness that came at a price. Now, only God knows how it came to pass that I dress the gentlemen of Dublin, it's Parliament, it's Bishops, it's Viceroy, a man who was the

Prime Minister of Britain, even the king himself." She hurried on..."your father would...." He cut her short, trying to be gentle. "My father hated the king, it's why he died".

"Your father was fighting a lost cause, G., THAT'S why he died". The Orange Order is now rampant in the North, we could have died. Up there, we were Catholics, pretending to be Protestants, why do you think you both have names straight out of a royal family tree?"

"And now, Mother, what are we now and what will we be in Wexford?"

"We are and will be whatever it pays us to be, G., the true laws of The Almighty are the laws of our own good fortune, Protestant or Catholic, we all worship the same God."

He could see his continued argument was upsetting her. He put his arms about her and she responded, kissing his cheek, feeling there the beginning of a stubble. Henry wedged into them, clutching her skirts and they stood there in her parlour, a little fortress, striving for its own commonwealth. She smiled through her tears, crying in little stifled sobs into his shoulder. "The curse of poverty left us no right to be happy, but we are now and will be further."

"Then there's no need to cry," he whispered in her ear. She touched his hair, "not crying over spilt milk, I'm crying that a man has just held me for the first time in a long time."

"Whatever you want to do, Mother, wherever you want to go, then we go, you're the general."

"Then you're my lieutenant." Hen tugged at her skirts. "And you are my little captain." The little circle broke. "There is something else, His Lordship said, that there is a revolution coming. The Orange Order is threatening to put an end to Catholicism in Ireland. The Catholics and the organisation called The Defenders are strengthening to create an army. A new group called The United Irishmen are forming for a rebellion and all this is going to happen in Dublin. There's talk of this man Wolf Tone, who, His Lordship says is a founder member and he's a danger to peaceful times."

She sat the two boys at the table and held their hands. "I will not have my boys having anything to do with any rebellion, do I make myself clear, Lieutenant, do I make myself clear, Captain?"

**

Bridie Rose Tansey had learnt that there was no security on this Earth only opportunity, and to create chances and to profit from those that offer. Firstly the Captain, then Rockingham had provided security, the opportunity, the chances and the profit. The motive for his staggering generosity , was something she chose not to dwell on. There was a slight infatuation of her, not overwhelmingly, like that of Bundy, but a cross purpose of intrigue and magnanimity, but most of all, his Lordship was immensely impressed. His generosity had a kind face and perhaps he was making amends for the scars of a nation in some small way, perpetrated by his ancestral benefactor. Bridie's gut told her that what you get free from a stranger can cost too much, there's sublime thieving in all giving and a method to it, to be sure. But the moment was now, the changes in her life were imminent and she would grab them with both hands. A man like Rockingham, for the most part, had an aristocratic disregard for the ordinary man, spawned in a world of silver spoons and lace, they reaped where they never sowed. She would grab the flower handed and bide her time until restitution might be sought, then weigh up the cost, bow to it or move on. It was the time to be practical.

The profit to His Lordship was clean. His agent in London will conduct business from there, directly to her, as soon as she settles. Orders from the agent will be sent to Dublin and Bundy will take care of forwarding. The agent will receive his 20% and Bundy will retain his as usual. Lord Rockingham..?, simply two sets of her best, once a year. She would keep Mr. Goldberg supplied to the best of her ability.

"His Lordship is a proper gentleman," she said to G., "so we won't trust him too much. Hope you know how to do this 20% thing in your little book."

Chapter 4

On 6th. May, 1793, the day of George's fourteenth birthday, Lord Rockingham's man came to Grafton Street to collect them in a perfect carriage, drawn by two fine horses. Belongings were carefully piled into the large luggage compartment and on the coach top, mother's three dresses, the boys' suits and the rest of their wealth, but especially, four rolls of crisp white linen and the threads and instruments of Bridie's trade. Mr. Goldberg wept at their leaving, his little prayer shawl wrapped about his small middle, especially for the occasion, the shawl she had made for him on his sixtieth birthday. Tearfully, the three young women closed the sprigging room door for the last time. Captain Bundy arrived early. With controlled emotion and reluctant acceptance, he made G. promise he would take care of his mother and keep in touch, trying to make light of the parting, in contradiction of his true feelings.

She felt the depression of a thousand days as they passed St. Stephen's Green and the paupers' pantomime on show. There seemed to be an even larger crowd than she remembered and a bigger need for the generosity of The Society Of Friends on a beautiful May Day in Dublin. The city, in it's new found wealth and in the expansion of its boundaries to rival London itself, was expected, like all great cities of Europe, to cultivate its own miseries, perhaps a necessary little fashionable unhappiness. His Lordship's driver was none too pleased when she asked him to pull over and the boys went with her to the railings, looking for the tall blonde man named John. Two years on and Georgie now so much more mature, was even more fascinated than then, that up to a few hundred, seemingly respectable middle class citizens, interspersed with a few drunks could spend a few pence and a wasted hour, watching the gluttonous devouring of offal, where every act, inside or outside the barrier is done to satisfy one hunger or another.

John was collecting pennies as usual and he saw her before she saw him. Tall, aquiline, like he himself could do with a substantial meal, he came to the rails, his grey eyes softening, the decent face in the beginning of a smile. Georgie shook the big bony hand, she handed him the little velvet pouch. "For your kindness, Sir," she whispered.

The vulgarians crushed against them. Amused, he opened the draw string and spread the pair of linen handkerchiefs on his open hand. The sprigging threads and scalloped borders spelt his name in laced detail. "John." Nestling there in the middle was ten silver shillings.

"I cannot accept, Madam," his smile widening. "We do not keep anything that does not belong to us."

"But they're yours, Mr. John, see your name is on them," insisted Hen.

They left Mr. John framed in the rails as the fine carriage left the sidewalk across the street. His face showed just a trace of surprise.

**

Lord Rockingham's bequest was a fine thatched single storied building. To say it was a cottage would be unseeming behaviour and an insult to its creator. It stood on a plateau of a good acre on the lower slopes of the magnificent Blackstairs Mountains. It looked like it had been newly whitewashed where the sun dazzled and the fine windows winked their welcome. Bridie asked the driver, Max, to halt the horses, half way up the laneway, just to take in the illusion. Shades of early evening scattered their purple through the setting sun, so that the scenery was human and personal. The everyday world was another country they had left behind and eventually, she reluctantly motioned Max to continue upwards. "It's a little mansion," she whispered. "We must make a name for it."

Her mansion was set in a little green oasis, which, obviously had been lovingly tended up to recently. Potato beds and strawberry stalks were rotting in the rich soil, the aftermath of last year's harvest, new shoots springing everywhere. Beyond a sturdy fence, the acre stretched away to a copse of young trees, interspersed with wild daisies and lavender. Somebody had made a stone seat under the young willow. Four windows faced south east offering a panoramic view of nearby Enniscorthy Town. Tiny cottages dotted the rough landscape, nestling among the rocks and crevices and the spruce trees, smoke curling like dark hair from roofs without chimney stacks. Bridie's house had a fine stack and an outbuilding as big as any of the hovels around.

The house, shining brightly in the sun, had five large rooms, all well furnished. Cupboards had been well stocked of bed clothes and towelling and the great fireplace with its swinging crane, had piled on its stone shelves, various pots and kettles and two new water buckets. The house had its own well.

She thanked Max for his great help and insisted he accept a stipend with her gratitude and when he had left, G. found her sitting under the willow. in a kind of ecstasy. Beyond the small fields, the wild land reached upwards to the mountain, purple with cross leaved heathers and wild thyme and the rocks patterned with stonecrop and lichen. Where the sloping hills turned into cliffs, trees and green tracery curved around the edges, like Bridie's lacework. The pink clouds on her first evening on The Blackstairs, soared above Mount Leinster in their last blush of a dying sunset.

"God bless you Lord Rockingham," she whispered.

The dirt path from the main road was dotted with holly, small oaks and fuchsia bushes, rowan berries, and scarlet red sloes ripened on the blackthorns. About the house, discarded blossoms and fern maintained the lustre of the place, where Bridie's little mansion looked down on the river Urrin and the sedge of the bog in the distance. Granite rock and limestone mounds stretched to either side, interspersed with shale and grit, and spruce trees abounded in the poor soil of the Blackstairs. Before the end of summer, all that once flowered would soon be fruit.

"Come inside, Mother," Hen called through the net of her drowsiness, "there's a room without a window."

Lord Rockingham had sent instructions ahead that the Tansey family was to be accommodated with help in any way they needed. It came in the colourful personage of Mr. Thomas Driscoll.

A dull sense of humour rested comfortably on Thomas Driscoll. The gravel in his voice suggested, not just the dust of the roads of north Wexford, but a larynx, long pickled in the fruits of Irish barley in copious visits to the whisky houses of a wide area.

On his arrival the following morning with a pair of helpers, Bridie soon saw in him a tincture of the stamp of acceptance with a kind of humour as a response to a hopeless and uncouth life, no other medicine but the humour. He introduced himself as simply Driscoll. A heavy set man, what was left of his hair straddled his shoulders like a torn nest, a greying ginger coloured mass, that suggested a foxy crop in his youth. His eyes were a vibrant blue and showed out the traits and personality of the man, a man with many faces.

"You'll be wanting the window put back them, Missus." His eyebrows, a bushy transplant from his locks, raised in what looked like surprise.

"Mr. Driscoll," she said incredulously, "I have never seen a room without a window, and such a fine room too, as far as the lamp can show."

"When we put back the windows, Mam, I said to the lads that four would be enough for now."

She gave him a quizzical look. "For now, you say?"

"There's not a cottage in all of Wexford with five windows, there's a church I know with only three windows."

She looked for some kind of psychological design to his argument, but not really an argument, she decided, as he wasn't looking for any victory to his opinion, he was simply stating a fact, forsaking her first question. "Sure only two months ago, it had only one, above the high altar."

The "lads" concerned, stood behind his heavy frame, blocking out the light at the door, humility like a feigned submission in them, their humility, as she soon got to know, a tough hide, as beneath shaded eyes, they wondered at this woman and her influence with Lord Rock himself. What's more, she came from up north, and nobody is to be trusted who came from anywhere north of Droghada.

"Now, Mr. Driscoll, one of us must have the last word," she said sternly, "otherwise we will never be done. Now, are you telling me there was never a window in that room at some stage, and somebody like you built it up?"

"Yes, Missus, I did."

"Mr. Driscoll", she said,evenly "I don't know why you built it up, but please put the window back, a house should have as much of God's light as possible, why would anyone want to block up a fine window space?"

He gave her a tolerant horse laugh, a touch of pity in its timber for her innocence.

"In Wexford, Missus, God has nothing to do with it, light comes with the rent and tithes, no rent, no light."

Two days later, the triumvir arrived with the window tied to a donkey's hip. The window space opened easily to give a glorious southern view to the river and the mountain. The spoor of light that burst into the room, turned the dust to gold as the rugged beauty of Mount Leinster assailed her.

"This is the size of two cabins, Missus, and another big place for you to clean, sure enough."

"This room is my sprigging school." She put her arm about Georgie, the other arm outstretched in welcome to the newly exposed splendour.

"A school is it Mam," Driscoll said in wonder. "O now Captain will have something to say about that, there's no schooling around here without Captain St. Ledger's say so."

"Mr. Driscoll....Thomas, it is the perfect name for you...doubting Thomas. I'm going to call you "Diddymus" from now on." She smiled, mischievously, "now go and finish my window, then come and have some tea." When the three left with their donkey, he could be heard muttering to the lads, "Diddymus, and what kind of a name is that, Diddymus."

In the lane their voices could be heard in unison, "Dinnymus....

Diddymus Driscoll," Thomas slapping at them playfully.

Diddymus had been employed to spend a day a week to attend the house of Mrs. Tansey, a good man with a child's heart, not even sophisticated enough to hide his naivety. He soon became like a family pet. However, his employer, Captain St. Ledger, local agent to a number of landlords including Lord Rockingham and tithe proctor to the Protestant Church of England, was a different kettle of fish entirely.

They say that youth is just the past, putting a leg forward, that time can be merciless. Enniscorthy, for theTanseys, became both a heaven and a hell. Bridie named the house "Thimble Hall" and after a few weeks, Diddymus found for her, six good women from the cottages of the mountain, who were willing to learn the craft of sprigging. All women everywhere had the experience of rough knitting work, especially here, where sheep were in abundance, providing the raw material and families wore cheap homespun woollens.

Contentment and a kind of happiness settled on Thimble in the first few months, despite the shadow of Captain St. Ledger, who, to Driscoll's surprise, did not yet pay a visit. Bridie found a school at St. Mary's, a Protestant school where Protestant orthodoxy was exclusive and where belief in its truth excluded belief in any other truth. It was to be consumed by all that the Papacy is not other than the ghost of the old Roman Empire. The teacher at St. Mary's, the Reverend Carrysworth, was an emotional and mental dirigible, obsessed with the saving of souls, provided they're Protestant.

"No man is a Christian who cheats his fellow man and perverts the truth," he would expound in his narrow little voice, a little man whose sharp tongue never mellowed, but grew sharper with time. A condition of their acceptance to this sanctum was to make public their faith in God and king and not necessarily in that order, two youngsters taking the oath to His Most Gracious Majesty, King George.

So Mother thought, will her boys' be Protestant or Catholic for now." She had seen what presented itself as a Catholic school, just off the square in Enniscorthy, and though she mulled over the question for some time, it wasn't for long. Her boys would have an education even if it be at the feet of the devil himself. Catholic education in Ireland was something of a monastic incarceration, where both teacher and pupil are unexercised and unaccepted. Thatched hovels and shaded copses were a refuge of a sort of an education, it's curriculum, constantly scrutinised and controlled by the authorities, it's purpose, to keep ignorance rampant.

Henry had little schooling, sickly, he remained restrained in his growing, though his condition responded well to the benign air of the

34

Blackstairs, thick and delicious with the whiffs and smells of rock and heather. George did have the benefit of the beginnings of his education in the North, where he was a Protestant.

Mr. Diddymus, his new name was always used out of earshot, would measure the boys against Bridie's doorpost to record their growing, however, Hen's illness pruned his body down and there were times when mother would notice the ailment attack the spiritual part of him, enlarging the dimensions of himself to himself, becoming his own exclusive object, becoming selfish and difficult.

A light cob horse and cart were purchased with Driscoll's help and he would take Hen away for part of a day, dropping George to school and Rev. Carrysworth's ranting.

In a place where drudgery was a curse, where ninety per cent of the people survived without hope, the people, for the sake of getting a living, by any means, forgot to live. For six women, Thimble Hall offered a release from boredom and need, a chance to fill the time and a reward, though meagre to begin with, made the pleasure twice as great. Early morning, G. would watch through the dawn distance, these women leaving their stone hovels where cooking smoke, like mother's lace, spread out from a hole in the thatch, their families fed the first of two daily meals, grateful bellies filled for a while, bellies, more interested in boxty bread and gruel than any kind of freedom or emancipation. Then a sop to their cold morning; warm sweet tea, freshly made bread with salted butter on Bridie's fine pine topped table, before a fireplace with a real chimney, where the raw thatch is hidden above a latted ceiling. Then, six hours in the sprigging room where three of them were quick to learn the delicate trade, the others, with callous hands, bred for bog cutting and the stirring of a few perches of scrub, were less delicate. The wheel of labour turned gently for them. "Mam,"as the woman of the house, would be respectfully referred to, though considerate ,Bridie could be heard once in a while, with a roughness to her voice in its criticism and it's scolding where a point of precision would be expounded. She would say they were like good horses, seldom sparred, when her eldest, her book keeper would count out their paltry earnings.

Bridie's orders of linen and threads were delivered to Enniscorthy on a regular basis and the coach back to Dublin carried her finished products to Bundy and Mr. Goldberg. As matters improved for Thimble Hall, so the six ladies received extra benefits, to their delight and Diddymus and Hen were the couriers once a month to meet the Dublin coach.

On sunny days, the school would work outside in Bridie's copse, as

G. would spend a few hours fighting dandelions in her garden, wondering how they can thrive in their gorgeous blooms, her eyes travelling in flight to where the wild flowers made corridors of colour between mountain and river, the rocks low and dark against the sun, where birds soared and sang, their songs carrying in the quiet day. Up there in the low acres was their playground; the brothers. Mount Leinster and Log Na Coille, with the two great peaks of Blackstairs, the beginning and end of all natural scenery. He would study her for a minute, knowing she was happier here in this place, than she had ever been in her life. Between the massive lumps of greenery, the river Urrin meets the mighty Slaney, shining up at him in its opulence in summer, a shimmer of liquid greens and blues, where they swam, he and his brother, in the cool depts. In winter, Slaney became a grey angry moving road in her effort to accommodate contributions from a delta of swollen streams below Black Rock and Clody, with power that would cut stones, growling to squeeze under the stone bridge of the town. Once a week, Rev. Carrysworth would read excerpts from the very English Daily, which at any time would be at least two weeks old, about affairs of the world, as seen by Threadneedle Street in London, on matters concerning the criminal activities of "that rebel rabble, the United Irishmen and all their fellow activities."These are despicable enemies of the king, and must not be accommodated," he warned, as he searched the newspaper. "Plots against His Most Gracious Majesty are being nurtured in these cottages and hovels all about us, inferiors, rising up, trying to be equal."

In a year when the Reign Of Terror engulfed France, when Marat, the scar faced friend of Robespierre was stabbed to death by his prostitute, in his bath, and another attempt was made on the life of King George, two more new states were named in America; Kentucky and Tennennee. In this year, Bridie Rose Tansey had established Thimble Sprigging in the big room where Diddymus's fine window looked out at her copse of young trees, beyond which Enniscorthy stretched eastwards toward cone shaped Vinegar Hill, a backdrop to the Market Square, the broach spire of Saint Aiden's Cathedral, the keep of the castle and the malt houses.

"I warn you all," continued The Reverend, "it is the essence of heresy to oppose the establishment and it's church, and it behoves us all to report such dissent. That fine continent of North America is now an example to the world of Britain's generosity and charity. His Majesty's government cultivated that pagan nation and its people, gave it efficiency, industry and wealth, before giving it its independence, and is as we speak, advising on matters of state."

G. wondered what newspaper Rev. Carrysworth got that piece of enlightened information from, even Hen knew of the American War of Independence, when His Majesty's forces ran before the Independents and are still running. And, he thought, with regards to those who live in the hovels of Wexford, who spend their days plotting the downfall of the king, those "hovellers," 'tis they who pay the rack tithes to the established church to keep the likes of the Reverend and Mrs. Carrysworth in luxury.

While he tried, out of courtesy, to memorise the names of the six ladies now employed in the sprigging room, Hen gave up early and simply gave them a number. Perhaps he was right. Women without identity may as well have a number instead of a name. The early morning breakfast table was where his problem was solved. The little morning feast at the big table would see the ladies sit in the same place, morning after morning, as organised by the one name he could remember. Hannah seemed to emerge as a sort of a mother figure, mainly due to her size, a comfortably built woman, soft faced and accommodating, whom Bridie came to depend on. Hannah wrote the names on slips of paper and for a week, placed the slips before each lady at breakfast. Hannah was number one. Number two was Elizabeth, quite an inordinate name for a woman without advantage. She would ask that everyone use her full name. Outside of her four children, her name was the only piece of delicate pride she had to mask her paltry life. Then, number three, May, a mother of seven, a softly spoken woman, mostly shy and withdrawn, who seemed always to be suffering all the misery of the shy. May had skin that seemed fragile as eggshell, still childlike with a mat of curling auburn hair. Rosie was number four, the youngest with all the excesses of youth. Daughter of Hannah, Rosie was a little older than George, she was skittish and Hannah would often say the girl was in need of a bridle. Numbers five and six, Teresa and Abhann, meaning river, were twins in their twenties, from a household of fourteen children, living on the far side of Enniscorthy. Hen insisted on calling her River, to her great annoyance, but the twins had hands, as delicate as their persons, and were mother's most productive workers. Hardly speaking, daily, they bent to the job before them, their objective, to afford a cottage of their own, away from the gruelling existence in a household, rabbit-like in its unplanned breeding and where accumulation of mere existence was swollen to a horror. River said that in her cabin, there was standing room only. "And who is your brother to be calling me a queer name", complained Abhann, pronounced, Awann, "and him and yourself to have names you wouldn't find on a dog's collar, G. and Hen indeed." George gave her a comforting laugh.

"You'll be Abhann from now on, Abhann, it's a lovely name. As for ourselves, well I never liked my name and Henry hates his, but enough to say they were a necessity at the time." She gave him a quick bold observance as his reply extinguished any light of understanding in her bright eyes. "Grand," she frowned.

Bridie had insisted she was not to know the surnames of those six women "The less we know of their tags and troubles the better," she said. "Our responsibility begins and ends here at our door, as does our discretion, so if the bailiff comes, for whatever reason, we know nothing, not even their names." And so, Hen had his numbers and G. christened the ladies; Hannah Spriggs, Elizabeth Spriggs, Abhann Spriggs, etc. etc.

Chapter 5

Captain Lawrence St. Ledger hated with a passion, the peasants of Killane and Enniscorthy. For all their grovelling poverty, they were too durable, that was the trouble. They lasted too long, as if their perseverance could conquer their fate. His abhorrence of over four hundred tenants, in the cabins of the mountainside and the overcrowded tenements of the town, subjected to his care, was a controlled savagery within him, to the extent that he had little respect for anything that couldn't hurt him. Their strength was in their silence.

However, an exception had to be made in the case of Mrs. Bridie Rose Tansey, mainly because she was a friend of Rockingham, and it puzzled him as to just how far their friendship had gone. She was, of course, a Protestant, she had been pointed out to him at service, the only one on the mountain.

Captain St. Ledger wore many masks, a form suitable to all occasions; for the conveying of the riot act, to the confiscating of livestock, to the drilling of his very own regiment of yeomanry, to the reading of lessons and scripture at St. Mary's, and a very special face for attractive women.

It was obvious he was taken by a woman who seemed to be unaffected by the weed of servitude, not to mention her considerable attractiveness, as in her obvious courage and self confidence. She presented a challenge. Her eldest son, to his amusement, had seen her take extra care with her appearance, as she had sent word by Driscoll that the agent might visit Thimble on his gale day, the day when he and his staff visited the area to collect rents and tithes. He would have had no reason to call, as the lady had free rent and being Protestant, did not pay tithes.

Bridie had found Hannah, agitated and fearful, in the morning. The buxom woman seemed bereft of her usual good spirits and energy, cutting short on a whispered conversation with Elizabeth, when Bridie walked into the sprigging room. Twigging that something was troubling them, she pushed Hannah until it was related that St. Ledger had threatened to evict all Bridie's spriggers from their cabins, as he had demanded a substantial rental increase, as there was now extra money coming from their work

So the day he came to Thimble, he had his "moneybags" with him, a small cowering little man, with a pitiful jaundiced face, a "terrible miser", according to Diddymus, a man who kept all his pomps and pleasures in his pocket. Gale day had arrived as it did every month and moneybags had set up his stall at daybreak in the town, to collect his rents and tithes. A Corporal and six redcoats from St. Ledger's private army oversaw the place of payment. Rents properly recorded, collected from pitiful hands, eager to discharge the obligation, rents into one greasy bag, the tinkling of solitary coins, a poor man's symphony. Tithes properly recorded, sops to the vanities of the Established Church, dropped into another.

Within minutes of meeting him, Bridie hated Lawrence St. Ledger, but she greeted him, pliant and affable, her party face masked to the occasion. That hatred, in their subsequent meetings, she never allowed to distort even one feature, but it seemed to her son, on observing her, to be almost a leisurely workout of pleasure, compiled with almost pity, though his treatment of the peasantry of Enniscorthy and Killane, added to her detestation of him.

St. Ledger was a man, it seemed who never rests, always finding more and more people to look down on. He knew, of course, of her situation in respect of Rockingham, how much in His Lordship's favour she was and the concessions afforded her; no rent, a labourer to labour one day a week, no window tax.

By now, contentment had settled on Bridie Rose Tansey, her contentment being from the enjoyment of herself and her boys and then from her work and from the friendship of her ladies. But she would often at night, in her comfortable bed, feel a draught of uncertainty, that, somehow her happiness had a temporary tinge to it, a shadow of happiness, she carried cautiously. St. Ledger was that shadow.

So his first visit was at her invitation. His aquiline austere face showed deep concentration, his eyes cool grey with a twitch of obvious acceptance. Here was the sort of woman he could never imagine living in any one of the cabins scattered about the mountain. However he maintained a difficult but certain doggedness and precocity in his authoritative swagger,but in his look of conscious determination, she saw, to her inner amusement, an awkward effort at trying to impress her with his fascination of himself. He was a tall man. To her surprise, he was younger than she had expected, given his reputation, perhaps a little handsome, she mused, dressed in black and but for the ridiculous wig could be regarded as presentable. For a while he seemed almost gracious, accepting her invitation to tea and some of the wonder bread that Hannah had perfected with her "secret" recipe and sweet basted cake. From the sprigging room, through a crack in the door, G. watched her spin her magic, the twins and Hen, ears to the jamb, straining to hear. St. Ledger had seen her at a distance, in church and in the town, with that heavy woman. Here, across her table, he was struck by her

40

looks, offering him, for a minute, a glimpse of the novelty of her courage and self confidence. She had little pompous mannerisms, mannerisms that were not without chllenge, he thought.

Before she poured tea, Bridie asked him politely, to dismiss his entourage. "You need no army at this house, Captain, to tell the truth, their presence offends me." Elizabeth Spriggs, Number Two, wide eyed and disbelieving watched the Yeos leave, the little collector of tithes in his private trap in close pursuit

Hannah nervously tended the table. He praised the variety of breads and Bridie invited him to praise the baker. Hannah started at the sound of her own name rang out in the big kitchen. He did nothing to acknowledge the woman.

"The pig," Bridie thought, "he should eat needles."

Daintily nibbling, he said "I'm told, Mrs. Tandy, you have had the pleasure of dressing many important gentlemen."

"My pleasure, Sir, but mostly theirs."

"Impertinence," he mused.

"Gentlemen like Mr. Grattan and Lord Leinster, Abercorn, the Lord Chancellor, the viceroy, Westmoreland. He raised his heavy eyebrows, she thought she saw a hint of admiration.

"I have many clients, my opinion of their importance is of no consequence." She offered more tea.

"And Lord Rockingham, Madam, what is your opinion of His Lordship?", his voice suddenly barbed and coarse. It delighted her to see a little jealousy, evident, feeding on suspicion. "His Lordship saw my talents and wanted to nurture them, Sir."

"Is it true, Madam that the king himself wears your creations?"

"One pair of shoulders is no different to the next, Captain, as long as I am paid for my labours."

"You have a charmed life, Mrs. Tansey."

"I work hard for that life, Sir, and you, Captain, where did your charm come from?"

Her dogged impertinence irked him, though softened by that enchanting smile.

"I am a St. Ledger of Doneraile, lord Doneraile is my uncle. I am a businessman and I am the proctor of these parts, and their landlord. I have leased these rights from Lord Rockingham."

His features darkened and said slowly, as if taking her into his confidence, "and if I had my way, all these cabins would be demolished and I would flood the mountain with sheep."

Well you would have to know, Captain, I would object most strongly to that notion, as I am sure would His Lordship."

41

He dabbed delicately at a crumb nesting on his lower lip and quickly changed the subject. "I wish to say, Mrs. Tansey, I am not used to being summoned to peasantry homesteads, but in your case...."

She cut him off. "In my case, Sir, and admit it, you have been curious."

He managed a trace of a smile. "Curiosity," she continued, "is simply to enquire what boils in another man's pot, as my great friend Mr. Bundy would say, but I always say that curiosity is a certain characteristic of a vigorous intellect."

Bridie Tansey wasn't a dragon of vindictiveness, though G. could see and hear through her controlled voice, her effort at a cool snub, discretely delivered, sufficiently effective in rebuffing him.

"Two matters I would discuss with you." She leaned an inch closer. Hannah had left the room.

Paying courtesy, to all intent and purposes, a peasant woman in a peasant kitchen, had him ill at ease and when she stood, he found himself considering his station and, and uncomfortably, stood almost to attention.

She motioned him to follow and a skirmish sounded in the sprigging room as they rushed to their places and the door opened.

"It's tea time, George." She threw her son a knowing look and the women, quietly devouring their work, glancing at each other under shaded eyes and conscious of his septic stare, put their needles down and followed G. to the kitchen. Hen remained in his corner and looked at her for comfort, she nodded to him in support and he continued wheeling bobbins. The women passed the proctor through the door, like cloistered nuns, some kind of dignity clinging to them with their rough dark dresses.

He looked about the bright room, felt it's industry, shelves full of neatly folded laces and crochets, linen reams, white and smelling of bleach, tiny cushions all along in a row, needles of all sizes, like silver straws standing out of their soft velvet hides.

Bridie stood at the window. Beyond the road, on the riverbank, cows grazed, lustrous hides shining between clusters of Sally bushes. With her back to him, she looked down on the little bothy huts, like sheep strewn between the rocks, small dark cabins where idle husbands sat in huddled bundles, in dark corners among the bundles of horsehair mattresses and straw and bunches of brown hens and wife and children moving about trying to find things.

"I'm told you are intimidating my knitters for extra tithes. I suggest you leave them alone, Sir."

G. listened at the door, ready in case she might need his help.

Though she said it with wintry simplicity, there was a world of feeling in her voice, challenging him. Her audacity stung.

"It's a simple matter of mathematics Madam," he said his voice rising. The mountain has to pay for itself. They are advantaged and every advantage has its tax."

"Tax is a prolific animal, Sir, and it is the part of a good landlord to sheer his flock, not to flay it".

"They do well, Madam, and are aware how well the Empire treats it's peasantry, they know that the virtue of adversity is fortitude". His annoyance was evident that she still had her back to him.

"Mrs. Tansey", his voice was suddenly conversational, almost friendly as he wove his arguments, "these people, on the whole are very simple, so simple that they take, literally, the things we tell them."

"Yes," she said to the window, and in your ignorance, you are creating two countries, one for you, one for them and they outnumber you by great numbers."

"Do not threaten me, Madam, our success over the years, is as a result of keeping them ignorant, keep them insignificant and contemptible. They just live, that's all."

Bridie clenched her fists in frustration.

"And the tithes, Sir?"

"The tithes are even more important than the taxes, they support our Established Church. Our tax system is the envy of the world, from their earnings, to their houses, the quality of their dwellings, the kind of roof, the windows...". She cut him off.

"I know all about your precious windows, Captain and to be truthful, they sicken me.Your power over the people is absolute, Sir, it's wedded to chronic fear. I have to say, I have seen the result of your power, the abject poverty in the town, on the hillsides and I believe it is a dangerous form of abuse."

He came nearer the window, her back to him was tugging at his nerve ends. "You do yourself no favours, Mrs. Tansey, by decrying your church and your state in one breath."

"Now, I hear a threat in your anger, Captain". She turned from the window, softening in her own control. "All religions united with government are incompatible with rights or liberty, and you know that very well."

"If I didn't know you better, Mrs. Tansey, I would wonder about your religious loyalties." She ignored the remark. "I will pay your precious tithes, on behalf of my six ladies and on behalf of Mr. Driscoll. Send your collector here for collection, I refuse to stand in line in one of your whisky houses."

St. Ledger was not married. It was known that he had many encounters, been seen with a variety of women from carriage driven ladies of some substance, on Sundays to tavern dwellers on Mondays.

Alone with her in the sprigging room, Henry didn't seem to exist for him, the Captain caught a new dimension of her, in the stream of light through the window, scattering it's silver banner among the linens.

The hopeful expectations that assailed him on seeing her in the town, at service and once in the tea shop in the square, would never be realised, that he knew now. They were each in one of those two countries, she had spoken about. Yet he couldn't but feel in awe of this woman, who, it seems found her own freedom, exploiting it in fulfilment of herself. He began taking greater cognizance of her, so that ideas and inclinations which he knew now to be reprehensible, were increasingly hard to banish and again he wondered at how she fulfilled what he saw as raw ambition. She had rebuked him, insulted him and his religion, he could have passions for her, other than fury, her next declaration sealed what was to be the perfection of that hostility, that was to remain as the kingpin of their relationship.

She was back at the window. She pointed beyond the cops. Elizabeth and Rosie were sitting among the shrubs in the afternoon sun, sipping tea.

"Seventeen acres of the lower slopes are mine. His Lordship omitted to inform me of this, until I received confirmation of his further generosity, from his agent in London, just last month. I've been here, over a year, Sir, and it seems you were to advise me of the situation on my arrival, yet you failed to do so."

St. Ledger seemed abstracted.

"I am not His Lordships messenger," he replied sheepishly.

"It's a meadow, Captain, almost free of rock, a meadow and well fenced on all sides, which I believe was the work of your good self. I wondered why you didn't put your precious sheep on it."

"Rockingham and my uncle simply didn't come to an agreement on it," he said .

"And yet you fenced it off, Sir, you trespassed." She gave him an accusatory smile.

He was hunting for words, his voice disappearing under growing tumult. "Madam, you would have no use for it."

She smiled again in a half contemptuous respect. "I have had meetings with my sons and with my ladies and believe me, Captain St. Ledger, we have use of it, great use indeed."

The red flag fluttered in his belly, as the black mood quickened in him. "It's obvious His Lordship has you greatly in his favour. It is said that a man who confers a great favour, would rather not be paid in the same coin" He looked at her with cold eyes, full of implication. "I cannot but wonder what was the coin in which you returned the favour, after all every good turn demands a good turn in return."

G. had been at the jarred door and now stepped into the room and stood by her, eyeballing the Captain.

His mother, he knew to be superior to all kinds of affronts, her reply to all hardships, even the hurt of such an insult, was patience and tolerance. He saw the raw animal heat rise up into her face, moisture stinging her eyes, as she turned again to Diddymus's window, then she turned again and looked directly at St. Ledger, her head tilted slightly at an angle of superb indifference. She walked from the room, his annoyance, evident at having to follow her like a servant. She had whispered to Hannah earlier, the result of which was a linen wrapped parcel of Hannah's breads ready for him to take with him. "My complements to Mrs. St. Ledger, Captain, hopefully she will enjoy the bread, as you seemed to."

He looked down at her in amusement, "there is no Mrs. St. Ledger, Madam."

"Then so much more for you and perhaps whoever you might be dining with tonight. Come again next month, Sir, in the mean time leave my ladies alone until we reach an agreement of tithes."

His driver had his carriage door at the ready. "And if we don't make an agreement?"

She fixed him with her business face, cordiality gone. "Eighteen acres, Captain, think how many cabins I could build on that, a hundred, two hundred. No rents, no taxes, think of the loss to your pocket and your uncle's. I do know, His Lordship does not want sheep on the mountain."

"His lordship is an unwell man, Mrs. Tansey," he scoffed, leaving his implication hanging.

Bridie saw the surprise in G.'s face. "You invited him back, Mother?"

They sat around the big table, St. Ledger's chair haunted by his aura. "Keep your enemies close, G., it's unknown the good that can come of a few fresh buns and basted bread." Then she collapsed her shoulders, in sheer relief that the conflict was over. "God what a pig the man is, he should eat needles."

"Is Lord Rockingham ill, Mother?"

"He's an old man, Georgie."

Hannah said to nobody in particular, "sure Ledger himself has a bad heart, you'll kill him with your soft talking, how blessed we are with you, Mam, but you'll get us all killed."

The kitchen party exploded with high mirth at the relief. How prophetic of the poor woman.

**

Wealth in the Wexford of 1794 was the holiest of Gods and the rich people of the Ascendancy minded their fortunes as a creation of their own for the sake of use and profit. Then there was the poor, where tithes and rents, forced them to live with the pig and the brown hen. But then there was the destitute, where an angle in the corner of the ditch of a field under a jutting rock, was home and habitat.

How providence has such wide arms, it drags you into never ending circles and annoys you at not being able to understand it.

Diddymus would come and execute his duties, one day a week, working in the yard, the horse's stable, the chicken coop or the vegetable patch and looked forward to the breakfast ritual, where, after much debate among the ladies, was eventually allowed to partake. Mother said she would never have to leave the house, so informing were the contributions on local gossip and events. Driscoll's friendship was an innocent well, overflowing and unseeking. Bridie came to rely more and more on him and the confidence of his help. He would stand the boys tall against the door post and mark their growing with his tobacco knife and he would tell them how grand and fine they were.

G. would often catch him looking at his mother, not in the way Captain St. Ledger looked at her, not in the way Mr. Bundy looked at her, with mild hope and expectance. There was a sort of a concern in the old man's observation like a wistful father for her well being.

And so, it was at one of the morning conferences, on a day when Diddymus and Hen were to take stock to Enniscorthy to meet the Dublin coach that she broached the idea to Georgie..

"We were in town this week, Driscoll, Hen and myself, and we drove the pony beyond the town on the road to Dooley's Gap and Kilcotty. We saw the unfortunate wretches in the ditches and also on the road to Killane. I want you to bring half a dozen of these families here to the Meadow, measure out a few perches for each and let them begin their own allotment. She cautioned him, "not until next week after St. Ledger's visit." She saw the concern in the old man's face. " The sooner we start, Mr. O'Driscoll, the sooner we stake our claim."

St. Ledger's visits had become more cordial. She had made an arrangement about the ladies debts, to their pathetic delight. In a heated argument, on religion she made a statement that she was to regret and gave him an ace in his sleeve and a stick to beat her with. For a man, obsessed with the spoils of his station, whose sum of all creeds was to hate man and worship God, St. Ledger found in religion, his literature and his science.

She told him she had been Catholic from her christening, that, religion didn't mean that much to her that whatever was convenience at a given time, then that was what she was.

"And what are you now, Madam?" he had said, stupefied at her admission, trying to find some kind of psychological design to her madness. "So you are, let me say, a Protestant of convenience."

One way or the other, Captain, it is none of your business."

"I have seen you in church, with your sons at worship, the words of our hymns rolling off your tongues, making God your accomplice. Do you realise, I can have your children dismissed from our schools, have you run out of Church."

He looked toward the sprigging room. "Have you ever worshiped in one of their churches, been at one of their schools?", believe me Madam, the idea of God ends in their paltry innards."

"I have been in their churches and their schools, Sir. It amuses me that you people bring your clothes to church, rather than your souls, your churches are clubs, stained glass to shut out the cries of the hungry and the hurt."

St. Ledger, to her surprise did nothing about her revelation and looked in both wonder and not a little awe at her brazen appearance at worship, hanging on the words of the Rev. Carrysworth. Frail cordiality abounded, however until the activity in The Meadow took his interest. By year's end, twenty families lived there, the mountain itself supplying much of the basic materials for a new set of family living. When timber was short, Bridie instructed them to dismantle the heavy fencing for roof struts while clay and wattles and reeds from the river bank made for a sturdy cottage. Potato seed and vegetables were brought from Wexford. A kind of agriculture flourished when the life in the ground found the seed. Through George's direction, the new tenants paid as much as they could toward the seeds, many unable to pay at all. A cooperative system was set up, where after first harvest, people came from around to buy produce, at a rate much inferior to that charged in town, at least, three if the markets, owned by St. Ledger, himself.

She had given them a means of self preservation and a semblance of value in their narrow lives, the means to make things good. Their gratefulness knew no bounds, often coming in the night, leaving produce on the doorstep, a few eggs, cleaned vegetables, a snared rabbit; the poor man's payment.

Orders continued to arrive, through the good offices of Mr. Bundy, who promised in his recent letter to journey to Killane very soon. The special seal of Lord Rockingham on his velum envelopes were a cause of great speculation at the sorting office in Enniscorthy. The spriggers were stunned but immensely impressed that two further orders of The Marletto design, were commissioned for His Most Gracious Majesty King George of England.

G.was convinced, that apart from his obvious obsession with his mother, it was this one phenomenon, the contact with royalty that kept St. Ledger coming each month. Outside of Hannah's breads, the sight of the king's attire on special hangers in the sprigging room, fascinated him, though he tried hard not to show it, nothing sharpening his sight like his envy, so at Christmas she presented him with a set of cuffs and a cravat, "just to keep him sweet," she said to G.

The boys had been forbidden to frequent the sprigging room, unless they had duties there to perform. Hen had become quite efficient in the more simple designs of lace making, like the rest of his body, his hands were delicate like a girl's. But he would warn his brother never to let on at school.

He had gotten to know some of the urchins of The Meadow and almost immediately, he felt an affinity with them. He took to running barefoot about the house, demanding his very worst clothes and somebody down there gave him the remnants of an old hat. G. would find him sitting in one of the newly built bathans, cross legged before a cooking fire, like one of the family, playing "stab at the stool". This was a dinner ritual with people who were content with nothing because they had nothing. An entire family, cross legged on an earth floor before a steaming pot of potatoes, with hissing and blowing at the potatoes, fingers and tongues stinging, you stabbed the morsel at the plate of salt which was placed on the only stool in the house, and it burned on the way down, as you eyed the next flowery ball. A specialty, was a can of buttermilk, passed from one to the other, dripping mouths in old and young, trying to catch up.

**

One day, against a household law, Hen stormed into the sprigging room. Hen had a slight stammer, not a stammer as such, just a hesitation in his speech. Today he had no impediment

"Mother, where did we get the horses?" He pointed through the window.

Down in the far end of the Meadow, where Diddimus had reported

48

the soil to be as hard as cows horns, hard and unyielding, a pair of marvellous shires pulled a heavy plough, their huge legs in white socks, grinding and pulling, the earth opening up in their wake. Children were running and jumping before and around the animals, Diddymus doing his best to keep them at safe distance.

Driscoll was not a small man, good height, his fifty something body, well into flesh. As the horses passed him by, the man at the plough, seemed, in the distance to dwarf old Diddymus, a good head and shoulders over the grand animals.

"Who is he," Bridie's frown deepened against the sun

"He's John Kelly, Mam," said May, in an admiring whisper. The twins were quickly at the window, River, a look of approval in her frail face, though Bridie thought she saw a little flush to her cheek, "John Kelly, Mam."

"Hmmmm!" grunted Hannah, and returned to her work, fingers tense as her mood.

Hen was soon running down the laneway, his floppy hat falling and tumbling before him. Later, when a great swath of mountain skutch and shale had turned colour from greens and yellows, to the rich browns of the Wexford soil, Diddymus brought the young man to her door.

G. could see her vivacity shining out as the two approached, Hen in their shadow

The man exuded a kind of animal sensuality, despite his youth. His blonde hair rested onto his shoulders, and curled on his forehead. His soft good face showed concentration of her, his eyes,blue and cool. A man spawned here on the mountain, sun washed, with steel below the surface, John Kelly was completely at ease in her presence, this woman who was slowly becoming a legend in Killane and Enniscorthy.

G. had never seen a man a couple of inches short of seven feet. His great shoulders strained against the confines of his shirt, and he would have had to stoop to come inside Bridie's door. Holding a soft cap in his hands, Kelly refused her invitation to have some tea.

"I would need to finish the ploughing, Mam, the horses are restless and I will need to get them back home before nightfall."

"Then I will have G. bring you down something to eat."

A slight courtesy and they were gone. She called to Driscoll. He strutted back to the door.

"Your fame is spreading, Mam," he said, dabbing the sweat on his brow and head, turning a bright shade of pink from the sun. "Sir George Palmer of Duhallow sends you his best wishes and he sends you the gift of the horses and plough for as long as they are needed. John Kelly and myself, we take work where we get it and Sir George is very good to us." Down below in The Meadow, the green sod was changing to rich amber under the team, as Kelly again bent to the task.

The giant stayed for a further two days, with his horses, setting out little habitats.The new owners worked around him, while Driscoll issued instructions, importantly, reporting to the house at the end of each day. Hen was slowly becoming a farmer, taking passionately to the big man, his asthma improving almost daily and when Mr. Kelly arrived at week's end with a cart load of potato seed, another gift from Lord Palmer, Bridie put pen to paper, a letter of gratitude, to be delivered by John Kelly to Duhallow. And yet another load of seed, this time with cabbages and turnips, but this time with the good wishes of one of the biggest landlords in Wexford, Sir Charles Mountnorris of Camolin Park.

Eventually John Kelly relented. Hen dragged him up to the house on his mother's instructions, or she was going down there and do it herself. Since opening the meadow, Bridie went there, only to make inspections, now and then. To be truthful, the pathetic attitude of the now, thirty families was an extension of their servitude, they would mill from their huts in waves of gratitude.

Hen's admiration for Kelly bordered on reverence and his worship of the giant was fed daily by fresh discoveries in his new found friend. Work done for now, he had brought a set of hurls, or camans as they were referred to, from his home in Killane and in the early evenings she watched him instructing the children in the game of hurling. The camans were roughly hewn sticks of ash, narrow at the handle, widening toward the base to strike at a hand sewn small ball of cow hide.

This man's frantic energy, awoke in her a kind of curious excitement and G. made a concerted effort with everyone to make him welcome. Mother's rising temperature brought an out of character blush to her cheeks and as he eventually agreed to join her with Diddimus at her table, all to Hen's delight, five pair of straining ears pressed to the door inside the sprigging room fought for a space, squinting through the cracks, hanging on his words, though few.

"The people are very grateful, Mam, for your great kindness." His voice was a second face, a second body, strong and all encompassing. He had good table manners, though the big hand struggled with the delicate cup handle. Next time, she would have something more acceptable,

"You and Mr.Driscoll have done much more for them, Mr. Kelly," he gave Hen an ironic smile, "and of course, the Captain here."

"The kindness of Lord Mountnorris and Sir Palmer, it is beyond kindness itself," she said.

Diddymus gave Kelly a knowing glance, amusement curling the edge of his mouth, under the stubble.

"Necessity, Mam," smiled Kelly. "Necessity turns a lion into a fox, it was Driscoll, he's the fox."

Diddimus caught his breath, his mouth full of cake. "It's Kelly, Mam, he's the fox."

The giant's face softened into a broad smile, the bond between the two, evident. Then the smile disappeared as quickly as it came. He stared at her, evenly and for a fraction of a second, hostility replaced his good face. Hen, jam and sugar crusting around his mouth, looked, transfixed at his hero.

"Remember, Mam, everything they have, these so called "Excellencies," these "Your Honours," these landlords and magistrates and proctors, everything they have is ill gotten, so don't be grateful for the crumbs from their tables. They have kept us poor for generations, six hundred years. Look at France to day, the poor rose up and the reign of terror is putting people like that to the chop. The poor of that great country flew a flag and it is only when we fly a flag that people like Mountnorris and Palmer should be afraid."

The smile returned, he pointed again at the old man, "all his fault, Mam." Laughter rippled about the table. They had forgotten Hannah was still in the kitchen. She threw him a savage look, rattled the plate onto the table and stormed out, but not before Kelly looked at her under his eyes, still smiling. "Mrs. Kelly" he nodded and winked at Henry.

G. looked at his mother and saw the question in her eyes. "Mrs. Kelly?".

Diddymus hurried on, "I'll tell you how you came by the generosity of them Lordships, Mam."

Pointing at Kelly, "that fella, told Sir George of your own generosity in such a way, that the good Palmer of Duhallow felt obliged, not that he's a good man and full of good deeds himself. Then we spun an even sadder story to Lord Mountnorris, and not wanting to be outdone, as the two are friendly rivals, Mountnorris fell for the bait." Hen clapped his hands in applause, staving off a coughing fit.

John Kelly stood to go, dwarfing her, looking at her with a tincture of anxiety.

"All these Lordship fellas are fools and obsessed with their own importance. They're easy to fool, but one you should be careful of. Be fearful of St. Ledger, Mam, and your fine house and your generosity, for he's a gombeenman of the worst kind."

"I'll be careful, Mr. Kelly, but you called her Mrs. Kelly?"

51

"Hannah is my aunt on my father's side, Mrs. Tansey," he replied, throwing Hannah a look full of mischief.

"He has been here for a number of weeks, coming and going and I think I know now why he shunned my invitations." Bridie scrutinised the woman in a shadow of a smile, as Kelly squeezed through the door.

"The relationship was made by nature, Mam, be sure I had nothing to do with it. Anyway, you always said you never wanted to know our names," she frowned deeply.

"John Kelly is the son of my brother. I heard him tell you to be careful of Captain St. Ledger, well let me tell you, John Kelly is a greater danger to you, to all of us, than any St. Ledger."

Hen and G. looked at her, in enquiry. He has funny and dangerous ideas of freeing Ireland from the grip of King George, with soldiers as young as Henry there. He has an army of gassoons, over there in Killane, teaching them all kinds of no good."

"Surely that's to be admired, Hannah," Bridie argued.

"From the hurling and the caman, to the pike and the gun, is a small journey. They say over two hundred youths are loyal to him, he drills them in a haggard in Killane, a field in the shadow of the mountain. John Kelly can't see beyond his nose, Mam, when it comes to fighting for Ireland, a block head and no more and what's more he'll get us all killed."

Mother smiled to comfort the old woman. "Then that makes two of us who will get us all killed, Hannah."

Hannah whispered to her. "My nephew sees all crime against the establishment as ligimate. John Kelly is taking young men from their homes, and giving them silly names like in the Yeomanry; Corporal, Sergeant, Captain and the like, and they play them as games over in Killane, and some day he'll let them out and get them all killed."

**

Bridie's charity took a step further, her philanthropy, soon to become an expensive article in the wrath of Captain St. Ledger. Her ladies had made three wedding gowns of virgin white linen, scalloped and laced, in three sizes. Young women, with little prospects of happiness before them, at least, walked to the altar on their wedding day, amply adorned and lovely in a new husband's eyes. They would come to Thimble, possibly in the unfortunate clothes, they slept in, to be stripped, measured and sized, with a warning to bring the garment back in its original condition. It was the first time, G. saw nudity in its female form. Rev. Carrysworth had told them that nudity is vulgar and should not be tolerated, that to be shameless is to be graceless before God. G. saw nothing graceless in what he saw through the open door of the sprigging room.

Her name, she said was Sharon. Her mother waited outside while the girl was been measured. Sharon's modesty was as scarce as her attire. Her mane of mahogany coloured hair was damp and shining, as her mother said she had just washed in the river.

"O child, have you no shift?", he heard his mother say, as the door to the sprigging room creaked open and he saw Sharon stand naked before her, the perfect form of pale shoulders, her backside toward him. As he stood, transfixed, mother gently turned the girl around, offering him full frontal in all its beauty. Bridie saw him over Sharon's shoulder, a curious look that suggested amusement, under her raised eyebrows The girl smiled at him with a certain precocity, like they were both looking into a big mirror, from opposite sides, a mirror that showed innocent sex and all other human activity, inextricably entwined, true innocence, ashamed of nothing. Life snapped back into full motion, as Bridie strode through the door in an unhurried motion, then closed it behind her.She swept past her son, to her bedroom, returning with some linens, that looked like a shift. He waited for a scolding. She put her hand on his shoulder and kissed his ear. "My Lieutenant is growing up," she whispered and went through to the sprigging room. Somebody had thrown a sheet over Sharon.

Within weeks, Bridie's three dresses were in constant demand. It was said, according to Diddymus, that young girls were embracing their nuptials early in their eagerness for a chance to wear a "Thimble Dress."

Chapter 6

In a place where God was dead or, at least, asleep, the god of war began to shake himself awake and roar his thunder, while the devil made more room in hell. Autumn of 1794 was in its last month, summer had not skipped her turn. Bridie loved Autumn, that there was a full moon every night, when all distant hills came into sight and the constellations above them. The Summer had left her bounty in the new plots and the residents began to think that maybe there was a God for them, or something like Him.

Word had been about that Captain St. Ledger had been unwell, shortage of breath and tiredness had kept him in his bed, and, it seemed there was a tincture of muffled celebration among the many who would wish him, no breath at all. But to "keep him sweet," the woman of Thimble Hall would send him a selection of cornmeal bread, offering wishes for his recovery.

How severe his distempers were, she never knew, but on an early November day, his carriage appeared at her door, complete with his outriders. He had tapped on the door of the carriage to halt on seeing John Kelly, hands on his hips, inside the ditch of The Meadow, where it bordered the lane. Hostility was there in the carriage like exploding gunpowder. St.Ledger threw an eye that was congenitally and eternally hostile over the activities in the Meadow, then tapped again and the horses pulled up hill to Thimble.

He looked paler, but otherwise seemed to be his pristine self, his very exclusive self. On two occasions, when he would send her his appreciation of the wholesome breads, which "outdid my physician," he had invited her to his house for luncheon, but she had refused.

"I see much activity, Madam, since my last visit." He remained in the doorway, casting a long shadow.

She ignored the remark. "I hope you have recovered, Captain, we are sorry to hear of your illness."

The Captain's fortunes were being rifled by the charity of this little woman on the outskirts of town. The gombeenman, to borrow John Kelly's pseudonym, had developed an economy built partly on the processing of agricultural produce from his vast acreage. Between Mary Street and the Island Road, his Malt Houses and Corn Stores and vegetable markets had become a nice profitable conglomerate, where he skinned the peasants and did it again and again. They were coming now to the little market in The Meadow, where a penny went twice as far as before and where the smell of a tiny profit was sweet and clean.

The mood and atmosphere in the kitchen seemed to be building up to some kind of war, it's pulse suspended in the air. Suddenly he seemed distracted and it was evident he wasn't going to stay, he had seen enough. It would be hard to ascertain exactly, which overt act over the past two years produced the exact reason for the hostilities; her constant snub at his early advances, his early snide remarks about her relationship with Rockingham, her success in all her endeavours, something he found difficult to tolerate in a woman, the slow rape of his industry or now, perhaps, a kind of jealousy at his finding the rabble rebel, John Kelly in her employ, or a madding combination of everything.

"There's a man in your employ, Madam, that you would do well to think again about continuing with a relationship that could cause you and your family, much grief. "And who might that be, Sir," she asked nonchalantly, "for outside of Mr. Driscoll, no other man is employed here."

"That one." , he spat, pointing his crop toward the Meadow.

"Captain", she said easily, like calming a cantankerous little boy. "Mr. Kelly is not in my employ, the work he is doing for my......neighbours, is strictly voluntary. I find nothing but goodness in the man."

And then, like times previously, this ungracious lout, showed his weakness, exposing his rudeness as an imitation of strength, and G. wanted to kill him there and then.

"And I wonder, Madam, do you pay him in the same coin as you have been paying Lord Rockingham?"

On previous visits, Hannah had brought the bread variety to the carriage drover. She had been nearby when the insult was hurled without mercy, tears stinging the old eyes, as he took the wrapped breads.

"He should eat needles, indeed, Mam,"she thought.

G. put his arm around his mother's shoulders that were tight with emotion. "I'm beginning to be afraid of him," she whispered.

Henry began to spend part of his weekends at John Kelly's home, where the big man lived with his mother, in a cottage on the slope of the mountain. It was a poor household. In a field behind the house, youths came on Sunday afternoons to play the hurling game and to drill with long sticks in war games. Strong youngsters would often object to being the enemy, when John Kelly would bind a red ribbon about their unwilling waists, and warn them to be "good little Englishmen, now, and we might let ye live for a while longer."

Time became a test of the pending troubles. The days came and

55

went like veiled figures at the door, healing grief's and quarrels, but soon became a merciless thing.

Bridie took to going, with Hannah, to town more often than before and there appeared, little bottles of medicine on her dressing table, with the name of a doctor, Doctor Mac Cabe, written on the label below a word hard to read, "laudanum". G. would see Driscoll studying her again. On a day after a night's drinking at Lousy Head's whisky house on Trasna Bridge, his observations would become more a scrutiny, focusing on her ailment, whatever it was, which he saw without any knowledge.

Bridie Rose got tired more easily and G. would find her, sitting outside on her stone chair, at night, looking at the skies, where the sanctuary of the stars peeked over the dark mass of Blackstairs. "See how they look down on us, Georgie, and how insignificant they make us look."

She moved closer to him, sharing her shawl, and he felt, for the first time, a kind of frailty in her, that her body was losing it's vitality and strength, that her boys, forever took for granted. He got the clinical smell of the medicine from her breath.

He said, "Mr. Driscoll told me, yesterday, to look after you, why did he say that?"

"Diddymus talks too much, G." She gave him that empty smile, that up until now, was never a stamp of her perfect features. "I think he fancies me, she smiled again, "anyway, he drinks too much."

"All men fancy you, Mother." He said taking her hand.

In the still night, the smell of eucalyptus rose from the tall trees down in the low fields. Smoke rose contentedly from the huts in The Meadow. As the moon rose further, the rocks high above were jagged silhouetted stag horns against the inky sky. Bridie moved to the house

"Hen asked me today, why you named us as you did, he said he would have liked to be named, John, like John Kelly."

"You tell him, I could have chosen a name like Tristan, or Theobold, or some other title. I think John Kelly is becoming too much of an influence on him."

Then she turned before going in. "Speaking of your brother, you will take care of him, won't you, always look after him?"

**

St. Ledger came to Thimble ,just one more time. Bridie's sickness came on horseback. The weekly trips to Doctor Mac Cabe became too much for her, so the good doctor came to Thimble with his medicines, which consisted of ether, for her pain. She insisted his fee should be ready for him, something he seldom saw among the poor, his payments mostly consisting of a few eggs, a small chicken or just a prayer for his kindness.

He told Georgie, her life was ending, a life that existed for her boys, only. "A physician can only parry the scythe of death, Mr. Tansey, " but he has no power over the hourglass."

G. had never been called "Mister" before and suddenly felt the weight of her impending death get heavier on his shoulders. She began to shed her leaves like a tree. He saw her beauty leave him and his brother, to whom it forever offered shade, comfort and love.

She would spend just an hour in the sprigging room with the ladies, but spend most of her time in bed. Hannah, would allow just one lady in turn, help her in the nursing in her bright comfortable bedroom. They would come from there, in tears. Hannah left the room on a day that G. felt the end was near, her sheets had blood stains on them. Hen would lie with her, his delicate hand clasped in hers, seeming to give her comfort.

It was an inhuman time. Three quarters of the county of Wexford lived, pitifully, in that time. Pauperism was rampant in the streets, where children and mothers were barefoot and often hungry.

Under the watchful eye of a government and a landlord system, debased by the stupid intolerance of the English priesthood, the country was marked by poverty and the poison of raw whiskey. On the weeks before Bridie died, a hopeless period of anger and frustration absorbed all that was left of G's. spirits and energy, that she should be taken from him, when all her efforts of the past few years were now coming to fruition. Diddymus hardly left the Thimble house, going over and over again, work that had been already done. Barefoot urchins, scraps of humanity would appear at the door with firewood, eggs, a rabbit, and the colours of the mountain crept slowly into the house, little girl children with bunches of heather, wild rock daisies, cocksfoot and cranberry and pimpernel and hogweed from the bogs.

**

At school, Rev. Careysworth gave fifteen minutes of his time, to reading to his students, The Times, a further indoctrination of young minds as to the benefit of being British, the only true religion in a country of two nations

Two weeks before Bridie died in early spring, he read for them of a place called Kentucky, which had become the 15th. State in the United

States of America. According to Diddymus, Kentucky was a place where no English were allowed to live, and suddenly G. wanted to be there, and for days Henry would roll the name around on his tongue; "Kentucky, Kentucky". G. promised him that one day, they would go to Kentucky.

Captain St. Ledger was at his most tyrannical. All cordiality gone now, this woman was out to, if not destroy him, certainly to destroy his reputation in the commercial life of Enniscorthy, to insult him and embarrass him. His arrival began the stirring of events, of a crisis coming to a head.

Waiting for Bridie's death, John Kelly would be found in early morning, sitting outside the door and would spend time with Diddymus, sitting in the copse; two minds, vacant and distressed.

St. Ledger's carriage drew up to the door in a sweep of importance, business like holding his crop. He breezed through the door, but not before throwing a sceptic look in Kelly's direction.

Looking for "Madam", his tone as usual authoritative. G. told him she was ill. He seemed disappointed, that the confrontation for which he had been prepared, would not now take place. It drove him onto more scornful oratory.

"How convenient, Sir", he spat, "then convey to Madam...."

G. cut him off, his voice shaking in passion and fearfulness. "My mother is dying, Sir", G. blurted and Hannah sobbed at the finality in the boy's voice, as she prepared St. Ledger's hamper. There was a purpose to the old woman's movements today, and today, above any other day, the hamper would be presented.

Obviously taken aback, the proctor took a minute to immerse himself in the revelation and somewhere in his fetid mind, he felt fortune creeping to his side.

"Then I will talk to you, Sir," he barked, concealing any feelings of sympathy, behind a facade of urgency and business. Kelly had heard the beginnings of controversy and came and set his huge frame outside the door."I have to tell you, Sir, that Lord Rockingham has died in London. As you and certainly, your mother will know, my uncle, Lord Donneraile had an option on the remaining lands, an option which we have taken up through his estate office in Whitehall. And before you might think of matters of His Lordship's will and testament, your mother is not mentioned in any documents, so that it prompts me again to wonder at the purpose of his great generosity, or his reason to hide his association with her. I have returned from London, just this week, on behalf of my uncle's business and I have to tell you, the property you now sit on, is now in my authority." He placed a signed parchment on the table, this house and all its land, including that slum you have built, is in my authority." Thimble and Bridie's garden and the entire Meadow was outlined in red like a blood stain, duly stamped and sealed

.

"All the grand formalities, look right, whatever about the moralities." Said G., his heart thumping.

"There's morality in everything, young man," said St Ledger, "all one has to do is find it."

G. raised his voice in a kind of desperation. "I will have this document examined....if my mother could...."

He matched the boy's voice. "Your mother set out to do me some damage, until the good Lord sought to teach her the ill or her ways, manifested here now in that room." He came closer to the youth, so the youth he could smell his foul breath. "If your mother were here, believe me, the whole lot of you would be out on the road now. You don't own a blade of grass, not a stone of this mountain, but I will be charitable and leave you here until...." he looked at the bedroom door, "until.. after."

He looked at Kelly, through the door. "And you, Sir." He pointed to the Meadow. " You will clear that of its vermin, and see to it that the boundary fence is replaced and that you level the ground as you found it."

At the door of his carriage, he beckoned G. to approach. "I have to tell you that your mother hijacked, our schools and our churches, while all the time, being a papist. As proctor, I have to tell you that there will be no burial on sanctified Protestant ground, such contamination, I will not allow, so spare yourself the ignominy of rejection at the gates. He looked again at the giant. "See that you carry out my demands, Kelly."

John took off his soft cap and wrung it in an effort to resemble modesty and subjugation. "I will, Sir, that I will, Your Honour."

G .deadened himself against the hurt, which was staggering, a wound that would be forever, a scar. He wanted to ask John Kelly to kill him there and then, the big man standing with his back to the cottage wall, his blue eyes were as knives, devouring the tyrant, his revenge would call for punishment at another time. Hannah, her ample rump on the little sill of the kitchen window, swayed to and fro in her terrible contempt.

When he had gone, Hen had a question for Kelly. "You called him your honour, John Kelly." Did his hero have a chink in his armour?

He put his big hand on the boy's head, his voice, suddenly wrathful, as he watched the carriage wind its way onto the main road. "Believe me, he will pay for today's little bit of business, and we won't wait until judgement day either. Now, about this "your honour", thing, Hen, you see, fellas like that give themselves credit for more brains than the good Lord ever gave them, fellas in love with themselves and their importance in the world, that he won't have many rivals for that love. Now, when we call them Brits "Your Honour", they're put into a confusion as to whether we praise them and give them due respects for being British and being our superiors, or whether we are seeing through the thick pigs that they are. But when we call them "Your Honour from England", that is to give them their true title to their ignorance. Well, Hen, my friend, that confuses them entirely. But heed me when I tell you, when you title them, do it with your head downcast, that makes them feel," he reached for a suitable description, "like Godlike. Do not ever eyeball him, Hen, the only time you eyeball an Englishman is when you kill him, now remember that."

St ledger, within two days, had closed off all commonage, just as his uncle, Lord Doneraile had done in Munster, a few years before in what was known as the Doneraile Conspiracy, whereby he built ditches and barriers around commonage, used by the cottiers and poor farmers for grazing and crop making. This gave birth to a secret oath bound society among the poor, their purpose was to plague the rich landlords. They were known as The Whiteboys, who wore white shirts as a uniform and out of which was born Irelands first army in five hundred years, when they changed their name to The Defenders.

But when Bridie was drawing her last, there was no such army in Wexford to protect her and within two days the destruction of the cottages began, not just in the meadow, but along the hillside toward the town. The Rev, Cope of Camolin, himself a magistrate and a friend of St. Ledger, sent reserves in red uniforms to control any objection that might occur among the peasantry.

Bridie Rose Tansey died in the first hour of spring. Holding G.'s hand, vicelike, concerned that it was St. Ledger's voice she was hearing, in and out of consciousness. G. assured her he had come to enquire of her health and if he could be of service. She made him promise he would do all in his power to keep his friendship, for both her boys, sakes. Poor mother, even then she was full of hope for her boys.

In the whispering crowded sprigging room, the ladies had laid her out in her rough box, it's crudity hidden in white linen and crochet shawls in an embroidered waterfall of lace. Diddymus had lovingly made her casket, outside in the shed, honing and shaping with his rough tools, like the work was liberating his soul.

"The box is pure," he whispered to Hen. "No nails to hold it together, but fine hidden dowels, a pure box, will hold well for her journey to heaven."

"Do you think mother will go to heaven, Mr. Driscoll?" the child asked.

The old man thought for a while, red faced, short of breath. Diddymus had spent many days in the whiskey house at Trasna, since Bridie took ill. "Well, she made them prayer clothes for Protestant and Catholic clergy alike, if one doesn't get her in, well the other will. Now God never told which one He likes the most, but sure I suppose, the Protestant is in it."

Many came to see the "kind lady" in her coffin, some for a customary weep, some to gape and eat. Hannah had employed two professional keeners, to strengthen the grief, with suitable wails and groans and double sets of tears.

John Kelly, Driscoll and the two boys buried Bridie in her copse, near the stone seat, with her head against the Hew, facing east, so she could see the sunrise for ever, according to Driscoll.

In his young years, George felt her loss, intensely. He felt the orb of injustice about to burst in his face, as he watched the cabins disappear one by one and he, himself would soon be evicted. Up until now, his childhood was a kingdom where nobody dies. He and Hen had been protected from the world that was Ireland.

For the destruction of Thimble, there was a magistrate present, as proper recording would be carried out in view of Lord Rockingham's influence in the place. A suitable austere pageant of importance, his voice croaked as he read the riot act. Kelly wondered where St. Ledger, was."In his counting house, no doubt," he whispered to G. A young officer, stiff-backed and confident, remained on his horse, while a dozen yeos stood half way to attention, and the navvy gang began their destruction of Bridie's palace.

"The two boys are orphans, Lieutenant Bookey", John Kelly, said, putting his hand on the horse's bridle. Lieutenant Bookey swung his crop, opening a gash across Kelly's face, opening a wound and a mood. Bookey became a rag doll, as John Kelly tore him from his mount, the huge body electric with passion and simply threw the unfortunate officer across the yard, where he rolled in a red and white ball, his scabbard and sword rattling a tattoo of indignity in the dust. Six of the redcoats restrained the rebel and before they dragged him away, Bookey, his hand shaking, tore the other cheek. "Captain St. Ledger is dead." he hissed. "You'll be dealing with me from now on, Kelly." Then he roared his instructions to begin and remounted his horse.

In his cocooned existence, there was so much George Tansey didn't understand, so many things he was ignorant of; the pig tax, the window tax, the riot act now having been read out, that from today, it was forbidden, under pain of hanging or transportation, that six people or more should assemble together in discussion, as a protection of the ascendancy. Why did mother have to die and indeed, Lord Rockingham, and why did Mr. Bundy in Dublin, not keep her up to scratch, and did he know that Hannah could have been responsible for St. Ledger's death, with "broken needles," in a way that mother described.

The ladies had left in fear, keening at the door before tearing themselves away, on the roads now with their families, oblivious to their future. Hannah remained, crying into her shawl, until she heard St. Ledger was dead. G. had seen her put a hand to her mouth, in surprise at the announcement. Henry, refused to leave the copse, in the mad turmoil, all his ailments ran into one; fear.

The Yeomanry they had become to know, in their sluggish minds and crude manners were rampant in their destruction, like young ones, allowed by a dysfunctional parent to break all the delph of the dresser. The machine, the killer of houses and homes, was constructed of a great pole, once a proud towering oak, inserted through the front window and if there was not a similar ope in the rear wall, one was made, so the unfortunate dwelling was skewered, front and back. Four fine Shires, gentle giants with too much power, patience and restraint, were shackled, two to each end of the pole and made to pull. Breaking wind, the horses made the ropes taut, then Thimble Hall groaned in protest, as the roof timbers tore and splintered. Then the slap of whips on flanks and rumps and Bridie's castle tumbled, the whole front of the building, in a contorted grin. Rocks, mortar and timber scattered in a patchwork to become fodder for the new Blackstairs inhabitants.

Hen cowered behind Bridie's seat, as his brother tried to gather the pots and utensils that were her joy. The cob horse in the shed became panicky and he made to free her and pull her to the cart, most of the finished linens had been taken to the Dublin coach two days before, by Diddymus, who now lumbered up the lane, protesting feebly. Driscoll was a well known character, to Lieutenant Bookey and his yeos, the old man having spent many a night as guest of His Majesty, incarcerated in the barracks in Carnew and Enniscorthy. His protests were quelled under a barrage of abuse from the uniforms, laughing and jibing at his familiar undertakings, to which they had become accustomed. He stank of whisky, his sodden eyes full of loss and misery. Like the peasants who, in the past few days, gave up with such grace and acceptance, Driscoll's weakness was to a great extent, biological, the condition of his culture. There was no battle here for him, no battle for John Kelly and none for the two bereft orphans. The evacuation from the mountain was total. Hundreds were suddenly homeless. Down on the road, they walked with head down, going in different and all directions, faces of adults and children, old and vulnerable, like church gargoyles and nobody looked back. Experience taught them there would be more ahead, not like slaves. Slaves can walk to their next dinner, the Irish, free can walk anywhere and crowd the roads with vagrants. Many were walking now toward the mines at Castlecomer, Rossmore and Arigna, where, if they got work, they got dinner. Over two hundred cabins had been destroyed, leaving an abattoir, entrails of transient shelters, without permanence, scattered on the heather and wild flowers, once pathetic castles, fit for man and animal, without hope. Hope in Ireland was a foul and deceitful thing. These weeping women and hard eyed men would now be everywhere but at home, like a million more in every county in Ireland.

The shed was cold, where they were allowed to stay for one more night. The cob horse was confused at having to share her stable, even more upset at Hen's coughing, which in the past week, had congested his breathing, mucus that had hardly touched him in the past year.

In the dark, Driscoll appeared, tired and older, a cold moon at his back. He was almost out of breath, leaning against the door pillar. He told them to pack and get out. Word is out that Captain St. Ledger had been poisoned, right here by the "Tansey Woman."

"But mother is dead," argued Hen.

"'Twas Hannah that did it", whispered Diddymus . "I broke the needles for her into tiny pieces and we baked them with the captain's bread. They said he died of a heart attack, which he did, but Angus, his driver found the half eaten bread and decided bread shouldn't be wasted, which it shouldn't, and when poor Angus coughed and squealed and heaved himself about the kitchen, and the captain laid out above in the parlour, they found the broken needles in his vomit."

"Is Angus dead too, Mr. Driscoll?", asked Hen.

"No son," he gave them a toothy grin, "but they found lots of needles in St. Ledger, when they opened his owl gullet."

The intimacy of the revelation found it's mark in all three of them, and there, in the midst of their loss and torment, the excess of their sorrow found it's mirth. They said goodbye to mother, Hen digging his hand into the earth above her, trying to touch her one last time. They left the horse with Diddimus, it would be recognised easily and the boys set off for Enniscorthy to join the dispossessed.

Part of the group that had left the mountain the day before, had rested under the Cotton Tree near the bridge in the centre of town. They looked for Hannah to try to find some sense in this unfolding puzzle. Like paupers on show, it came back to G., their days in St. Stephen's Green. They tried to melt into the group of about one hundred. Some had thrown them a disinterested recognition, most ignored them, sullen faced and hungry, struck dumb by the regular recycling of their adversity.

In the early morning, there was a business hum about the town. The Market Square was preparing for the Saturday fair. Livestock, tethered to railings chewed on their cud, stall owners, setting up outside the Market House, with its strategic location at the convergence of five streets. It was common knowledge that St. Ledger was dead. There seemed to be a levity to their labours, as if sensing the prospect of a distant good. After a while The Society Of Friends came and set up a kitchen to the side of the bridge and soup and bread was handed out to pathetic hands. Hen thought they might see Mr. John, their benefactor of St. Stephen's Green. Paupery had returned to the Tanseys.

The redcoats suddenly appeared, coming up Castle Street. Usually, a loafing disgruntled mob, many heads, few brains. This morning, there was a bristle to their step, no loafing today, things to do. Two urchins from the house in Killane were loose, the house where Captain St. Ledger met his drop. Five pounds awaited the one to bring them before a magistrate. Barefoot ruffians in rags, formed a mob of their own behind the soldiers, laughing and making faces like dancing dogs. Startled, G. saw Diddymus and the horse and trap coming past the Duffry Gate. Within ten minutes, his brother Hen and the old man were to seal their fate.

Driscoll pulled in behind the huge tree, beckoning on the boys to climb aboard. Hen ran to meet him and the prancing urchins recognised the frail asthmatic frame, the Protestant blonde haired boy who snubbed them on his way to school. Thomas Driscoll, a well recognised character, a red faced lumbering drunk, usually the pawn of ridicule in the town, would have often be seen driving the youth. The soldiers moved in.

They spent the next two days and nights in a cold cell at the pleasure of King George. G. worried for his brother, who seemed to shrink further into himself like a frightened kitten, that became as a lion when a doctor tried to tend him. He would lose his breath in fits of passion until he became exhausted and then slept. In the mornings, the yellow light of dawn shone bravely through the little bared window, but did nothing to lighten the gloom.

After three days they were brought before a magistrate and accused of the wilful murder of Captain Lawrence St. Ledger.

G.'s anger and hurt exploded in the crowded courtroom and he cried out his objection, to be told to keep his peace, until a gentleman, suitably wigged and adorned, stood as representative of "those two boys." He told the court that he had been instructed by Sir George Palmer of Duhallow Park. The name sparked a small memory in G.'s head, that he was one of the two landlords to send much needed help to The Meadow.

Lord Doneraile had employed counsel, who charged that his nephew had been horribly murdered, in a manner that could only have come from a house of industry, where needles like these found in Captain St. Ledgers gullet, causing him heart failure, were the tools of that industry. There are only two residents of that house, and they stand here before the court.

Debate went back and forth, as to the ages of the accused and their ability to commit such a crime. However, nobody else was in the frame and their counsel, a Mr. Philpott-Curran established the fact that six women and the woman of the house, a Mrs. Tansey, who is since deceased, and a rough fellow, a sort of a handy man, all would have a motive, "as it seems," advised Mr. Philpott-Curran "would a few hundred more who occupy the lands of Lord Doneraile."

The assizes decreed that the youths should be held in incarceration until further investigation and an effort was to be made to interview the six ladies concerned and the so called handyman.

Hen was suitably sick, trumpeting a spoor of vomit over the dock's railing, onto the powdered wig of counsel for Lord Doneraile

Chapter 7

He would remember, forever, this time and it's dark spirits. G. always had a retentive memory, which can be a good thing, but could sometimes, be damning in his ability to forget. Spring had come around again and the protective garment that Bridie had wrapped her boys in, was quickly torn away, and they were to witness, for the first time, the true meaning of injustice and villainy, committed in the name of the ascendancy.

In the previous century, after the great battle of Kinsale, poor King James The Second of England, was left with thirty thousand prisoners, so he decided to sell the Irish, as slaves to planters and settlers in his New World colonies, from the great Amazon River in South America, to the silver mines in Mexico, to Hudson Valley, even to Markesan in India. The disappearance of a few hundred or a few thousand Irish, now would not be a cause for concern or alarm, where that trade still existed and wandering urchins, especially orphans, were rich pickings for those traders.

Such an agent and trader, was Captain Oliver Wharton of a place called "The Richmond", a house of industry in Carlow. A dark grey mass of a building, Richmond was a jail, a house of care and an asylum, all rolled into one. Despite Mr. Philpot-Curran's efforts on their behalf, they were dispatched to Captain Wharton's asylum to await His Majesty's pleasure, while an obviously feeble effort would be made to hunt for the elusive six ladies, who by now were wandering the roads of any one of four or five counties.

G. looked for it to be as acceptable as Mr. Bundy's house in Dublin, but as Richmond opened its gates to receive them into a so called house of care, a place of rogues, thieves, insanities, self preservation quickly became paramount with him. There was no Bridie here to work her magic.

Here, his dreaming was haunted. At night, he would be quietly insane, where illusions became faithful interpreters of the daytime drudgery, a daily nightmare of the weed of slavery, to be abused and compelled, by violence, to suffer wrong. He could see all about him, the pleasures that shone in the faces of madness, and soon realised that less harm would come to him and his brother, in being mad among madmen, than in being sane all alone. Through a narrow crack, he allowed a sane eye to peer from inside his self-imposed lunacy. Not to be mad in Richmond was in fact another form of madness.

Captain Wharton's Richmond was a sprawling prison on the lands of Baron Donoughmore of Munster, handed down from the plantations by Elizabeth , Stuart and Cromwell, a Jacobite heritage. Wharton, a tithe proctor and keeper of the facility, oversaw this house of correction on whom the law cannot be enforced. He was the law's enforcer in South Carlow. Wharton, had become a good and faithful servant to the establishment and was well rewarded for that. He had his own yeomanry, mostly left over's from the American wars, who served their captain with a mercenary zeal. They cleared the roads and ditches of the rabble peasantry, and it was from here that Wharton spun his web of slavery, a constant stream of bondage, mainly young men and women, heading for Wexford and deportation.

The boys broke stones in the heat of the day, in a quarry near Brown's Hill, where ancient Dolmens, the altars of Irish ancestors were reduced to chippings to build roads that went, mostly, nowhere.

The work kept them exhausted, weariness to seduce the body, better than any drug. In a corner cot, which they shared at night, they would share their malady, batten down and confide and plot the downfall of the horrid captain and Hen said he wished Hannah and Diddymus were there with more needles.

At roll call in the great yard, the praises of King George, of England and Ireland would be expounded before the new day, with the raising of the red standard. In his child's bewilderment, Bridie Rose Tansey's baby, observing men in red menacing uniforms, rifles at the ready, pummelling the rough flag stones beneath that flag, calling out their loyalty to someone who lived far away, before a few hundred glassy eyed, drooling jawed unfortunates, where male and female were hardly distinguishable, through that wily crack of sanity, how he would have thought the whole world, full of simpletons, that you don't need to seek madmen in madhouses, they're roaming free with wigs and guns.

And sure, wasn't King George himself, mad as a brush, Diddymus told him once. And what an object of dread it would be to his young mind, that on a day when "recruits" were being singled out to be pampered and uniformed for the so called Regent Corps, that in dread of being chosen, he would steel himself to control, once again, the painful menses that savaged the excretory tract of his frail body. To soil himself today, as happened before, would result in a dousing in freezing salt water, a colonic irrigation of immense physical intrusion and a special diet for a week to tighten his bowls.

Nor would Hen have known that far away, the King of England was being attended by six physicians with a similar diet, each offering his own opinion on the size, smell and quality of His Majesty's excreta, when the royal shit would give up the secret of his dementia.

The new recruits for The Regent Corps, so named for The Prince Of Wales, sometime Regent in Ireland, when his father's reason would fly, these recruits would require little or no training in military art. You were required to stand up straight and to walk with little or no difficulty. Accuracy in firing a weapon, though preferable, was not a fundamental requisite.

There were the beginnings of Nationalist unrest in the northern colonized counties. Boys and young men were being dragged from institutions like Richmond and made soldiers of the British Army. Swanky uniforms, warm boots and guns were issued as thousands of naive plebeian have-nots and half wits were marched to the nearest barracks or garrison for a hot meal, swear an oath to the king and pledge to kill the scouring horde that threatened to unseat him in Ireland. Villains and imbeciles, the pathetic members of the scavenger class, the untouchables of Ireland's society were given a shilling and an hour of glory at the front line of some marching column, to take the first onslaught from their brothers, first to die for king and country.

The finger of specify had not yet pointed at them. Perhaps it was because Henry was, as yet only eleven years old and looked even younger, small of frame, with the delicacy of a girl. Wharton, a brute with an immobile and merciless face, would study the child and Hen would cower under his scrutiny. G. had been unable to hide his deep hatred from the gluttonous captain, who found a sort of lust in his recognition of it. So much worse a reprobate than the late St. Ledger, G. hated something in this Englishman that was part of himself and it was as if both of them were prepared to set feelings aside for a while, to be nurtured and fed, but G. knew he was sowing thorns, often allowing his shield of dementia to slip.

Wharton took to satisfying his venereal delights in the ranks of the inmates. A boy or a girl, it didn't matter, would be chosen at a whim, when he would be drunk in the night and G. knew it would be only a matter of time before Hen was chosen. At roll call in the cold mornings, G. would prompt his brother to massive wheezing and coughing fits, but the pendulum soon swung in their direction, when the captain took a sick boy into his bed, his delicacy only heightened the challenge.

It was a long time afterwards that Hen was able to bring himself to talk of the matter, and even then it was relayed in a hesitant and whispered stringing of words, an oblique hint in which he would try to tell all. After that night, Henry was never the same. He became quick to temper, with a sharp tongue, like an edged tool, that could get them into trouble. His torment began on that night, his invaded fragile body speared helplessly under the huge scarred demonically male body. G.

knew his brother would suffer a life imprisonment unless they were able to get out of Richmond. Hen did have one weapon, however; his ability to throw up his insides at the drop of a hat. When he was sent for again, he vomited all over the captains bed, before he took his pleasure and Wharton's ranting could be heard echoing through the dark corridors.

It was a week after Hen's ordeal, that the chance presented itself, a chance to escape. His body was healing, his mind a cesspool of hatred and torment.

On a morning in early June, Wharton recruited twelve youths for The Regent Corps and three dozen were called for the day's work in the quarries of Brown's Hill. Captain Wharton would ride out on some days to inspect the work, as he did on that day. A dozen lazed about in the languid early simmer as the chain gang worked on the useless and irrational slave wheel. The yeomen made a business like effort at Wharton's arrival, the magnificent grey stallion, the pride of his stable, stomped and moved about, restless and anxious to run, a thoroughbred brute. A number of the inmates were hunched together for a few minutes and for a precious few minutes were unsupervised, as the soldiers stood in line to answer Wharton's grunting demands and requests for progress. G.'s weapon was a fine piece of ancient dolman, fitted into his hand, it's sharp edges, a comforting assurance. He prayed to the god of horses to forgive him. The missile aimed at the enormous flank of the horse, and found it's mark. But Hen, in tandem, had seen his brother's intent. A small sharp flint stone winged from his delicate fist, in an effort, much more productive than that of his brother. The horse's fetlock splintered where sheer bone, sinus and muscle holds the animal upright. The stallion, wide eyed and raging, roared like a human and suddenly Captain Wharton was being dragged through broken stones, his leg strapped to the stirrup.

Simpletons jumped up and down, eyes wide like the stallion's. While the yeos tried frantically to wave the horse down, he continued to bolt downhill, over boulders and through thicket, to come to rest in a pool of pale water.

Yeomen covered the workers with heavy rifles, looking confused, but any one of them could have spooked the horse. G. whispered to Hen to keep his head down. He was blushing furiously in his guilt as the heat of his blood rose into his usually pale face. G. noticed a sergeant taking a special interest in him, with a questioning observation. He was the one who came for Hen on that awful night of torment.

Captain Wharton did not die, but would be in the infirmary for quite some time. The report through the mad throng was that Captain

Wharton was being measured for a new skin.

G. was taken aside on the following morning by the sergeant. A tall man, mature in age, with a local accent and, agreeable looking for a yeoman sergeant, told him he knew they had spooked the stallion, and one or two more would testify to the fact, as soon as the captain was well enough.

"I've put your names now forward for transportation," he said and saw the youth's surprise, stupefaction assailing him.

"You cannot stay in Ireland," he insisted. "You'll definitely hang", and throwing an eye toward Hen, "who'll take care of him? You'll hang," he insisted, "or at least you will be made a soldier of the Regent, so you will die anyway."

He hesitated further. "My name is Kelly, John Kelly's older brother. Your mother was good to him, over in Killane, he has been asking me to look out for you."

Here was the Irish tragedy, the varying offensive, that pitted brother against brother. This man, wearing the king's uniform, and would have taken an oath to protect him with his life, while John Kelly was out there, somewhere, with just one ambition, to put an end to that king and all belonging to him. Both men, spawned here and from birth, finding life's odds stacked against them, survival, a daily challenge, crime everywhere. A man like Sergeant Kelly, perhaps with a warm cottage and a family, for a man like him, there were no alternatives, for a man like Sergeant Kelly, alternatives grew on imaginary trees.

Chapter 8

The medieval town of Wexford had, for centuries, been the gateway to Europe. Boasting a picturesque and safe harbour, it was the conduit through which passed ninety per cent of the merchandise which filtered daily into the town from the counties of Wicklow, Carlow, Kilkenny, Laois, Most of Tipperary and west Waterford and Wexford itself.

Nestling in the sunny heel of Ireland, the town spread itself along the western side of The Slaney inlet, in a line of cobbled stoned quays and jetties, about ten miles inside the Hook Of Rosslare and the open sea and two day's journey from England. Green lush pastures spread outward from the town, north to Arklow and the highlands of Wicklow, north east to The Blackstairs Mountains and then westward in a great green blanket to the harbour of Waterford and the great delta of New Ross. This golden triangle, together with The Golden Vale Of Munster, stretching through Limerick, Tipperary, Cork and east Kerry, Galway, Roscommon and Longford, because of the gentle climate in the turning of the seasons, yielded a superb harvest, in some areas, a double harvest, of enough corn, butter, pork and beef to feed the entire British army, her beggars, her jails, even her royalty and their horses.

**

A slightly built man, with almost feminine features stood on the deck of the packet "Vixen". The caressing circuits of the off shore breeze were heavy with the scents of bog earth, wild grain and tall grasses, and he drank in every part and tag of it, stroking his senses, cleansing them of the dust and heat of Paris and the cloistered damp conditions of the crowded ship.

Wexford harbour was alive with activity. Paul Quay could barely accommodated the ship and only a super feat of navigational wizardry allowed her to slip gently past the points of Raven and Rosslare, between a horde of sloops and frigates that choked the narrow waterways of the inner harbour.

Before he disembarked, he caught sight of the tall figure of his friend, dodging and darting through the busy quayside, resplendent in unaccustomed civvies, tanned and welcoming. The passenger had not yet acclimatised himself to seeing Thomas out of uniform, now that the retired officer had taken up the very respectable position as magistrate of Dungannon. It had been said in the authoritative circles of Dublin's levelling clique, that the handsome Corkman and practising Anglican had been so honoured, in order to take him out of the corrupt communications and manners of the man on "Vixen" and the troublesome fledgling republic movement, The United Irishmen.

The place was a ferment. G. watched through the dust of the late June afternoon, the huge ship settle against the pier, below the Stonebridge jail, light air bubbles swirling in her wake, to fall away beneath the massive black stern; bubbles of illusion, fading away and leaving no trace, gone, gone away. The scene matched his torment, that by the end of the day, there would be nothing of himself and Hen, to say they ever existed, save for a scrawl by an ignorant hand across a page of a ship's manifest to say that George and Henry Tansey and a hundred other prisoners, enemies of the king, were accepted on board a prison ship in the year 1794 to be transported to a place called Jamaica, there to live and work forever at the pleasure of his Most Gracious Majesty, King George The Third, scraps of Irish humanity, to be sold into the British slave trade.

Through the heavy air, thick and oppressive, the scene was an illusion, a visual fallacy , like a painted backdrop in the heavy afternoon, all motion seemed arrested and framed in a powdery veil. Many of the prisoners, strapped to the rusting railings of the Stonebridge, were asleep, a sleep of resignation. The tethers were strips of cow hide, tied to a heavy chain which was padlocked to the rails. The hide, tightened in the hot sun and cut at the wrists until they would slacken again when the jailer would douse them with water, cool and welcome.

Even the rats were free in Wexford, G. thought. His fears, especially for Hen were sharp sighted, so acute now that he could hear the rats scurrying about under the great timbers of the quayside. He could picture them, button noses, curious creatures, sniffing and finding their way into the holds of ships, to be transported like Hen and he, anonymous tingummy bobs, caught in the net of life, they to go to labour, the rats to spread their disease in the new land.

G. moved in the line, trying to find some ease, the curve of his back ached in protest and again, the ligature chewed at his wrists. He spoke to her in his half dream, that somehow her boys had come to this when her protection was taken from them, and yet he felt her nearness. She had said to him once that destiny lies half inside you and half outside, that it was like a chain, only one link of that chain can be handled at one time, and he wondered if she was feeding him that chain now. "The rats are free, Mother, 'tis not a sin to escape.".

Since she died, the axle of evil on which they spun was framed to some perfection, as to render it impossible to avoid, but in so many endeavours to break free the power of whatever character was left within him, seemed to weave itself within her shadow, working it's solitary way through a thousand obstacles. He felt her presence now in the heat haze, no death, but her beauty, her very breath at his ear, never quenched against his own will. The tissue of Bridie Tansey's life, she wore with colours all her own, even the beauty of her sayings when she would string her words of comfort and encouragement on a thread to make everything seem alright

Hen was in repose, like he was in a calm interchange with her, G. believed, his eyes closed tightly against the day. His face bore a half smile, but G. moved against him, stunning him out of his vapour.

The slow moving inhabitants of Wexford town hardly gave the string of urchins a second glance, a throng of inattention, in their ignorance and indifference. Pork, cattle,corn,whiskey,butter, humans, the scene was a daily one, all for export. A young one would cry out, echoed by another and another, that in some kindly face there might be salvation.

The six yeos sweated in their coarse kit, exhausted as their charges, after a tiring journey from Carlow in lumbering trundles, over roads, unyielding and unsympathetic. Impatient to rid themselves of the troublesome curs in their charge, the alehouses of Wexford town beckoned, the best of their miserable lives, but intoxication, tempers hot and short in anticipation. Hen whimpered and tried to push nearer his brother. Being close to him would ease his convulsions, and maybe he would stop shaking and stop crying and maybe he wouldn't shit again or get sick up and upset the guards, and maybe the same guards would leave him alone and maybe they might try to kill the redcoats, like they did, Captain Wharton and he churned inside, remembering that piece of his existence, that in his child's mind, was the devil's design, and maybe, compared to Richmond, the prison ship might not be too bad after all. Maybe they would go to Kentucky .

G. cupped the small frame in his own, but there was little slack to the chain. They both felt the comfort in the closeness. They closed their eyes, shuttering out the world, the killing of the yoes, put on hold for a while, they swayed in a rocking swaying motion of sibling intimacy. For a time, G. must have slept. In semi consciousness, veiled figures, sent from a distant friendly communion passed by. He reached for the gifts they offered, but they passed on and were lost to him. In his stupor, he tried to call them back.

Suddenly, he jerked himself standing. Somebody was standing over him. Grey eyes, still and vital, were dogged in their observation of him, but G. saw no contempt in the pale angular face, but a sort of gentle curiosity, and he thought he was still in the gentle cloak of sleep and one of the communion had returned.

"You don't want to bother with that one, Sir," the Yeoman said, in a voice, thick and coarse. "That one broke away too often, he did, the troublesome little bugger."

The stranger ignored the limey, his voice, unhurried and authoritative. "It's alright, Corporal, my friend is a magistrate."

The stranger's companion, a tall man of very handsome appearance, was moving along the chain, handing out coins to some of the prisoners. Foul hands reached out for the offerings, straining their hands against the chain.

"They'll not be wanting a penny where they're going, Governor," the corporal croaked, "nor will they have a pocket to put it in, where they're going. Move on now, Sir, you and your friend." The man with the grey eyes maintained his observation of the two boys.

"Why are you bound, son?"

"Bound your honour?" G. remembered what Diddymus had instructed, about being respectful to the English gentlemen.

The man frowned, "please don't call me that." Then, that half smile again. G. strained himself upward.

"Bound for that prison ship, Sir," throwing a furtive eye toward the oppressive bulk, her huge stern turned to them in provocation, a crouching brute, waiting for the off.

"I mean, what is your crime?" he said

Hen squinted up through the piercing orb of the sun that gave the man a kind of halo, shrouding his face. There was more than a trace of pride in Hen's delivery.

"Georgie killed Captain Wharton," he piped.

"Hush, Hen," G. whispered, "you'll get us killed." Henry never knew it was his piece of flint that spooked the horse. G. had let him believe it was his stone that caused the damage, for the youngster's protection.

"Well he's not dead yet, Sir, but he will be soon," argued Hen.

In an Ireland that spawned incessant poor, the man with grey eyes suppressed an inclination to soften that smile further, that two urchins, bedraggled and hungry, should be subjects of a bureaucracy that had long developed into an autonomous spiritual life, where the public itself is it's enemy. Transported, not for the stealing of a loaf of bread, or a chicken from the pantry of some rapacious landlord or proctor, but for the killing, or the attempted killing of one of His Majesty's chauvinists, well......???

Passersby were now beginning to take an interest and the guards were becoming agitated, the corporal being short with the tall companion. "They'll be fed when I say so, Sir, and that's when they board."

The gentleman pressed closer to G.

"To kill a captain indeed," he said softly. Then he took something from inside his immaculate green waist coat. Half hidden by the satin frill of his shirt sleeve, he pressed it into G.'s cupped hands

"How old are you, Son?"

"I'm fifteen, Sir."

"They would have hanged you, if you were a year older".

"O no, Sir," piped Hen again, " Mother wouldn't let them."

"She was there?, your mother?"

"Oh no Sir." The gentleman looked perplexed. A vulgar Redcoat was at his side.

"You're doing a good job here, Corporal." He didn't look at the soldier, but held G. in that all encompassing observation, a pattern of expression that the youth was to encounter again in time to come.

"She sent you, Sir." G. allowed his voice careful inflection , conscious of the yeos.

"Thomas.....the call had a light lilt to it. The tall man caught up with his companion and the boys watched the two move toward the Bullring and the town centre, immaculate and at ease with their stations. A boy pulled a barrow of luggage over the cobblestones in their wake The heat wave was a veil of gossamer that slowly consumed them.

His hand shook as he parted two fingers, then three. Lying between his sweating palms, the little tobacco knife glinted bravely up at him, delicate butterfly wings in the mother-of-pearl handle. Like the butterflies dancing in the copse over Bridie's grave, the butterflies that count time, not in months or years, but in moments, the gentle creature that takes it's time.

The Redcoat sergeant fumed, a rough dog of a man, with thick guttural , fluent in foulness and complaining that nightfall was almost arrived and yet nobody had claimed the prisoners and they would all spend the night under the stars. The chained gang had been moved down to Cullimore's Quay, their miseries forgotten at the mention of food. They were made to sit near a mountain of casks and hide bales. Even now in the half light, the quays were busy, ships going and coming, forever dragging and draining the country of its life, forever satisfying the avarice of England and it's insatiable hunger for bounty.

The wool bales and the hides stank of the carcases that once inhabited them, but in the dark, G.'s senses awakened to an odour far beyond that of stale offal; the freedom that now was biting with keener fangs than any tethers, than any hunger.

Sour buttermilk and boxty bread was being devoured in a savage gluttony, while the new complement of guards from the ship were transferring documents with the disgruntled redcoats and when the little knife cut the cowhide strips on Hen's wrists and ankles, his lungs tightened inside his chest with emotion and with shaking hands, he cut at his brother's ties.

A lanky youth, who had been the subject of intense speculation to the gang ever since they left Carlow, and who twice tried to flee his captors, speculation because he refused to be involved in any kind of conversation, so that Hen maintained he was a dummy and christened him so, now, his mouth dripping milk like a dog with distemper, copped to their endeavours. He held out his wrists to G., his eyes wide and pleading. G. hesitated. The yeos were still arguing in the darkness. The prisoners paid little attention, food for now, more important than freedom.

G. cut at the dummy's straps.

Chapter 9

The young English journalist was possessed of a keen mind. Already successful as a freelance, he could spend his life in the filtered purity of fine offices, but his nostrils would always be filled with the smells that permeate life's struggles, the challenge and the controversy that chomps at the very heart of man's existence and the fight that will ensue, simply because man meets man, walking in different directions.

He had visited both Ireland and France on a couple of occasions, and got to study and compare the complementary ideals of those two countries and became fascinated in how the Directorate in France and the Society of the United Irishmen would secure for themselves, freedom and reform, through the doctrines of Liberty and Equality.

"County Wexford," he wrote for The Journal, "and its surrounding counties, occupy the most fertile lands in all of Europe, perhaps in all the world and ships are on a continuous mission of gluttonous extortion and abrogation, and one can only wonder at the ability of such a small nation to cope with the haemorrhage of the essence of her propagation, as a daily pageant of sail outward beyond The Hook Of Wexford and the little country turns her back to them in a kind of grief."

Military presence was everywhere. Scrutiny stood at every gangway, documentation, checked and re-checked. It was the climate they found themselves in. Two youngsters on the run from His Majesty's forces, would find welcome shelter in many a cottage or hovel in Wexford.

The Dummy, surprise and wonder, suddenly began talking. A surging monologue exploded from his gasping lungs as they crowded through the stinking hides. Wrathful, almost unintelligible, the lanky youth wheezed out his new found ambition; to go into Wexford Town and from there to Waterford City, find an old musket or a fine blunderbuss, join the rebels and become a good Irish scoundrel and a patriot and fight for Ireland.

In the darkness, they separated at the entrance to the Bullring, the rebel heading through the Ring, into the Corn Market and toward the centre of town. Trying to blend into the clutter of the Custom House Quay, they headed westward beyond the huge artillery park, where the king's army exercised by day and billeted by night. G. could see through the railings, guards on watch, but could find no indication that three runaways were yet reported missing. They stood for a while at the great timber mass that was the Wexford Bridge, to look back at the prison ship. The ghostly hulk had had her lamps lit on her decks and in the cabins. He could just make out, hunched forms on board, some more climbing the rope ladders from the jollies, soon to be incarcerated in her bowls, to live the rest of their miserable lives in a pipe dream, that someday they would return, the only means to give life to the whole misbegotten trough of madness. They could soon be missed when a headcount was taken.

The generosity of the poor to the poor was a splint to the festering sore of society. With a pocket full of barley and a swag full of cold potatoes each, a cottier's wife had wished them God's speed and blessing, their bed for the night, a shared straw mattress, with her three sons. Four daughters were discretely moved out to the stock house, no doubt, the good lady, having many good protections against temptation, believed he surest one being a handy distance. Hen was sick in the night, to the annoyance of the sons.

The town of Wexford began at the walls of the quays and stretched back through three parallel thoroughfares; Main Street, Back Street and Selskar, then beyond the medieval town wall to John Street. In between, lay an artery of smaller streets and laneways, constantly congested with carts and wagons on their way to the waiting ships. There were three artillery parks, one at either end of the town, the third in its pulsating heart, where the militia presence was a constant impediment to normality, a daily drudgery of a foreign presence, misunderstood and mistrusted. A combination of the double centre points of Wexford Town, was The Bullring and The Corn Market, two vibrating hearts joined by a narrow laneway, coming from Main Street and Back Street.

It was a cloudless Sunday morning. The early sun cast strands of warm light across the town, as it threatened another day of stone heat. The summer breezes, coming through Raven Point from the South Atlantic were a purification of the air and he got the wonderful scent of freedom in his nostrils. Hen wanted to know why his brother was smiling. G. was drawn back to the town and was relieved to find the dreaded ship had already sailed. He felt for her sorry cargo, some would die on the long voyage. He fondled the little knife in his pocket, stroking the curves of the butterfly crest, the kaleidoscopic little weaver that would, forever be the epitome of his liberty. On what would be a quiet Sunday morning, he sensed an air of expectancy, a stirring of mild commotion, even.

People began milling in and out of the houses and the shops on Selskar and Back and as the Catholic Churches emptied of their faithful, the artillery park off Slaney Street was busy with military manoeuvres and drilling. Crowds began to gather and loiter, an illegal occupation in Ireland, where no more than a couple of peasants were allowed to gather in conversation, or for any other purpose. The twin circles of Corn Market and Bullring were beginning to fill, anticipation abounding in the Sunday faces.

The poor of Wexford, seventy per cent of its inhabitants for whom hope and prospect was greater than possession, spend the best part their lives counting on what is to come, broke today with onerous subjection and defied authority. The crowds increased as did their eagerness and impetuosity , as the day took on more than normal military policing. What better for a couple of cur escapees, than to melt into the pushing swirling intimacy of the rabble throng.

G. looked around and suddenly, the euphoria he had felt earlier, evaporated and he knew that to survive here, he must be beyond age, to grow three years in one.

Since Mother died, their childhood days went with her. Necessity was now him, moving from one remote ledge to another, where he would have to run to meet any opportunity half way, or simply go and find them. She would say,"when the storm blows, don't argue with it, find a blanket or go out and dance in the storm, for want will turn a lion into a fox."

They found an elevated spot at the entrance to the Bullring, a vantage point from where they could see back along the quay toward Selskar and all the way down to the Custom House Quay. G. felt safe in the closeness of the crowd. The noon sun was now up and peasant ladies abandoned coarse frieze, in their opposites, while grandeur and haughty of hearts, having so many to look down on today, sweated and persevered, their importance in the world, a necessity to their discomfort. Bravery was rash today as peasant ventured to jibe at the privileged, when tall hats, feathered bonnets and sun parasols blocked the peasant view.

A quietly spoken tall young gentleman said, "here, lad, stand by me, here," and he made room for the two urchins on a broken ledge of the wall. There was nothing artificial about the superbly dressed man's humanity, but a benevolence that was, at once at ease with his obvious breeding, a simple gesture, a fair distribution that a small delicate boy would see better from a higher vantage point.

"Thank you, Your Honour," wheezed the boy, as the stranger helped him onto the ledge.

The stranger shook his head and smiled. James Attridge took a note pad from inside his perfect tail coat, pushed the loose frills of his perfect silk cuffs up inside his coat sleeve and began writing.

Attridge, after a number of trips to Ireland, still found it difficult to understand that title that he found unanswerable. "Your Honour," offered to an ordinary individual because of his appearance or accent, to abase instead of elevate, a trick of the Irish peasant, using it as a calculatedly jibe or a studied insult. His scribbled shorthand laboured across the page of the pad, the charcoal pencil denting the paper into crevices and G wondered how he could express the images all about him in childlike moon shapes. Hen was mesmerized. The gentleman smiled at the boys' obvious wonder.

"It's called shorthand," Attridge smiled

Leaflets were being handed about the crowd, G. reached for one.

There were many, possibly a majority in the crowd who could not read. The Englishman seemed surprised when the older of the two boys began to read the message.

In the Ireland of the dying century, to cause a meeting to be convened, where thoughts of discontent are threatened with publicity, was an illegal act and a affront to king and regiment. Let the Irish fight all they want, but keep them ignorant and stop them from thinking.

A column of Ancient Britons, led by a group of fencibles, the most dishonourable and ignorant of the Irish and English regiments, had been at drill at the Artillery Park, now stomped the rough surface of the cobbles in a phalanx of strutting, stomping grim faced fever.

To many, the flyers meant nothing, a shadow of words on cheap paper, no pictures to untangle the message.

"I didn't think......," Attridge began, as the youngest of the brothers began reading the leaflet.

"Oh we can read, Your Honour, and write too," Hen said, with cold wintry simplicity. "We read The Times", he boasted, running his eyes over the page.

There it was again, the "Your Honour thing," and the visitor smiled inwardly, as ever intrigued by the artful subtleness, the ability of the Irish culture, to open at the twinkle of an eye, a sense of beautiful condescension.

"Government reform and emancipation for Catholics, Defenders, Protestants, Presbyterians, alike..."

In bold script, "An Argument On Behalf Of the Catholics of Ireland."

Suddenly, treason makers and heroes were all about. Then a great pounding noisy desperation burst from The Corn Market into the Bullring and Hen stretched to see. A surging crescendo of voices pierced the morning, a thunderclap of noise was an impertinent interruption to the military rasping confrontation between a sergeant and a fully rigged yeoman captain on horseback.

Captain James Boyd was ready to explode, his heavy square body, rhetorical and wrathful, that his Sunday should be interrupted by the rabble of the town. His surprise was evident as he looked into the Bullring and for the first time, saw his town, which he controlled with an iron fist, fall into turmoil.

Captain James Boyd, of His Majesty's Wexford Militia and Chief Magistrate of the county, was to have lunch today with the Catholic Bishop Caulfield, who was known to appease the captain, from time to time, often at the price of the little cleric's honour. There were often compromises passed between entree and pudding that often put a good rebel behind bars, or worse, the Bishops motive, an elegant incognito , for the sake of peace and tranquillity.

The stomping stopped and Mr. Honan, the unhappy sergeant, presented himself in a flurry of exaggerated blazonry and Boyd offered a pathetic gesture in reply. The shouting , surging crowd was led from what must have been some meeting place outside of town, through Main Street into the Corn market by a line of well dressed gentlemen. Banners, bunting, boughs, even pinafores, dragged from mothers waists became a canopy of green. There was an abandonment to providence as a voice in the crowd shouted, "Wolfe Tone, Wolfe Tone." It was taken up in pockets here and there, it stuck in throats for a fearful choking second, then it burst on the warm air. The Englishman sensed the undercurrent of hysteria in the gathering that was increasing by the minute. Here in Wexford, a fuel was being prepared and the spark that would set it alight was a slightly built man, to whom the masses called again, "Wolf Tone, Wolf Tone."

They had prepared some kind of platform and the man they called "Tone", stood above the crowd in the amphitheatre, his voice surprising in its strength, full of energy and purpose.

He turned toward the quays, raising his arms for silence.

G. gasped in total astonishment and the half remembered dream of two days ago came rushing back. Hen's small face was angelic in his recognising of the man.

"It's him," he whispered and Mr. Wolfe Tone began to speak.

"The Lord Lieutenant of Ireland and the most gracious and understanding King George, have allowed, in their wisdom, The Society of the United Irishmen in association with The Catholic Committee, to develop from a secret society, to come into the light as an entirely constitutional and legal organisation...."

The crowds' good humour increased as it sensed the speaker's resolve, wrapping their poverty and captivity in this waking dream of hope.

G. took the knife from his pocket and looked again at the shining instrument and it's little butterfly. James Attridge looked at him with a hint of suspicion. A ruffian, though with some education, with barely a shoe to his feet, that knife was worth six months wages to a poor man.

"That's a good knife." He said.

"It is surely", said G., looking beyond the bobbing heads of the crowd to the man on the platform.

"He gave it to me."

Attridge looked from one to the other. "Mr. Wolfe Tone gave you this?" Eyebrows raised in disbelief, "Why?"

"Is that his name, Your honour?"

The words of Mr. Tone's strong oratory continued......"the constitution of the Society of The United Irishmen, reads in it's opening paragraph......"

"Why?" Attridge repeated

G'.s reply was unintelligible, long and stretched, " I...Hen and me....we were.....". He looked at the stranger. "I don't know, Sir."

"......... for the purpose of forwarding a brotherhood of affection, a communion of rights and a union of power among Irishmen of every religious persuasion and of none, thereby to obtain a complete reform, in the legislature founded on principles of civil, political and religious liberty." Mr. Tone's voice rose in its emotion. The Englishman scribbled his notes, enthralled.

In the presence of the army, the crowd continued to swell. Today, fear and trepidation did not exist in Wexford. Hearts today were warm and affection dwelt with danger. The man's words were being translated, brother to brother, mouth to ear, whose limited capacity for understanding, might diminish the essence of the grandeur of his message.

Magistrate Boyd bristled with anger, stood on his stirrups and circled the Bullring with a thunderous stare and the Welsh Regiment suddenly heard themselves in reference. Attridge had long before copped to the genius of Tone, having read all of his pamphlets . He had little tricks that seemed to allow his oratory embrace everyone present or who read his writings.

"The men in the red coats, bayonets at the ready, we are all brothers today, Celtic brothers of the proud land of Wales. Many of you are Irish indeed, brothers of the Motherland and you have nothing to fear from this day. We have the pleasure of the company of five Magistrates of His Majesty's Courts here with us, which includes our great friend, Mr. Thomas Russell, up until recently an officer in his Majesty's Army, also Mr. James Napper Tandy, Magistrate and secretary of our legitimate organisation."

Hen pointed at the tall man who was giving out coins to the chained gang at the Stonebridge. The handsome Russell raised his arms, recognising the crowd. As a contrast, Mr. Tandy had, an older man with a rather graceless look, face and shoulders, sort of hanging down, a man designed with a kind of solemn ego. Three others of equal importance, acknowledged the assembly.

Tone continued to Boyd's annoyance. "These magistrates and their bailiffs will monitor these proceedings, and any misconduct or incitement to rowdiness on the part of any person, in or out of uniform will be properly noted and will be immediately handed over to Captain Boyd and dealt with severely."

Boyd and Honan looked uneasy as a thousand heads turned in their direction. Suddenly, feeling low on assurance, the magistrate of Wexford eased himself back into his saddle and as the crowd erupted in applause and the sun got even hotter, the captain cursed inwardly, that this cocky little barrister from Dublin should pick his patch to start his war, for war it was, as far as he was concerned, that any man would bring thousands into the streets in a pageant of disobedience. A mad king in London and his Lord Lieutenant in Dublin allow proclamations to be read and distributed that stink of treason and sedition. The shell of his discomfort tightened when he saw Mr. Wolfe Tone look directly at him in a posture that suggested mild belligerence.

"Our great Presbyterian friends in the north of Ireland, in the city of Belfast, established our movement which now embraces two thirds of the people of our country, in all denominations in a democratic peaceful movement for reform. That movement must now be constitutionally recognised, peaceful in all its endeavours and respectful of existing laws until these laws can be reformed, through negotiation and debate." Pointing out the man with the hanging down look, he continued, "I quote our secretary, Mr. Napper Tandy when he wrote, "in the state of abject slavery, no hope remains for us, but in the sincere and hearty union of all the people for a complete radical reform of our Parliament."

In the crowd, moving among it, people were distributing the leaflets, among them a tall man in black clericals and taller again, G. saw the huge blonde figure of John Kelly. These two were among many present who would relish, right now here in Wexford, a little rebellion. It had been long enough a thought in many minds. Mr. Tone was creating a revolution, but whoever heard of a peaceful revolution, how could it be non violent? Kelly and his friends were of a turbulent virtue, they could muster a thousand men here and now, while hopes and dreams are loose in the streets. The man in black; Father Philip Roche felt the pang of expectancy dissipate in a kind of betrayal. He and Kelly had come to Wexford for this rally, full of hope and possibly a call to arms. John Kelly of Killane looked more despairingly at the speaker, then continued his task.

Hen, in his excitement at seeing John Kelly, slipped from his perch and the Englishman helped him back to his place. Attridge had been writing furiously in a hand his two young companions thought could never be a masterpiece of literature, yet he assured them that here in what looked like a crumpled mass of lint, was an account of history in the making.

The voice was coming at them in bursts of staccato, now and then losing some words to the shouting and the beginning of frenzy.

"There is a marvellous reform happening in the world. Unjust and incompetent governments are falling, colonies are being made independent and democracy and pluralism is being born. I have just come from France." A great cheer went up and the crowd settled again. " The revolutions in America and in France, have made peoples everywhere more aware of their rights to freedom and equality. But our struggle will be peaceful. We have begun in Belfast, today we are in Wexford, in two days, Enniscorthy."

James Attridge marvelled at the ability of this slight unstaturesque man to command the respect and the beginnings of devotion of this mass that had the ability and the potential to be a mob. In Belfast, six months before, he told them, he and Mr, Thomas Russell were guests of the first open meeting of The United Irishmen. He told them of men like Mr. Robert Simms, a merchant, Mr. William Sinclair, a linen manufacturer, men like Richard Mc. Cormack, along with Dr. Mc. Nevin, Dr. William Drennan, Simon Butler, a barrister like himself, Thomas Addis Emmet, now standing here with him.

"These volunteers of Belfast, the spawn of our glorious society, walked with us through the streets of that great city and fifteen thousand souls took up the march."

Not for the first time, in an hour, Boyd looked uncomfortable under the scrutiny of the speaker. Pomp and noise burst from the crowd, as many of the privileged left the scene, many complaining to Boyd that such savagery was allowed to be abroad on a day of worship. Sergeant Honan and his Ancient Britains, bristled in the heat.

Suddenly the mob became a procession, bursting onto the Custom House Quay, at the very spot where two orphans sought and found their freedom, thanks to the man now at the head of the march. No word of command came from the Magistrate of Wexford, though his frustration mounted at the audacity of the events now unfolding before him, almost becoming dismounted when the crush against his horse spooked the animal. He would not have hesitated to have his men open fire on such dissent. Policeman, soldier, magistrate, judge, jury and hangman, his power was absolute, but two factors pushed him toward frustrating inactivity; the front line of this herd, this mass mind of emotion consisted of fellow magistrates, at least three members of the Dublin Parliament and a dozen factious influentials , who would monitor and report on the day's events, and notwithstanding the fact that further trouble awaited at junctions of Brede Gate, Ferrybank, St. John's Gate and Selskar, to swell the crowd further to, perhaps, twenty thousand.

Doors and windows were being thrown open to the revellers and the fine line of well dressed gentlemen, with Mr. Tone and Mr. Russell and the man with the funny name and the man called Emmet, waved to upstairs windows, with shouting, laughing faces like pictures in frames. There were exceptions to this hour of bewitchery, like The Rev. Miller and Rev. Edward Stone of Main Street, where the grand houses were locked against the crowd. As also were the town mansions of the feared Lord Kingsborough of The North Cork Militia and the parsonage off The Bullring and the Catholic mansion, from where Dr. Caulfield himself watched through half drawn drapes with trepidation and with great need to be afraid. Caulfield, like a number of his fellow Catholic Bishops, like Dr. Moynihan of Cork, were quick to excommunicate any members of their flocks who would raise a hand or a rebellious word against the ascendancy. The town house of Captain James Boyd on George's Street, was, naturally appointed enough protection to warrant the king himself.

Having circled the town, the marchers pressed feverishly to meet the members of The Committee. The Englishman had long since melted into the crowd, back at the Bullring, but as the purple shades of evening began to settle on Wexford, the fires, south toward The Three Rocks and beyond the bridge to Castlebridge, raked the dusk, yellow and black and pale and then hectic red as the flames took and the wind eddies off the sea fanned them further in their circuits. Boyd's wounds of pride were still open and revenge, always a strong principle in tyrants, would help him to heal. The Ancient Britons were firing the empty cottages in the hills. Peasants scurried from the town to their burning homes.

Hen wasn't satisfied until they found John Kelly. They found him, desolate, sitting on a low part of the balustrade of the bridge, looking across at the burning cabins. Surprised and delighted to see them, he warned them to stay out of sight of the yoes, though he could not tell

85

them whether or not they had been missed from the ship. His brother had told him of the affair with Wharton and the decision of the magistrate to deport them. He had come to Wexford, four days ago, waiting for the prison ship to dock. When it did, he slept on the pier for three nights, but when he saw the prisoners on the quayside, he found no trace of them.

A great smile broke on the good face. "By God, Hen, what a man you are, and you taking on a despot like Wharton, what a pity that man Wolfe Tone doesn't have your guts, sure the man is all talk." He lifted the delighted youth off the ground. "What a soldier, Hen." The youngster was aesthetic.

"What would you have done, John Kelly?" said Hen, unable to hide his pride and his great affection for the giant. "There were six big soldiers tormenting us."

"Well my soldier friend, I would have torn them apart." He gave G. a cold calculating look, and G. saw there in his eyes, instead of the usual warmth, a change in his barometer, hostile and embittered. "I have two hundred fellows here with me, Georgie and believe me, we could do great damage here today"

"You would be foolish, John, you wouldn't stand a chance, mother often spoke about Mr. Wolfe Tone. He's a good man, I'm sure of it, it was he who freed us." Kelly looked from one to the other, his face incomprehensible. G. showed him the knife and related the story.

"Well then, maybe his trip to Wexford was worthwhile after all, because a fat lot of good he did here this day, except to put the people in hope, ten thousand souls with ten thousand hopes and burning homes." He looked again at the fires.

"How did you escape that trouble with Bookey, John Kelly," Hen asked

"Father Murphy worked his magic, Hen my friend." The name ment nothing to the youth.

"What do you want Mr. Tone to do , John?"

"Raise an army, Georgie, the country is living on hope for five hundred years." He looked about at the dispersing crowd. The boys would be naked of cover without the throng. "You need to get out of here, lads. Go through the bridge, follow the crowd, then go north to maybe Camolin, or Boolavogue, yes go to Boolavogue, keep to the ditches and I will come across you there in a few days."

Where is Mr. Driscoll", asked Hen.

"He's in jail somewhere," replied Kelly, "for disturbing the peace, no doubt. Don't worry Hen, lad, old Diddymus will come to no harm."

G. saw the Englishman engaged in conversation with Mr. Tone and his friend at the entrance to the Bullring, just across the road from the bridge. Fondling the knife, he steered Hen nearer, his intention; to return the knife. He stood off, shy to interrupt. Wolfe Tone looked in their direction as people waited to shake his hand, but there was no sign of his recognising the two urchins.

"You're very persistent, Mr. Attridge," Mr. Russell was saying

"I promise, Sir, nothing will be printed or recorded without your permission. I write for as many as five newspapers, here, in France and in America, I can be your voice, Mr. Tone, I will be pleased to let you see my credentials."

Tone hesitated for a minute, then put a hand on the younger man's shoulder, "are you staying in Wexford, Mr......."

"Attridge, Sir, James Attridge, and yes I am staying as long as necessary, and I am then going to stay with my friend, Sir George Palmer of Duhallow Park and will be staying with him, indefinitely."

Russell looked at his friend, he laughed long and easy, confidence spreading on the warm features." Our very own journalist, Theo." To Attridge, he said, "meet us later this evening at Whites. I feel you're going to write about us anyway, and I fear the pen that assumes its own direction, so I will prefer to keep you in my sights."

G. caught Mr. Tone's gaze again as the three shook hands and others pressed to meet him. Again, despite Hen's childish smile and a half wave of a hand, there was no recognition.

G. had second thoughts and they moved to the bridge. That name came up again, he thought and wondered at the coincidence, Duhallow and Sir George Palmer and he remembered the generosity to his mother.

The Quay had long been cleared of the hides. The cobbles had been washed, but carelessly, as congealed blood and water had settled between the stones in a mosaic of red and purple and an army of dead and dying flies littered the little rivulets. Peasants crowded across the huge expanse of the bridge. Hundreds would sleep in the ditches to night in Allah and Blackwater and Scullabogue, and for many nights to come.

Hen caught his brother's hand and dragged him toward the centre arch. A kind of altar had been erected there, a rough structure on which a dozen candles fluttered in the breeze, sending hot grease into little pools at their base.

The crowd was indifferent to a dozen prayerful figures on their knees beneath the gibbet from which four bodies hung, but then the people of Wexford were accustomed to such sights, their only interest being that the victims were none of their own.

For G., the villainous sight clawed at his senses. Hen's empty stomach went into spasms until he was breathless. He hadn't been sick up now for two days. The scaffold groaned where the ropes moved on the monstrous timbers, that cut and dragged the twisted necks, the distorted angle of each head was hideous, the eyes lifeless and turgid. Hen seemed to be drawn to it, one of the corpses taking his interest. This time he spewed Mrs. Carty's corn and boxty in an eruption against the battlement. The Dummy hadn't made it, to fight for Ireland after all. His skinny frame, too light for the hangman's pleasure, so that a bag of stones had been tied to his feet to enhance his weight.

They stayed with the running crowd until deep ditches and bog land gave welcome cover. Stone- walled cabins burned, the air, thick with the smell of burning thatch.

Chapter 10

James Attridge was lost. Perhaps not so much physically, but mentally he felt that the major factions of his tired brain were suspended in some kind of animated limbo and the events of the past week were as a dream in which he lived with strangers, cut off from his everyday habits.

An Englishman, posted to Ireland just two weeks ago, providence and some would say dogged perseverance had brought him into the company of some of the most unusual and wonderful people he had met in all his twenty three years. He had walked in many a dangerous path, looking for lucky and unusual occurrences, but none so mystifying and pleasurable, as he had found in the town of Wexford on the last week of June in 1794.

Fate leads the willing and drags along the reluctant by the hair, the proverb says, so what was it that drew him to the picturesque town on a day that the agitator, Theobold Wolfe Tone, addressed twenty thousand Irish peasantry in The Corn Market and on the quays and in the streets and led the heaving mass, with green banners and cockades, singing and dancing through the narrow streets, while Militia and Yeomanry stood by, paralysed with indecision. Tone himself had given him a green bough and an Englishman had walked with important Irish freedom seekers, after which he was given the names for his records; Russell, Harvey, Tandy, Jackson, Shears, Emmet, Fitzgerald and the other Fitzgerald, the Lord Edward and many more. In the great swell of emotion, euphoric tantrums, fits of mad hedonism had consumed the crowd. The noise, the revelry, the imagination and the bewilderment, ignorance and blindness, had found a sort of animal gratification in safe and collective action.

In an alehouse the previous night, in the town of Enniscorthy, a fellow had told him he should leave the mail coach at a place called Trasna Bridge and he would be directed by "any owl dog" to the estates of Sir George Palmer of Duhallow Park.

The coach rattled northward to Gorey, leaving the stranger standing in a cloud of dust. He was confused, there were little by roads leading in all directions and he felt like a fly clung to a wheel axel.

The bridge comprised part of the main road so he assumed the estates of Sir George Palmer would be located somewhere along the main artery, but east or west, there was no "owl dog", to tell him, a pilgrim on the road to Damascus, waiting for his Samaritan. The place was deserted as a moonscape, only the silver voiced river underneath broke the silence. He leaned over the battlement and lazily watched it eddy and shimmer in its flow, immersing himself in it's warm tranquillity. Noble thoughts of Liberty and Equality, the message of Wolfe Tone swam about in Trasna'a cool depts, the lively voice rising like a spawning salmon against the flow.

In a few minutes, he began to wonder if he might find just one brother in this solitude. Isolation can kill a man. To the left of the bridge, on a junction to one of the by roads, an isolated building suggested life. A name over the small window said "Peoples" and then "Whiskey and Ale." A number of cottages and cabins, packed in small crevices in the hillside, struggled in clusters upwards, dotting the slopes like motionless sheep. Lifting his heavy carpet bag, he decided to walk to the whiskey house and see if anyone was alive, so far life seemed extinct.

The door was locked and nothing seen through the little window suggested there might be someone inside. As he neared the first piece of settlement, something began a metamorphosis out of the noon haze, a slow oscillation of beast and rider, unhurried and lagging in the clammy atmosphere. He dropped the bag and waited, life at last.

Slowly the mirage divulged itself in a curious and wonderful presentation and the fallacy world that had consumed him in the past week, manifested itself a step further.

Mary Kate Keohane was mounted on a small long horned sauntering milk cow. Her legs, to her knees exposed and sun tanned, yawned across the girth of the animal, just behind the grinding shoulder blades. There was a provocation at the edge of her innocence, a child's challenge of one that has just discovered her own nature.

Attridge clung to the apparition. He had found Mary Kate Keohane at the very end of her youth, womanhood was there, waiting. She had stunning hazel eyes, smouldering pools of magnetism, inquisitive and bold. Her hair, tossed and wild curled, was sloe black and glistened like the hide of the splendid animal beneath her. A more than generous mouth, tightly closed in her inspection of him, for he was standing in her path, now gave him a heart stopping smile. Her voice was a second face, bright like a tide of sunshine from behind a storm cloud. She had the curved bone structure of some Eastern princess, he decided, a Palatine beauty, come to his rescue.

"Will you open the gate for me, Sir."

The docile animal chewed on some previously procured meal, a small hen perched contentedly on the flat area between her horns. Every now and then the sharp beak would dart in various directions across the cow's forehead, eyes and ears and relieve her of pestering flies and other flying vermin. The bird had only one eye, so that it's

90

head twisted in outrageous angles in pursuit of prey. Right now, the head was in profile and the eye was eying him suspiciously.

James reached out to stroke the cow's forehead. "I wouldn't do that, Sir, don't put your hand on Queenie....." It was too late. The eye stalked the hand as it rose to the bait. "I believe I am lost," he said slowly, "perhaps...."

The hen's head jerked forward in a spastic movement, the fly splatting beak burying itself in the delicate cuff of his shirt and the soft frill. The girl's magnificent face cascaded in mirth as the stranger tried to extricate himself and what was left of the material from the bird with the evil eye, that continued to ogle him.

"The wicket Sir, would you mind opening it, my brother is supposed to have it open for me."

Suddenly, three youngsters appeared inside the green hedge at either side of the gate and James became aware a woman standing in the doorway of the cottage. He was enjoying her childish exhilaration.

"I was told to get off the mail at Trasna, I'm afraid I am lost, I'm sorry."

He went to open the gate and couldn't believe she was going to steer the animal through, without dismounting."

"No, Sir, 'tis I am sorry for what Blind Eye did to your fine shirt, she can be very contrary in the heat."

The girl suddenly became shy, even demure, and a new personality unfolded, enchanting him further. "You're in Trasna, Sir."

She found him affable, even interesting, his acceptance of Blind Eye's onslaught. The lace hung in a torn sliver form his sleeve. Any other Englishman with expensive clothes would have caused a commotion and the law would be threatened for having two wild animals on the public roadway.

"I need to get to Duhallow Park." He smiled.

"You're IN Duhallow, Sir, this place is part of Duhallow Estate, and you'll be looking for Lord Palmer."

He had the gate open back for her. He was even more interesting and come to think of it, very handsome, taller than Raefil with longer hair and very delicate features. The hen was pecking away merrily. It's surprising Sir George didn't have Paddy to meet him with the carriage, but then in the past few days, what with the commotion in Wexford, a lot of strange people are about. She pointed to the west, the village of Boolavogue is just a mile and you'll get a spin from there."

He wiped his forehead with a shining white kerchief. "I couldn't help wondering where everyone is, the place seems deserted."

"They'll be at the hurling game, Sir, thank you."

91

The beast eyed the open gate and the step beyond. Then with head down and the hen's wings fluttering to keep balance, all three made the combined effort. There was a consorted "Yahoo,Yahoo", from inside the ditch, and suddenly the gate swung closed with a shudder. Like a huge frigate in a churning sea, Queenie swayed and bucked away from the gate, sending bird and rider sprawling in two directions. It was then James saw the length of string, tied to the gate. Blind Eye landed safely, while the Palatine beauty, now showing more than just delicate knee rolled, unceremoniously in the soft margin. She began to shout and rant in a strange dialect, which only fuelled the boys to further jubilation. It was obvious the prank had been played before and, gallantly, the Englishman come to her assistance, which only spurned her more, and dropping her guard momentarily, she allowed him to see the child within, another sweet identity. She strode, with venom in each step, through the gate and vanished inside. Queenie had become disorientated and was running awkwardly, her udder full of milk, toward Trasna Bridge. A youngster, thinking better than to tempt the wrath of his sister any further, bounded after the distraught animal.

Attridge picked up the carpet bag again, somehow it seemed lighter than before.

**

G. felt every path was dangerous, as he waited for lucky occurrences , however, as the days went by and the nights where he found ditches and sheds for their means, the pressure of trying to stay invisible, eased. Yet someone continued to guide their luck and sent it in strange and wonderful ways and images. Bridie Rose Tansey, from her exclusive heaven, couldn't have chosen their second deliverer to be more remote than the first.

Philip Roche was a priest of the Holy Roman Catholic Church, ordained to manage the spiritual affairs of the people of Monageer Parish. A man of great provocation where his broad hat didn't necessarily cover a venerable head, on the day his horse drawn cart picked up two youths on the road near Ballagh. Spread across straw bales, his large frame seemed to take up the entire dray. He was well intoxicated. The hat half covered his pickled face from the sun and he pushed it across a shock of dark brown hair, to observe the youths, as his driver, a short youth of sixteen, made room for them up front. The driver, with straw shoots in his red hair "clicked, clacked", at the horse, and the animal, drowsy as the day, continued his sluggish drag.

"Holy Mother of God, but 'tis a hot day, surely."

"Surely 'tis, Father," replied the youth, and he gave G. a look, as if he had made that reply a few times before. "Surely 'tis Father Philip."

The priest settled back into the straw and squinted at the sky. Little feather clouds, jocund wisps of gossamer, circled the almost clear sea within his fuzzy focus. "Y'know, lads, we don't look at the heavens enough," he sighed.

"For sure, Father."

"Y'know, lads, the Holy Bible tells us that the heavens declare the glory of God and the firmament showeth His handiwork...psalm....19, yeah! I believe it's 19." He squeezed the sentence through a throat, restricted by the awkward angle of his head and the malt in his larynx. "I think it's verse...one..."

"'Tis, surely Father."

Hen had, already found a comfortable posture and was resting, half smiling at the grinding haunches of the horse. Roche pointed Heavenward. "See the little baby clouds, little fellows. They circle around us, displaying their eternal splendours and all we do is look at the ground." He made an imaginary circle with his finger. "Look at them, up there, where no human race is, and they're looking down at us and they speak to each other about how insignificant we are, in the long eternity of time."

"'Tis true, Father Philip." The red haired driver teased the horses stern with the stick, the animal responding with a prick of one ear. Roche gave a long sigh, maintaining the mood and pulled the hat down over his face. "It's a pity there's not more of them, faith, keep down the heat, so where are you two youngsters on your way to, now?"

G. was suddenly jerked back to reality from his warm acquiescence. "Wherever you are going yourself, Father," he said, feebly.

The priest propped himself on an elbow, studied them for a minute. "'Tis a bad time for young people to be abroad, especially when they don't know where they're going."

"'Tis, surely, Father." The foxy had taken off his boot and was now scratching the rump with a bare foot, to the horse's delight.

"We trust in God, Father", G. said, throwing a cautionary glance at Hen, knowing his reply rang empty and inadequately.

"Yeah!, Son, scoffed the priest. "Trust in God by all means, but be sure you tie up your horse." The proverb fell flat. "There's very little of God around here. The Almighty has been replaced with so called respectability, who think He is here for the asking." He lay back again, the great hat falling to one side and it was then G. recognised him, the tall priest handing out the leaflets with John Kelly at Mr. Tone's rally in Wexford Town. "Instead, God is the immemorial refuge of the

93

incompetent, the helpless, the miserable, the down trodden, I'm afraid he's the god of immorality."

"G'wan there"." The horse didn't quicken.

Chapter 11

Duhallow Park, by its bulk and size, was, for its owners, a task for life, an autobiography of a haughty architect, a great stage on which it, in years past, had been a place of pomp and grandeur, of great births and deaths, of marriages and adultery, of war and peace. Built with granite from the Wicklow Mountains and the deep red of Wexford sandstone, it was a harvest of stone, that had dulled over centuries, even a hint of decay in places.

Duhallow faced south onto the sweep of the Trasna river, where it found The River Bann in a symphony of brimming opulence, a pair of hurrying sisters, to meet the great Slaney, all three to feed the gluttonous harbour of Wexford. Wide threaded steps swept up from the carriage sweep to where the avenue widened before the house. The steps led to the main casement, on which stood stout limestone pillars offering a great gothic arch to the skies. The steps were skirted on both sides with a flanking colonnade of gothic pillars holding a broad balustrade which was repeated on the broad wall capping that held the roof guttering. Animals, mostly lions,carved in the black marble of Kilkenny, strutted, sat and reclined on limestone mountings, sentinels of time, frozen in another century, with a leprosy of chipped snouts, ears and scarred gnarled faces.

Attridge stood back in the great sweep before the house, in admiration. He was aware of workers in the lower fields below, near the river. Air scented, atmosphere serene along winding paths, the rhododendrons stretched past magnolias and early azaleas' tall larches, black beech and clusters of camellias in sheltered ditches of furze, sycamores and helm oak. Through the pines and eucalyptus, he could see out buildings, nearer the house, frames holding cherries, flanked by rows of plum trees, by borders of cutting flowers, and off to the side, vegetable plots, with rhubarb and raspberry canes. "Father would love this," he thought.

In the distance, a marvellous woodland stretched along the river bank, a multi coloured carpet of greens, reds and browns in waves of colour. His father had been for many years, estate manager at Duhallow, and his home now at Winsor was almost a replica of what was spread out before him, though in a miniature form. And then the house; the panels above a hundred windows were of the same black marble, that seemed there like eyelids, observing him. He felt Duhallow to be a place of ghosts.

From a young age, the history of Duhallow and its geography were a part of his growing, as his father would recount on his experiences of the estate and the child would steep himself in its mysteries and it's mythologies, bringing down something from heaven, in their often too lonely existence. From the time of the Scandinavian invaders, the lands of Duhallow were in Norse hands and even when Brian Boru, the High King of Ireland defeated the invaders, eight hundred years before, the original Duhallow was left intact. His father had told him of the pishog, the ancient belief, that it was a sacramental symbolism above the doorway that protected Duhallow against the Cromwellians. He never said what the symbolism was.

"The Irish cannot be without their ghosts," Arthur Attridge used to say.

Cromwell was one hundred and fifty years gone, and much of the grandeur of Duhallow, gone with him. The house had long dispensed with liveried footmen, grooms. stewards, parlour and chamber maids and valets, in their fetters of bonnets and starch. So as James Attridge, His Honour from England, pulled at the bell pulley, that sounded like coming from a mile inside the house, he noticed, high up on either side of the great door, a set of carved plaques, embedded in the wall. Less exposed to the weather, their profile did not decay over the years. The faces on the naked declining women, though intelligent, to say the least, were frozen in what he thought to be fear or anxiety. James decided on the latter, for their huge breasts were spread to either side of their chests, almost under their armpits, armpits as widespread as their short legs, akimbo, in the act of masturbation. Venereal delights at Duhallow Park. His father never said.

A short round woman opened the door to him, a white square of linen crochet on her grey head, a look of insistence and expectancy on her scrubbed face and ushered him inside, a touch of nervousness about her.

James was more than pleasantly surprised at the contrast to the somewhat facade outside. Antiquity, full of praises of past generations was everywhere. The sun was an adventure pouring through the atrium of coloured glass, sending rainbows down through three open landings onto the impressive foyer below. The twin stairways, like necklaces of polished newels and banisters swept upwards to spread out in search of rooms and suits, many uninhabited for a century. Portraits hung in abundance in heavy gilded frames. Again ,Father never said. Serious men and women in grand finery and polished livery looked at him through faded centuries and none of them at all looked like Sir George Palmer when he bounded into the parlour to meet his guest in a flurry of welcome.

"Ah my dear boy." His voice was like a polished relic, a baritone deep and rich, unexpected in a man of his small stature. It had an endearing mixture of an old aristocratic grandeur and a seasoned trill and roll of the Wexford burr.

Attridge knew why the peer bore no resemblance to the gallery of rogues at repose in the landings, it was because he was not one of them. Palmer had married ancient dynasty in the person of Lady Pamela Southwick, a direct descendent of the Earl Of Stafford, who in the reign of Charles The First, like many English monarchs, often strapped for cash and who turned to Ireland to rescue them from the poor house, was handed Duhallow and 30,000 acres in return for a substantial donation to the king's housekeeping, while the original owners, the Delaneys and the O'Duggans were destined to roam the roads. At that time, many an ancestor hanged himself in the loss of hope and expectation, while Grandpapa Southwick favoured his "treasure", Pamela, who cut the halters when she married George Palmer, a Presbyterian landowner of a thousand acres of sheep slopes and heather crevices on the western base of Mount Leinster.

"Nobility, cheaply bought," an admission often uttered by Palmer in moments of resignation and reflection. Sir George Palmer was a squat balding man with an agreeable pudding face, that lighted at his obvious approval of his visitor. His eyes, behind small rimless spectacles, danced in their vitality and his voice came short and breathless. "My dear boy."

He ushered the younger man to one of the great windows of the parlour, where the hot summer sent a spoor of powdery light, filling the room with gold. He squinted up over the glasses in a long searching inspection.

"Yes.....by golly", his voice faltering. Your mother, I see your sweet mother in it. "Emotion flowed through his hand, strong on James's shoulder.

"I'm supposed to be like her, Sir, so my father says, all we have at Winsor is a small cameo."

"We were expecting you earlier, James". His grip was still vital. "Come with me, Mrs. Laffan is making us some tea." They were back in the great hallway. A small portrait, the size of a serving tray hung to the right of the entrance to the parlour. Away from the company of the old ghosts that climbed the stairway, it seemed to enjoy a pride of place, equal to another larger painting hanging in tandem to the other side of the doorway. Palmer pointed to the first, a realistic depiction of a plain woman, looked out at him. It showed an innocent and quiet face, where the artist and the subject sought no frills or embellishments.

Lady Pamela Palmer had an aristocratic disregard for the machinery behind the management of materialism and vanity. "A simple woman without airs and graces," his father had told him.

"You wouldn't have known her, of course," Palmer said, respect and affection, deep rooted.

"She did have ambition as anyone would, shouldering a place like Duhallow, but her ambitions were lawful, never climbed upward on the miseries or credulities of others. She used to say that no bird soars too high, provided he soars on his own wings."

"My father thought very highly of her, Sir," James whispered reverently, as though she were listening. "I feel I know her , just as I feel I have known you all my life, Father spoke of nothing but Duhallow and Wexford."

"And she of him, my boy, and she of him, they were a good team. In his time here with us, Duhallow was perfection itself. It's different now in those troubled times. I have a manager, a good man, lives in Enniscorthy, but it isn't as personal as when....." He trailed off "Arthur lived here in the house, one of the family."

"I used to ask him why he ever left, but never got an answer that made any sense. His farm in Winsor was more a retiring place for him, I always thought, but who retires so young. I don't think my mother liked the place, though, I suppose I was too young to understand before she died."

The old man guided him to the other portrait. "She was Pamela's bird of flight, the daughter we never had." The old man saw the immediate approval in his guest. "Your mother was beauty itself, James."

A feeling of almost intense heat at the back of his neck threatened to make him breathless. She must have charmed and confused the artist and held his imagination in a hungry ecstasy, for through his eyes, Heather Shanahan made her appearance in a thousand difference utterances of his creative mind. Her eyes, deep set and dark, at first pensive until, on scrutiny, you were allowed to see the character within, which manifested itself in the softening of the brow and a sign of devilish mischief at the edges of her beauty, which could, to any man, be almost unbearable. Her hair, a raven's cowl, a ciborium of dark fleece, cascading onto bare shoulders and on looking closer, what seemed at first, to be clusters of ornate heraldry, were in fact, little golden straw flutes, like he had caught her at harvest time.

"You have her looks, Son, her very good looks."

Attridge woke from his trance, his eyes moist. "Nobody is that good looking, Sir." He replied

Reluctant to leave her, he made one last study, closer now. The background of the work, clouded in a semi darkness, seemed to him, confusing. Outlines of bits of old furniture with a suggestion of a fireplace of some kind, lots of blue and red and gold and purple in the flames, lively burning in the distance at her back. Her incredible beauty was a stark contrast to the unlikely background, except for the fire, perhaps the artist saw it as an equation to his subject.

"It's not signed." He tried to sift his eyes through the dark areas at the edge of the canvas. "It is not indeed", said Palmer, heading back to the tea. "Indeed a chap would want to parade something so lovely, don't you think....some travelling fellow, my Pamela knew, no doubt, it was so long ago." James saw the peer studying him again, as if he had left something unsaid.

"You've come to Duhallow at a very interesting time, young Attridge, interesting and dangerous. We sent a carriage to Trasna to meet the mail yesterday and the day before. Mrs. Laffan and myself thought you were lost."

James began to apologise and the old man waved it aside. "Fact is, Sir, I got waylaid in the affairs in Wexford."

He gave James a look of caution. "Ah yes! I've heard about Wexford. Don't get caught up in these affairs, my boy, dangerous times, United Irishmen, Defenders, Whiteboys and the Orangemen, dangerous times." He saw the lovely light of young exuberance , that would be a crime to dampen.

"I've received my first major commission, Sir, my father explained to you in his recent letter, my scholarship."

"Yes he did, and very proudly written, may I say."

"Even the New York Times will take my reports, the Massachusetts Spy and The Boston Gazette. I am to report on the so called troubles in Ireland, for The Times and the Journal, though I'm sure The Times of London will watch me closely, they will undoubtedly censure as they choose."

Palmer went to the window again. It was a vacant stare that brought him beyond the great green sloap of the lawn to the river beyond. "Then you will have to digest these experiences like you would, your roughage, because you will have tough morsels to swallow. As I have said, Lad, tread carefully. Journalists are treated with some scepticism in Ireland. Beat a bush and you'll find a cynic. He can be either Catholic or Protestant, loyalist or nationalist. He's a parasite of civilisation, a fellow who knows the price of everything and the value of nothing."

"Like Mr. Wolfe Tone, Sir?" Attridge threw the question on

impulse, eager for an answer. Palmer frowned, his heavy eyebrows knitting. "Ah yes!, Wolfe Tone....now there's a fellow."

James hurried on. "I believe, Sir George, that Mr. Tone's theme is honourable; emancipation for the Catholics and the reform of the Irish Parliament, and all peacefully done, no arms, no war."

He apologised. "I'm sorry, Sir, just that it seems so simplistic, even naive, you would say, I don't mean to be cynical."

Palmer looked again, wistfully at the river, his cup sitting precariously on the edge of the saucer. Don't take Mr. Tone's ideals and promises with too much levity, a great many people have died for them and many more will, I fear." He tugged at the gold chain that straddled his ample midriff, releasing the fob from his waist coat pocket. "You're not being cynical, James, you've hit Duhallow at a most entreating time. In the next week, you will meet some fine cynics here. You will find out soon enough, I mix my dinner guests, like I do my drinks, a little bit of everything."

His bright eyes glistened mischievously. "Now, to your room, a little rest after your journey and later we'll talk again, about your father and Windsor."

In the hallway, Mrs. Laffan studied the visitor, as he looked again at the portrait and she wondered where all the years had gone. Slow to break his concentration, she said gently, "I'll take you to your room now, Mr. James." He insisted on taking the heavy bag. On the sweep of the stairs, Palmer called to him. "How many"

"Sir?"

"At the rally, how many?"

"I believe fifteen thousand, perhaps more."

"How many expected at Enniscorthy and then in Dublin?"

"Same again, Sir, even more."

Sir George looked up over the spectacles, "and you say he has no army?"

In the hall below, a scruffy red headed youth with a field of straw in his hair was suddenly at the door. Palmer stood before him, hands clasped behind his back. "Well, Paddy, and did you bring Fr. Roche home?"

"I brought him almost near Boolavogue, Sir George", pronounced in his colourful articulation, "Ser Garge", "where they arrested him"

Resignation stormed through the hunched shoulders of the peer. "Yes!", he stormed.

"Well to tell the truth, Ser Garge, Father Philip was drunk, so he was and he called the king of England a name."

"A name?"

"Ranach ramhallach" the youth said, carefully.

Palmer struggled to contain an undercurrent of amusement, at the innocent look of concern on the face that had, by now, become as blushed as the crop above it.

"And why would they arrest him, sure they wouldn't know the meaning, as indeed would I." He squinted at Paddy, "unless maybe you did the translation."

The young voice was in respectful protest. "Faith I did not Ser Gerge, Father Philip tran... transferred it all by himself for them." Palmer sighed heavily, "put the horse away and go down to Gobnait and she'll feed you, then go over to Father Murphy and tell him what happened."

James looked enquiringly at the housekeeper. "A ranting jennet", she said, "he called the king a ranting jennet." She wore a face that showed no amusement, as James smiled. "That man, so called a man of God, will surely come to grief, and now, Fr. Murphy will have to go on his knees and plea for his release." Her flushed face softened. Mrs. Laffan had been on tender hooks since hearing of his planned trip and spent time preparing the special bedroom, pestering poor Dreoilin that everything be perfect.

**

Father Philip Roche's respect for the law and order of the militia of the Barony of Kilcormack, existed in precise relationship to the size of the contents of the Sunday collection box at the door of his church, when he had a church.

When the small company of yeomen, under the heat of the sun and the care of Corporal Frances Mc. Donagh, stopped the sauntering horse on the outskirts of Boolavogue, for no other purpose than to "cause devilment in the pursuit of calamities," it woke the priest from his slumber. "You have nothing else to do," Roche shouted, "but to cause devilment in the pursuit of calamities."

"We'll have no disturbance on the king's highway." The corporal's voice had little cordiality in it, though there was a tincture of inflection for a kind of mock respect, creating the antagonist in the cleric. Propped on an imbecilic elbow, he focused on the redcoat and a spark of recognition lighted the leaden face. "Ah sure 'tis yourself again, Mac. Donagh, and you to be promoted to Corporal now."

"I was Corporal last time as well when I warned you of consequences if I found you drunk and disorderly in public."

The three subordinates sweated in their tunics. One prompted, "let

101

him go, Corporal, sure there is no trouble in him."

The priest speared the young recruit with a daggered look. "And sure, I know you too, you little sleevene. To think I was the one to hear your first confessions, the both of you, and give you your first Holy Communion, that God should strike me dead for the doing of it, and you in the bloody uniform of our oppressor." Roche was on his knees, now in the straw and G. feared they might be recognised.

"I know your parents," the cleric ranted, his passion rising and G. thought he saw the crazed eyes fill with tears, his voice, breaking, "and now you're taking the king's shilling. King's highway indeed, Mac Donagh, 'tis your ancestors and mine that built these roads, mostly with their bare hands, for they, like us , were under the same yoke and not that German excuse for a king, the ranach ramhallach, and that Sir, to your ignorant ear," he addressed the third soldier, who had all the hallmarks of an imported mercenary, "translated, means a raving jennet." Then he struck out with the crop the redhead was using to tickle the horse, lost his balance and cascaded onto the road

The mercenary sprang from his horse and levelled a tirade on the drunk. "Bloody priests, papists and scaremongers, the lot of them." His accent was a sharp belch of words, cut off at their ends, hardly decipherable, a limey Londoner, like many of his so called "mates," a jailbird in his own country, hated by oppressor and oppressed alike.

"Get back," shouted the corporal as G. was about to run to the priest's aid. The driver put a hand on his shoulder and shook his head in warning. "I'll ask for your opinion when I want it, Soldier", continued Mac. Donagh and the limey pouted his discontent. Roche struggled to his feet, half a foot taller than his attacker. He turned to Mc. Donagh, ignoring the Englishman. In a faltering voice, he spat ." Misery acquaints a man with strange bedfellows, that's Shakespeare and as for you, Sir, you're worse, even than that." He jerked his head to the Englishman. "You, Mac Donagh, are a traitor and traitors are odious, and that's Don Quixote. This simpleton strikes me on behalf of his king and his country, so what is your excuse?"

Mc. Donagh called to the redcoat, who was about to remount. "Get off your horse, Soldier, help the priest to mount, you'll take the horse's head."

As if seeing the two youngsters for the first time, Corporal Mac. Donagh asked them where they were bound. Roche, slumped in the hard saddle, his temple bleeding, saw the look of bewilderment in them. "They're on their way to Father Murphy of Boolavogue, they're his new altar servers." Roche seized the redhead in an understanding regard. "See they get there now, Paddy, or John Murphy will have my head and thank Sir George for my perambulation."

"For your per.........and Father Murphy, to be sure, I'll do that, Father Philip, to be sure," he frowned.

"Will you be alright Father?", G. said

"I'll be fine, Son, it won't be my first time as guest of His Majesty, so hand me my hat and tell Father Murphy, I send my regards." To the disgruntled redcoat he said, with not a little bit of sarcasm, "see to the horse now, Your Honour and I hope you and he have no secrets." The English man's scowl was palpable as he kicked small stones ahead, in sweeps of emulation.

At Trasna Bridge, the company with their prisoner headed north to Carnew. The redhead was more urgent now, with the horse than before, he turned west for Boolavogue. "We'll be at Father Murphy's in no time, suppose he'll be expectin' ye now."

"Who's Father Murphy?" Hen spoke for the first time.

"You can leave us off here now, Sir," said G., ready to slip from the cart.

"It would be more than my life would be worth, faith, if I don't deliver you. Father Philip has a fine temper, anyway, the way that fella Mac Donagh looked at ye...." The rough features, spawned of hard construction, a youngster without privileges, made by life, a master of distrust, sized the strangers up, taking their measure. "Besides, two strange lads, walking the roads to nowhere at all could be fodder for an English bastard like that one." His green eyes lingered, had a touch of mischief in their depts. "Boolavogue it be then."

**

The corridor on the first floor was wide and stretched away on an ornate runner carpet toward a gable window in the distance. He was conscious of heavy doors, ornate masonry and carpentry and carvings on side tables, gilded wall paintings and beautiful, though worn upholstery and old archery weapons and instruments like trophies. Mrs. Laffan opened the door to a large bedroom and to the smell of candle grease and musty informality, a sort of a friendliness to everything, the grandeur, long gone. The great four poster bed filled but a small space in the room. A selection of floor tapestries covered the polished boards. Occasional chairs and a small dining table with carvers filled the front facing windows and a chase longue, in reclining splendour faced the marble masterpiece that was the fireplace. Despite the old opulence , the mixture of colours, predominantly red and rich ochre, the scenery was human and personal, a room that, despite its size, could be warm in

103

winter. The air was thick and delicious with the odours of freshly cut lilies, lavender and sun dried linen.

"Mrs. Lavan, he said cautiously, this is far too...., surely another room, one not so important, this room is fit for some dignitary perhaps."

The old lady, her breath returning, sat for a minute on an arm rest. "Sure what's a dignitary, Mr. James, only some jumped up corporal and Ireland is full of that kind. It was himself that agreed with me that this should be your room."

She looked about her, eyebrows lifting the curtains of her eyes, revealing a bright, almost youthful observation. Her memory might be infirm and faltering, but here her relics were no hazy dreams, but light-beamed and preserved. Her eyes filled, emotion deep in her throat.

"You were born here, right here in this room, on December 12th. Twenty three years ago."

"I never expected anything so grand," he said. "My father never said."

"Your father was a man of few words", she sighed, the memory seeming to hurt. She moved to the door, "but he's a good man, good and kind to your mother. Right there in that bed, you saw the light of day for the first time. Sir George and Mr, Henry Attridge were down below in the parlour, a bottle of grog to each of them. It was Her Ladyship and myself that brought you into the world for 'twas shortly before Christmas and Doctor Stanford was his usual long quaffing self, taking on the seasonal graces earlier every year. Doctor Stanford was marvellous for drinking every ones health while spoiling his own." She laughed at the memory, then looked longingly at the bed "There was the lovely Heather and you already birthed and propped up in her arms for the world to see and the fire, lively and welcoming for you ."

He stood looking down on the bed, his fingers, stroking the crisp linen of the pillow. "Thank you," he said.

"I should live twice, Mr. James, an old one like me to be able to remember the past for my memory is becoming a dark page. Nowadays 'tis a thing that the Lord gave me to forget with instead of remembering." She took a step back into the room and a spoor of yellow light through the window caught her in it's track. "But I do remember everything about her, her growing up in Lady Pamela's shadow and how we all loved her."

She put a hand on his arm "And now you're here and she's here too, for I can see her in you. I'll send the rest of your luggage by Paddy when it arrives from Wexford."

Chapter 12

Father John Murphy had a restless night. This Sunday had little promise for him. He would say his Mass here in Boolavogue at 9 a.m., officiate at his parish priest's Mass at 11 a.m. in Monageer and attend to half a dozen sick calls in the afternoon. The reason for his unrest was a scheduled visit in the afternoon to the home of the Rev. Roger Owen, Established Church rector of Camolin, a man for whom he had a perverted hatred and as far as John Murphy was concerned, the very core of evil that had been allowed to permeate North Wexford.

Today, for some reason he had a mind to remember his two great friends and mentors; the Jesuit, Andrew Cassins, who influenced him since a child and the great loyalist before God to the Catholic Stuart monarch in exile in Rome; Bishop Nicholas Sweetman who ordained him and arranged his education in Spain. The old man, though in his 90's was sadly missed for his understanding of the often unrest and sometimes, revolutionary aspirations of his impoverished and wretched flock to want to strike out against their oppressors. A champion of the cause of the poor, he unambiguously branded the de facto monarch entrenched in London, George 111, a usurper and a thief.

Wexford's new Bishop changed the whole complexion of the Catholic Church and helped, in no small way, the establishment of even more discontent among the peasants, on finding that now, as in counties like Waterford and Cork, they had no champion to speak for them. Doctor Caulfield maintained that the reconciliation to the government and all political realities, were incumbent on the Catholic Church. A new situation on diocesan affairs had to take place and his priests were to put before their flocks, unambiguous guidelines concerning complete loyalty to their government and to the Protestant king of England, his laws and his regime. The unalterable circumstances of the peasant was to continue, unchallenging, as being the decree of Almighty God. And then there was the situation of a pair of orphans, sent to him with the complements of his friend, Philip Roche, and what to do with them.

John Murphy had a lodging room at the home of John Donoghue and his wife, Mary, a Catholic tenant farmer about a mile from Boolavogue. Despite the summer month, he felt the emptiness of his life in his dark little room, where he reads his futilities among the cracks in the ceiling and the walls. He washed and dressed, and slipped out of the house, unseen, his landlord long since at work on his small holding. He walked the mile to his church, people calling to him the goodness of the day, through open cabin doors. Livestock scratched and picked at the dry soil and children were being washed in the sunshine, preparing for Mass.

The parish church at Boolavogue was the ultimate allowed by the authorities of the established state church. A converted barn, a place of worship to a selective God, uncaring and indifferent, who bestows few blessings on the days and nights of the underprivileged. He pushed through the heavy double doors. Mary Donoghue, the wife of his landlord, had already arrived to wake the two orphans, where she had made up a bed for them in the sacristy.

The priest sat on the last bench and focussed on the little red light over the altar, the tiny beacon that said God was at home. He thought of the magnificent Cathedral of Seville, where he had spent five years. The wonderful College of St. Thomas Aquinas, the pomp and ceremony under the Dome of the Cathedral, with its golden pillars, arched minster and grandeur of marble altars and acres of stained glass, contrasted depressingly with this morning's surroundings. Yet God was at home there too and he wondered what his rector, regent and his professors of sacred theology and arts in the venerable major college, would say to him now. How would the Venerable Francisco de Aquila Ribbon advise him on their philosophy of passive obedience and of the Divine Rights of kings.

If ever a mind's construction should manifest in the face, the body or the demeanour of individuals, it did so in the two prelates, in the palm of whose hands, priests like Father Murphy were, daily twisting and turning to their whims and manifestations. Bishop Nicholas Sweetman was a big broad pet of a man, with a generous mind to match. He had been the father and the protector of his diocese, without pretention. As a contrast, the new bishop, James Caulfield was a small narrow man, with high spiked white hair, parsimonious in mind and mouth and bureaucratic to the point of fanaticism.

The little chapel was sparsely furnished, with rough bench seating. It had five windows, the maximum amount allowed, two on either side and one over the altar. Mary Donoghue came from the little sacristy and began to dress the altar. On hearing the sound behind her, she squinted through the dull interior. "Ah 'tis yourself, Father, I'll light the lamps now".

"Not just yet, Mary, there's still an hour," he whispered. "Sure enough, 'twill save the oil."

The broad, red faced woman tiptoed halfway toward him and whispered, reverently. "The three women are here for the churching, Father, and make sure you bring the two ladeens for their breakfast after Mass."

And there it was again, define the indefinable, which comes as an accepted part of the cosy philosophy of Melchoir Cano in the splendid other world of Seville, but which, in the cabins and potato patches of Kilcormack and Boolavogue, the cold light of reality is that the Almighty dispenses justice in His own dispassionate way, heaping deprivation and suppression on His subjects and then sits in judgement on them.

"Three for churching." Ritual purification of women who had been through childbirth, because someone somewhere, in a Melchoir edict, suggested there was impurity associated with the creating of a new life, where the intimacy of a husband and wife, in the act of procreation, degenerates into a coarse and a sinful act, that in the giving of birth, the devil enters the ravaged body, when every nerve end is raw and open.

"Father Almighty, You who brought all things out of nothingness into being, we pray to You and implore You to cleanse this, Your servant, that she may be accounted worthy to partake of Your holy mysteries."

The little red lamp at God's front door, fluttered and John Murphy raised his head to the crucifix and asked for His forgiveness for blaspheming, in another morning full of troubles.

The three women had been churched before at Boolavogue, though they were not of his parish, as many women travelled outside their own jurisdiction in a self imposed humility until they were cleansed. They knelt now on the dirt floor, just in the entrance, in what was known as The Sarum Rite in The Order of The Purification of Women, unfit, until purified, to approach the altar. John Murphy was one of the few ordained for Wexford to dispense with that Rite, one of his many little revolutions. He heralded the women to the altar and asked Mary to light the lamps. Did the Lord not know that man is also involved in the act of procreation. George and Henry Tansey stood in the open doorway of the little sacristy, lost in their new friendless existence.

**

He had thrown himself on the big bed, pressing his tired body against its pillows, savouring the down softness that once upon a time, was his cradle. He thought of the painting downstairs, imagining her here, in the big quiet room in the early hours of his life and that he should be in this place that now, was becoming a part of his life again.

He slept for a while and in the late afternoon, James went downstairs. There were some sounds of business coming from the kitchen, somewhere to the back of the house, otherwise the house was quiet, like it was having its own siesta. He let himself outside, gently closing the great door and again, the succulent odours of blossoms and sweet grasses and the lustre of Duhallow, assailed him. He strolled around to the rear of the building where a great yard housed a number of out buildings and all the provisions for a house, always hungry for the fuels to keep its heart beating. Hay sheds, three quarters empty now, as the harvest was still a month or two away, blacksmith's store, a carpenters workshop and a lumber house, a dung pit and what looked like a steel mill, with a stack of lengths of iron bars and carriage wheels and a line of horse stalls made a business square, that in all the big houses would comprise a home industry of considerable proportions. In a haggard an immense animal snorted his objection to an intrusion in the sleeping afternoon, and James thought it better to go no further, as the bull moved lazily into a dark shed, out of sight. Hens walked and fed freely. Potato pits lined along a walkway, like grave plots. The gravelled path sloped downward to the river, to where the land levelled out and the great summer blossoms trailed off to a slowly wandering dirt track, where nettles and fern grew. Beyond further the river disappeared under a canopy of sally bushes, where cattle browsed in the shades, their horns catching in the flimsy twigery. He stood and again took in the avalanche of colour of a hundred acres of woodland, like a forest fire, the dancing tongues of flame spread out before him. All around, he felt the life in the ground, the narrow ridges, the open and closed furrows in the fields. His father had often told him that the lands of Wexford were the most fertile in the whole world.

In the warmth of a summer afternoon, Wexford propped up it's bounty to him, and he wondered how come half of the people of Ireland, the most bounteous country in the world, were hungry.

**

The two turf burning stoves sat like old black elephants in their corners, their bellies, empty and smelling of last winter's cinders. In the heat of summer, the heavy body odours, aggravated by the blanket of thatch, would waft up to him, so that Father Murphy had a little receptacle of constant burning incense on his altar for the duration of Mass to neutralize the stench. Today, he was alone, his parish priest was to send him a deacon from Monageer, to help with communions etc., but nobody had come. He hoped, above all that Lord Mountnorris would be another absentee, as he had insinuated he would arrive to Boolavogue, "one of these days," to address the congregation.

Unhinged jaws, grotesque expressions, tongues projected through stained teeth and sucking naked gums, accepted the Sacred Host. Murphy's sermons often took the shape of public discourse, they were never dull, but always able to still, for a while, the personal griefs and strifes in his listeners.

Today, when two young men were preparing to leave the parish for far off America, to find the new life, the priest spoke to them of the feats of Saint Brendan, known in history as God's navigator. His basic skills of sailing from the ridged coastline of County Kerry, riding the rollers in a scallop shell boat. The saint had studied fables from distant lands of mysterious beauty. The crowd lived on his words, ignorance fed and provended on the illiterate, as Murphy brought Brendan to life. The monk and his followers fashioned an oversized curach , made of willow ribs and wicker and cased in oak and tanned hides, a huge triangular sail and a dozen spoon shaped oars. He stored, in the larder, water skins, dried fish, grain, roots and sea moss.

"On the epic voyage", John Murphy continued, "the trials Brendan and his fourteen companions, had to encounter; Mermaids, Monster Fish, Black Dwarfs. They recorded for posterity, the mythical Isle of Fleas and Mice, The Island of Perpetual Day, and Satan, himself hurled hot iron at the ship in an effort to deter the saint."

John Murphy seldom used a script. He sought out now in the congregation, the subject of his message."The Keane brothers, those who are about to follow in the steps of Brendan, will sail shortly to the new world, with our prayers and good wishes."He sought them out, standing to one side of the church, their shoulders against the wall and many faces in the crowd, showing mild concern. "However," the priest smiled, "providence prevailed and the navigator landed his little band in safety, in a place he named "Hi Brazil," and which we know, today as America." There were smiles of relief as John said to them that this epic took place over a thousand years before Mr. Columbus was even born. "And I read that another new state has been named in that grand country, called Tennessee, and so we pray for the boys and ask God to smooth their journey as He did Brendan's." The brothers, shy and uncomfortable, simply stared at the earthen floor and sweated further as the sun, outside reached for his zenith.

The priest then opened his arms in an all encompassing gesture, a habit they were well accustomed to, when he had something important to say. The imparting of this message always stuck in his craw, hesitant and apologetic, he laboured the account.

"For this week and next week, there will be no collections in this church."

A murmur of discontent spread through the crowd. They knew what was coming.

"The end of harvest is around the corner and rents and tithes are due in the next week, and I ask you to try your hardest, to meet your commitments. I shall speak to Lord Mountnorris about some leverage in the rents, but the tithes are due immediately to The Rev. Mr. Tottenham and to the Rev. Mr. Owen." He left the weight of his message settle for a minute, then carried on wearily.

"There have been rallies in parts of County Wexford in recent times. Such rallies are better off, not attended and especially, I want to say to you that such ideas and promises should not be listened to. These men fill you with false hope. I say to you, before Almighty God, such aspirations are wrong and will lead only to more hardship and violence."

Argumentative rumblings began at the rear of the church and a tall angular man stood into the isle. Big and menacing, he stormed toward the exit. He stopped at the door and turned to the priest and in a voice, shaking with passion and a dark look that showed unblinking hostility, the elder of the two youths,sitting to the left of the altar, that it was rumoured, Father Murphy had adopted, saw, for the first time, the reason for Wexford's discontent.

"You talk of harvest," the big man stormed. For a man, poorly dressed, his voice and deliverance were not equally attired, the tone authoritative and absolute. "What harvest, in God's name. The crop has nothing to do with us, we work it, harvest it and then watch it sailing down the Slaney for the great houses and the English army. The golden grain of Shelmalier is for their horses." Saliva glistened on his stubble as he tried to control himself, the military were outside, as they were, every Sunday, in every parish in Ireland at some pretence at policing. The priest's sermon is sifted for any reference, no matter how remote, which might be suggestive of incitement to disobedience or lawlessness.

"You say your Mass in a barn," the big man continued, " fit for pigs, yet you ask us for our pennies for the grand churches and the wealth of the ministers of a foreign religion, which has no God, a Church that pays homage to wealth and power and hates us and hates you, Murphy. To Hell with them."

"Raefil Keane, the elder brother of the two who were for America, joined the ranting man at the door. He beckoned to them and they followed, reluctant and shy, and then another, the youngest, a ten year old, a wily mouse of a brat, audacity in the unwashed face, in the shadow of his big brother. More joined in the protest and G. saw Diddymus in the crowd. He nudged his brother who, already had a broad smile of recognition on his face.

The priest simply bowed his head. "O'Connor," he whispered, like a prayer, "your anger only tortures yourself."

The blacksmith of Trasna collected his cudgel from behind the open door, an ash branch with a metal cap at its base. It stood the height of himself as he confronted the six militia. The party of about thirty which followed him from the church stood nervously by. Raefil Keane sided up to the blacksmith for support. The euphoria of his outburst, not yet dispelled, the young soldiers, aware of O'Connor Devereaux's reputation, gave him a revered silence. He said nothing, just stood at each one evenly, his face, cold and pitiless, raised the stick and brought it down and the metal protector sparked on the slab. Then, for a second, the ice in his eyes melted and a half smile played about the edges of what could be once, a generous mouth. The man was known to have a brutal way of amusing himself. He kept the other half of that smile in his sleeve and strode to the road.

The young Englishman who had come to stay at Duhallow, had watched, with interest, the happenings inside and had followed the big man into the sunlight, but not before he had seen the apparition, he had encountered on Trasna Bridge, yesterday. She had been sitting beside the young man who had followed the blacksmith in protest and had tried to restrain him on leaving.

A Presbyterian, though lapsed in some years passed as a regular worshipper, James Attridge would more likely be at Rev. Tottenham's service in Kilcormack, where, according to Sir George Palmer, the hymn books resound with a melodious cursing of The Almighty, and the shutting out of the hurt in the world. "That hour on a Sunday," he said at breakfast, "is the most segregated hour in all of Ireland. Go down to John Murphy's Mass at Boolavogue, much more interesting, for there is more of God in that shed than in all the temples of the ascendancy.

James was an inch or two shorter than the blacksmith as he approached him. "Excuse me, Mr, O'Connor." The cultured tone stopped the blacksmith in his tracks. He had heard of the young visitor to Duhallow and hesitated before turning.

"I'm a journalist, Sir, and wondered if I might have a few words." James was taken aback by a new expression that assailed the carved face. His eyes took on a curious fixed glare, like the colourless shining of glass, intent and, Attridge found, disturbing for a moment, almost like he was expecting him. "Your opinion on the tithes...I write for The Journal and The Times."

O'Connor Devereaux studied the stranger for what seemed an age.

He seemed abstracted, then without answering, he stormed off, heading toward Trasna, the cudgel matching his great determined strides. Raefil Keane, a well built ruggedly handsome individual grinned his satisfaction, his eyes, hostile said to the stranger, "O'Connor Devereaux won't talk to you, you're wasting your time, this is no place for you."

Then he saw her again, framed in the doorway; the cow girl, her true beauty that he dared again to admire.

Last night, Lord Palmer, over a quiet dinner and a reeling in the years, had said, in his summation of his ideas on religion, "Protestantism is the ejaculations of a mad king of England, while Catholicism is just a toy, for there is no sin in the world but ignorance and it abounds here on both sides."

**

Father Murphy ate a hearty breakfast at Mary Donovan's table. She would tend the church, then hurry home to prepare the meal and the priest would sit with her and her husband, Tom and often their son, Sean. This morning, two hungry orphans added to the party and it was decided to sleep the Tansey boys in a room over the hayloft, to earn their keep, working on the farm and in and around the church.

Fifteen years earlier, the entire Donovan family of the present generation, had succumbed to greed and avarice, took the oath to honour the king and embrace the ascendency in all its forms, to be faithful to bear true allegiance to His Most Gracious Majesty, King George. Crossing the floor, for the Donovan clan, resulted in the acquisition of a tract of land the size of a town at Tobergal and the title of Squire, which never fitted prettily with the fine Celtic name of Donovan. Tom would say, he never could find God in that place, that for those who were born under the yoke of monarchy, to believe in God, was a kind of freedom. "Every Catholic in Ireland," he said, over his boiled eggs, "thinks God is on his side, the rich and powerful know He is." Tom, born a Protestant, eventually embraced the Catholic faith when he married his Mary and was quickly ostracized by his cousin, the Squireen. The split caused him great concern and he lost considerable wealth and status. But he and Mary were content in their reduced holding, on which stood Father Murphy's church. The building of the church caused further strife, as Cousin John, continually vowed to seek permission from the landlord, Lord Mountnorris to demolish it.

**

Father John Murphy, the curate of Boolavogue was a poor man. In his mid forties, he had few privileges , that his new altar server could see, except the respect and a cautious fear, from his flock. Because of that, he was practical and prosaic. Most of his choices were made for him by a power beyond himself, where he could sink or swim at the whim of his landlord. He was not a tall man, two inches under six feet, about the height, of G. himself, but he had a powerful body, that he could see, when helping him to don his vestments for Mass. Murphy had a broad spectrum of interests, all associated with the lives of his parishioners. In the flat fields of Kilcormack, he played hurling with them and on the narrow roads, he brought up seasonal competitions in the road game of bowling. However, there was just one extravagance allowed him. Because he was a superb horseman, Mountnorris supplied him with his wonderful black mare. That horse, however, had a long string attached to her, namely the acceptance of the authority of The Earl, whose often friendly soft words made hard arguments.

G. soon recognised that there was a lot of craft in John Murphy's compliance. He rode with the Camolin Hunt, owned and controlled by Lord Mountnorris and often dined at his table at Camolin Park, as he did with Sir George Palmer of Duhallow. Palmer had no such hold on him, the peer simply admired the cleric and thought he was wasted on his devotion to his flock.

On the day the brothers arrived at Boolavogue, Paddy had introduced the brothers Tansey as Father Roche's friends and quickly scampered. John Murphy looked at them with trepidation, two more statistics from the fringes. Father Philip's conscience is well bred, but that conscience had of recent times, become an expensive encumbrance of his fellow cleric. Since they took Roche's little church from him, It had become a regular occurrence that the stranger and the poor would knock on Murphy's door, with Father Philip's complements.

This morning, his parish priest would do without his services at Monageer. There would be repercussions. A curate's height of ability consists in knowing how to submit to the leadership of others, but Murphy was content in the knowing that by yielding a prudent obedience, he was able to exercise, at least, partial control. Mountnorris knew this, his parish priest knew this, many pastors of the Ascendancy Church knew this and were often jealous of his popularity among, not just his parishioners, but among the many liberal landowners of the region.

**

"Now I've been studying you two since you arrived at my door and we all know around this table, that you are not the general run of young fellows seen tramping the roads of Ireland. It seems to me, that education and reason of birth forbid you to do things unlawful and ill, so why do I find two young gentlemen of some decorum, let me say, needing the shelter of my humble church, because, to tell the truth, you interest me greatly." The priest waited, giving G. a look of encouragement. Tom lit his pipe and passed the jar of tobacco to Murphy. The room filled with the scent of freshly cut tobacco.

How a good meal reconciles everybody and Mary Donovan, while endowed with a generosity and a serenity in her own mode of life, waited for the outcome. The memory of his eviction, the murder of St. Ledger, the hunger of the past few days, their hiding and cowering from the authorities, the black spectacle of the prison ship, the strangled figure of the dummy on Wexford Bridge and above all, the emaciated figure of their mother and having to leave her grave unattended and the monument above her and their lives, without a goal, without her, seemed suddenly bearable in the comfort of the house and the good face of Mary Donovan, when suddenly G. found, somehow, sweetness and relief in a flood of tears. Young Sean Donovan bowed his head, embarrassed that a fellow bigger than himself should cry at all.

Composing himself, G. spoke openly of what was most intimate in him, astonished at himself, giving them a brief history of his journey.

Mary sat enthralled. "The Irish," sighed Murphy, "always find pleasure in hardships, heard told." The story of the king's cape gave an edge to the telling. "Imagine," Mary said, her eyes filled. "She made a cloak for the king of England."

"My mother called Georgie her lieutenant," quipped Hen, " and I was her captain."

"I like the telling of this Wharton fellow," Tom smiled, sitting back in his chair in a little zone of satisfaction, "pity you had to hurt the stallion." He said to Hen, warmly. "I bet the horse is alright now, Sir, but I'd do it again," said Hen.

"Then 'tis a pity it wasn't the king of England that was on his back." Laughed Donovan. He looked at the priest through his heavy eyebrows. "Sorry Father."

"So, Mr. Georgie", said Father Murphy, "today I go to Camolin on an errand I would wish not to have to put on myself. So today, you'll be MY lieutenant and help me with the mare. Your brother will stay with Mary and help set up your new quarters, until we'll see what to do with you."

Chapter 13

Camolin, the seat of Lord Arthur Charles Mountnorris, was situated half way between Enniscorthy and Gorey and lay to the north of Boolavogue. It was the centre point of a great plateau, that was washed down from the hills to the east, in the dawn of time, and laid out in a fertile plane like a foot rug before the rolling hills of County Wicklow. This Wexford garden stretched a hundred miles, north to Arklow and Avoca, south to Wexford itself for another one hundred miles, east to the lowlands of Cahore, Courtown and Blackwater and westward to Ferns and the Slaney River. This opulent network of rich streams, meadows and pasture land, endowed it's owners with lavish harvest, unequalled anywhere in the world, a sea of golden corn, vegetation and fruits, would spawn twice in a year.

Lord Mountnorris and Sir George Palmer, shared, between them, a considerable slice of this hallowed land, with Mountnorris having two thirds of the region. They weren't the worst of landlords, affording their tenants, a kind of existence which would place them a step above the subsistence of many less fortunate. Palmer of Duhallow was known to be more liberal than most. An agnostic, he had no preference for Catholic or Protestant and confounded fellow land owners that he continually conferred favours to his favourite clerical friend, Father John Murphy of Boolavogue. George Palmer was known to render a service to a friend to bind him closer to him and to an enemy in order to make a friend of him.

But such men as Lord Mountnorris, in their gargantuan comforts and shabby gentility, could become easy prey to the mysterious power of flattery and calumny. In their world so remote from reality, they could be induced to follow anything, provided it was sufficiently seasoned with praise and prayer and especially if such solicitudes were delivered by a high collared clergyman, with copious daily promises of unconditional redemption. Foolish credulity often spares a powerful man the ordeal of thinking for himself. Such thought often spun about in the thinking mind of John Murphy's waking hours, and worked for him like a balm, when the monotonous graft of his day would be swilled out of his system in something that God never denied him; a good night's sleep.

Two such men with high collared solemnity lived in the life of Lord Mountnorris. The Rev. Roger Owen, Established Church Rector and magistrate extreme of Camolin, was one of them. Owen had come to Camolin, ten years before, worked on the many weaknesses of

Mountnorris, supped at his table and bedded his servants for the greater glory of God. A man, grey and drawn before his time, existing on the edge of a holy madness, with neurotic impulses, Rev. Roger Owen was a compulsive worker, an energetic player and when sane, possessed a genius for commerce.

Camolin, from the ancient Gaelic, meaning Bend of Eolan, was, when he arrived, simply a bend in the road and now, as the two steered the mare and rig through the town, Murphy wondered at the rate in which the place had grown in a short few years, and felt a pang of conditional praise for his arch rival. Camolin was now a thriving agricultural paradise. Owen had established Camolin as a massive intervention centre for the entire grain and wheat harvesting of north Wexford and south Wicklow. He built silos in strategic locations and within a few years, his enterprise controlled the movement of every grain of cereal , every head of vegetable and every basket of fruit. Small and large producers became victims of his monopolies. As magistrate, Mountnorris gave him a free hand and on Owen's arrival to power, evictions on a massive scale were carried out in the area. In the past two years, John Murphy believed that Owen had reached his full level of competence, with the recent rumours that he was now carrying out his own executions and administering punishment for the least of reasons with impunity.

The other high collared solemn persecutor was another senior member of the Established Church; The Rev. Richard Cope, magistrate of Carnew, a tyrant who needed no excuse of madness to perpetrate his own brand of justice. G.'s education into the tyranny of the imposition of imperialism upon a whole people, sitting in darkness had begun.

They tied the rig outside of Rev. Owen's Church of Saint Malachy, which he named after the County Down Saint It was situated near the town, while Owen himself inhabited a sumptuous mansion half a mile beyond Camolin, on the Arklow Road. The town was quiet on a warm Sunday afternoon. The church had been newly refurbished and re-consecrated since Father John had last visited. Growing up in Tincurry, where his schooling just happened under hedges and in barns, it had been a sin for Catholics to enter the portals of a Protestant church. From a young age, he had committed a venial transgression, as often as the mind would take him, and when nobody was watching, just to see what "their" God was like.

The extravagance took his breath away. Father Murphy knelt before the altar, while G., conscious of his own unease, remained in the shadows of the entrance. The church was empty. Murphy's depression which began with O'Connor Devereaux's recriminations, three hours before, deepened and he felt a childish spark of jealousy at the new velvet kneelers, the rich tapestries, the carved woods and gold plated ornaments, the expensive panelling all around. He bowed his head and tried to find God. If God were here, then He was the richer brother than the one this morning in Boolavogue. He thought of the poor unfortunate women who had knelt before him and asked either the rich or the poor God for His cleansing, His forgiveness for the birthing of a new soul. He asked Roger Owen's God to take the stone from his heart, to forgive his discontent and the abject hatred he had for the man he was about to encounter.

Speaking almost to himself, but in G.'s ear shot, the youth strained to hear. "All this gold and velvet and coloured glass brings me back to Seville in Spain, where I studied, and the great Cathedral, the hallowed halls of the College of Saint Thomas. Treasures, sent from the Americas for Spain's Catholics. Treasures were sent to Ireland too, but were confiscated by the Ascendency Church."

G. stood and went further up the aisle, courage mounting, drinking in the grandeur. To the side, between two stained glass windows, a mosaic of what was supposed to be of Jesus, G. thought, "what terrible eyes, perhaps Jesus would prefer to be someplace else.

The young woman looked familiar. Her head bowed reverently, she tiptoed from the vestry to a side table, from which she removed a small ornament and spread a laced cloth on the table, then replaced the icon. He recognised Elizabeth, the young sprigger from Thimble. She started on seeing him, then hurried away. "You shouldn't be here Georgie," she whispered. He touched the cloth and was not surprised to recognise Bridie's trade mark; the sprigs of the hawthorn. How necessity knows no faith.

Commotion wafted from the vestry and a young man in black frock coat burst onto the altar. "You must go now, you there," he called, loud enough to wake Father Murphy from his thoughts. He immediately recognised the priest, "you have no right to be here, Father Murphy." G. bounded from the altar, certain the youngster was about to strike the priest, an act quite acceptable, in finding an intruder. G. stood above him, taller and ready to act.

Murphy stood, his face cool and affable, put his arm about the youth's shoulder. Like he was being contaminated, he tried to pull away but felt the strength, like a vice.

"Who are you , Son?"

"I am the Rev. Owen's Deacon."Then he pulled away, "and his nephew, Sir."

As they moved to the door, feeling his contempt, Murphy said, gently, "take care Deacon, you wear the cloth of your God, but your conceit, you wear as an armour. Take care not to boast of little things."

The heavy door screamed shut on it's hinges. "God is gone for His siesta, Georgie," he smiled, gave a little whistle and the mare perked her ears. "Onward and upward, girl."

"Where are we going Father?", asked G., still shaking from the ignorance of the upstart.

The priest gritted his teeth in a forced smile, "to free a fellow priest, G., that is if he isn't already dead. You drive, I'll navigate."

**

"'Tis a very bad day for you to come, Father John." A youth about G.'s age, hurried toward the locked gates. Beyond the bars a fine house basked in the sunshine, skirted by immaculate lawns and pathways, blossoms everywhere. The young man spoke to the visitors through the bars. He sweated in the heat, his rugged mountainy frame, garish and ridiculous in butler livery, suitably braided, a white wig sat on his head, from under which his dark unruly crop peeked. "Rev. Owen is entertaining."

"Every day is a bad day to have to come to this place, and Holy Mother of God, Simon Carty and what have they done to you, you look like a lamp post, and does your father know you're here dressed like a performing monkey, and worse still, does your uncle Jack Keohane know you're here?" Murphy was incensed. "Now go and tell Mr. Owen that I am here to see him."

"I'm not allowed to talk...to address The Rev. Owen, Father." Under the priest's scrutiny, the youth from Trasna cowered further, his face flushed with the virtue of a child. "Then find someone who has that privilege, Son, for like you, my friend and I are becoming lamp posts, rooted to this spot, now there's a good lad." Simon ran to the house, the wig slipping further.

It took a further ten minutes before they were allowed through the gates. "Rev. Owen will see you in the west garden, Sir." This steward was well tutored in the role of disciple, he was not unhappy in his fetters of mechanized automation. Young Carty took up his station inside the bars, caged.

The youth was right, Father Murphy and his lieutenant couldn't have chosen a worse time to come seeking favours.

It had been known in the County, that some of the magistrates of Wexford met on a regular basis, to compare notes, and to communicate affairs in their own jurisdictions. In the garden, a score of immaculate men and women were being pampered over a lavish feast by a team of stewards, and valets, running to extravagant demands, butlers holding parasols and fly swatters to protect the ladies from the unkind elements. Hysterical voices full of empty talk wound down to a whisper as the guests became aware of the figure in black standing on the terraced steps. The women were all in bloom, like the flowers in Rev. Owen's garden; dainty buttercups and daisies, draped in petals and lace. They turned their comely faces to the intruder, each movement, stiff and corseted. Epidemic efforts to give grace to deformity and vulgarity in Owen's lawn, so called fashion, was simply an abortive issue of vain ostentation and exclusive egotism, born to conform to every whim."God, what a circus", thought G., standing in the priest's shadow.

Four or five of the County's notorious commanders, were more aware than others about the table, of John Murphy's presence. The priest recognised them, for what they were, tyrants and despots, each one with a sickness, rooted and inherent in the nature of that tyranny. All magistrates, against whom laws cannot be enforced, who themselves were the law's masters.

Magistrate Hawtrey White, the hunter of the east country, and a sworn advocate of the total abolition of all things Catholic, with a special abhorrence of priests, according to the doctrine of The Orange Order. Sweating under an outrageous wig, Murphy's presence added to his discomfort. Magistrate Hunter Gowan, from North Wexford, known for his commercial prowess, especially in the sale of mercy. Prisoners in his capture could buy their freedom at a price, no matter how notorious. Archibold Jacob of Enniscorthy, known for the bringing of his own executioner to his assizes and James Boyd, who persecuted his own area around Wexford Town

Mrs. Owen motioned to the boy with the parasol to move closer and keep her in the shade while, inwardly chiding her husband's naughtiness for ignoring the dust covered visitors, it was becoming embarrassing to her guests and to the two. Eventually Roger Owen left his chair and stood with his back to Murphy, while ogling the merry makers, with a wry smile, rich in his satisfaction of the priest's discomfort. G. wondered what Father Murphy would do next, as his own unease turned to anger. He looked at the cleric, the man was studying the sea of pomposity before him with half contemptuous respect. He had full control of himself, and instant of irritation he might have had, gone. Under the scrutiny of each individual in a personal searing observation, G. felt a slight change in the barometer of their demeanour.

"Make him go away, Uncle." A little petal, already heady with wine, her pouting precociousness floating like acid, "I don't like the way he looks at me."

"Get rid of him, Owen, I never understand, you spoil these blasted priests." Her father, The Rev. Cope came to her rescue, coming behind her chair and patting her shoulder. "Never fear, my dear, no harm will be allowed come to you." She giggled into her fan and G. thought, looking at petal and the tall angry man standing behind her, and then thought of the upstart that accosted them at the Church earlier and felt a kind of sorrow for them, that they and their peers, destroyed by imperialism, would never know decorum or respect for anyone but their own, that their impudence and folly would never have bounds.

"What is it this time, Murphy." Owen asked, playing to his audience. The refined woman sitting next to Jacob, a woman, it would seem, easily troubled, whose natural occupation would run counter to normal life on any day, croaked, "who is he, Jacob?"

"Hush my dear." Jacob looked at Murphy, fire in his eyes.

"I've come for Father Philip Roche."

"Roche is a menace in our roads, he's a drunk and a cur." Owen addressed the priest for the first time. "I have sentenced him to a month at His Majesty's pleasure, it will cool his ire."

"At least he's alive," scoffed John, "he'll be dead in a month, your prisons aren't fit for dogs, Sir." Murphy's voice was alarmingly calm in the atmosphere, it irked the gentlemen and perturbed the ladies.

Mrs. Owen chided further. "Really Roger, I don't know how you tolerate this man, and on Sunday and before our guests." More giggles, little interior convulsions, coquettish men and women, believing they were immortal and their society eternal. G. thought again of St. Ledger and of Wharton and wondered, perhaps, compared with this circus, they were not so bad after all.

"Your Roche fellow accosted one of my corporals, that alone, Murphy, is a death sentence consideration." Owen looked at G. for the first time, as if, 'till now he hadn't existed and the youth took it as his cue to speak.

"That is not how it happened, Your Honour."

The total sound in the garden suddenly became a combined intake of breath, as four mighty magistrates were taken by surprise, not to mention Father John, himself. A raggy youth, without the required downcast eyes, dared to address them. Stupefaction persisted with the ridiculous women until it became pure stupidity, fans working overtime. This boy, his voice had confidence, his stature and assurance, contemptible before them. Seeing there would be protests, G. hurried on.

120

"I was there, Sir, and but for the corporal, your soldier with the foreign accent, would have killed Father Roche. Yes, the priest was drunk, but he was asleep on the cart, when your soldiers came along the road."

Murphy moved forward on the steps, leaving the youth in the shadow of the portal

"And who might you be, youngster?"

"He's one of my altar servers, and I am as anxious to leave here as the ladies would wish, so I am asking you again to release Roche to me. He's of no use to you, he is harmless and you know it and you also know that as time goes on, he'll become more difficult and cause your jailers some difficulty."

"This Kelly fellow, last week, Roche today, I am running out of favours, Father Murphy", Owen spat.

"Owen moved toward the step and Murphy came half way to meet him. "Stay where you are, Sir," Owen demanded. He was tired of this priest, forever digging for favours, forever knocking at the door of his sensibilities and frail emotions. He took a sheet of paper from inside his swallow tails and shoved it before Murphy's face. "Take it, I had already, knowing you would come begging, to rid myself of this cur, now get him out of my sight."

Magistrate, Rev. Cope seemed to be taking little interest in proceedings, pretending to be tiring, dabbing his narrow face with silk. Father Murphy knew otherwise. Cope suddenly laughed hoarsely, his eyes venomous. "I cannot understand your patience with this man and this urchin with him. I would have Roche hanged by now, desecrating the name of the king, obstruction to our military in the pursuit of its duty." Turning to Murphy, " and as for you, Sir, go and tend this rebel and give him a little red banner to wave for his little revolution, then go and tend to the poor, after all, that is your calling, or indeed, I would........"

Murphy cut him off and slowly moved closer the table, side stepping Owen and eyeballed the despot, his voice rising just a decibel , "....would have me .....pitchcapped, Mr. Cope?"

Ladies looked over their fans, bewildered, men and women looked at one another, searchingly. "Is it not true, Mr. Cope, you have employed the services of a man called Hempenstall and his rabble for that purpose."

G. had no idea of what the priest was talking about, but he could see there was some enjoyment registering on the good face, taking all by surprise. "Pitchcapping, ladies, the horrific word speaks for itself." Then to Cope, "let me warn you, Sir, you speak of the poor, the poor which you have, with others, created". He looked about the table accusingly. "You speak of revolutions, of banners and little flags. Well great revolutions are never the fault of the people, but of the government. Poverty is the parent of revolution and crime, and I warn you, all of you, beware of the poor waving banners and flags."

He walked about the table, further discomfort registering on pathetic faces, Cope, silent and seething at the affront. "Mr. Owen, knows only too well, my worth to my government, to your establishment to your king. My parish is the most loyal in the whole of Wexford, my flock gives you order and conformity at my behest, which weighs heavily on them and on me. You would be wise to cherish that and nurture it."

Then G. saw the man within, a man who would believe that anger only tortures one self, he struck out at the crucible of his ire, bringing his fist down on the corner of the table. Bottles of the very best vintage of Owen's magnificent cellar, tumbled and a woman cried out.

"At my Mass this very morning, I asked, with my heart in my hand, that my parishioners gather together, their few shillings to pay for all this, the tithes that sit you all in comfort and self indulgence, and I had to lie to them, as well they know, that the money is for God."

Then he smiled, his arm about the young fellow. "Let's go and collect Philip, Georgie, like you, I didn't expect to burst in on a fancy dress party."

They headed for the exit, not before he stood facing them again, daring any one to conront them.

Cope, in their wake, chided his host again at the threatening insubordination of this priest "He IS important, my friend, he's one of the few that conforms totally, he keeps in line, so I meet him half way. Conformity, acceptance, even humility, though you didn't see too much of that today, he has all three, though they come at a price. He's also, let me warn you all, held in high esteem by Lord Mountnorris and Palmer of Duhallow treats him like a brother."

Murphy sat back in the little rig, suddenly exhausted after the encounter. "What is this about Hempenstall, Father."

He looked evenly at the boy, it was evident the confrontation had disturbed him, he looked tired. "Evil, Son, evil has come among us, so much more terrifying than before."

"What kept you," was the greeting, the big priest croaked as he climbed aboard.

Murphy ignored the pleasantry, "they beat you again." He had bruising and lacerations to his face, one eye, swollen. He put a pair of bruised knuckles up before them, "not half as bad as I gave the bastards, and there's a limey cur in there and he won't walk for a month, and that's for sure."

G. smiled, feeling a little self satisfaction at the thought.

"Roche looked at the youth. "Do I now you, laddie?"

"You'll get us all killed." John had no levity for him.

"Ah, you'll be all right, John, nobody toes the line as well as yourself." He pulled his hat down over his eyes and sighed, "O Lord, if there is a lord, save my soul if I have a soul."

He lifted a piece of the hat, "you sure I don't know you, Son?"

G. gave him a knowing smile and the tired battered cleric simply smiled back, then closed his eyes.

Chapter 14

September's harvest was saved, packaged and sent across the channel. Father Murphy's dues were delivered, by supportive parishioners to his digs with lavish generosity, in many cases, as much as they could afford. Henry and Georgie helped to stock his turf store, in the yard, cart loads of winter fuel. He would protest that he had more than plenty, but still they came, enough for the little fireplace in his room and for the two stoves in the church. They were shown, by Tom Donovan, the skill in preparing his potato pit and tend his vegetable plot. Father John's chicken coup needed extending as three hens, delivered on his birthday, with the complements of Gobnait Brennan, Sir George Palmer's cook at Duhallow, added to his clutch of twelve. All this generosity found its way in many directions and allowed him to be comfortable in his own generosity, when much of the bounty would find its way to his alms table in a dark corner of the church of Boolavogue. Freshly laid eggs, cabbages, potatoes, would be spirited away with closed dignity in the exodus of Mass. Every Sunday evening, late, he would leave he side door open, have the table replenished for those who would wish to partake of his generosity under the cover of darkness.

The boys did become servers, learning the wide words of Latin, without needing the art of translation. "The tongue of man is a twisty thing, so says Homer, in his wonderful Iliad and that was three thousand years ago," said Father Murphy. "You boys learn fine and fast."

Hen remained his puny self, with little growth, but his health improved under Mary Donovan's coaxing, and her saintly patience.

**

"They're like a clutch of old rooks up there in the parlour, with the clergy sanding around in their frocks."

Mrs. Annie Laffan stood in the middle of her huge kitchen, fretting more than her usual. Two more had arrived, two extra guests, and she wondered through what window, common courtesy had fled, that prior notice is no longer received or required. Manners in today's Ireland are as idle as a scare crow in the desert.

The place smelled of boiler steam. Potatoes and vegetables sat in harmony in great shining copper pots, their lids like half cocked hats, allowing little puffs of steam escape up the chimney shaft over the hot stoves. Joints of Duhallow lamb, tender legs and cutlet ribs, had been taken from the main oven, allowed to breath out of the boiling lard and now rested in the "cosy", a cool oven where Gobnait Brennan kept her little muslin bags , filled with her choice of herbs from Luther's garden. The cook of Duhallow had a rich rule of taste that surpassed all opposition. A fish kettle, with heavy brass handles, a present to Gobnait from Conor O'Connor Devereaux The Forge, to give him his full title, had been set aside the great range. A fine salmon, still in his jacket, lay submerged in his cooking water, waiting to be stripped and trussed on the great silver platter, a tray of prepared lemons, sprigs of Luther's parsley and tomato crescents lay ready for the decoration of his bier, to be presented by Kate Keohane, in a feast of epicurean grandeur, the only grandeur to be found in Duhallow, these days; it's table. Kitchen maids , their starched caps askew in the final moments of preparation, scurried about in their fevered duties under Gobnait's onslaughts, so the conveyor system, as always, is immaculate, beginning with the broth of young nettles, to the sorbet, lying ready in the coolness of the larder, then through the gastronomic adventure that it was to sit at Sir George Palmer's table. That was the only grandeur in Duhallow, as Sir George had long since dispensed with the services of valets, squires and pages, the imperial attitude that you own everything, where as Lady Pamela would say, she would not wish the house and it's servants to own her. Twice a year, Duhallow had it's meitheal or working party, party being the operative word. One hundred boys and girls from the village would spend the day scrubbing and cleaning under open windows in a hundred rooms, when the smell of carbolic and disinfectant assailed Duhallow. Meitheal would end the day with a party in the lawn for the workers, young people danced and sang to Sir George's delight and Mr. Sanquest the estate manager would send an assistant from Enniscorthy to pay them their shillings on leaving. George Palmer would say the day's doings were generating the simple goodness of life. Nothing simple about his famous dinners, however, as James Attridge was about to witness

**

He had been introduced to the few regular staff, mainly kitchen workers, under Mrs. Brennan, a pot girl, an assistant cook and a dairy maid, while Mrs. Laffan had a chamber maid to tend laundry and the few bedrooms needing daily attention. Since Mr. Attridge happened on Duhallow, a second maid had been appointed. And then there was Mary Kate Keohane and her sister Droleen. Droleen, he first encountered on the nettle path, on his way to browse. The woods seemed nearer the

125

house than he imagined, it depended on the time of day, when the sun, setting or rising can play tricks. Whoever planted the woodland in another century, had in mind to build a cathedral of lasting beauty, an atrium of wonderful foliage like a prayer to the heavens. From the end of the nettle path, an avenue of Cherry Blossoms wound its way to the entrance. Like huge sentinels, Oak and Ash soared to the sky, where spoors of coloured light shone through the canopy. Beyond toward the river, Alder and Willow Sallies, in the marshy areas, the slopes to the west, covered with Aspen, Elm and in the centre of the pathway, one mighty Yew, where a seat had been built in its shade. The solitude of the place in a warm afternoon, made him tip toe, feeling a pang of veneration seize him. On the far side of the Yew tree, the figure, which had been blending into the foliage, so that he was almost upon her before he realised her presence, moved in a sort of a swoon dance, arms outstretched, barefoot, her head to one side, the figure breaking the light beams.

"I'm sorry, I disturbed you," he said, "didn't think there was anybody about."

She stood before him, head down, almost afraid, and slightly out of breath. "You dance very well." It seemed to embarrass her further. "Do I know you?"

"No, Sir,", she hesitated, "may I go now?"

"Certainly not", Attridge smiled, she had dared to look straight at him. "You were here first, 'tis I should be going."

She had an angular good face, about seventeen, he reckoned. A strong body that suggested a working girl, but he had not met her, but then he was at Duhallow only these past couple of days.

"I must be going now , Sir, my sister will be looking for me." The girl reached for her shoes and seemed to float through the growth and was gone.

His official meeting with her sister happened in Gobnet Brennan's kitchen, where, almost from the first day, he took to having a morning or afternoon tea with her and Annie Laffan on the huge scrubbed table. The cook, a woman of few words, could show her approval or disapproval of a matter or a person, just by her demeanour. James was immediately comfortable in her presence and felt he was of no intrusion in her patch. Mrs. Laffan delighted in his company, of course.

He sensed a presence at the larder door, as the girl took the notice of Annie Laffan. "Ah, there you are, Kate, well on time as usual, there's some tea in the pot for yourself and Droleen." The old lady continued her discussion with James, but he was lost to her, as the visitor took two cups to the range. Droleen watcher her sister's hand shake, the spout of the teapot beating a tattoo on the rim of the cup.

He bristled with surprise and evident appreciation. "It's you, isn't it, the girl with the cow?"

"Ah sure you haven't met, I'm sorry James, these girls...."

"Oh, we've met all right, Mrs. Laffan, both ladies indeed." His face lighted with amusement. "In fact, you might say, we met under rather...", he hesitated..."unusual circumstances, nice circumstances."

Looking at her again, her beauty had a breathtaking expression, her demeanour almost meek, yet meekness, he felt was not common in her. She studied her cup like it was going to talk to her, then looked directly at him, moving to the table. " I must apologise for my brother's behaviour, Sir, and I hope you were able to get a lift to Duhallow." Her eyes returned to the cup.

" I followed your instructions and yes I arrived safely, and by the way, there is no need for apologies, though I might say, an apology to you and to your cow and not forgetting Blind Eye, would be appropriate, Miss....."

"Mary Kate Keohane and her sister, Droleen ." Mrs. Laffan quipped

"Ah so you're sisters?" Annie, though amused at Kate's discomfort, Kate was never caught for words or explanations, had a lost look about her and wondered what was going on between the three.

"You'd better go up now, Kate, a lot to be done." Gobnait handed her a scrap of paper, it was the menu for to night's dinner and the list of guests. Droleen bobbed in a kind of courtesy and they were gone.

"They're lovely girls," mused Attridge.

"Yes, she is." Gobnait Brennan of few words looked at him under her eyes.

"I met the younger one in the woods. Kate, I met on the road on Saturday and at Father Murphy's Mass on Sunday", he explained. "Had no idea she was a part of Duhallow."

"A big part of Duhallow," said Mrs. Laffan. "These two girls live over in Trasna, looking after her aunt and uncle and her brother, Brian. Sir George won't have a dinner party without her, he has been known to cancel if she isn't available. He's at her to come here to Duhallow, but," she whispered, throwing an eye to the door, "the aunt isn't too well and the uncle, Jack Keohane, well....we all know that..". This time the knowing eye was thrown to Gobnait and the contentment in the understanding between the two women was evident. Then the good face softened. "Mary Kate's mother died only four years ago, her father is long dead, as a young man he was, and a young family to him.

"I declare", sighed Annie Laffan, checking for the tenth time, her guest list for the evening's dinner table, " but the man is totally gone out of his mind."

The diminutive Gobnait Brennan, a woman of fifty years, showing strength and artistry of a cook, half her age, threw her friend a knowing look in a determined set of her puss, as she whisked the egg yolks for his Lordship's hollandaise.

If Kate Keohane had worry beads, she would have them in her hot little fist now. The cross- section of guests read like a council of war; Priests, Rev. Misters, Politicians, Soldiers, the Usual old agitators and a Lord or two thrown in. In his mixumgatherum dinners, for which he was notorious, this one took the biscuit and she had wished she was somewhere else this night. Her fear caused her to lose her temper more than once with Droleen, when they set up the grand table.

**

"He's got clergy up there in all shapes and sizes, men in black, each thinking he has a god of his own and not to mind that scoundrel priest Roche, half drunk as usual. And there's half an army up there in the middle of them, wearing their good clothes and weighed down with their accessories and their importance."

The housekeeper wrung her hands in distress. "if this night won't end in chaos, I'll be no judge of the human race, or any other race indeed." She called to Droleen in her own importance, "mind that delph, now, child, how you handle it, for 'tis older than your grandmother and twice her value."

Droleen Keohane was a girl of limited graces, pressed into service at Duhallow, by circumstances not of her own making, as, until the age of ten, she thought she was a boy, consumed with doing boy's things. Her entire being as a woman, she always thought was a secret, for didn't God make women to match men, so she always wanted to be a brother to her brother and a brother to her sister, Kate. Content to be the runt of the family, in the tiny Keohane farm, west of Trasna, even her school days at Boolovogue was a distraction from her love of the land and the animals. Her great passion was for the trees, the woods and the folklore and mythology attached to them. She would spend hours with Luther in the garden of Duhallow and in the woods beyond the nettle path and in summer would become a recluse whenever possible, in her make shift camp in the sallies.

So Mary Kate, her older sister by three years and indescribably more beautiful and full of intuition and wisdom, dragged her off to Duhallow, put a starched cap on her head, once a hiding place for farmyard compost, to re-construct her sister, where presentability might eventually germinate. How Kate wished Lady Palmer were here to take on the task, as she did with Kate herself, taught her the finer things in life, led her through the right path, not by severity but by persuasion.

In the Ireland of the dying eighteenth century, where Mary Kate Keohane sauntered her lazy cow, an animal with a tinsure of royalty about her, named Queenie, into her stall for milking, then dressed herself, befitting a fine servant girl at Lord Palmer's table, where a young Englishman found himself, by some quirk of fate a guest at one of Wexford's formidable estate houses, when a young barrister took the garrison town of Wexford, which, for six centuries and more, was a social dish, not built for the desperate, a place of slaves, compelled by violence and servitude to suffer great wrongs, the young barrister, Tone, who took it in a short morning and shook it, so the rattle of its chains were heard for a thousand miles, in that Ireland, a complex regime of uniformed and rude militia, a sort of a mob, many of them out of British jails, a mob without direction, let loose to serve a mad king sitting in London, in that Ireland, the young man from Windsor in England felt the huge occasion batter his senses.

James was aesthetic when Sir George invited him to have his new found friend, Mr. Tone to be among the guests. Wolfe Tone had been in Enniscorthy the day before, when he granted yet another interview to the enthusiastic young journalist.

**

The tall priest was a fascination to the young journalist from London. James had remembered seeing him in Wexford and his reputation as a hellraiser, his condemnation by Mrs. Laffan and the fact that he was a rebel of whom Sir George had quipped, that disobedience in him was the most courageous of his virtues, but at times was indistinguishable from his laziness and his neglect.

"London has perfected it's occupation very well, my young friend," Roche instructed, "but the culture of that occupation, as their culture perceives it, is a tragedy being weaved over half a thousand years. It consists in nothing more than the pounding of an entire nation." Philip Roche's eyebrows heightened in the good strong face. The cut above his left eye, evidence of the day he spent in Rev. Owen's prison.

Owen of Camolin would have been on the list of invitees, however, Sir George, on hearing Wolfe Tone, the new agitator was coming, opted for the more senior, Rev. R.J. Cope of Carnew, a shrewd and able debater, and he wanted to test the reputation of Mr. Tone, which, according to James Attridge, supersedes him, where ever he goes.

Roche continued, "Now firstly, you have the army and it's different corps and regiments, as the established English forces. Then you have the Militia, only recently drawn up, because of the unrest in the country, you see and the many wonderful rallies being held all over the countrysides. Now this fine bunch of hooligans was invented for the purpose of containing riots." He looked across the room to where a young officer, Lieutenant Bookey, was in conversation with Rev. Cope, and raised his voice for the lieutenant's benefit.

"A bunch of hooligans, Sir, they specialise in evictions, confiscating of properties, livestock and children, and so on." Bookie looked severely at the unfrocked priest. James glanced about the room as Roche continued, and Mrs.Laffan's palpatations soared in concern that Sir George's mixumgatherum would sit soon.

"Now, the Militia officers are chosen from an extreme core of Protestant bigots, while the rank and file, believe it or not, are Catholic." Roche pointed to his own breast. Now you see, Mr. Attridge, they would be, so to speak, our crowd, taking, as they say, the King's Shilling, and hunting and killing their own brothers for the earning of it."

To preserve the malice in his voice, and Sir George looking to him to open the night's proceedings, knowing Roche to be a true disputant, who was always right when it came to the ascendancy, Roche sauntered to the great sideboard, helping himself to another decanter of wine. Kate Keohane stood nearby, wishing they would sit, as Gobnait too was beginning to fret that the meats might spoil. The priest gave her a splendid wink, "Kate, darling."

She bobbed, "Father Philip."

Back at the fireplace, where James waited, the priest re- filled the glasses. Attridge watched her move about, checking things, a hidden innocence to her vivacity; her gift, as she moved about the table, a shining creature, confusing him again.

"Now, the Yeomanry, now that's something different entirely, that, you see, is a commission from the crown, His Most Gracious Madness, etc. That crowd are, mostly part time and can't soldier for nuts, sons of large and small farmers, you'll know them by the dung on their boots and between their ears."

He smiled broadly at James's amusement on the colourful descriptions. The smile continued over James's shoulder as Roche bowed his head in courtesy to Mr. Tone, who was in conversation with another clergyman, Mr. William Jackson, who Mr. Tone had introduced as a friend, just home from Europe, and who he had brought along in place of Mr. Thomas Russell, who was indisposed because of his new appointment as Magistrate duties in Dungannon.

"While we wish to change the constitution of Ireland," Mr. Tone was saying to Sir George, "we must still earn a living, I am here for the assizes in three districts, hoping to save poor wretches from injustice, saving Ireland is just a part time job."

Back at the fireplace, his elbow resting on the mantelpiece, Roche continued his lesson."With the Yeomanry, these Protestants regard it as a means to a legal armed force against the Catholics, which must cause great confusion to someone like yourself, Mr. Attridge, as Catholics are encouraged to join the Yeomanry and take the accursed "king's shilling," Roche continued

"The King's Shilling," James echoed.

"Because it IS Ireland, Sir, chaos turns to benefit sometimes." He turned into the great mirror over the fireplace, curtailing his strong baritone "It is our belief and especially the belief of senior rankers like your uncle, that Catholics have infiltrated the ranks of the military for the dual purpose of reporting back to organisations like the United Irishmen," he nodded toward Wolf Tone,"the activities of the corps."

"Sir George is a Yeoman?" James looked incredulously at Palmer.

"But of course, my friend, you see, good and evil lie close together. Let no man presume to think that he can devise any plan of extensive evil, un-alloyed to unadulterated good."

The dinner party stood in little knots of conversation about the room. Admiration sparkled in Roche's eyes. "Palmer is at the head of four hundred part timers and while he's there, scroungers and despots like Mountnorris, Cope, over there with the soldier, Owen and others will mind their P's and Q's. To be a tenant of George Palmer is to be privileged compared with the lot of the vast majority. The lands and people of Duhallow are, at least for now, content. They treat him with a respectful caution in which fear is not a component. God grant him a dozen lives, for where would we be without Duhallow, a refuge for poor sinners like myself and Father Murphy, over there, not to mention the food and hospitality."

Attridge, laughed, "He's not my uncle, Father Roche. I shall try to remember the different corps, what a complex country you have, Sir".

For anybody who cared to listen, the big priest said "this country is fine, Mr. Attridge, it's the lice and vermin that inhabits her is the problem."

Sir George saw personally to the seating arrangements, a responsibility in great houses usually carried out by some starched footman or butler, then a slight argument with himself that it met with his approval, before asking Father Roche for one of his famous prayer before meals.

"When a man's stomach is full, it makes no difference whether he is rich or poor." Philip Roche, stood on ceremony, his wine goblet raised. His tired intoxicated eyes swam in warm candlelight, he looked more than his forty two years. "To Ireland's innocence and beauty," he looked at Kate Keohane, busy about the table, "beauty before God's presence, and to friends, "he continued, looking invitingly from one guest to the other, and with some scepticism.

Sir George, setting the tone for a debate, the favourite part of his evening, interrupted, "unless, of course, you gentlemen should find an impediment to those aspirations." He laughed through his congestion. Some of his guests tonight were sworn enemies, here only because of Sir George's influence in the region. Many of these at his table, men so impatient of inferiority, that their obligation is painful to them. This is grist to the peer's mill.

William Jackson, a balding cleric, mid fifties, in the cloth and the collar of the ordained, stood, as was the custom on Duhallow's dinner table, visitors for the first time, were required to introduce themselves to "The Claret."

"May I say, gentlemen, my name is William Jackson and I am here as guest in tandem, of Mr. Theobold Wolfe Tone. I am a retired rector of diverse places and my complements to your house, Sir and your kind hospitality."

Mr. Tone, stood to continue the pleasantries. My name is Theobold Wolf Tone, I am a barrister and am here for the assizes in Wexford, over the coming week. I am pleasured to be here at Duhallow, thanks to your hospitality, Sir and new found friendship with Mr. James Attridge, a journalist of repute, even at a young age." James nodded his appreciation, then stood. " James Attridge, who was born here in this great house and at present a house guest of Sir George, an employer of my father, once upon a time and friend, so much appreciated".

Sir George looked enquiringly at the young officer. Bookey was on his feet, looking splendid, thought Cope. "I am Lieutenant Bookey of the Yeomanry of Lord Mountnorris and I am here to fulfil Sir George's invitation to his Lordship, who is indisposed." He waited for a comment, there was none and he couldn't help feeling a pang of annoyance at his evident dismissal.

Proclamations of newcomers to Duhallow, complete, as all others had been to the estate before, some more than others. The Rev. Cope looked darkly at Jackson. "We know who you are, Sir, a defrocked priest, as indeed is another here at this table. I'm surprised to see you back in Ireland, so soon after...."

"My notorious divorce, Sir, my spell in prison, my life with that Duchess in France, Mr. Cope, take your pick."

The group felt the tangle of words tighten between the two and Palmer threw a knowing glance at James, a glance full of mischief and expectancy. Nothing the old man worshiped as an argument , where forbearance and temper became entwined. He had explained to his young house guest, the benefit of his "male only" dinner parties. "Tempers can be let loose, mostly without restraint and in deference to, because of their beauty, women have the right to be ignorant of everything, but will not keep still. My dear wife, of course, was the exception."

"I refer, Sir, to your open sympathy with the Madgets, the Morats and the Robespiers of this world," Cope continued.

"Ah you mean the revolution in France?" Jacksons voice was encouraging for more conflict. "I have had the privilege of living in that fine country for a number of years with my dear friend, Elizabeth Chudleigh, but then you know all about that, you being a collector of gossip in all its forms." He hurried on, as Cope was about to protest. "Did you know, she was maid of honour to the Princess of Wales, but surely you know that too, she was exceptionally beautiful, Mr. Cope, you especially would have been impressed, but contrary, Sir to common gossip, I was not that lucky, the lady was never my mistress."

"Oh what a shame," Palmer made a face of exaggerated disappointment, throwing an eyeful of mischief at James.

To people's amusement, Sir George would engage the lovely servant girl in conversation, but obviously to the annoyance of Bookey and Cope, who were used to wigged valets and footmen fussing in all directions. Lord Edward Fitzgerald was certainly amused at the lack of vain ostentation as existed in the great houses, even in his own at Leinster House, a time in Ireland when if you were not in fashion, you were nobody. He felt comfortable in this old house that it seems, had turned its back on all of that.

The old man would put a hand on hers and issue some request about the wine, most of which he would pour himself, leaving his seat, as if to help her. She would whisper, like everything is alright and urge him to be seated. "Don't forget to tell Mrs. Brennan," and he would whisper to her. "I will Sir George", and "I surely will Sir George." "The hunt tomorrow now Kate, everything will be ready." She would give him that magnificent smile of complete tolerance,"It surely will, Sir George." Her sister would go about her work uninterrupted. The girls wore a presentable black dress, well flared, overhung with a white pinafore, laced cuffs and frill to the neck, all for easy movement. No mute servility here, servility without names, in starched shackles.

Philip Roche looked challengingly at the slightly built barrister. "Mr. Tone, was in France, is that not so, Sir?, I'm told you met senior officials."

Attridge's journalist juices began to flow. The young Lieutenant sat back in a small private zone of cynical expectancy.

Wolf Tone thought for a minute. Other pieces of conversation had now dried up. He would chose his words carefully. There were people in this room who, through misconception of his answer, could have him arrested. He felt a tinge of anger at his host and at this drunken priest for singling him out. He wondered at Palmer's politics. After all, he was a Yeomanry Commander. A census of those around him filled him with apprehension. Clerics in this part of the country, though Catholic, were in the pockets of the establishment. Experience had told him to know his audience, every one, and for the past two hours, through fumes of tobacco and liquor, he felt he had their measure. He was aware of the two young girls, standing back in the shadows and wished Palmer would send them away, dinner being served and finished.

Lord Edward Fitzgerald, potentially one of the most powerful men in Ireland, could be a perfect leader of his people, money, status abounding. He had been offered important roles to play by the authorities, but always refused to the chagrin of his powerful family. A sheltered and pampered life left him, in Wold Tone's opinion, too cushioned against the elements awaiting him, should he show his hand. The result; a pleasant, extremely cautious gentleman. At thirty years of age, the handsome Fitzgerald was no stranger to Paris and as an officer in the English army, had been wounded in the American campaign, after which, he was elected to the Irish Parliament. He had a new young wife, who demands all of his time though he WAS at Wexford. Tone had no fear of him. The fact that he was at the Wexford rally and walked with the throng, was encouraging, his membership of The United Irishmen would bring status and respectability, but would stop there.

The priests; Father Roche, he had met at Wexford. An open book, he was already a martyr to the Irish cause and the Irish whisky, but a danger to himself and those who sit with him.

Father John Redmond. How Palmer loved extremes in his company. A middle aged Catholic cleric, precise and articulate, the parish priest of Camolin. In conversation,Tone found him to be passionately law abiding and subject to the establishment and the King, and demanded, with an iron hand, that his parishioners should be likewise. As a consequence, a faithful servant and well favoured by his bishop and well rewarded.

Now, the Rev. R.J. Cope of Carnew. His fame had gone before him. A magistrate and land owner, feared and detested, according to Roche, in a radius of a hundred square miles and an ardent admirer of the rampant and demented Protestant clergyman in the North, Theodore William Bruce. This dear clergyman of Carnew, boasts his own small army. A man to fear, a man without scruples when words should be spoken carefully in his company. He sat, waiting for Tone's answer, knowing well the barrister's affiliations and his fight for Catholic emancipation, a great wrinkled crevice over his eyes, knitting his brows together, the face of a fanatic.

Then, Captain Isaac Carnock of Ferns Castle, a magistrate, fighting in the Scarawalsh Yeoman Cavalry. Tone had found in him, a certain amount of liberalism toward the Catholic question, though a powerful and respected leader in his community. Captain Carnock's liberalism would be well tested in another forum.

Not likewise, however, the second soldier in the room, the young Lieutenant Bookey, who, not like the Captain, was dressed in light blue swallow coat, with darker blue britches and deep red waistcoat. He was heavily decorated with a stock of accessories pinned to his lapels. A red fireball waiting to ignite, Bookey looked cheap and gaudy, in the midst of so much greys and blacks. Palmer had insisted he remove his sabre and gave it to Kate to put away. His estate at Rockspring, a training camp for marauding yeomanry had become notorious, from where his nightly sorties set out to cause havoc and fear among the peasants.

Then the other Roche; Edward Roche of Garrylough, also a captain in the Shelmalier Cavalry. A thick set man of fifty, a heavy face set on broad shoulders. Tone had been taken by his evident astuteness and obvious worldiness, well educated, it seemed. What Wolf Tone did not realise at time, was that the fifty year old, prosperous tenant farmer and miller, was active in the fledgling ranks of the United Irishmen.

Almost finally, there was Anthony Perry of Inch, five miles north of Gorey, between the Wicklow Hills and the sea, a member of the local yeomanry, and an infiltrator and organiser for the United Irishmen in North Wexford. Perry was an ignorant agitator, like the priest Philip Roche, he walked a dangerous path and like Father Roche, would start a rebellion all his own.

The remaining Catholic priest left little impression. Tone could see that Sir George had a favouritism for the middle aged dark haired cleric. Father John Murphy of Boolovague, who seemed to play his cards close to his chest, sat quietly conversing with those who wished to engage him. Wolfe Tone had no measure of him, a peasant priest, he saw him in conversation on and off with the peasant serving girls. Boolavogue, seemed to the barrister, when he was driven through the hamlet, that afternoon, to be almost an afterthought, a few scattered houses and cabins, representative of many hovel hamlets, the hallmark of the poverty and oppression imposed at will by so few on so many. Father Murphy was, as their curate, equal in every way, to their poverty and oppression.

"France?", he said, measuring his words. "I agree with Lord Edward earlier, chaos exists in France, but it is almost a new country now, there are many adversities to be overcome and it will be later rather than sooner before Mr. Robespiere brings together, all the civil and military reforms needed in a democracy, factions like the Jacobins and the Gherondists."

He addressed the big priest. "Senior officials, you say, Father, I was not so privileged. I was there on the business of The Catholic Committee, to visit the Irish monasteries, established over two hundred years ago, when the Irish were the enlightenment of Paris and of Europe. Monasteries like Sainte Genevieve, right on the mountain top overlooking the city, on a street named Street of the Green Horse. I also spent some reflective time with the priests at the college Des Lombardes in it's beautiful surroundings on the banks of The Seine. I was to meet there, Mr. Thomas Pain on appointment, but our paths did not cross, it was my loss."

Bookey, stiff and upright in his chair, put his glass slowly on the table, he did not look at Tone, but at Captain Carnock, like he was about to score points.

"I have it on good account that you visited The Tuilleries Palace, the seat of that corrupt government, that you were entertained by high ranking officers,"he said.

Tone, calm and collected, said, "As a tourist, Sir, everyone visits the Tuilleries, also the Royal, even Versailles. Now if you would call Mr. Nicholas Madgett, a good clergyman of Kerry extraction, an official, then yes, I was welcomed by the gentleman. Mr. Madgett is an official in the troubled department of foreign affairs and is interested greatly in the affairs of Ireland."

Palmer's pleasure in debate heightened when Bookey made a further effort at impressing his peers. "And, Sir, who gave you the mandate, or the right to be an ambassador, to sip and associate with an enemy of your country, and with, though you say you did not meet a troublemaker and a drunk in this Mr. Pain?"

Oh! Oh!. Laughed Palmer, while Roche, the priest bristled at the audacity of this brat. Palmer called to Kate Keohane and whispered something to her. She replaced the decanter of port and melted into the background. Attridge, though hanging on the brutish charge of the lieutenant, followed her with shaded passionate eyes.

"By God, Tone, croaked Palmer, what was your carry on in France, that this young maverick should have had you followed?"

Wolf Tone smiled, " "I can only say,I am flattered, Sir George, very flattered." He then seized the officer with that opaque look, down dressing him without hardly changing another feature. He sighed loudly, like tiring of the upstart. "Any man who is capable of writing a bible for peace, such as Mr. Pain, on the Rights of Man, is anything but a troublemaker. This Irishman is held in great esteem all over Europe and in America, where despotic monarchy is crumbling and human rights and liberty for all is becoming the order of the day. It's called democracy, Lieutenant....sorry I've forgotten your name?"

"Bookey," he spat.

Tone threw a dismissive hand toward him, "Bookey then." Then addressed Rev. Cope. Lord Edward Fitzgerald made little contribution as did the other priest, Murphy.

"Yes, Mr. Pain is a martyr to the drink." He turned again to Bookey. " "I'll wager, his intelligence would outweigh that of an unknown lieutenant any day of the week."

Bookey smarted at the insult and Carnock became concerned. Often in the past, the senior officer had had to curb the younger man's temper and indiscretions.

"Well then, Mr. Bookey, indeed Mr. Pain is addicted to drink, but then he's Irish, where eighty per cent of the people are martyrs to something or other, drink, like Pain, religion like our clergy, power like yourself, but mostly in Ireland, Sir, to injustice. Some of us go to great extremes in our perversions." He extended his glass to the soldier, "democracy, Soldier, where all men are equal in the eyes of God, democracy, I recommend again to you, try it sometime."

Father Redmond, the Camolin priest, eased the mounting pressure, which it was obvious, Bookey intended to stoke further. "And Mr. Tone, there is another bible, as you call it. I recommend to you, the bible by Mr. Edmond Burke, another good Irishman, in which he castigates the revolution in France as demonic for its terror and murder."

"Mr. Burke is a fine politician, Father Redmond," Tone continued, "Indeed as they say, as an Irishman, he's a great Englishman. He advocates that with the impending war with Spain, Ireland should fight on the side of England, to become nothing else, but the King's gun fodder. Why? I say, Ireland has no truck with Spain, why should we fight a country which has been good to us over the years, where our Catholic priests are educated. Mr. Burke's world is a world of aristocratic order, a world of Emperors, Kings, Queens, a place allocated to everyone and so called, anointed by God. Burke condemns the right of the French people to rise up out of a thousand years of deprivation and slavery at the hands of the dynasties, corrupt and cross bred."

Rev. Cope broke from a conversation with Lord Edward. It was evident to James that this clergyman would object to the company of half the guests at Palmer's table. "Doesn't it trouble you, Mr. Tone, that mixing with such officials could result in an enquiry into your motives. Do you not think that we might, those of us who are simple passive onlookers, might see the beginning of treason in your efforts?"

Father Roche scoffed loudly "You Sir, simple and passive, you say, you Sir, judge, jury and executioner, detester of all things, non-Protestant, judge, jury and executioner...." Caught for words, his fellow priest interjected. He had been holding interaction with just Father Redmond at his right and Anthony Perry to his left, otherwise, made little contribution 'till now.

"Please, gentlemen, no more politics, no more arguments in respect to our host. I, for one will be looking to the hunt tomorrow, we should be in our beds."

"No! No!, I insist, the host shouted, pounding the table. The intelligence is too immense to be allowed to filter into such mundane matters as horses. Go on Murphy, go on."

"It's unfair", John Murphy chided, "that you continue to stir the coals of unrest that smoulder in the hearts and minds of such conflicting ideas and so called ideals as sit about your table, my dear friend. Wine loosens our tongues and allows us to drop our reserves. One of these evening, you will allow matters go too far."

"And do you have reserves, hidden reserves?" Bookey harassed.

Father Murphy stood and Sir George, to his delight, applauded inwardly. John Murphy could take his place in any company, any debate, but he's like an old clock, he needs to be wound up every now and then. James Attridge had been influenced by his oratory in the church and now waited, in anticipation. To the ascendancy in the area, power mongers like Cope, he was a bit of a thorn and was simply a nuisance when it came to securing favours for his flock.

"Yes, I do, in fact, Lieutenant. I have reservations about corps of marauding drunken soldiers in full battledress , traversing the countryside, inflicting pain and deprivation on a pauperised and helpless people, feeding on their dependency and poverty and ignorance."

Bookey flared. "You dare Sir."

Ignoring the soldier, Murphy looked at Wolf Tone, his face full of accusation." And I have even greater reservations about organisations, whose chiefs go about the land in mob rallies, inciting that ignorance and promising new horizons, new reforms and new tomorrows."

Lord Fitzgerald, to Palmer's right, helped himself to the port decanter. He was uncomfortable, it was evident, at the cross presence of so many diverse opinions in a small company and doubted if he would accept any further invitations to this very unusual house. It was his second visit. When Lady Palmer was alive, much more acceptable then, not nearly as dangerous.

"So tell me, Father Murphy," his voice as cultured as himself, "would you have it that your people remain down trodden and, as you say, ignorant forever, or do you see anything good in what Mr. Tone is endeavouring to bring about?"

Roche didn't wait. "Look at you, John, look at you," his voice rising again. "A priest, a respected scholar of divinity, a theologian, for God's sake." He looked about the table in a kind of pleading. "This man tends to some of the poorest peasants in Wexford." He stopped at Redmond. "Fellow priest, Father Redmond here, in a fine house in Camolin, surrounded by many fertile acres of land...."

Redmond cut in, " given to me by my Protestant brothers in Christ...."

"Your Protestant brothers in Christ never owned the land in the first place, Sir, or is that the reason you're refusing absolution in your confessional to known and unknown sympathisers of nationalism, even refusing them last rights?" He continued, blocking Redmond's feeble attempt at answering. "This man, John Murphy, like many of the priests of Ireland, who are not courting favours from a corrupt establishment, rents a tiny room in Boolavogue and lives on the charity of good loyal Catholics. John Murphy is subject to a parish of paupers. An ascendancy church all around him would prefer he didn't exist, but without him you would have chaos in the whole of Kilcormack and beyond, a poor agitator, as poor as the mice in his excuse for a church, an agitator for small favours for his flock and with a cowardly bishop who is in the pocket of your ascendancy.

Murphy remained standing and was insisting. The candles were being replenished by the two girls, the younger one always in her sister's shadow.

"I'm content in my station, I simply don't want my people to be intimidated and harassed by the military and I do not want cosy

139

promises for a better tomorrow. Generation after generation have had their heroes and their martyrs and yet we continue in a servile dependent state. I will continue to insist the peasant of Kilcormack remains law abiding and God fearing for as long as is possible."

He looked at Lord Edward, a kind of pleading in his dark eyes. "It's almost sixteen years, Sir since Mr. Grattan and the Volunteers promised new reforms for the ordinary people. I had just come home from Seville and I thought that God had bestowed this great miracle in recognition of my ordination. How naive is that? The revolution of seventy two, backed by the guns of the Volunteers promised us a heaven on earth and how naive was that?"

He sat, exasperation draining him. Wolfe Tone warmed to him. Quiet and almost withdrawn all evening, the genial priest was surprising in his knowledge, his ethical common sense, steel somewhere underneath.

"I think the priest is right," insisted Cope, at least that we agree on."

"Ireland is now a nation, Mr. Grattan says in Parliament," said Mr. Tone, to nobody in particular , " that the 1790's will be a decisive decade for Ireland. But I fear for Ireland, Rev. Cope, I see something ominous ahead, unless we remain unresolved in rebellion and resolved to continue to be the pawn of Britain." He continued, eying the two military men. "Let it be said here and now, I seek reform, only, irrespective of creed or persuasion, and I want you to know that I do not condone the antics of the Defenders or the Whiteboys and the other factions cropping up, and I do NOT condone the ethics of Orangeism. I do not condone violence in any form, from any side and I do not oppose the king, contrary to common beliefs. Lord Edward will confirm, I have been offered an opportunity by Mr. Grattan, himself, to take a seat in Parliament. That very notion in itself is undemocratic. I will do that when we have a democratic system and a simple Irish Catholic peasant can put his mark under my name for election, when every man and woman in Ireland, Protestant, Catholic, Presbyterian alike can vote and not in our present restraints, where one in fifty has that privilege, I look to the age of reason."

Cope laughed, a barbed sarcasm. "For heaven sake, Mr. Tone, you're an intelligent man and a respectable Protestant of the ascendancy and yet you mention the Irish peasant and the age of reason in one breath. There IS no reason in this animal, man. You cannot lead or drive him, for he never reaches that age. And as for a vote for women, for God sake Sir, have some sense."

Kate Keohane stopped short on leaving the room for the kitchen, hurt clouding her expression. Edward Roche's strong voice followed her. "In one toxic breath, Sir, that ridiculous expression dismisses four million people, how very sad."

Captain Carnock, slurred through his wine, "I believe my friend did not mean that remark, Sir."

Bookey cut in. "You snubbed me earlier, Mr. Tone, however in the spirit of the evening, I forgive you. Now, in Father Murphy's wisdom, he should be of counsel to you and those who seek status above their station. Leave well alone, I say to the agitators, be grateful that His Majesty should look on Ireland with such kindness and affection. But your efforts at your so called Catholic emancipation, is nothing but an effort on your part to break the connection with Britain". He turned to Lord Edward, "Sir, Britain has been good to you and your family." To Tone, "you can thank His Majesty for your fine education, and you, Sir," this to Edward Fitzgerald. You sit on a fine estate at Garrylough, and who is to thank for that?"

He had gone too far, thought Lord Edward, as the room fell to silence. Both Tone and Fitzgerald exploded in mirthful ridicule, Carnock knew the younger man had made a chronic mistake. Oh! The witless dandy.

Containing his amusement, the man from Garrylough raised his eyebrows, but the dandy continued. Kate Keohane was back with Gobnait's wonderful after dinner pudding. She placed it, as she was told to, very gently on the sideboard.

"You want a democratic assembly in Parliament," he spat, annoyed at the composure of the barrister, "a rabble of land leaguers and fenians, paid agitators and pauperised adventurers, rape mongers and pillagers. Is that your vision for Ireland, Mr. Tone?"

"I believe you describe yourself very well, Lieutenant and let me reiterate, I have never expressed a wish to sever our tie with England, however I do say that our king and our government have much to learn of democracy."

"Rape mongers and pillagers, Sir," repeated Bookey.

Edward Roche said, pensively, taking stock of the younger man, "It's so sad to see such anger in a face not much more than a boy."

"I have learned my trade well, Sir, my age has nothing to do with it."

"Ah," quoted Sir George, "poor little men, poor little strutting peacocks! They spread out their tails as conquerors, almost as soon as they are able to walk. Go on Bookey, by God, continue to entertain us."

Bookey continued. "Your silence is somewhat disturbing, Mr. Roche, where do your affiliations point to and I take it you are no relation of the priest?"

Edward Roche had an established maturity about him, like a justice or a philosopher. He put both hands on the table and sized the upstart. "You see, unlike your good self, Lieutenant, I have very little to crow about, so hence my relative silence. Now tell me, nay, tell us all, because we are all ears. Who owns your estate at, I believe, Rocksprings."

The soldier frowned, " I am the own....."

"No, Sir, I mean the real or original owner of Rocksprings, this place you call home."

"My father," he spat, confused.

Wolfe Tone smiled, seeing the virtual greed for banter in his host's face.

"And his father before him," fumed the lieutenant.

"The fact is that you have only the right of a squatter to that land, Sir, is that not so?. You are just like the majority of landlords in Ireland and, as Mr. Tone said, you describe them so well, as rape mongers and pillagers. You acquired these lands through an ascendancy created one hundred and fifty years ago, an ascendancy of terror and confiscation.

Edward Roche was unhurried. "My great grandfather, Sir, owned the estates and property at Garrylough to the south of the county. I am at present, paying a handsome sum annually to Captain Le Hunt of the Shelmalier Yeomanry Cavalry, of which, I myself am an officer, for the pleasure of renting lands that are rightfully mine. I am, Mr. Bookey, what is known in Ireland as a wealthy tenant farmer and miller. My estates, which one day should be owned by my sons, on the fertile plains of Shelmalier, east of the River Slaney were given to my ancestors in the 12th. century for services rendered to the proud king of Leinster, one Dermot Mc. Murragh. We built Artramount Castle, where my landlord Le Hunt now resides, we built Drinagh Castle, the abbey at Selskar for the Augustinians , we were created knights, sheriffs for the county and enjoyed the life and titles of nobility until Cromwell came, and all the great Irish landlords suffered at his sword, the O'Moores, O'Carrolls, O'Dempseys, O'Riellys, Mc. Carthys, Fitzgeralds, The Geraldines..."

"My great grandmother was the only survivor when Strongbow's armies came, killed her parents, her seven brothers and sisters, and all the servants and farmhands. Bodies hanged from trees and rafters as an example to all of Garrylough. I pass the great oak every day and see them like ripened fruit, hanging in the wind. Two years later, she was bought at a hiring fair in New Ross, by a small tenant farmer and eventually married a son of the house. Le hunt's ancestors were given Garrylough, to whom I pay rent today and who refers to me as

"Roche."

He slugged at his wine, the graft of the indignity of his existence, swilled out of his system in a burst of self control. "So you see, young man, with fire and hatred rampant in your belly, you really don't know who you are, except if truth be known and acted out, you are a man of no property, as like a usurper of a day long gone, when your ancestor, some mealy mouthed Cromwellian lymie corporal pitched his dirty arse on the sweet grass of Rocksprings and stayed. Where as I know exactly who I am. So let my silence disturb you and my thoughts provoke you, for in them, there is no room for a tiresome lily faced boy, who's direction is both dangerous and provocative."

The dandy was caught for words. "I keep the peace in my patch, Sir, I have been decorated accordingly. Camolin and Enniscorthy are being plagued by so called Croppies, Defenders and Whiteboys, so that we are unable to sleep in our beds at night, but the Croppies, a new army of troublemakers, or are they another wing to your organisation, Mr. Tone?"

Kate was back in the room, every now and then she would return to the kitchen and relate the goings on up above.

"Croppies," said John Murphy, his face flushed, slow to shake the tree of weighty controversy.

"I'll tell you what the Croppy is, Lieutenant. The Croppy Boy is an enigma, a ghetto born ruffian, who is looking for a place for himself in what he hopes will be a new Ireland, as promised by our guest to night, Mr. Wolfe Tone. The Croppy shears his head in the style of his counterpart in France, though the poor devil is ignorant if it's whereabouts. The Croppy Boy is tired of centuries of depreciation , and has seen, through these centuries, the cycle of the life of his ancestors, from cradle to grave; outcasts. The Croppy Boy sees his mother cry daily, his father broken and without hope, often hungry, while cart loads of food passes his cabin, daily on its way to England. The Croppy Boy has a sister, who has been raped and a brother who has been subjected to a new outrage against the innocence, the pitchcapping, he has a sibling with the suffering of malnutrition, he has seen suicide and he has decided, enough is enough. But he is resolute, now. The Croppy Boy, through that resolution is now resolute, has become hardy and tenacious, and is looking for leadership and direction."

For the first time tonight, Murphy was assertive, when Rev. Cope said, "that Croppy terrifies the respectability , he is a destroyer of property, will steal at will and our womenfolk are terrified."

"Just a while ago, Mr. Cope, your young friend did not put too much store in womenfolk, or was that just Catholic womenfolk, for the tree casts it's shadow on all, even the wood cutter. I believe, as Aquinas tells us, that whatever way by which one frees himself from fear and tyranny of others, is a natural good. These words were written before Christ Himself walked the Earth. In "Summa Theoligica Quest", Saint Thomas tells us that, if a need is so great, so pressing that, clearly the urgent necessity has to be relieved, then a man may lawfully relieve his distress out of the property of another, openly or secretly."

The priest of Boolavogue sighed wearily, looking at Cope, "and they are sending us to perdition for stealing a chicken."

"And tell us, Father Murphy", Bookey interjected coarsely, "will you be the leader, the one to lead the Croppies into the Promised Land?"

"He's contemptible," thought Attridge.

The big cleric rose wearily and sauntered to the sideboard where Kate Keohane was about to cut Gobnet Brennan's beautiful strawberry pudding into sumptuous portions. He gave Kate a dark look, no wink this time. He took the knife gently from her hand. Returning to the table, he stood behind Lieutenant Bookie and Kate thought he was going to do damage. He dwarfed the Redcoat, placing the wedge shaped blade before him on the table. She stood petrified, and Palmer wondered if he had allowed matters go too far. Roche pushed the handle of the knife toward Bookie's hand, but Father Murphy eased it out of harm's way. Before Roche moved away, he hissed through an angry mouth, "I'd prefer to kill you now, Bookey, than to think that providence might favour you with such a task, for there is no doubt, you could start a revolution all on your own."

But Cope continued, while Bookey tried to hide his upset and contempt for a man , an enemy who is too formidable to be opposed one to one. "Enough of the roulette, gentlemen, I believe again that Father Murphy and myself are of a similar opinion."

Murphy held his tongue, there will be many a favour entreated for in days to come. In Cope's book, interest works night and day, debt knaws with invisible teeth.

"Your forthcoming rally at Enniscorthy can only invite the pot of dissent to overflow, Mr. Tone. Mr. Russell, a fellow magistrate, I believe, is very foolish in his organising of this meeting. Wretches will live on its promises, promises that have no substance. Father Murphy and all the Catholic Clergy of Ireland should know and appreciate what we in the ascendancy have done for the masses. The priests would do well to remember that the new seminarian college at Maynooth, is presently under construction at the total expense and endeavour of London on land owned by the authorities, solely for the education of young Catholic priests."

"Let's have another lesson in fact here," barked Philip Roche. Firstly, Sir, you or the authorities do not own the lands at Maynooth." He pointed at Lord Edward, "that gentleman is the rightful owner of Maynooth and all the fertile lands west of Dublin, confiscated at the pleasure of Elizabeth and of course, Lord Cromwell. Secondly, your seminary is yet another move to shackle further the entire priesthood. Maynooth is to be a place of imprisonment and a den of brain washing to six hundred indoctrinated half wits whose education will be controlled in accordance with the terms laid down by the authorities and the Bishops, so that the country will be awash with arse lickers like Redmond here, a submission that makes slaves of men and of the whole human frame. I shouldn't live to see the day, Irish priests will wear the uniform of John Bull. And as for the endeavour and expense, the endeavour will be the slave labour that holds us fast and the expense, well don't worry, the king of England will find another fine tax for his purpose."

Attridge, all evening, had the feeling of being on the edge of things, with little or nothing to offer to the proceedings. He felt at one with the gentlemanly quietness of Lord Edward Fitzgerald, and what seemed to be the inadequacy of Father Redmond, whose duty, it seemed was to comply with everything R. J. Cope had to say. He asked to be excused for a while, being warned by a merry Sir George, to remember everything that took place, " for posterity". Bookey was saying, "I suggest, Sir George, you clean up your social list, it's wearisome and dangerous, there's treason in this room."

Attridge hesitated at the door waiting for Palmer's reply, it was worth the waiting. "Nothing that happens or that is said at this table, tonight or any night is for public consumption. What you do beyond the boundaries of Duhallow, in your so called duty, is the business of yourself and Rev. Cope, though I have to say that your notoriety upsets me. Should I find that you are unable to hold the fire in that belly of yours, as to who sits here and what their opinions are, I shall have you evicted from your beloved Rocksprings, your ill gotten estate and shipped from Wexford harbour, for like yourself, I sit on an estate to which I have no call, no doubt some great Irishman's inheritance is my benefactor."

Cope stood to go, Palmer stood with him, unsteady arm about the cleric's shoulder, to his discomfort. "Now R. J. here knows exactly what I am talking about. A great lump of his tithes come out of the pockets of my tenants, a fine stretch of his lands is of the generosity of Duhallow, a little agreement between my late wife Pamela and

Mountnorris himself, but not written in stone, is that not so, R.J.?"

John Murphy stood with the tall Philip Roche. "I can see trouble in the tea leaves, Philip." Then he went to shake the hands of all, even Bookey " Yes, John Murphy, and not like yourself, when it comes, I will welcome it and a great shout will go up and it will be heard the world over. Our ancient roots will rise themselves from their slumber and their seeds will stir up into our souls." The big priest had a special warmth in his hand shake for Tone and Lord Edward.

**

Always complementary to her cooking, James sat at the great kitchen table, when the visitors had gone to bed. Lord Edward, Mr. Tone and Mr. Edward Roche, were guests for the night. Gobnait Brennan was an assistant cook at Duhallow when James was born. Since he came back, though she seldom showed any signs of emotion or favour, in her enclosed life, it was surprisingly evident to Kate Keohane that the cook liked what the child had become.

"Man's destiny lies half within himself, half without, Mrs. Brennan, but I fear for the future after tonight's business. There are many willing for a rebellion, but many more will be dragged along in its wake, and there are two or three about your table tonight who are capable of pushing that button. Poor Father Murphy."

"O that a man might know the end of this day's business ere it comes", James quoted.

The cook of Duhallow ground her sparcely spread teeth together in a grin of acceptance, trying to decipher what surely were words of great importance.

Chapter 15

The stirrup cups were being charged and Lieutenant Bookey had cornered Wolfe Tone on the terrace. When Kate approached with her tray Bookey was already immersed in his own importance. "So you don't hunt, Mr. Tone. Only those who appreciate the finer things in life can call themselves huntsmen." Resplendent in his hunting gear, Bookey continued, taking a cup from Kate Keohane. " A fine human pleasure, Mr. Tone, that should you partake, might temper your mind from matters of politics that do not concern you. Believe me, Sir, a canter is decidedly a cure for all evils."

Tone helped himself to a cup, smiling at her, he said, "do you never sleep, young lady?" Even in the early part of the day, the stunning young woman could enthral. He remembered how Attridge seemed to find her highly infectious during dinner.

"I envy you your happy pastime, Lieutenant, but canter a horse, I am well able, however over ditches unnecessarily is a cruel imposition on my frail constitution, even more cruel on the unfortunate horse."

The horn sounded below on the sweep to the house, hounds impatient for the off, scurrying about in the hedges and under the bellies of the sweating horses, dogs, almost as illiterate as man, how they feed man's colossal vanity, he thought.

"However", he continued, "I could never understand that the paucity of human pleasures, as you perceive it, should persuade us ever to call hunting, one of them. After all, when caught, the fox is worth nothing, just fools following for the pleasure of following, you can't even eat the damned thing. However, again, Lieutenant, better defenceless animals than the human kind, eh?"

"You seem set on insulting me, Sir," seethed the soldier, "you don't want me as an adversary."

Tone's face remained almost tranquil, only the grey eyes remained fixed. "For goodness sake, Mr. Bookey, I have much more important enemies who privilege me with their contempt, than a country upstart at the head of a questionable band of ruffians, he calls a regiment. Now, Sir, I suggest you go and play."

There was a sudden, almost reverend interruption to the proceedings as three score heads turned toward the stately coach and pair, complete with outriders and a splendid grey stallion coming up behind. Steps were brought to the carriage for his exiting. From the time the carriage door opened, the imperial attitude settled on the drama, as if he and he alone had the right to be selfish. Lord Mountnorris had arrived and immediately asked if the priest John Murphy had come.

Before Bookey had a chance to continue the conflict, Sir George Palmer bounded across the terrace and caught Wolfe Tone by the arm. "Take no notice of him, Mountnorris loves the drama."

"Why does he look for the priest, Sir George?" asked Tone.

"You might not think so, Tone, but Murphy is the finest horseman in these parts and he has been Mountnorris's champion for some time. John Murphy is a sportsman of considerable stature, even at his age, road bowling, and the field game of hurling. He has an army of kids who follow him like he is a god in their innocent eyes."

John Murphy and Lord Mountnorris were in conversation, no doubt about tactics, etc., when Palmer said, "there is somebody here who knows you, leave this youngster to find his own troubles, he's good at that." Bookey seethed further and went to find his horse.

A man was leaning against the balustrade. "Gerald Hill", laughed Tone, recognising a former college mate. They shook hands warmly. Palmer seemed pleased. "Hill tells me you two were in Trinity together."

Palmer moved to meet the visiting peer, a stirrup cup in each hand.

Sir Gerald Hill, only one of two who were wearing wigs that morning, precise and immaculate, sized his friend up. "You look well, Tone, a little thinner perhaps, but well nevertheless". Tone remembered the spoilt aristocratic schoolboy who had servants strutting about him seeing to his every need and comfort. Hill had fallen into flesh, looking more than his thirty six years.

On the terrace, James Attridge had introduced Wolf Tone to a number of the visitors, Lord Edward had left in the early morning. Sir George, delighted in bringing the barrister to every attention fuelling his insatiable lust for political controversy, relishing the embarrassment in the faces of many members of the ascendancy, pushed by Palmer to press flesh with an agitator. Palmer knew he had landed a great fish and he would be forever grateful to James and whatever providence that brought Tone to Duhallow. He marvelled at the calm unobtrusive way in which the visitor handled favour and controversy alike, polite to his fingertips, few saw the steel underneath.

Hill was immediately condemning. "My God, Tone, you were brilliant at college, the only one who didn't have to cram for exams, medals for oratory, and those pamphlets, though ill advised, were brilliantly delivered. London's Middle Temple, and you could be, if you chose, Ireland's leading barrister. I remember, you once had aspirations for the British Army." He raised his voice, attracting attention "Damn it man, you would be a general by now." He put an arm about the narrow shoulders, "Edmond Burke, himself, a native Irishman heaped praise on your writings, though, again not in agreement with some of your aspirations. Only God knows what dementia has invaded that brain of yours, embroiling yourself in this nonsensical pilgrimage for the damn Catholics."

"Please, my friend", Tone cautioned, conscious of ears nearby. "We had enough politics last night here to last us a fortnight at least. They've sounded the horn."

"Theobold," Hill's voice was pinpricked with caution. "These people cannot be given the quarter you seek for them. My estates in the North, are constantly under siege from the rabble that call themselves Whiteboys, Defenders and so called United Irishmen, and this troublemaker Monro in Antrim, who professes to know you." He pressed on, his voice rising again, frustration at its edges, " and now I come south to find you're their leader." He scowled "you should go into Grattan's Parliament, man, you'd be excellent."

Tone's eyes brightened. "Gerald, thank you for your praises, coming from you, praise indeed, but Henry Grattan and I will never sit together in Parliament or in any assembly....". He broke off, looked about him and pointed to the girl moving about the guests, carefully holding her tray. "You see that lovely child there, dispensing the cups, Henry Grattan and I will sit in Parliament when that girl and all of her family will honour me with her vote, and when Mr. Grattan stops bringing his knitting to Parliament. Mr. Grattan can have my application to contest membership, when the King of England allows the Catholics of Ireland to vote for me. It is only then will we rid ourselves of those night raids on your estates. Give the people due dignity and you'll have law and order, keep them underground and you will have anarchy. Read Mr. Pain's book, Gerald, he says Edmond Burke has discovered a world of windmills and that monarchy is arbitrary power in an individual person."

All cordiality gone, Hill insisted, "then I take it, Sir, that you object to monarchy in Ireland?"

"I have taken the oath to His Majesty", Tone said, that was conditional on taking silk, but on the whole, yes I do, because in the main, it is ill gotten and corrupt."

"And are you including in that, The King of England?"

"Again I quote Tom Pain, Gerald, that the nobility of France, the aristocracy of England and the Ascendancy in Ireland is evil, because it all came from conquest."

Hill was incredulous. "So you sympathise with the revolution in France, then?"

Tone sighed politely and made to move. "You have mentioned Edmond Burke and I really do wonder where his sympathies lie. The French nobility was the most corrupt in Europe and don't tell me you don't know that, and a symbol of that corruptness is a woman whose full scope of ignorance has yet to be mapped. Marie Antoinette, the wife of the Dauphine, your Mr. Burke wrote of her in '73, that she was like a glittering star, full of life and splendour and joy, all this while her subjects died in the streets of hunger. Mr. Burke, to my mind is a poor judge of character, Gerald."

The horn sounded again

"We know why your friend was in Paris, Theobold. We know who Jackson met and we know his ambitions to bring the French to Ireland. He's sloppy and adventurous, he won't get far. And what of Lord Edward Fitzgerald and Mr. Napper Tandy?, what was their purpose with the French?"

Sir Gerald Hill, his heavy face in slight palpitation, said, "most important, you, Sir, you above all the others could pull it off".

Tone shook his head. "Fitzgerald is aristocracy, the French hate aristocracy. Tandy?, well the poor man has erroneous perceptions in a free Ireland. As for me, Sir, I believe England to be a tyrant, do you think I would replace one tyrant with another, by bringing the French?"

"You've been to France, recently, Theobold." Hill's eyes were full of mischief.

"On Catholic Committee business, nothing else, I visited France to further the cause of the Catholics."

"But you're a Protestant, man," fumed Hill.

"I'm Irish first, Sir."

Hill stormed off, his horse being attended by two stewards and Tone saw in the set of his shoulders, the slap of the crop on the rump of the unsuspecting horse, an enemy in the making, the pouting audacious brat who learned his craft from birth.

All around him, people walked in dangerous paths, while the superior man is quiet and calm, waiting for the appointments of Heaven. Wolfe Tone made his way inside, where an early lunch awaited him, as he acknowledged the courtesy wave from the hand of the one uncomplicated man in all of Wexford; Father John Murphy. A youth in a black frock coat, too young to be ordained, stroked the black mare as the priest climbed aboard. The youth looked up at the terrace, brought out the little butterfly from his pocket and wondered again to be so bold as to approach the man in the centre of attraction all morning, with the knife that had given him and his brother their freedom, but Mr. Tone had gone inside with James Attridge and the occasion was lost to him.

Chapter 16

As in every year, the rampant harvest is saved, packaged and sent across the channel. Father Murphy's dues were delivered by members of his flock who could afford it, to his digs with lavish generosity, mostly more than they could afford. The Tansy boys helped stock his turf store in the yard, cart loads of winter fuel. He would protest that he had more than enough, but still they came, enough for his fireplace in his room and for the two gluttonous stoves in his church at Boolavogue. Donovan showed them how to prepare his potato pit and tend his vegetable plot. Father John's chicken coup needed extending as three more hens were delivered on his birthday every year complements of Mrs. Gobnet Brennan, Lord Palmer's cook at Duhallow. All this found its way in many directions and allowed him to be generous in his own generosity, when on Sundays much of the bounty found its way to the alms table in a dark corner of the church. Baskets of fresh eggs, turnips, cabbages and potatoes would be spirited away after Mass.

The boys had become servers. They learned the wide words in Latin, without needing the art of translation.

"The tongue of man is a twisty thing, so says Homer in his Iliad and that was three thousand years ago," said the priest, you boys learn fine and fast."

Looking, especially at G., Father warned, knowing he might have aspirations to the priesthood, he had the gentle nature and the fortitude essential for the calling, "pure religion and undefiled before God and the Father is this; to visit the fatherless and widows in their affliction, feed the bellies of the poor and keep oneself unspotted before the world, so says the Bible, my young friend, a tall order indeed."

Hen remained his puny self, with little growth, but his health improved under Mary Donovan's coaxing. They had had a good childhood and were now at the stage of passing that subtle stage from childhood to adulthood and for G., the arrival point in the process was when he discovered that core of strength within him that helped him to survive the hurt of recent time. Not so, Hen. His consumptive condition left him querulous and unhappy, like the purpose in his young life was to have a grievance, often, it seemed, against the whole world. Mary would strive to satisfy his many whims, assuring G. that the boy's unhappiness was never anything but a form of fatigue. G. would scold him and tell him his fits were dangerous and bad, that he was only looking for attention and that Mother would not approve.

"Yes, well she's not here is she," he would argue. G. had come to realize that nothing would fill the void in him left by her death, nothing soon. He would still cry in his sleep at night, mentioning Captain Wharton's name in his nightmares.

Chapter 17

John Rudd was feeling good about life. His business was flourishing. Rudds Inn, the main hostelry of the principle town of Enniscorthy had snared a wonderful and profitable cherry. When Bridie Tansey would take her two boys, in her trap, from Killane to Enniscorthy, tea and Johnnie Cake and doughnuts were a treat in the posh dining room, where people sat in their tea time tables, with white linen and little floral posies. She would say that some degree of affectation was necessary to the mind and to the body, but never to over act, one of the many occasions when they would " put on their Protestant Faces." "You know what happened to the frog....... the frog tried to be as big as the elephant and what happened?.... he burst."

Today, G. looked and felt very different. Almost as tall as Father John, in his new frock coat, from the priest's closet in his sacristy, he was to accompany Father John to the conference in Rudds Inn. Business that John Rudd had been courting for some time had landed gloriously on his doorstep, with the election to high office of the new Bishop of Ferns, one James Caulfield. The Bishop had brought the Catholic Church and all its commercial advantages, to Rudds, to the chagrin of the Catholic traders of the area, that Mr. John Rudd, a Protestant, a devout Loyalist and a member of the fledgling Orange Order, should be favoured by a Catholic Bishop, anxious to be seen to show solidarity with government, ascendancy and London. To this end, the diminutive cleric publicly urged his priests to reconcile themselves to the political realities of the time and it's inevitabilities, a complete contrast to the ideals of his predecessor, the genial Bishop Nicholas Sweetman, who would entertain the conference at his residence at Ferns or in Wexford Town.

A conference to accommodate the priests of north Wexford would convene at Rudds Inn, twice yearly, at which refreshments and lunch would be served as part of the Bishop's new doctrine. The little man, in full regalia, arrived in an immaculate coach and pair, complete with outriders, a gift, it was reported, from Dublin Castle, with the complements of the Lord Lieutenant himself, a king's bishop, well installed and well plumed. Like a royal pageant, the wispy wraith of a man floated through the foyer. John Rudd bowed and scraped before the church's new prince, the nervous staff at his elbow.

It was the year 1795 and Bishop John Caulfield was to send out an edict from the town of Enniscorthy, that was to contribute in no small way to the ventilation of a new antagonism among his flock and a sense of trepidation in his priests. In the big comfortable dining room of Rudds Inn, Caulfield distributed a new dossier of rules and regulations regarding the future administration of his clergy and how they should relate to the people and to the authorities and especially as occur in the course of moral theology.

G. sat in the rear of the room with half a dozen deacons who would be there in attendance, like himself. He really wanted to wait in the yard with the mare, but Father Murphy had paid for his ticket, he was to pretend he was a deacon in his black frock coat and white neck kerchief. G. watched him associating with fellow priests, but felt Father Murphy really didn't want to be there, knowing he had little respect for the new Bishop.

For two hours, Caulfield laid down his guidelines for political conduct, as Roman Catholic priests, their behaviour in the face of lawlessness, intercourse with the authorities and the king's commissioners should be strengthened and matured.

John Murphy sat and listened to the do's and don'ts of Caulfield's new edict and saw him sow the seeds of a forthcoming rebellion among his subjects. Dissension very well directed, dividing even the true hearted of those already wearied and dust covered clerics was becoming a mighty stream of waters, dividing what was once a mountain of solid rock.

"I want you," the prelate emphasised clearly, the voice bigger than the man, "to impress on the people of Wexford, to reconcile themselves to their unalterable circumstances. There is to be an unambiguous transference of loyalty from your many associations with so called nationalism, onto the divine shoulders and person of His Gracious Majesty."

For some reason, John Murphy got the impression that the bishop scoured the room, settling on him. "I forbid the public pastime of road bowling and field hurling, where no good can come of an accumulation of so many hot blooded youngsters, their tempers open to the world." All about, heavy bodies stirred restlessly in their seats.

"All turbulence, disturbing the public peace and good order, opposing the King's government and legislature, or violating the established laws of the land, is to be marked with detestation and reprobation. You are to instil loyalty and fidelity on the part of the peasants, to the gracious King George, so that, from here on, obedience to the laws of His Majesty's Government is to be a religious, conscientious and indispensible duty of every Roman Catholic."

"The eleventh commandment", somebody whispered. "Honour thy King."

"It is your duty as priests of the Catholic Church, to ensure that all tithes are paid on time and your parishioners should be encouraged to work harder and longer to witness self mortification where necessary in order to meet these obligations. Should you find hardship among the peasantry, then you should endeavour to be of assistance from your own resources."

Faces turned incredulously to one another. John Murphy simply stared at his own clenched fists, fighting for control.

"I charge you that the downfall of this once proud nation is heading toward an apocalypse on the backs of two maladies; intemperance and drunkenness, and you will strive to disencumber your flock of same malady by showing perseverance and temperance in your own lives."

In his own humility, the bishop was greatly aware of the unworthiness all about him, but of a tiny beacon of redemption in the morass before him, a kind of saintliness, that of his own.

"By the grace of God, my entire life has been devoted to such mortification, and I have included in my message to you, a simple prayer to the God of understanding and forgiveness, to be said daily. Read it, have it copied and distributed. Instil such virtues of which I speak and your people will benefit greatly in the acceptance of their circumstances." Then he named publicly, the twelve priests he had sacked since coming to office, for embracing the deformities mentioned."

John Murphy looked about him at his colleagues, high complexioned horsemen of various ages, the younger among them, child faced and innocent, like the deacons, pushed by a mother, assuring her of an entry into Heaven. He felt an emptiness for them, a fatherly concern, that wanted to send them home to that mother with the unveiled ambition to climb upwards on the miseries of her chosen one. If they came to Enniscorthy for comforting, to immerse themselves and refresh themselves in the healing and understanding balm of Mother Church, then this sharp faced little man in princely garb, was yet to be another disappointment. They would find no tolerance, no tenderness or loyalty here, no crutch for the trials and crisis of their narrow lives. A crowded room of Irish Catholic priests, who were not allowed, by Parliament, to own property of any kind and whose measure of wealth, was to rent for their meagre comforts, one room in a designated boarding house.

His friend, Father Philip Roche, in a fit of sobriety had lamented for the want of just one leader in a country that once had a hundred and twenty kings and he thought of Roche now, banned from the convention and possibly drunk in a corner of People's Whiskey House at Trasna, as he looked at the purple clad traitor before him and whispered the poet's lamentation, "I am in Hell, isolated from God."

He told them he had arranged a list of the commercial traders of Wexford, to be used by them and recommended to their parishioners, for personal requirements, like shirts, shoes, clerical outfitters and the printing of books, stationery, pencils. "These traders are recommended by the authorities to me and I can arrange a small discount."

The newly printed book of rules, together with recommended traders, was distributed and the logo on the cover, surmounted with the crown of the House of Hanover, "George Rex 111, Ascendancy Scribner, printers to the Government and The Crown."

Diminutive, unattractive though he was, Caulfield had a kind of aura about him. In the foyer of Rudds, he moved through the crowd and young priests bobbed and smiled nervously as they bent to kiss his ring.

G. felt a pang of nervousness as the bishop seemed to approach, but his target was Father John.

"If I might have a word, Father Murphy."

They moved to a corner under a portrait of King George, the artist found the madness in the eyes to perfection. They were in G.'s ear shot, Murphy a good five inches taller.

"I didn't think you would know me, Lordship." Said John.

"Well now, and why wouldn't I know you, Father, I'm getting to know all my priests, the loyal ones and the troublesome ones." He hesitated, waiting for a reply. There was none. "We all know, that if the late Bishop Sweetman had his way, 'tis you'd be wearing the purple, not me."

G. heard the remark and looked over the bishop's shoulder at Murphy, his surprise evident.

"Hardly," replied Murphy

"He had great time for you John, without a doubt, you are well qualified, a theologian at the age of thirty." The sharpness in his voice softened.

"I had great time for him, Bishop." He left the complement hang.

"You turned it down, I'm told, may I ask why?"

"It's something I prefer not to discuss, begging your pardon." Father Murphy's voice was cold, not forthcoming, something G. had not witnessed before.

"I wish to know, Father, it's not easy being a poor country priest when you know you could go much further."

"If I had wanted an easy life, Lordship, I would have remained at home in Tincurry with my poor family, and you know, Sir, that a recommendation from your Bishop is not enough, it has to have the blessing of London."

" Of Rome, Father."

"London first, then Rome".

"So?" invited the bishop.

"So," sighed Murphy, "I will be a priest at my mother's wishes and I praise God daily for her influence, but a Bishop at King George's pleasure?, hardly."

G. sensed the beginning of conflict. "Have you no ambition to get off the bottom rung, man?" His patience jarred at the other's temperance . "In the next year or two, we shall be designating assistant bishops to a number of dioceses, such an appointment could take you off the roads and place you in a position of power and respectability. You're a theologian, for goodness sake, you could do so much for the good."

Murphy made to move. "Not in Ireland, Lordship. "In Ireland we have confused power with greatness, it has become a desolating pestilence, polluting all it touches and I have seen that manifest itself here today."

"Before you go, Sir," the bishop was losing control, "I want you to know I take great exception to the way you have infiltrated the penal system, contracting and bargaining on behalf of law breakers, drunkards,near-do-wells. Because of such favours, I am being sought after for reciprocal courtesies. You have become uncooperative with our brothers of the ascendancy of the area, you have become an embarrassment to Rev. Roger Owen in recent times."

Those nearby were aware of a pending calamity, a country priest squaring off to the Bishop of Wexford.

"You also know what I have said about games on the roadways and in the fields."

"Don't have any fear of the innocent games we play, Lordship. They fill in the lonely hungry hours of a people stripped of hope and dignity by a nation of demagogues. It is poverty and not road bowling and field hurling that is the parent of crime and revolution."

G. saw Murphy step away. "Believe me, Bishop, in me you will find no better servant, but should you embark on such inadvisable action, then that is where you will find your revolution."

The purple storm savaged the doorway and the Bishop went and immolated himself on the unfortunate coachman.

Among the clergy, there were mixed attitudes to Murphy's conduct and a number of them gathered up their belongings and left.

A fellow priest put a hand on John Murphy's shoulder. G. was introduced again as "my lieutenant" by Father John, who seemed

158

pleased to meet the stranger.

Father Michael, was a low size rugged faced man, younger than Father John. He showed a certain doggedness, even precocity.

"Glad to see you showing a bit of dissent at long last John you know, of course, that is the essence of a heretic." Michael had a warm smile, showing certain affection for his senior.

"You're not supposed to be here at all, Michael, he just sang out your name, yourself and Roche...." John whispered.

"I'll be anywhere I chose to be, brother Murphy, the fact that my bishop chooses to send me to coventry is not a burden on me, indeed 'tis a blessing. I have no church any more, but then the church was a prison and Caulfield held the key."

"He'll put you in prison," said John. "This fellow is listed as a rebel rousing renegade," he explained to G.

Father Michael put a friendly arm about his friend. "Wherever anyone is against his will, John, that is to him, a prison. I say my Mass every morning at The Three Rocks. A rock is my altar, as God Himself is my rock. What is a church but a roof and a few bits of furniture, where the idea of Caulfield's god ends in a paltry cattle shed." Now, he slapped Murphy's broad back, "you're taking me for a few ales, but not in this place," he frowned, and turning to the few dozen frocked assembly, he called to them. "My good friend, John Murphy , The Bishop of Boolavogue, is going to sup with me, together with his trusty lieutenant....., what is your name again son?" Caught off guard, G. stammered, "George, Sir." Michael's eyes popped in pantomimic disbelief, "Holy God, Son, surely nobody ever threw holy water on that." He turned to his audience, about sixty clerics showed their amusement. "Did any of you villains baptise this fine fellow in the name of the King of England?"

"They call me G., Sir".

Father Michael frowned. "Well, sure, the whole world is founded on compromise, let's put it this way, G., you might have dispensed with the horse, but you still have the saddle, now, we're going to that fine establishment, the welcoming hostelry of Mr. Maurice O'Callaghan, beyond in the square and ye had better follow." Before storming through the door, he unhinged the portrait of the king, put it gently on the floor, face to the wall, then pointed to the notice to the right of the entrance, " No Catholics." He pulled it from the wall and went back into the tavern, where a further twenty or thirty clerics were watering their wits. He held up the notice. "Now do you want me to translate this bit of heresy or have you all lost your self respect." Then he shouted above the din, "you're Catholics, for Christ sake, you shouldn't be in

159

here," dashing the framed notice against the fireplace, glass shattering.

This very strange cleric, obviously well known and just a little feared and admired by all, put a hand on G.'s shoulder. "C'mon George," he smiled.

Mr. John Rudd saw the death of his day's business, as in one sweeping accumulated motion, seventy frocked clergy spewed past him into the street. Extra staff, he had taken on for the day's bumper business stood idle. Two priests, he would take note of and he would mark for future mention to Rev. Owen of Camolin, when he would visit and look for the progress of his half share of the business. He would want to know, after all his courting of the wispy bishop of Wexford, why the day was a disaster.

In Mr. O'Callaghan's low ceilingd tavern, tobacco smoke and general smog drifted up to the heavy beams, the audience was fifty per cent of the atmosphere . Michael became more voiced as the hour turned. But what was in his heart was soon on his lips, as drunkenness never keeps a secret. He began, to Father John's annoyance, about the sovereignty of the people, under the yoke of ascendancy and the right of the people to rise up.

O'Callaghan never had such a night's business as a hundred cloaked clerics crowded his thatched ale house. The so called Catholic Committee has resolved that they were the only body, competent to declare the will and the sentiments of the Catholics of Ireland and they are adamant that we, the pastors of the people have no interference in politics. Wolf Tone and Napper Tandy and the others refer to a vote that may tend, and I quote, "to alter our present happy constitution under which we have all, so long prospered."

Rage creased his flushed face and he looked directly at John Murphy. " Now, what kind of Irishness is that, John Murphy, and we barely surviving here in Wexford, under a cowardly bishop, but then you're one for turning the other cheek, are you not, my friend?" Sarcasm was rooted in his unhappiness.

"Be careful", whispered John, "the walls have ears."

The Defenders are rising up in Ulster, God bless them." The rebel continued and G. could picture him as a pulpit thumper, the hammer of God and could understand, perhaps why he was silenced. " They're spreading all the way down to us, Monro in Antrim, Joy Mc. Cracken in Tyrone, they'll be looking for us John," he turned to the crowd, "for all of us." His eyes filled with passion.

Father John stood and looked at G., motioning toward the door, but addressed his friend before leaving. "You bring your hopes and dreams onto the streets and roads and thousands will die and what will you do then, Michael, lock your door and your window and lay low until it's all over, until your tree of liberty dies in the dust?"

They made for the door. "The tree of liberty must be refreshed and nurtured from time to time, Father Murphy, shouted the priest, "with the blood of patriots, tyrants and crooked landlords, and I won't be behind shuttered doors and windows, when it happens."

"And do you have someone in mind to make it happen, Michael?" asked John quietly.

"Well it won't be Wolf Tone, for sure, for he's all old guff and if truth be known, he's a loyalist." He gave John a broad smile, "and it certainly won't be you, Father Murphy, for I know you're a man of peace, but mark my words, peace comes at a great price." They shook hands and G. felt the strong grip of the man. "Good night to you Mr.G, and you take care of this fella."

"You then?", smiled John Murphy. "Will you start your little rebellion, Michael?" They made for the door.

The priest tried to find comfort in the small trap, as G. steered the mare onto the road for home.

"That man will come to no good, so help me, he's a hundred times worse and more dangerous than Roche, so he is." He sighed wearily. "We'll go to Duhallow, Georgie. Give her a little tug at Trasna Bridge, she'll find her own way."

"Right Father," smiled G., he liked going to Duhallow. He had become friendly with James Attridge, who allowed him to read his reports at times. There was always something nice to eat in the pantry behind Mrs. Brennan's kitchen and there was always a chance to meet Kate Keohane, just to look at her.

Chapter 18

The River Slaney is deep and wide at Enniscorthy and it is navigable all the way to Wexford, eddying into shaded places along the way where the Marsh Harrier speeds slowly along the tops of reeds and the humped backed Breen languishes in the weeds and the sand banks, while in the fast flowing torrents, Gudgeon, Roche and Trout are in abundance, a river as fertile as the woods and the meadows that border it. The historic town is dominated by the Drum Tower Castle, built in the thirteenth century and given as a thank you gift to the Poet Laureate Spenser, by Queen Elizabeth The First, for some favourable notations, he had written about her. Enniscorthy staggers quaintly on the gentle slopes of the Wicklow Hills, which rise in waves of greens and browns, to the north and the Cathedral Town of Ferns, sheltered on the west by the peaks of Mount Leinster. The majestic Blackstairs Mountains is a protective rib of granite, running south to the perimeter of New Ross. Like a great garden wall, the mountains, where the Honey Buzzard and the Sparrow hawk soar on flat wings in their hunt for prey, protect and shelter the fertile gardens and plains that stretch south and east to the sea. Plains of cultured fields, full of harvest and autumn colours, spread westward, then rise gently at first, then more urgently to The Scullogue Gap, a great platform, like a high altar in the cathedral of The Blackstairs.

It was two months since the rally called by Mr. Thomas Russell took place in the town and close on fifteen thousand turned out to hear Wolfe Tone speak. Few people know of his whereabouts today, except those close to him. James had received a letter from him, by special courier. Tone was in Paris on "matters political" that was, of course not to be mentioned in dispatches.

Today it was the turn of the Orangemen, a spectacular event, the first of its kind in the south and the visiting lodges, as they called them, from Dublin, Belfast, Antrim and Tyrone, had spent the previous days, setting up their tents and stalls.

Philip Roche was in jubilant mood, relishing the thought that, before the day is out, disobedience and a touch of lawlessness would descend on the festivities to enflame the crowd and he and Jack Keohane and a little private army would be there to light the flame, wherever the opportunity might present itself. John Kelly of Killane had the whole programme set out. Father John Murphy had a different point of view, as he and his now familiar young companion made their way to the centre of town and met the big priest.

Murphy wasn't open to levity to day. He felt the euphoria in the atmosphere, but in him, was an erratic nervousness and a taut anxiety, that there was going to be trouble. He pointed his great blackthorn across to the other side of the river, where otters played about on the bank, and where the carriages of the privileged were assembled, liveried stewards and horse attendants busy in their chores. "That crowd are not discussing the weather, over there, nor the price of corn. Their agents and gombeenmen are busy about the place and names will be reported, should there be trouble, and when you and Mr. Tone and the rest of you, who are about to change the world, when you are satisfied that you have opened the hornets' nest, the hornets will fly and poor wretches and their families will suffer, and all those who are going to protect you, will have scuppered back to the safety of Dublin and their respective committees."

"May I remind you, John Murphy, some of that crowd over there, as you call them, are friends of your's, and by the way, the poor wretches you talk about are well used to being burned out of their hovels, and we look for nobody to protect us, we are well capable of doing so, ourselves."

Murphy winked at G. "They have their uses, Philip, as you well know."

The big priest put an arm about the youth. "When they priest you, young Tansey, make sure your bread is buttered on both sides, like John Murphy here, that way you will live a long life."

G. smiled,"think I'm going to be a priest, Father Philip?".

Roche patted the blonde head in assurance. "Sure you are, Son, for sure you are."

He sensed her presence, even before he came onto the bridge. Military presence was everywhere, but little notice taken of them in a sort of a carnival atmosphere, in the noon sunshine.

**

She was sitting on the wide battlement, her legs dangling, heels slapping against the stone. She was in the company of a number of young people, including her sister Droleen. Raefil Keane was leaning against the wall, as near to her as he dared in public, looking up into her face, like nothing else existed around him. Droleen came all over shy when she saw Attridge. Kate Keohane caught his approach, like she had been expecting him.

Keane was rubbing, tenderly, the back of her small hand with his, and in a spasm of mild indignation, she slapped it away.

The crowd pressed past him, down the quay and onto the bridge on their way to the centre of town. James had to push out of the stream of bodies to get to her. Her companion, sensing the change in her attitude, turned. Raefil Keane had a good face, weathered and broad like his shoulders. His sleeves were rolled up to his elbows, he displayed with modesty, a body of power and strength that would have few limitations. His hair, dark and thick was tied back with a green ribbon.

Slightly breathless, not altogether from the brisk walk from Vinegar Hill, just outside the town, where the huge camp site had been built ,but rather her immense beauty, once again caught him off his usual composure.

"Hello, Miss Keohane."

"Mr. Attridge."

"I didn't expect you to come all this way for an Orange meeting, didn't know that you would be interested," he mused.

"Well I did, and I'm not," she said, her smile almost a secret.

Attridge gave Droleen a warm smile, she blushed profusely.

"You know Raefil, Mr. Attridge and a casual gesture to her friends "Mr. James Attridge," she introduced. They studied him with a mixture of careful distance and mild surprise, that Kate should be so composed in his company, at his distinct accent, a curiosity in its explicit friendliness with Kate, edged, of course with obvious admiration.

Keane was immediately hostile and nodded in quiet and obvious disapproval, while Kate ran off the names of her friends, but they were lost to the visitor. "And what would a gentleman like yourself be doing in Ennis today, you'd think you would have something better to do, like hunting or some such gentlemanly pastime?", Keane quipped.

"I'm a journalist, Sir, reporting is what I do, it's how I make my living, and if Mr. Wolfe Tone came here today, would you not be interested in what he has to say?"

"Promises, promises," spat Raefil, it's months since we heard him in this town and all times before and after. If his promises were milk and potatoes, we would be well starved by now."

"Raefil Keane," she rasped, "I'll thank you to be civil to anyone I see fit to bring into your ignorant company, so there."

"I didn't mean to preach or offend, but you're a Catholic, Mr. Keane, don't you want to be allowed to vote for yourself, your friends here and Kate?"

One of the young girls in the company giggled nervously. Raefil fumed inwardly that he should be so familiar. "If Mr. Tone succeeds, life will be better for all of you," James argued, pointing to the far side of the river, to where the military were assembling. "No more military policing, no intimidation, you will have a democracy."

The young faces around him were suddenly blank, expressionless, ignorant and uninformed, like they had no idea what he was talking about, the pathetic acceptance of generations mooned on the lovely faces.

"A lot you care about our future, Sir," Keane continued. "Take a look around you and see what Mr. Tone and his likes can give us."

With a further look at Kate, he stormed off in the direction of Market Square, soon lost in the procession. "I'm afraid I've upset your friend, Miss. Keohane."He helped her off the wall.

"Don't take too much notice of him, 'tis his temper, when it stirs in him, he forgets his manners."

They walked behind the little group of friends, every few steps, they would look back in amusement and skip onwards.

"There was a time, I'd be burnt at the stake for talking to you, socially, Mr. Attridge," she teased, looking up at him under her dark eyes.

"Is he your .....friend?" he asked.

"Well, of course he's my friend, just like the others, and I bet you don't remember their names."

She smiled at her shoes, peeping from under her grey skirts, pleased at his interest. In the privacy of his thoughts, the slightly erotic picture presented itself of the girl on the lump of a cow, more than her shoes exposed.

"I mean, special friend, do you see much of him?" "Too much sometimes," she replied, teasing him further. "He's very fond of me, I know that, he tries to protect me from interfering English Gentlemen."

Attridge thought better to leave the subject for now, there being a mild suggestion that the matter was none of his business.

The Slaney was festooned with gobbards and other small craft, bobbing in the swell, mostly used to carry grain from north of the county to Wexford and New Ross.

**

A few yards from Rudds Inn, they caught up with Raefil Keane. As they came abreast of him, and James was thinking he should move on, find a vantage point for the meeting and leave the fiery Irishman alone with his girlfriend, a small company of local yeomanry , marched busily, in and out of step toward the square. As they got nearer, the amusing spectacle took shape. Outside of the corporal at their head none of the King's yeos were more than twelve or thirteen year's old, new recruits, waiting for manhood. The red uniforms, made for bodies twice their size adorned the motley crew. At their head, looking very important, a low sized corporal in reasonably good attire, "humped, humped , humped" through his nose in an effort to keep them in step.

Attridge was about to make another effort at pleasantries, when Keane sprang into the path of the approaching "army." At about half way in the phalanx, he reached into the middle of the confused youths and yanked one of them, and a bundle of red and white lay sprawled on the road, rifle, kit- bag in total disarray.

To James's surprise, he heard Kate laugh, then fight for control as the young soldier rolled in the dust. A crowd had gathered and began to cheer with delight, as Raefil dragged him to his feet. The youngster lost his hat and a shock of dark hair cascaded over his face, as Keane began to shake him like a rag doll, then dragged him helplessly to the front of the marchers. The very unhappy teen roared and shouted in protest and most of all in embarrassment. James remembered the youth from Father Murphy's Mass.

"It's his brother," whispered Kate, in amusement. The crowd began shouting encouragement, while Keane the senior remained steel faced, confronting the corporal. Young soldiers of the crown giggled into their enormous sleeves. Keane began to tear at the tunic jacket of his brother, almost hanging him in the wide kit straps, the youths protests, unheeded, and again the crowd began to jibe and dance in support. Raefil Keane was known to the majority of the assembly, it struck Attridge; popular no doubt. With his free hand, Kate's boyfriend caught one of the corporal's lapels in a huge fist. At this stage, Keane junior was down to his britches and stained vest.

"I'll tell you just one more time, Murray, keep your rotten hands off my family, and I'll tell you just this once, if I find him any more in this uniform, I'll hang him and you by your bloody kitbags."

Corporal Murray fumed in his discomfort, his colour rising, himself no more in age than his tormentor. Raefil dropped his unfortunate brother and he fell, face down in the dust. Murray heaved a kick at the new recruit, the effort leaving brocade and gold stitched lapels in Keane's fist.

The corporal almost cried in frustration. "I keep telling him to stay at home, but he keeps coming back, so he does, so now in future, spancil him to a fence, for I'll have no more to do with him."

Murray tried to kick him again, but the youngster, realizing he was free, scrambled to his feet, shouting obscenities at his brother and threatening all kinds of plagues. The crowd exploded in laughter, uncontrolled, when the youngster tried to get away, his trousers, minus his belt and braces, fell about his knees, his bare backside exposed for all to see, as he skipped and fell and skipped and fell again, and hopped trying to protect his modesty.

Raefil watched the fleeing figure of his brother scampering down the lane to the side of Rudds, then scowled at the corporal. "They're filling the youngsters with nonsense, about being a good English boy, Mr. Murray and if I find that you made him take the oath...."

"He took the shilling fast enough", growled Murray. The company shuffled uncomfortably in their ill fitting boots. "He was paid his money sure enough, are you going to pay His Majesty back now Raefil Keane?," he spat.

Keane tore the remnant of the tunic from the floor and began to search the pockets frantically, unending the kit bag. He felt the heat of frustration at the back of his neck. "Well?" said Murray.

Attridge saw the pain in Kate's eyes for her friend. He dug into his pocket and pulled out a fist full of coins. "Take your damned money", he said to the corporal

"No," stormed Keane, "keep your money." He softened for a minute, "I'll not be taking your money."

Suddenly the clinking of coins against a tin can broke the silence. It was passed around as people called, "here, here. over here." The coins were dropped from pockets already empty, a reasonable kindness that needed no thanks. The man they called Sean, sided up to him, a cunning smile on an impish puckered face. "I was collecting some debts, Raefil, for you, there now, give him his owl money."

Without looking at his benefactor, and holding Murray in his septic stare, he said, " how much is in it Sean?"

"Enough Raefil", said the little man.

"Then count me out twenty four halfpennies, there's a good lad." He didn't take his eyes off the soldier as Sean went through the collection, with help. The tiny copper coins lay in his fist for a minute. "Fully paid, in case His Majesty should have the need." He threw the coins at Murray and the crowd again roared its approval, as the King's splintered shilling was lost in the corporal's tunic, most of it falling to the ground.

"We'd better be going," somebody said. Coming off the bridge, with a dozen yeos cavalry, was Lieutenant Bookey. Here was nothing to play about, here was anarchy with a sting and immediately the loitering crowd dispersed. Murray managed to get his crew into some shape and was marching off as Bookey dismounted and climbed the steps of Rudds. He nodded stiffly at James Attridge, ignoring the others, while a king's ransom lay in the dust.

It was to be a day of shame for the town of Enniscorthy, a day without any tender sentiment, a day that sewed another seed of anarchy and rebellion.

Chapter 19

"It's said that hatred distorts a man's features," whispered Roche, then, by God, there's a lot of ugliness in Enniscorthy, this day." He watched, with apprehension, at the manic preparations in every corner of the town, in fields, in yards, in the barrack square, even in the Cathedral foreground. The base of Vinegar Hill at the far side of the bridge had been selected as the camp site for the visiting Orangemen and their families. Since early morning, the crowds were milling toward the town, Military and Yeomanry were everywhere. From mid day, the peasantry were allowed nowhere near the Vinegar fields and the camp site.

At two o'clock the Orange parade would march through Templeshannon, Abbey Square, Mill Park Road, St. John's Road, from the east side of the river, over the bridge and out to the far end of town, turn in a prepared field, then back the same route. A rostrum, decked with bunting and flags had been set up outside Rudds Inn, where dignitaries would sit and an address would be given in praise of the King's birthday, after which the parade would return to Vinegar Hill for celebrations. A parade in honour of King George's birthday, was a yearly event in one or other town in Wexford and peasants were obliged, under pain of retribution to come out, in force to swell the tribute, so it could be reported how greatly His Majesty was loved.

Today, however, a new heathenism was introduced to the people of Wexford, a fetishism and a new colour that had nothing to do with the pigmentation or the ethereal magic to be found in a rainbow, but a symbol, a fountainhead of evil and corruption that was to make patriotism loyal to London, an excuse for murder and pestilence, that was to plague an entire nation for generations to come. Like an optical illusion, an orange cloud of banners, flags and plumes formed itself from the narrow exits of Vinegar Hill Lane and spread in a golden fusion onto the wider road of Templeshannon.

It seemed, to the crowds on the west side of river, that it moved slowly, like a cortege, but as it neared the bridge, there was a military style purpose to the marching, defiant, jaws set and distorted in what seemed to John Murphy, was a perfect hatred at the world. The marching body was not military, but ordinary men. Each one had an orange cockade in his hat, with a length of orange material about his waist, as a sash. They were in perfect step, but it was a staccato stomping motion, meant to intimidate the onlooker. The marchers were interspersed with bands of fife players and a new instrument of fearful noise was foisted on the people, making its first appearance outside of the North. Not an instrument, but a kind of weapon, bearing its name from the place of its origin; Lambeg, a little village, south west of Belfast.

A massive drum of fifty pounds in weight, carried by two men, one in front, to give it balance, the other with its halter around his shoulders. That man carried the instrument's septic soul, a pair of curved Malacca rods, that brought out the marching rhythm, in an ear shattering impertinent desperation. The huge banners carried portraits of King George and William of Orange, but as they turned off the bridge onto Abbey Street, the full force of the insult hit the crowd.

The feet of the two thousand marchers, were wrapped in the green of Ireland. The patriotic symbol, was being trod underfoot in a gesture of contemptuousness and affectation. The marchers were accompanied by a thousand military, three hundred of which were on horseback and the insult manifested itself a further step. The horses were similarly shod, while a portrait of The Pope, in caricature, hung from beneath their tails. There was a stifling atmosphere of unreality in the whole scene and the crowd took on a semi-catatonic state, like their senses had been pulverised and they had simply contracted out.

John Murphy was in despair and he prayed the crowd would not react. In the shadow of Ferns, Ireland's ancient royal and episcopal city, once the capital of the kingdom of Leinster and centre of divine worship, a new idolatry was manifesting itself in the glorification of a king who died a hundred years ago and a living madman of The House of Hanover, living in London.

Dignitaries applauded from the rostrum; Owen, Cope of Carew, Thomas Hancock, Hayden, Jacks, Captain Pounden, the devil of Enniscorthy of the town's garrison, Bookey and Carnock.

Banners heralded the Orangemen of Cork, the dreaded North Cork Yeomanry, lodges from Belfast, Newry, also Dublin, Carlow and towns, close by. The parade crowded before the rostrum and the notoriously dissenting clergyman Rev.Theodore Wm. Bruce made his address. With a mouth as big and as ear piercing as the three Lambeg drums, full of rasping, his message rang out over the huge square, entreating God to show the peasantry, the way of true religion and to instil in them the piousness and humility of the Saviour, in embracing the authority of His Most Gracious Majesty, King George.

It seemed to G. that the peasants, who lined the roadway to the square on both sides, had been preparing for their own demonstrations. Stewards were busy flitting in and out among the crowd, distributing what seemed to be little squares of black material, about the size of a pocket kerchief. Bruce ended his oration to great applause, as he beseeched God to bless His Divine Majesty with wisdom and good health on this august occasion. "Poor God," sighed John Murphy. As the marchers fell into line for the return to Vinegar Hill, the drums started up again, the horses stirred in the heat and the fifes commenced their thin infestation of sound. There were a number of priests moving among the crowd of spectators, Michael Murphy, Roche, Mogue Kerins, Dixon, the one armed Esmond Kyan of Mount Howard, the big blacksmith; Devereaux, Raefil Keane and Kate Keohane's uncle Jack Keohane and a score of youths, the bowlers and the caman players of the district, G. had come to recognize. Then his heart leaped in alarm, Hen was among them close by to Jack Keohane.

"I warned him to stay at hom," G. said to the priest.

"Jack Keohane will look after him," said Father Murphy. "Jack's a good man behind it all."

Some sort of a command rang out, and echoed down through the ranks of the spectators, a guttural rasp, uttered in Gaelic, "turn about, turn about", and five thousand peaceful objectors, on a single pulse, turned and faced the river on one side, the houses on the other.

G. looked at his companion and Murphy nodded in the inevitability of the moment. They joined the flow, knowing this calculated rudeness would be looked on as a studied insult and would be well avenged. Suddenly the crowd united in a mass mind in their fear and contempt and began to run toward the bridge. Billows of smoke was belching from the low fields of Vinegar Hill, sheets of flame were devouring the tent village, that had housed the Orangemen for the past three days. People were shouting with delight, hostility replaced with frantic running and gesturing. Tents, kitchens, beer halls, stables were aflame. A thousand peasants lined the ditches and laneways, skirting Vinegar, shouting, dancing in their delight, their black kerchiefs of protest, now banners of victory.

In each of a hundred infernos, the bulk of charred buggies, carts, floats stood out in stark profile against the flames. Frantically, the Orange fraternity, men, women and children, ran about the fields, their importance gone, shouting obscenities and trying to save something of their belongings. They were left with nothing, save the banners to their kings. All animals had been set free by the arsonists and were loose among the fields and ditches, dogs, chickens and hogs and horses, wide eyed among the chaos.

Father Murphy sat on the mare, on the edge of a field and suppressed a fallen thought for the day. He couldn't help but smile inwardly, his heart lifting erratically. The spectacle of tormentors in torment created a quiet euphoria in him and he tried to hide the evidence from his young lieutenant. It would soon be dispelled in the naked retribution that would certainly follow.

**

She had cried, like many of the women about her in the crowd at the affront and the insults of the Orangemen. Her eyes smarted now as she stood close to Attridge, he welcomed that closeness, no matter what the reason, as they looked up at the inferno, at the stupid Orange men and women chasing animals all over the place. Kate was crying again now, with unashamed satisfaction. He heard her whisper as the crowd pressed them together. "Well done, Raefil, good lad."

However, there had been a fatality of a kind on the day. Diddymus Driscoll had been seen in the town from early, very under the influence of drink. He had caused a few skirmishes, trying to get into Rudds Inn, where no Catholics are served during ordinary business. Henry, now well ensconced in the brotherhood of Jack Keohane and the Kellys of Killane, and who had grown two inches in their company, or so he thought, had seen Driscoll generally making a nuisance of himself, a dangerous game, in the company of so many military. On the return march, Diddymus had pulled a rider from his horse, the soldier receiving concussion in the fray. Driscoll was carried off to jail, another mission of mercy for Father John Murphy.

Chapter 20

A bright day was a deathly and depressing contrast to the interior of a thousand cabins in the baronies of Kilcormack, Bantry and Shelmalier. One might be of a superior quality above another, but only for the simple fact that it had a proper fireplace with a chimney shaft instead of a hole in the thatch or that it might have two windows instead of one, or none at all, or indeed a table to sit at and not the floor. The census of 1793, a few years earlier, recorded that in the whole of County Donegal there were just 700 chairs, at least there were twice that number in County Wexford, Lord Mountnorris having 200 himself and "only one arse to him," said Master Dunn.

Kate had already introduced him to the Master, a name lovingly christened on him by the hundreds of children he had taught as their school master over the years. She was on a "message," to the old school house on behalf of Lord Palmer and invited Attridge to come with her in the little buggy

Urchins, barefoot and smiling bounded in and out of half doors and peasant women greeted the pair as they drove past. If there were men about, few were seen, imagining them to stay inside with their own dark dignity and their desire for anonymity in a pitiful existence. Lord Palmer was well known and appreciated for his charity to the peasantry of Father Murphy's parish, though he was not their landlord.

Master Dunn's school house, compared to the hovels scattered across the hillside outside of Boolavogue, was an exception. The long low building had four fine rooms, four fire places and a solid slate roof, a prosperous interruption to the poverty all about. It stood on a flat table of granite, the slab of its foundation, stretching out in front of the house in a natural stone floor. Flower beds and creeping roses gave it a chocolate box look, mature trees sheltering the house to the east and the north. It looked like a sort of a sentinel, looking down on the cabins, James thought, and a sweeping pathway rose from the western side of the building, up onto a small mountain, like nature itself offered the little place of learning her own kind of protection. However, this little place of learning had been burned out on two occasions, this structure, rebuilt with the generosity of Duhallow. However all learning had recently been outlawed by the authorities . It was now the home of the Master and his lover, Norah Scully.

Word had come that they had hanged Thomas Driscoll in Wexford. It was said they had tortured him for the names of dissidents, and it was unknown if old Diddymus had squealed. Henry Tansey had locked himself in his loft for two days in his distraction, while John Kelly moved a step further in his resolution for revenge. The whisky House on Trasna Bridge seethed with resolve and Lousy Head Peoples, the inn keeper poured a plethora of pints of ale, as the old poet, Dempsey said his poems with a new resolve to dump the British.

The door was open and they stepped inside without knocking. "I saw you coming the road and welcome". It was a large bright room, full of colour in the cushions on the two settles and the curtained windows. A table that would seat ten took up half the space, scrubbed so that the tongues and ligatures of the bleached wood stood out in textured profile.

A tall shape was bent in two before the open fire, so that the head was virtually in the coals.

A pair of long legs and a narrow backside welcomed them. "The kettle will sing soon." Then the figure straightened, surprisingly supple for a woman of her age. Norah Scully was a tall thin woman, dressed completely in black, her white hair tied back severely over her ears, giving her an oriental look. A smoking clay pipe protruded from her stained teeth. Skin, like parchment was tightly drawn over a prominent bone structure, an aquiline austere face, not all together unpleasant. She took the pipe from her narrow mouth and the image softened.

James remembered his previous visit with Kate, Norah Scully's big hand, rough in her hand shake. " We brought the grog, Norah, Sir George says we should have enough."

The tall woman cupped Kate's face in her hands and kissed her forehead. She looked into the azure moist eyes of the younger woman, an unhurried inspection. "We're blessed with Sir George, child, and he's blessed with you." She moved toward the door leading to another room. " And now, I'll wake the maneen himself and we'll have the tea."

James had seated himself on the settle, near where some roughly made shelving stood from ceiling to floor. The shelves were laden with a surprising collection of books, not neatly stacked, but randomly strewn about, many interlaced with scraps of paper, while several mounds of creased bits of manuscript lay piled one on the other. On the bottom shelf, three cardboard boxes overflowed with scraps of writing paper, brown with age and turf smoke on which notations had been scribbled and put there for some kind of reference.

Norah Scully stopped in the doorway. "I see you're in his office, Sir, and you'll excuse the dirt of his corner, but 'tis the one place in the house where Norah Scully is not allowed to touch, for himself is afraid I'd be lighting the fire with his bits and scraps of carry on."

"James is a writer, Norah," said Kate.

"Then you'll have plenty in common, for I don't read or write at all, for I think the best writers are them that don't write at all."

Mr. Dunn has some extraordinary books, Miss. Scully, I'm honoured he allows me to peruse them."

"I'm just Norah Scully, Sir, and you're welcome to take them all home with you this day". Attridge smiled from Master Dunn's corner, "then I am just James and I appreciate your kindness."

She went through to the inner room, leaving the door ajar . A huge bed filled the ope. A mountain of bedclothes stirred as something moved beneath them.

Amusing himself, Attridge leafed through the well bound books, careful not to disturb the pieces of notation which were everywhere. The big black kettle hissed contentedly on its cradle and Kate, familiar to the surroundings, began setting the table. Norah Scully called from the room, " the good table cloth now Alana."

"In your honour," she whispered, holding up the linen cloth.

Francis Cornelius Dunn was about half the man, Norah Scully was the woman. She stood behind him in the doorway, towering five or six inches above him, throwing her eyes to heaven and trying, furtively to get him into his sleeveless vest, which was refusing a safe passage over the loosely fitting linen shirt, over black pants, their legs which stopped at a heavy pair of boots, laces dragging the tiled floor. He wore no socks.

"Isn't it a wonder I never married in this life," he complained, "and a woman like yourself to torment me." They seemed to be stuck in the doorway, as she pulled the last remnant of the vest down his back.

"Faith, 'tis well Norah Scully would be doing, O'Duinn," she always used the Gaelic when she referred to him, "to torment you in this life, for the good God knows only too well, that you'll be most terribly tormented in the next life, and that this is only a trial for what is to come and the reason why He left you live so long is that you're left here to mend, while the good die young."

The little man had a good big round face, well whiskered, with bright lively eyes. His grey hair was sparsely strewn in many directions, and hung, limp onto his shoulders. Round and pot bellied, he looked like an aging gnome, the nose, set flat, was a beacon in the middle of a busy face, where even now in his half waking senses, were on full alert.

He spoke to Kate in Irish, holding her with his eyes, running the back of his hand along her cheek, in an endearing gesture. She replied to him, shyly, furtively looking at James. Though he didn't understand it, Attridge had slowly become more and more tuned into the language, it's dulcet tones of expression, and the gift that the Irish had for its use in the softening of tones, compared with the so called correct English.

The old man held his visitor's hands in his own. "Welcome again, and I was telling Kate Keohane, how she gets more lovely day by day, sure as you know, she'll soon be as pretty as Norah Scully.".

The clay pipe was back in her mouth, as she filled the teapot from the singing kettle, her rump to them. Master Duinn inspected the buggy with its contents. Whisky, port wine and a score of bottles of ale and the black porter, complements of Sir George Palmer, for the waking of Diddymus Driscoll, when they bring him back from Wexford tomorrow.

"So, I was thinking, the last time you were here and when you left, you were born at Duhallow Park."

The Master poured his tea into his saucer and slugged it through his moustache, squinting at James above the rim, "when was that now?."

"Twenty three years ago, Sir, my father was estate manager at Duhallow Park, for Sir George."

Dunn threw a quick glance at Norah Scully, it might have been an oblique hint, a significant pause, before saying, "I remember the man well, my school was well up then in these days. A fine gentleman, I remember, and indeed, your mother, what a beauty she was. There was a picture of her in the big house."

"Thank you, Mr. Dunn, it's still there." The two men went outside and Norah Scully brought them a dram from the whiskey bottle.

Without invitation, O' Duinn began, the first sip, loosening his tongue. "Yourself and myself will now begin the wake for poor Driscoll, they'll be many here tomorrow to send him on his way, what a fool he was, to carry on before the yeos. I was going to change the world, once, wake up the nation from six hundred years of slumber."

His old eyes opened wide with the forgotten wonder of it. I spoke in every tavern, every whisky house, every crossroads and outside every church and often was trounced for it, with my poems and songs and my speechifying. I was no stranger to the insides of jails." He frowned into his glass. " Sure I was only a young fool, a poor man from a poor race and all of us fooled by demagogues." He gave a phlegmy laugh, " It made for lovely poems and songs, though, I'll have to admit, for all our poems and songs are sad, even when we write of love."

"Have you heard of Mr. Wolfe Tone, Sir?," Attridge said.

"Yes, I've heard of Tone, I've heard of his messages, full of promise, with a lot of if's and but's and maybe's." He squinted across to where the hills sloped down to caress the distant sleepy town of Ferns. "Mr. Wolfe Tone isn't the man. Pamphlets and great eloquence are not the tools for freeing a nation, Mr. Attridge, a nation where men starve and dogs are pampered. Poor mens' reasons are never heard, but that poverty is the parent of revolution. We're the fools of Europe, Sir, we dance and prance in our imposed poverty. I'm sorry to have to say, we don't need a Mr. Wolfe Tone, we need a soldier of the peasant stock, a man who won't mind getting his hands dirty."

James marvelled at the man's eloquence, at the tone of his voice and imagined him as a youngster, stirring the minds of his listeners. He looked, almost accusingly at the visitor, a smile at the edge of the stubbled mouth. "The English are a fine people, my young friend, fine people, if they'd only stay at home and mind the house." As on his previous visit, James left the School House with a manuscript, with a promise to have it returned.

Chapter 21

Norah Scully had prepared the old fodder house at the east end of the building, for the reposing of Trasna's first martyr. The shed was cleaned and freshly white washed for the occasion, a shining sepulchre to repose him, where, for the next few hours, amid keening and praying and ululations, the crowd would extol all the new virtues, Thomas Driscoll acquired in death.

His widow soon took pride of place at the head of the crude coffin and due homage was paid to her grief, while three of her nine children clung protectively to her skirts. Later, as the sombre whispering of prayers floated on the calm evening, a promenade of dark lamenting bodies filed past the box, appropriate condolences offered, ostentatiously.

And so, it began; the burial service that took on a meaning all its own, paying homage to the living, rather than honour the dead. Here was the setting up of a hero and Attridge, from the fringes, wondered at the hypocrisy in a display of homage all around and watched in disbelief, as well dressed men, mostly strangers to all concerned, and certainly unknown to the widow, who accepted their condolences in pathetic piety, climbed the steep hill to the school house, the rebel priest Father Michael, among them. Father Philip Roche welcomed them vigorously, comrades of the Organisation of the United Irishmen, come to honour a fallen friend. John Murphy seethed inwardly at the show of vulgar self-importance. " I doubt any of these fellows ever knew Driscoll", he whispered to James, "when they came to shoe the horses," he quoted, "the beetle held out his leg."

Among them, a dark haired man in his mid thirties, seemed to attract much of the interest and Father Michael introduced him as William Dwyer, the leader of the United Irishmen in county Wicklow, a man named William Baker, all the way from Antrim and a colleague of Henry Monro. John Kelly of Killane, who was one of the few who could boast of knowing Driscoll personally, when their meetings at work or at play, were always filled with a sort of a mock hostility and confrontation, when the object of their argument was never more than a two pound lump of iron on a byroad or a hurling ball in a flat field. The Tansey brothers spent the night, keepers at the gate of repose.

John Murphy's tension mounted, when down below on the road, a company of yoes halted in their patrol, but moved on again toward Boolavogue.

John Murphy cornered Father Michael as they were leaving.

"You're a crowd of hypocrites, Michael, Tom Driscoll was never a United Man, he hardly knew what you fellows were all about".

Michael studied his friend for a minute, then with an ironic smile he whispered, "he is now, John and as a dead hero, he's much more valuable to us than if he were alive for ten lives. The burial Mass, two days hence, I'll be coming down to celebrate with you." He hesitated for a minute, "and I'll be bringing Mogue Kearns with me." He gave John a playful pat on the back, "sure you'll be needing all the help you can get now."

They stood outside the white washed mortuary, where lighted candles sought out crevices in the stone, and Driscoll's head, separated from Driscoll's trunk seemed to move in the flickering flames, making the whole thing a hideous show. "There were few accolades for the man when he was alive, few houses that would welcome him, now they come and gape and go." He moved toward the house with James. "Maybe Norah Scully will oblige with a dram or two, he held the younger man's arm. "Young Tansey is upset it seems Driscoll was good to his mother".

Father Philip Roche took up the prayers, his voice loud and beseeching echoed from the shed. " Beseeching thee O Lord, for peace in our times." But as the big man moved about, to the praises and tributes, the prayers for peace seemed to John Murphy, only on a sort of tacit understanding that the remarks should not be taken at par.

The curate of Boolavogue moved heavily toward the School House and Master Dunn's fireside. " Come with me, James," he sighed. "God what hypocrites. Great fleas have little fleas upon their backs, to bite them, and little fleas have lesser fleas on their backs to bite them and even lesser fleas, and so on ad infinitem."

"I like that saying, Father, might use it somewhere with your permission."

"Use it," the priest droned, "for you'll find plenty of opportunity in Ireland, God knows."

Nora Scully lit the lamps and a warm, comforting glow fused through the windows onto the slab outside.

Kate had arrived late. She had been tending table at Duhallow where Sir George entertained Father John and Father Philip to lunch. Palmer loved the company of priests, especially rebel priests, so he had insisted Philip would bring along, Father Michael, again savouring the debate of John Murphy, contrasting the opinions of the other two, who clearly wanted war.

Dusk was falling and the lamps had been lit in the cabins, a single lamp or candle shining bravely in the dark interiors, children playing about in the semi darkness, while here and there the beginning of gregarious ardour was threatening to overflow the solemn requiem.

For now, the quiet orderliness of prayers, keening and craw thumping in Thomas Driscoll's whitewashed quarters, while elsewhere in Francis Cornelious Dunn's copious domain, other emotions were stirring and Raefil Keane's two young brothers were slowly becoming the influence to induce in the gathering, a kind of parallel fervour in the evening's sentiment. The brothers were setting out in the wake of Saint Brendan. Tomorrow, they would begin their journey to Queenstown in the port of Cork and from there on the long arduous journey to America.

Half way up to the school house, Kate Keohane stopped and looked at the scene in wonder. With the windows alight and the mortuary doors wide, lamps and whitewash shining through, the whole scene was like a reflection of somewhere else, a painted backdrop or a pastoral.

Musicians were playing in a corner somewhere, squeezing their instruments in a slow quarter time in a haunting kind of respect. This would change as the night went on, latent life to be the reality in death, death to be asked to step aside for those without preparation for it, famous words used by Father Murphy to James, where more respect should be afforded the dead.

Children came out and danced around her, barefoot and uplifted in the glow of the occasion up above, little phantom spirits, not yet ready for the kingdom of sleep. Kate was their heroine due to her fortune in the eyes of Sir George Palmer in the big house. She had brought many of the disadvantaged urchins to Duhallow, watching their awed wonder at the magnificence of the house and Gobnait's kitchen

She passed by the door and for a reason, not self explanatory, she was pleased to see Mr. Attridge seated near Father Murphy, in what, in an Irish cottage, is a place reserved for special visitors, the upper half of the settle, nearest the fireplace. A group of neighbours engaged in conversation with the newest visitor, The Master himself, the conduit of that engagement. Once again, James was interested in the great selection of books.

Fortune turns everything to the advantage of those she favours. James Attridge's advantages seemed to be without tax and condition. In the eyes of most of the people in this close knit community, the young Englishman had two profits to his sufficiency in Boolavogue, profits, long since his arrival, discussed over pints of ale and smoky firesides. A guest at Duhallow, often seen in the company of Kate Keohane, a regular guest at the School House and often a Massgoer at Father John's chapel, though, as an Englishman, he couldn't be anything but a

Protestant.

Others, however, tired of being duped all of their lives and long since, lost the power to be magnanimous and distrust their only defence against betrayal, saw in his pious rightfulness, the raw material of some bad action.

Attridge had the capacity to listen, to agree and to immerse himself in their rhetoric and to be swept along in the almost childlike innocence of their simple psychology, which, on his mature analysis, was never childish and far from infantine.

The makeshift mortuary was still filled to capacity. Kate worked her way slowly to the bereaved family. Hands grasped her's in warm affection and in appreciation of many favours, she would have interceded for them with Sir George. The widow, children still clinging to her, every now and then, at the sight of a familiar face, showing genuine condolence, would cry out in a recharged manifestation of grief, as she did with Kate Keohane. The distraught widow told her, in choking bursts, how Thomas Driscoll had always said what a fine girl Kate Keohane was, and how he'd be glad and proud that she might marry one of his sons, someday.

"I've just come from Duhallow Park, Agnes," she whispered. "Now you mustn't worry about anything. Sir George will talk to Father Murphy and in a day or two, they will look after you."

The keening continued in slow protracted monotone, and trying to blot out the martyred face of Diddymus Driscoll, she was glad to find fresh air. Driscoll was stirring in his own tragic twilight and the heavy smell of his corrosion was becoming more and more oppressive and revolting. He had been dead now for over a week.

Chapter 22

Raefil Keane had been drinking. She found him slouched against a rock, out of the run of things, two large empty bottles at his feet, a third, half empty in his fist. He was studying the flat acres that stretched away into the pending darkness, his eyes full of pain. Kate sat by him on a soft divot and pulled her knees up under her.

"I hate this", she said softly. "I hate Thomas dying like this, for all his fault."

He wiped the lip of the bottle with the palm of his hand and passed it to her.

"What is it?", she said.

"Porter."

"I hate porter," she slugged, grimaced and swallowed. She took another sip and handed it back. " Yuk!, hate that."

"How was the journey?". She looked out into his private world.

"God d'you know, but no man should have to die like that, and no innocent man at all, at all."

"Don't drink any more, Raefil," she said carefully.

Ignoring her suggestion, Keane continued, like he was reading from a script in the distance. "When we got to Wexford, Tansey, Father Murphy's altar boy, Georgie Tansey and me, Father Currin had the body ready for me. Boyde's men were after tying Thomas's legs, bent back like a trussed chicken. When the priest found him, he was after stiffening up, so we had to break his legs to get him into the box, his two arms were already broken." His voice had no malice in it, it was choked with emotion. She began to rub his hand and entreat him to stop, but he continued, turning his own hand over to grasp her's. "They wouldn't give us his head. For hours, we stood the horses outside the jail. The head was on a spike above the entrance to the Stonehouse and the yeos were dancing around and jeering and mocking us. But for Tansey, I would have destroyed the lot of them, but then what good would that be." His voice faltered again in tearful frustration. "Father Currin found a man named Harvey, a powerful man in Wexford and he helped us and after a long while they took it down."

Keane put the bottle on his head and finished the dark liquid. "Twice, they stopped us on the road on the way home and made us open the box and spill poor Thomas onto the road, in case we were carrying guns." He sobbed, "God, Kate, he must have suffered a powerful lot. Do you know that that bastard Owen had him tortured, even before he sent him to Wexford. Imagine, poor Thomas, drunk out of his owl skull, and they raking his chest and his back with a garden scythe, sure he had to be mad with pain and fear before they hanged him."

He rolled gently off the flat stone and lay his head in her lap. She stroked his hair, feeling the strong strands caressing her fingers. "A crowd of them were Irish, not English at all, at all. They spoke like me, looked like me, except for that terrible red uniform they have to wear. Imagine, fellas with names like Carty, Moloney, Sullivan, Brady, imagine a Peadar Sullivan in the colours of the king of England, and he hanging his own?"

He reached up and stroked her face with the backs of his fingers. "You're my girl, aren't you, Kate?" Her breath was warm and sensuous against his hand, her thighs, a supple cushion for his aching head.

"Well, I'm nobody else's Raefil Keane."

His hand crept downward, brushed against her full breast and lingered there for a second or two. It was significant, a sop to his intolerable depression.

Raefil Keane hardly ever knew a day that he had not seen Kate Keohane, that he had not wanted her company, to be in her shadow. Earlier, she was a girl-boy, chasing rabbits into burrows, running through the pastures and hills of Boolavogue, hunting renegade heifers, barefoot in trees, swimming in rivers, through haggards, caked in dung, suckling small animals. Together, they shared the delights in the beauty and happiness of childhood, hiding the great mysteries and myths, they uncovered daily from the scepticism of elders, inventing and enacting lovely falsehoods.

In their teens, their close harmonising of ideas continued until she began witnessing in herself, mixed sensations of the beginning of womanhood, and certain activities ceased, to his boyish annoyance. The swimming in the river, the scene of his awakening to her flowering, the horse play at threshing and the fairs, when her features became suddenly too refined for the pulling and dragging in the once spontaneous and delightful occupations, became no more. "No longer", Lady Palmer insisted, the tareaway should wear shoes, a young woman should be properly shod, else her feet will spread, no more, tormenting thorns and prickles. And there are toys for all ages, and he began to concentrate his fragile hopes and unsure mind on pleasing this new and exciting awakening. Keane matched her maturing beauty with his supreme performances in all things sporting, and became to savour the new smells and approving gestures that permeated this new being. But, watching her develop busily, he was less industrious in his own maturity and the schooling and the guidance of Lady Palmer brought out in her, a kind of finesse and superiority and a confidence that wasn't there before. Kate could already cast that shadow in which he felt inadequate.

She pulled his hand away gently and pulled him to his feet.

"It's the stranger, isn't it?"

"No it isn't". She said it too quickly to be convincing. "The music is brightening," she said, thankfully the darkness hiding her guilt. Cause me to blush and you'll lose me.

"Dance with me, you like the hornpipe."

He pulled away from her. "You were always my girl, until now." Keane staggered down the boreen. "Always," he said over and over.

**

The two young Keanes were leaving for America on the morrow, and the betrothal ritual became later, a centre piece of the late evening. Their two sweethearts, full of wild innocent allure were dragged to the large bedroom, while the music climbed slowly to fever pitch. There in feint protest, their giddy secret souls, loving the opportunity to sacrifice themselves, the two girls had their under drawers dragged from them and a tuft of pubic hair delicately sheared off. The procession bearing the intimate potions, cascaded through the house, to Norah Scully's delight, the Master, crunching up his old face against the noise. Room to room it went in a running skipping frenzy before ending up outside in the warm night and forming itself in a circle about the two new emigrants. Each relic, in a soft velvet little purse, made especially for the purpose, was ceremoniously draped about their necks and a flowing lilting lingo rang out, a solemn testament to the girls being left behind, to be faithful to their commitment until they marry one day beyond the sea.

In a mixture of superstition and pride, special etiquette and generic humanity, the crowd danced in and out of the circle, in the good humoured philosophic state, that Attridge continued to find all around him, and the beauty of its flame, again enthralled him. Cheerfulness and adversity seemed to be a habit of mind with the people, a marriage ritual and a solemn wake, inextricable in the pouring out of emotion. Theirs; one great muscle, a heart like a ship heaving in the wind that blows from all four corners of heaven.

**

They walked beyond the mortuary shed and the turf shed and onto the climbing pathway that swept in a half circle above and to the east of School House. Breathless, they reached Kate's "most favourite place in all the world," a platform of a soft downy grass, like a shelf, a stretched palm of a hand that oversaw the valley in three directions. To their backs, was a wall of limestone interspersed with wild rock flowers, around which the path continued to the summit of Ceim an Athair.

Breathing heavily, Attridge said, "and where's YOUR betrothed, and does he have a little sachet about his neck?"

"I am not betrothed to any man, and if you mean Raefil Keane, Mr. Attridge, well he's gone home, find and drunk for himself, and he has nothing 'round his neck, nor will any man wear a part of my body, like a trophy."

James threw his head back and laughed, his breath still coming in short stabs. "It's not what he thinks", he teased, "I see the way he looks at you."

" Is it how you look at me?" She stood at the edge of the clearing and with her hands on her hips, she drank in the night air like she was not just feeling it, but tasting it.

"How DO I look at you, Kate Keohane?" She turned to face him. The moon was a yellow scintillating ball at her back, a huge harvest disk, that sought out her profile as she turned toward him and bathed her in a golden splendour. He felt like he had, on occasions, in the past few months, a gentle panic and a feeling of incandescence, that she seemed to have the trick of blending with nature, taking all its beauty to her own, without any effort on her part. Now, in the extraneous Moon's glow, there was a feeling in the pit of his stomach of almost a separation from normality, so that, if she were to step away nearer the edge, she would float and the mystic orb would consume her.

She teased again, "maybe like I want you to, James Attridge, and by the way, you're beginning to develop a fine Irish accent, so you are." Her face darkened for a minute. "Raefil is a holy show when he has drink taken, but he's very upset for what happened in Wexford."

She sought out a flat stone ,like she had done so a thousand times and he looked down at her with a host of mixed emotions.

"Look how small the School House is from up here, find a place to sit, James."

"I'll stand a while, this is a most beautiful place, I agree". His head swam, Norah Scully's whisky insulating his thoughts. "I hadn't realised we were up so high. Do you know, young lady, that, thanks to The Master's hospitality, Mr. Driscoll's wake and the marriage rituals of four young and lovely people, I'm half full of Irish whisky, and then you drag me up a mountain."

She hugged her knees, then touched his arm as he found a place to sit next to her. "See there." She pointed into the east. "That's Duhallow."

He squinted into the powdery haze and found the bulk of the house, like a great grey headstone rising out of the gentle slope of the valley. "I had no idea it was so near", he whispered.

" From a height, everything seems nearer, 'tis only half a mile by road, but a sparrow would half the distance. See, Mrs. Laffan has the lamps lighting in the parlour, she'll be giving Sir George his night time drink now."

"You think a lot of Sir George, don't you, Kate."

"Only for the Palmers, I'd be like one of those mud larks down there on the river bed. My parents died one after the other, when we were young, my brother and myself and we live with Uncle Jack and his wife. They have no children. Lady Palmer came to our class one day when The Master had us reading poetry and she took a fancy to me, for whatever reason." She threw him a side glance, the mischief in her eye suggested her confidence, shining out. "I was given a part time job at the big house, but Lady Palmer had high notions for me and was always kind to me and my family. There was a girl in my place once, and I always felt sure she wanted me to be like her, though she never said. There's a painting of a beautiful woman in the big house, I think she's the one, she went away a long time ago. If you press Mrs. Laffan she might tell you about her."

"I know the picture," he said, containing his anxiety to tell her.

"They want me to make my home at Duhallow, me and Droleen, but my brother Brian is still troublesome and I need to be at home for another while yet, my Aunt Sarah is quiet and dependent, for Uncle Jack is always out somewhere saving Ireland.

The moon sailed in a black empty sky, and as it rose up from the East, it slowly became smaller and brighter and like the heavenly lamp keeper had lit another million candles, the whole valley became bathed in a pale shadowless radiance. Kate stood again, looking out at the black firmament.

"When I was a small girl, I used come up here because I thought God lived here, even more than he did in Father John's chapel in Boolavogue. I used feel sorry for God that all the world was so foul and bad, that He never ventured any further than Ceim an Athair, that all His infinite grace and goodness stopped up here."

She sat again on her perch and he looked at her for a long while. The moon on her face, it's beams entangled in the richness of her raven hair, the small white folded hands on her lap, brought him suddenly close to her, to the wounds and the pleasures of all her encounters. He wanted to have been a part of all of them and envied anyone who had.

"Now," she said, brightly, "the moon is fully up and we can see everything. The tide is out at Cahore."

Attridge could see westward for several miles. Trasna and the eastern end of Boolavogue were swathed in a cosmic fall out, so the roads, cabins and ditches stood out in salient detail. To the east, the severe focus of the moonlight brought Duhallow Park, burnished and fairy- like ,within touching distance.

"Cahore is thirty miles away, Kate," he said gently, still absorbed in the eerie scene.

"But I can hear it," she said, even above the music coming from the School House."

"Hear what?"

"The Mudlarks," she said

She pointed toward TheTrasna and where it flowed below Duhallow, stroking the air with her finger, along where the coiling blackness marked the river's course. Below the great house, was the beak of the Black Swan, from where the house gets its name, where the Trasna splits; one leg to join The Bann, the other to flow to Cahore. "When the tide is out at the sea and the river falls, the swan rises, a huge mudflat in the middle of the river, in the shape of the big bird. The Master showed it to me first, long ago, he called it the Water Spirit. The mudlarks know this and they come all the way to feed off her back". She saw the question in his eyes. "An Ealla Dubh." She explained, "somebody Englishized it to Duhallow, some poor Englishman who couldn't get his tongue around the sweet word, according to my Uncle Jack."

"Listen," she palmed the air. "They're like complaining old women, or I often think of them when I hear them complaining to one another, like hens, half asleep in their huts, tiny little whistles and warbles and complaints before sleep takes them. Then one staggers or is interrupted and the whole lot go into confusion, then settle again, whispering, purring and arguing."

As she brought her hand back to rest, he caught hold of it. She looked up at him in undisguised defiance, but without protest. "Are you going to marry Mr. Keane," he said, cautiously.

"I'm not going to marry him, not going to marry any man."

"You surely are, Kate, what a waste that would be if you were not to marry."

"Waste is it," she scoffed. "It's when we marry, ' tis then we're wasted. Every girl and every woman in Ireland, mistresses and nurses,

187

that's all we are. To women in Ireland, marriage is only a sad sour cup and we take it only for the dread of loneliness in old age. We spend our lives impaled under heavy bodies, our youth and beauty dragged from us, like the child we produce every year. We grow old before our time, our days given to the wondering how we're going to feed them and protect them, so they can grow up and be like us and start the whole thing all over again, crippled and disfigured, our youth stamped in wrinkles and our lives in the worst of woes."

She sighed heavily. "God, but Ireland is a terrible place for a woman, no matter how good her man might be, for his religion makes him a pauper and he is shackled to it, already serving his term in hell."

"Are you embittered," he asked, feeling her distress, "because I feel you're a little different from many of the ladies I have met."

"That's thanks to Lady Pamela, she paid for extra lessons for me in Enniscorthy and I am never short of money for my needs, as Sir George has come to depend on me, as does Annie Laffan, they're getting old. And yes, I suppose I am embittered. A woman with children in this country is God's own mistake, so to be unmarried, for me 'tis to be in the very best of health, Mr. Attridge."She gave him an assuring smile as if to say, "don't you worry about me now."

She looked down at the School House. "Look at Mary Driscoll, down there and her husband in his crude box, now the Widow Driscoll, a damning tag, tied to her for the rest of her life, with her nine children, for her sins, because, Mr. Attridge, in this country it is a sin to have a child and she has had to be churched nine times by the priest, to ask God to cleanse her, while her husband swilled his own sins away in People's whisky house. It will be up to poor Father Murphy to rescue her from insanity for sure, when he goes knocking on the door of Mountnorris."

There was silence for a while as he drank in the almost unreal atmosphere of the "special place in all the world."

"I'm privileged you brought me here."

"And so you should, 'tis few I allow beyond the path, it's my very own place. I was missing for a whole day, once, when I was small and the whole village was out looking for me. The Master told them where I would be. They found me here, just getting dark, fast asleep."

Somehow, it seemed important to him, that she should bring him here, more than she realized.

"It's called The Priest's Leap, Ceim an Athair, see here where I'm sitting, the shape of a horse's hoof in the stone. In the time of Oliver Cromwell, a priest was being hunted by the army. Any soldier who brought the head of a priest back to barracks, with his collar and sacred

188

stole, would earn for himself five pounds. The priest's horse came down over the top above, landed here on the flat stone and leaped from here all the way to Log na Coille in the Wicklow Mountains, leaving the shape of the fine horse's hoof in the stone forever."

"It's a fine story, Kate Keohane," he laughed.

"It's a true story, James Attridge," she insisted, heading down the pathway to the music. "Sure, we were persecuted back then too, I don't know why I should be talking to you at all, Mr. Attridge." She grabbed his hand as the ground gave way in the steep incline. "D'you know what this fellow Cromwell said? My uncle Jack had me pestered when I was young, to learn the terrible words, until I had them off by heart". She pursed her handsome lips, raising her head importantly, and in a forced strident tone, quoted, "I meddle with no man's conscience, but if by liberty of conscience, you mean a right to exercise the Mass, I judge it best to use plain dealing and let you know, where the Parliament of England is concerned, that will not be allowed."

"The cheek of that," she scoffed, then Uncle Jack says the chief of the Roundheads went and killed half a million of us."

"Your uncle Jack is right, Kate."

"He has me learning the new one now, the oath of the Orangemen, something about.... In the awful presence of God, etc, etc." His voice lifted above her's, mimicking her accent, glibly. " Etc. Etc., and do further swear that I will use my utmost exertion to exterminate all the Catholics of the Kingdom of Ireland."

"That's it," she cried out, do you know it too, you're not an Orangeman into the bargain?"

"There's evil in that text," he said, ignoring the jibe, watching her hips sway and gyrate over the rough path, and the folds of her skirt bobbing against her heels.

"The cheek of them," she fumed, playfully, "wouldn't they leave poor God out of it, hasn't He enough to do. C'mon, I'll show you to hornpipe. Are you sure you're not an Orangeman, now?".

Chapter 23

If a thousand came to receive old Diddymus home from Wexford, in two pieces, five thousand came to bury him. Captain Isaac Carnock of the Camolin Yeomanry, feared the consequences of the enormous crowd and the mass mind, full of eagerness and impetuosity, rising and falling as it grew.

Having a column of only four hundred men, he was soon fortified by the barracks of Enniscorthy, from which was sent a company of two hundred Hessian Dragoons and the professional tormentors; the hated Ancient Britons and the Welch Fencibles, under their commander, the little package of tyrannical arrogance, Captain Timothy R. Wrenne. The four priests seemed to Mary Donovan, to fill the little sacristy, wall to wall, Father Murphy, the rebel, Father Michael, Philip Roche and, as promised, the huge frame of Father Mogue Kearns. When Henry Tansey saw the priest earlier, his heart jumped, this man was almost as big as John Kelly, but then there's nobody as big as John Kelly.

Dismissed by his Bishop for rebel activities, Mogue Kearns had been in France as a student at the height of the revolution and had been hanged from a lamp post by the mob in the streets. His massive size bent the lamp post and his feet touched the ground. He was saved by a caring doctor until he returned to Ireland and became involved in the fringes of the political unrest. The marks of the ligature, he carried like a trophy, and would put them on display when drink would awaken his patriotic juices.

John Murphy was boiling inside, that Michael should have brought a well known agitator to his church where he strove daily to conform to rule and regulation.

Hundreds of militia in "all sorts of uniform," according to Henry, were drawn up outside the church. Thousands who couldn't gain admittance to the ceremony, had been pushed back onto the ditches and into the fields and a rude military swarm had assembled in the wide roadway. Murphy stood on the step of his church in defiance. Captain Carnock, upright and officious, but with a respectful reflection to his voice, introduced the senior officer of the day from Tullow, Captain Wrenne. John Murphy sized the diminutive officer in the green and grey uniform and cockade of the dreaded corps. "I would ask you to move back, Captain, while we bring out the coffin, your presence will cause confusion and confrontation. Passions are running high here, this man did not die of influenza."

Wrenne, thick voiced and intolerable, a man who loved the bristle of bayonets, cut through the quiet respectful atmosphere. "There will be no moving back. I am here on the orders of General Sir James Duff of His Majesty's forces. What I see here is nothing short of incitement, the crime for which your victim was rightfully executed." He looked down from his tall mount, his stirrups shortened to their limit to accommodate his short legs, a blunt cold observation, devoid of any kind of respect. "Now get your schismatic doxy over with, I don't take lightly to being dragged into some kind of ceremonial sorcery on a day set aside for my rest. We'll be watching you."

Carnock fumed, "you'll have respect, Captain," throwing Wrenne a foul look.

Murphy stormed back inside among rumblings of discontent and he was conscious of the anger all around him, an anger he had been starving for some time now. Conor O'Connor Devereaux the blacksmith had the green flag of The Organisation of The United Irishmen, over the coffin and Murphy found Lieutenant Bookey in the dark crypt studying the banned emblem. Without hesitation, Murphy dragged the cloth from the box and threw it at Devereaux. "I'm trying to keep sanity here, Conor, put it away, there will be no emblems of sentiment here, or there will be no funeral."

The blacksmith scowled at Murphy, irked by the smug smile of satisfaction on Bookey's face. "That flag is not sentiment, John Murphy, 'tis the embodiment of our territory and our history, and it seems to me that you don't have gumption to admit it, nor do you care. I'll take it outside, where God Himself will unfurl it."

"Save me from bloody patriots," John Murphy said into his chest as he led the coffin into the sunlight, the three co- celebrants close behind. Mogue Kearns, bent his head a little closer to Murphy, "In here, you're boss, out there, you have no jurisdiction, remember that, matters are in preparation."

Father Murphy looked back at the big priest, quizzically and saw only contempt there, as in the face of his friend Michael. Father Philip gave him a fine warm wink.

Rough commands stung the warm day, as Captain Wrenne, sweating in his regimentals, cursed the ceremonial doggerel of recantations of goodness and liberty. The confounded ceremony had taken almost two depressive hours, while the peasantry all around, with nothing really belonging to them but time, sat or lay back listening to the heavy voice of Father John's orations, the saying of prayers and the stream of virtually everyone in the parish taking communion. The ones in the fields simply lay back in the crab grass looking at the sky, mumbling their replies.

The soldiers of the crown, dry throated and bleached in the parched humid dustiness, gritted their teeth in search of saliva. Their torment was more exacerbated with the slugging at jugs and bottles, not all of them containing water or milk and the incessant munching of food, the dinner the peasants brought, knowing the day would drag. How a good dinner and feasting, reconciles everyone, thought Roche. The cavalry, about three hundred of them sat, drenched in their saddles while the mood of the peasants became a sort of a tantalizing and goading high spirited carnival to sharpen the spur of the military's envy.

Chaos slowly crept into the proceedings. Innocence, wisdom and ignorance pranced hand in hand, as a thousand peasants ran behind the cortege, the nose of the mob in a rushing , pushing herd, cutting the soldiers off in a confused disgruntled mass. Wrenne swore as his mount reared, almost unseating him, and soon the army was wedged into the narrow road, with the crowd split into sections, half before them, half, behind. People scuppered and tripped among the horses and soldiers, as they crowded and pushed their way through the laneway, upsetting mounts and riders. Infantry men narrowed their shoulders, as rough men and women pressed heavier and heavier against them, so soon the phalanx of military might became disjunctioned and began to disperse and be pushed, unceremoniously this way and that. "Divide the fire and you will soon put it out", mused Philip Roche

Green hats and shawls and cockades appeared and figures, hooded and anonymous, made their way through the by roads, over hills and across streams to swell the torrent and the Captain, from the slums of Liverpool's hatchet quarters, felt a nauseous sensation twist his insides. Timothy R. Wrenne, for the first time in his military career felt control slipping away from him. This was no army as that which he had to contend with on his campaigns in India and America. This was an opposition of a goading boisterous mob, women and children, without weaponry, without strategy, and without, it seemed, a leader. They danced to imaginary music, cannoning and jibing, the unfortunate animals kicking and hoisting and threatening to bolt. Wrenne's horse was being pushed sideways and it broke through a ditch into a field, so that, when he forced his mount back onto the road, he was isolated from his men, and for a few minutes, the little officer feared for his life. In the distance, uniformed men were falling from their saddles, others, with their head gear askew, began to flail at their tormentors in an effort to keep mounted. Rumps were spiked from under loose shawls and sweating horses became a danger to rider and pedestrian.

Wrenne felt that he could die here, the victim of some woman's kitchen knife, but knew that if he drew a sword, retaliation in waves would result

The graveyard at Trasna was a long low meadow, shaded to the east with a rolling hump of high ground, which, on the far side it fell away in a sweep of soft heathers and wild grasses to the sallies on the river bank. Fuchsia and honeysuckle were in bloom, splashes of red and orange shone from the hedges. Clusters of spruce and ash made it a peaceful place. Diddimus couldn't have chosen a finer day for his departure from this world. Rough headstones and hewn crosses among crannied walls and flowering beds marked the places of Trasna's dead, more for the glorification of those who live than that of those who died.

The priests had reached the open graveside, where the sun had caked the damp earth to gristle powdery clods and parts of Thomas Driscoll's ancestors were relieved, for a short time of their stern sentence and basked in their hideousness among the pods of clay. Yet another rosary began and James Attridge, from his vantage point on a high section of the ditch between the army and the burial couldn't help but feel a certain elation and a flippancy about Captain Carnock's demeanour in the obvious discomfort of his fellow officer from Tullow. Little beach pebbles were the rosary beads of many, ten well polished gobs, one for each Hail Mary, would be passed, reverently from one patch pocket to the other and back again, to pray the five mysteries, fifty transactions in all and Wrenne fumed at the third rosary so far. Diddymus was reverently lowered into his grave and five thousand heads bent in prayer, for today, their most potent instrument of action, for the army it was obvious, after almost three hours were slowly becoming a less force than when they initially set out.

It was then, Attridge was to see for the first time, The Wexford Pike, not just one but a hundred and more. The latest refinement of science: a javelin like spear, a good ten feet in length, had a spear and a sharp hook of tempered steel that would open a horse's belly with one stroke. He had become mildly aware of something about to happen, a suggestion of expectancy all about him. Raefil Keane, who had been with him and Kate, was suddenly missing.

"Look." Kate shook his arm, but he had already seen the spectacle. For a minute, the sun in his eyes, they stood in silhouette; a line of pikemen, across the summit of the hill, behind the army. Like a massive flock of passive ravens, they stood, stiff backed and defiant in the sunlight, then on a hoarse command, goose stepped a few paces down the incline, to be replaced from behind the hill by another line. Now, with the green sod behind them, the shadows became substance, the illusion, real. Big rough men of bog and mountain, green banners and cockades in abundance, down faced the Hessians and Attridge felt the raw animal heat of their contempt, as he and thousands more looked up in disbelief at the men of Killane, Shelmalier and Bargey. They had come to pay tribute to a man whose death, tomorrow should have been forgotten, whose death would have been but a whisper to the living, who in his little life, if he had control of it, would have been snuffed out by nothing more heroic than liver failure. Raefil stood up there, big John Kelly at his side, in reverent silence, wild things, waiting, challenging.

Kate Keohane felt a curious awakening excitement. Her face lit up and exploded in a rush of nervous laughter as danger and delight mingled in the tempest about to happen. The whole crowd erupted and John Murphy was suddenly aware of the undertone of hysteria in the mob. He saw what was undoubtedly raw satisfaction in the faces of his three fellow priests."You all knew about this," he spat. Father Michael smiled. "If a pike needs piking, then I'll do it, as Kearns says, you have no influence out here, John."

Mogue Kearns put a hand on John's arm, his face like carved granite, there was no amusement in it, as the first stirrings of panic seized the crowd. A red line of yeomanry quickly positioned along the base of the hill, just inside the low wall in front of the Hessians. "What's happening, in God's name," shouted Father John. "That, there, up there, is the new face of Ireland, Father," said Kearns, pointing to the sky and you will have nothing to say on the matter."

"You're all mad, shouted the man from Boolavogue". As he ran for the ditch, his white robe threatened to trip him up.

Three hundred riflemen were at the ready. A command from either above or below, one word in angry command and untold slaughter was assured. Kate put her hand to her mouth, stifling a cry. Carnock, Wrenne and Bookey had their swords drawn for the signal to fire that would come from the little Captain from Tullow.

Murphy punched the air in a fit of frustration and began running toward the gate. He seemed abstracted in fear, pushing people aside, Father Roche, hot on his heels. Someone took up his stifled call, it was a woman, running before him. More joined, squeezing through the gate, the more agile, scaling the low wall onto the road.

Hen Tansey, in his altar clothes became excited at seeing his friend, John Kelly in the front line of the rebels and began running. G. shouted to him to remain by the grave side, but his call fell on a convenient pair of deaf ears. G. saw Kate Keohane leap from the ditch and a thousand men and women scrambled through the line of soldiers, assaulting the hill, right in the line of fire. Attridge shouted to her, but she continued, calling for him to follow, she soon became swallowed up in the climbers. People were falling to their knees, righting themselves then falling again as the mob approached the pikemen. The two priests positioned themselves, arms outstretched, between the rifles and the pikes, the crowd followed suit, shouting at the Hessians and in a minute, the pikemen were out of sight.

Attridge stood in wonder, "Jesus," he prayed.

Children were now on the hill, as the human shield grew in numbers. The army, perplexed and frustrated, would have no alternative, but to stand down. John Murphy shouted at the top of his voice, "Wrenne, Wrenne". It was simply to jolt the officer back into reality, but the entire mob took up the chant and his name rang out over the burial mounds of Trasna and beyond, the word, which today had become a byword for all things bad and evil "Wrenne." The Hessian captain seemed transfixed, rooted in his indecision and Captain Carnock, sensing the possible danger of an erratic reply, ran through the lines shouting to the men to stand down and immediately an atmosphere of relief settled. The little upstart, to Attridge, seemed almost relieved himself that someone had taken the initiative

As quickly as they had appeared, the pikemen vanished from behind the crowd, spirited into the day, their show of defiance finished for now.

Murphy eyeballed the little officer, simply acknowledging Carnock, while Bookey fumed at a chance missed to show his prowess before a visiting officer, that might stand him in good stead whenever an opportunity might present itself. "Put your sword away, Mr. Bookey, there will be no showing off toda." Then to Wrenne, "you can thank the people of Kilcormack this day, Sir, for you would have died along with a thousand more, with women and children."

I'll thank nobody", grunted Wrenne, "as far as I can see, there's an army primed and ready here, and a sweep will be carried out in every quarter to root out those weapons and the owners chastised, and I'll thank you for your cooperation in the matter. They tell me, you're the one with the influence."

Diddymus was still to be put to rest. "In God's name where did all this come from." He turned to Roche, the armoury, where did it come from?"

Roche raised his eyebrows, nonchalantly, with a half smile. "What armoury, John?"

**

He found her with Raefil and her brother, Brian. They were lying on

195

their backs in the tall warm grass, where the army of rebels had stood earlier, near the top of the mound. The youngster was transfixed like he had been in the company of angels. He saw Attridge approaching. "Did you see me with the pike Mr. Attridge?, I was a pikeman with John Kelly and Raefil and my uncle Jack."

Eternity was born for a fifteen year old, a day he would remember for the rest of his life, the day he took up arms, be it just a sturdy ash cudgel, side by side with John Kelly against the king of England.

Kate remained prostrate, looking up at the blue expanse above her. Flushed and ecstatic, her voice coming in short spurts, she said, "wasn't it wonderful, the feeling when we ran the hill with Father John, sure they were powerless behind us."

The neck of her full dress was open to the sun and she rubbed her hand against her craw, in a slow lazy caress and James, again felt that tightening in his chest. Her eyes followed a jocund wisp of cloud. "It was like God was up there calling us, no fear, no fright." She sat up suddenly.

"You could all have been killed, the lot of you," Attridge insisted.

"We're not at war enough," said Keane, "that those bastards would fire on women and children, though that reprobate Wrenne, you wouldn't know what he might do."

Young Brian had scampered down to the road. Captain Carnock and his corps had stayed behind until Driscoll was suitably buried, all his virtues acquired by his death.

Wrenne's company of Dragoons were still at the mercy of the crowd. A thousand ahead of them, a thousand more behind him, they still dictated his pace in their grip. They would remain fastened to him, his men and his horses for a further two miles to Trasna Bridge.

"The day was just a demonstration, Mr. Attridge," Raefil said, looking down at Wrenne and his frustration. He laughed heartily. "Will you look at him, if there's one thing an Englishman can't abide, ' tis the close pressing of a Irishman against his person."

He gave James a half smile. "No war today, Mr. Attridge, maybe tomorrow, tell that to Wolfe Tone, next time you see him. Kate felt a tinge of amusement, that Raefil was softening toward the stranger.

James threw Carnock a knowing look, when the trio joined the marchers. Perhaps the Captain didn't recognize him in his turmoil. However, Lieutenant Bookey did. "I hope, Mr. Attridge, you're not getting yourself mixed up in this sort of thing," his voice cold and compelling. "You, here at a rabble funeral, I shall have to report personally to Sir George Palmer."

"I came to bury a hero, Lieutenant," he said to the mounted officer, which, by the way, you and yours helped to crown. It's my business to report on such matters of interest, about poor people, poor soldiery, desecration of hallowed places and the disgracing of His Majesty's forces at the hands of a country priest and a few women and children."

"And will you also report about incitement to war, the danger perpetrated by an army of a thousand savage pikemen?"

"Army, Sir?, I saw no army, no threat to His Majesty's forces. What I saw, was a group of simple peasant men, ready to protect their women and children. What I did see, Lieutenant, was the insanity on your face, when you were not allowed to fire on them, the same of Captain Timothy Wrenne, and but for Captain Carnock, shouting to stand down, we would now be opening many more graves, including, no doubt, yours, Sir."

Attridge stroked the horse's forehead. "Good day to you now, Lieutenant." Bookey was beyond rationality, pulled at the reins, venting his anger on the animal, who was not allowed to go any faster.

"Where DID the pikes go, where have they been?" James asked his two companions, "Raefil?."

"That's for a clever Englishman like you to find out." A childish smirk lighted the good face, "James."

In several meetings, neither had ever referred to Christian names. "I know," said Kate, teasing him.

She looked at Raefil. Attridge saw the parallelism of their lives, a single soul between them and James hoped that the strain and tension that might have existed in his relationship with Keane, by now might have dissipated, as he noticed the intimation of an ironic smile playing about the iron set of his jaw. At least, he appreciated the use of first names now.

Chapter 24

The relationship between Sir Charles Mountnorris of Camolin Park and Father John Murphy was always based on a sort of mutual exploitation, a kind of mental and physical barter.

Mountnorris, the leading Ascendancy landlord of north Wexford, had a roll of the dice in respect of his twenty thousand tenants. He knew the pleasure and the pains of power, and wielded it in an energy of omnipotence for which he had a special face, but often in the influence of the pauper curate of Boolavogue, the peer achieved it's responsible use, for which he had another face. In John Murphy, Mountnorris had a friend whom he loved and hated in turn, loved for his pensive simplicity, his genius as a horseman and athlete, though now in middle age, hated often for his influence with the people of Kilcormack, more respected than any man in the parish, more feared than any landlord or bishop. In the abstract knotted web of their relationship, they would find warmth together. In a counselling, when the priest would scavenge through the peer's confused and scrambled intellect, looking for favours for the downtrodden masses, Murphy would insist in the headiness of an excellent claret, that his friend's strength came from God, and he should hold himself in modesty before Him and before His subjects. There were nights, not too often, when Murphy's mare would be the source of his safety, on the way home to his lonely accommodations. "Be strong, but be merciful if you would have the respect of your neighbours and not their fear," the priest would counsel his influential friend.

If truth be known, Mountnorris was a little jealous of the priest's influence with the masses. There were people in Kilcormack would die for this priest, if so called on.

It was two weeks since the so called "shame of Enniscorthy," two days after the funeral of Thomas Driscoll. Murphy went to Camolin Park, on a mission, not nearly a social visit. The heavy bodied peer would walk up and down his small private dining room, small in terms of Camolin Park, complaining of his poor circulation, then return to his table and slurp some more wine.

"I'm told this fellow Driscoll was a hobo, a man always looking for trouble. The magistrate demanded the prisoner be released to them and my captain had no option but comply."

"Captain Carnock is in your own yeomanry, Sir, the least you could have done was send me word," argued Murphy.

"Yes, for you to have the whole judiciary system climbing the walls, with your arguments on his behalf. He was a troublemaker, John."

"The magistrates of north Wexford are a hoard of terrorists and no laws can be enforced against them and if their savagery continues, the people will have no alternative but to follow a path of action, led by some hot tempered rebel, looking for notoriety, and I don't know if I can contain them," the priest pleaded.

"You must speak to them." Mountnorris raised his voice in demand, "for the sake of our friendship, for the sake of humanity."

Murphy pushed his meat around the plate, the luncheon was more than adequate, but his appetite was elsewhere. "The magistrates like White and Owen are killing at random, between them they will start a revolution in these parts."

The priest looked at his host, fingered the rim of his glass and said, cautiously, "Charles, I want you to disband your own corps."

There was an undercurrent of hysteria in the older man's voice. He strode about the room for the second time."Disband the Yeomanry?, my God man you can't be serious."

"If you do so, the others will follow."

Mountnorris looked for some kind of psychological design in the priest's request. Murphy rushed on in a torrent of words. "The others respect you, if we rid ourselves of the Yeos here in north Wexford, the unrest will pass. Your soldiers are killing their own without compunction. The demonstrations at the funeral was a frightening spectacle, more such demonstrations will follow".

"Yes, and your lot was the cause of it, and I'm told that but for your effort, there would have been carnage." He sighed heavily into his wine and Murphy saw the enmity and vituperation of a depressed mind, struggling to stay whole in his own troubled world. The only incurable troubles of the rich are the troubles that money can't cure. "In '72, you persuaded me to stand with the liberals for a better deal for your people. Bagnal Harvey of Wexford and I and others fought the good election and we lost. Since then, I have been ostracized by the authorities and my person casts a very short shadow on the ground. They have begun to see in me, the essence of a heretic and yet my heresy signifies no more than my opinion that your Catholics should be represented in Parliament." He raised a finger in caution, "not by Catholics, mind you, it is certain, they can never be in Government, but by those of us whose right it is to do so."

Father Murphy felt again, the sense of disqualification, the dreaded solitude, even here with a kind of a friend, for the people, the great losers whose score in the game of life is always zero.

"I must tell you, John Murphy, there is an armoury being built here in Wexford. We know the peasants have a hoard of pikes and swords and cudgels and God knows what, hidden away and now we have seen them displayed in public." His eyes darkened and held his guest in their caution. "I must, of need, end my disadvantage with The Lord Lieutenant." He was suddenly stiff backed, his agues forgotten in the importance of his egotism. Like the other ascendancy landlords of Ireland, unsafe and tremulous in their status at the whim of government and in their inheritance, at the acceptance of the disinherited, conceit to their character, what salt is to the ocean, it helps them to endure.

"Struggles are eternal, John, mankind has grown strong in their depts. God Himself has said that the poor will always be with us. I will increase my Yeomanry in size and someday you will thank me for it's doing, for in doing so, I will maintain peace."

"Where there is no brotherhood, there is no peace, Sir," insisted Murphy , wearily, making to leave, compatibility gone.

"You're a peaceful man, Father Murphy", said the peer, "leave the politics and matters of government to us. Go and manage our spiritual needs, use your own kind of logic that cries for miracles and occasionally gets one."

The affection between them, mostly muted over the years, with an asterisk of stipulation about it, fragmented on that day. The damaging implications of the situation, stamped the relationship between Lord Charles Mountnorris and Father John Murphy from then onwards. The camaraderie and mutual respect that had flourished to a shared benefit for ten years, died at the open doorway of the Camolin Mansion.

With Murphy, there was always a condition, Sir Charles fumed inwardly. Damn the fellow, it's always conciliation and appeasement. Damn him for a fine horseman and huntsman again and again.

Mountnorris called from the steps as G. brought the trap alongside. "Sunday then, we start the hunt from here."

"What about the family?, you made me no answer," Murphy called.

"Are they a brood?"

"You created nine orphans, Roger Owen has put then on the road." Murphy climbed aboard

Again, conditions. "You'll lead the hunt on Sunday, I have a Member of Parliament as my guest, I might get you some favours."

"Is he liberal?" The priest managed a half smile.

"Yes."

Before Murphy could reply, Mountnorris called, "that Condon place is available at the western end....."

"I know where it is, Sir," the priest winked at Georgie. "She can't afford a rent," teased Murphy.

"Until her brood is earning then," annoyance bordered on desperation Murphy gave a token acceptance, the wound of their previous encounter, set aside for now in the small victory. "The windows, can we open windows?"

"Damn the windows," exploded Mountnorris, "do as you wish." Murphy looked at G., pursed his lips and wondered if there was another nugget to be plucked.. A liveried boy came down to the trap and handed the priest a cloth purse. Coins tinkled expensively. "Sir Charles says for the widow, Father John."

He weighed the coins in an open palm, throwing a furtive eye at the doorway as Mountnorris went to go inside. There was a world of meaning in the simple nod that flowed between the two and G. saw a sadness in the Murphy face, a depression in the middle of a triumph and his eyes filled as he looked away to the distance. As they sauntered the mare to the gates, John Murphy said, "Charles Mountnorris could be a man for good, but he hasn't the courage enough to appear as good as he really is."

In the darkening day, John Murphy could feel the beginning of turmoil, out there in the hills and the villages. The cold balance of probability stung at his back in that he felt the premonition of the full flavour of the happenings of the past few days, an opaque mirror, through which he could see the dim outlines of pending chaos.

"Where to Father John?"

"Just take me out of the shadow of Camolin, Georgie."

**

"There now, you know what to do." G. was to carry out his first act of charity. Father Murphy stayed in the trap as the youth strode elatedly to the door of the cabin. It was dusk and a tiny window reflected a single lamp. The hut squatted, cold and dark in its friendless existence. To G.'s surprise, there were some eight bodies inside, on straw cushions and rough cots that surrounded the one roomed hut. Someone in the semi darkness rushed to make a seat for Father Murphy's server, whom the parish got to know, though few knew his name. Today he was bringing bounty, a double favour to the Driscoll brood, as Sir Charles called them, though as John Murphy, sitting outside, the prime mover in the lives of so many, knew; there is always a sort of a sublime thieving in all giving. Mountnorris will come looking for favours another day.

Tansey had his hands rung off their sockets, even kissed, when the full force of the message found home. The widow, simply came to the

201

door, where Murphy saw a deluge of appreciation and understanding in her drained face.

"Mr. Tansey will borrow Donoghue's dray tomorrow and bring you to the Condon place," he called to her. Her eyes filled with tearful gratitude.

"What a funny old world it is, Georgie." Murphy leaned back against the strip of cushion. "That house she's getting has no windows. You and I will have to plead her case, to allow the light of day shine through. There will be a condition, that she and her little family take the oath to the King of England, just for the benefit of God's daylight."

John Murphy laughed, a tincture of contempt at its edge, "the king your sainted mother made a jacket for."

"I told that to nobody else, Father," G. said shyly.

"Perhaps it's just as well, Son, your secret is safe with me." He laughed again, this time, ringing heartily.

Chapter 25

On the night after Thomas Driscoll's funeral, a crowd had invited themselves back to The School House, The Master had sent out word that there was still a power of drink left and he was afraid Norah Scully would make a beast of herself. He had told Kate, to inform Mr. Attridge that he had found the book of which Mr. Tone had referred to; Tom Pain's The Rights of Man," "a book," said Master Dunn, to be chewed and digested."

The Master, as always was holding court, many of those hanging on his words, were, onetime his students, learning more now that the school was no longer, than they ever did before. The night was full of the talk of the funeral and the spectacle of the day. Faces turned to the Master in masks of bewilderment and ignorance. "So, you see, death, the most dreaded of all evils, is therefore of no concern to us; for while we exist, death is not present, and when death is present, we no longer exist, - Epicururus said that in the third century."

The first feeling of an event stirring, was the breakup of a convergence at the doorway and suddenly Jack Keohane, menacing and alien stood in the centre of the crowded room, bastard drunk and belligerent. "I bear no disrespect for this fine house and the grand people in it," he slurred. Middle aged and middle sized, with a body like it was carved from Blackstairs granite, he projected rancour and hostility, good and strong and it took James Attridge, who was standing before the door leading to Nora Scully's bedroom, a while before he realized, through the pall of tobacco smoke and body matter, that he was the source of Keohane's ire. Drink, combined with the death of his friend, had dislodged his very limited capacity for composure and in that state, Jack Keohane always needed to strike out.

"You," he shouted, "you and your kind." There was no design, psychological or otherwise to the statement. Then he said, focusing on the Englishman, "'tis you're like that killed him, a simple foolish man with nothing in his brain but temper and childishness."

Apprehension and embarrassment filled the room, discordant babble in corners faded as Attridge put his drink on a table and faced him. "I have no wish to have a confrontation with you, Mr. Keohane," he said calmly. I'm a guest in the house of Mr. Dunn, and I have no wish to abuse his hospitality, however...."

A heavy resonant baritone issued from outside, where he had been standing in the evening's calm, but he stood now, facing Keohane, dwarfing him and Conor Devereaux gave him a knowing look, an understanding eye. For a big man, the blacksmith of Trasna, he could be quite softly spoken. His body was lean despite his age, which James put at mid fifties, which was also belied by the heavy shock of dark hair, tied neatly at the nape of his neck. Only his face was the contradiction. Onetime, undoubtfully handsome, it was like carved driftwood, dark and creviced. His eyes were vital, the plough of time had encased them in wrinkled beds and had clefted his cheeks, his mouth, generous, his stance, now quietly arrogant. For a thin man, he had massive shoulders and in the heat of the room, where his sleeves were rolled up to his elbows, his arms and hands were like a brace of armed weaponry. That Conor O'Connor Devereaux carried authority was evident, and why wouldn't he, quiet and inoffensive, with metal barely below the surface.

Still holding his little friend in the grip of a cautious eye, he said to the stranger "you must forgive my friend, his patriotism sometimes leaves him brainless and his politics takes him in all directions." There was a swell of nervous laughter here and there. Dunn, with a half smile focused on Conor, over his spectacles. Then he gave James a long lingering look, like he had done that Sunday outside Father Murphy's church, like trying to see beyond him or inside him and the exercise seemed to side track him for a minute or two. A good measure of drink had been taken. "But, Keohane, like the rest of us, has lost a friend in very tragic circumstances and we are a bit outside ourselves for the crime that has been committed." In his dark frown, there was a heap of understanding when he said, "go home Jack, there's a good lad."

Frustration creased the arrogant face and Keohane stormed to the door. Kate stepped in front of her uncle, her eyes smarting. He side stepped her. "Your wrong, Uncle Jack," she protested.

The blacksmith nodded courteously and The Master observed the drama. Devereaux seemed to look for a reason to stay, then asked someone to find his coat. "Thank you, Sir," said Attridge, about to make an effort at a hand shake, but with a nod to Norah Scully, the big man followed Keohane into the night.

"I'm sorry about Uncle Jack," said Kate, "his temper will get the better of him some day, and he'll end up like Thomas Driscoll or worse."

"There's nothing worse than that, Kate," he said.

"Yes there is, for he could start a war all by himself, I'll kill him when he sobers up. My father used to say, Jack was a petty little man with a petty little mind."

"The blacksmith, he seems to hold respect," said James.

"He's respected all right, nobody would cross him, but he's a good man, maybe I'll take you to his forge." The crowded room returned to the conversations and the business of what after funerals are all about, the atmosphere lightening and a fiddle began tuning up. "Conor is a kind man, people think him a bit strange until they get to know him. He used to come to Duhallow often, and eat with Gobnait in her kitchen. Sir George is very fond of him, but he would never go beyond the kitchen. Recently he is staying away, despite Sir George's constant invitations. If shoding is to be done, he would have Paddy light the Duhallow furnace in the anvil house, come to do his business and leave. It's strange, but Gobneait and Mrs. Laffan and even Sir George, seem to understand his staying away, and I don't understand, unless there was a row or something, or maybe it has something to do with his grievance with Father Murphy, who, as you know, loves Gobnait's kitchen as much as he does his altar."

Chapter 26

Chaos reigned, especially in the northern counties, and the authorities stamped it with a seal that would make it rightful order. Theobold Wolf Tone wrote to his friend, James Attridge, whom he hadn't seen for some time, inviting him to Kildare, where he would have much to report. He had been summoned to Dublin Castle, where a tribunal would have "some questions," for him.

Chateau Buoe, with its tower and idyllic surroundings looked as welcoming as ever. Matilda Tone, dainty and pleasant as before, seemed to James to be even more frail and on this occasion, she presented her four children, two of them, presentable enough now to sit at table with visiting guests. Attridge had sought permission from Father Murphy to bring along young Georgie Tansey and advised Tone, beforehand that he would be accompanied by the youth who had become interested in the noble profession of journalism. Stupefaction almost became stupidity in G.'s eagerness to meet Mr. Tone, face to face and to show his appreciation for favours past. Henry was not too displeased, as to G.'s great relief, he didn't have to to wet nurse his young brother anymore. Hen spent most of his spare time in the company of big John Kelly, often staying with his hero at John's mother's house in Killane.

The house was still in mourning. Mr. Tone senior had died some months before and in the troubled climate, Wolfe Tone had decided to keep his passing a low key affair. Leaders of the United Irishmen and the Catholic Committee had paid their respects, coming and going at Chateau Buoe, almost in single file. A collection of the leaders, whose names were already engraved on the list of the Convention Act, to be seen in great numbers, would be perilous and an invitation to trouble.

"Young Tansey, here, is a friend of Father John Murphy, whom you met at Duhallow," James explained.

"I'm afraid the good priest holds me in doubtful esteem," Tone smiled

"Mr. Tansey has something to give you, Sir", said James. G. took the little tobacco knife from his pocket and handed it to Tone. "You saved my life, Sir and that of my little brother."

Tone's face lit up in recognition. "It was a part of a shaving set from Paris, it seems it did its job very well."

"G. is Father Murphy's right hand man, he calls him his lieutenant. We are inclined to think that he might follow his mentor in a vocation." G. shook his head, as Wolfe Tone fondled the knife, studying the youth. "I don't think so, Sir, G. said. "In Ireland, I fear we think more and more about religious tolerance, than religion itself. I see Father John struggling day after day, torn between the two churches, where in one, like that of Mr. Owen and Mr. Cope, he sees no tolerance, even in his bishop, while in his own, nothing else exists BUT tolerance. I believe Father Murphy has pure religion, I doubt if I could have it. Growing up, I was neither Catholic or Protestant, it was whatever suited me or my mother, our name was often our passport."

"And now, Son?"

"Now," smiled G. "I'm learning journalism, thanks to the generosity of Mr. Attridge and Sir George Palmer. I work on the farm of Mr. Donovan and help at Duhallow, I like to work in the fields with Sir George's farmworkers."

Wolfe Tone handed him the pocket knife."Keep it, Mr. Tansey, who knows, it might yet turn out to be the first weapon to strike for freedom. I do recall two boys in a crowd of children, trussed up like turkeys in the heat of Wexford, it was a while ago. Mentioning the butterfly knife, Wolf Tone said that it was part of a shaving set, given to him by his brother, Matthew.

"Two years ago, Sir, it was you gave me that freedom, it's my intention to put it to some good," said G.

**

In the small library, the den where Mr. Tone prepared his pamphlets and carved his dreams for an Ireland, free of tyranny, their host, after a welcome dinner, set about his purpose of James's summons. He had a file of considerable bulk, ready and bound for the journalist, to take with him.

"Simply," he commenced, moving some papers about the desk. "There has been a secret committee set up by Lord Chancellor Fitzgibbon of Dublin Castle. It compels witnesses to give evidence on oath. He has introduced what is termed, Star Chamber Proceedings, which has already created spies, informers and gombeen men into all facets of life. Blood suckers for profit have infiltrated the common system of life, for the sole purpose of discrediting the Catholics and the Presbyterians, by implicating them in the outrages, now becoming rampant. The process allows Fitzgibbon to prove his opinion to William Pitt in London, that the Catholics are untrustworthy, a danger to the establish-ment and has pushed forward the doctrine of the Orange Order, that,"these dark conspirators", as he calls them, should be heavily dealt with and once and for all, annihilated."

Wolfe Tone reminded the youngster that all details were contained in the file, but G. explained he wished to keep up with the practice of short hand which Mr. Attridge was teaching him.

"Now," continued the host, "Fitzgibbon has brought up before his secret Committee, a final solution to rid the country of its three million Catholic Defenders.Trouble is brewing with France, so to supplement the army in Ireland, he has recruited a newly paid militia under his own control. With the Prime Minister's blessing, the jails of Britain have been emptied of its most foul inmates; murderers, sadists and madmen in uniform and are to be let loose on the country with unrestricted discipline. Volunteering is suspended and the Convention Act is to be pushed through the Houses of Parliament, making illegal, the holding of assemblies of any body of people, consisting of more than one half dozen. There are paid spies everywhere, under the, so called Star Chamber. Our entire organisation, including Lord Edward Fitzgerald and Thomas Russell, is compromised to a perilous degree and set in place, a code of distrust, even among many, we thought were on our side."

Mrs. Matilda Tone brought them tea and savouries and a carafe of brandy and invited G. to be mother.Wolfe Tone opted for the brandy, as did James.

"You will remember, James, Mr. William Jackson, had dinner with us at Sir George Palmer's house, the one I recommended to your hospitality, for which I regret greatly." To the other's expression of recognition, he continued, "the ex clergyman."

"I'm sad to say, he has committed suicide in prison, as a victim of said Star Chamber, at the hands of two spies, who secretly endeared themselves to the establishment and the pocket of London. I befriended Jackson, knowing him to be an important activist in the revolution in France. The man came well recommended by Mr. Nicholas Madgett, a west of Ireland man and now a respected member of the French ministry for Foreign Affairs. The two spies, Leonard Mc.Nally,a brilliant lawyer, once imprisoned with the fire of revolution in his belly and in his passion for the Society of the United Irishmen, fought three duels for its honour. The other, a John Cockayne and a close friend of Jackson, was directly in the pocket of prime minister Pitt. Knowing Jackson's penchant for loose women and strong liquor, they plied him with both on one of his trips from Paris, bearing important documents from Madgett to my friend Thomas Russell. Before he died, he sang like a canary and put us all in jeopardy."

He looked from one to the other, sighed heavily and took up a letter from beneath a file. "I will read you a letter, which I have hidden from my wife, but spells out the density of our troubles. It's a letter our people has intelligence of, written by Mc. Nally, to his co deserter, Cockayne, there is a copy in your file, hand written by myself and you will forgive the dreadful hand."

Tone quoted "I have reported to The Prime Minister, that it would be prudent to allow Mr. Jackson ample rope and to treat him like a minnow. The circle which is capable of instigating a concrete arrangement with the French, does not include Jackson, he has no metal, no influence."

Tone looked sternly at Attridge, G. kept scribbling. "The ones to look at," the letter continued, "are Hamilton Rowan, Oliver Bond, William Drennan, O'Connor and especially, Theobold Wolfe Tone, he has the influence, the intelligence and the ambition. Tone has been to France, at least twice, as has Lord Fitzgerald, though they travel separately and as far as we know, they seem to have separate agendas. My source tells me His Lordship is being involved to play a responsible hand in the affairs of The United Irishmen, but so far, prefers the company of his wife and his privileged surroundings."

Wolfe Tone put the document down, sipped the brandy and tilted another drop into his glass. As always, his anxiety and frustration flushed to his face, emphasising his acne. "The restrictions are causing us to lose much of our momentum, all further rallies are outlawed, people's lives would be put in danger. Our membership remains loyal and is increasing by the day, but we are, once again, underground, and playing a waiting game. Waiting can spoil hope and agrarian outrages between the poorer classes of Catholicism and Orangeism, continues, mainly in the north. Doctor Drennan and Rowan are in prison but I'm sure they will come out alright, Philpott-Curran is their defence. My friend Tom Russell has relinquished his job as magistrate for Dungannon and is now a librarian in Belfast. The general disintegration of affairs has left him depressed and retiring. He meets with Mc. Cracken and Monro in Belfast, along with my brother, Matthew, who in his naivety, believes the whole matter is something of wonder and could easily become a marked man. I am at him to return to America. I was in America. I could make a living there, the Americans need good lawyers, but it wasn't for me, my wife craved for home, as indeed did I. America is busy, cleaning up after the British. My children would have liked to have stayed."

"So." he sighed, "I'm back on the circuit, one has to make a living. I've been a neglectful husband and father, James, liberty comes at a great price. One thing I will say in grateful appreciation, to the tragic Mr. Jackson, his escapades in France took their attention off myself,

209

while I went about my business."

Tone had a sudden intensity in his voice, laying a background anxiously. "If anything happens to me, this file contains many of your accounts of my endeavours, if anything happens, you may print as you wish."

He hesitated,"I will lay great responsibility on you, by telling you that I have met with Robespiere and Marat in Paris."

He saw the surprise consume his two guests. "And two prominent senior officers of the army, Hoche and Bonaparte, I have become very close to Hoche, Bonaparte is a different kettle of fish altogether."

Chapter 27

Taking another letter from his pile, Wolfe Tone continued. "For almost three years now, I have been in constant contact with General Hoche, seeking help for Ireland. But matters have changed greatly in that time. France is now governed by what they call The Committee of Public Safety and Robespiere's days, I believe, are numbered. The country is completely in the hands of the Jacobin revolutionaries. Our problem is that Jacobinism is hostile to religion in any form, so it stands completely in the way of Catholicism. The Catholic Church in Ireland abhors the revolution, but our peasantry wants it copied here."

He smiled and shook his head in frustration "The Defenders of Ireland want Catholic Faith and French ideals. France is at war, not only with England, which our Parliament here supports, but also with Netherlands, Prussia, Austria and Spain."

"This is a letter from my friend, Russell, he writes – "I sent word to Joy Mc. Cracken and Monro, that two ships had left a small port in Wales, bound for Larne, heavily laden with troops and I had it on good authority that Mr. Pitt had foraged in every cesspit and jail and pound to find them. Mad men and curs of Britain are being pardoned of their heinous crimes, given arms and are being unleashed on us. I joined my two friends on Scabbard Head and watched the great bulk of H.M.S. Robust in full sail, rounding the head of Donaghadee, skirting Copeland Island. The eighty gun ship of the line, one of the biggest of the British fleet, was both majestic and menacing in the waters of the north channelas the second ship, the frigate, Melapsus, with forty guns brought up the rear. So help me, Theobold, Henry Joy Mc. Cracken, a man of robust and happy personality, as you know, his voice cracked in his throat as he felt the hard core of hostility and antagonism, assail us."

"Shall I continue, you do not have this in your file?" Tone sipped his brandy. G. wrote feverishly.

" Please, Sir."

"On the sickle shaped promontory above the harbour at Larne, we watched the huge ships unfurl their canvas. Before they docked, I wondered again at the beauty of our land and this place, the head known as The Curran curves round toward the south, to the west, the Sallaghh Braes, to the north, the Slemish Hills, sheltering our beautiful harbour, was now being desecrated before it's Architect, with the presence of evil." Tone hesitated as if reading it for the first time. "Two thousand men disembarked, like animals that had been in captivity for a long time, who had known deprivation and despair in stinking jails, who knew no bounds, suddenly had freedom thrust upon them. I left my friends under cover and sauntered closer and joined a crowd of mostly peasants, fascinated by the spectacle, never knowing or imagining it's consequence. The colonel with his corps of dragoons, followed by a phalanx of yeomanry, of the garrison of Larne and Carncastle, stormed onto the quay, a welcoming committee for the new immigrants. Colonel Lumney urged his horse forward and the unkempt visitors, standing at all angles and postures listened to his address with priggish indifference. They were advised that they were coming from one kind of prison to another. Their term of training and drilling in the hills of Antrim, Down and Tyrone, would be arduous, to a point where they would wish they had never come and if it takes two years, backs and spirits will be broken, "until you will hate this country and everyone In it". Russell finished with a warning. "This tide of iniquity has been let loose on us, my dear Tone, and as Mac Cracken at our meeting of strategy has warned to take care of our houses, our sons, our women, because, until these people are engaged in real war, they will seek other means of enterprise and enjoyment."

Wolf Tone put the letter down and took another sip."My friends in the north are somewhat disappointed with my journey to America, that I couldn't succour for Ireland, but think of it, gentlemen, they have no more truck with King George, they've kicked his royal backside out their door forever. Oh! How I envy them."

"Now," he clapped his hands in finality. "I'm before the Tribunal in two days," as if enjoying the prospect. "I'm before a school of fools, have your pencils sharpened and alert, because I will want you present, James."

Chapter 28

A crisp February morning announced the spring. James had left G at their accommodations, who was none too pleased at not being included in the day's drama, before the Tribunal, Attridge being conscious of overstepping the trust offered to him personally by the friends of The United Irishmen. James promised him they would arrange his reports for publishing when the time was right.

He sat with Thomas Russell, Addis Emmet and Wolf Tone at a small Inn, just off a junction of Cork Hill, across the road from the main entrance to Dublin Castle. It was not at all a castle, more a sprawling mansion behind high walls, the only part of the medieval keep still standing, were the two round towers and a portion of the old curtain wall. Gone with the centuries, were the draw bridges, the moat and the monuments to ancient Celtic wraiths and Norse occupation. The ridge with accommodated the Upper Castle yard was the site of the old King John's castle and which became in Elizabeth's reign, the residence of the Lord Deputy or Viceroy and now was the headquarters of the British administration in Ireland.

"Are you under arrest?" asked Emmet

"I don't know," replied Tone, lightly, it's possible I might be after today's business," he laughed.

The four looked through the window of the Inn, their faces, tranquil, almost indifferent. Attridge was fascinated at the matter-of-fact attitude of, especially Tone himself, about to be summoned before a tribunal instigated by the most powerful man in Ireland, Lord Fitzgibbon himself, The Lord Chancellor, a passionate campaigner for a complete union with Britain and a sworn enemy of the Catholic Committee.

"Fitzgibbon, himself is going to chair the tribunal," said Russell. "You should be honoured."

"You're held in high esteem, Theobold," smiled Emmet.

"It's he should be honoured," said Russell, despite the levity, the big man showed a tincture of concern. "Be careful, my friend."

Attridge watched his friend study the colourless limestone walls, pallid and lifeless in the chill morning. Inside stood the The Birmingham Tower, the State Prison and yards, tragic scene of countless executions and the pillory of Red Hugh O'Donnell, the sixteenth century chieftain.

"They used to hang us inside those walls, they now hang us in the streets and on bridges." Tone sighed, then sprang to his feet and stormed into Cork hill.

"It's time, James," he said abruptly and shook hands with his two friends.

"Careful, Tone," Russell called.

**

The room was a high ceilinged panelled auditorium with few comfort furnishings. An arena, Wolfe Tone reckoned, where poor devils fought for their lives under the penal authoritarianism for half a Millennium. It was a courtroom with tiered seating along both walls and at the head, a raised dais, with an ornate desk, at which sat The Lord Chancellor Fitzgibbon and the chief Secretary, Robert Hobart. A smaller desk to the right, was occupied by two civil servants, while a dozen men or more, sat in the first row of seats. Other than that, the room was empty.

"Poor enough reception committee," whispered Tone to James, as the journalist took a seat further along the second row of seating. Wolfe Tone introduced James, simply as a friend. Outlandish wigs and cockades everywhere as faces like stone gargoyles gave him a quick inspection, then ignored him.

Mr. Tone was directed to sit in a sedan chair which had been placed in a central position, but he refused the courtesy, saying if the house didn't mind, he would prefer to remain standing. James smiled to himself, he could already see that the man had them at a disadvantage already, firstly refusing to be seated then speaking without being invited.

"May I ask the tribunal, if I am under arrest, and if not, the reason why I am here?"

The Chief Secretary replied, already indignant at the seemingly trite attitude of the barrister. "You are not under arrest, Mr. Tone. This is a tribunal of enquiry into the activities of a number of organisations, to which activities, your name has been credited, we speak, firstly of your involvement in the so called Catholic Committee. May I say, that in the concessions granted by his most gracious Majesty, many blessings have been bestowed on our Catholic peasantry, however, there is great unrest in the country and we have reason to believe that your considerable influence in these organisations and factions, is cause to give us concern and to impress on you, the grave error of your disposition toward the established government."

Lord Chancellor John Fitzgibbon, now in his late fifties, the son of a Catholic who turned faith, because as a Catholic, he could not be a part of the legal profession, sat like a judgemental owl, hunched forward in a probing gesture. The blanket like wig, grey and musty, covered his

214

ears and hung like a blanket to his waist, Tone thought he could smell the sweat underneath and the lice that lived there. A most detested advocate of a complete union with England, he was arrogant and bitterly hostile to the great majority of his own countrymen, corrupt and corrupter in the name of the crown.

Hobart made reference to those present, hoping for some kind of remorse in his victim. "This desk is representative of government and Mr.Henry Grattan, himself an untiring advocate of emancipation for the Catholics, together with some members of the Irish Parliament and we are pleased to have, with us, representatives of the Catholics of Ireland in the presence of Lords Fingal and Southwell and Gormanstown and Kenmare. These honourable gentlemen have found it necessary to establish, on behalf of the Catholics, their most firm attachment to His Majesty's Royal person and to the constitution under which his Irish Catholic subjects live in contented happiness. They come today to impress on this tribunal, their rejection and that of the Catholics, on the whole part, any countenance afforded these factions that have sprung up in the country and hold forth no hostility to the established and elected order of government."

Hobart looked at Fitzgibbon, as if seeking encouragement. The Lord Chancellor nodded his agreement and the Secretary continued. "Mr. Grattan and many members of his parliament hold you in kind esteem, Mr. Tone. You have friends, many friends who recognise your talents and who have sought to help you in the past."

Fitzgibbon interrupted, his voice coarse and condescending, as much as his massive ego would allow him to be. "Mr. Gratten gathered around him the original Volunteer body, a powerful police force, consisting the very best Protestant Yeomanry, which helped bring about the glorious revolution, with admirable efficiency and without bloodshed. Now, an alarming measure of drilling is taking place among the lower classes of the populace, so there is an irresponsible effort to arm the poverty and the beggars of the kingdom." He raised his voice and was suddenly, condemnatory, as Tone, simply clasped his hands behind his back and took a step forward, then a step backward, like he was paying no attention. "That, Sir is not what Mr. Grattan's parliament strove for. He believes, as we all do," then he scoured the audience with a look that was full of purpose and the voice lifted a further decibel, "that the political movements of Ireland, should be in the complete and absolute control of the gentry." From under his eyes, Wolfe Tone watched the powdered heads nodding in fevered support and he seethed inside. Then he raised his head and gave the audience a long searching look, especially the "Four Evangelists," mentioned earlier, the Catholic arse lickers whose tongues were not long enough to show their loyalty and their appreciation of their charmed lives.

Then he looked furtively at Grattan. "My Lords, I wish it to be recorded that I and my colleagues hold Mr. Grattan in high esteem, and establish him to be nothing but a supreme Irishman. However, we differ in the lengths to which we go in the interest of this nation, in that it is my belief and the belief of the Catholics of Ireland, whom are NOT represented by Lords, Kenmare, Southwell, Gormanstown and Fingal, that no reform of the people is practicable that should not include the Catholics, together with the Presbyterians AND the Protestants. My writings proclaim it openly, we are about to place it, in sacred request, at the feet of the king, himself, the great measure, essential to the freedom and prosperity of Ireland and an equal representation of all the people in Parliament."

Rumblings of disagreement and contention began in the rows of pathetic submission. Fitzgibbon sifted through a mound of papers before him. "You have said, Sir, that the Irish Parliament is.... and I quote,.... a bought and pensioned retiring home of corruption". More rumblings. "Careful," whispered Attridge.

"I have said so, my Lord," said Tone, clearly and without hesitation, "and I repeat it here now before this assembly, as being a victim of it on my own part. I was offered a peerage and a seat in the Irish Parliament, without a vote being cast in my favour by the people and I challenge the house to set forth, proof of democratic procedure in the circumstances of representation in the house, by legal means. I predict that seventy per cent of members will be found wanting.". He pointed accusingly at the four Catholic Lords. "And yet, the four most influential landowners in the country", and he called out their names for emphasis, "who between them, own a third of the most fertile land in the country, are refused entrance to The House, on the grounds of their religion and they sit, wasted, before us."

Lord Fingal shouted that they are well capable to speak for themselves.

Tone raised his voice above the din. "And yet again, there are fellow Catholics on their vast estates, who starve and shiver their way through winter after winter."

Accusations flowed fast and furious and James feared for his friend, away from the fray, he continued to make sparse notations. Like a centre of gravity, James felt the core of contempt light on the narrow figure, still strutting defiantly and now and then he would shake his head in answer to Fitzgibbon, while groans of protest and annoyance would burst from the audience.

Hobart's condemnation increased."The Catholic Convention, of which these Catholic Lords," pointing to the four, "here present, were substantial and law abiding members, until you, Sir, took over its destiny, have declared their intention to unite their efforts with the friends of Parliamentary reform. You, Sir, through your efforts, have libelled the House of Lords, and I have reported to The Lord Lieutenant, that, in my opinion, your ultimate object is to bring about the separation of this country with England. It is the opinion of this tribunal that these people have voted you generous amounts of money as their cabinet minister and advisor, who first proposed alliance between Puritans and Catholics."

"Here, here," and "shame," from the listeners.

Fitzgibbon consulted his notes, leaned toward The Secretary and Hobart, feverishly whispered in the honourable ear. "We refer to your paper, Hibernicus, there are words here, according to our Secretary, that constitutes conspiracy."

The tribunal was weakening, as The Lord Lieutenant strove to confirm his accusations. It was evident, to Attridge that he had not read Hibernicus.

"You charge me with conspiracy, My Lord, yet at no time have I advocated such measures at to break the tie with England. It is obvious to me that you have not read my papers, and obvious that The Lord Secretary has misread or misunderstood my reasoning. I repeat here now, that a connection between our two countries would be beneficial to both, only if it were one of perfect equality, equal law, equal commerce, equal liberty and equal justice, and only if and when the enormous absurdity and injustice of the Irish tithe system has been removed from the obligations of the poor. You, yourself, Sir, have refused to grant a committee to even investigate this great evil."

More whispering, but before any further grievances could be uttered, Tone continued. "I admit responsibility in the drafting of our pledge which we are taking to the king, and we do appreciate very much His Majesty's kindness in allowing us audience. We prepare before him, three simple endeavours, none of which are treasonable or objectionable to any fair thinking and democratic institution. We require a cordial union among all the people of Ireland, a radical reform of the Irish Parliament and it should include Irishmen of every religious persuasion and of none."

Tone strode nearer the bench. "I repeat, My Lord, whether I am under arrest."

"You are not under arrest, Sir," Fitzgerald's voice raised in frustration. "However, I will have your thoughts straight from your own lips, on the dependency of your country on the generosity and the support of your sister country."

"I'm sure you have before you, my letter on that subject, published in Faulkner's Journal for all to read, that I protest against the principle, that, as an Irishman, I owe my allegiance to Great Britain, or to the king of Great Britain. My allegiance is to the King of Ireland, and I would resist, to the last drop of my blood, resist the claim of any king or any nation, who should dare to exact any obedience from me."

There was abject silence for half a minute, then the rumble began in quick succession, a babble of discordant sounds of protest and condemnation. Fitzgibbon was on his feet, hawk faced, his eyes on fire. "I say to you, Mr. Tone, you will no longer find sustenance for your endeavours in either The Catholic Committee or The United Irishmen. You can consider yourself lucky there is not a warrant issued forthwith, and but for your obvious influence in high places," he looked searchingly at Grattan, "you would be a guest of the nation this very night. You may go."

Attridge clenched his fists in disbelief, as Wolfe Tone continued to address the assembly."You should know, Sir, for I believe you do not know, of the existence of a vile and destructive committee whose sole purpose is to discredit the Catholics of Ireland and the United Irishmen, by implicating all of them in the outrages committed in the countryside. The conduct of the nation rests on your shoulders, the aim of this committee is to discredit the Catholics and the United Irishmen, by implicating all of them in outrages committed by the Defenders. I have no allegiance with the organisation that calls itself The Defenders. But I say to you, My Lords, that the destruction being wrought and the wedge that is being driven between the various factions of our society, that has lasted for five hundred years, will last for another half a millennium, if you continue to allow the gates of suspicion and distrust, to be left open.

Tone turned on his heel and strode purposefully to the exit. James stuffed his notes inside his pocket. "Don't look back," whispered Tone, as he quickened his step.

They returned to the Inn, and found Emmet and Russell still there waiting, a flagon of ale, ready and waiting.

Wolfe Tone sighed heavily, his voice hesitant and tired.

"It's over," he sighed, "after all the work and the preparations, I believe, our trip to the Court of St. James will be a waste of time and energy, I can see it in the mundane face of the Viceroy of Ireland, and the grey breath that hangs over this house of tyranny."

Chapter 29

Dinner with Thomas Addis Emmet helped to alleviate the tension of the day and it was at the lawyer's house in Rathfarnham, that Wolf Tone was to meet his friend's younger student brother, Robert.

He simply burst in on the party with a young friend, when after dinner drinks were on the table. Unlike his brother, who was always composed and agreeable, a sort of gentleman, one could never imagine other than behind a desk, or dispensing his lawyerism in a courthouse, Robert seemed to have a current of life within him, dogged and precocious. He shook Tone's hand warmly and welcomed him and James to Rathfarnham. Russell seemed to be simply amused, as he always was, when meeting the young brat.

"I told my brother to wish you bon voyage when you go to London, Mr. Tone, with your delegation, and so I do now indeed, however, if I might be so bold......"

"I think I know what you have to tell me, Mr. Emmet," laughed Tone, "your good brother has told me often of your revolutionary ideals, I'm afraid they will have to wait a while."

The tall, good-looking youth persisted, bringing Attridge into the conversation and introduced his friend. "This is Mr. Thomas Moore, he's a poet of outstanding capabilities and he has written of Ireland's struggles."

"Are you a revolutionary also, Mr. Moore?" asked James.

Moore was a small man of about eighteen, with a head of black curls and a face of a cherub. He was wide eyed and shy, unlike his friend. "No, Sir," the poet replied, "I doubt if my stature would suit the paraphernalia of a military," he patted his midriff apologetically.

"No," interjected Robert Emmet, "but he could cause a revolution all on his own, with his pen. With Moore's poetry, Sir, you could paint the wind, or put a whole battalion at the ready, words in their very best order". He looked, keenly at Wolfe Tone, full of frantic energy, that could be overpowering in its intensity, like his mind was winging to a distant place, partly on the liquor he and Thomas Moore had consumed before breaking in on the quiet party at Rathfarnham.

"I've been to Paris, Mr. Tone, as I know you have," giving him a suggestive observation,"and I've been to Versailles, thanks to the generosity of my brother Tone looked at Emmet Senior, a wry smile breaking on his relaxed features. Thomas gave his young brother a stern look of caution. "And I have been to Saint Patrick's Hall in Dublin Castle, and you are about to set out to visit Saint James's Palace in

219

London, and I tell you Sir, nothing compares to the grandeur of Saint Patrick's here in Dublin. The apartments of the seat of The Lord Lieutenant of Ireland are the very essence of grandeur and magistracy, to equal and surpass that of Emirate, Sultanate, or Tsardom in any part of the world. It is common knowledge that the only court without a king or queen in it, is the envy of royalty, worldwide, and the protocol and pomp adhered to in Dublin, compared only to that of Versailles at the height of French court splendour."

Emmet Senior went to interrupt. "No," Wolfe Tone said, "please let your brother continue, he'll make a great orator someday." "Yes," chided Thomas Addis Emmet, "if his mouth doesn't get him into trouble before that day comes."

Despite his brother's discomfort at the hijacking of the party, young Emmet continued, loving the attention. He sat nearer to Tone and held the visitors enthralled. "Mr. Tone, it's obvious you have never been in these apartments. A portrait of King Henry the Second, receiving the homage of the defeated Irish Chieftains, the first English Monarch to annex Ireland to his crown, five centuries ago, hangs in the Great Hall, along with the most recent abomination, George The Third, supported by Liberty and Justice."

He raised his voice in emphasis, Moore, smiling through a tipsy haze. "And the banner of the Knights of Saint Patrick adorns the lofty cornices, along with the flags of the nations colonised by Britain over the centuries." His eyes moistened and to Tone's surprise, he saw there, where emotions were not new to the youngster and he saw there, a heart that had room for everything.

"Did you know, Mr. Tone, that Saint Peter guards the north door and Saint Patrick and Brian Boru, the east." Robert Emmet sighed heavily and suddenly seemed older than his eighteen years.

"They have Christ everywhere, poor Christ, His arrest, His trial, Christ before Caiphus, Christ before Herod, Christ before Pilate. They have the King of England presenting the keys of Heaven to The Almighty Himself, or perhaps it's visa versa," he frowned. "Now how's that for arrogance, Mr. Tone, you tell me. My friend Moore has put it into poetic parlance." He looked at Tom Moore, reverently, "a masterpiece, though I don't like to read it." Moore rocked from one foot to the other, still standing and gave his friend a look of compliance.

"I'm afraid our debating society at Trinity has deduced that this whole thing you and your friends have for the mad King of England, is simply a waste of time, a supplication that will have no favourable outcome, or no outcome at all. I have read where you have written that the American situation was settled in six months, surely, ours is more complicated, it's old and rusted. They had a fine revolution to sort matters and sent Cornwallace packing back to London."

At the door, he turned, bowed respectfully and said, "when you are ready, Mr. Tone, for your revolution, Mr. Thomas Moore and all my debating society will be there for you, and I'll get you a million men to stand with you."

They were gone. "They have the fuel, the fire, I wonder who'll set the spark," Russell smiled.

"My brother wants to change the world," Emmet mused, sipping his brandy.

Chapter 30

The committee, chosen to "prostrate themselves at the foot of the throne" in a final and exasperated plea for reform of Ireland's parliament and emancipation for three million Catholics, were ushered down to the state salon of the packet Nordland, where hot punch awaited them. It was very cold. The arctic waters of the Lough lapped the bows gently and a winter northern wind from the Fjords, an impassive faced tyrant, seemed ready to stab at any time, the warning circuits, cold and treacherous, already accumulating in tenebrous masses over Ratlin.

Lord French, a leading aristocrat and a committee member of the United Irishmen and the Catholic Committee had been chosen as chairman of the expedition, a man, it was felt, would be acceptable for his liberalism and his membership of the House of Lords. Around the polished table on which was laid out, the declaration of the Catholic Committee and the aspirations of three quarters of the entire population of Ireland, to be placed before His Majesty, stood about a dozen members, among them, Russell, Teeling, Mc. Tier, Mc. Cracken, Keogh, Addis Emmet, Wolfe Tone and his friend Attridge.

Tone opened the largest of the cabin's portholes and the boisterous beating of drums, the shrill call of the fifes and the clamour of voices, raised in coarse adversity, filled the room. The English Prime MinisterPitt, acutely aware of the dangers of granting any kind of reform to the Catholics of Ireland, had endeavoured, through his agents to re-kindle the fires of religious bigotry, and on the eve of the historic audience with the king, rumours were disseminated of fighting and rioting, perpetrated by the Catholics on " innocent and fearful Protestants."

The passion of Protestantism for the villainous King William The Third, The Prince of Orange, Stadtholder of The United Provinces, King of England and Ireland, over a hundred years ago, was the platform from which William Pitt The Younger chose to unleash one of the most iniquitous schemes man had ever devised to pitch one brother against another brother. He chose the diminutive Dutchman as the hero to be worshiped as a celebrity by the Orangemen in the north, who, starved for a hero, clutched at a straw.

"I heard Bruce speak in Dungannon," said Russell, looking onto the quayside where the Northern Clergyman was preparing to address two thousand Orangemen. "Bruce talks about God, like God were his wine butler and talks about King Billy, like he was God; the glorious revolution of 1690, the divine presence of the Godlike King William of Orange at Auchrim and The Boyne and the quietening of Sarsfield at Limerick, offensive stuff indeed to anyone with nationalist pretensions. King Billy, he said, was magnificently healthy and robust, a king of supreme stature and prosperous features, benign, affable and sweet tempered and a God to his people and to us."

Russell looked at James Attridge. "If ever the violation of truth be known, it is in the deification of William of Orange, a typical case of people like Bruce there, believing that repetition transforms a lie into truth." He sipped his punch and rolled the warm sweet liquid around his mouth. "William of Orange, Stadtholder of The Provinces and King of England and Ireland, stood all of five foot and three inches in his raised heels. He was thin like a pipe cleaner with a deformed back, which, God help us, made him spin slightly on the heel of his right foot, so that he came toward you, sort of sideways." Russell raised the unfortunate gait in emphasis, a grin of mischief on his handsome face. Faces about the salon spread themselves in tight grins of control and drinks were slugged loudly.

"Our Billy was a chronic asthmatic and as a consequence, an irritable, short tempered little package of arrogance, propped up by the kind of sick propaganda you are about to hear out there. A hundred years on and it's hard to have to listen to such absurdities, he was bisexual, but a homosexual and part of his arrogance stemmed from the fact he could not produce an heir."

Wolf Tone cut in. "He favoured the company of young men."

Somebody broke the control of the room and it rocked with laughter and Tone smiled boyishly, enjoying the levity of his friends. All the work had been done for the London visit and now the tide and the ship were ready and impatient, as a small nation held its breath for the outcome, on a day when His Most Glorious Majesty was having one of his seizures and the farthest thing on the mind of Prime Minister Pitt was the Irish Catholic Question.

Earlier in the day, their carriages had been stopped on their way to the quayside, the horses were unshackled and in their enthusiasm, the people of Belfast pulled the carriages amid pomp and revelry to the ship, only to be met there by an organised Orange rally, under the direction of The Rev. William Bruce, the North's most obsessive Orangeman.

Nielson, Sinclair and Mc. Tier, of the Catholic Committee, stood on the port side of the Nordland and called to the crowd for calm and restraint and to resist the goading adversity of the Orangemen. A line of about two hundred of the Dumbartonshire Cavalry, supplemented by a similar number of Yeoman Riflemen, kept the green and orange armies apart. Lambeg drums, the size of cart wheels and shrill sounding fifes heralded the lantern jawed clergyman. The drums were appalling instruments of war, designed to incite and provoke, growing keener and sharper with each stroke, jarring the senses to boiling point. Beaten incessantly with a pair of rods that twisted and bent with the pressure of spastic like movements from elbow to fist, it cut the air in whistle sounds and slapped the skin of the instrument in sharp salvos that drowned out everything else.

Samuel Nielson stood behind Wolf Tone at the window. "So that's Bruce," said Tone.

Nielson had to raise his voice above the din, outside.

"That's the man, puppet of the loyalists and high priest of bigotry. Under the banner of King William and with the bible in hand, that fellow is responsible for riots and sectarian killing all over the province."

He had two thousand ranting followers, hate gripped between their teeth, features distorted.

"Your true enemy is not necessarily in London, Theobold," Neilson said, "the man in the palace would prefer peace in Ireland, albeit on his terms. Out there is your real enemy. Your words of peace and reconciliation for all men, only inflame the fires of hatred that lie in that heart. Peace is an obstacle to Rev. Bruce's welfare and fortune."

Wolf Tone remained eye to eye with the clergyman, with a look of serenity, almost sympathy for the spittle filled maw and the staring eyes. "What enmity expressed in one face, so much for the saying that great hatred can be concealed in the countenance."

Then Tone smiled broadly through the window at Bruce and the huge guttural vocals assailed him, like it was coming at him through a barrel of slurry. The party began to split up as non travellers prepared to leave the ship. Good wishes were extended in prayers and praise for the five delegates who would sail; Wolfe Tone, John Keogh and Edward Byrne, well to do business men, also James Devereaux, Christopher Bellew and Sir Thomas French, all but one were Protestants, fighting for Catholic Emancipation in the Court of St. James. Tone smiled at the thought, but felt no grandeur in their efforts, he feared the whole expedition a waste of time and effort.

As the five saw their friends off, Bruce's voice rang out, the green army had been moved back several meters to the rear wall, out of any cause of danger.

"..... and I say to you, 'tis a danger to the true religion, to all the Protestants of Ireland, that the Papists of Ireland, if allowed any kind of freedom, would establish an inquisition. It would give us a Catholic Government in Dublin, deceive us of our liberty and forbid us of our loyalty to King William and the sacred person of our most glorious Majesty, King George." Bruce's guttrel was a bellows of incitement to mass hatred.

It irked him to see the disregard those on board, showed him and he shouted in a pitch of almost hysteria. "Do you want scavengers and reprobates and drunkards in your parliament....., do you want your rights and codes taken, word for word from their bible of The Rights of Man, written by a drunken maniac?" He wiped the spit and lost no momentum, calling on God to smite all Papacy, pagan worshipers and idolatry.

"Poor God," sighed Russell, as he disembarked. "He is the immemorial refuge of the incompetent, the helpless and the miserable. Poor God; You who everyone knows Thy name." The huge canvases were unfurled and Nordland moved slowly into middle channel, and Rev. Bruce continued his rantings, his anger always making him a prisoner of his own mind.

Chapter 31

Dignitaries from seven nations assembled in the large state room, west of the Chapel Royal. Spain, Holland, Austria, even The Vatican were there. Fevered knots of conversation spread about the immaculate chamber, at the top end of which, a dais and gilded throne stood unoccupied.

King George the Third had not yet made his entrance and Prime Minister Pitt fumed inwardly, not just being kept at His Majesty's pleasure on a busy day in Parliament, but that he should be made to share his audience with trinket bearing ambassadors, pompous aristocrats and purple clad legates. Mr. Pitt the Younger knew this to be simply a fob off, a slap on the wrist for the rejection, last Monday of the king's request for finance to buy the magnificent new house, being built by Lord Buckingham at the upper end of the Mall, for a sum of twenty eight thousand pounds. St. James's Palace was too confined for the daily dissertation of state affairs. It was totally inadequate for the ever increasing numbers attending Court and with fifteen children and a household staff of two hundred, the Queen had her mind set on a new palace at Buckingham House.

The Irish delegation was standing to the rear of the room, Keogh and Byrne, with their backs to the wall, Tone, alone at a window, further up the side isle, wanting to get a closer look at this Prime Minister Pitt, the cause of all his woes, James Attridge and Lord French further up to the centre. Tone moved up to the next window, closer the dais. The window looked down onto a courtyard. A delegation from Ireland had never attended an audience with a reigning monarch for the purpose of discussions on reform of any kind. The splendour of the surroundings seemed to free them of the erratic nervousness, first witnessed on entering the Court of St. James. Now they fluctuated between hope, anxiety and expectation.

Wolfe Tone was disconsolate. Like Lord French, he had expected a private audience with the king and perhaps a minister or two.

There was an urgency in the pulling back of the tall ornate double doors and the long corridor outside, stretching away in a shining marble and velvet artery, was suddenly filled with a surging torrent of near hysteria. Six young to middle age men bounded into the chamber in a flurry of energy, purpose and importance, breaking the stifling tense atmosphere. The centre figure, sizing up his entourage, dismissed, with a flurry, all but two of them, then took in the contents of the room in a condescending inspection. Magnificently dressed men bowed magnificently. All flounces and frills, a lace handkerchief held delicately in one hand, he dismissed their attentions and bounced excellently toward the Prime Minister. Mr. Pitt and his three ministerial advisers stepped back reverently in courtesy.

Prince George Augustus Frederick, the eldest of the king's fifteen children and gluttonous campaigner for his father's committal, on grounds of insanity, was a strikingly handsome man, with a shock of dark hair. Egotistic and self-opinionated, the thirty year old had secured for himself, a reputation as part of London's sub life, a womanizer and libertine and a great embarrassment to the king, who, as an erratic and questionable monarch, was an unblemished husband and father and both pitied and loved among his people.

As he drew nearer, Tone noticed the carefully made up face, the blusher on the cheeks and a dark shading of the eyelids and he wondered what the world of men was coming to. "Prime Minister," the Prince of Wales had a commanding voice, cultured and authoritive. "I must impress on you, the urgency that I again, become Regent and this time finally to succeed. It is grossly unfair, Sir, that I should be Regent one minute, because my father might take a turn, and then be kicked back into irrelevance again if he shows a tincture of improvement, a sort of a caretaker on half pay."

William Pitt, the great manipulator and carpetbagger of the unsuspecting, bowed gently and said, in a voice, full of psychological design, a prime minister at twenty-four years of age, Wolfe Tone couldn't but feel a pang of jealousy at the confidence and authority, even before the Royals.

"Your Royal Highness understands the immense role you play as prince regent. In the king's absence, you keep us on the track to greatness."

"But I am not now, again Regent, the doctors say the king is recovered. Do you know, Sir," the prince looked about furtively, some ears were bending cautiously toward the debate, not least the Irishman "do you know, Sir, the king was missing for fourteen hours, day before yesterday. The palace was frantic, delegates sent home, he was no place to be found."

Pitt gave him a long troubled look, aware of the visitors. "Has His Majesty been found yet, Highness?"

"Of course he's been found," the prince hissed and trailed to a whisper, "in one of the nurseries under my little sister's bed, playing with her dolls, I declare. I will only say, Prime Minister, you know that my father's bowel movements have been causing his physicians great concern," putting the scented kerchief to his nose.

Pitt continued to pamper. "Your contribution to foreign policy is invaluable, especially that of four years ago on your opinions on the troubles in Ireland. As Regent then, you were invaluable". The future George the Fourth looked suddenly perplexed. "Really, you say so?"

"Your Highness is aware that the Irish parliament has entertained the idea that, while you await the final call to coronation, that you might honour them as the Lord Lieutenant of Ireland.2 Pitt mused with the idea that England might be rid of the troublesome heir for, at least a while. Tone saw it in his eyes. Pitt is a cunning manipulator, he thought.

"Would I have to live there, in Ireland?" The idea broke on his crimson cheeks, like in a new awakening.

"Of course, Sir, the people love you with a passion, 'tis a most pleasant country."

The Prince of Wales stood stiffly and demanding and said smilingly, "how do you know this, Sir, you've never being there, I've heard it's nothing but bog and bog men."

"I believe otherwise, Sir," said Pitt, "remember we have owned it for five hundred years, we have surely instilled some kind of civility in it."

"That long, Mr. Pitt?" The Prince was about to continue, when he moved to the screamer board, running his eyes down the list of visitors.

"They're here, Mr. Pitt," he called from the doorway and the Prime Minister frowned at the vulgarian. "Save me from royalty," the youthful prime minister whispered under his breath.

"Here, Highness?"

"Yes, yes, the Irish, they're here for the audience, why was I not informed?" He stood in the doorway, a royal pageant of self importance. "Please show yourselves, the Irish people."

Wolfe Tone remained at the window, the courtyard, still the object of his attention. He simmered in his discomfort, remaining defiant and self restraint, a loud din in his head to hide the urge to storm from the room.

"Show yourselves, I am the Prince of Wales." He gave them a severe observation as foreign delegates moved aside. He then eyeballed Sir Thomas French, the only one of the delegation from Ireland wearing an insignia. The prince seemed to look through the aristocratic French. "Tell them what I have said, Prime Minister," he called to Pitt and was gone in a haze of perfume, his two aids bowing and frantically trying to lift the tail of his ridiculous cloak.

**

228

Normality returned, but only for a while. It was now an hour and a half since the audience of a hundred had prepared itself for the king's presence. Somehow, Wolf Tone was comforted in his frustration on seeing the discomfort in the face of William Pitt, and the waiting, suddenly became less of a burden. God, how they put such great value on themselves, he thought as to set none at all on others. For people like the prince of self indulgence, egotism is an anaesthetic to dull the pain of their stupidity. Lord Lieutenant, indeed.

King George the Third moved purposefully in a cauldron of strutting attendants, secretaries and half a dozen of his children. In a surging deluge of words, waving his arms in huge dramatic gestures, he floated into the state room, a heavy ermine cloak billowing around him. At the door, he stopped suddenly, a dark blank expression, savaging his ageing face, like he was, momentarily lost. Then, squinting at the screamer board, the occasion seemed to hit home and there was a world of feeling in his shout of recognition and the procession continued in and out through the bobbing, genuflecting dignitaries in waves of welcome.

"He IS mad," Tone sighed to Attridge, who had moved away from French as the king approached.

Insanity was the hallmark of the first ruler of German stock to be born on English soil and great fits of massive irresponsibility had often resulted in great misfortunes for his country. But now, Mr. Pitt had a tight reins on the homely monarch, and the old man, still only fifty five, but besieged with neurosis and latent lunacy, looked fifteen years older. George Rex depended on the pampered advice and counsel fed to him by the Pitt regime.

The king recognised nobody in particular, except the Papal legate, and shouted at the unfortunate Italian to remember him to dear Pope Giovanni. He waved his hand dismissively, not sure how far down the line of Giovannis, Giovanni was.

"It's Pious, Majesty," whispered Pitt, "Pious the Sixth."

"Yes!, Yes," he waved again down at the legate, "Pious, Pious, of course."

George the Third looked and smelled like he hadn't washed for a month. The buttons to the shirt beneath the velvet cloak had been left undone, exposing a stained grey-white under garment. As he stood before Pitt on the dais, a young prince tried to put the matter right and his father stood there, his chin in the air, trying to converse with his P.M., over the boy's head. His wig had slipped down over one ear, in the effort, exposing wispy dead tufts of grey hair, congealed in sweat and matted powder. "Your shoes, father," the boy said, and, with the help of an aid, removed the royal slippers and managed, by propping up His Majesty, to slip the brogues onto his bare feet.

As he turned his back further, he said, "I do miss the queen, why does she pick a time like this to be in Germany?" He sounded pathetically lost, almost insecure without her. "I would have seen you privately, Prime Minister, but it's been a devilish morning, what with Charlotte away, she's in Germany, you know." The young prince managed to make his father a little more respectable, by straightening a lace and crochet half cape, where the rich velvet of the cloak emphasised the intricate needlework.

"Your Majesty," Pitt insisted, "as I have already mentioned, I believe you know my feelings on the Irish question, it's imperative Your Majesty makes no promises today. With the French war looming, the powerful Catholic lobby among the peasants is taking on momentum. The royalty of Europe is fighting for its life and the established order is being threatened by revolutionaries."

George had now taken his seat, and this private whispered conversation continued between the two, while a hundred delegates waited in silence. "But our subjects in Ireland are most composed, revolt would never come from that quarter."

"Indeed, Sire, they love you dearly, they are here to tell you so." He moved before the king, his back to the audience and Tone moved slowly to the next window, within ear shot."Mr. Edmond Burke and the Secretary of State and myself; we believe that some minor reforms might be made to the Irish, so as to win them over from sympathy with The French aspirations of so called liberty. Nothing near full reform, Sire, should be promised, but a sop to conciliate any ideas of revolution."

Tone's insides churned as he felt the momentum of the day, disappear.

"There will be no talk of revolution, Mr. Pitt, not in Ireland. It is inconceivable, as inconceivable as the idea that we reform them and leave them to the wilds of the world, without our direction and succour and sustenance. It would be a shirking of our responsibili-ties before God and a violation of the sacred oath of our coronation."

Wolf Tone, in his torment, watched two men, strangers to him, who had never been to Ireland, had no conception of her brutalised existence, stand in huddled conclave, designing her future for a further century and building a tomb for the orphan of Europe. The vast futility that pervaded the spirit of past heroes, intensified like a slab of grey granite over his own and he felt desolate and alone.

King George threw his eyes over the assembly as Pitt moved to one side and Attridge couldn't but catch the Prime Minister's demeanour, sheltering behind it, something like a mild contentment.

The king motioned for the Irish ambassador to approach. Sir Thomas French moved to the throne and went on one knee, his leather bound book of aspirations in his grip. King George continued to address the Prime Minister, while French rocked in his attempt to remain prostrated.

"We have received, Mr. Pitt, on good account from Dublin, that in the continuance of the present arrangements with our Catholic subjects, the landlords of Ireland will introduce new levies for fair taxation in order to help you with the war effort with France, thereby in their efforts, bringing them closer to our cause and our person."

Taking the bound manuscript, he handed it to an aide and looked on the bowed head of Sir Thomas, then gave him a nod of acceptance. His eyes clouded over for a minute in a glazed expression, like he was trying to think of something appropriate to the occasion, some magnanimous gesture, some historical utterance, that would be recorded for history.

George the Third fixed a stare at a timid looking man standing off near a window and, in a flurry of unintelligible sophistry said, "there was an Irish dance, I think they call it a jig or a jug or some such name.....a dance....at our coronation. Of course, the Queen wasn't there then, she would have been most pleased....fine dancers, the Irish, I'm told. She's in Germany, you know, so tell them in Ireland."

Lord French's address of humble appreciation, rang out in the silenced room, appreciation, that, for the first time in history, through innumerable difficulties, the plain people of Ireland were able to prostrate themselves at the foot of the throne, to bring before His Majesty, the humble petitions of three million of his loyal subjects, their sufferings, their wants and their wishes for his well being.

King George then dismissed French with an unaccustomed hand shake and a warm smile, then continued to accept the delegates of Rome and India and others, in quick succession. Wolf Tone looked down into the courtyard. Tears of anger and frustration welled up in him and in his mind's eye, he followed the leather bound pages, now pushed up into the sweating arm pit of some civil servant, to be filed away in a morass of bureaucratic indifference and ineptitude. He thought of the endless meetings in every county to get a mandate for this expedition, and the futility of the exercise, how it crushed his spirit and energy. The blank imbecilic face of King George was kind and homely, a face that held no promise or ability to deliver even the slightest sop of pity or understanding of Wolf Tone's cause.

James Attridge put a comforting hand on his friend's shoulder, as Lord French and the rest of the Irish delegation made their way to the exit, after the royal procession breezed through the corridor, His Majesty's voice echoing back to the audience, a speech pattern of clusters of staccato long breathless sentences, full of stretched words strung together.

"Christ help Ireland," sighed Wolf Tone "The king is ill, we could have the Regent in power again before long."

Chapter 32

It was a day of simple enjoyment of simple friendship and conversation with uncomplicated people. As James walked the Nettle Path to the woods, the tranquillity of the passing moment, was helpful in the blotting out of the miseries, the highs and the lows of the past few weeks. The chariot of his life was changing gear, it had become a ceaseless churning process and he strove to keep up. He had not heard from Mr. Tone for three months, not since returning from the sham that was the trip to London. "You won't hear from me for a while," Tone had told him. "I am going away for a while, and since that tribunal in the Castle, I fear I could be in danger and worse, a danger to my friends, that includes you, James." James had taken an interest in the everyday running of Duhallow, feeling he needed to show appreciation of Sir George's kindness to him.

The young sister of Kate Keohane, the one with the unusual name was in her leafy boudoir, barefoot and dancing to her imaginary music, the fairy music as she called it. He gave her a wide berth, respecting her privacy, taking the outer path past the columns of Horse Chestnuts and Ash, where the crocuses at their mighty feet had lost their purple and yellow and while garbed for another year, the fuchsia and honeysuckle were still in bloom, and the only sound was the drone of bees wings. He walked for an hour and was surprised, on his return to find her still there, this time sitting on her special seat with the gardener, they called Luther. He had come to know Luther, his quiet unassuming attitude to all things and his evident love of the soil and all that springs from it. Luther looked like he was spawned in the soil, with seed and manure in his veins. Beloved of Sir George, James would often find the peer sitting in the middle of a plot of vegetables with him, having a packed lunch, lovingly designed by Gobnait.

They stood on his arrival into the clearing. He said he hoped he wasn't disturbing them. Luther remained standing and insisted Attridge be seated. "I'm giving Droleen a lesson or two on matters of the soil, Sir, he looked at her fondly, "she's a very good student."

It was then James saw his countenance change, a sort of an affection without demand, as he looked at her, then it was gone, as quickly as it came. He saw Attridge looking at him, "I'll be going now, Sir, Mrs. Brennan will be looking for her vegetables for the week end."

Droleen looked into the ceiling of the forest, where the shot beams of light penetrated the green arches. She hardly noticed Luther's exit, after shaking James's outstretched hand. "I'm not disturbing you,

Luther?"

"No, Mr. Attridge.", and he was gone.

"Did you know, Mr. Attridge, that trees can speak to God, for they're always reaching up to Him ?".

"I'm sure you're right, Droleen."

"And did you know that The Oak tree, it feeds the animals with its acorns, but to pull a sapling of Oak about you, it will protect you from the fairies, and did you know that The Elder Tree, though it has black berries and can smell terrible, for it's the home of witches and all things evil, Mrs. Brennan can make ointments for rashes and inflammation of your skin from the berries. You know that The Ash Tree is a good symbol, that it brings lightening down on itself, to protect the animals, Mr. Devereaux makes hurleys from the timber of The Ash, Father John's altar in Boolavogue is made from it, made by Mr. Devereaux. Never pass an Alder Tree on a journey". She wasn't to be disturbed as she continued his lesson on tree folklore, to his delight, like here in her own place, she had a new personality of confidence and self assurance, that was never evident in the shadow of her sister.

"The Alder wood is white, until you cut it, then it turns red, the colour of blood. And The Willow and The Sally, put a sally rod around the milk churn for the making of good butter, and did you know that Brian Boru's harp was made from Willow, and The Cherry Blossom, with it's lovely fruit, that the Cuckoo never sings until he eats three cherries and shake the Cherry Tree and the amount of berries that fall will tell you how long you live. The Hawthorn, Mr. Attridge is the one to watch, it's a lonesome tree, loved by the fairies, so we hang ribbons on it to keep them away."

Her face darkened as she rose from her seat and went to the huge Ash Tree, a few yards away, embracing the girth, rubbing it's bark, stroking the rough surface. "The Ash is not just for hurleys and altars, they hang people from it. The Ash branch never breaks, it bounces up and down under the weight and sometimes the victim's feet touch the ground, but he springs up again, so it takes him a long time to die."

"Luther taught me all about the trees," she smiled, then, aware of her ramblings, she apologised.

" I'm told his name is NOT Luther, is that right?" James asked, dismissing her apology, "I'm delighted and thank you for the lesson."

"Heavens, his name is not Luther, his name is Martin, but there was another Martin on the farm, so he was called Luther." She said so matter of factly that James couldn't keep from exploding, to her delight. "Just like me, she continued, sure my name isn't Droleen." He looked at her, mystified, " what IS your name, then?"

"Wren."

"Wren?"

"Yes, Sir, after the little bird, who ratted on Saint Stephen, the first martyr. He screamed and flew away from the bush where Saint Stephen was hiding when the soldiers came. I was born on the Saint's day, the day after Christmas". She saw the question coming."Droleen is the Irish for the Wren, it's pronounced DREOILIN, but strangers don't know how to spell that, it's the same with Gobnet, above."

"Gobnet, are you saying that is NOT her name either, Droleen?" He waited and she sighed impatiently.

"No, Sir, but they spell her name in a different way, like they do to mine, her's is GOBNAIT, you see."

Through the Nettle Path, Attridge shook his head in disbelief, Gobnet who isn't Gobnet, Droleen, who isn't Droleen, and Luther, who is not Luther.

**

James had a little writing room to the rear of the kitchen, which he had chosen personally, rather than the room where Mrs. Laffan thought he should use, a small parlour next door to Sir George's study. James argued, the kitchen was the more appropriate, where he could eat, when not dining with Sir George, also, it was to the other side of Gobnet's warm stoves and fires were not needed in the cold weather. His den had a small window looking onto the huge yard of Duhallow, and away beyond, he could see the haggard where the prize bull of Duhallow had his domain. Old Cantankerous, as he was called, with his indolent expression and endless patience for just standing and waiting, would seem to stare back at him, at peace, until disturbed, a giant caught in the net of life and time.

He had long since taken a liking to the young deacon, no matter how often Georgie insisted he was no priest in the making. In G.'s spare time, he would read and help the Englishman, sort his notes for publication. James always made for himself, a deadline to meet the Mail to Enniscorthy. Attridge was impressed further on finding that he was a part of the duo he met at the Wexford rally, two years ago, the child that still had in his pocket, a tobacco knife, given to him by no other than Wolf Tone himself. Here was a young one of seventeen, able to read and write, as indeed could his younger brother, an intelligence, characterised by a natural comprehension of life. The youth who read The Times, no less.

Georgie Tansey got to dine at the table of Sir George Palmer, once the most sought after dinner table in all of North Wexford, where he entertained the peer with stories of the North, his mother, St. Ledger of Killane and the gifts from Duhallow, of seeds and crops, which Sir George had sent, with John Kelly and Mr. Driscoll.

**

Coming back from his magical encounter with Droleen, he found G. waiting for him and decided to give an hour or two, streamlining his account of the London expedition, among notes he had written on the efforts of Mr. Tone. He stood for a while looking out at Cantankerous, crunching away, the huge animal looked depressed. "That fellow calms me, G.," he said.

He gave the boy a set of notes "Will you read these back to me, please."

James remained at the window, eyeballing the bull, while G. began the piece. "Like Mr. Nielson in Belfast, Mr. John Keogh, the shrewd municipal Dublin politician, rallied about him, the men of trade, the so called rabble of obscure porter-swilling merchants, without property, pretentiousness or influence, the committee which met in holes and corners according to the aristocratic Lord Kenmare, from the floor of the House, where good oratory will make anything acceptable, and where his speeches are usually measured by the hour rather than by their content. With Mr. Wolfe Tone, Mr. Nieson has endeavoured to bypass these autocrats like Kenmare, Lords Trimleston, Fingall, Gormanstown and others, among them, Lord Kingsborough, in favour of a democratic and forward looking Directory like Mr. Emmet, Henry Joy Mc. Cracken, Mr. Stokes, the Shears Brothers, Mr. Napper Tandy, Mr. Thomas Russell and others."

G. began to titter from behind the page. "Glad you are amused," said, Attridge, "all these efforts might soon be obsolete, G."

"Mr. Wolfe Tone," the article continued, "has quoted the classical diamond uttered by Mr. Samuel Johnson, at the signing of the American Declaration of Independence, of their common enemy, the King of England, saying we must all hang together or as assuredly, we will all hang separately. How good and how pleasant it is for people to dwell together in unity, said the new President of America."

Tansey found James studying him, with amusement. "So what's so funny, Mr. Tansey?"

"Just that a number of people mentioned here, my mother dressed them."

"Dressed them?"

236

"My job was to measure them."

"Measure them." Attridge was stupefied.

G. fingered the names on the pad. "Kenmare, Gormanstown and there, Trimleston, Ponsonby, even Mr. Grattan, Mr. Grattan came to our shop in Grafton Street, and Lord Rockingham, it was he who gave us the house in Killane."

"You had a shop in Grafton Street in Dublin, your mother dressed the elite of Dublin, and, now Lord Rockingham, one, no twice, the Prime Minister of Britain?" What do they feed this lad for breakfast at Donovan's.

G. ran on, in a matter-of-fact tone, without pretence. "I can show you the neck measurements and the cuff dimensions of many more, Lord Flood, Lord Charlemont, The King himself, all their details are in my mother's book."

"What about the King Himself?" mused Attridge, "did you measure His Majesty and is that in your mother's little book, and don't tell me he came to your shop in Grafton Street." James was in disbelief, showing just a little scepticism.

"We made a crochet cloak for His Majesty, with his name on the back of it, little harps and shamrocks and sprigging all around the edges. That was, of course, AFTER we had left the Workhouse."

James exploded in mirth for the second time in an hour, his papers scattering to the floor. "O Georgie, my friend, you just must tell Sir George, you simply must, and bring your little book, it's worth its weight in gold, surely. You deserve tea and cake for that, we must tell Kate. What is this about Workhouse and who gave you a house in Killane, I'm all confused." He put an arm 'round G.'s shoulder and steered him to the kitchen. "Let's tell Mrs. Brennan."

Chapter 33

The chapel at Boolavogue issued a surprising and welcoming draught of heat at the door. The stoves of the thatched building burned cheerfully, Henry Tansey, in his altar clothes had fed the black bellied furnaces, with sods of granite like peat piled up for further consumption. There was a brace of tables to the rear of the church, set with cups and utensils, jugs of milk and what seemed to James, to be platters of bread and meats, covered against the smoke of the fires.

Father Murphy was vested in red for the celebration of the birth of Christ on this Christmas morning and stiffened shoulders loosened of their tension in the warmth and closeness of the atmosphere. As the church filled, palls of pungent vapour rose from the cold wet bodies, the coarse, unrefined clothing, filling the air with gas, a fetid malodour that mixed with that of the belching peat stoves and soon became acceptable, almost pleasant. However, as in the heat of summer, when the heavy thatch pressed down on the sweating body odours, Father Murphy brought an incense filled burner to the side of his altar, purifying and easing the intensity of the fetor.

His sermon was to equate poverty with the Catholic faith, simple and uncomplaining, that vividly comprehends the deep mysteries of Christianity. Only through God's grace can we learn to endure what sometimes seems to us to be the complete absence of hope. Today, in the all encompassing beatitude of the Child of Bethlehem, he quoted Amyl; that the beautiful souls of this world would have an art of saintly process by which bitterness is converted to kindness, the gall of human experience into guiltiness, ingratitude into goodness and insults into pardon. And while the curse of poverty leaves us no right to be generous, so that we begin to lose our links with the world, we must remember that Godliness is the witness to the basic side of life, to have heartbreak and heartache once in a while, else, how can Christ enter in. How many of us observe His birthday, how few His precepts.

"If society cannot help the many who are poor, then it cannot save the few who are rich. Poverty is an awful thing, a degrading thing and rarely any good ever comes of it, but with God's help, we rise up to the goodness in the world, in spite of adversity, not because of it." His words often went over the heads of many in his congregation, but he felt they set them in proportion to the week ahead.

About a hundred stayed behind to avail of Father John's Christmas treat. Hot tea and victuals were quickly consumed in pathetic gratitude. Whole families moved in haunted order about the tables, one of many phases in succession of their life's humiliation. At John's insistence, Attridge joined him near a stove for a tinsure of whisky, before they left for Duhallow, where Christmas dinner, as a long standing custom, was served in Gobnet's kitchen, the numbers, overflowing to the pantry, when the farm workers, those without families to share Christmas with, would become a part of the family, Sir George himself, overseeing the operation, a host in his own kitchen every bit as much as in the great dining room with the elite.

"A though provoking message, Father," said James. John had invited Devereaux to join them, but the blacksmith seemed to prefer to remain with the throng, where bottles of porter and a whisky bottle was evident.

"It's an insult to push bits of philosophy across an altar rail, James, for 'tis poor consolation to a people who are cold and hungry."

The old door creaked in protest and the cold savaged them, like a razor's edge.

"Would you look at them," Murphy called. Attridge squinted through the frozen morning. "Go home to your families, I say."

About a dozen redcoats were huddled against the ditch, six grazing horses, moved the snow about with their snouts, looking for grass. The men looked like they had been soldered into the bleak landscape, their faces, raw and sore.

"D'you think we'd be talking treason or plotting the downfall of the British Empire in Boolavogue, this holy morning?. Come inside, I say," the priest spat angrily, "God Almighty, doesn't the British Army have overcoats, even mittens?"

The eldest of the King's Yeos would have been no more than twenty, their red uniforms, soiled and ill fitting, hands, death like, locked on the cold rifle barrels.

"They'll be no weaponry in my church, leave them out there against the wall, or don't come in at all."

The youths shuffled past James, the warmth inside alien, after two hours in the arctic conditions. Somebody called to shut the door and James found himself back inside and watched the cameo unfold to his amusement. People moved to avoid the soldiers and complaints reverberated about the place. Murphy called for hot tea, heralding them toward a fire. Seasonal goodwill was not a feeling that evoked the minds of the congregation, and Attridge felt the dissention in all quarters. The Tansey brothers brought the hot beverage and the rumblings of resentment were sullen and bitter.

"There will be no animosity in the house of God on this day, or any other day, these boys are neighbours and sons of your friends," Murphy

239

called. The big blacksmith slapped his mug of whisky onto the table and stormed to the door. For the second time, Attridge saw Devereaux, unequivocally call his priest down.

"I'll not spend Christmas morning in the company of my oppressor's uniform, no matter who wears it." He set his teeth like clamps, his big frame clothed in that great coat, tied at the waist with a thick leather belt, so he looked like a garrison keeper.

"They're just boys, Conor," pleaded Murphy

"Boys is it, John Murphy. You preach that we accept the will of God, in our poverty and destitution, we do. You ask us to keep giving to God, and to ask nothing in return, we do. You ask us to rise up to the goodness in the world, despite adversity, we do. Sometimes we get tired of your pious supplications and turning the other cheek." His severe gaunt features darkened further. "But to sup with my enemies, who watch me pray to my God and plague my every move, I will not, Sir. Only this past summer, they pointed their weapons at you and you praying over the coffin of Driscoll and would like as not have destroyed you."

One of the youths protested, a small figure in the shadow of the smith. "We were not there, Father John, I swear we weren't." He stood up, narrow boy's figure, cup in hand. He had opened the laces of his boots and removed them to bring his feet back to life. He was stockingless and his feet looked raw and chaffed and dirty.

"You're good at swearing, laddie, I would say, good at swearing to the oath and taking the shilling for the doing of it." Devereaux stormed out. Like before, a few followed him, but not before copious bits were stuffed into damp pockets and great gulps of milk or whisky swilled in a fever.

Outside in the colourless winter sunshine, James approached the blacksmith, to invite him to Duhallow for Christmas dinner, on the instructions of Sir George. Conor O'Connor Devereaux softened his stance, nodded a sort of an appreciation, looked back through the door and said, "tell Palmer, maybe next year." His eyes moistened in bloodshot sockets, the cold, biting. Then he looked at the horses and the ditch where the yeos were standing, then to James's surprise, he gave him a half smile. " Blessing of Christmas on you," and he was gone.

There would be hell to pay. In a country, arming for rebellion, there is little thought for birthdays, even the most important birthday of all. Truth, sound theology and scriptures fade into insignificance, when the only truth any man has, the only hope, is to endure. In the Ireland of the new century, about to dawn, an ordinary man can win nothing, unless he has, first understood, that he must count on nobody but himself, that any device whatever, by which a man frees himself from fear and tyranny is a natural good. James laughed heartily against his frozen breath as he mounted his horse, recalled the verse he had read somewhere; "If you ride a horse, sit close and tight / if you ride a man, sit easy and light."

The twelve rifles had disappeared, the six horses, stripped naked of their leathers.

Chapter 34

Edward Lewins had, by 1796, spent almost six years in France, on a single mission; to secure an armada for Ireland. As a consequence, this Irishman had a price on his head and William Pitt the Younger would like nothing more than to drag him back to Dublin and make an exhibition of him.

He had entertained such emissaries as, Mr. Arthur O' Connor, Napper Tandy and Lord Edward Fitzgerald in the past, but found them lacking in passion to suit his own and dangerously flaunting their ambitions in public. He found, in the slightly built, unassuming barrister from Dublin, who had been recommended by none other than Mr. Nicholas Madgett, the American Ambassador, a man of commitment and supreme intelligence. Through Lewins's influence, Theobold Wolf Tone had met, on a few occasions, members of the French Directory and the senior staff of both Army and Navy.

In February of 1796, in General Bonaparte's headquarters at The Tulleries Palace, General Clarke, the Chief of Staff, chaired a second meeting in a month, named Armee d'Irelande, at which a considerable representation of the forces of France, were present; General Napoleon Bonaparte, and General Lazarre Hoche, the two most powerful officers in France, Le Peley, the Minister of the Marine, Tullyrand Perigarde, Minister for Foreign Affairs, and who had by now, aspirations to the seat of Prime Minister, Ambassador Madgett, also Colonel Shee, the ageing soldier turned diplomat, General Desaix, the young up and coming genius in the field and personal friend of Bonaparte and half a dozen senior officers. General Clarke, himself of Irish extraction, chaired the meeting.

The man who came to Paris, without credentials, his only mode of introduction were his files of testimonials and with ninety pounds in his pocket, now showed an audacity before Europe's most powerful Directory, that slowly became, in Napoleon Bonaparte's opinion, nothing short of insubordination. Homer said, it is the bold man who, every time does best, at home or abroad.

The Chairman read the requisition for Armee d'Irelande, which Lewins referred to earlier as Wolf Tone's shopping list. Forty ships, with a total minimum of four hundred guns between them, at least 20,000 troops with the requisite ammunition and armoury, plus Admirals and Generals, "as seems appropriate".

The room remained silent and Clarke looked about the table for a response, then continued. "For an expedition to Ireland, it would be important to chose an Admiral of repute and, of course an experienced General, I suggest either Pichegru or Jourdan."

Clarke allowed for some discussion and Tone asked for permission to speak. "It might surprise you, gentlemen, that we are aware, in Ireland of your many successes and failures in the field and while we would welcome the idea of General Pichegru or Jourdan, we are also very aware of General Hoche's many victories and would ask him to consider the possibility of taking the expedition."

"General Hoche already has a heavy schedule at Sombre et Meuse", warned Clarke, looking at the general, who was the only officer not in uniform. Tone noted the look of surprise on Hoche's handsome face, who had yet to exchange any words with Bonaparte, who sat pensively and characteristically moody. Bonaparte seldom stood in the company of his fellow officer. There was what looked like a yard in the difference of their stature and a mile in their character and presentation. Tone wondered how the lovely Josephine favoured The Little General above Hoche, but then he always felt that a woman's reason to be non fathomable, like dreams, they exist, only to confuse.

Ambassador Monroe interjected, wishing to make some kind of contribution, though Tone wondered at the credibility of the man who recommended William Jackson as an emissary to Ireland: the drunk incompetant who put so many lives in danger. "I believe, we have a number of fine Irish officers in the French army, Sir, like Generals Kilmain or Harty."

"I believe," replied Tone, that a French officer would be more appropriate, there would be no discrimination and the novelty in Ireland would swell the ranks of the volunteers."

Bonaparte, obviously irked at the Irishman's specifics and at being left out of the proceedings, so far, sprang to his feet and glancing at the map, spread out on the table before him, fumed, "you must remember, France is not yet at any strength on the seas. Our Navy was ninety per cent royals and we are still only learning the trade."

Nicholas Madgett irked the general further when he said, "it seems, General, you, yourself are not wanted in Ireland." A titter lapped about the room.

Ignoring the banter, he waited for the attention to return, momentarily surrendering his irritation. "I have no intention of subjecting the Irish people to a liberator for whom they have no regard." He looked at Tone, without actually seeing him, a disrespectful slur, then raised his voice in emphasis, " nor do I have the urge to subject my armies and navies to a confrontation with Britain over an insignificant island on the edge of the Atlantic Ocean, from which no benefit can accrue to France. You require a city of men and a fleet of ships, and what are we to get in return, Mr. Tone." For the first time the general seemed to address him straight on, his voice, full of implication.

Lewins sprang to Tone's defence, while the tall Hoche sank into his chair, seething at the slur. "You do my friend an injustice, General. I believe he has put forward a good argument in favour of an expedition, something I personally, have been seeking for over five years. France owes us a helping hand, Sir."

"France owes you nothing, Sir," Napoleon fumed, his patience, flagging. He took a note from his jacket pocket and consulted it for a minute. "You know these names, Sir, Lord Edward Fitzgerald, Mr. O' Connor and," he hesitated on the name, Mr.Napper Tandy?"

"I know them," said Tone, in surprise.

"These gentlemen were in Hamburg, last week and met with our agents there. They say that 1,500 men and three or four ships would suffice." He returned his note to the pocket, and looking at Desaix, said, "we have conscripts being called up, daily, perhaps we could meet that request, which seems to me to be much more reasonable." Desaix nodded in support, throwing an eye at the Irishman, and seeing there, in the controlled features, the beginning of conflict.

Lewins interjected, "with respect, General, Lord Edward knows nothing of military affairs, though I admit, he fought in America, the man is an aristocrat of privileged stock, he's a dreamer, a romantic and, at times a fool."

Tone spoke slowly, Bonaparte's snub still echoing in his ears. "There are 100,000 British Military of one form or another, in my country. As we speak, there is a curfew in operation and poor men are being hunted if they are found to be missing from their miserable cabins after eight o'clock in the evening. The military; some of them, pardoned by William Pitt from the jails of England, are rampant. It's open season on the peasantry, and Fitzgerald asks for a handful of men, sufficient against the biggest army in the world. Surely, General, your vast experience in the field should suggest otherwise."

Lewins stiffened as he saw Tone dress down the general, as he would a school boy, and he feared that the Irishman could lose everything, if he allowed those changing waves of his Irish temper to manifest itself.

"I know my country, General Bonaparte, and her people and I will not have them brought into battle against impossible odds. I know you would wish a prolonged offensive to keep the British occupied in the West, while you seek new dynasties and empires in the East." His eyes brightening with verve and emotion, Tone continued. Hoche delighted in the slight Irishman's turn of mind and phrase. "I have said the Irish people are ambitious in their quest for liberty and in that quest, they have studied well, the prowess of French Military under your good self and General Hoche and others. Your personal history, Sir, is that of a soldier of great power, an adventurer, wielded by an abnormal energy, but with little regard for casualties. I could list every battle you have fought and the casualties within the French ranks, outnumber that of your fellow generals, two to one."

Lewins sat, red faced, while Ambassador Madgett continued making notations. General Hoche smiled into his notes. There was an undercurrent of concern about the table, as Bonaparte bit down on his ire.

Clarke interjected, quickly. "General, you did say yesterday, you had an alternative."

"It's not of my making, but if the Directory insists on helping the Irish," he looked at Le Poley, the Marine Minister, collecting his thoughts, any cordiality that might have been present recently, gone, "at present, we have ships standing at La Rochelle, Nantes, Brest and at Le Harve de Grace." The minister nodded, "we have, General."

"Because of my activities at Toulon, on the Mediterranean, the British have a squadron under Warren at Gibraltar and another at Biscay. We have fed them intelligence that we intend to invade England through the Straits of Gibraltar." He sighed heavily and looked at Wolfe Tone for reaction. "We can slip out of Brest and Nantes with Armee d' Irelande, within the next month and sail directly for the Port of Cork. Pichegru tells me it is an immense harbour, poorly fortified, with one narrow entrance, barely a thousand yards wide. We can bombard the ports of Portsmouth and Plymouth and the strongest of English ports along the way. We will install ourselves inside the harbour of Cork. Pichegru says, two ships of the line would defend the outer harbour while we reinforce, then proceed eastwards and northwards, to take the country."

Among the younger officers, there was an immediate nodding of heads, in nothing short of acquiescence and Hoche looked at the Irishman and Tone saw the raising of a handsome eyebrow, in the shape of a question, what now, Irishman? The big general was not disappointed.

"And what then?" Wolfe Tone's question was immense in its simplicity, and for a minute, Bonaparte had to dig deep.

"Well, we would......we would fortify the whole country and set up a new French garrison, training new recruits for the task ahead."

"What task, General, you would have liberated the country, the task for which you came, and who would be at our head?"

"The French army, Sir, a recompense for your liberty. It will give us a bold face for when we seize John Bull, when we are ready."

"So, what you mean, General Bonaparte, is that Ireland should be the butt of England's bombardment, that we simply change one oppressor for another. We become a French colony, like Austria, and Italy and Egypt, will, if your savage campaigns succeed."

Edward Lewins, without hesitation waved a finger of caution. "That can never be, General, Mr. Tone is right." Madgett was becoming less and less impressive, wiping his brow. "Perhaps The Directory should give the General's suggestion some thought."

Wolfe Tone stepped back from the table, his face, cool and relentless. Lewins and Madgett had heard of the mastery with which the Irishman could dominate a situation. As the party watched now, they could detect no hint of strain or tension in the narrow face, indeed there seemed to be only one register of feeling there, the feeling of being in complete control, it was beacon bright before this important Directory. Lazarre Hoche was to be more and more impressed as the source and the cornerstone of the Irishman's confidence shone out, and he reached into his sub conscious for a verse he read of the cockerel who said to the horse, "let us agree not to step on each other's feet now."

Tone went to the window and looked out into the gardens as if speaking to himself. "It is four months since I left my home and family. I have a child I have yet to meet. There is a price on my head in Ireland and I am to be hanged as soon as the British authorities who occupy my country can get a hold of me. They know well, my purpose here, there are assassins here in Paris in the pay of England. I have spent five years preparing for this day, to see my country independent and free of England's tyranny. I did not endure the hardships and the dangers so as to make Ireland a French colony, an outpost for French dominance of Europe and a drilling field for her military."

Napoleon Bonaparte went to intervene and for the first time, Tone raised his voice, turning to the audience and stretched an impudent hand to silence the general. "I will NOT replace one tyrant with another". The silence in the room was palpable. "I did it in order to arrive at your doorstep, now for the second time in four years". He hesitated for a moment, finding composure and looked squarely at the one impediment to his endeavours. "I did it to collect a great debt, long owed to my country by France and I feel no sense of guilt for the asking, for indeed the demanding of it. I could now be in India with my sweet family, where my brother William is second in command of the

Infantry of the Maharatta State. There is a position there for me, worthy of my talents and qualifications."

Monroe looked up from his notes."Here! Here!", but looked cautiously at the others and caught the beginning of a smile creasing the face of General Hoche.

General Clark, the Chairman, hid his pleasure. This man has Napoleon's gall, the rapid glance like half an eye of the rogue Irish. His grandfather Clarke used refer to making it almost an endearment, cutting you to pieces with a bonnet plume.

"Yesterday and today, I had in my hand, a begging bowl, and for a while, forgot my purpose and even my dignity. I ask you for 20,000 men, a fraction of the brave Irishmen who died for France in the past one and a half centuries, one million men, Generals, I say to you."

Tone raised his voice to a pitch and never before had any of the party, present, who knew Bonaparte since a corporal, seen in his face, usually sullen and commanding, such a collapse in the metal of his demeanour. The Little General seemed to disintegrate under the sophisticated barrage of the Irishman, the deluge of statistics, catching them broadside, leaving the room reeling.

"It amazes me to learn how ignorant the British are of their history and indeed also, the French. My father used say, names are but noise and smoke, they can cut out heaven's light". He looked at them with that rogue's eye, "my mother used say that names are the light that glows on the sea waves at night." He thought for a minute, his fingers on his chin, dramatically. "I hardly know where to begin with names, General. Ramillies, and the Irish Dragoons, under Lord Clare, who became gun fodder, so the mad king of France, who built the vulgarity that is Versailles, and his army would not become totally decimated. You will remember, General Bonaparte, or perhaps you will not, as, of course, you are not French, the great Marshals of this country, Marshals Brown, Tyrconnell, the Major O'Mahoney, the brave generals Lawless and de Lacey, carrying your tricolour, pinned to the green of Ireland. They fought and died for you and won for you in the greatest battles Europe has ever witnessed."

He took a breath, then continued like replenishing his memory."The Irish defence of Cromona, Marsaglia, where your precious French retreated at the sound of the trumpets and which we ignored, took the twin hills of the city and the day with it. Barcelona, saw 600 of us dead, your precious Toulon, General Bonaparte, which you claim now to be your own personal city, was won for you by the Irish, Spires, Almanza, Villa, and the great Irish carnage at Fontenoy." Bonaparte was about to intervene, his pulsating pitching respiration, evident, but the Irishman continued, his voice rising in emphasis.

"And don't forget Menin and Ypres, where a thousand of us died in a day." Then he spat in a pang of frustration, "and you will, of course have heard of Sarsfield from our noble city of Limerick, when at Landen he cried that his dying was not for Ireland, but willingly gave it to France."

He looked ,sorrowfully at the table, his eyes smarting with emotion and his tolerance finally snapped. His hand swept across the mound of papers, sending them to the floor and Lewins thought, "He's going to be arrested." Hoche looked, for the first time, uneasy, looks of disapproval greeted the outburst.

"One million martyrs, Sir, and you offer me a handful of conscriptions, most of which will consist of the rabble and putrification of your jails, with a few royals thrown in. We already have bourgeoisie curs in Ireland from British jails, don't insult me further."

Bonaparte addressed his Chief of Staff. This time there was a kind of appeasement in it's delivery. "Mr. Chairman, it is my intention to proceed with the Italian campaign, after which, I am prepared to pay our debt to Ireland and prepare an expedition."

Clarke nodded slowly, Lewins breathed a sigh of relief, a young officer began to applaud. Napoleon Bonaparte would still control matters, always ready to stamp his authority.

"Pichegru is needed in Holland, Kilmain is too old for such a task. I will consider Hardy, perhaps Jourdan or Battier, or perhaps, Humbert."

He threw Tone a look full of malice, though his words were made tolerable by an almost friendly monotone. Wolfe Tone had already apologised for his outburst and the youngest officer was re arranging the mound of documents. "It will be in a year or two, Sir, and you shall have your armada."

The Irishman was not finished."General, if we wait a further two years, half a million of my countrymen will perish. Our patience has been exhausted and all the different factions will begin to consume one another. Mr. Pitt of England has commenced to unleash such a period of terror, abuse and slaughter, from which we can never recover, unless we take matters in hand now. We have delayed too long and it's your revolution that has lit the flame in Ireland for its own rebellion. The Little General wondered if there was no pleasing this troublesome man from Ireland. He began his strutting up and down the room, once again, consulting a little time fob, where it's gold chain adorned his waistcoat.

Further arguments threatened to engulf the proceedings, when a patter of light tapping, grew louder and more urgent, until attention was drawn to the tall Hoche. His small cane continued the tattoo on the floor, as he stood. He looked at Clarke. "With your permission, Sir, I will embark on the Irish expedition. I can be ready in six months."

Wolfe Tone dared to hold his breath. "But your armies are needed at Sombre, we cannot leave The Rhine without cover," argued The Chief of Staff.

"I have three armies there, Sir, one can be spared. I have 10,000 men in and around Brest and two regiments here in Paris and at Quiberon." For the first time, he locked attention on Napoleon Bonaparte, the Corsican returning the observation with a trace of a smile, though it was evident it was in contradiction of his true feelings. "The General is correct, our Navy is poorly equipped and trained, not like England, but if any man can get us to Ireland in such circumstances, it should be Admiral Latouche Treville, he's the best in France." Bonaparte interjected, he had already secured the services of Treville for Toulon and his expedition to Italy. For the next ten minutes, the two leading soldiers of France argued and General Clarke, once again not relishing the task of overseeing another confrontation between the two, was relieved when Hoche said he would find his own Admiral. It was well known, these conflicts were based, as much on personal civil wars as much as for the glory of France. Lewins looked across at his friend, trying to study his reaction and saw little registered there, except a softening of the features that had made a brave assault on, possibly the world's most successful warlord of the eighteenth century and won. Little did Lewins know that Wolfe Tone's insides were churning with relief and tense expectancy, but found an appropriate attitude for the occasion, one of mild controlled acceptance. He wanted to jig about the room and hug and kiss the big handsome Hoche, who reminded him of his friend at home, Thomas Russell, but he would reserve that for another time. Instead, he shook every hand in the room, which was accepted warmly, except that of Bonaparte, who made an apology, bowed stiffly and made for the door.

"I wish you and General Hoche success, Mr. Tone, but I believe your adventure untimely. The Bible tells us, to everything there is a season and a time to every purpose under heaven, your endeavours are untimely."

Tones voice softened. "So is this a time for Italy, General?. Why Italy at this time, why Italy at all, it is no threat to France?"

"I go to Italy to make France great, Mr. Tone, what do you suggest I should do, with your immense experience in matters military, when should I do it?"

Tone thought it was an odd reply. He gave the little Corsican that twinkle in the half smile. "Don't do it at all, Sir, leave it alone."

Bonaparte's face opened in a wide titter and he saw, for the first time, a kind of a boyish attractiveness, a smile in Napoleon was a rarity, a laugh, a primeval phenomenon.The simple innocent reply from the Irishman caught him off guard.

"Sense can be very unreasonable, General, you go to the East, to make a great nation even greater, and I wish you God's blessing, for the desire for greatness is a godlike sin. I go west to make a tiny nation free, no more, no less."

"Mark my words, Sir," Bonaparte said, liberty is the hardest test God can put on a nation, many crimes are committed in its name, however, I know of no man on earth who deserves it more, or no nation that is worthy of the man." This time he extended his hand, the handshake, prolonged and warmed to Tone's surprise. "Would you be king of Ireland, Mr. Tone?"

"I'm just a simple pamphleteer, General, an out of work lawyer. A king is created out of audacity, he seldom represents his people, or subjects, as he likes to call them, he's nothing but a shadow in the sunshine. My friend, Mr. Thomas Russell says a throne is a box, covered by a piece of velvet, a crown; a hat with a hole in it."

Laughter filled the room, the Directory, now an audience. "And your friend, would he be king, a king with a sense of humour?"

Tone's features darkened. "Mr. Russell, I am told, has been arrested, I fear for his safety. No Sir, Ireland will be a democracy, with a president and its own assembly."

"Will you be president, then?", Hoche asked, smiling.

"Our president is in Hamburg, General. General Bonaparte spoke of him earlier, a noble fellow of the first family in Ireland, Lord Edward Fitzgerald."

"And you, Sir, when this is all over and the John Bull is harnessed?" Bonaparte teased, the smile now incongruous in him.

"I have no wish to harness John Bull, General Bonaparte I simply wish to send him home. Since spending some time on the plains of Princeton in America, I have taken a liking to farming. The life in the land can do wonders for a man, it goes into his life and stirs it up. It's a good life."

Napoleon put his hand on the handle of the door, looked about the room. "I believe it would be a waste, but then may I say, that, should you be stirred with any more life, then God help France." Loud laughter saw off the Little General and hands grasped hands again in a show of solidarity and good will.

The big man stood looking down at the map, running his fingers over it and stopped at the little island on the edge of the European mass.

"Let us find some ships, Mr. Tone, and some soldiers and send the John Bull home. I think I will like Ireland, it is so.....remote, on its own out there in the Atlantic. Is Ireland a good place? It's a good place, General, folklore says it was born on a night when a star danced, Ireland will like you."

"Take no notice of Napoleon, Mr. Tone, France will not dominate you, however, I can see us coming to certain diplomatic and trade relationships, to our mutual benefits, we must pay for the logistics involved." Lazare Hoche fixed the Irishman in an all encompassing observation that, for Tone seemed to lighten the adversity of recent days and a friendship was born that, sadly was not to last very long.

General Clarke had been engaging the others in a circle of discussion out of ear and suddenly he broke rank and approached the Irishman. "It has been decided that there are renegades in the pay of the king of England, right here in Paris. For your safety and in the interest of anonymity, we have decided to secure a uniform for you in the rank of Adjutant General. The regimentals will be sent to your lodgings, ready for this evening's dinner at de Whites, we'll make a Frenchman of you yet."

Chapter 35

Innocent wonder in the countryside, hand in hand with cynical worldliness in the great houses, greeted the Christmas of 1796. Thoughts, however of war and destruction, just a few miles off the south coast of Ireland, were otherwise than the birthday of Christ, where fifty ships and twenty thousand men struggled to find shore in one of the worst storms in their living memory. On that day, Wolfe Tone was to write later, if the weather had been kinder and command more efficient, the face of Ireland would have been changed forever.

The marvellous Lazare Hoche was true to his word. For six months, he and his agents ventured through the coastline of western France, conscripting men for the Armee d' Irelande and soliciting local merchants and businessmen for funds, with the promise of franchises in Ireland. The towns and villages were filthy, mused Wolfe Tone, as he became a General with a begging bowl. Rennes and Brest represented cities in turmoil, not yet having benefited from the revolution, like the Northern provinces.

Admiral Morard de Galles, a tall thin middle aged man with a Van Dyke beard, that gave him a long austere look, was to be the one to lead the fleet for Ireland. A friendly man, honoured that General Hoche had chosen him for the task, he didn't hesitate to impress on Wolfe Tone, that his allegiance to France was absolute and came second, only to his native Holland, now named The Batavian Republic, after its defeat by France, two years earlier. Tone was concerned, fearful of the oncoming winter and the equinoctial gales that would plague them out of Biscay.

"There need be no consequence," said the Admiral, in a cordial and easy confidence, "I have negotiated storms before, even the south coasts of The Americas."

"You have never seen the Irish coast line in winter, Sir," impressed Tone, his voice blunted with concern. "There are moods of weather on our coast that even you will have never witnessed, storms that can whip the blood in a man's body, enough to blow the hair off a dog, as we say." The choice of de Galles was to prove the first of many disastrous decisions, no least, the fact that he seemed poorly in health, consistently congested and short of breath.

To add to his woes, Tone had received a message from James Attridge in Wexford, enclosing an article from The London Morning Post of September 24th, which had been copied from The Northern Star, confirming the arrest of Mr. Thomas Russell and Mr. Sam Nielson, for treason. They had been campaigning in County Antrim with Henry Joy

Mc. Cracken, when, it seems they were visited by the Marquis of Devonshire, The Earl Of West Meath and the notorious John Pollack, the Crown Attorney. Pollack would almost certainly look for the death penalty.

He was to receive another communication in the form of a letter from the Directory in Paris. Napoleon Bonaparte had taken Italy. In one month's campaign, he had forced the Sardinians to a peace. He conquered The Austrians separately, and Italy was left at his mercy. The Pope made peace at enormous expense to Rome and the King of Naples negotiated terms.

Hoche was silent for a minute, after reading the document. "The Italians were no threat to us, as you so advised Bonaparte. I do not understand the General. His enemy is here on his doorstep, yet he turns eastwards. A brigade of men under a single sergeant would have taken Italy, yet, the word is Napoleon lost upwards of 30,000 men." He sighed in frustration, "that enemy will live to destroy him, if his ambition, warped as it is, will not do it first. That enemy will destroy him if he keeps turning his back on him." He lifted a glass of wine. "To victory in Ireland, my Irish friend, let us match the Little General, but surely for a greater cause."

On the last week in November, Wolf Tone finished his inventory of arms and ammunition, his pen, shaking under the magnitude of the armoury. He felt the moment of commitment, accompanied by not a little dread, as he committed the manifest to paper; the barrels and boxes of destruction that would end five hundred years of tyranny and restore his country to a quality of life, denied to her for so long. He kissed the clipboard where the little emblem, now, well known to all concerned; the little gold harp, then read the list again, of the latest refinement of science, the instruments of mass destruction; 85,000 stand of arms, 40 pieces of field artillery, 25 of siege, including mortars and howitzers, 120,000 barrels of powder, 9 million musket cartridges, one million flints, sabres, pistols, the list seemed endless. He was ignorant of the proper usage of this mountain, but the terminology sounded wonderful to his ears and on a number of boxes and barrels, he had chalked the messages; "To King George" and "For King Billy, With Love", and "To The John Bull."

In his account which he sent to James Attridge, later, he wrote, "On a cold day, December 10th., in my uniform of Adjutent or Chef de Brigade, as many of the men would refer to me, I climbed the hill, overlooking Brest Road and the harbour. From where I sat, high above the almost inhuman scene, I had the huge expanse of the Brest Basin in my sights, all the way out to where the harbour divided into three underwater channels, hazardous and beckoning. A light vaporous cloud had settled over the fleet. Like ghost ships, the long sleek vessels waited quiescently for their riders, stocked high with provisions and ammunitions.

I made some kind of a prayer to some kind of God. I am thirty three years old, I told Him and want for talent and want for opportunities, but if I succeed here, I may yet make some noise in the world. I am confident that the cause to which I am devoted, is so just, that I shall never have the need to ever approach myself. At my age, Alexander had conquered the world, my mission not being so ambitious, but surely, more worthy of Your blessing. I do know, also, that at my age, You Yourself were hanged for your mission and it is said you died for all the just causes in the world. I have amassed the finest army to bear the finest cause, let it be not in vain, that there be no disappointment.

But there was disappointment in abundance, James, not least of all, God, who from the outset seemed to be absent outside of His universe. Even in His limitless ocean of mercy, how He disappoints. How fortune can be a whore, recently giving of her benefits in little parcels, now, in one week, takes it all away in one swoop."

Chapter 36

18,000 troops, aboard seventeen ships of the line, each carrying upwards of eighty guns, fifteen frigates, each with forty guns, ten corvettes, nine transports, two powder vessels and a few small ships, left Brest, in the shelter of darkness and a rising easterly wind to aft, on December 15th. Under General Lazare Hoche, 29 year old veteran of a hundred battles and sailed through the straits into the Atlantic, headed for Ireland.

The three leading vessels sought out the exit of the basin, under tenebrous clouds; General Hoche, with Admiral de Galles on the frigate, "Fraternite". Second in command and on the frigate " L'imortalite", was General Emanuel Grouchy, the thirty year old hero of the battle of Vendee, himself having been a royalist before the revolution and commanding "L'imortalite" was Admiral Bouvet, also, once a royalist. The third ship of command, "L'imdomtable", a huge ship of the line, with 87 guns, was under the command of General Cherin, on which Wolf Tone himself sailed.

The 15th. December 1796, had no goodness in it. It became a prologue to disaster. The affliction began in the treacherous and difficult pass, The Razz de Seine which is only three miles wide and corrupt with currents and rocks. The wider channel, The Iroise, was avoided as word came that Captain Pellew of The British Admiralty was outside with his squadron, as Britain had been fed through intelligence released by General Hoche, that Portugal was to be the venue for the new armada. When the wind turned westerly and a ghostly fog enveloped the entire Brittany coast, in a pall of chastisement, de Galles, ill on his first day out, signalled the fleet to take the wider channel, Iroise, but with the blackness of the night, the signal was lost.

Soon the fleet was in chaos. "Indomptible", cleared the rocks, with only inches to spare, but the huge ship of the line, "Seduisant", foundered with the loss of 1,200 men, still in sight of land. In the mayhem, only seventeen vessels managed to clear Razz and made open sea and a further seventeen made for Iroise channel, thirty miles to the south. On December 18th., the wind asserted itself, further stabbing at the huge square sails, demanding the larger ships to tack over and back, making little headway. Within ten hours, it was established that "Fraternite", with Hoche and de Galles aboard, was missing, along with the other vessels. Twice in four days, the fleet split in an ocean that held no enemy, not a British ship was sighted, no enemy but the wind.

Wolfe Tone was to learn later, that in that week, there were just four British war ships in Dublin Bay, one prison ship in Wexford Harbour and two frigates and a few traders in Cork. On the 19th., the gales had set firmly to westward, making the troops sickly and impatient. On board "Indomptable, General Cherin opened the sealed dispatches of instructions on a signal from Grouchy from the frigate "L'immortalite". Presuming Hoche to be lost, the orders directly from Paris, aggravated the situation further, sending Wolfe Tone into a spasm of whipped fury. The destination for the armada was to be Bantry Bay, in the south west corner of Ireland.

Stragglers caught up with the fleet. The huge war ships, with their square rigged sails, vulnerable to every whim of the elements, could not sail nearer the wind, than six points or 67 degrees without disaster, so a journey, which in ordinary events, would have taken thirty six hours, was now, four days in the passing. Soldiers milled about the decks, impeding the efforts of the sailors, the constant tacking making the army warriors, pathetically ill.

Eventually, thirty four vessels reached the vicinity of Bantry, amid a reckoning that nineteen ships were missing. Studying his charts, General Cherin couldn't help but wonder, with a tincture of amusement, at the audacity of providence, that the long narrow basin, south of Bantry Bay, outside which he found himself, was named Roaring Water Bay.

Without the two commanders in-chiefs, plans, money and proclamations, indecision was rampant. It was hell's cauldron out there, when the wind became even more adverse and was dead ahead on entering the Bay. Several ships were far to leeward and were pushed too far west onto Dursey Head and by December 22nd. Just fifteen vessels managed to enter Bantry Bay. Sometime in the night an inhuman gale from the east, blew all but six ships out to sea and many had decided to return to France.

Wolfe Tone was to write to Attridge in the coming month. "I felt the vast horrible futility of the past week. It hung over me like a pall over my senses. How I cried, alone in the dark deck of "L'imdomtable", feeling the pulse of Ireland labouring under her tyranny, yet within jumping distance, with victory in sight, she wouldn't let me land, so near to her, I could throw a biscuit ashore. I tell you, I felt her resignation and her desperation, which she pulled down over her, like the mists and clouds of Bantry. I felt my country abandoning her pride.

The French were like brothers. In the huge salon of "Indomptable", General Cherin, the youthful second in charge of the military, led a toast to Citoyen Wolfe Tone and Armee d' Irelande to a roar of reciprocation from the officers above the sound of the storm and Indomptable's creaking timbers, and to even louder applause, Vive Irelande and Liberte d' Irelande. Heavy foul smelling Frenchmen embraced me to the faint purr of a pipe, played by a young able bodied Breton.

However, I have to say, there is little accounting for the actions of the inexperienced General Grouchy, the chief, now that Hoche was confirmed missing, and even more so, that of the new Admiral in charge, Admiral Bouvet, on "L'immortalete", during the early hours of December 24th. I had suggested to Charin, we sail around to the mouth of The Shannon, but whether the command ship ahead of us got the message or not, and I am convinced it did, Bouvet and Grouchy decided to cut lines and called the entire armada to sail for France.

My friend, cowardice is the infirmity of human nature and until the test comes, it's hard to be sure of one's courage. But there is valour in all of us and it lies somewhere between rashness and cowardice. General Grouchy seemed, in the past two days to be a man caught in the wisps of a nightmare and I had become concerned at the physical and mental damage that had been wrought on the new commander. He was consumed by the fear of the satanic rocks, scraping at the hull of his ship, he seemed in a nightmare from which he could not flee nor wake.

My armada failed and we limped into Brest on January 1st. 1797. Almost fifty ships sailed for Ireland, impeded by nothing but weather. Not one British warship was sighted.

The good General Hoche and Admiral de Galles, were never taken. "L'immortalete", eventually returned to Rochfort on January 14th. And their going missing on the first day of the voyage is something that concerns me greatly and I intend to know how Europe's greatest Admiral could get lost on his way from France to Ireland.

I am wondering if you might come to Paris, James. There will soon be a triumphal celebration for General Bonaparte, sometime in the next month, you might wish to report on it, also I do have further documents for you. My wife and children are here with me, thankfully and we live in Nanterre, just outside of Paris. I have a job with Lazare Hoche on The Rhine, where he has command of the army at Sombre et Meuse. He is anxious to bring up another expedition for Ireland, but right now, I am concerned for my great friend and advocate. Lazare has consumption."

Chapter 37

Having received the account of the failed expedition, Attridge couldn't but wonder at the decision to chose Bantry for the landing. As details unfolded, the sentiments of Father Roche, John Kelly and Raefil Keane and others, shone out beacon bright in Tone's memory, the lack of leadership and communication within the United movement. Theobold Wolfe Tone had the ability to do great things, to set up mountains of hope and to deliver that hope, to take by the scruff of the neck, an institution and shake it to its foundations, all that, but by his own admission, was incapable of command. Tone was content to pave the way, but failed the final test that would have made him great.

James Attridge prepared his text for the American Press.

"Why Bantry, in the south west, where, even in Summer, the harbours are unfit to house so many ships, where landing areas would be confined to narrow choices, but where the coast line in Winter is constantly pounded by the elements. But, most of all, the unsuitability of the whole of the south west was evident to everyone. It is a cesspit of rogue yeomanry and militia and a terrified peasantry, under the command of General Dalrymple, where any United Irishman who dared to put his head above the parapet, was named from the pulpits of the Catholic Churches and where the Bishops, especially Bishop Moylan rampaged through the dioceses, calling down destruction from heaven on them, handing the authorities a readymade register of local suspects, leading to widespread floggings, burnings and executions. It was open season for Dalrympal's infantry and dragoons.

This reporter has learned that the Yeomanry of North Cork is among the most notorious and villainous blackguards in the entire army, their ranks consist over half of Orangemen. The North Cork Militia, under their commander, Lord Kingsborough sought out the town lands of Castletownbere, Crookhaven, Dingle and Caheragh, for special treatment in the rumour that the peasants knew of the French Armada, and would have joined Wolfe Tone. It is this reporter's opinion that this is a rumour without foundation and substance. The whole country waited for The French, but nobody knew when or where and nobody was prepared. Caharagh in the west was the first to be targeted. Not a single cabin was left standing and a thousand souls were left homeless in winter. It was here at the cross of four roads, once the location of what is commonly known in Ireland, as a Pattern: an outdoor peasant dancing area, that this reporter witnessed public flogging and for the first time saw in practice the demonic torture called pitchcapping.

I have to report that the atrocities being committed here in the name of the King of England is something you cannot balance on any scales. All the wonderful violent passions of the people are quelled and the consequence for Ireland will be worse than all her previous calamities and misfortunes. This is the beginning of a tragic age and famine is becoming a regular happening. I visited a place called Barley Cove, where a French ship went down in the Christmas storm. "L'impatient" sank with the loss of seven hundred men. Just a few made it to shore, but were shot or piked at water's edge.

England commits, daily a kind of genocide and the English Parliament has created a nation of paupers. The failed French invasion, instead of creating an aura of celebration and self congratulatory proclamation on the part of the authorities, became a spur for further penalisation. It created a responsive pulse through the ranks of the oppressors, where the new Bills of Indemnity and Convention, were unashamedly exercised, driving more and more Catholics into the ranks of the United Irishmen. Protestant and Presbyterian roughnecks stormed the country in the guise of Orangism and Yeomanism and Ireland's own reign of terror progressed a pace.

A fearful persecution of Catholics now is rampant, especially in Armagh and Tyrone, where Mr. Mc.Cracken and Mr. Monro had whipped the Unitedmen into shape, with the help of Mr. Thomas Russell.

The County of Wexford did submit, outside of small skirmishes, to the fantasies of their oppressors, mostly with the submission of sheep. A slow process of social and civil denial has wound the people down to a low gear, believing the old adage trumpeted from the pulpits at Catholic Sunday Mass, that truth is on the side of the oppressed. From a wearied and indignant race, the new regime under General Lake, the Commander in Chief, exacted it's dues and has absorbed all that is left of what was once, it's energy and high spirits.

The war against France and the extra garrison and port security required to dissuade them from another invasion is proving expensive for the exchequer. The ever increasing demand for money, has put the overdrawn peasant, who has by now, paid for the Queen's purchase of her dream home at Buckingham House, under further pressure. Landlords are being pressed for major contributions, resulting in increased rents and tithes, so that inventories are kept in every household and every farm item or farm animal which might be deemed a luxury, was either confiscated for the war effort or severely taxed. The result of this madness has become an act of similar madness, where pigs, brown hens and other farm animals are now living indoors with their owners for fear of thievery at night, when peasant is pitched against his peasant neighbour. Horses are now being conscripted into the army, so that now, one hundred tons of corn has been assigned daily from the national crop to feed them, almost 6,000 in this the first month of 1797. This is not to interfere in any way with the continuance of stock for England. Food shortages are becoming chronic, especially in the midlands and in the western counties, where crops are forced to meet the new demands, so that the rough lumper potato, which the horses reject, is slowly becoming the mainstay diet. The bland diet is slowly robbing the peasant of a balanced carbohydrate intake and sickness is coming at a gallop".

James Attridge – 1st. February 1797.

"Saoirse."

**

Father John Murphy believed that the devil tempts idleness. To do nothing in the world is to foster lawlessness and contempt, so he constantly nurtured time consuming activities, all of which were now illegal. He had meticulously handpicked the particular road that ran from Trasna Bridge to the hamlet of Ballycanew as the best road in the area for the game of Bowling, as he had done in four other areas of north Wexford. Around each area, he had had organised and promoted the sport, but with some modifications on the multi participation game of ancient times, to a more sophisticated stratagem, involving teams of limited numbers, as he had done with the even more ancient game of hurling in the low fields. Clubs formed around the sports and competitions were regular happenings, the combative instinct in the young and not so young, aggressive and often savage. Massively skilful games, there was more to hurling and bowling than just strength, though it was a factor. Brute force and agility had to be controlled and fashioned into craft. In hurling, a team of up to thirty players on each side, strove to control a small leather ball, made of cow hide, and, the object, to score between two posts, ten paces apart of the opposite side. The bowling craft was concentrated in getting a two lb. ball of iron from starting point to finishing point, over a course of some three miles, in as few throws as possible, to twist and turn the bowl so that bends of the road, dykes, hedgerows and other obstacles are negotiated with dexterity.

Kate Keohane had served lunch at Duhallow, where Mr. Sanquest, the estate manager had come from Enniscorthy. It seemed no longer to be unusual that after her work, she would often walk with Attridge,

260

sometimes through the nettle path to the woods, or, as today, to catch up with the bowling. They came on the game at the far side of Trasna Bridge. Mr. People's Ale House was having a brisk day. Pulling the trap to a stand, with an advantaged view over the crowd of supporters, Kate beckoned to half a dozen urchins to climb on board, who sized the stranger with grave suspicion. The ditches and dykes were crowded with observers and, to his surprise, James saw John Murphy in conversation with the huge figure of John Kelly at the head of the crowd. They seemed to be commenting on matters of strategy. John Kelly, his team from Killane, recognisable by their green sash about muscular midriffs standing in line, waited for his instructions. The Trasna team, with their red strip, behind the priest, concentrated on the priest's every word.

Father Murphy signalled and Raefil Keane came from the Trasna line amid back slapping and shouts of encouragement. Man and priest were in deep discussion, animosity which often erupted between them on matters other than bowling, forgotten for now. A straight ribbon of road stretched out before them for about 150 yards, then turned right on an angle of 45%, for a further ninety yards, before turning again. Clusters of supporters and advisers were eying the course, heads sideways, eyes squinting, arms outstretched, measuring the distance, everyone an authority.

Attridge's fascination deepened. The priest who, on Sundays and all other days, takes on the management of their spiritual affairs and, on their behalf, cries out for miracles and sometimes, creates them, was now giving them their fill of important input, heeding their suggestion, for what seemed to be the final two throws of the tournament. The visitor had grasped, under Kate's instruction, the essence of the game.

The Killane boys were growing impatient, making restless signs to the stewards. John Kelly, who always had great respect for the priest, was patient, lobbing his bowl from one massive fist to another. John Murphy smiled inwardly on seeing with his green sash about his middle, his young altar server, Henry Tansey, in adoration of the giant of Killane.

A steward nodded his consent to Kelly and the Killane man lumbered up to the mark, a bone crushing arm held out before him, the lump of iron, held like a weapon, scarlet determination distorting his handsome face. With the groan of an expiring steer, the run and the force of the bowl, catapulting from his fist, extracted all the wind from him. Two lbs. of swirling flying iron sang as it passed the gallery. Kate whispered, "it's flying too low, all power, no direction." The missile dug itself into the shoulder of the road where the ground fell away, a full thirty yards short of the hairpin bend.

Father Murphy smiled a knowing glance at Raefil Keane, an assurance that they had it all worked out.

"Hold his coat."

"I'll hold your coat, Father."

There was a scramble to hold the priest's coat and some fellow held the privilege. Somebody shouted to "show him the road"

The priest was heavy chested, but beneath the coat, surprisingly slim waisted, and on rolling up his sleeves, up over olive skinned biceps, he presented a figure, ten years his junior. Attridge looked about and caught the approving glances of, not just a few of the ladies. He had noticed, earlier, to his great amusement, that, before a team member would throw, a fellow contestant would carry out a quick kneading to shoulders and arms, while the athlete himself would go through a ritual of hand wringing, arm shaking, elbow flapping, accompanied by stomping of his bare feet and sucking and blowing. Coughing and clearing of throat and spitting out, heavy burping and breaking of wind, was an accepted preliminary, in a sort of priming and pruning of body. However, he noticed that such familiarities could not be afforded to the ordained, though, should he require, Attridge had no doubt, John Murphy would have found many a willing hand for his embalming.

"There's a cluster of tall trees wedged into the acute turn of the road, he's surely not going to try to clear them," said Attridge.

"See, beyond the turn, what do you see?" she said.

"Somebody moving."

"That's the target, Father John must aim for that fellow," she smiled.

"Over the trees?", said James, incredulously.

"Through them," she whispered.

"He's forty years old," argued Attridge.

 "So?" Kate hunched her shoulders.

One of the urchins, without taking his eyes off the bare armed priest, said, "Raefil threw the first bowl, he's the best in all the world."

"Raefil always throws first," said Kate, matter of factly. James caught her looking at Keane, her admiration and approval shining out in a mild passion. James pretended not to notice.

Holding the bowl lightly, Murphy stood studying the green barrier, blind to the road beyond the turn, throwing a furtive glance at the man, who could only be seen through the lower branches. Cuteness prevailed, he wore a red shirt which screamed "I'm here, I'm here, hit me." The gallery had moved up to the bend of the road, so they could see Murphy to their right and the home run straight ahead to the bridge. Murphy's run was short. He stood for a minute, studying the green barrier, like he was praying to it, fixing in his mind, the road beyond, every inch of which he knew. The spruces dwarfed him. When the bowl left his hand, the measured projectile found the valley in the trees and it scorched through the gap.

"Now," he shouted, and a hundred panting supporters cut through the ditch where the belt of trees ended. The youth with the red shirt who marked the road for the throw was there to welcome the lump when it hit the road and ran on and on, willing it a bit further.

James Attridge balanced himself in the moving trap as all followed and wondered at this quiet unassuming man, who spoke very little except to decry Mr. Wolfe Tone at Sir George Palmer's dinner table at Duhallow and for whom it was obvious, Palmer had a great respect. Here was a man, a theologian, equally at ease among the extra refinement and the grace note of the privileged, as with the crowded masses of unknown ranks. He sensed now, the undercurrent of the crowd's affinity with their priest, this man who had become a cherished beacon in their miserable lives. Father John Murphy was becoming a very interesting individual and the journalist was already building up in his mind, fitting notations for a future story on this priest of Boolavogue. Little was he to know how the turn of events, about to unfold, would fill, not only a good story, but an entire volume.

A dozen burley youths lined up respectfully before John Murphy, now back attired in his tailed coat. One of them would be the last to throw. Eager to be the chosen one, to save the honour of the boys of Boolavogue, the competitors began the now familiar motions; dancing about, puffing and blowing and waving of arms like a flock of mating swans. The priest eyed each one in his pretence at indecision while Raefil Keane whispered in his ear, as an indication who it might be. He then made his way to the trap, which had pulled into a verge.

He said to her with wintry simplicity, "you weren't here before, you're always here for the start." He gave Attridge a regard of dismissal.

"We had to stop off at The Master's on the way, Raefil," Kate explained, with a hint of tension. The trap more crowded now than earlier. "You know I like you to be there at the start." He moved back to the front. "He always starts with the first throw", she explained again. The boys in the trap called to their hero.

Will Pat Sinnot, a wiry resilient peasant lad, one of a family of ten, whose presence at home was sometimes forgotten and often discarded, was the choice of Raefil. Will Pat never had glory in his young life, until the day, two years ago, Father Murphy began coaching him and four of his brothers, the art of the bowl. He grasped that peach when the priest picked him for the youth team of Trasna and Boolavague, and he vowed to justify the priest's faith in him, devoting his days to developing his skills. He would be seen on the roads alone, his sister marking the course for him, often his string of a body under the donkey cart, his father's tired old ass strolling behind him. Now, trusted with the awesome task of saving the honour of the senior team against the roughnecks of The Blackstairs.

Raefil began rubbing and slapping the narrow shoulders until they tingled.

"Big breath now, Will, puff now and blow out, a good cough now, there's a lad. Cough, a good cough now." The youth blew and sucked and coughed to oblige. Raefil narrowed his mouth, "do you want to fart now, 'tis o k to fart."

The young face reddened with stress, thought better of it. "I'm alright now, Raefil, just show me the road."

Will Pat did the business. In the respectful silence that suddenly descended on the tense crowd, the boy's endurance took root and the propellant, and James could hardly imagine where the strength came from, sang past the galleries toward it's glorious reward, wrapped in the prayers of all Trasna, the blessings of Father John and Raefil Keane's spittle. The iron ball was half way home when Will Pat Sinnot hit the ground, flat out and remained there until the roar went up. A thousand pairs of bare feet danced around the lump as it crawled to its resting place, well beyond the finishing line, east of Trasna Bridge.

"Goats of men, we are, Father John," sighed Kelly, that we could lose to a slip of a boy." Sinnot was raised on the shoulders of his admirers, looking for that all important wink from the priest and it came, to his delight, over the heads of the crowd.

The aura of goodwill was like a sunbeam from behind a dark cloud, the happiness of a passing moment. Jack Keohane was drunk. Standing on a barrel outside of Lousy Head's Whisky House, he was one of the first to see the militia coming west from Boolavogue. Adversity was the only path in Jack Keohane's life. A man, whose past evils, present evils and future evils will come together as his true touch stone when he's drinking. He was calling to the militia to "come on down."

Lieutenant Bookey was always easily recognised. The scarlet and black of the doublet with its gold collar and the trade mark bouquet of peacock feathers from his exotic hens at Rockspring.

"He has barely a dozen men with him, surely he's not going to attack," said James.

"Yes he would," said Kate, squinting into the sunlight, "for he's so busy making himself important, that he forgets how stupid he is."

Attridge stifled a smile, despite the tension all around. Her ability to dress her words, her thoughts, in a style that never showed a sign of effort, was a fascination to him.

She went to climb down from the trap as her uncle continued his barrage."He'll get us all into trouble," she whispered. The children all around were ashen faced, as one of the military rode away beck the way they had come."They're sending for reinforcements," someone said.

"John Kelly whistled, a loud call between forefinger and thumb and a hundred mountain men melted from the crowd and formed a phalanx of protest, crudely armed with cudgels and implements of their sport; hurleys.

Kelly approached the priest. "I know you're a man of peace, Father, but we were half expecting this today. If you would just leave the bridge, take the women and children with you and leave the rest to us. They attacked us in Killane last week, but we'll break heads this day, as God...."

"Leave God out of this John Kelly," warned the priest. "What you do over in Killane is your own business, but there will be no breaking of heads here". Murphy called for someone to bring his black mare and a sense of fear gripped him, a fear that would be powerless unless he acted quickly.

Kelly's men had been joined now by Raefil Keane's Red Ribbons, as he called the sportsmen of Trasna and raw rude bodies were stood up, stiff backed, the young bodies no longer their own, with courage borrowed from the mass, so their mothers, in a moment didn't know them.

The journalist watched the scene unfold, as his friend, G. brought the horse. The priest mounted very slowly, easing himself into the saddle in a heavy tired motion. He steered her through the throng and out toward the company of Yeomen. Silence fell in his wake and little whispers stirred in the dying sunlight of the late afternoon. "They'll kill you, Father," Raefil shouted and Murphy gave him an intense look, allowing the horse to saunter outwards and Bookey became confused, the priest alone, what's he at?"

The throng looked at the rise beyond the bridge, where Murphy seemed to be in conversation, rather than confrontation with Bookey and suddenly astonishment was rampant as the army turned and disappeared onto the lower road, leaving the priest in silhouette against the western sundown.

**

Father Murphy was to Duhallow before the two, sitting at the kitchen table, Georgie was in the pantry with Kate's sister Droleen and Paddy.

"How, in God's name did you manage that, Father Murphy?" Mrs. Laffan had put food for them and Gobnet sat, absorbed in the story, related by the young deacon, in her mind, the next curate to be installed in Boolavogue, God help him.

"We were breaking the law today, James," the priest sighed, I just wanted one more game on the roads of Trasna. I warned Bookey that there were a few hundred ready on the bridge to confront him. Thank God he's a rank coward, and I made it easy for him." He looked at Kate across the table, his brow creased in a personal agony. "I promised him there will be no more sporting in Trasna, in the whole of Kilcormack, for the foreseeable future. I will go directly to Rev. Owen tomorrow to make my own report and suffer one more humiliation. I have always maintained my own report before the authorities, before a colourful and exaggerated account of the military. He looked under his eyes at James, a half smile relieving the tension. "I'll have some anxious moments explaining that to the blacksmith," and looking at Kate, he laughed this time, "and to Raefil Keane too."

Gobnet Brennan saw the irony in the message and a look of recognition and understanding passed between herself and the housekeeper.

Father Murphy concentrated on the meal before him. "I'm afraid there are many more lions in my path than those two." He smiled apologetically. "I have a whole parish to placate that their games are forbidden."

John Murphy wasn't to know how loud that lion roar would echo around the world in time to come.

Chapter 38

Arthur Charles Annesley was made first Earl of Mountnorris in 1780. The House Of Lords in Westminster, decided, for some reason, that he was not entitled to inherit his father's titles in England and so, to placate, they gave him, as compensation, half the County of Wexford, complete with mansion at Camolin Park, a private army called the Blue Corps and a horde of well paying tenants in lands once owned by the Mc. Morroughs, the Kinsellaghs, the Redmonds, the O' Murphys, the Fitzstephens and the Morgans.

Father Murphy prayed to God in thanksgiving for His creation, for the creation of new shoots of harvest springing from the earth, even in winter, the earth is ready again to create, when only weeks ago saw the scattering and sowing of seeds.

James Attridge saw the priest hesitate and felt his distress, knowing that his announcement that all road and field games were to be cancelled, and trying to soften the blow, said "for the foreseeable future." James looked about the crowded church, if she were here, he would know, but Mrs. Laffan had said Kate had gone to Enniscorthy for a few days to care for an aunt. James was conscious of a disappointment nagging at his innards, that she wasn't here.

The message to the congregation reverberated around the church, another crime in the cynical Irish calendar. Before there was a protest, James, from the rear of the church watched the usual antagonists for reaction. A commotion of some sort erupted outside. John Murphy looked doggedly at the open doors beyond which, the usual group of Yeomanry were seated on the ditch at the far side of the road, now called to attention, stiff and expectant.

Immediately, Murphy knew what was coming. He had a little pulpit to the right of the altar, but seldom used it, likewise a special chair for the eventful arrival of his Bishop, which the priest never sat on, preferring to speak to them from the three steps in front of his altar. Mountnorris filled the doorway in all his pomposity and John Murphy raised the palms of his hands against the peer, preventing him making a step forward, while he told the peasants about Mr. Cato. "Have you heard of Mr. Cato?"

James saw again, the great current of life in the priest, burst forth, as Murphy raised his voice, rousing his congregation. He had, what few Catholic Clergy had; the ability to stare the odds of life straight in the face and pull from the surrounding norm of crime, tyranny and challenge, an advantage to his great spectrum of interests on behalf of his flock. Attridge saw Mountnorris stiffen in his contempt.

"Cato, The Elder," Murphy continued. "In the second century before Christ came on this Earth, said that if you do one thing late or wrong, you will be wrong and late in all your work. I can tell Mr. Cato, that Kilcormack is never wrong, never late in her harvest, due to her commitment to hard work, though for little return to her own benefit."

The audacity thrilled Attridge, as Murphy beckoned to Mountnorris to proceed, but he continued to speak, to the peer's annoyance. "I regret the cancellation of our games, and I maintain that our games are not a contravention of the new Act foisted upon us, I look at it by way of a thanksgiving prayer by our communities for the harvest, a pageant."

Georgie Tansey rushed to open the little gate at the centre of the altar rail and that aristocratic disregard for a lower class shone out as the bulk of cape and satin squeezed through and he went and assiduously sat on the Bishop's chair. The crowd sat transfixed, many had never seen him before, just his tithe and rents collectors and the flurry of gombeenmen in his pay.

Father Murphy made a cold suggestion of welcome, before the uneasy congregation, knowing that Lord Mountnorris had already visited all the Catholic churches in the region with his message, and knowing what was coming, steeled himself for the onslaught, as the visitor prepared to talk.

The voice rang out to the thatch with a nervous tinge, the object of the tinge was not the mask of mass suspicion that was obvious on the faces before him, but the closeness of John Murphy, his face expressionless, no doubt angry at not being forewarned of the visit.

"I have spoken in a number of your churches in the area and out of my great respect of the people of Kilcormack and especially, your priest, Father John Murphy, I have allowed this church of Boolavogue to be the last on my list." The lack of response in the congregation unsettled him for a minute. "The governments of London and Dublin have received great intelligence that preparations are far advanced for a second effort on the part of The French to land an armada in Ireland.. We are aware of accumulating incidents that can no longer be regarded as coincidental, like activity at night time, barking of dogs from dusk to dawn and the likes. Blacksmiths are working around the clock, gates and railings of our estates are being dragged from their foundations, for, we believe, the making of arms. Wexford is teeming with pike making units, swords and knives hidden in thatched roofs, all making ready for the French arrival."

A ripple of discontent floated from the rear of the church and James recognised the gravel voice of Conor Devereaux among others.

268

"I have to say to my friend, Father Murphy and your's, that if matters continue, he has to contemplate for the first time, military violence approaching Boolavogue and Trasn." Mountnorris continued, his voice strengthening. "Through the exhortations of our Lord Lieutenant, of my fellow landlords of North Wexford and your own Bishop Caulfield, the meeting of these landlords, last week, has passed, by a great majority, the proposal to proclaim sixteen parishes which includes, Monageer, Boolavogue and the whole of Kilcormack."

It was met with scuffles here and there, as brave men made to stand in argument, only to be pulled back by frightened wives. The Lord of Camolin, hoping his efforts here would go as easily as in most of the other churches, had yet, a bigger fester to impose. His voice rose in emphasis and the yeos outside took a few steps nearer the entrance.

"You should come in now, this day, and surrender to the magistrates, your arms, guns, muskets, pistols, blunderbusses, swords, pikes and any other warlike or hostile weapon in your possession."

Tension mounted further. "You will renounce and abjure with sincere contrition any and all unlawful oaths, of combining or conspiring with the so called United Irishmen, and give solemn and satisfactory assurance to these magistrates of your loyalty, submission to the establishment and the very best of kings and his family. Your Bishop asks you to comply with these requirements, he is asking his priests to exert all their energy, industry and zeal to bring back all of their flock who have been led astray, to go, if necessary from town to town, from village to hamlet, house to house, to exhort the people in Jesus Christ."

He held Murphy in a stare that was insistent and pugnacious, encompassing the unsuspecting Tansey, thinking, possibly that G. was of the cloth. James saw the youth lower his eyes against the onslaught. Mountnorris called for attention and summoned one of his aids from the bottom of the church, who brought a folio of a quality paper. He held it up before them. "I ask you now to adhere to this document of a hundred words, conveying your allegiance upon the Holy Evangelists, to our Most Gracious Majesty, King George and to the succession of his illustrious family, to the throne, that you will support the constitution, hand in all arms, suppress all tumult and report on any secret conspiracies. You will sign, on leaving this church, the oath of allegiance, that you are not a United Irishman and you will never take the oath to that organisation. All of you will swear here, in the presence of God."

He shouted above the beginnings of agitation in many quarters, stood up and shouted them down again.

269

"Else I will be obliged to warn and caution you against the most imminent and most dreadful dangers to which you will be exposed, in the first place, a military force to be sent on you, on free quarters, who will be warranted to commit the gravest excesses, to burn your houses, to destroy and consume your stock, your corn and hay and every article of your substance."

The flood of rage subsided when John Murphy himself, signed the document, to Mountnorris's relief, knowing, ninety per cent of his flock would follow. About fifty peasants stormed into the morning sunshine, the usual objectors, Devereaux as always in the lead. They will be well marked, thought Attridge, that and surely this is the end of relationships, in many directions.

Storming through the isle to the exit, Mountnorris sized the Englishman. "I am a subject of the king, My Lord, I signed at birth," said Attridge. However, Sir, it is my belief that you, all on your own here this day, have drawn the first sword of a rebellion and I also believe Father Murphy can no longer keep the people in harness, on behalf of His Most Gracious Majesty."

"It's time Palmer sent you home, Sir, you do him no honour coming to a place like this, and if I had my way....". James cut him off. "Have you ever met the King, Lord Mountnorris?"

"No, Sir, that has not yet been my pleasure."

"Well, Sir, I have, and believe me, Sir, it is no pleasure, none whatsoever."

The Peer would report his victory to Dublin Castle, his name and reputation on the up. He was tired of being a liberal. John Murphy was disconsolate.

Chapter 39

James was at the School House, with Master Dunn when Conor Devereaux was arrested. At Dunns invitation, James had spent many hours brooding over the Master's great collection of old books and letters. A dusty old leather bound manuscript was spread before the two on the scrubbed kitchen table, a great book of wonder tales by Airt O Muirgheasa, outlining the origin of the Celtic tongue, a part of a collection of languages, originating in many areas of central and northern Europe, going back to the fifth century before Christ. On the Master's shelves, stories of grand folklore and accounts of great Irish battles and their heroes abounded, how the great warrior, Cu Roi was slain, the literary tale of Eadaoin and the Donn Cuailgne, when a boy became an apprentice to a magician, the escapades of the hero, Oisin and the narratives of Fionn Mac Cumhaill, his grandson, Oscar and Brian Boru, himself.

Norah Scully had been busying herself outside on the slab in a pleasant afternoon, which had gentled down to a soft breeze coming up from the river. Norah was washing the old man's under drawers in a sudsy bucket, when she heard commotion coming up from the cabins below. She dried her hands in her apron and going to the edge of the slab, the urgent call of the youth hit her. There was no understanding what the youth was saying. He was on horseback, bareback and calling into the cabins, he spurred the horse up the hill, shouting all the while. Madness in his eyes, the horse splintered the granite surface and James ran to the door.

"The blacksmith," he shouted, "they're taking Mr. Devereaux, burning the forge."

"Your horse is saddled," Dunn called to Attridge "Norah and myself will follow." He began to lace his boots.

James followed the lad, then left him behind as the boy turned off Trasna Bridge to other hamlets with his message. There were people already hurrying toward the bridge and many were choking the narrow lane leading to Conor's house.

Recently, a new menace had come on the scene. Young Tansey had told James of the new captain of the dreaded Hessians, who had been sent from Kildare, and was already a thorn in John Murphy's side. "A little wasp of a man," G. had said, "barely up to my shoulder. His name is Captain Wrenne, the authorities up there think Bookey and Carnock are too soft on us."

Attridge recognised the captain instantly, amazing how some little people can stand out in a crowd. A little terrier, Captain Wrenne stood, barely the height of his stirrups, the green Hessian uniform, the feathered cockade, striving to make him look bigger, he was shouting his directions at his men, while Bookey stood off, his own men ready for trouble, as the crowd thronged into the clearing before the forge. Yeos were ransacking the forge, bringing everything out onto a pyre ready for torching.

Wrenne1 ranted his orders. "I want you to find weapons, powder, bring them out. Keep the bloody peasants back, keep them back, or by God there will be blood." Conor had been working on the hurling camans. They were heaped up onto the pile, many, still in their raw state, many still finished and honed to perfection, the curved sticks of ash the high lights of the knotty wood shining out. Oil was poured on the pile. It burned and crackled, the flames devouring Conor's festival of form, as they added picture frames, wood carvings, crafted scythe and fork handles, undoubtedly ready for a pike to to be attached. Not a pike in sight and people often wondered where he kept his famous horde. It was like burning a self portrait and James caught sight of the big blacksmith. He was shackled to a tree, glassy eyed and motionless before the inferno. It was evident he had put up some kind of defence. A gash over his right eye was bleeding profusely, threatening to blind him, while four Redcoats stood guard over him. James came around the far side of the tree, but was not allowed near him. Devereaux threw him a look of despair.

A company of Yeos, on Bookey's orders were about to attack the cottage and Devereaux shouted to leave the house alone. The door gave away easily under the ram, when the shout echoed from inside the forge, they had found four pikes. A corporal held them up like trophies, their blades newly sharpened.

Captain Wrenne barked further instructions and five torches were prepared. Attridge managed to get nearer the smith, now calm and reconciled. He hissed at Attridge, "don't let them fire the cottage, James," a pleading in the creviced face.

Norah Scully came running into the yard and joined the group of women, still multiplying , as more and more came. Ashen faced and suddenly furious, they shouted their contempt and a girl, defying and unafraid, ran through the barricade of redcoats and swabbed at the blood on Conor's face. It was Kate Keohane and a crude and obnoxious Lieutenant Bookey scoffed to leave Mary of Magdelaine do her work.

The torches were ready for firing and a sergeant shattered the windows of the cottage with the butt of his blunderbuss. Six more pikes were brought out from the forge and Wrenne shouted, "Burn it."

Kate had bound Conor's head with the linen. Then, in a frenzy, she called to Norah Scully to "c'mon Norah," as she ran toward the cottage. There didn't seem to be a psychological design to her effort, until she burst through the broken door and ran inside the house. Norah echoed the call, "c'mon, c'mon." Thirty women stormed the cottage as the first of the torches was lit from the pyre. Three more pikes were found and the crowd increased. The little cottage choked with a powerful onslaught, as more crawled through the broken windows. Children were handed over the cills, as Kate, standing in the doorway, called for more. For the second time in half a year, the captain of the German Hessians was confronted by the women of Boolavogue. Physical provocation and raw animal effrontery stared quietly now, out through the door and windows of Conor Devereaux's cottage, for the crowd of two hundred protesters went suddenly silent, as the dry heavy thatch beckoned to the torchers.

His emotions in turmoil, Wrenne roared to the women to come out, for it is going to be fired. Bookey stood near the captain, waiting for the order. "At the count of three", said Wrenne, "small minds feel no pain."

Jack Keohane ran from the crowd to the doorway. "The bastards are going to commit mass murder." He faced the gallery of peasants and soldiers, his arms raised in supplication. Sibilant whispers were heard inside the cottage. "Hail Mary Full of Grace, the Lord is with thee....."

"Three," shouted Wrenne. "Now don't wear out your boots, soldier, fire the thatch." The five torchers stood motionless, in a state of confusion and hesitancy. "NOW!," roared the little captain and Bookey gave them the nod to proceed.

Suddenly, James Attridge appeared on horseback, breaking through the cordon of Redcoats and took up position before the door of the cottage, next to Keohane. Prayers continued inside. Attridge called to the lieutenant of Rockspring, ignoring Wrenne. His heart racing, James felt the terror all around him. Half a dozen Hessian rifles were trained on him.

"Lieutenant Bookey, you know me."

"I know you."

Wrenne was rooted, frustration and malice tore at his nerve ends. "What is this," he roared, "I said fire the house, they'll soon come out."

"Then I'll have you know, Sir, you are about to destroy the property of Sir George Palmer, a close friend of Lord Mountnorris, and I certainly hope you will shoulder the blame for what you are about to do. You have found what it is you were looking for, I suggest you deal with it in a manner befitting an officer and a gentleman and if you have something that warrants the attention of a magistrate and a court, you

273

should arrange proceedings accordingly."

Wrenne fumed. "A devil," thought Kate, from inside the window "A devil in human form." He strutted toward Attridge , who completely ignored him and called louder to Bookey. "In the mean time, these properties and the land you and your army occupy belong to Sir George Palmer. The blacksmith is merely a tenant, I therefore suggest that, rather than cause ill will between him and Lord Mountnorris, whose Yeomanry you command, that you desist from this murderous act and leave here with your prisoner, who is a friend of Sir George and who, no doubt, you will treat with respect."

Wrenne was aware that this man, whoever he was, would be somewhat apart from the rabble about him. Attridge then addressed him. "There are no trivialities here, Captain, you are about to kill a hundred women and children in the name of Sir Charles Mountnorris."

Bookey hesitated and began a whispered argument with the little Hessian, then beckoned to his men and to everyone's relief, the torches were thrown on the fire. Their argument continued and eventually, Bookey, in the awful light of revelation, was suddenly in command. He was heard to say that he was in charge of the militia here or something to that effect. The pikes were loaded onto a cart and Conor Devereaux was frogmarched through the lane amid calls of support from the crowd.

James dismounted and stood head and shoulders over the bantam Hessian

"You won't be so lucky next time, Sir, when you will find more guts in me than in Lieutenant Bookey and when there won't be a hundred women to protect you."

"I'll take my chances with you anytime, Captain and without your green bellies to protect you."

They danced out through the broken door in celebration as the dozen Hessians followed the Yoes through the lane. The women came and hailed the Englishman. Kate Keohane stood back in her own private zone of admiration, an admiration that continued to be fed with fresh discoveries between them in a perpetual succession of happenings, and what next, he wondered.

**

Father Murphy had gone north to Tinahealy to spend a day or two with his sister. Help came from all over and willing hands doused the fire and already the door and windows were being made secure.

Inside the cottage, she found him sitting in the warm kitchen, two sketches of a woman in rosewood frames, set out on the table. He was lost in his scrutiny of them. "These are of my mother, he explained, I brought them from London on my last trip. Mrs. Laffan persuaded me to let Mr. Devereaux frame them for me, I found them here when I came in." He lifted up the two pictures for a further scrutiny. "I said I would agree, but only if she did the asking. I don't think Conor Devereaux thinks too much of me, he's uncomfortable in my company, or maybe the other way around, he never said they were ready. The frames make them even more beautiful."

She looked at them over his shoulder and hesitated."Why did you do that, James, put yourself in danger with that captain fellow?"

"It was you and the women took the risk, he would have fired the thatch as soon as look at you."

"Such a funny feeling it was." She smiled, a look of childlike defiance crossed her face, "in the darkness of the cottage, all crushed together, praying." She thought for a minute. "Would he have done it?. What worries me is that Bookey would have done it, I think it was the prayers to the Virgin that stopped it. Whatever they say about Mountnorris, he would not condone mass murder. It was you that saved the day, James Attridge, and you know it."

He stood the little frames before him and smiled. "If there's one thing that will stop a soldier bent on destruction, it's a hundred women shaking their petticoats at him."

She looked again at the drawings."You brought them from England?"

"Yes, my father gave them to me to bring to Duhallow," he said, studying them again.

"But that one is already here, in the cottage," she said, pointing at the bigger of the two.

"Here?"

A tiny backwash of concern crossed her face. She loosed the shawl tied across her waist and gave him a dark look, a conflict of emotions, at odds in her.

"Have you been here, before, James, here in Connors cottage?"

"No."

"This cottage is over twenty years old, but nobody has ever lived in it."

His curiosity became more assiduous. "Kate?"

She sighed, reconciled to continue. "Conor never lived here, after building it with his own hands, with the best that everything could buy. He lives behind the forge, has always."

"And then?"

"A shrine to a woman he once loved and who left him."

He said slowly, "and the woman, who was she?"

"Nobody knows, though, I'm sure plenty know and won't talk about it." She sought to change the subject. "Gobnet Brennan says your father is not well in England, do you miss him?"

"We were never that close. I was mostly away at school, he was always a lonely man after my mother died. He's a good man, everything he did was for me. I'll be going to see him soon."

"I miss my mother," she continued, "she too was a quiet woman, not like me." He laughed gently, watching her eyes misting over."Sure 'tis stupid to be quiet in this world. Luther always says that if you handle a nettle too gentle, it will sting you, that you can frighten a bull from inside the window. I prefer to go out and look him in the eye." She looked through to the other room, to hide her smarting eyes. "Some people go on living from day to day, half frightened, always looking behind them.There's nothing worse in the world than to be indifferent to what's going on around you. Maybe to try, is to die, but not to care is never to be born. Lady Palmer taught me that."

"You liked Lady Palmer," he said.

"Lady Pamela and Master Dunn. They set me up for the world, what world there is, but I miss Mammy, she was one of those women I told you about, a woman of Ireland, God help us, died in childbirth when she was told never to have another. My father, a man of Ireland drank himself to death, always thinking he was responsible for her death."

People were busy boarding up the broken windows. The door had already been taken off it's hinges.Her back was still turned to him as she came back to reality. He began to make words of comfort. "It was a long time ago, there's just my brother now and Droleen. "And how lucky they are," he smiled.

"Do you know who this woman is, Kate, the woman of this house?"

"Not until now." She hesitated again, then made a decision on what would be surely a breaking of a confidence and cutting a knot that was tied a long time ago.

"Come with me, Mr. Attridge, you're a big boy now. Your mother was very beautiful, bring the drawing with you. She turned to him in the doorway. "She's already here." Then she guided him through the little parlour and through again to a bedroom. The furnishings had a quality never seen in a peasant cottage in any part of Ireland. A beautiful hand carved dressing table occupied the far wall from the doorway, the highly polished wood suggested many hours of sanding, honing, polishing. A mirror in delicate framing, drawers with handles and nothing to suggest that it was a room, prepared for none but the little vanities of a woman. The bedstead, a combination of intricate iron work and brass was unmade, the well sprung base, it's coils, taut and scintillating in the sunbeams poking through the shattered window. Items of Conor's crafts were all around, from rough charcoal sketches to full coloured portraits, water colours and heavy oils. Master Dunn and the crow faced Norah Scully, Father John, recognisable in a random scattering of framed lines and squikkles, like done in a hurry. The beautiful Kate Keohane smiled at him from an ornate picture frame at a place of pride through the parlour door.

She pulled a linen cloth from a bulky object on a side table. James's breath shortened. There, as large as a horse's head was the bronze of the lady in the picture, the eyes, mystic apertures in their metal sockets, the features, sharp and acute, yet painfully pensive.

She watched for his response and saw there his incredulity. "She' very beautiful, James and if the lady under your arm is the same as the bronze......then?"

"You've seen this before?" he asked, his voice cracking.

"Yes, my mother, Droleen and myself were the only ones allowed into the cottage, outside of The Master. We cleaned it and kept it in the condition he wanted, like one day the lady would return."

"I don't know if I should have....." she frowned. He put a hand on her arm. "I'm a big boy now, remember, I can never thank you enough."

"Then come to the forge, there's something else." She said. He followed her outside.

The furnace under the canopy was still flaming, a young boy was turning the bellows, delighting in the jumping flames. It looked like Conor had been working when the military came. Attridge didn't have to move beyond the huge doors of the forge. He felt he had been here before, but he hadn't.

In his surprise and wonder, he bagan to understand. He had seen that scene daily since he came to Duhallow; the furnace, the huge canopy over, the huge rough dresser in the dark background, the ropes and the pulleys and the great anvil itself, all the natural objects of the blacksmith's craft. It caught his breath in a kind of a strangled laugh and his eyes filled.

"All it needs is the lady," Kate said gently, "the lovely woman at Duhallow."

He remained transfixed in the doorway. Jack Keohane was repairing the cottage door in the rear of the forge. Jack, a little of his customary icy tension melting with a quick handshake, told James he had done well or something like it, that constituted a complement. Attridge accepted warmly, to Kate's delight. "I'm going to Camolin in the morning, Mr. Keohane."

"Fat lot of good Mountnorris will do for you," snorted Keohane, "for they've taken the smith to Carnew."

"Why Carnew," said Kate.

"Because the Reverend Mr. Cope is out for blood and anyone carrying weapons. That little scrawneen Wrenne is in the pay of the Protestant." Then he lowered his head, in self reproach. "It's my own fault, Kate, I was to come to the forge yesterday to take the twelve pikes to Duhallow, but I was drunk, I thought another day would make no matter." With a nod to the Englishman he returned to his task.

"Duhallow, what did he mean ?"

"Why don't you go and tell Sir George about today. There's a lot of work to be done here," she whispered.

**

For over twenty years, Conor O'Connor Devereaux reconciled his life to fate and never feared to look fortune in the face. In maturity he had a great hate of that life and therefore, was its master. He could accept whatever came, regardless of the consequences, unafraid and proud. A man who gets strength both from hope and despair, he stood gentle and alone, his strength, like tempered steel, caressed and moulded on his anvil. He was now at the mercy of a man who had no mercy. Rev. Cope will pontificate that he is handing the smith over to God's mercy, while having none himself. Poor God.

Chapter 40

Young Henry Tansey had found new interests. He was becoming less interested in matters of religion. Though growing in strength and the malady that had invaded his frail body for the first twelve years of his life, seemed to be almost a thing of the past, it was due mainly to the long and productive days spent at Donovan's little farm, but to his brother's anxiety, Henry was spending more of his spare time with big John Kelly and people like Jack Keohane and Raefil Keane, and with the hurlers of Boolavogue and Trasna, who, despite Father Murphy's insistence, they continued to play their games, contrary to law and defying curfews. The younger Tansey would pester James Attridge to persuade Mr. Wolfe Tone, to make him a United Irishman, the sacred oath rolling off his tongue. G. often felt, seeing him through mature eyes, that his early sickness seemed to enlarge his dimensions of himself to himself. He was slowly becoming his own exclusive object, that, often supreme selfishness was his main duty. Even now, at fifteen years of age, he would wake in the night in a stupor, shouting the name Wharton.

On one of the rare occasions when he agreed to attend Mass, he and Georgie walked ahead of Mary Donovan to the chapel. G. thought it was a stack of old rags left on the steps of John Murphy's church. The wide road and square outside the church were still empty as the village stirred itself awake. Hen began to pull at the mound obstructing the doorway.

The Blacksmith moaned and suddenly his body went into spasm at the interruption. Mary cried out in despair. She folded her shawl under his head and sent Hen to call for Father John, only to meet him half way.

Conor's body had been whipped out of recognition. His shoulders, back and buttocks were stripped almost bare of skin, tissue and wounds allowed to fester. The long body was covered in a gruesome mass of nematodes and insect larva, so his back was a quivering sliding colony of maggots, with a life of its own.

Somebody procured a small cart and a few of the early Mass goers helped to put him inside. Women, many in tears donated shawls and wraps for his comfort. Old Doctor Seamus Hyde, tut-tutted to himself as he examined Conor. "Thank God for the larva," he whispered to G., "these little fellows have managed to keep the infection in check, might have saved your wretched life," he whispered in Devereaux's ear. With a little whiskey for the patient and a bottle for himself, he began cleaning the awful wounds. The doctor remained with him all day in the comfort of Father John's sacristy and Sir George Palmer, on hearing of the situation, insisted he be brought to Duhallow, where a good clean room was prepared, as near to the kitchen as possible, knowing the Smith would be uneasy in any of the guest rooms above stairs.

"It's over twenty years since he spent any worthwhile time here. If it's the only way I can get him back into my house, unconscious and half dead, then so be it."

He hired an old nurse from Enniscorthy, to tend the smith day and night and for two weeks, he instructed Doctor Seamus to call every day. He was, at times, delirious, calling out in his torment, then relapse into unconsciousness. The nurse would force feed him at times. "He's an obstinate man, I've never seen more. Obstinacy and dogmatism are the surest signs of stupidity", she would complain. Gobnet Brennan didn't take kindly to the medics efforts at taking over her kitchen, dictating, even to the cook of Duhallow on the finer points of a sick man's diet.

"The most stubborn are the most intelligent, or did they never teach you that at school, that you can never be good without a little bit of obstinacy in you", the cook would argue. Her menu differed daily, with the best from Luther's garden; Bean Porridge, Boiled Trout, Calve's Head Soup, Meat Pasty, Bubble'n Squeak, Flummery, Hotchpotch. Only Sir George was allowed to sit in the bedroom, who paved the way, almost by negotiation with the old nurse, for James and Father Murphy and the others. Kate Keohane challenged the old nurse, to refuse her visits at her peril.

Two weeks after Conor Devereaux had been dumped on the steps of Father Murphy's church, Sir George Palmer walked into the kitchen at Duhallow where James and young Tansey were sipping tea with Annie Laffan. A racking cough had kept him awake in the night. He moved stiffly with the help of a cane. He told the housekeeper not to fuss, when she scolded him for going the stairs without assistance, jumping to her feet to help him to a chair. He announced he would have lunch at two o' clock in the small parlour, and addressing G., who was on his feet, said he would love to hear more about the king of England, another time, as James and he needed to speak alone."Pick a nice wine, James, he said, in a shortage of breath, throwing a dark eye at Gobnet Brennan, "we must talk."

The Chateau Barton glinted in the crystal as Droleen had finished serving lunch. Before going, she stoked the fire, which sparkled into life, the friendly flares reflecting the rich dark redness of the Bordeaux. "Good wine, James?", Palmer raised an eyebrow. "Excellent wine, Sir, too good, too expensive just for lunch."

The old man looked out over his glasses, that twinkle, stubborn and endearing. "It's only the first bottle is expensive, Son, the French say that." He thought for a minute, studying the liquid, "besides, there is something I need you to know." Then he returned to the wine again. "How well you picked this wine."

James laughed. "I must confess, I was fed information by Mrs. Brennan, she told me it was Kate's favourite, so I automatically chose it."

"Kate knows a lot about wine, she learned a lot from my wife. Pamela adored that girl. Kate was a good learner, almost the incarnation of your mother. It gives me great pleasure to see her in Pamela's clothes, though Kate wouldn't hear of it at first. It was Mrs. Laffan's idea, so they have a new life now, though mind you, she draws a line at the ball gowns and anything pretentious," he chuckled, "most of the wardrobe was given to charity."

He looked mischievously at Attridge. "I've seen how you look at her, approvingly, I would say and I believe, she approves."

"She's a very special lady, Sir, I should be so lucky to have her affection."

"O, I know all about her affection, James," the old man teased. "Kate has spoken to Mrs. Laffan." That twinkle again, outshining the sparkle in the wine. "And Henrietta Owen, what about the lovely Lady Owen?"

"Spoilt and arrogant," said Attridge quickly.

"I've seen how she looks at you, too, the very criteria for today's society lady, people stand aside for women like that."

"Stand aside and walk on, Sir," replied James, "she needs a good spanking, what I know of her. I've met her only twice in all."

"Would you marry her, James?" Palmer's voice was suddenly authoritative, orthodox, and James wondered if there was a prerogative.

Attridge frowned into his glass. "She's a pretty young thing, Sir George and I am sure the subject of many a man's desire, but she's an Owen and I would become an Owen, perhaps living in some vice regal lodge in India, or pushed through the back door of Dublin's Irish Parliament, or worse."

"Would you marry Kate Keohane?" the question came fast, despite the levity.

"Miss Keohane says that Ireland is a terrible place for a married woman."

"So you two have broached the subject?," the old eyebrow raised itself again.

James laughed, "I suppose so, but only in general."

Palmer laughed heartily through the phlegm. Attridge was suddenly serious."Sir George, my life has been hectic since the day my father suggested I call on you and I thank him daily in my mind for opening that door to me and especially you Sir, for your friendship which I treasure most of all. I have met wonderful people, from priests, blacksmiths, revolutionaries, every kind of militia and all in between. I am half English, but my Irish roots are, I believe, more deeply set. I'm like a potato plant in Luther's garden, the best part of me seems to be underground. I don't know what fate brought me here, but daily, I try to figure it out."

"Fate is not an eagle, James, fate creeps like a rat." Palmer sipped at the wine.

"You know that Mr. Tone is back in France, Sir George, after the failed expedition. There's going to be a revolution here, I think it's unavoidable now, what with the military running amok in the country. I intend to be a part of it. I have written world wide of the injustices that exist and am published where my stories are accepted. I hope to continue to do so, to inform the world or perhaps carry one of Mr. Devereaux's pikes, but I fear you might disapprove."

"Let your pen be your sword, Son, and write Ireland into the new century. Let them read about it in America, in France, even in England, for the English peasant is most ignorant as to affairs in his own country. "Now," he said, rising, "hand me the shawl, 'tis a cold day out there and as far as disapproval is concerned....well let us go pay old Cantankerous a visit."

He smiled at the younger man's surprise. "Good that your young friend is gone. I would not want Father Murphy to see this, we'll go through the kitchen."

James kept his thoughts to himself. Father John knows all about the bull of Duhallow, as everyone does, far and wide. He wondered if the medication that he takes to make him sleep was scrambling the old brain. Cantankerous was in his three acre playground, cordoned off with natural boundaries and stout fencing. Like a Lord in his pile, the massive dark brown creature, with an undulating throat, stirred himself at the sight of the approaching couple. The beast enjoyed the privileges indicative of his status, born mad whose nature was to roar and fight, a god of venom and aggravation and a glutton in the process of creation. A corner nearest the house, consisted of his living quarters, a fine iron shed, which was one of a half a dozen more structures, housing the milking parlour, the forge, the fuel shed, the dairy, where in his indolent expression during milking, Sir George said of him, that he would stand there looking over his secure fencing, contemplating the one difficulty in his life; his alternatives, especially his desirable alternatives, of which he had many.

The fenced off area before his mansion was empty and the bull had been moved into the adjoining meadow, out of danger's way. Luther signalled to Sir George that everything was OK and opened the gate to Cantankerous's shed. It smelt of dung and fresh fodder, the animal's heavy breath still hung on the air, so heavy, you could almost see it. Still puzzled, James followed his host to the rear of the building. A heavy door, padlocked and almost hidden behind the bull's feeding trough was set into a dark corner

Palmer gave him a key. "Open these James."

Attridge looked dubiously behind him and wondered if the animal was out of mischief's way, then unlocked the door's two heavy padlocks. Beyond was a long narrow tunnel of a room, running the length of the whole line of outbuildings. It had a few small windows looking onto the hill behind Duhallow, heavily curtained and Sir George pulled aside the dust encrusted material to allow a space light into the tunnel.

James stood motionless, a small sensation of heat creeping up inside his collar. Almost beyond rationality, he thought it was some kind of an illusion brought on by Mr. Barton's fine Bordeaux.

A thousand, perhaps two thousand pikes lined the walls of the armoury. Ten and twelve feet high, they stood like sentinels down the length of the walls and across the end gable in the distant darkness. The pike heads, some of them a good three feet from top of the ash handle to the razor like vortex glinted in the rush of light. Hundreds of rifles, muskets, blunderbusses and bayonets littered the centre of the floor space and what looked like crates of grape or ammunitions were neatly stacked under the windows. His eyes tried to take in the indescribable. A mound of lengths of raw steel, not yet tempered, together with iron gates and pieces of old railings were stacked, waiting for the hammer that would give them another life, for which they were never previously designed.

"Kate asked me to let you in on our little secret. She said you were asking questions, something her loud mouthed uncle said. I think it's only fair, you should know what is going on. The peasants have their night missions as well as the military. I buy steel, it's a big estate." He chuckled hoarsely, " however, many gates and stanchions and lengths of railings have recently gone missing in the estates of north Wexford. Devereaux and smiths like him have to be congratulated."

Attridge took down a pike and levelled it out in front, ill prepared for the weight, the point dipped to the floor. "Hold it more centre ways and get the balance, so that you have a terrifying blade in front of you and a stout cudgel behind." "I didn't know you were a patriot, Sir", said James, returning the weapon.

"Patriot?, is that what you call it, James?" He sat on a crate, picked up one of the muskets and toyed with it. "Samuel Johnson said a few years back, that patriotism is the last refuge of a scoundrel and I believe it to be so, especially when it relates to me. Let's lock up and let these fellows go back to sleep for a little while longer."

When they were finished, Cantankerous was ushered back to his domain."Visitors stay well away from this lad. He's the keeper of the arms," smiled Palmer. He gave Gobnet a knowing look as they went through the kitchen. She had made fresh bread on which her butter melted into the soft innards.

"I'm going to France, Sir,", James said. Mr. Tone has asked me to make the trip. He's going to try for another armada for Ireland and I am privileged to receive his request. I had fears for Mr. Devereaux, but now that he's on the mend, I feel I can go. I think you know about his home and what Kate Keohane and I found there and I do know about the portrait in the hall, which I believe you knew about all along." Palmer looked intensely at him, searching for events beginning to stir.

"Ah!", the peer shrugged, "sure every able bodied man in Trasna and Boolavogue were in love with Heather Shanahan, poor Devereaux had to stand in line, Arthur was the lucky one."

"I've received a correspondent from my father's friend, who looks after our farm at Windsor, that he has been poorly of late and it's my intention to stop off on my way back. I shall be away for a while."

"We'll miss you, James. Take care, our blessings go with you, I'll have a letter ready for you to take, this place still misses Arthur."

Chapter 41

Paddy waited for him in the hallway, bags ready to go. James had been able to spend an hour with the Smith almost every day, both knowing that something special existed between them, a kind of hidden mutual understanding that would be discussed at another time.

She met him at the open door. Kate seemed subdued and he wanted to think that her mood mirrored his, the disappointment at not seeing her for some time to come. He would have made an issue of it, taking her to the Priest's Leap and making a big deal of his going, but even now he was apprehensive of her opinion of him and he had seen how she put Raefil in his place for taking her affections for granted. "When I'm here, Kate, I'm in a better place," he whispered.

She put a finger to his lips, then kissed him very gently on the cheek, her look, full of implication. Then she walked quickly back to the kitchen, her eyes smarting.

Attridge had been worried that couriers had been coming and going from Duhallow with despatches which authorities could use, if found, for their purpose, after "A letter to the editor," in The Journal quoted an American periodical as saying, "Mr. Attridge is the natural enemy of the Ascendancy in Ireland, as the whore is of a decent woman. This man is more to be feared than a thousand rifles."

George Palmer put his mind at rest. "You do not gain freedom by silencing one brand of ideas, James. Let you be the censor, for no government should be without censors, and in America where the Press is free, no one ever will. Let them sensor your writing, lad, for all it is for them is patching fig leaves to hide the naked truth."

**

A velvet mantle of soft sunlight settled over Wexford as his coach picked him up at Trasna Bridge to take him to Wexford Town. It was an early departure, the place seemed a world apart, engaged in the brown earth, the air heavy and delicious with the odours of heather and gossamer and the strong wafting of brine and seaweed as he neared the great bridge at Wexford docks. Workers were in the fields and cattle moved slowly toward milking parlours and the villages and hamlets on the road were preparing for their day's work and it was difficult to believe the turmoil that existed beneath the fragile surface of a country soon to be torn asunder.

"How Le Harve stinks," wrote Wolfe Tone "and Paris itself in the warm weather and I won't mention Brest. My God to compare with your beautiful Slaney and her silver opulence and her clear cool depts. I hear her voice, it will be the first song of celebration should my endeavours succeed. The women of northern France are ugly as sin, James, but value for money is marvellous because of depreciation of French currency against Sterling. Two guineas buy very adequate accommodation for a whole month, four pennies, a superb seat at the theatre and a good wine is virtually for nothing."

On board the package, Pegasus, James read again his friend's account of Paris. "Though the Seine stinks, the city is clean now. All the gardens which had been trodden on and neglected are now refreshed. The Northern Bank, with it's fashionable streets and shops, the Champs Elysees, Plas de Louis XV, the home of the Guillotine, The Louvre and Scare Coeur, is all now a heaven for the discerning while The Left Bank houses the Government Offices and the intellectual life of Europe's new vivarium. It's hard to believe, as I write this at my new home in Nanterre, outside the city, that the revolution happened only eight years ago, just eight years since Bastille."

Attridge had prepared an up to date account of, as he headed it, "And So Begins Ireland's Own Reign Of Terror," for release to an agent in New York, where it would appear in half a dozen newspapers, among them The New York Times, The Boston Gazette and The Massachusetts Spy.

"Robespierre, the instigator of France's Reign Of Terror has become, himself, a guest of Madame Guillotine, as has his lieutenant, Marat, the man who had half his face eaten while living in the sewers of Paris at the beginning of the revolution.

In Ireland, the new Viceroy, Lord Camden is installed in Dublin Castle and ousted cleanly and clinically is the more liberal Lord Fitzwilliam, the likable Scotsman, whose reign lasted only eighty days, in which time he had raised the hopes of three million Catholics, to achieve for them, the emancipation that Wolf Tone had dreamed of. In his sacking of Fitzwilliam, Mr. Pitt, in his London office, had established his determination, once and for all, a union with Britain and govern this unfortunate island from Whitehall and drive the peasants into open revolt and give legitimacy to the text of the oath of the Orange Order; "to use my utmost exertion, to exterminate all Catholics from the Kingdom of Ireland."

Daily, the lodges of the North ring with ballads and verses, glorifying their idol, King William of Orange and the streets of Newry, Belfast, Londonderry and major towns and hamlets are now the stage for the most macabre enactment of sectarian hatred and religious bigotry. Their orange banners and cockades parade with drums and fifes, calling on God Himself to help them in their quest for an ethnic cleansing of all things Papist. This corps of corruption, which membership carries a special decoration from the king, in the form of a specially commissioned tin medal and an orange ribbon is amply named the "Battalion of Testimony," a battalion of fools, who carry out atrocities on both sides to pit Catholic against Protestant, to establish fact.

This had the effect of driving over half a million men to take the oath of The United Irishmen, a pledge of reconciliation and brotherhood; " ....in the presence of God, I do pledge myself to my country, to forward a brotherhood of affection and identity of interests, a communion of rights and a union of power among Irishmen of all religions and persuasions, for the freedom and happiness of our country." Mr. Pitt has sown the seed of rebellion and the die is cast. This reporter has seen at first hand, thousands of Catholics being hounded from their remote cabins in outlying hillsides and at the edges of bogs and ditches, in the pursuit of Union. In County Antrim alone, eight thousand souls have been hunted, disposed and many killed while the red shades of the Union Jack, like a great blind has begun to be drawn down across the land. Septic villains have been pardoned for their crimes by King George and emptied of the jails of England and infiltrated among the militia and the Yeomanry of Antrim, Down and Donegal, and given a posh name of "Elite Corps." 1797 in the year of the Generals in Ireland; Lumney, Clavering, despots like Stapleton and Matthews of the York Fencibles, the Ayreshire Highlanders, Nugent and Barber and the Monaghan Regiments of the notorious Hillsboroughs. None of these gentlemen have compunction or scruples when it comes to mass slaughter of the natives. Fires of bigotry and discriminating rumours and accounts of hangings, massacres and evictions, so called and perpetrated by Catholics on Protestants and vice versa, resulted in a thousand dead at The Diamond, Irishman against Irishman.

Further south to Meath, Offaly and Laois, the colour red lightens a little for the time being while further still towards Kildare, Wicklow and Waterford there is still a restless kind of peace, with anarchy barely bridled and lying just beneath the surface.

However, in the areas of Meath, Kildare and Dublin, Generals Dundas, Gosford, Sir James Duff, with their Hessian, Reay, Kells and Navan Yeomanry, Militia Fencibles, brought south this so called Elite Corps to join them in their drilling, while the most vile and unscrupulous blackguards were sent to join Lord Kingsborough of the "North Corks," the very dregs of the Orange population of Cork and the most merciless employee of British tyranny, In any of her colonies across the world.

In Wexford, Colonel Le Hunt, Generals Lombard, de Courcey, Colonel Pounden, the "Dog Of Enniscorthy," General Eustace of New Ross, Fawcett, Grogan are relatively quiet, adamant now, with the help of the Catholic hierarchy, that the population of these counties, once subdued, should remain so.

This tiny country is awash with ,military, strutting generals and the phenomenon of power, but the most remarkable facet, is the tranquillity of the greater part of Catholic Ireland in the South and West, in Cork, Kerry, Limerick, all of Connaught and Donegal as well as wide tracts of the midlands. This, at a time when Ulster is brimming with dissention, disorder and chaos. This is due, in part to the loyalty of the under trodden peasant to his landlord and his priest, but it is mainly the result of apathy, handed down through generations of persecution and disqualification, having yielded all he has, and with nothing more to yield, eventually getting peace from his acquiescence. In Ireland, the peasant knows that, having no hope brings no despair."

James Attridge, reporting for The Sunday Republican, The New York Times, The Boston Gazette,

Chapter 42

Theobold Wolfe Tone longed again for the company of Thomas Russell and indeed Thomas Emmet, with his superb mind and calculating ability. How they would be a comfort to him now for the meeting that is about to happen, to steel him against what will undoubtedly be a dressing down at the hands of Bonaparte, who, no doubt has been taking the Bantry disaster as almost a personal triumph, in that General Hoche, as Commander of the expedition, left a lot of questions to be answered.

He arrived at the Tulleries an hour early. James Attridge had arrived in Paris in the early morning with arrangements to meet in a nearby cafe. Standing on the Pont Royale, Tone gazed down on the murky waters of The Seine and tried again to formulate the meeting in his mind. It's possible General Napoleon might decide to snub him, as he is known to have done to persons of more importance than a simple Irish barrister, for who does Mr. Tone think he is, having lost us some seven ships and over three thousand men, when he couldn't find his way to his own country.

Looking down the river to the Ile de la Cite, the magnificent bulk of Notre-Dame de Paris loomed over the river, it's island splitting the waters. The flying buttresses and majestic portals had beckoned earlier and Tone, an agnostic and detester of Popes and Bishops had spent a half hour before the six hundred year old altar, the huge rose window showering him with multicoloured ingots of light and hopefully, some kind of supernatural inspiration.There, in the twilight atmosphere of the great Cathedral, he felt the quickening of his pulse and the beginnings of mild panic. His great friend Lazare Hoche was dead, but he told himself there's courage in panic, so he would use it as the element with which he would evaluate his progress and be as good as the little French general, now termed "The Wolf of Europe."

At least he welcomed the fact that his friend Edward Lewins, the most senior member of the Society of the United Irishmen would be there, the man who had won the respect and cooperation of the new French regime, from Carnot himself to the rank and file of the diplomatic corps, to the point that he was now referred to as the Irish Minister. Madget would be there, the Irish member of the Ministry of Staff, Colonel Shee and of course, General Clarke, the head of the war department, all of whom, despite Bantry, were solidly behind Wolfe Tone's second effort at an armada. He was hopeful that Mr. James Monro would attend the celebrations, a man who loved all things

French and tipped to be a future President of America, but also a friend of Ireland.

For half an hour, Attridge brought him up to date with affairs at home, especially in Ulster, where the whole province is "brimming with revolt"....James was careful not to dwell too much on the Bantry question but, Tone was quite prepared to talk of the matter, he had done much investigating in the past year. Attridge thought his friend looked tired and had lost some weight, despite the value for money on food and wine. Despite everything, James felt again, the kinetic energy shining through

They spent the late afternoon at Tone's new home at Nanterre, where James was again impressed by her almost saintly patience and understanding. The enigmatic character of the dainty woman, who married Wolf Tone when she was just sixteen, enthralled him, her small decent face, yielding, he thought, to the intricacies of her life, a woman older than her still young years, should demonstrate. His children, William and Maria gloried in the wonders of Paris, the house at Nanterre was a pleasant Elizabethan farmhouse, once owned by a minor Royalist. It was planted in a shaded lane on a tiny tributary of the Seine, an hour outside Paris. Matilda Tone, still a supreme encouragement to her husband's endeavours, hoped sincerely he would take early retirement. Though she had to admit, she always softened in that determination on seeing him in his regimentals as a French Adjutant General

At Nanterre, she said to Attridge, over a light snack in a shady copse where her garden sloped down to a narrow stream, that she could have been anywhere, in her beloved Kildare, only with a much more agreeable climate, the one deficiency she would admit to, being the absence of the rich pungency of the damp heathers and the rich mosses and all the other bog land essences that blow up from the Bog of Allen in late Summer.

"I'm content, Mr. Attridge," she said, though in a significant pause, he detected a hint of strain or tension in her face. "I want this to be all over." Theobold's outburst at Bonaparte last year does him no good. I persuaded him, as did Mr. Lewins, to apologise to the general and eventually he did, committing his sentiments to paper, with his good wishes for a successful campaign in Italy. However, Bonaparte never got it, by the time it had arrived in Toulon, the armada had left for the Italian campaign." She gave James a look that held concern, anxiety, he knew by now to be the normal course of her existence. "I pray there will be no more discord between them, Mr. Attridge. General Hoche, his great friend is dead. General Bonaparte is a very powerful man and demands due respect. You will see this tonight, when the crowd will treat him as a god."

Chapter 43

Six weeks before, Commander Duncan of the British Admiralty, with only three ships and a few small vessels, destroyed ninety French ships laying at the Texel. A triumph of audacity and courage, he destroyed the entire Dutch Navy in one attempt, which was under the command of France. Tone was always aware that such a disaster would put paid to his Batavian adventure of securing another armada for Ireland, but he would have to admit, that, sheltering behind it was a tincture of satisfaction, that if the great general of France was not away in Toulon feeding his insane perversion for another invasion in the east, it might not have happened. When Duncan struck, Napoleon had a hundred ships in Toulon Harbour along with his new warship, the love of his life; the massive " l'Oriental" preparing for the invasion of Egypt.

General Napoleon Bonaparte had returned from his Italian campaign in triumph. A purge was being conceived against Lazare Carnot and his Directory and the little Corsican was quickly becoming the embodiment of the New Century in Europe.

The Irishman was to have his final confrontation with the budding dictator and the magnificent Palais Royale was the venue for same and for one of the many victory celebrations.The whole atmosphere was thick and flowing with jubilant and congratulatory triumphalism.

The cream of French military and naval personnel in ostentatious regimentals was received by special invitation and Tone was surprised to receive delivery of a gilded command at Nanterre. He, and a friend were to join the party of General Desaix for a state banquet "in honour of the triumphs of General Napoleon Bonaparte in Italy."

"Mrs. Tone is concerned for your.......", Wolf Tone cut in, smiling, as they walked through the great hall, "my lack of tact, James, I promise I'll be very good."

"May I have that in writing, Sir."

**

Six hundred admirers were treated to the very best that Paris had to offer in cuisine and entertainment and the adoring crowd bristled with passion and concordance in the immense spectacle. Surrounded by his campaign officers and Directory officials, Tone noticed the presence of Bonaparte's own family, already being brought to prominence. The magnitutade of the occasion did not sit comfortably with his Corsican peasantry siblings but they were seated in splendid supremacy to the right of the main top table; eldest brother, Joseph, also Lucien, Louis and Jerome. His sister, Marie Pauline and mother Letizia, were not present, the occasion, being strictly military.

The victor was praised in song and dance. Lays, the leading French baritone, together with Madame Pontriel, performed from Mozart's Figaro, and the newly written Magic Flute. The programme read, Mademoiselle Gavauden and the Napoleonic favourite, Clotilde, performed singularly, and the dancers, the renowned, Vestris and Goyan in grateful and admirable dexterity, all praising the victor.Tone remembered the call , four years ago, when he was in Whites and a less auspicious banquet, " Aux Armes Citoyen" called out in rough celebration when the revolution was in its infancy. Here again the drawn swords, the banners and the tricolours proclaimed, not only the new democracy, but the new conqueror of Europe.

Bonaparte was twenty eight years old, and the Irishman, in the midst of the joie de vivre tried to ignore little pangs of deprivation, even jealousy twisting around in his belly. He felt alone among his smiling friends, mourning the death of all his endeavours. Hoche was dead, he had no pillar in France, the cause of the United Irishmen had been stifled and proclaimed, all its leaders, dead or in prison and tyranny stalked the land of Ireland. The failure of the Bantry expedition weighed heavily on his shoulders. In jealousy and envy, nothing is more frightful than laughter.

After the festivities the room filled with heady excitement as Bonaparte, with a small entourage of personal staff, moved among the tables. Senior officers and their nervous juniors rose to meet him in waves of welcome offering words of congratulations. The walls and cabinets were festooned with treasures of art, angelic and saintly. Cherubs and ancient faces stared out in variations of human and sub human personality. Many an Italian grotto and holy place had been left bereft of their ancient archives to the benefit of Parisian museums and galleries. Priceless relics and masterpieces from Parma, Modina, Niece, Mantua and Malta adorned the walls of The Palais, while cellars lay chick-a-block with bounty from Rome itself.

"If there's anything worse than a robber, James, it is a bigger robber. If you put your hand into the sugar jar, make sure it is in ,up to your elbow at least."

The wine had settled his nerves and Tone now waited for the little general. He was pleased to be seated with some of the officers of the failed Bantry expedition. Some had felt less than comfortable at meeting him again, especially Admiral Bouvet and the two generals, Cherin and Grouchy, but Wolf Tone put them at ease, with promises of further endeavours. It had been decided, shortly after the death of Lazaer Hoche, that General Desaix would be responsible for any further effort for Ireland. He had met again, the first time since Bantry, fellow officers of the expedition; Hedonville, Dufalgo and Generals Watrin and Mermet. Attridge were impressed at the esteem in which his friend was undoubtedly held among the elite of the Army. The two Irishmen were introduced to, as General Desaix, proclaimed, an up and coming leader, the tall dark haired General Humbert, who had already expressed a wish to be included in any further Armee d'Irlande.

Tone was inwardly amused to find Bonaparte furtively peeking in his direction through heads and shoulders of his admirers, as all the time the august procession wound its way toward his table.

"I believe, Gentlemen", smiled Tone, raising his voice above the din, glass in hand as he stood, "that Bantry was not all together a failure. I believe, in the foul weather, that ours was a superb feat of seamanship, that we were able to take fifty ships out of Brest and under the very noses of Admirals like Colpays, Brideport and Pellew, without being detected. So help me, Gentlemen, they were chasing their tails all over the South Atlantic, while, but for the weather, we would have outclassed and outsailed them."

There were ripples of agreement all around and he asked them to raise a toast to General Hoche, And there were ripples of agreement all 'round. "Lord Shannon of Cork, himself being an Englishman in my country, was heard to sing on the banks of the River Lee;

"Oh by my soul 'tis a Protestant wind, Lillibulero, Bullen-a-lee.

"So I finished the verse for him and wrote, as I cannot sing, Gentlemen:

"The next one that comes will be Catholic bound, Lillibulero and Ireland be free."

Further laughter and suddenly Napoleon Bonaparte was standing there.

His authority was painfully evident, deferred by his peers. He looked older than he did, a year ago, more a sense of restraint about him. His hair was cut in a boyish style, short to back and sides and a fringe combed forward to hide a receding hair line. His uniform was of black silk jacket, with red braiding, matching his britches. The high collar was heavily embossed in gold crochet delicate design as were the epaulettes, the black boots, laced in gold. Wolf Tone thought the general looked very famous indeed, for there was a hint of regal dynamism in his approach, through which a glimmer of magnanimous benevolence was allowed to seep through.

The little general has spent too much time in the company of Popes, thought the Irishman, monastic incarceration has given a kind of altruism to the stoop of his head.

Attridge saw in the general immediately, a man overwhelmed with his own prestige.

Despite General Grouchy's failure at Bantry Bay, Bonaparte shook his hand, his benevolence shining out, addressing him by his first name; Emmanuel, then the others, alternating between their rank and "citoyen". He ignored Bouvet completely, to the admiral's annoyance. It was already abroad that he blamed the Admiral's lack of commitment and fortitude for the failure, in the absence of de Galles.

"Well, Mr. Tone, we meet again, and I see they found an insignia for you, Adjutant indeed."

The spark, already lit with half a sentence. James saw Tone bristling and felt the sweat at the back of his neck.

"May I congratulate The General on his success in Italy." There was no handshake and as the Irishman resumed his seat, others dithered in indecision as to follow, and were rescued when Bonaparte himself decided to take a seat. Snub for snub, thought Attridge, Napoleon had no choice but to sit. His aids scurried to pour wine for him and Tone recognised in one companion at least, the sensitive manifestation of the General's latent homosexuality. Tone's obvious interest in the young handsome man unsettled the Frenchman and Bonaparte dismissed the youth immediately.

"Thank you, Sir, but then you never understood my going there, if I recall."

"I still don't, General."

He was again on the edge of provocation by this cool, impassive, unshakable Irishman.

"And gone to Ireland instead?"

Tone smiled matter-of-factly. "It was your decision not to General, yours to make."

"Yes, it was, but then you had Hoche and I am sorry for your loss, he was your friend."

"Thank you," Wolfe Tone acknowledged.

"But also a fool, a fool that he was unable to execute a landing in a deserted backward country with an armada of fifty ships, and nobody to oppose him."

The smile was incongruous in him and suddenly he dropped it and, looking from one to the other around the table with aristocratic disregard he tightened his little mouth in emphasis.

"Better had he died in glory under a ship's bow or on a rock crevice in this Bantry, than in his bed. His disastrous campaign to your country,

Sir, I say, put an end to him at any rate."

General Grouchy interrupted sheepishly, "I believe the General is being unkind to Adjutant Tone and to General Hoche, if any blame is to be apportioned, it should be....."

"Blame?" Napoleon's eyes blazed, his voice rising. "Blame?, it was downright incompetence and cowardice, Citizen, he was the Commander. Fifty ships, twenty five thousand men and nothing to show for it but a clean pair of heels. Cowardice, Sir, rank cowardice." He threw a jaundiced look at Bouvet and the big Naval Officer, ten years his senior, cowered under the onslaught.

The half smile returned, full of implications. "Tut-Tut-Tut, I say, half the ships half the manpower. A commander doesn't get lost at sea, Gentlemen. I have read the report of the department of the marine, 'tis but a Sunday's sail."

"He does, Sir, if the ship's captain under whose care he sails is in the pocket of the enemy." Tone was circumspect with great difficulty, remaining courteous all the time.

"And can the Irishman prove the allegation that the Captain of the Fraternity was in the pay of the British, it is a most serious accusation, Sir, against the French Navy."

"I said the enemy, General," said Tone, easily, but his composure was slipping.

"Irish then," spat the general.

"Even French," quipped Wolfe Tone.

Bonaparte's frown darkened further and he looked about the table in enquiry.

"The same Captain now sits on your senior staff in Toulon, where you prepare for your invasion of Egypt. You hold him in high esteem, yet as a senior Naval Captain, while his Admiral was ill and I'm told delirious, managed to get lost between Brest and Ireland, with General Hoche, who never was a sailor, at his mercy. Tone smiled, tut-tut-tut indeed General Bonaparte, for indeed 'tis but a Sunday sail."

Euphoria around the table heightened and as this was the only table Napoleon chose to sit at, ears close by were bending to what was looking like a confrontation.

Knowing, that he was never going to get another armada through the offices of Napoleon, the Irishman turned the knife further. "Your Captain Villaneaux purposefully lost the Fraternite for which he was highly paid and praised. He sailed as far north as Newfoundland in his efforts to discredit Commander Hoche, all the while blaming the weather. You see, General, I too have done my investigations, but, it seems, more thoroughly than yourself, with respect."

Bonaparte turned to Grouchy. "Is this correct, Emmanuel?"

"It is commonly said, General," said Grouchy.

Without looking at any of his aids, he said, "see we look into this matter of Villaneaux," then addressing Tone again, "I say you were ill governed by General Hoche, whose whole purpose in the matter of Ireland is questionable. You have heard of Fustador, Mr. Tone.

"I know about Fustadore., General."

"September, the month of the fruit harvest in France."

Wolfe Tone felt the undercurrent of tension knot his insides further. The first stirrings of contempt before the enormity of what Bonaparte was about to say, churned in him, and he threw a quick glance at the others, for he had heard stirrings of rumours set about in propaganda.

"It is also the name of the coup d'état on September 4th., while I was away, that your benefactor and friend was involved in a conspiracy to restore the Bourbons to power and to his bed."

The Irishman's face turned to one of indifference, as if he hadn't heard and the French General was goaded to further oratory. "Citizen Barras, himself a leader in the coup, promoted your Hoche to War Minister," he shouted, playing now to the gallery.

Then the Irishman smiled. In a voice full of riducule, he said, "your contempt for both men is admirable, but understandable, but the object of your ire has nothing to do with political affairs, or with a coup. You spend too much time out of France, General."

Big men shifted uncomfortably in their seats, as Wilfe Tone continued.

"In the time of Furstidore, General Hoche was dying in his bed and I was with him constantly. As a recognition for his bravery and genius, he received his seal of office from the Directory, on the same day, he received the Last Rights." Then he said, raising his voice a decibel, "look for your perfidy and your enemies somewhere else, General."

For the first time, Attridge saw, what he recognised as a beaten man and The Little General said, furiously, "should I look for it in Ireland, ADJUTENT?"

"Look for them in France, Sir, and they are most certainly in England, not in the East. You continue to pursue your personal dream eastward, when France's enemy is on her doorstep."

In the background, Beethoven's Piano Concerto belted out and yet more were moving toward the conflict.

"You criticize my adventures in the east." Bonaparte looked to the others for support, with a septic half smile. It wasn't forthcoming

"What then would the Irishman have me do about Egypt?", he asked, mockingly, accepting wine.

297

Wolfe Tone, sipped from his glass in tandem. "I have once before, when you were preparing for the Italian campaign made you an answer to that question, Sir, and I repeat now, "leave it alone, General.""

The simplicity of the reply was audacious and more so with the genuine broad smile that delivered it in its perfection and a nervous titter went up, here and there a brave laughter.

Napoleon's voice was almost exaggerated, a quiver appearing at its edge, it was a battlefield across a square of white linen

"You persist with this talk of a great debt owed to your country. You make us sick with your constant talk of the Irish at Ypers and Cremona and Landen with the so called Irish Brigade. We are tired of it, Sir, it is all in the past, this obsession with Fontenoy. You found an easy shoulder in Hoche and even Robespierre. We have more pressing business in the preservation of France and we might talk of Ireland at another time." He stood to go.

Then James Attridge saw a part of Theobold Wolf Tone he never knew existed, another soul side, seldom shown to the world, but it manifested itself on the floor of The Palais Royale there and then. Tone's eyes smarted with emotion, all cordiality gone. He stood up in a spastic dogged movement. "I talk of Fontenoy, General, at your displeasure. Whether we fought for royalists or revolutionaries, without thirty five thousand Irishmen at Fontenoy, when we took the day, the British, the Dutch and the Hanoverians would have gone on to carve up this country, just fifty years ago and there would have been an end to the French Nation, and you would be now on your four acre farm in Corsica milking a few sick cows."

He raised his voice in emphasis. "There would have been no need for a glorious revolution in France, General, for there would have been no France to liberate."

Looking at him now, in his finery, a king in the making, before his adoring and fearing public, Wolfe Tone remembered another day, some five years ago on the Pont Royale, a young lieutenant, his lank dark hair resting on his collar, matted and greased, the print of his hat, a tracery on the crown of his head,his uniform; ill fitting. He was in command of a company of dragoons, escorting a tumbril full of sorrowful and terrified royalists to the Guillotine. The victims, seven men and four women had matching numbered tags, one pinned to an ear lobe and a matching one, to a lapel or a bodice. A youth in the crowd had explained to the visiting Irishman, who that afternoon, had a meeting with Robespierre and Marat to borrow a few ships for Ireland, that the reason for the tags was to match the severed head to the body after execution.

A group of faction fighters had suddenly appeared from a delta of streets, off Rue Saint Hanore, armed and bent on destruction. The little lieutenant's reply was swift and ruthless. While his men engaged in a street battle, Bonaparte and one dragoon climbed the rungs of the cart and shot the condemned prisoners, like fish in a barrel. The little man's rasping voice pummelled the air in an all encompassing control of the army and citizens alike, who cowered before his verbal onslaught. He was a bully then, thought Tone, he's a bully now.

For now, the General was on the receiving end of an Irish onslaught. "You amass a huge armada at Toulon for an expedition to Egypt, while only twelve hours away, the British destroy ninety of your ships at Camperdown and the loss of fifteen thousand men. In your quest for glory, you denuded The Texel of security. While the entire fleet of The British Admiralty was in total disarray and in mutiny at Spithead and Portsmouth, you chose to march to The Alps, into the opposite direction, and you speak of commitment and cowardice. It is true, General, you do not wish to engage the British on the seas, they would destroy you." He smiled affably, through his anger. "Lazare Hoche wasn't afraid," Napoleon was still silent. "I am told your new ship – l'Orientale- aptly named, is the biggest in the world, accommodates three thousand men, that ship will never come home, Sir."

Attridge was transfixed and felt the raw animal heat of the blood on his face, yet, Tone showed no signs of the troublesome acne that usually invaded his features when he was upset or anxious about something. He was all of one piece. He had crossed the threshold of all his emotions. There was no fear, no necessity to appease or placate. In a few sentences, the Irishman had brought to stark confutation, the victories and the conquests, the admiration and the decoration that had been heaped on Bonaparte in the past few weeks since his return, for his sortie through the art troves and vineyards of Italy

Attridge felt the discomfort all about, but when Napoleon said, "you insult me Sir, at your peril", and to unload his ire, Tone interrupted again. "I have not finished, General Bonaparte, I have nothing to do with your campaigns, though I will serve France if I cannot serve my country. I am not afraid of you, Sir, nor of your bullying. I come from a country over run with bullies, I have learned long ago to ignore their rantings."

To the surprise of all about, the generals temper seemed to mellow for a minute, when Wolfe Tone's voice gentled down to a kind of politeness.

"The King of England is a mad king, Sir, and therefore, possibly the very worse of them all. We have been their doormat since the eleventh century, through all their houses, from William The Conqueror and the House of Normandy, to the House of Plantagenet, Lancaster, then York, then Tudor, Stuart, the Bloody Protectors to today's House of Hanover. George the Third is the spawn of centuries of bastard monarchs, he headed the coercion that led to the glorious American Revolution, when he refused in his dementia to accept the olive branch."

Tone made to leave, to James's relief, but he wasn't quite finished and breaths were again being stifled in anticipation. "It is already said that you favour a single currency for all of Europe, General, with possibly, your profile on the coinage. King George the Third of England occupies my shilling." He took a silver coin from his breast pocket. Then he unclipped a tiny badge from his lapel and slapped it down on the table before Napoleon. The little gold harp shone bravely on the white cloth.

"The people of Ireland are dying for want of an ally. Give me a fleet with a committed commander and I will put your head on British Sterling. The Harp remains for Ireland."

Cordiality remained for a further minute."Engage England, or they will follow you into the Mediterranean and they will snuff you out. Come to Ireland and I will stand a million fighting men at your side, without pay, their price is only freedom."

Before the irate Frenchman could reply, Wolf Tone stormed from the room, his companion hot on his heels

The General's voice rose in dudgeon all the way back to his table, his anger, spilling over to his cowering subordinates. Cognac and platitudes did nothing to quell his anger and his sense of humiliation.

"Damned Irish," he roared, "full of ghost stories, fairy tales and goblins." His voice staggered on a pitched note of enragement and the performers stopped in mid concert."You have to be totally confused in your mind to even try to understand them at all. I'll have nothing to do with Ireland, make that clear," he shouted to nobody in particular.

Gerard Humbert, the dark haired quietly spoken general, slipped the little harp emblem into his pocket. On the steps of The Royal, frustration creased his face. "Get me to a tavern James, before I explode, and don't look behind, remember what happened to Lott's wife."

"You promised me a story, Sir, but WOW." James DID look behind.

Chapter 44

James remained at Nanterre at Tone's insistence and needed little persuasion on the part of Matilda, who gloried in the presence of someone from Ireland, the love of her country, an indulgent, though Attridge had to remind her on more than one occasion that he was an Englishman, after all.

"An Englishman by adoption, James, she insisted, an Irishman by the grace of God." He was to regret these extra few days of pampering, when he, eventually sidled up the Thames and took the Mail to Windsor.

**

The Royal Borough looked resplendent. Everything seemed to lie in the shadow of the enormous castle, spread out on a site beyond the arched bridge, a site, chosen personally by William The Conqueror, six hundred years before for the accommodation of successful monarchs.

The Royal Landscapes, Royal Tattoo, Royal Ascot, Royal Windsor, Eaton, the Victoria Barracks, the Corn Exchange at The Guildhall, all built at the pleasure of a line of monarchs, anxious for blessedness after death, anointed in their audacity. The castle, the burial place of Henry The Eight and his favourite queen, Jane Seymour and home of the famous Queen Mary's Dolls House, was changing its guard as he stepped from the coach and retrieved his bag.

England was at war with half the world, he thought, yet the nation remains obstinately and zealously obsessed with pomp and it's ideology. James recognised his father's single carriage in the waiting line, as the Windsor Castle Guard marched up Windsor High Street to the castle from Victoria Barracks, strutting to the accompanied music of their military band. Young boys played about the battlements of the bridge, while young girls fed the ducks and the swans.

Genuine Grief was nervously expressed on the good stubble face of William (Lummy) Fairchild as he removed his hat respectfully before shaking hands. His rough hard working hand like a talon, but the grip was warm and generous, and James knew he was too late. Arthur Attridge was dead these past three days.

Lummy and his wife had been in the employ of the Attridges for as long as James could remember and before, on the modest one hundred acre farm outside the village of Cookham on the banks of The Thames. Living on a cottage on the farm, the Fairchilds were employee, neighbour and friend to Arthur and his son. Anne and Lummy were virtual members of the family, having no children of their own, so affection was heaped on young Attridge, Anne playing mother, spending more time in the kitchen of the large farmhouse, than in her own. Lummy, a strong quiet grey-haired man never seemed to leave the fields, the haggard or the outhouses always among the animals, knowing all the while that his wife had more than a tender affection for Arthur Attridge. Between the two men and a few part time labourers, the farm was always kept at maximum production, manicured as a lady's dressing table , the house never lacking the touch of a woman's hand since James's mother died.

"Arthur was pretty well, up to a week ago," Lummy offered. They hadn't spoken since setting out for home, leaving the younger man to his wretchedness. "Anne had the doctor attend him day and night, but a seizure took him in the end. We hoped and prayed you would make it on time, James."

His misery had company in Lummy and his wife. "I'm sure you and Anne did all you could, Lummy, but I could have left Paris earlier, you gave me timely notice."

"We weren't to know he would go so quickly, he was often sick, so now don't be beating yourself."

Small boats bobbed on the river as now and then, busy barges, passing by, would disturb them on their moorings. Across the river, the great bulk of Eaton, his alma mater, came into view as the horse turned off toward the country, along the familiar street, the road, the village and soon the house, submerged in its own tranquil pastures, and rolling meadows, the home that once was a cherished beacon in his life, but now gave him a sense of imminent changes in his life. As the horse sauntered through the drive, he felt his association with the place, coming to an end, now that his father would no longer be there.

Arthur Attridge had made few friends in over twenty years in his secluded homestead, once a gift from Sir George Palmer of Duhallow in Wexford, on Arthur's leaving his post there as estate manager. Looking at the sad house now, again, as often before, James wondered why his father had left Duhallow, and especially as he had now seen the wonders of Wexford. All that time, James knew, Arthur had missed Ireland, pined for it. After his wife died, he would choose a friendless existence in his parlour, after his day's work, where he had this solicitude for things and but for Lummy and Anne, he fenced himself all around with imposed silence. Growing up, young Attridge saw and respected how his father had been unable to live in society, a man, totally sufficient for himself, even extended to his son. Eaton was only

302

a couple of miles away, yet James became a boarder by design, to fly from the solitude that only Anne Fairchild was able to penetrate. James often found them before the parlour fire, a tray before them and his father seemed, at times, to be happy in her company. But Arthur's heart withered, often seating himself at the window, looking out, without seeing, as his mind shrank away, hearing only the echoes of his own thoughts and finding no other inspiration. The young student wanted for nothing but a common denomination with his father that always seemed out of reach. Arthur was uneasy with any affection shown to him and was equally reticent in showing it to others. When James would work on the farm during holidays, he would always find an excuse to work alongside Lummy. Affection with Arthur had become a mixture of admiration and pity, a mere habit or duty. Father had love in him, but it was always disguised in a complex character, helplessly unhappy.

She sat on a straight backed chair, stiff and upright, hardly leaning against the backrest. Anne Fairchild was a tall woman. She would have had a beauty about her, one time, a beauty with something masculine in it. Now in her fifties, the housekeeper, in whom James always knew, from his use of reason, had harboured secret dreams when it came to his father. She was chief mourner now, dressed in mourning black, a square of delicate lace covering her grey head, her grief, fully expressed, her eyes pinned to the corpse of Arthur Attridge, transfixed in their bloodshot sockets.

Lummy, standing behind James at the parlour door, whispered, respectfully, "Anne, James is here." He called to her again and suddenly she awoke from her trance, and stood and embraced the visitor. He felt the tension in her narrow body relax. She held his hand, moving together to the coffin under the window. Arthur Attridge was going to be buried in the tokens of luxury. Silky frills and crochet tapestries adorned the bier, his father sinking into its luxury, like he was at rest for the first time rather than the last.

"We would have had to bury him without you, James", she sighed. "Thank God you are here."

Lummy had left the room, the strongly build veteran of the earth, his purpose, forever, just to please. He was always aware of the knot, the web, the mesh into which his wife's relationship with the dead man was tied, but he never questioned this muted affection that existed between the two. Her austere face showed concentra-tion as they looked on the marbled features of his father. Almost unrecognisable in its fleshless death mask, all its beauty, gone, pain and the plough of years had cleft his sunken cheeks, the mouth between them, a tight, stern and forbidding narrow line.

"I loved your father, James. "She stroked the grey, brow. Decomposition had begun to show at the edges of his mouth and at his nostrils.

"I know that, Anne," he whispered.

"I want you to know, it stayed at the door James, William Fairchild is a good man."

"I would welcome any comfort extended to my father, Anne, even outside the confines of duty, he enjoyed little of it in life, and I want you to know, that, you and Lummy are safe here in this farm, little will change."

"He called for you toward the end in his delirium, said he had things to say to you."

"We said little to each other over the years, you know that. Did he leave any note?"

"He asked for writing paper and a pen, minutes before his final stroke. When I brought it, he didn't know me. Your solicitor is coming tomorrow, there might be something there." She made to leave " I'll leave you with him now," she whispered, tearfully, "Arthur was a good man to William and myself."

A heavy odour hung in the warm room. For some reason, Anne had lit the fire in the grate and heaped it high. "You might ask Lummy to help me seal the coffin now," he called after her, then we'll drive to Saint George's Chapel to make arrangements for burial."

In his inside pocket was the sealed letter from Sir George to Arthur. He had no need of it now.

PART TWO

Chapter 45

While Theobold Wolfe Tone pursued his dream in France, by the end of 1796, from his modest digs in Ann Street in Belfast, Mr. Thomas Russell, born of a British army family, of Anglican persuasion in Dromahane, Co. Cork, had completed his transformation from Army Officer and Whig, to passionate republican radical. By now he had endeared himself to the people of Belfast, openly proclaiming himself a sympathiser for reform and meeting with fellow radicals in the taverns and meeting halls. By year's end, the witty fundamentalist, Matthew Tone, Theobold's younger brother, had returned from America and in his brother's absence, renewed his relationship with the handsome Corkman, enjoying ballads, elegies and bawdy songs with talented musicians like William Bunting. However, behind the facade of jollity and often, frivolous pursuits, Russell had spear headed a potentially superb vehicle for an eventual strike for freedom. With Henry Mc. Cracken, Henry Monro, Sam Nielson and many other influential Northerners, he forged links with the Catholic Defenders, all over Ulster and North Leinster. Tens of thousands had taken the oath to the Society of the United Irishmen, while the Catholic clergy ranted their loyalty to King George. With Mc. Cracken, Russell set up societies and clubs even as far as Donegal, westward to Connaught and even south to Cork. The United men were soon joined by the Jacobin Society of Belfast and trojan work was done among the Presbyterians, who swelled the ranks, even the Freemason Lodges presented many members.

So who would eventually light the flame?, who was the spark. There was none here, he was in France, seeking foreign aid. He left behind, the will and the conviction, but without a superman to marshal and to point the way, there was nobody to carry the nation, a nation that once had over a hundred kings. So the meetings and the speculation and the debates continued and while the Caledonian's September shipment of goods and wayward urchins, sold for the slave trade, unloaded at Fishguard, much of the manifest for the benefit of William Owen of Camolin, a crowd of more unrefined villains left that port in British regalia and retched itself, vile and uncouth, on the beach of Fair Head, in Ballycastle, County Antrim.

A Star Chamber expert, a convoluted pseudonym for a crowd of spies had sought to win favour with the establishment, folded away his barrister wig and gown in his private lock-up in Kings Inns in Dublin and prepared his monthly report for London, as to the situation in

Ireland and who was who, in her proposed strike for freedom. Mr. Leonard Mc. Nally, had oiled his way into Lord Edward Fitzgerald's trust. His closing note on the Corkman read, "It is our opinion that Mr. Thomas Russell, a former officer in His Majesty's Army, should be quietened, as he can now boast upwards of one million men embrace his cause. He is a personal friend of the agitator Tone, who is, of course, courting French intervention, once again. I suggest we leave Lord Edward Fitzgerald alone for now, the gentleman will lead us to bigger fish."

**

James had been away over four months, working from Windsor and settling the Fairchilds into the farmhouse, when he made arrangements, superbly beneficial to the pair. They would own the farm for as long as they lived, but with accommodations for him when he would visit. It would be rent free, but he would receive twenty five per cent of revenue from the very productive farm, Lummy already knew the best markets, and on their retirement or death, all would revert back to James.

He had arrived at Duhallow late in the evening. Mrs. Laffan was delighted at his return and Sir George was evidently relieved that he was safe, but the old man looked tired and decided to hear the visitor's report on France and Windsor in the morning.

He shunned the big dining table, preferring as always, to have his breakfast at Gobnet's kitchen table and was surprised to find the big blacksmith at the table, his plate emptied clean before him, his mug of milky tea being replenished. He stood at James's entrance, and to Attridge's delight, Conor Devereaux moved to shake his hand in welcome.

"You look very well, Sir," said James, evidently surprised at what looked like a complete recovery. When I went away, I thought..," he looked sheepishly at Gobnet, seated in her chair by the range.

"Thought I was going to die," smiled Conor. "Thought it was going to take longer, Sir, I've never seen such ....barbarity."

"I had the best of attention," said the smith, "but I have the anxiety to live on in days like this and nothing can be meaner in the world than that anxiety, to live on anyhow and in any shape at all". He hesitated, "I'm sorry to hear of Mr. Attridge's passing, you'll accept my condolences."

"Thank you, Sir."

Again that dark look, like the blacksmith of Boolavogue was

looking beyond his eyes, this morning his baritone was a polite pleasant hum. "He was a good man, God rest him."

"You knew him, Mr. Devereaux?"

"Yes, I knew him, sure was he not Palmer's right hand man, he was well known."

"He was a good father, Sir". James's voice faltered for a minute. "He took care of me and my mother, but she died when I was very young, you see, so there was just the two of us and a housekeeper and a farm hand. I feel I haven't mourned him enough".

"I can see your mourning, Son, the dead sleep in their night, let your business now be with the living, these things are in the hands of God . So now, what's for you?"

"Now, Sir, I continue my work as a journalist, especially if Mr. Wolf Tone remains in need of my services."

Attridge looked across at Gobnet Brennan. "It's been like an anonymous adventure, my coming here. My father seldom spoke of Ireland and I don't know why he ever left here, Wexford is a wonderful place."

The big man stood to go. "Wexford is a fine place." Conor gave him a sterile look, "without The British, and I'm afraid your Mr. Tone will be going nowhere with his talk and with his pamphlets and I say it with great respect, but we can do without pamphlets and despite our love for a peaceful life, we cannot do without guns. You cannot fight an enemy with pieces of paper."

He turned at the back door when James called, "I wish to thank you for the framing of my mother's sketches." James's tone was a pinprick of mischievous expectancy, for now he wouldn't mention the sculpture in his cottage, nor the portrait in the hall. "I insist to pay you, they are works of art."

Gobnet Brennan looked at Mrs. Laffan then sat back, a line of thought, a conduit between the two.

"They tell me you saved the cottage. "It's I should be finding a way of payment," Devereaux said from the doorway. They shook hands again and the smith left.

The housekeeper began clearing the table. "I cannot believe how well he looks, after his ordeal, I really thought Conor Devereaux would hardly walk again."

"As long as I know him," Mrs. Laffan ran on, "Conor Devereaux has been in some kind of trouble or other, though I have to say that life has dealt him blows, too many blows, all of which, I suppose only strengthened his resolve against his adversaries. He was going to get better, if it killed him".

Gobnet cackled in a seldom seen burst of humour, showing the gap left by the loss of two lower teeth, which she always said was caused by nibbling at the bone of a hind leg of a hogget."Never roast the hind leg," she instructed then to her kitchen maids, "for when a sheep wants to climb, he uses his hind legs to lift him up, so that's where all the old muscle comes from. Always boil it, until the flesh falls off"

Laffan continued. "His grandfather's lands were confiscated in the last century, like so many more. Conor would have been a big landowner around Graiguenamanagh and Kiltealy, north of New Ross". Gobnet took James's breakfast from the oven and made some fresh tea, her freshly made bread, a meal in itself. "He came to Kilcormack, thirty years ago. Brennan and myself were only apprentices then to Lady Pamela. He was only twenty two then, without a penny. He studied his craft under a famous blacksmith in Enniscorthy, a fellow named Moses Kiely. I remember, Kiely was a great blacksmith, not just as a farrier, but a maker of gates, ornamental fencing, all kinds of weapons, swords and the likes for the nobility, pikes for the peasants, bronze and hardwoods were like baker's dough in that man's hands. Kiely could tell a whole story or a parable with a hammer and chisel and a flat tablet of teak.

"And Mr. Devereaux?", James asked.

"Well, Conor opened business for himself, here in Trasna and found a great friend and benefactor in Sir George. Moses Kiely came over from Enniscorthy to try to persuade his best apprentice to go back with him, making him all kinds of promises, but this part of the world needed a good forge, Sir George wasn't about to let go, and built him a fine forge on two acres of land at no expense to Conor."

She hesitated when he said, "and ?"

"The forge then was three times the size it is now. They came from all over, not just with horses, but, for his other stuff, because he turned out to be also, a wonderful artist with half a dozen apprentices."

"What happened, Mrs. Laffan?" James said, enthralled.

She looked across at Gobnet and James saw in the face of the cook, an oblique look, a knowing glance. "I'm sorry, Mrs. Brennan," he apologised, "it's the journalist in me, inquisitive to the last, especially in matters that do not concern me."

"Conor had a falling out with us here at Duhallow, with Sir George, he threatened never to set foot in the house again."

"But he's here now", smiled Attridge.

"Sure that's the grand thing about it," Brennan said, stoking the fire of the huge range, himself and His Lordship made things right between them while you were away, and of course, the fact that he spent almost

310

two months here, getting himself better,"

Laffan tittered. "Kate Keohane had both of them pestered to put things right and she would try to bring them together, after Conor was attacked, though it was sticking out that that was what they wanted all the time". She laughed again. "There are times in Duhallow, when we all do as Miss. Keohane says, even Sir George himself."

"I intend to go and see The Master Dunn and Norah Scully, tomorrow, I've brought him some books from London, do you think I could go and visit Conor too?"

"That would be splendid", she said, "bring Kate with you, she'll be here in the morning."

"I haven't seen Kate in four months." He had it out before realising what he had said. "Don't forget, you haven't seen any of us in four months," scoffed the housekeeper.

**

James pulled the horse to the gate and was about to dismount when young Keohane came to the half door of the cottage. He pulled it open and tripped down the short pathway.

"I remember you," said James.

"I'm Brian, Sir, I remember you." He smiled broadly, the mischievous child face had gone, the heavy dark looks, blossoming in the quality Keohane features.

"You've grown."

"I'm sixteen."

"So you are."

They stood in silence for a minute.

"Are you looking for Mary Kate, Mr. Attridge?" Attridge raised an eyebrow, the innocent directness, catching him unawares. He smiled, "yes, I am, Brian."

"She went west for Queenie, 'tis her milking time." He looked at the visitor under his eyes, "the cow, Sir, but she could be at the strand now." He pointed in the direction of the river, through a low gap across the road. "Take the horse through the gap, 'tis two fields to the river, she might be on the bank, near the sallies."

Attridge eased the mare through the little gap across the road and sauntered through the meadow. The late April sun was warm on his back and without dismounting, took off his coat and slung it across her back. A wide open gap left him into the second field, where he had a clear view of a mile of river bank, bunches of sally bushes off to his right. He went nearer the sallies, but there was no sign. Perhaps he

311

should go back onto the road. He looked eastward toward Trasna Bridge. Beyond the clump of trees, Queenie was grazing, the blind hen picking contentedly at the daring flies along her back. His pulse quickened at the familiar sight, palpitating, he lowered himself gently from the saddle, and not wanting to spook the cow, tied the horse to a tree stump. There was a long red scarf tied around the milker's neck. He laughed to himself and shook his head at the audacity and at the animal's acceptance of the garment as if she were quite used to the adornment.

He stopped abruptly. Kate Keohane stood, barefoot on a little sandy bed, proud of the river's flow. He held his breath, for fear the slightest puff would dilute the sublime conception before him. She had been in the water and her only garment, a sheer white linen under shift, flimsy as a butterfly's wing, clung provocatively to her magnificent body. The sun's reflection on the running water played about her beautiful contours, seeking out and displaying to him, her luscious innocence. He stood, transfixed. She entered the water again and the loose gown billowed up around her. Like a water lily, she eased out into the middle of the stream, laying her head back into the folds of the garment, then brought her naked thighs up to float on the surface. She stayed like this for only half a glorious minute, as the water was pulling her downstream. She found her footing and stood, waist high in the water, her full breasts straining at the clinging material. Again she waded toward the little island, this time turned toward him. She stood for a minute, classical statuary, the likes of Botticelli's Birth of Venus, leaving the waters of Paphos. The scene was that unreal, almost absurd and suddenly he felt a mixture of lechery at her exposure and disadvantage and an intense emotional excitement. She hadn't yet seen him. Reluctantly, he turned to slip away and perhaps wait on the road until she had finished.

"Don't go James." Kate was standing on the low bank, facing him and for a brief minute her innocence was gone, and unashamed, she exuded an animal sexuality. She stood, one leg before the other, the line of her left hip jutting provocatively. Her hair matted in wet curls, hung to one side and she frowned through the sunlight.

He walked toward her, his head and his heart, pounding and as she came more and more into focus, she was more stunning, more beautiful than he had ever seen her. His eyes moistened as he became embroiled in that beauty and the exquisite reversal of things. In one glorious moment, bad became good, pain became ecstasy and all the ugliness of Paris and Windsor disappeared. He felt his shirt and the front of his thighs getting wet as she put her arms up and around his neck and he clung to her. They could have dried there in the warm sun, they stood for so long, motionless and pillared. When they eventually broke apart, she looked up into his face.

"Why, Mr. Attridge, I believe you're crying." Tears flooded her dark eyes and she sobbed gently into his shoulder.

"I just needed to see you, Kate," he whispered into the wet mane. It was to be a day of revelation, when secrets would be pried out. In an atmosphere of grief and pleasure, a day he would remember for the rest of his life, and not just for the Birth of Venus on a river bank at Trasna.

**

Sir George had asked him to dine with him in the dining room at four, he wanted to hear all about Paris and Windsor. The image of Kate still embedded in his mind and vision, he changed for the occasion, bringing from his room, some gifts he had purchased and the unopened letter, Palmer had given him for Arthur.

"They've made Mr. Tone an Adjutant General," James began his report. There were just the two of them at the huge table and possibly because he had been away for so long, Attridge felt there was an atmosphere of occasion about Palmer's invitation.

"I will be preparing my full report, Sir, and it would please me if you might read it, though Wolfe Tone has asked me to keep it to myself until he gives me permission to release it."

"The occasion at the Tulleries Palace was immense and Mr. Tone was hailed by all the officers, engaged with almost constant conversation, all eager to know about Ireland and many insisted they be included in his second attempt at an armada. I tell you, Sir, even I felt the frantic energy in the great hall. There was a sort of villainy in the crowd, many of them irregulars, but everyone in a uniform of one kind or another, even myself in the blue and red strip of a captain. I learned later, that our uniforms were mainly to be some kind of camouflage for our own benefit, as they told Mr. Tone that England had spies everywhere. Also, of course, Tone has excellent French, while mine is just so, so."

"There was a polite disorderliness, which seemed to increase a decibel or two, every half hour and as the night went on, I felt again, the almost hysterical gaiety. High spirits extolled the now familiar message, all over France; " Propriete Nationale – Liberte – Egalite – Fraternite."

Palmer was an attentive listener and insisted on pouring the wine. A fruit pie of Wexford's early strawberries, and sugar crusted apples was a reminder of how he had missed the food at Duhallow, as he

313

continued.

"Wolfe Tone, with tears of emotion, said he could feel the destiny and a pride at being present at the birth of a new democracy."

He leaned forward in emphasis and could see his old friend was enjoying the colourful description. " Then, Sir George, a simple but wonderful thing happened. The huge orchestra eased down and played very gently, a philigry of sound, sifting through the chatter, and suddenly excellent order was maintained for an exquisite dancer, her name; Mademoiselle Clothilda. She was Napoleon Bonaparte's favourite. His table was nearest the stage where he seemed enthralled by the lady, entranced by her artistry. Then without enticement or solicited provocation, six hundred revellers were captivated in a superb orchestration of movements and pirouettes. Superb French and Italian opera singers and the crowd showed equal appreciation to noisy applause. On any day, since the revolution, when a hundred people would die at the Guillotine or in the streets of Paris, I was struck with the warmth and obvious tenderness for a tiny dancer and I must say I wondered at the cynicism. Tone said into my ear, they kill at random, yet are wet eyed before a little dancer."

James smiled into his glass when he said, " before I could make a comment, Wolfe Tone whispered further, "If the thousand ascendancy landlords that occupy my country, if they were marched into Dublin Bay, if these parasites who live off the poor and destitute in the bogs and mud cabins were publicly pitched or hanged at the crossroads of every town and village of Ireland, if Mr. Guillotine would set up his excellent killing machine in the centre of the city and do his business, would I go to the academy and watch a Mademoiselle Clothilda?" He gave me a cynical look, "would I indeed, and let me tell you, James Attridge, that goes for your friend and benefactor, Sir George Palmer also."

Palmer exploded in mirth, bringing on a fit of coughing. "The man is right," he laughed.

"You'll read about it all, Sir, but one of the young officers, by the name of Humbert, raised his glass and, uninhibited, called for a toast to "Armee d'Irelande" and two dozen officers, among them the cream of French army and navy stood to recognise Mr. Tone."

"Then, suddenly the word " Aux Armes, Citoyens" rang out and the stage was full of the National Guard. They came from both sides of the platform in precise steps, bayonets fixed and sabres drawn. A wall of tricolour banners formed a backdrop to the tattoo as a phalanx of coordinated aggression pounded the boards, to booming drums and whistling fifes. The effect was awesome, Sir, wild and uproarious. Mr.

Tone said how he wished, with all his tired being and fervently craved such a scene of mass triumphalism for the halls and the theatres of Dublin."

Palmer sighed, "you paint such a picture, James, I fear Wolf Tone has a lot to answer for in his influence of up until two years ago, what was an innocent youngster from Windsor in England."

James frowned, " it has been my privilege, but the night was not to end very successfully, which you will read about, when Tone gave Napoleon a lesson in history."

"Was Bonaparte interested in Irish history?" Palmer looked surprised. "He owns Italy now, for goodness sake."

Attridge laughed at the thought. "French history,Sir, we gave Napoleon a lesson in French history." Palmer's wine glass stopped half way to his mouth. James continued, "they have an anthem called Marseillaise, a song full of gusto, a marching song, a good one."

The old man was suddenly in a change of mood. "And Windsor, James, tell me about that."

"To my shame, Sir, I didn't realise how serious my father's illnes was. He had been unwell for a long time."

"The eternal Footman comes to us all, Son, you had matters of the living to attend to."

"I feel now, Sir, that I could have been more forthcoming, to complement him for the good father he was, and to thank him, not least bringing me to this place."

He sipped his wine. "I have put the farm in good hands."

"I know the Fairchilds, they have been good workers."

"And now, tenants, Sir, we have a good understanding, but I never got to talk with my father at the end."

He took the letter from his inside pocket and pushed it across the table. "Nor did I have the chance to deliver your letter."

The peer did likewise, taking an opened envelope from his jacket. "I've had this letter for over a year, James, it's from Arthur, seeking and giving advice and instructions, you recognise his hand writing. You may open my letter, but firstly, read this."

The huge standing clock was the only sound in the room, James was aware of the sound intruding in on his stupefaction, like an icy code of weakening excitement, the clock and the message reverberated around his brain. Palmer looked at him, concernedly, unsure of what would happen next, now that he had entered the moment of commitment.

"What your.....what Arthur had to tell you is in that letter, where he asks me, in the event of a sudden death, to reveal to you, the whole affair of twenty three years ago. I wondered at the wisdom of such a move, but it was Arthur's wish."

Palmer was pleased to see, what seemed to be an acceptance of the message in the face of the younger man. He sighed deeply and continued.

"I have often, in the past year, sat alone here, wondering how it would be to undo the past, but that is denied, even to God Himself, the power to undo the past. All the obligations, the hatreds, the loves, the injuries, the remorse, if they could be blown away to begin again, but it can't and all we can only do with the past is to make it useful for the present and for the future."

The old man looked across at James, as if for comfort and encouragement, then returned his heavy eyes to the glass in front of him. "We can't let the past alone, James, my boy, 'tis sitting here behind us, waiting to be invited in."

He sighed again, then continued. "It's a boy meets girl story. Twenty three years ago or there about, the hardworking Steward of Duhallow, swallowed his nervousness, draped his courage about his collar and asked the lovely Heather Shanahan to marry him. I have to admit, my wife and I encouraged the liaison. Attridge was a most accomplished fellow, and my right hand, with an excellent future. Heather Shanahan was the product of a highly respected farming family from over Bantry way. Her father was a disciplinarian of the old school and looked very favourably on the match, she being his only child. But Heather had other ideas. Stubborn as she was beautiful, Heather was in love with a young artist, a wild fellow, who was learning his craft at Enniscorthy, and by all accounts, destined for the academies of Dublin or even London."

Palmer stopped to get his thoughts together, then laughed loudly, as a hidden memory peeped at him out of the past.

"We were then, as we are now, an open house, to staff and traveller alike. Heather brought Conor O'Connor Devereaux to Duhallow, to the disgust of our housekeeper of the time, Mrs. Forbes, at that time, Mrs. Lafan and Gobnet Brennan were young assistants. The housekeeper made Conor eat his meal in the pantry . He would make a habit of coming here, uninvited, however, Arthur was always civil to him, though he had the authority to throw him off the property, and when, eventually Arthur decided to execute that authority, there was an almighty fist fight, which Devereaux had been blooding for. He was a most handsome devil, at that time, big and brawny, electric with devilment and charm."

Palmer stood and walked to the window, his old bones aching. James thought he looked ill, yesterday when he arrived from London, today frail and more consumptive than ever.

"Attridge was no match for him, I had to intervene and just for the day, I got them to shake hands, and we finished a bottle of wine and a bottle of brandy right into the dawn." His face clouded over and he returned to his chair.

"Old man Shanahan, Heather's father, threatened to take her back to Bantry, if Devereaux was allowed to continue with his pursuit of his daughter, saying Conor was a social climber and a vagabond."

Palmer hesitated, then stabbed at the core of the story. "Heather Shanahan became pregnant and hell and heaven came to Duhallow; an angel in the shape of a lovely baby boy, a devil in Conor Devereaux."

James stared at Sir George, looking for meanings beyond the mere obvious. He intensified his focus, a gape of wonder and expectation.

"Heather was disowned by her family and Arthur Attridge and she were married at the ascendancy church in Carnew. She spent her confinement here and Lady Pamela, who adored Heather, found light work for her, until you were born. We were forced to have a pair of armed guards at the front gate, day and night, as Conor Devereaux went wild and sometimes was found senseless and drunk at the gates. A depression fell on him and his drinking became uncontrolled and for a time, his spirit and his mind faltered. Sadly, your mother's love and admiration for him turned to rejection and fear, until I disinherited my small holding at Windsor and gave it to them and I built a forge for Conor on two acres of land at Trasna."

James was silent, the revelation stifling any reply he might have.

"In his ramblings, Conor built the cottage, thinking she might return to him, but never lived in it. The day Heather and Arthur left for England, he tried to burn Duhallow. For two years, he never left the forge and his mind slowly returned, but he had a complete change of character and never forgave me for my part in the matter, though I have to say, he is softening in recent times. Arthur loved her to the extent he was prepared, with her father's consent, to marry her and accept another man's child. There was no question of marrying the blacksmith, a man without money or status and not in touch with the real world. I have worked hard to befriend him, always aware of his pain and his loss, the loss of a wife and a son. It wasn't until I persuaded him to move his pikes and the armoury which he and his co- smiths had accumulated over the years, to Duhallow, that we became anyway close, but it was your arrival that possibly sealed his return. He has his own keys to the sheds and he has his own forge here. I know the girls spoil him, thinking I don't know. Kate treats him like she would a father, and I know he sees Heather in her."

James rose and relief opened on the old man's face, James put his hands on the old shoulders, his emotions threatening to overflow.

"You might not think kindly of me for the telling of it, lad, but your father, for that is what you will always remember him as, told me, many years ago, shortly after your mother died, that it would be his intention to tell you. His instructions to me are all in the letter." He turned his sad old eyes to the younger man.

"This old country is fighting and dying for it's very existence. Old farts like me, the so called society, full of all kinds of folly and indulging in all kinds of vices and dispossessing the righteous, are the true bastards of this world. We are the diseased teeth and the decayed bones, and it's time we were extracted. People like me have no rightful inheritance, Palmer, Mountnorris, Eli, Tottenham, Owen, Cope, Le Hunt, and a thousand more, are here by greed and default, and in the judgement of God, have no rights, our river is without source, our tree, without roots."

He stood to face James. "Happy the man who can recall his fathers with joy and pride. The two men in your life are good God fearing men. Too often, at my table, when pushed on the subject by Philip Roche or John Murphy, too many heads have bowed in frustration and shame, because too many of us were spawned by reprobates, roundheads and tinkers. Most of us do not know or have chosen to forget our ancestry. I have no right to deprive you of yours."

Attridge held the old man close and felt the relief in the old shoulders. He said nothing, but left the room.

Mrs. Laffan stood aside in the hall. He stopped for a minute, tears smarting to break free. Then he bounded down the steps onto the gravel and headed for the stables. The big brown mare still had cud in her mouth as he spurred her through the avenue onto the road.

The housekeeper stuck her head around the door. "You told him then, Sir?"

"Yes, and please God I've done the right thing by him."

"Don't fret yourself, Sir, for 'tis what Conor himself wanted, when he was recovering. With your permission I'll go and tell Gobnet Brennan, and then there's Kate, she'll be doubtless, very happy."

"I'm inclined to think, Kate will know very soon," he whispered, sitting to finish his wine.

The mare's hooves raked the small stones and he called loudly to the cottage. Kate Keohane came to the door and beckoned to him to come up to the cottage.

"No," he called, "come and sit up behind," tapping the horse's broad haunches, "and bring a wrap." She ran to the wicket, the long grey shawl trailing behind her. She could see he was upset, little tucks of breath catching in his throat.

"What's the matter, James, is it Sir George?"

"No", he said, slapping at the rump, get up here."

She put a foot on the stirrup stone and rose onto the horse's back, feeling the heat of the animal, damp against her thighs. She ran the long wrap at her waist, handed him the two ends which he knotted in front of him. She clung to his broad back as they went at a gallop through the bridge and onto the Trasna Road, until the reckless pace of the mare frightened her. She called to him through the hiss and the thunder beneath her to have a care. There were people on the bridge and a small crowd had gathered outside of Lousy Head's whisky house in the late afternoon sunshine. Her shawl and her hair cut a wash behind her as the horse pricked her ears and drove at Feisty Dunn's hill, forelocks bucking at the steep slope. James spurred her onto the slab and through to the barn and upwards again to Kate's narrow path to where God lives. Norah Scully rushed to her door, just in time to see them disappear through the growth.

James undid the knot and helped her down. She looked down over the valley, breathless as the horse, her hands on her hips. Without looking at him, she repeated, "is it Sir George, James?"

He shook his head, "no", she whispered, her breath returning. "It's Conor, isn't it, is he dead?" She frowned, "he was grand yesterday, Doctor Seamus....."

Attridge was standing under the horse's head, his arms stroking the mane and saturated neck, his own head, close to the probing eye. He whispered to the proud head. "Sorry, sorry." The horse stood still like she was hypnotized. "Do you know this one's name, Kate?"

She came nearer and put her hand on the wet snout. "She's Sally, and by the way, I was more terrified than she was."

"Then maybe Sally will explain life to me. You have a fine intelligent head on you, Sally, perhaps you can explain life to me." Then he cried silently into Sally's sinewy glossy flesh.

"I'm afraid, James, why are you like this?" she whispered.

He turned from the horse and held her very close, very tightly, until she could hardly breathe. She raised her hand and stroked a lock of his hair back into place. She felt his sweat. Suddenly he soaked himself in healing melancholy and his crying was a succession of soft whimpers. Then he broke away from her and his crying became a hysterical laugh and he threw himself on the soft grass and asked her to explain life, because Sally didn't seem to know. Kate sat on her smooth stone and looked at him. "There's nobody dead then!"

"No, except your mother and that was a long time ago, I am told, and my...........Arthur Attridge."

"Yes, but we have done our grieving, we have given them to God." Her eyes moistened for a minute, "so why the crying?"

"Darling Kate." He crossed the clearing and the bend of the river caught his attention. "The tide is out at Cahore, Kate, your black swan is up and your mud larks are on their way for feeding." He looked down at the grey battlements of Duhallow Park, soon to slip under the golden dusk of the evening's blanket. He sat at her feet and propped herself against her knees.

"I'm crying for the pain, for all the wrong turnings we take in life, even before we walk."

She stroked his head delicately.

"You say God is up here, then maybe He can explain life to me and why it demands such a high rate of interest, why He makes life so short, yet lengthens it with its ills, it's toils and tribulations. My friend Wolf Tone used to question the brave victories of life that seemed so splendid, but which are never really won."

She didn't interrupt him, just kept petting him.

"How she must have felt, Kate, in love with one man only to be swept away by arrangement, with another, to be imprisoned in a foreign country, while her lover was left to his madness. I can feel their pain, all of them, and is that what killed her, chained to a loveless marriage. And what about him, Arthur Attridge, I hardly knew him, but he was a good man and a kind father to his wife's lovechild. When he looked into her eyes, whose reflection did he see there, yet he kept the portraits."

She leaned forward over his shoulders. "Your surely talking about the blacksmith."

"Yes, my father."

He got to his feet and looked again through the velvet mantle spread out before him. "I'm illegitimate, Kate, born out of wedlock."

"Don't be ridiculous, James Attridge, no child in the world is illegitimate, you could be the only child in all Wexford born out of love."

The lovely shaded dusk settled on the eastern plains of Wexford. For all its beauty, he felt the crushing sadness of his surroundings. "They would have walked through all of this together, like you and I, climbed the hills, rode a horse together, maybe up here to the Priest's Leap."

He looked all around at her little heaven. "This is the magic hour of legend and lovers, Kate, who knows, I could have been conceived up here with God."

She had her hand to her mouth when he looked at her again, then she took it away and her face radiated into an all encompassing smile. "Think of the romance", she whispered, "he was her prince, she, his princess. My mother told me once that Conor O'Connor Devereaux was the most handsome man, most dashing man in all of Wexford. Titled ladies vied for his favours."

She stood by the mare, stroking her forehead. Then, the surprise in her voice, clear and gushing, as the realization struck her. "My God, James, you're not English any more, not even half English." She dropped the reins and came over to where he was standing, looking down on the Dubh Eala and the birds beginning to land. He looked down into her upturned face and the tears welled up in him again.

"You're the son of Irish nobility," she whispered; the O'Connors of Connaught and the Devereauxs of Leinster, and Mr. Wolf Tone is wrong if he said that about life and the wrong turnings and everything. It's what Master O'Duinn says about life is the truth, that all human foibles, the love of living is the most powerful, he says that life is a great bargain, that we got it for nothing.

They walked toward the horse, her eyes wide and staring in her curiosity. "We should go down now, she'll buck at the path in the dark." He stood very close to her.

"Will you marry me, Kate?"

She felt the insanity of tender emotion stopping her heartbeat for a instant, the cross purpose of her own desires, flagging in the turmoil that had exploded onto his life. That life, for him had suddenly become a whole new conception, violent and sublime, a breathtaking reversal of things, bad to good, pain to ecstasy, emotion and excitement consuming him.

"You honour me, James Attridge." She stood closer to him, the horse's long back, warm against them."But too much has been trust on your broad shoulders this day, besides having to contemplate marriage into the bargain. "I'll mark this day well in my heart and you won't need to ask me again, for when the turmoil is over and the dust has settled, I'll remind you of your proposal."

Her kiss was a promise, as she speared herself against him in an agonizing spirit of delight. Her mouth and tongue moved wildly and libidinously against his in an aching spasm, full of implication.

"I love you, James Attridge, or whoever you are." She broke away, laughing nervously, shocked at her own audacity. "Here you are, a fine one indeed, proposing to an innocent girl and she not knowing what to call you."

They called at the door of The Masters for a minute. Despite the warm invitation to stay, James "promised he would call tomorrow, he had some books for O'Duinn.

"Something tells me James knows," the old man said to Norah Scully.

**

"Tell me about them," he said, pushing his papers aside as Mrs. Laffan brought him his afternoon tea to the library. He was preparing his reports for the American papers and one or two in London. Nobody in Ireland would print his contributions, not even the Journal.

The housekeeper asked for permission to sit. "Those two were free as small birds," she began. There were two cups on the tray, as young Tansey had been working with James, but had gone. Sir George was napping. James insisted she join him and she poured for them. "He'd call for her here at the yard door, on a horse, wild and frenzied like himself, and off she would spur up behind him."

She frowned and shook her head. "They were too alike, two dashing beautiful people, they drove through the world like it was never going to end. Her face would light up at the sound of his voice and she would call through a window to go home, she was too busy and could lose her job and he would sit on the wall for an hour or more, waiting for her and they would go on some adventure or other. Conor felt confident in Sir George's admiration for his skills and the fact that Lady Pamela showed great favour to Heather.

But they broke Devereaux, broke his spirit and he took to the drinking. We would find him asleep in ditches after she was taken to England with you."

"But why didn't he fight for her, I mean they were in love?,"James insisted.

"Romance is the privilege of the rich, James, still is, today. Sure he had nothing, not even a house, he lived behind the old forge, with the old blacksmith, as he does today, now that he is recovered. As soon as he could, he went back there. Heather's father threatened her, that if she didn't accept Arthur Attridge, Conor's body would be found in a ditch. Sir George, eventually made up to Conor, but things were never as you would say, friendly, not until you came back. But he has never come beyond Brennan's kitchen in over twenty years. That shed out there is his second home, he comes and goes as he pleases. I often think he feels her presence here still, God help us".

Laffan sipped her tea, then put the cup down, laughing into its emptiness. "He used climb onto the roof, by way of a ladder from one of the balconies at the back of the house, for maintenance and that, and would threaten to jump unless she came with him, it could be at any hour of day or night, or he would call to her to dance for him in the yard as he looked down at her, and she would, if only to keep him quiet, not a dance to batter the floor, but she would spin and sway and turn gracefully. He would lilt a tune and she would get the mood of it, all smiling and laughing. Then he would shout down to her again to marry him."

"Was she very beautiful?.," he asked, a tightening in his voice.

"She was that, very beautiful, daft and beautiful, she was."

"Sir George was young enough at the time, did he love her?"

Laffan shot him a surprised look. She hesitated, raised her eyebrows. "Yes, I believe he did," nodding her head. "She was only a parlour maid, but she wanted for nothing and she would, shamelessly take advantage of his affection, even teased him, with her beautiful figure and her chestnut hair and haunting eyes. I believe he saw the same qualities in Kate Keohane almost twenty years later, different emotions, no doubt, but I often think he sees her as your mother's....."

"Reincarnation?" Mrs. Laffan.

"Yes, that". She replied softly.

"Was she as beautiful as Kate?" He tried to cloak the furtiveness in his voice. The housekeeper didn't seem to be surprised at the request.

"I don't think anybody is that beautiful, James, your mother was exceptional, her mould came from another place. But where does beauty begin and where does it end, for her beauty was tragic. Kate Keohane is exceptional in another way, beside her beauty, she's intelligent and favoured in a different way. She's wild enough, but not in the way Heather Shanahan was wild, she was irresponsible in her wildness and paid the price."

The housekeeper looked directly at him."I suppose too, I and the rest of us were a little jealous of her, of her looks, the wild Irish colouring of her and her favouritism with The Palmers."

"Mrs. Laffan, I have asked Kate to marry me."

"And her reply?" Again there was no hint of surprise in her demeanour.

"To wait a while, until we can all adjust," he replied.

"As I've said, James, intelligence." She smiled, "but don't wait too long. God sends us many gifts in His silence, if we do not use them, He will take them back."

He stood to go, held, her hands in his. "Thank you for everything."

"Remember, not too long", she repeated, "though we would surely miss her."

323

There was a movement in the hall outside, the sound of a chair being moved across the floor. It had been dragged into position before the painting of Heather Shanahan. Sir George and Conor Devereaux were sitting very close together, a glass of brandy to each of them. The two stood in the open doorway of the dining room and listened. The old woman smiled mischievously, narrowing her mouth.

Heather looked down through the dark pools of her eyes, with an aristocratic regard, like she were standing judgement on them. "A fellow could cower under that stare," said Palmer, sipping his brandy, "that posture you gave her is a sort of a posture you would find in a famous place, like a palace or a great house."

An enigmatic, she floated down to them, in their mixed emotions, a mental perception streaking through the time barrier." My God, Devereaux," said Palmer, "you were always the tinker, the crucifier of convention. It's only you would sit a goddess before a filthy fire, an unknown background, you can only barely see the anvil, at least that would suggest something."

"So you're being the critic now are you, you old roundhead." Devereaux's voice, it's strength and baritone timber, fully returned, the sarcastic dart of wit, without any sting. "You never got the message, did you Palmer, but sure then romance to you was only a business."

Looking up at her he said, "you see, Sir, goddesses are born of fire, she was the vortex of my creation." Then he raised his voice in emphasis, "She IS the anvil."

"You'll need to talk to the boy, Devereaux," said Palmer, softly.

"I will".

"Soon, Conor," Palmer persisted.

"Soon."

Somehow, James was pleased to see him going from the house. He was cautious how he or Conor might approach the subject and he didn't think he was up to such a discussion on the past, and preferred to let Conor introduce the subject in his own time.

"Behind it all, "Mrs. Laffan said, "he's a shy man, maybe tomorrow."

Delighted to see a semblance of affection between the two men in the hallway, out of sight, James thankfully hoped to wait for another time.

It happened the following day.

**

After breakfast, James went to trade concentrations with Old

324

Cantankerous. It had become almost a daily ritual over the past year. In the mornings, the bull was always noncontroversial, beautifully coordinated and all at rest. Resting in the early sunshine before the heat came up to torment him, he would sit there in his front garden, like he was collecting his wits for the day. His calmness, godlike, something brutal about his good temper, as he would chew his cud, outstaring his morning visitor. A place to achieve serenity, it had become, for Attridge, until the glare of passion would rise in the huge animal's eyes and the day would pass the meridian.

Strolling past the forge and the milking parlour, he noticed the secret back door to the armoury was without its heavy padlock. He tried the door, it was locked from the inside. The big voice rasped from inside, "who is it."

"It's James, Sir".

There was a long delay and he was about to leave when the heavy bolt was drawn and Conor stood in the doorway, a blanket draped over his bare upper body.

"I didn't mean to disturb, I ....."

"It's all right, lad, Palmer told me you know about this place, though I wasn't too pleased that he should put such a burden on your shoulders, the less you know, the less your danger."

An iron crossbar was suspended from the ceiling, to about eight feet from the floor. It was already swinging lazily over and back. Conor stared, for a minute, at the floor like a boy caught in some mischievous act. He indicated a pot of jelly like ointment, a green and brown sludge, suspended over a candle flame.

"Norah Scully's anointing", he said, with a half smile and half the contents of Luther's garden."

"Here, let me." Attridge began to remove his riding gloves.

"No". Conor was spiked into action, tightening his grip on the blanket, "you don't need".

He put his hands on the older man's shoulders, "please let me, how can you get the balm onto your back, Conor, I'd be honoured, please".

It's not a pretty sight, now, it's a job for a nurse," Conor said.

"Yes, well the nurse isn't here, I'm told you sent her home some time ago, with a flea in her ear."

"Old battleaxe, that she was, she was curing my body while she was dementing my mind."

James laughed lightly, slowly taking off the blanket. "Let's see now, then".

"Leave the glove on then", said Conor, frowning at the idea of his terrible injuries being exposed.

"What, and ruin a good glove?, besides, the leather is rough. He closed his eyes for a second, holding his breath.

The flesh had drawn itself together in gnarled lumps and nodules and little canals of tissue criss crossed his back. It was multi coloured in deep red and purple where blood had congealed. The mutilation reflected the agony that he must have endured, but the most devastating of all was the red raw ring around his neck where the hanging rope had squeezed the flesh in a concertina like pattern. Even his buttocks had not escaped the savagery.

"The world was full of savagery, one time, but then it became civilized, all over the world, except here in Ireland, barbarism still has its pleasures here". As he spread the gunge over the torn flesh, he thought conversation would ease what remained of the tension between them

"No doubt, you've seen man's inhumanity in France." Conor hissed through the pain. "You're not hurting me, don't be afraid to rub it well in." He stretched his arms to allow James access the under parts.

"No, Sir, the system in France, even when dealing with their darkest enemies, it's a quick and clean execution. No floggings, no hangings, the guillotine is a humane method of execution, no savagery like our friends here seem to glory in. Mr. Wolfe Tone calls it the Brand of Cain. At his first meeting with Napoleon Bonaparte, Mr. Tone described the barbarism that is carried out here. He praised the maker of the Guillotine, who ends life in one single act. In Ireland, he told the French general we do everything in quarters. Napoleon was amused until Tone explained, we half hang, half drag, then quarter the victim, all while still alive, before we tear out the heart and innards, so we kill a man from inside out."

"I bet Mr. Bonaparte was not impressed." The blacksmith reached for the bar, and to James's amazement, he seemed to summon all his strength, leaving the floor and bringing his chin above the bar. "My muscles were all locked," he groaned, the arteries around my shoulders were severed."

There was a yard and a half between his shoulder blades. Though still emaciated in the long recovery, the fifty year old body was still magnificent. Lanky and intense, the upper body gathered itself into a waist that a girl's corset would fit, the proud Irish head, dogged in it's stubbornness his movements against the bar more supple. He lifted himself a dozen times instructing James to continue the massage. "It's good, very good," he hissed again.

His voice, unequivocal. James said, "Conor, this outrage must be avenged"

"Patience, Lad, a bitter plant, wait until it sweetens, 'tis not the time." He began putting his shirt on.

"But Sir George told me what they did, even the Rev. Cope, himself, laid into you."

Conor sighed. "Let our patience plod along, son, I have demanded nothing be done for now.

"You saved the forge." He looked directly at Attridge, a kind of pleading in his dark eyes.

"The women saved the forge, Sir, and the cottage."

"'Twas a brave thing to do, but then it's amazing what the Roundheads will take from an Englishman", he smiled, " now if you had been an Irishman, you'd have joined me on the gibbet".

James straightened the collar and helped him on with his leather waist coat. " I am an Irishman, remember, Mr. Devereaux, and you have known that for much longer than I. I bet you knew from the first day I set foot in Duhallow".

" Yes, there's no mistaking you, when I think of her". He became serious, a dark line over his eyes, showed pain and James recognised, not of the body kind. "For a while, after she went away, my punishment was greater than I could bear, but, sure, the old Roundhead up there in the house was right, I would have made a poor husband and father. Arthur Attridge made a good job of you. To make a child in my image would have been a capital crime, for my image is certainly not worth repeating."

He held out a hand the size of a dinner plate and grasped his son's hand warmly. "We'll just be the very best of friends, James, just Conor and James, I have no right to have you bear my name, I don't deserve that honour, Arthur Attridge does."

" I want you to know, Sir, that I have asked Kate Keohane to marry me, so it's important I have your blessing, you're the only relative I have in the world. When I told her last night about my new father, she said she didn't know what to call me now. I've put her right as I am so doing now with you. I told her, when we marry, if we marry, she will be called Mrs. James O'Connor Attridge".

The big hand tightened further, Conor nodded, his eyes filling. "Think she would approve".

Chapter 46

Attridge had been working on his columns while in Windsor for The Spy, The Sunday Republican, the Boston and New York newspapers and he had managed to find an agent while in Paris, for the purpose of translation and distribution to the French periodicals; Ben Informed, La Monde, and Le Moniteur. He had taken Sir George's advice to write under a pseudonym, from now on, for the sake of safety; "Saoirse", the Irish word for Liberty.

" Ireland, 1798".

General Abercrombie, the Commander-In-Chief in Ireland has, by now been replaced and ridiculed for his humane attitude to the Irish Catholics and his protestation of the bloody repression of the people that Mr. Pitt's Indemnity Bill and The Insurrection Act brought. The General returned to his native Scotland, saying he would not be a hound for King George, and would not be a part of the "ruffian soldiery", that scavenged the country without restraint.

And so, Prime Minister Pitt found his hound. General Lake became the new commander and so began the fearful yoke of Martial Law, that hung like an all encompassing shackle over the country and spawned a sickness inherent in it, that makes a man not trust even his brother or his friend. Mr. Pitt, Lord Castlereagh, the Chief Secretary, Lord Camden, the Viceroy and General Lake made up the quartet that bloodied, like ravaging hounds, one faction against another.

This reporter has read the proclamation issued to outline the danger of Catholic Emancipation and Parliamentary Reform which would lead, it maintained, to the inevitable annihilation of the entire Protestant Ascendancy. A triumvir of sadism and totalitarianism entrenched itself in Dublin, for the purpose to carry out Britain's plans for the eventual union with England and the proclamation was designed for the sole purpose of genocide, with religious bigotry as it's weapon.

God is to stand by, while a million Irishmen slaughtered one another in His name and for His greater glory. Every law which protects the rights of the subject has been suspended, making God Himself the accomplice.

With tenacity and commitment, the commander-in-chief, General Lake, a despot of associated vices and noxiousness, has taken on the mantle of executioner on behalf of King George The Third, and has issued his proclamation of evil, and I quote;

"In the obedience to the order of The Lord Lieutenant of Ireland, in council, The Commander-In-Chief, commands that The Military in all its forms, do act without waiting for direction from the civil magistrates, in dispensing unlawful assemblies of persons threatening the peace of the realm and the safety of the lives of His Most Gracious Majesty's loyal subjects, wheresoever collected".

" Saoirse".

**

Sleep hadn't consumed the priest for weeks. More a sombre inertia, it left him drained. Once, his great nourishment for his daily task, the blessed balm of nature had deserted him and his sleep had only been a troubled and torpid languor. Would he resign to a bohemian life, like Roche, like Mogue Kearns and dozens of rebel priests, free of all responsibility to a deranged authority and a thankless population. As he continued to bombard his flock to comply with the rules and regulations meted out by his bishop, the people became more and more inattentive, the new sanctions, robbing them of any purpose there might have been, to their restrained and tight existence.

He felt as old as the century, as he dragged himself through the early morning activity. Hungry and fasting, he would go to his chapel for the first of Sunday's Masses. The young deacon, Georgie Tansey, who had by now decided on the priesthood, despite Father Murphy's cautionary advice, would be preparing the altar and Mary Donovan would be waiting, recently troubled by the priest's temperament, feeling the weight of the great burden of his responsibilities.

Murphy stood at his lectern for what seemed an age, before commencing his sermon, conscious of the fact that the Hessian Military had wreaked havoc and torment on a random list of cottiers who had, last year, agreed to sign a document of conciliation and hand in all weapons, all under the direction of Father Murphy in this very church. People were stealing anything that might be construed as a weapon from his neighbours, in order to seem to be abiding by the demands of the authorities, just to get a document. But now they were being burnt out just for having a weapon in the first place.

"I want you to have restraint", he said to them, among ripples of unrest and murmurs of strained utterings. The cabins and cottages in Trasna, Cromha and the Oulart road will be rebuilt, and in the meantime, I expect kindly neighbours to assist those who have been dispossessed. We can be thankful that it is almost summer and the severities of winter no longer plague us."

Murphy raised his hands in supplication and James Attridge once again felt sorry for the cleric, a man who, of late, has had to bear, with composure, one heavy mischance after another.

"The situation in the north, and as far south as our neighbour in Kildare is serious, where entire villages have been burnt out and public hangings have become common place. I have secured money through the generosity of Lord Mountnorris and Sir George Palmer to help with the rebuilding."

He thumped the lectern. "You will abide by the rules of Martial Law and be inside your homes by nine o'clock in the evening. I say to you, that I am warned by the government that they will send the Army at free quarters, to do as it pleases, into any village or parish that fails to comply". He raised his voice further, knowing he was losing his power over them. "There is one more message", he said. Eyes, blind with anger pinned to the priest. " I have already asked you, over the past six months, to cease public games, I am sorry to God I ever introduced such pastimes to you, for they will be your undoing, and finally, a procession and declaration of loyalty is to take place in Enniscorthy at three in the afternoon on next Sunday, to mark the birthday of King George. Under pain of losing your homes and belongings, you will be there. Patrols who find homes occupied by able bodied men and women during the hours of three and six in the afternoon, will be empowered to burn them and dismantle the walls."

As was expected, Conor O'Connor Devereaux was framed in the doorway, again on his way out and from many quarters, was joined by his usual little army of dissenters. As Raefil Keane passed by James, standing in his regular place near the back wall, the young rebel, to his surprise, shook his hand and offered condolences on " the death of your father in England."

"We have been like sheep, John Murphy", Conor called out, "strings around our ears, following you, your venerating animals. But this day, you and your bishop have taken away from us, our dignity and the gods of our fathers. Be assured, John Murphy, we will find other gods to praise."

A dozen yeos, who knew almost everyone, were busy calling names to two secretaries in Hession uniform as a hundred men bounded out into the sunlight, before Mass had ended.

**

Sir George Palmer was hunched forward in his great chair. Annie Laffan had lit a fire in the cosy, the little lounge next door to his office, which had now been taken over by James and his sometimes assistant, G. Tansey. New dispatches had come by courier. Palmer came out of a doze. "Tell me about them", he invited. There was some wine left after dinner. "Devereaux is down in the kitchen, James, bring him up. I believe you're helping him with his recovery, it's a generous act".

He's almost back to full strength, Sir, his energy is unbelievable."

Still uncomfortable in ascendancy comfort, Conor preferred the homely convenience of Gobnet Brennan's world. He accepted the wine, usually more partial to plain ale, especially the dark one from the brewery of Mr. Arthur Guinness at old Lousy Heads on Trasna Bridge. Devereaux had long ago left off drinking whiskey, which one time, almost killed him, more potent than the desecration to his body by Rev. Cope and his henchmen.

"My source has informed me of the atrocities that have taken place in the north, over the past two months, some of them before I went to France." James opened some papers and continued. "These happenings are coming nearer to us all the time, people are being killed, in many cases for no reason, but for complying with the authorities in handing up weapons in return for a letter of pardon by some magistrate, a pardon which a Hessian or a Yeo, will comply with at his own discretion. Carnew, Narraghamore, Kilcullen, Stratford, the huge massacre at Dunlavin, on the streets outside Dublin castle, Naas, Prosperous, Old Kilcullen and Slane. These happenings are on our doorstep."

Attridge hesitated before opening his most recent report. Sir George chewed on some imaginary morsel. The blacksmith rose and stood in the window, looking into a dark country which had become bereft of common sense. The glass shook in his hand and he emptied it for fear it might spill over. He came back and filled it again.

"This is an account of Carlow, where four thousand rebels camped on the lawn of Sir Edward Crosbie, all with his permission."

Palmer raised his eyebrows in disbelief. "Four Thousand?"

"The Carlow garrison had already been ratted to and they were waiting for the rebels. Many of them had surrendered, but the militia slaughtered them, even those who had surrendered. They hanged Crosbie and used his head as a football in the square. Then they sought out the so called safe houses and over two hundred cabins and cottages were burnt, many with the unfortunate people inside them. My contact, I quote; "it was barbaric, a slaughter on a mass scale."

"I knew Crosbie", said Palmer, "a good sort." His eyes hardened toward his fire, as if seeing it in the flames. "They'll be nobody use my head as a football."

"Faith no," said Devereaux, and gave the older man a look that showed the kind of muted affection, despite the complex implications

331

of their long relationship.

"However, Wexford is not in revolt", said Palmer, comfortably.

"The rebellion is at our border", insisted Conor. "It will be in Wexford tomorrow. I've said to Father Murphy, the people will not thank him for stripping them of any source of defence". There was deep frustration in his voice. "A dozen little revolutions have taken place in the past seventy two hours and already, over two thousand have died, and God only knows how many in Antrim and Down. There is nobody to direct strategy, the whole thing is without direction. Men of lofty desires, like Mac Cracken and Monro prepare the revolution while the little ones carry it out."

There was a quiet knock on the door and Mrs. Laffan introduced Father John Murphy, The priest caught the last of Conor's word; "is it true that in the absence of Mr. Wolfe Tone, there isn't a man great enough or wise enough for the people to surrender their destiny to?"

Murphy looked quietly into the fire. "James has been reading his reports, John Murphy", said Conor, it's terrific stuff, Sir". Murphy patted the broad shoulder in supplication, but said nothing.

" John Murphy, you spoke, from your altar, while Mountnorris stood at your shoulder about God and His judgement, and how on the day of judgement, he won't be looking for trophies and bank accounts, but that He'll be looking for bruises and scars. Well, John Murphy, judgement day is here, scars everywhere. I wonder if we have enough for Him. The whole Directory and whatever leadership we had is either dead or in prison, waiting for hanging, without ever holding a gun or firing a shot or carrying a pike. "Devereaux sighed, "O for a King, for a Taoiseach. 'Tis you will have to bury us, by the thousand, if this evil is allowed to come into Wexford."

James moved some papers aside, chose one and continued. "I am quoting here from my source's report; "In the aftermath of the slaughter in Kildare, Dublin and Carlow decided to end their struggle in the face of such odds and ill fortune. About two thousand of them under a Mr. Anthony Perkins, assembled on the hill of Knockalwin in The Curragh of Kildare and, on a unanimous resolve, dispatched a message to negotiate terms of surrender to General Dundas in Dublin. All weapons were to be handed up in return for clemency and Dundas, readily agreed. It is said that Dundas is a humane character, more so than most of His Majesty's officers."

Conor broke in, his eyes burning, "Dundas is a red coated British General, in that organisation, Son, there is no humanity, tell that to your source."

Murphy smiled at the "Son", part, having been both confused and delighted at the news, imparted to him by an aesthetic Kate Keohane, earlier.

"At the same time," Attridge continued reading. "It has been reported, General Gosford, was to go to Kildare to accept terms, but it was Major General Sir James Duff, who was on his way to Limerick and who was aware of the mass surrender, re-directed his march to The Curragh. The weary peasants, hungry and forlorn, had been joined by members of families, including many children, bringing food. Duff's forces opened fire from all directions, on approaching the hill. The insurgents were totally without cover and eight hundred were slaughtered. It is now estimated that over three and a half thousand have been killed in various skirmishes and executions. Pitchcapping is rampant and torture is meted out at random as a source of warning to those who might have inclinations to revolt, or those who have taken the oath." James put down the report.

"Nothing can be done, only to comply", sighed the priest, accepting wine."You had great expectations of Mr. Tone. Now he's gone the way of others, and who would know if the French would be as bad, or worse than the English, would we be the anvil or the hammer." He threw a queried cold look at Conor.

Then Sir George Palmer, like for the moment, he felt the depression lifting, looked at Murphy, a long searching observation. In his old head, there was a sense of events happening, and he wondered exactly what the priest meant by that last remark.

"James", he said, cautiously, looking at Conor for a reaction, "take Father Murphy to see Old Cantankerous".

"I know that animal, Palmer", laughed John, not within a mile, thank you." He frowned, "and what do I want with Cantankerous at this hour?"

The blacksmith looked in amazement at the peer, thinking he had lost his reason. "Before the light fades, James", Palmer nodded, I had one of the men shift the bull earlier."

"You'll regret this, Palmer", Conor said, "for God sake man!"

"I don't think so, go with them."

"What is going on?" Murphy followed the younger man through the kitchen, Devereaux following. Brennan heard the priest say, "what a name to give a bull, anyway." Conor looked at her, concern darkening his features and she wondered what the matter was, until, through her little window onto the yard, the bull missing, she saw them going through his quarters and her heart tightened.

James had taken one of the heavy lamps from the overhang. He opened the secret door at the back of Cantankerous's quarters and locked it again from the inside. Almost immediately, the farmhands carefully tempted the bull back into his own space, locking the gates to the outer meadow. James saw the concern in the priest's eyes. "It's all right Father John, we'll be exiting through another secret door."

They could hear the massive animal moving next door, his breath, in spurts against the wall. The lamp lit up sections of the armoury and the priest looked about in wonder. Like tall assiduous sentinels, the pikes, as many as three thousand of them, looked down at him, the proud spears and curled sharp hooks, some glinted in the lamp's light, others less bright, coated in a dust film or rusted metal, in their long confinement. Murphy squinted beyond the lamp's power and Devereaux studied his reactions, especially when they became accustomed to the half light and the priest looked with wonder at the stacks of muskets and ammunition, rifles and blunderbusses in heaps like bundles of disbanded sheaves.

To the questions written on the face of the priest, Attridge said, "ten years, Palmer tells me, Conor and others like him have been making, stealing and carrying."

"Others?" Murphy looked at the blacksmith.

"There are twenty seven blacksmiths in north Wexford, John Murphy, and not all of them are just shoeing horses, in fact some of us are so busy in other directions, the creatures are often going barefoot. It's all for the protection of Wexford."

"It's madness", stormed the priest. Old Cantankerous moved in his bed. Murphy took down a pike, a full ten feet long. He held it out in front of him, jabbing at the air, the great length and weight of it pressurizing his strong shoulders.

"We had a lot of help, half your hurling heroes and your glorious bowlers. We have weapons under mountains, in potato beds, even in our own beds, John Murphy, and 'tis fearful I am that the weight of this knowledge will persuade you to apply to that sanctimonious conscience of yours."

"Madness", he repeated, " and all the iron, the steel, the guns, who paid for all of this?"

"Gates, railings, the grand estates, stripped in the darkness. The anvil and the fire do the rest. As for the ammunition, most of it is stolen." Conor allowed himself a half smile his triumphalism shining out. "In one night, our people took a mile and a half of Le Hunt's railings and five gates from his fine estate. It is said that his prize herd was found half way to the Wicklow Hills."

"They'll need to be cleaning these muskets, the rifles, on a constant basis, they can be dangerous otherwise". The priest's voice was like a separate thing. He was almost philosophical, like a compendium of thoughts, flooding in on him. "An unclean barrel can explode in your face." He jabbed again with the pike. A foot from the savage point of the metal head, was a little hook like curved blade. He fingered it, cautiously. "It slides inside the horse's saddle strap and cuts it, unseating the rider, unfortunately, it cuts the horse as well, spooking him," James explains.

"In a war, a horse becomes a soldier, must suffer the consequences." The two men were more than surprised at the priest's matter-of-fact attitude. "Devereaux was always thorough," he said to the pike. "It would tear a man asunder, even standing a dozen feet away." He jabbed again, like he was warming to the idea. This time, the butt stubbed against the wall and Cantankerous came out of his stupor, raising his great bulk onto his front legs, his indolent blind expression, devouring the wall behind him.

In the Cosy, Sir George sifted through the papers left by James Attridge. The two men had left. Palmer asked, "Well, how was he?"

"Surprisingly accepting of the whole thing, Sir, he advised Conor that the rifles should be better maintained, wanted to know all about the pikes, and where they came from, the metal, the steel."

Palmer was holding another of the reports when James said, "It's a copy of a letter from Lord Lieutenant Camden to the Duke of Portland, let me read it for you, it's stomach churning, considering the massacre in Kildare and Dunlavin.

"It says, I have to inform Your Grace, that I learn from General Dundas, that the rebels on The Curragh of Kildare have, at last, laid down their arms and delivered up a number of their leaders. I have the pleasure of informing Your Grace, that Sir James Duff, who with infinite alacrity and address, has opened the communication with Limerick, that with Cork, being already open, had arrived at Kildare, whilst the rebels had possession of it, completely routed them."

Attridge threw down the paper. "This is The Viceroy of Ireland, speaking, Sir, the propaganda is sickening, these peasants were sitting down and eating their scraps, when they were murdered. The women and children had already joined them in their surrender."

Attridge sat before the fire, after stoking and feeding it, his concern showing. "Devereaux told us that Raefil Keane, you know, Kate's friend, has been arrested along with a dozen more in Carnew."

"More work for Father Murphy, I expect," said Palmer.

335

Chapter 47

It was on the day Father John Murphy struck his first blow for freedom. So used to feeling the pain of impotence and the frustration of being powerless, with no language but to obey, he felt crushed in the splendour of Rev. Cope's quarters. James and Kate had come to Carnew with him.

The British garrison of the border town of Carnew was situated in the attractive 17th. Century castle on the outskirts of the town. The ball alley, where John Murphy had won many of his Leinster competitions, comprised part of the domain, as did, part of the jail and courthouse. Situated on the border of Wicklow and Wexford, Carnew was heavily garrisoned due to the consistent activities of rebels in the nearby hills of Wicklow, surrounding Bunclody, Clonagh, Shillelagh, Clonamon and the towns of Gorey and Tullow.

It seems, Reafil had assaulted a yeoman, leaving him half dead, in a twist of fate in the struggling tides of his life. The yeoman Corporal was his brother, the youngster, Raefil had made a show of in Enniscorthy, two years before. Almost a man, the youth had sworn his allegiance to the king, changed his religion to the Ascendancy Church and taken the Orange oath. Raefil tried to kill him and so, warranted the death penalty, without doubt. Having sentenced him to death, Magistrate Cope handed him and a few dozen more to Sir Frederick Flood for execution.

At Cope's headquarters, the three had managed to get access to an interview with the magistrate, on a busy day, filled with the affairs of his personal state. They waited for him for almost an hour. Affectation, as necessary to Rev. Cope's grey little mind as expensive dress was to his body, he bounded from his office to meet them in the outer landing, looking down on the courtyard, the immaculate gardens and the ball alley.

They had met, of course, several times at Duhallow, though he hated having to spend time in the company of a priest, let alone having to dine with him.

Like Roger Owen, Cope was well governed in the art of ostentation, especially here, on his own patch. On numerous occasions, they had hunted together at Duhallow and at Camolin Park with Mountnorris. Despite their different background and persuasions, there was a kind of friendship of consequence, thrown together by the influence of circumstance. William Cope had admiration for the priest, but only in his athletic abilities and especially his superb horsemanship. Other than that, he saw John Murphy as a beguiler of position and of favour, turning to advantage, his repute and influence with the landlords of North Wexford, for the benefit of his troublesome peasantry. Once the priest of Boolavogue kept his horde at heel, he would be accepted, but grudgingly.

It was a week of long assizes in Carnew and Roger Owen had come over from Camolin to assist his friend in over sixty hearings in all, in similar offences or singularly for more offensives against His Majesty.

Cordiality gone, that look of discrimination that always existed in Rev. Cope, was brighter today and it shone out when Murphy pushed for his favour.

"May I remind you of our friendship over the years and of the insignificance of the misdemeanour committed by Mr. Raefil Keane," said John Murphy sensing already, the antagonism building up between them. He had come into the hallway to meet them, knowing what Murphy's visit was all about; to secure the release of some vagabond or other. "Stay here," the beak nosed rector said, in much irritation. Irritation was everywhere, Cope had purposefully kept them waiting over half an hour, knowing that noon had been decided on, as time for retribution. He returned with a clipboard, running his fingers down the list. "Keane, Keane" he said, importantly.

He looked over the board at Murphy, an undeniable insistence in his eyes. "Friendship, Sir,? between us there is no friendship, there never was and there never will. There can only be friendship between equals." Looking at Attridge, but ignoring Kate, he scoffed, "and you, Sir, it's about time Palmer kept you in line, and demand you associate with your own kind."

James moved toward the cleric, but Murphy put a hand of caution on his arm. "Your rudeness, Sir, is the weak man's imitation of strength, Father Murphy is superior to any insults which come from your septic mouth, but you will apologise to Miss. Keohane, or by ....."

"Leave it James, he's not worth it," interrupted Murphy. But Kate was looking through the window, at activity taking place in the ball alley. The main gates to the roadway were locked and a crowd had gathered outside, coming to plead on behalf of the prisoners.

Cope seemed a little on edge, wishing to rid himself of this intrusion. "This fellow Keane, half killed one of His Majesty's military. The fact they were brothers only strengthens my resolve. If this vagabond can do this to his own brother, think of the havoc he can cause among us. It's my intention to protect my subjects against such possible tyranny. Now, I am busy and you will excuse me".

As in the previous few days, like pouring water on a drowning mouse, a Barabbas would be released to the waiting crowd, embolding the sin with a magnanimous show of mercy. The one prisoner released was allowed through the gate to freedom, leaving it open wide to reveal the condemned, who were either marched to the town's square for public flogging, pitchcapping or hanging, as so ordered by the magistrates, who were now on free quarter along with their officers.

Dismissing the party, William Cope advised that Mr. Keane's dismissal or otherwise, now rested in the hands of his colleague, Rev. Roger Owen and their attention was once again drawn to the activities down below. A number of prisoners began to come into the alley in procession form. About thirty bewildered and lifeless individuals, hands and legs bound, allowing limited movement, stood about bewildered.

It happened very quickly. Kate screamed at the window, "look, O Jesus."

The Barabbas character had been chosen, a man of advanced age, who was remonstrating with the captain of Sir Frederick Flood's company, that he should be left and pulling Raefil Keane from the line, he wanted the younger man released. It was well known that there never would be a young Barabbas, to go about causing damage. The old man was manhandled through the gate, while the Yeos cordoned the group into the back of the alley. The prisoners had spent six days in a dark deep dungeon on straw, wreaking in urine and vomit. Hardly able to focus in the sudden bolt of daylight, they were hardly aware of sixty rifles trained on them.

"They're shooting," cried Kate.

To Murphy's abhorrence, Rev. Roger Owen appeared in the second line of riflemen, his gun spat with the others in his line and the front line of kneeling assassins. The last thing Raefil Keane saw, before he collapsed was the face of his brother in the firing line, one eye closed above the bolt, that and Father Murphy's hand raised in blessing from an upstairs window of the castle.

Kate ran to the stairway, and unafraid, bounded across the yard to the alley, even when the soldiers were reloading for a second assault Attridge seemed nailed to the floor while John made to follow her. Then he turned and faced Cope. The first blow caught the magistrate straight in the face, the bone of his beaked nose, disintegrating under the heavy fist. The second pummelled his chest bone, taking away his agonised breath in a sickening infusion like his windpipe had shattered and as he fell, the third caught him in the side of the head, shattering an ear drum. For the rest of his life, Rev. William Cope, would have less than half the capacity to hear.

James, wide eyed, applauded inwardly, but Kate was already half way across the square. Guns were still trained as she found Raefil. He was prostrate across the body of a youth, no more than sixteen years old, his cropped head matted in blood. When James got to the scene, he stood directly in front of the firing line, hands on hips, daring them to do it again. He called out to Owen, who gave the order to disband and he heard the sergeant shout to the crowd outside to come and take away their "belongings." The gate was thrown open and the crowd, wailing and throwing their arms about, began sifting through the mangled staring faces.

Her face creased in agony, she began stroking the cropped head, calling his name, over and over, his unseeing eyes seemed to focus on her as if in a final attempt to see her face, the face, that from a child was the solace of his expectations, today had no language for her.

Roger Owen had disappeared and William Cope was unconscious upstairs in his castle. There was nobody accountable, except a sergeant or a corporal offering abuse.

Her beauty, distorted in a mixture of fear and condemnation, she walked slowly along the broken line of Yeomen. Some looked straight ahead, over her head, others, caught up in the venom of her scrutiny. Eyes dropped before hers while others looked at her in spurious disregard, scoffing at her pain. Suggestive remarks were passed along the line in crude vulgarity, vile and carnal. It was then she saw the cowering figure of young Keane, and the hatred in her broke into a roaring flame. Suddenly, she hit out with brutish abandon, flailing like a mad woman. He tried to move backward, tripping himself and she continued scratching and hitting out in near dementia. The Yeos, laughing and jibing at his discomfort, began to muscle in on her, but the youngster shouted above the din, to leave her alone, tears flooding, and like a wounded pup, he followed in the steps of Rev. Owen, into some dark conclave John Murphy was kneeling among the dead, offering last rights. The favourite Catholic cleric of Camolin and Carnew, stood by at the gate and approached Murphy. "These men have been excommunicated from the Catholic Church, John", they are no longer to the mercy of God, you have no right to exercise the sacrament of Unction."

Murphy made no answer until he was finished, then stood to him at the gates. "I hope I will be around, Father Redmond, when you will be beseeching The Almighty for the last blessing. There are six martyrs here from my parish. They will receive their just rights, so help me."

**

339

Arrangements were made to bring the six home, the distraught mother of Raefil Keane, in her choking grief, cradled her son on a bale of straw in the back of a cart, all the while holding Father Murphy's hand for comfort. "You gave him the last rights, didn't you father?"

"I did, Nonie, and he will have a Catholic burial, for your son's death has opened the eyes of many."

"They'll come looking for you, John." Attridge couldn't conceal a half smile, "didn't know you had it in you." He clenched his fist, holding it up, "that right pile driver!"

"Rev. William Cope is the least of my worries, now, James, I can tell you."

Tired and frustrated, Murphy accepted an invitation to a light lunch at Duhallow, after which they sat for a while in the cosy, among James's papers. Sir George seldom made an appearance downstairs, before mid afternoon.

"Young Tansey has become a great help to me," Attridge said, sifting through the papers. "He writes as well as myself and is very articulate, he's a bright lad."

Murphy looked at his host under his eyes. "You mean too good to be wasted on the priesthood, I bet you're right, but he seems more adamant day by day."

"Mr. Nielson of Belfast is a great source of information to me and his reports help me to formulate my column, but his dispatches are a maxim gatherum of words and, as an owner of a newspaper, he isn't very good to decipher. G. is a great help in that situation."

"This is a report to date."

"There are now, a half a million men committed United Irishmen, and the same again, ready and willing to participate with the French on their second effort. The counties of Antrim, Down, Derry, Tyrone, Meath and Kildare, committed to the revolutionary dogma of Wolfe Tone, while the major part of the province of Leinster, outside of Dublin, though sympathetic, would bide time, apathy playing a great part in their stagnation. Lack of leadership is painfully obvious".

James looked at Murphy. "This is rubbish, Father, I have just returned from Paris. I have seen the confrontations between Tone and Bonaparte. There will be no second armada, at least not in the near or distant future."

"Listen to this", he continued Neilson's report.

"Two weeks ago, a pair of codgers, known as Renolds and Mc. Nally, both barristers who had secured for themselver,over the last year, positions of trust within the senior ranks of The United Irishmen, led the authorities to a premises owned by one, Mr. Oliver Bond in Bridge street in Dublin. The result was the arrest of the entire Leinster Directory, with the exception of Lord Edward Fitzgerald, it's Commander-in-Chief. All papers relating to the membership of the society, together with the preparations for a revolution, were confiscated. Names and addresses of the national officers were made known and all the missing links were filled in by the two spies. It's ironic, that Reynolds is the brother-in-law of Mr. Theobold Wolf Tone, the brother of Matilda Tone."

Signed Nielson".

"Shall I continue, Father?, this piece is written by Deacon Tansey."

Murphy nodded, deep in concentration.

"The violence is swift and sudden." James broke off for a minute. "And this, before today's massacre, he's referring here to Kildare and Dunlavin."

"The violence is swift and sudden. It leaves waves of hatred and malice as well as fear in its wake. Thousands of Catholic Yeomen have been sacked from the military and replaced by the so called " elite regiment", the low life of British jails. Vain and vile, the machine of cowardice is grinding its way through the nation, picking at random, it's victims. Practicing priests continue to harangue their parishioners for the surrender of weapons, but as with a personal and much loved friend of this reporter, this priest begins to realise, that, if there is one pike in a household of four men, then there must be another and another, until a house is totally ransacked. They're stealing, even buying weapons to hand into the weapon dumps in order to satisfy the magistrates. The persecution continues, despite signed documents that are supposed to guarantee protection. Fear stalks the land, afraid to rebel, afraid not to."

Attridge hesitated, G. has a footnote, you'll like this, John."

"Mr. Edmond Burke, who is known as Ireland's best Englishman, has said it and I quote. "No passion so effectually robs the mind of all its powers of acting and reasoning, as fear. Prime Minister Pitt, The Younger said of it, "spare me the details, just get on with it, have it over quickly. King George said of it, "what rebellion, where?"

"Heaven protect us", said Murphy.

"The very words uttered by Mr. Tone, in Saint James's Palace, two years ago, Sir, in the company of a man, a king, who, it seemed to me, hardly knew what country he was domiciled in , never mind the fact that he ruled a quarter of the civilized world, a man, gentle as a dove, or so they say, plays with his daughters' dolls, and he has many daughters."

"It's all written down, James, maybe somebody will tell the story in years to come. I am away now, Paddy tells me there is some activity at the bridge, I need to get home, we have funerals to prepare."

James continued in the quietness of the room. "In this month of April, on a day when three dozen and more, died in a hail of bullets in the ball alley of Carnew, Wexford Town has been proclaimed, with the introduction into the town of the dreaded North Cork Militia. With great pomp and military aggression, a circus, bedecked with colours of the British Empire and Orange plumage, with drum rolls and fifes, at their head the strutting pimp of Westminster, lord Kingsborough. The three companies of regiment brought their wives and children and whores, vulgar and indiscriminating, and lavishly festooned with orange favours. The plebeian horde shouted their anti Catholic slogans and carried banners for the glory of King William of Orange and the mad King George, on rampage through the narrow streets. Not to be undone, it is reported that companies of the North Corks were also posted to Enniscorthy, Gorey, Arklow and Ferns. Eventually, the war on the peasantry has come to Wexford.

It is this reporter's opinion that three major factors have become now, the harbinger of the revolution which could burst on the Wexford scene at any time, in this year of 1798.

Firstly, the sacking of the Town of Wexford by the hated and feared Lord Kingsborough and his North Cork Militia and the introduction there, as I write, of a rigid and brutish totalitarianism. The world should shiver that a political establishment can put such instruments in the hands of men of hate.

Secondly, the establishment of a directive, that, even where weapons are being surrendered, one in every ten rebels is being executed anyway, and where there is no surrender, all suffers.

But pivotal to this reign of tyranny, has to be, at the age of thirty six, the recent appointment of one, John Jeffreys Pratt, the First Earl of Camden, to the office of Lord Lieutenant of Ireland. This spoilt son of a Lord Chancellor, and friend of William Pitt the Younger, is a devout opponent of all things Catholic and professes publicly, his Orange sympathies and his desire for a complete Union with England"

"Saoirse". 1798. Wexford.

**

The first targets of the North Corks were the young men who had shown solidarity with the revolutionaries in France. In preparation for the coming of Napoleon Bonaparte to Ireland, they had shorn their heads in a cropped style. Now, easy targets, they were hunted down, often dragged from groups of frightened youths on the roads, or working in the fields and towns, chased into bogs or cul-de-sacs, little frightened piglets. Pitchcapping was the invention of the visitors, and Sergeant Thomas Honan, along with Captain Swayne, had perfected the art. Honan, in his notoriety was named "Tamas Diabhalta," or Tom the Devil.

Through the window of the cosy, James saw Foxy Paddy coming at a gallop through the avenue. His heart lunged when he saw that the lad was riding father Murphy's black mare. James threw open the window. "They're hanging people on the bridge, Mr. Attridge," Paddy shouted. The youth was ashen faced and red eyed, holding up a crumpled piece of parchment. "They're hanging the Croppies, Sir," he cried, they're killing them on the bridge."

Luther and Droleen were coming through the nettle path and Paddy called to the gardener, "They're killing them Mr. Luther."

James asked Luther to prepare the trap, while Paddy vomited on the cobbles. "I was to meet Kate on the bridge, Mr. Attridge." Droleen looked up at him through sheepish eyes. "I'm not too sure it's safe, Droleen, if what Paddy says is true." She continued to plead, her eyes with a steady lambent light.

"Climb up, then", he said, when Luther had delivered the trap. "Paddy, you take the reins." He opened the sheet of paper, smoothing it against his thigh. He read the text quickly, his stomach churning; " By order of the prosecutors and magistrates of the courts of Camolin and Carnew, in the Barony of Ferns, retribution to be administered in the public view, for atrocities committed against His Most Gracious Majesty, King George, in the persons of whose names here inscribed...." About two dozen names sprung from the page, by order of these magistrates, under the seal of Camolin and Carnew; William Jonathan Cope, Roger Reginald Owen, date and seal attached.

A surging monologue, like a pathetic babble of sound was flowing from the youth. "They pulled Father Murphy from his horse, Sir, and he shouted to me to take his horse to Duhallow....they'll kill Father Murphy." He began to cry and the girl cried in tandem. There was the first stirring of hysteria before the enormity of what they were about to witness.

Fate has a terrible power that no one, small or great, can escape, how it lays its hands on men. As the trap turned onto the Trasna road, the magnificent coach of Rev. Roger Owen, in the company of his wife and niece was being driven eastwards from Enniscorthy, complete with two outriders and a coachman in the attire of a prince. On seeing Attridge in the open trap, Owen tapped for his coachman to halt the two supreme horses. James was surprised to think that, with, and again if, what has come to light is true, atrocities are about to be committed in his name, Owen would hardly be out on a Sunday drive without protection and in the company of his spoilt ladies. As the minutes passed, the magistrate, it seemed, had no idea of what was going on. The buxom wife, Annabella, as eve, caressed in flounces and airs, and the petite petal, their niece, Henrietta, remained disinterested. Again, James Attridge, for a time, accepted as a possible suitor for the hand of the daughter of the assistant governor of India, rode in the company of staff of Duhallow on a Sunday afternoon, betraying his function as some kind of relation of Sir George Palmer, and what was he thinking. Still smitten by this most attractive of men, Henrietta inwardly bemoaned the fact that he had no interest in her whatever.

Droleen, the pain of anxiety and neurosis, the normal course of her life, but when she is in her heavenly copse, sat with her hands in her lap, her eyes downcast, wishing they would go away. Attridge saw again, through a mist of frightening recollection, the cleric with his rifle trained in the ball alley, and wondered how anyone could explain the eccentricities of a man that dons his best attire, and brings his wife for a ride in the countryside, just a few hours after causing the slaughter of innocent peasants, like he had a set of attitudes designed for appropriate occasions, a man who adjusts his tie when he speaks of murder.

"I'm told you were in Carnew this morning, Sir." Owen spat the words, more a statement than a request.

Hiding his surprise, Attridge said, "yes, Mr. Owen, I was."

"I was hoping to meet John Murphy on the road", he continued." You can tell your friend that I shall be making enquiries as to the damage caused to my colleague, at the hands of this priest, and but for the fact I have the ladies with me, I would visit this church of his, with consequences."

Mrs. Owen shrugged her mountainous shoulders and scolded her husband about dallying on such a lovely afternoon, ignoring all the while the fact that other beings were about. Henrietta simply looked straight ahead and wondered if she should forgive Mr. Attridge for his uncultivated mind and being so ignorant of the world he lives in.

"May I ask you, Mr. Owen, where you are going?"

Owen looked at him in contempt, but to Paddy's amazement, James continued, "it's just that Paddy here tells me there is some disturbance on the Ballycanew Road and if there are faction disturbances, it could be uncomfortable for the ladies. If you are going to Camolin, may I suggest you go through Trasna Bridge, Sir, you cannot be too careful in these times." Attridge showed enough concern to convince, ignoring

Paddy's look of incredulity.

"Sir?", the coachman called to Owen." He hesitated for a minute and to James's delight, Owen grunted, "very well" and tapped the step of the door with his cane.

"Don't look at me like that, Paddy, whatever is going on there, I want him and his ladies to see his handy work, don't follow for a few minutes, now." The coach disappeared in a canter and Rosie cocked her ears at Paddy's "click" and they followed at a slow pace.

They had reached the bridge. Consternation was rife, the place in a cauldron. From his vantage point on the trap, James could see into and beyond the melee. People were being cordoned back at bayonet point by the military and, already there had been injuries.

The Owen carriage, had sped on ahead and seeing the crowd, the coachman decided to gallop the horses beyond the crowd, having no idea of what was going on. Crowds were no longer allowed to assemble and Roger Owen said to his wife, above the noise, that there would be consequences for this breach of the peace, he would send in the army on reaching home. But the horses were spooked by the confusion all about, a shot rang out and the driver lost control, sending the huge carriage sideways into a dyke. Petal screamed as she was thrown against the door, the carriage almost on its side against the ditch. An unfortunate outrider was jammed between it and the wheel.

She seemed to come from nowhere in the crowd. James was relieved to see her moving slowly toward the trap and eventually climbed aboard. Droleen, her face in turmoil, put her arms about her sister and cried again.

The horses were whipped again and again in the coachman's frenzy to get away from the mob, but the wheels only dug deeper into the soft margin. Stopped only a few feet from Owen, Attridge, didn't restrain his sense of pleasure, as a primitive sort of satisfaction assailed him at the cries from the big carriage.

The crowd had swelled to several hundred, as many again could be seen running through the byroads to the spectacle. Just beyond the bridge, a high knoll of ground was the platform.

The Owen ladies, petrified and imprisoned, tried to conceal their fear behind a facade of indignation and verbal minatory, the sabre rattling and threats of authoritarian reprimand, lost in the tumult, while Owen, red faced and furious, tried to call for assistance, on seeing a uniform or two. The position of his carriage in the dyke would not allow him to see the real picture.

From her perch, Kate sickened at the sight. Father Murphy, blood flowing from a head wound, was tied, his hands spread and tied to the shafts of a cart, his ankles tied together. For one sickening violent moment, through a haze of ghostly ennui, she thought he had been crucified.

Six men were tied to a gibbet, their necks, strapped to a rail at their backs, to keep their heads steady. The smell of boiling pitch assailed her nostrils, coming from a huge pot hanging on a tripod over a blazing fire. Two motionless youths lay trussed like turkeys on the cobbles.

James recognised the diminutive figure of an old friend of Boolavogue, the bold Captain Wrenne, who had come back again to stamp his mark on a scene where he had witnessed defeat and humiliation in the past. He stood now on a barrel and called out in a clear voice, like grated sulphur, his face contemptuous, as his vigour increased. Wrenne had worked for a month on the preparations for this day, to bring a lesson of civil obedience outside the walls of prison yards or dark dungeons, into the light of day for the public to witness. He had courted favours among the military and local yeomanry, to build a sizable corps for the event. Outside of his own Hessian Regiment, he had a scattering of German Dragoons and Welsh Fencibles and Hompesch reinforcements. A shilling would buy their services on a quiet Sunday, a patrol duty in search of weaponry would give them carte blanche to pillage on the journey home.

He read out the proclamation, copies of which were pinned to trees and railings, without knowing that it's author was only a hundred yards away, in the depth of the crowd, in a ditch. Finishing, he warned, "we will hang the priest if anyone among you decide to break through the ranks, and we have over three hundred armed military to preserve peace. You see before you, eight of twenty seven felons who escaped from Stonebridge Jail in Wexford, caught in Camolin, judged by a magistrate and accordingly condemned for offenses and outrages against the government of this realm. We extend the occasion to you, to witness our means of dealing with such felony so you will see the wisdom of cohering to the laws of this kingdom and that the so called Croppies will cease their campaign of disobedience and dissension."

Father John seemed dazed, his head hanging in despair. Conor Devereaux was suddenly at the carriage, which was still unrecognised by the militia. He put a big hand through the carriage door, pulled the curtain aside, which Mrs. Owen had drawn for security and The Rev. fell back against the cushions, petrified, not just at the threateneing manic stare of the blacksmith, but realising he was in mortal danger as soon as the mob recognised him. Owen had not seen Devereaux since his colleague William Cope had half killed him, five months before.

"If the priest dies," he hissed, "you and your ladies will die here and

now, I promise, and I am prepared to suffer the consequences."
Whimpering in chorus came from the innards of the carriage.

Then the North Corks were introduced to the town land of
Kilcormack in a pitiless and malevolent orgy of cruelty that pervaded
all nature and reason. Within the next ten minutes, a force of evil of the
supernatural kind was visited on Trasna, with such commitment and
virulence, as to dislodge the very souls of the petrified peasants.

He looked like he had been standing with a group of jeering officers,
to the right of the knoll, until he stood to his full height. Sergeant
Hempenstall, a great mountain of a man laboured to centre stage. The
seven foot giant allowed a solid beam to be placed across the expanse
of his massive shoulders. Two aids dragged the crumpled youths to the
walking gallows, their quivering bodies flailing in protest. A short rope,
attached to both ends of the beam were looped about each neck, while
Hempenstall squatted, his branch like arms, steadying the human
gibbet. Then the massive thighs strained, as his bulk eased itself
upright. The short ropes tightened and the youths were suddenly
hanging.

"They were half hanged before, Mr. Attridge", cried Paddy," and
Father John tried to stop it and now they're hanging them again."

A great roar went up, while women and children cried out in horror.
Kate's face was a mask of intense despair, in her hopelessness, blotting
out her pain in the murder of Raefil, just hours before. Droleen slipped
to the floor of the little trap, rolled up in a forlorn attempt to make
herself invisible. Paddy tried to comfort her, she pushed his hand away.

A scream came from inside the carriage and Roger Owen, in a final
attempt to find help, called across the heads the name Bookey. Surprise
burst on the face of the lieutenant on recognising the magistrate. With a
bodyguard, he pushed his way toward the carriage, as the Croppies on
the human gibbet, jerked feebly, then went still. Hempenstall gave out a
great gasp, then dropped his sorry load to the ground, to shouts of
applause from his gallery. One had still life in him and was consumed
by sudden spasms in his final moments. He trashed about the road, like
looking for merciful death, until a sergeant finally shot the Croppy. The
horse jibbed at the noise and Kate went down to comfort her, turning
her face in against the horse's warm neck, not able to look any longer.

Conor Devereaux had three rifles commissioned to train on him and
Jack Keohane lay on a ditch, his head, bloodied and wrapped in a cloth.

Owen roared at Bookey. Mrs. Owen cried out for someone to free
the carriage

"What is the meaning of this, Lieutenant," cried Owen.

Bookey saluted. "Sir, Captain Wrenne has your instructions. The

Captain chose this place".

"The ladies are petrified, get us out of here, or I will have your head." The Rev. Owen was beside himself. "Sir", the officer called above the din, " your instructions were to chose a public place, for the executions. The captain chose this place."

It was too late to avoid the final atrocity.

The six youths, with eyes like horses eyes, their heads strapped back onto the beam, were brought into focus. Captain Swayne, the anointed centurion of the pitchcap and his lieutenant, an uncommissioned officer, Thomas Honan, who had become icons of destruction in the Dublin area and surrounds, had prepared a helmet like cap for each victim. The tripod, with its cauldron of steaming pitch, bubbled contentedly. Pain in waves was everywhere as the caps were filled and upended quickly and expertly and pressed downward on each horrible head, in one flowing accurate movement. Endless torment that would live with each victim, the rest of their lives, if they survive this day, began in that diabolical few minutes. Screams exploded on the air, as petrified hair, scalp and membrane gave way. Ears, nose, eyes, mouth and throat were consumed in one searing execution as boiling pitch and boiling flesh coagulated quickly. The agony continued in the youths and in the crowd, for a few minutes, then cold water was poured over each crown, to help quicken the process.

Even Bookey, who had so far, not witnessed this new form of torture, was momentarily mesmerized at the sight, as he and a dozen of his men tried to free the carriage from the dyke.

Women and children in the crowd, ran about like whipped dogs, out of touch with reality before them. Men were in a frenzy, but three hundred rifles were trained on them. Father Murphy strained against his bonds, calling out for mercy for the croppies.

Little Petal Henrietta Owen was transfixed. The spectacle held her spellbound, then she began to tear at the door handle, trying to get out. She was about to be sick, her speech, unintelligible. Then a mighty roar of anguish forced her attention back to the platform, and Bookey and his men stopped their efforts. The six had been cut free of their bonds and like young goats, they were still held captive, by the twin handles on each cap, as strong hands tried to pull and drag at what was now a helmet of solid pitch. Great lumps of tissue and scalp came away, an ear, a nose, all the way down to the shoulders.

Henrietta collapsed. Mrs. Owen, who had witnessed the scene in Gorey, the week before, had become very silent and looked through the far window, along the river, shutting out the whole affair.

Attridge, tears of mad frustration blinding him, held Kate Keohane in his arms. Droleen remained motionless, she had not witnessed the atrocity, still in foetal position on the floor of the trap. The croppies were being chased, choking and blind, through the bridge by a dozen marauding North Corks, led by a red haired thug, his Scottish wild guttural, a surging bombardment of malice, until the youths drove themselves headlong into the battlements of the bridge, or passed out, mercifully in the ditch. One mounted the wide fortification and fell headlong into the river below. The Orangemen were bent on further mischief and young Georgie Tansey, a cut on his forehead from the butt of a rifle when he tried to release his priest, tried again, as Wrenne and Bookey were summoned to the large carriage in the ditch. This time, he managed to free Murphy, as nobody seemed to have any further interest in him. Guns were let off into the air as the army prepared to leave, their shilling well earned.

Captain Wrenne greeted the magistrate with a smart salute. The carriage had been righted and the horses hitched.

"You will report to me of these proceedings, Captain," fumed Owen, the ladies are ill with the spectacle, now get me out of here."

Wrenne was calm and evidently satisfied with his afternoon's work. "Rev. Cope has instructed that executions and recriminations are, in future, to be carried out in public places, Sir, and your Excellency's name is attached to today's proceedings."

He gave Owen a wry smile and moved closer, "you really shouldn't have brought the ladies, Sir." Then closer still, he whispered, "she who is afraid of every nettle, shouldn't piss in the grass," pointing at his nostril, "but then, perhaps your Excellency came for the entertainment".

"You will have respect, Sir, or by God, you will regret it. Take care you will not be sent back to that cesspit you came from."

Wrenne sobered quickly. "Rebels are brought before you, Rev. Owen, as a matter of courtesy. The army has free quarter when it comes to dealing with these croppies, and don't you forget it."

Somebody threw a stone and shattered the window in on the ladies, leading to more screaming from Petal. Madame Owen sucked on her smelling salts, as the carriage was about to come under assault. The driver slapped his reins and the team sped, as Lady Owen puked sick all over her aunt's printed gown.

The half mad croppies had been recovered and were being attended to, as was Father Murphy, while he performed last rights on the two youths, hanged. Two of the pitch capped had died and a third was to choke on a mouthful of pitch before the day was out.

In the fleeing carriage, when she had stopped her heaving, Henrietta found some kind of a voice and spat at her uncle. "This is all your doing, isn't it Uncle, your name is put to this atrocity."

"Still filled with panic and anger, Owen controlled an urge to swear. "These people are vermin, Henrietta. I do this cleansing of our society for King and country."

"But you're my father's brother, they were just boys. What did they do, steal a sheep or something."

She began to heave again, her aunt plying her with kerchiefs. He eyeballed her across the puke and the smell and raised his voice, bringing the conversation to an end. "For King and Country, my dear, just like your father is doing in India."

Chapter 48

The shades of evening dropped slowly over Trasna. The air, a doldrum of dejectedness weighed down the spirits of the people.

As soon as it was safe, little bands of peasantry, little families and half families limped onto the gruesome scene and took away their dead and maimed. All the victims were from other regions, imported victims of Trasna and despite James's invitation to bring some of the injured to Duhallow, he was politely snubbed, their sons would die at home. Norah Scully and Doctor Seamus laboured to comfort the torn bodies. Father John had slight concussion and accepted an invitation to stay the night at Duhallow.

At about nine o'clock, the secret door of the armoury was pulled aside. A dozen shadows entered. A small dray pulled into the yard and thirty pikes were carefully loaded and covered with sack cloth and straw. Mrs. Brennan looked through her kitchen window, chewed further on a stringy piece of meat, with her paltry teeth, nodded in contentment, replaced the curtain and continued making Father Murphy's broth.

O'Connor Devereaux gave Jack Keohane his final instructions. About fifty of the military took over Lousy Heads public house, forcing him to open immediately after the pageant. Four armed corporals were chosen to take up positions at the door, for their safety.

The dray passed by the Inn and was stopped by a sergeant. However it looked innocent enough, a grey haired tired and suitably cowered woman and her three wide eyed children, on her way to some hovel. Norah Scully kicked the rump of the old horse and sauntered on, heading across the bridge and headed for Ferns, three miles away, where it was established, forty of the Hessian Dragoons of the execution party were staying the night, with their Captain Wrenne. Out of sight, she urged the horse to pick up speed, leaving the rioting excursionists to poor Mr. People's care. Curfew was in operation. A male peasant found abroad, would be shot on sight.

One hour later the party set off from the Inn and most of them died in the shadows of the old Norman Castle and the holy well of Saint Moling, above the town of Ferns, where, four hundred years earlier, it had been the victory site of another O' Connor- The O' Connor in his conflict with Dermot Mc. Murraugh. Before returning home, Conor Devereaux and his night travellers, hid their pikes high in the crumbling walls of the ancient tower, for use at another time.

At midnight, James heard the back door to the kitchen rattle lightly.

He had been waiting for it and kept the fire in the range, alive. Father Murphy had gone to bed, his wound dressed and his belly well warmed with Brennan's brew of brandy and wheat wine.

The tall figure stood in the shadow of the pantry door. "I didn't think you'd be still up, lad," his voice tired and coarse.

"I waited for you, I knew you would come. I have some hot toddy on the boil, it's very good, Father John and Sir George had their fill earlier."

"Is he all right, the priest", asked conor.

"Yes, he's in bed now, the house is quiet."

Devereaux eased himself into Gobnet's great chair, near the warm stove. He looked tired and drawn, and closed his eyes for a minute. Attridge studied the fine frame and could see in it, the specimen so well described by Mrs. Laffan. The strong body and character of thirty years ago was still there. The powerful hidden current of life that had sustained him and conditioned him in adversity was there in the chair, defiant and independent.

"Word came a short time ago by Paddy. There's been a mass killing of the Carnew militia near Ferns."

The eyes remained closed. He moved in the old chair, finding a more comfortable angle for his long legs. James brought him a mug of the steaming liquid. The blacksmith opened his eyes at the welcome aroma and cupped the tankard in his hands.

"Be careful, Conor", Attridge frowned. "If you were there, you could be a marked man."

"I'm marked anyway, lad, all blacksmiths are." He sighed, long and melancholy. "My Jesus, that savagery on the bridge today, 'twas a Calvary and nothing else. The Romans were there today in all their murderous vigour. In this day and age, nowhere else in the world is such savagery wreaked by one nation on another. We thought we'd get that big fella, that walking gallows."

"He's hardly human," said James.

"He's human all right, some woman gave him birth, he bleeds like the rest of them, he's just another one of their instruments." He sighed again and sipped the liquid.

An awful light of lechery came into Conor's eyes, venomous and bloodshot. "It's not the death that's so terrible, it's the dying that is so obscene. Thirty two of the bastard Roundheads, died with the names of the croppies on their lips. That big carrot head, you saw him chase the youngster into the wall of the bridge, that carrot Roundhead went to his maker with the child's name in his throat."

He gritted his teeth and his voice shook with emotion, the mug threatening to upend. Tears welled up in him. "Sean Ban Mac Carthaig, I shouted at him, say it Roundhead, say it, Sean Ban Mac Carthaig, I shouted again. And he couldn't get his thick Scottish tongue around the beautiful name. I shouted again, say it, say it, ask him to pray for your soul. It was the last thing he said, that he would ever say." His tears said it all. "I've never killed before, not an animal, they're turning us into killers, James."

"It's open revolt now then?", James said easily

"Aye. 'Tis the whole thing now, it can't be avoided, they'll create havoc after tonight's business. We're forever waiting and waiting. Half a million, I'm told would rise up if the French came. It's a leader we need, where's your friend Mr. Tone, all the big names are in jail and most of them will hang; the Shears Brothers from Cork, Stokes, Emmet, Bond, O'Connor, Lord Edward Fitzgerald, our so-called Commander-in-Chief, word is he will die of his wounds, found, once more in a back room consulting and meeting and consulting and meetings, and going nowhere. Rowen, he's in America, Tone back in France, where he'll stay, no doubt. Rowan, he'd be a good leader, Mr. Khan, from Shelmaleer, he's a one armed man, fought in France and in America, he'd do."

Attridge, glad to see the enthusiasm returning, said, "there's a man in Wexford Town, Bagnal Harvey, Beauchamp Bagnal Harvey, to give him his full title, they say he is possibly the man to head a rebellion."

Devereaux shook his head, "I know Harvey, he's not the calibre, he's as likely to lead a rebellion as.......a priest....as ....", he reached for a comparison...." as John Murphy."

"Don't go home tonight Conor," James pleaded. "Stay here at Duhallow".

The older man stood and put his hands on his son's shoulders. "You're a good lad, your sweet mother would be proud of you. Stay away from the fight if it comes, somebody has to write about our struggle. Remain a Protestant, if that sweet girl agrees to marry you, 'tis a terrible thing to be a Catholic in Ireland this day. I'll be home in no time, across the old bog road. If they come and I'm not there, they'll burn the cottage, if they haven't done it already."

At the door, James said, "Kate Keohane says that, about being a Catholic in Ireland." He gave Conor a searching look. "She said something else, Sir. On the bridge this evening, after the mayhem ceased, she accepted my proposal of marriage. She said she's afraid to marry in times like this, but more afraid not to. I wanted you to be the first to know".

"The old eyes filled again. He held his son's hands in his, and nodded in grateful consent. "Then today's is not altogether the devil's work."

"Catholic and Protestant, Conor?" Attridge smiled.

"John Murphy will think of something, 'tis all he's good at." Then a smile invaded his weary features. "I heard he crowned that fella Cope, broke his head?"

James laughed, "I was more surprised than the Reverned, Father John was like a prize fighter."

**

The priest's lieutenant scraped his boots free of the dung of Donoghue's haggard and left them on the steps of Father Murphy's chapel in Boolavogue. Summer could not come too soon, the April growth left the trees no longer naked as they had been in their frosted beards, the bitter blast of winter, gone.

Father John lay prostrated on the altar steps, his arms spread out in the shape of the cross, deep in concentration and prayer. G. slipped into a pew, careful not to disturb his friend. He knew that John Murphy's heart lived in the grace of God, but only on one other occasion did he see the priest in this gesture of entreatment, it was when his mother was dying.

After what seemed an age, he came to a kneeling position, the effort releasing the end of his prayer, "I beseech Thee." He remained on his knees for another ten minutes, head bowed, he seemed distracted, then became aware of his young friend. "How long have you been here, Georgie?" His voice sounded tired, even the strongest have their times of fatigue.

"Long enough to know you are troubled, Sir, I tried to pray with you." G. said.

Murphy placed his hand on the boy's head and G. saw the turmoil in eyes that evidently hadn't slept in the night.

"You've been a good friend, Georgie, a comfort to me, without complaint."

"You gave Hen and me a home, Father, saved us from transportation."

Murphy smiled, putting an arm about the young shoulders, guiding him to the sacristy where they would often brew tea after Mass.

"Tea, Georgie, something I wish to show you." He hesitated, "and there was I thinking it was Mr. Wolfe Tone it was that saved you."

"We did have a little help from him, right enough," G. smiled.

One of the turf burning stoves had been lit in the early morning and a kettle soon sang. Murphy held the cup in both hands, feeling the warmth of the liquid, then sipped. "It's good Georgie." He took a sheet of velum from his drawer. "I'm going to read you a letter, Son, a communication from a Bishop, words that have come from a so called holy man, but a dogma designed, surely in hell." It was an expensive sheet of paper with a crest imprinted at the top. It looked important.

"Have you ever heard of the Rite of Excommunication, Georgie?"

"I read about it once, but I can't say I understand it, Father."

"You are about to hear the very christening of evil, and I pray to God it never becomes the lot for you to have to impart it on any congregation, if and when you take holy orders. It's taken, in part from a letter called Patriotism and Obedience, first devised by Bishop Troy of Ossery, almost twenty years ago, and recently by Bishop Moylan of Cork, and now sent to me by my bishop to consider and work upon it. He calls his flock to loyalty, not to be deceived by invaders who promise emancipation and the lure of so called equalising property, because they come only to rob, rape, plunder and destroy, he says."

Murphy looked under his eyes at the youth."You see, this is characteristic of the Catholic Hierarchy, because of their views on the revolution in France."

He continued. "Of these who participate in rebellious activities in any form, we exclude them, their accomplices and abettors from the participation and the communion of the precious body of Our Lord, from the society of all Christians and from the threshold of the church, in Heaven and in Hell, there to burn with the Devil and his angles and all the wicked."

His frown deepened, laying the abominable edict on his audience. "Let their children be carried about, vagabonds to beg and let them be cast out of their dwellings, and let strangers plunder their labours. May there be none to help them, nor none to pity their faithless offspring. May their posterity be cut off in one generation. May they be continually before The Lord and may their memory perish from the Earth. We forbid the Faithful to speak or communicate with such individuals, in our public sentence of excommunication."

"Will you read it out?", asked G., frowning.

"More tea, Georgie, there's a lad."

"May I show it to Mr. Attridge?", he asked.

Ignoring both questions, the priest accepted a second cup of tea. "Now about this priesthood, young man."

"Father?"

"Mary Kate Keohane says Ireland is a terrible place for women, especially women with a brood to bring up. Well, let me tell you, it's ten times more terrible for a priest, especially one with principles, so think on." He folded the bishop's letter. "Take it to James and when he's finished with it, tell him to burn it to hell, for that is where it belongs."

Georgie opened the day's diary. "Today is for churching, Father, but nobody came."

"You do it, Georgie, one or two will come, they always do."

Murphy saw the look of concern cross the young face. "It's just a prayer or two in Latin, Son, over the head of a woman. She won't understand a word you're saying, not the need for it. You've seen me do it often enough, you're as good as myself at the Latin, a candle for her to hold and your face to show proper reverence." He smiled and said, "I'll have you conducting baptisms before long."

At the door he called back to a worried G. "Make a drop of tea for her, Georgie, don't forget the tea."

**

Both had the scars of three days before, slight head wounds to remind them of the massacres of Trasna and Carnew. Murphy would again visit eight cabins of mourning, his business now with the living in their ceremonies of gloom.

Mary Donovan had the doors already unlocked, her good face, dark in anticipation of his mood, as latent as his vespers.

G. Tansey was preparing the altar for Mass, the black vestments ready for the Mass of The Dead. Father Murphy had slept in his sacristy overnight, his personal tribute to the eight martyrs, brought to the church the night before. They lay now in their crude coffins in the dark alcove at the bottom of the church.

The young Deacon, had by now decided on the priesthood, despite Father Murphy's cautionary advice, to think on. Two new altar servers had been taken on, they stood in nervous anticipation at the sacristy door, hands folded, their white soutannes, crisp and starched as themselves. It was a morning of silent prayers and necessities uttered in controlled whispers., as the priest donned his vestments. Mary was aware his breathing had become laboured and heavy under the great burden of his responsibilities.

"And still they come", he thought. "Dejected and beaten, and yet they come for.... I know not, for I and my God have rejected them, and yet they come."

Standing at his lectern, looking down over the crowded church, he was conscious of the fact that the Yeos had wreaked havoc and torment

356

on a random list of cottiers, who had last year, agreed to sign a document of conciliation and hand in all weapons under the direction of Father Murphy, in this very church. Retaliation for the deaths of over thirty militia, at Ferns, would be avenged in the days to come.

He spoke today of the great Saint Columcille, a kinsman of the Ui Neill kings of Tyrone and Tirconnell, and who's mother, Ethna, was a descendant of Cathair Mor, founder of the Royal Line of Leinster.

"Columcille would have made a great Chieftan, but he chose instead, Christ as his commander, his motto being, "God's eye to look before me and God's wisdom to guide me."

There was a ripple of unrest when he continued. "The saint continually prayed for his enemies and left retribution in God's hands. When his enemies burnt and pillaged his houses and monasteries, he wrote," Murphy consulted his notes:

"My house, my little oak tree,

My dwelling, my mansion of prayer,

O God in the heavens above

Bring woe to him who plunders there."

At the gates, the militia stood about with their captain, heavily armed and ready for any event. They had, as always, demanded the double doors to the church should be left open. The mid May sunshine had already crept into the lower areas of the thatched building.

John Murphy put away his notes, then to the surprise of the congregation, he stepped from his altar and called for assistance to vacate the front pews, have them moved aside and the eight coffins to be brought up front of the altar.

"Boolavogue has become a haunt of whipped dogs, the blunt instrument of the law has left us bereft. Bring the coffins up here into the light and more, more candles, the innocents in our midst will no longer languish in the shadows."

Willing hands, confused but resolute, eagerly bent to the task and the eight boxes soon lay before the altar. Then, in an impassioned sermon, in open mouthed surprise, the crowded church heard their priest beg for their forgiveness.

"I have, in my ambition, to please my superiors, left you vulnerable and naked before your enemies. Because I believed it was the will of God, I have stripped you of your defences and even your dignity. I believed there is only one truth, one hope and that is to endure."

Conor Devereaux was in his usual corner, in the shadows, Attridge and Kate Keohane, nearby. The blacksmith looked at James, a deep frown showed an undercurrent of concern, that there was a change of mood, a new context.

"Well, I was wrong", continued Murphy and Devereaux moved to close the church doors. There was a protest outside.

"I was wrong, because, in life's extremes, truth serves only it's slaves and fills us with hope and with expectations and fulfils none of them."

As the priest looked down on the crude coffins, Kate thought, for a minute that he was about to lose control, his physical misery and mental anguish, painfully evident.

The door was being forced from outside. "Open the doors, Murphy called, it's for all to hear."

Devereaux threw open the doors and stood there in defiance, filling the opening, his eyes daggers in perfected hatred.

"Move aside, now Mr. Devereaux." His voice full of warning, Murphy continued, louder now that he had momentum. "The authorities have sought to impose savage and barbaric vengeance on our people and they have succeeded, even beyond their wildest dreams, until all decency, all moral values were gone. The night patrols have intensified the military, whose way of talking, we can hardly understand, continue to burn, shoot, hang, pitchcap, pillage and rape, in places where they know all weaponry has already been surrendered and in most places, never actually existed. I say to them, Wexford has been loyal to the king, that, I have, even up to last week, urged you to abandon all things revolutionary. I have gone to your cabins and pulled old pikes from the chimneys, from your thatch and taken them away the very farm instruments you need for your very existence."

His eyes filled and his voice, with malice exploded in a deluge. "But no more."

The silence was like a climax in the crowded church, as his messages fastened themselves together and Attridge thought on the priest in the armoury, his expression as he handled the pike.

"We are weary of trying, so, no more. A friend said to me, last night, as I tried to console him on the loss of his fine son, lying here before us, that this Irish nation could become extinct. We are a nation of saints and scholars, we have taught the world, the love of learning and we hold onto it as if for fear of losing it, though we cower under hedges for classrooms in our search for learning. We cannot become extinct. What will the next generations think of us if we allow ourselves become the ghosts of their dead past."

"No more", he shouted again. "Mr. George Washington, the President of America said that to be prepared for war is one of the most effectual means of preserving peace."

He lowered his head for a poignant moment then stepped down

between the coffins and touched each one reverently. "Frances Wade, Jeremiah Burke, Cornelius Synott." Loud wailing greeted each name...." Raefil Keane, died because he loved his freedom to excel in every kind of innocent activity the Almighty visited upon him. What is it that every man wants?" He looked pleadingly around the thronged chapel. "To be secure, to be happy, to do what he pleases, without restraint and without compulsion, for freedom is the fruit of self sufficiency, it is the supreme good. These sacred words were uttered by a slave in the second century and his words hold true today, no matter what the King of England says, no matter what Mr. Pitt says, no matter what Lord Mountnorris says and no matter what John Murphy says. We ask only to be free, the birds are free".

"Patrick Corbett,", he continued, stroking the rough timbers, "Sean Mac Carthy, Frank Costelloe, Anthony Mac Guire. Victims of barbaric and extraneous laws, are not criminals, but martyrs and they have gone down the road to meet their maker this day, a road we must all travel, even our tormentors. These boys loved this land, they will soon lie under it. Justice is the right of the weak and God is the great dispenser, but remember, the sword of heaven is double edged and He brings it down on the unjust."

Kate Keohane, rushed from the church, in choking grief, demanding James stay behind. He knew where she might be going, saying he would follow later. Within the hour, Trasna and Boolavogue buried their dead amidst the mire of a large military presence.

**

He pulled the horse at The Master's, but Kate had "gone up above". Norah Scully took the horse and tied him, as James struggled against the path to be with her, a warm rug over his arm. The moon, brighter now, played about her, making for her, a long narrow shadow on the worn grass. He sat by her, on her throne and spread the shawl across her shoulders.

"It's chilly, you shouldn't be here all alone, there's a wind coming" he said, "you've been here hours."

"It's the Night hag", she whispered, a tincture of respect in her voice. "The Master used say that when the whisper of a light wind comes over Boolavogue, in the early part of the night, just when the day puts on his nightshirt, 'tis the Night Hag, looking for a place to rest. The hour of cockshut, the Master used call it. What a funny people we are, James Attridge."

"Funny indeed", he whispered, tightening his arm about her. He felt her breath faltering. "In all your travels, you've never been so entertained, have you?. In Ireland, we play for real, real bullets, real dead."

"The mud larks aren't coming." Her voice faltered.

"The tide is out Kate love, the Dubh Eala is up, the mud larks will come," he consoled.

"No, the larks won't come, they're afraid to come," she cried, pointing down to the river's delta. She stood, "see, it's out out, but they won't come, because they're afraid, little wild things, they see us all as devils, they'll never come again to Trasna, the monks won't let them." She began to weep, her cries coming in uncontrolled spasms, grief that had no language..

It was an age before he said that he had promised Norah Scully they would stop for tea on the way down.

"He used to want to come up here with me." She stood near the edge. The moon was full now and the sinewy crepuscule of half an hour ago had receded and the valley was swathed in an acute cold brilliance, like the whole vista was covered in snow. "Sometimes, I wouldn't let him, because I wanted to be alone, or to tease him, maybe, and he would wait below on the slab or on Norah Scully's settle, for an hour or sometimes, more, until I came down and there would be no complaining in him."

"Because Raefil loved you, Kate, he gave you unconditional devotion. I often thought he must have hated me forever existing."

"At first, yes, he could have killed you, but later, he told me that he learned to accept. It." She looked through her tears, directly at him. "I have a small confession to make, James. I told Raefil that we were going to marry, before I accepted your proposal. I brought him up here to the Priest's Leap and we both cried and he told me, in a way that he was almost relieved, because he would be all his life, afraid he wouldn't be able to please me, that he was a rebel and would become a croppy and he would, most likely die soon and make me a widow."

She began to cry again, her sorrow, incompatible with hope and the future. "He said James Attridge was a good man, considering he was only half Irish." Then a sifted laugh came into her anguish, "and that, maybe I could arrange a conversion of some kind through Father Murphy and the king of England and maybe, make you a whole man. I told him there and then, who you were, that your were Conor's son. I hope you don't mind. It seemed to lighten his burden and settle him but he asked me not to have him at our wedding. Now there will be no necessity."

She got up to go, clung closely to him. "We could get married now, very soon, in a few days. I spoke to Mrs. Laffan and Sir George. We are going to have a meitheal, for all of Trasna. Sir George wants to open the whole house from top to bottom. He says he wants to give us a house on the estate.

She saw the questions, but ran down the path before him. They sat for a time before The Master's fire. Norah had tea ready in her flowery teapot. Master O'Duinn insisted a drop of whisky be added, "for it helps us to justify God's ways, an edict of death and destruction, made in hell, a union of marriage, made in heaven."

The Master had some books for James, one, a small copy book, with frayed edges. With his old teacher's hands, he, lovingly opened the cover and Kate, her face flushed with the first sip of the whisky, put a hand to her mouth to stifle her surprise. "O no," she laughed.

"It's Kate's first master work of literature, among other things," smiled the old man.

In childish script, written along prepared lines on the paper, he read the blurred script, like the pencil had needed a sharpening, all these years ago;

"This is my copy book, my very first,
I will fill it with blessings for which I thirst."
Mary Kate Keohane, 1782

The pages were filled with the meanderings of a child's mind, drawings, baby arithmetic, the names of her siblings, page after page reaching out in preparation for her future and her expectations.

"I was a terrible writer," she said, shyly.

"I can read every word", said Attridge, taking her hand. Looking at O'Duinn, he said, "thank you Sir, I shall treasure it always."

"The day she wrote that first line, it would have been in a hedge school, for I didn't get a school until two years later, through the goodness of Sir George, and indeed there would have been no church in Boolavogue, Masses were celebrated on flat rocks."

Norah Scully, sitting back on her settle, her usually stern features, softening, said, "worse days than them are coming, faith. Look what yesterday brought, imagine what tomorrow is making for us." She lowered her voice as if someone was outside on the slab listening. "Don't wait for the banns to be read at church, for tomorrow there might be no church, if what John Murphy said this morning is to be taken seriously. Marry now, let ye, tomorrow, don't wait. It was wise to be patient, once, but here and now it's folly."

Kate brightened. "We're going to have a meitheal, Norah, the whole village will be at Duhallow, it's Sir George that wants it."

"Tomorrow, then", Scully smiled.

Kate looked at him. "It will take a few days, Norah, but yes, sooner than we had intended," Attridge said. O'Duinn nodded his agreement, then reached for the bottle.

** **

The kitchen at Duhallow was in a turmoil. Since the announcement of the wedding, everyone was in a skittish mood, least of all, Palmer himself, that the house should witness a time of love and happiness, a moment of bliss to repay unnumbered days of pain

Gobnet Brennan was not skittish, Gobnet Brennan was seldom skittish, her mind was on the numbers to be fed at the meitheal, though Sir George had insisted, with Mrs. Laffan that caterers were to be drawn from Enniscorthy, along with serving personnel, as the staff of Duhallow, the house staff and the field workers were to be guests, this was insisted on by the bride herself. All around, temperatures were rising, the euphoria of the forthcoming occasion, not yet dispelled since it was announced that Mary Kate Keohane was marrying Mr. Attridge. However, Brennan had insisted she remain in her kitchen for most part of the day, "those foreigners cannot be trusted with my things, and Luther is to attend the fires in the great range."

Mrs. Laffan delighted in explaining a Duhallow meitheal to James, not since Lady Pamela was mistress, had they a meitheal at Duhallow. The wedding will take two days duration. "On the first day, the people of the village will come. The house will be thrown open to them. The windows of the house will be opened, front and back and the dust of the last few years will be wafted into God's sunshine. Fifty and more will scrub and polish the place from top to bottom, linens will be washed, that had been washed before, carpets and curtains dusted and fireplaces and stairways and corridors will get their Spring cleaning, and each will receive two day's wages. The second day, will be set aside for the wedding and all the workers will be greeted as guests." Laffan's eyes moistened, as she recalled, days that had gone. "Lady Pamela's yearly meitheal was the event of the year, though the fine houses of Wexford criticised her and Sir George for, as they said, turning Duhallow into a workhouse and socialising with the peasantry."

Mrs. Laffan laughed at a further memory. "I remember, Mrs. Owen of Carnew, one afternoon some years ago, scolding Lady Pamela for the way she ran Duhallow, her friendship with all her staff and the lack of culture distinction. Her Ladyship dismissed the woman, even then, gross in her body, as I am now, and not entirely pleasant to look at, replied, that before God, we are all naked and in our birthday suits, and tell me now, Mrs. Owen, she said, if He is looking at us now, which

362

one of us gives Him the most pleasure, You or I, in our grandeur, or that sweet child cleaning my banisters." The housekeeper smiled in the thought of the little triumph. "The banister girl at work was your Kate, James."

In the third week of May, 1798, the preparations for the wedding were complete. John Murphy, never as much a slave of dogma, as he had been a slave to authority, purged his brain to secure a blessing for the marriage of Kate and James Attridge. Sir George Palmer, untroubled by a blessing of the lack of it, suggested to Kate, she should consult young Georgie Tansey, whose mother embraced whatever religion was beneficial to her and her boys, to suit any particular necessity. Catholic or Protestant, though the latter was supreme in all aspects on Earth and in Kilcormack, God is the god of all, god of want and god of satiety, god of the villain, god of the saint, god of the mosque, god of the synagogue.

On the day of the meitheal, the day before the wedding, James stuck his head through the kitchen door. Sir George wanted them both in the library.

Father John Murphy was with the old man, who seemed, of late, to be yielding to frailty by the day. The priest had discussed the ceremony with the bridal couple, earlier, but Palmer had asked him to have tea with him, there was something he needed Murphy for, later.

Mrs. Laffan had opened the door to a man, she had met, only on special occasions at Duhallow. He was in the library with Palmer and John Murphy, when the two knocked and were called to enter. Mr. Mac Manus looked every bit, the barrister, at ease with whatever business that brought him to Duhallow. Kate recognised him, he had been here only a week ago, and she had attended to him on his other visits.The heavily built lawyer stood as they entered, heavy spectacles resting on the tip of his nose in a face, full of litigation. Kate felt uneasy in the room, where a casual business like aura had settled. She stood near the door, like she was ready to serve a tray or something, but she noticed a side table had already been served with fresh afternoon tea. Sir George beckoned for her to sit next to him, patting her hand in assurance. James was being congratulated by the lawyer on his forthcoming wedding and John Murphy gave him a bland look as if to say, "I don't know, James."

The old man cleared his congested pipes, as much as to give him relief as to open proceedings. " These two young people have given you a small problem, Father Murphy, James being a Protestant and Kate, a Catholic, now believe me, it is no problem for me, however...."

"It is no problem to me, either, George, if that is their only difficulty, facing into the new century, then praise be to God. They will be properly married, take my word for it, how they worship after that, is their own business," assured the priest.

Palmer continued. "However, there's no comfort, no security in being Catholic in Ireland at this time, Father Murphy, your faith has lost its basic conviction, it's obligation to support its followers in their common struggle. Your bishops have abandoned you."

Murphy agreed with little conviction. "It is their lot to harmonize their flock with the order of things, Sir, and they will maintain that that is exactly what they are doing."

Palmer became more forceful, encompassing the couple. "And what are these young people going to do, and can you advise them." He addressed Mr. Mac Manus. "A landowner is best served by the ascendancy church. I know that religion should be disentangled as much as possibly, from authority and metaphysics and allowed to rest honestly on one's shoulders, but this is Ireland being dragged heels first into a new century, where to be Catholic is to be third class, no matter what the privilege of property."

Kate smiled, looking at the expression of surprise on James's face. "But God help you, Sir George, sure James has no property here, save a small farm and that's in England, so that 'tis a case of we living there or find a house in Kilcormack."

Palmer exploded in exaggeration. "Heaven above child and what would Duhallow do without the both of you?"

James shook his head slowly, throwing a furtive glance at the priest. The old man was losing it, becoming more contrary by the day. Mr. Mac Manus smiled, more a legal frown and nodded back.

Palmer hesitated for a minute and pressed his hand on hers, where her fingers were entwined on her lap. "My dear wife and I were never blessed with children. It's a century since a child walked these old halls. Never did I hold a child by the hand that was mine, nor for a child to hold my heart. Pamela and I were never in that world where little children have their existence."

Her eyes moistened at his obvious regret that life had failed to fill that void. He looked at James. " But we came near to it when you were born here in this house, only for circumstances to take you away again. Arthur Attridge was a good friend, a loyal employee and the circumstances of your return to Duhallow have certain connotations of destiny about it. Providence smiles on me further when you marry the sweetest girl in all of Wexford, a child favoured by the departed mistress of this house and to whom Kate was kindness itself, all through her illness, while her own mother was dying, and kinder to me in my increasing difficult old age. That horse doctor Hyde, says I'm not long for this world, unless I give up my smoking and my drinking, a lot he knows. However I do feel the Reaper's sting in winter and the summer isn't warm any more."

Kate's eyes filled again and he moved to comfort her. "Your father was the best dairyman I've ever had and 'twas here he courted your mother, who left my parlour to marry him. Pity I must say, that God took those two to make more room on Earth for his brother Jack Keohane to do his mischief."

"Now," he said, looking at the lawyer, "I have made my arrangements for your wedding gift. Mr. Mac Manus has made all the necessary papers and documents and they're here with him now and Father Murphy has agreed to be witness." Murphy raised his eyes in surprise while Mac Manus spread the papers on the table

"I suggested to Kate, last week that you should have a good house here on Duhallow land. Well, there is one, ready for you to walk into."

Attridge stood to examine the documents and as Mac Manus pointed to a relevant paragraph, his face paled as the paradox opened out before him. Kate, her hand still in the old man's warm grasp, looked at her fiancé, frowning at the pallor on him. He stretched his hand and she came and stood near him, his hand, ice cold in her's.

"Duhallow, all it's lands, tenancies, rents, properties thereon, bequeath to James Arthur Attridge Devereaux, including four financial accounts, numbered......"

She began to sob quietly and felt the priest near her, begin to read, his eyes lurching at the magnitude of the gesture.

Palmer eased himself from his chair and stood between them, smiling at her disconcertment and her tears. He hugged her shoulders gently and she turned into him, feeling his frailty as he looked over her shoulder at Attridge.

"I, we cannot accept this, Sir, I am totally unequal to it, not deserving." James was virtually transfixed.

"You take control tomorrow on the day of your wedding," said Palmer, ignoring the protest. "You have been working with my agent, he's a good agent and will be a great help to you. He already knows about this and is prepared to continue in your employment.

He stood before the fire. "Fill this old house with music. Fill it with parlour maids, bedroom maids, footmen if you wish, it is said I ignore all that kind of stuff, but fill it with the music and the laughter of children, let the sound of them ring through the corridors and let the old place live again."

It took Mac Manus almost ten minutes to read further details in respect of matters like livestock and tenants rights and the continued employment and protection of the existing staff.

Looking down at his boots, Palmer pulled his thoughts together, then raised his head, a touch of lechery shone under his spectacles. "You might have often wondered how it is that I am, though a virtual outcast as far as the aristocracy is concerned, never interfered with by those who would be regarded as the upper classes, people like Mountnorris, Cope, Owen, indeed how they sit at my table at my bidding and you will never see a Redcoat fowling my lands". He took a pair of documents from Mr. Mac Manus. "It's because, I....you, James now, own three quarters of the property both Owen and Cope sit on. Twenty five years ago, I leased five hundred acres in Carnew and Camolin to those two gentlemen, knowing even then, they had militia in their command. Cope has three hundred acres and Owen has two hundred, on leases of five years duration, to be renewed at my pleasure. I have kept them dancing on strings ever since, especially when the terms come up for renewal. In all that time, I have never renewed my rents, their lease is not much better than a peppercorn, but Duhallow receives a quarter of their harvest, to do as I please with. I sell it mostly, such an agreement suits me and my tenants reap the benefits in many ways. Mr. Cope's fine mansion is on your lands, which he built without my permission and contrary to the terms of his lease, and I'm told Mr. Owen is to build a house for his niece Henrietta on the Belturn spread, again without permission." He laughed at James's incredulity. "It's a fine stick to beat them with, whenever you wish."

Palmer had already discussed the whole matter with Mrs. Laffan. She had come for the tray and stood now in the jamb of the door, smiling through her tears.

**

The marriage should have been a happy occasion for John Murphy. Duhallow, the house he had grown to love and become a part of, bristled with happiness and though it was only the happiness of the passing moment, as a rebellion waited around the corner, Murphy's cloud threatened to eclipse the sun of the day, his melancholy today, not being just a form of fatigue, but a premonition of the blackness to come and how he needed to sink into its depts. He made his apologies to the new Mistress of Duhallow and her husband and before he left, joined Sir George in his cosy for a drink. He told the old man of his intention to resign, that his attack on Cope and his sermon at Sunday's Mass, had gained the attention of the authorities. There were matters he had to attend to, however.

To his surprise, Palmer was overjoyed at his decision. "A man of your intelligence and drive is wasted in that barn of a church, John," he crowed. "You're an academic, for God's sake, write a book, take up residence here at Duhallow, James will help you, that collar will get you killed or banished to perdition."

Later, he was asleep in the old chair in his vestry, when Georgie Tansey, reluctantly woke him, with a letter delivered by messenger from Lord Mountnorris.

"A company of Yeomanry will be dispatched from Carnew on the morrow, in defence of what have been an attack on a magistrate and an incitement on your part, to wanton destruction of the peace which exists in Kilcormack. I cannot protect you in regard to our relationship and I suggest you leave the district immediately. I will be pleased to accept your resignation and on having same, I will endeavour to intercede on your behalf."

Having read the edict for him, Georgie asked, "what will you do Father?" The concern and fear for the man he had come to love and respect was evident.

Murphy sighed wearily, putting his hands on the youth's shoulders. "I want you to promise me something, Georgie."

G. nodded, his eyes filling, "anything Father."

"If anything happens to me....now listen, don't come back here after I've left.They won't bother you, Son, stay at Mary Donovan's, or go to your friends at Duhallow." Then he gave him a look that mixed compassion with demand and the lad felt the strong hands tighten into his shoulders. "Secondly, be a priest if you must, but not just yet." He took a folder from a drawer. " And when the time comes, if it does, don't go to Dublin. Stay away from Manooth, like Father Philip Roche said, recently, go to Seville, all the details are here. I have kept in touch with one or two of the abbots, they will see you right. It's not much, but I had some money put aside for you."

"And your church, Father, what will happen to your church?"

"Will you fetch the mare for me, Son, there are a few things I must take care of."

**

When G. came back from Donovan's with the horse, he found the priest in the little garden beyond the gravel path at the rear of the building. The fresh earth had been dug in between the shrubs and Murphy was staring into a hole about three feet in debth. On a square of canvas, the

367

sacred crucibles of Mass and Benediction, sparkled in the sunshine; the Chalice and Paten, Ciborium and Monstrance, together with the altar cloth and condiments. He wrapped them reverently in the canvas placed them in the hole and shovelled the earth carefully back into place, spreading dead leaves on the newly turned earth.

They went before the altar, where the little door to the Tabernacle was left open. Murphy knelt on the steps. The youth knelt respectfully as the curate of Boolavogue prayed silently and waited for the appointments of Heaven. Then he rose and smiled assuringly. "Now, Georgie, pull down the altar lamp and quench the flame."

G. hesitated, the altar lamp is never extinguished, it resembles the presence of God.

"Out the flame, Georgie."

The youth blew gently and the light of Heaven died.

"Now, it's no longer a church, I have decommissioned it before God. The Church is more than a building, Georgie, they cannot desecrate it now."

Quietly and calmly, he collected a few cherished items and put them into the mare's saddlebag.

"Where will you go, Father?"

"Maybe I'll go and see that scoundrel Mountnorris".

"They'll catch you there", said G., hysterically. Go to Duhallow."

"They'll catch me anyway, if they want to, I would not want to be arrested at Duhallow," said Murphy.

As he pulled the mare before the doors of the church, he stroked her mane and inched her under the little stained glass north window. The little steeple cast it's shadow on them both. The horse stood motionless, a benighted creature who seemed to feel there was some kind of reverence in the exercise, while Father Murphy prayed, his head against the warm gable wall.

Then, without looking back, horse and rider headed smartly down the road toward The Harrow and Camolin. Georgie Tansey felt the depression weighing him down and wept openly.

Chapter 49

"In your lifetime, there comes a moment when destiny calls, when it seeks you out and finds you by some insignificant accident and eternity is born. The tiny acorn, fertilised by one drop of rain, becomes a tree on which a man can be crucified".

These cautionary words of Father Philip Roche at the dinner table in Duhallow, four years previously, when the big priest turned the point of the knife in on the red breast of the pompous Lieutenant Bookey and invited him to begin the rebellion of Wexford, where there was no waiting around some corner, to be enacted in his prophesy, rang out on the day Father Murphy decommissioned his church. That rebellion was to be found in the most unlikely source.

In the afternoon, the road to The Harrow, on the way to Ferns, was like a place of pilgrimage. The programme of surrender continued in return for certificates of protection. About fifty men from various parts of the town land of Kilcormack strolled wearily into the assembly yard near the jail in Ferns, careful to arrive in groups of not more than four personnel at a time. About four dozen militia and Yeos were sitting about in the sunshine, "in their sleeves", thought Phelim Crotty, " just looking for mischief."

In an iron shed, they made their contribution to the pile of weapons, supervised by Captain Carnock, The Rev. Turner and the Rev. Birdshaw. As the surrendered weapons dropped on the pile, the soldiers cheered with dog barks and pig snorting. Ungenerous tempers began to amuse themselves, the bulk being locals, but a dozen Hessians engaged in crude banter, which soon received support from all sides. Crotty, who had stopped with Paudge Smith and Francis Carty, at Lousyhead's whisky house in Trasna for a stimulant before their journey began, felt his ire rising. It was incumbent on all who surrendered, to wear a white scarf or sash, to show conformity. Forcing the group to wear their emblems of shame on their heads, the Hessians proceeded to jab and taunt them into a run through the gates, chasing the stumbling peasants through the town, jeering and shouting, their swords drawn.

Phelim Crotty turned, managed to avoid the sabre and pulled the vulgarian from his mount. Crotty was a big man and could have killed the Englishman, without need of a weapon, but a Hessian sword came from behind and ran the Trasna man through and he died in the street. To establish their grievance, the fallen horseman was pulled to his feet and Francis Carty was held upright, so the Hessian could skewer him and regain his pride. At the high road on the Ferns side of Milltown, the army turned back and the peasants, who had witnessed the massacre sank into the ditches, terrified.

Paudge Smith begged the loan of a small cart from a cottier and with help, began to drag the two bodies onto the road to Trasna.

John Murphy was about to turn the mare off The Harrow road to Camolin Park, where we would submit his resignation to Lord Mountnorris, more as a gesture of their friendship, but also knowing, it would buy him time to put his affairs in order. It had crossed his mind recently that he might go back to Saville or perhaps go on the missionary fields, even to England, where a Catholic priest would find safety, something not guaranteed in Ireland today. At the turn of the road, Tom Donovan and a group of about twenty called to him. They were coming up the road from Boolavogue, while, from the other direction the demented fugitives from Ferns reached him first. Donovan and his friends were heavily armed, but carried their flags of compliance.

"We're to Ferns, John," said Donovan. "They've threatened me and Mary."

Paudge Smith and his sorry load broke through the second group and related what had happened. Looking on the corpses of Crotty and Carty, John Murphy thought for a minute. "Don't go to Ferns, Tom, the British forces are out of control, to think this sort of thing could happen again. Was Captain Carnock there?"

"He was, Father", cried Smith," him and two clergy. Them two saw the whole thing and did nothing."

"Hold your weapons, all of you, they'll come again, best to die, defending ourselves than to die like dogs in a ditch. The night patrols will be about shortly."

Donovan had his head on his knees, his back to the stones. He raised his head slowly at a new and unfamiliar tone in the priest and sensed an undercurrent of concern. Many of the two groups tried to disguise their surprise in little shy courtesies. Father John Murphy, the pulpit thumping advocate of authority, in all its corruptness, the man, some called saint, some called traitor, after his sermon at Mass for the dead, and now, talking treason. Donovan looked up and watched the solitude of the priest's innocence shine outward from a child's heart, a man, who, only a short time ago, was on a mission of submissive imploration and supplication.

Murphy looked from one to the other, eyes now beginning to meet his in a kind of mild defiance. Tom smiled up at him, an eyebrow raised, waiting.

"What's going on Tom?"

"As you say, Father Murphy, we are not indeed going to wait to die like dogs in a ditch."

"Then why are you going to Ferns?"

Still seated, a glint of mischief danced in his blue eyes. "I'm....we're going to Ferns because we are proper citizens of the crown. This is my third visit in six days, some of these fellas go almost daily now. Devereaux, John Kelly, Keohane, have been to Camolin, any old iron bar or busted pike or scythe that we can find to keep them happy, while we're busy elsewher."

Suddenly their minds were open books. "To think I've been breakfasting with you for ten years, and you, all of you, you took the oath." Murphy feigned surprise. "Who's in charge here?"

Without thinking, a few pointed at Donovan.

"Faith, no leader at all at all, John, I'm a bit of a local organizer, a stringer man, a small man by any account, myself and Conor Devereaux, Jack Keohane, a few more."

"And Sir George Palmer?". Murphy poked further, thinking of the armoury at Duhallow.

"He's a good old Roundhead, you'll never know how good," said Donovan

"You know about the armoury at Duhallow then?", John Murphy asked.

Donovan laughed heartily. "I built it with the blacksmith and a few dozen more, even Kelly and old Diddimus of Killane, even the Master Dunne, even Norah Scully, half your bowling team, Raefil Keane, God be with him, every second smith in the county, I could go on. We have half a dozen like it, but bigger."

He smiled up into the fading sunshine. "Have a place for everything, Father John, but remember to keep it somewhere else."

"There are over fifty of you here on the road, you could be shot for an assembly of this size," Murphy warned.

"I have lookouts in front and behind," said Tom, climbing to his feet. He stood for a minute, drinking in the scents of the ripening harvest all about. He sighed heavily. "I should be at home, minding my little farm, and you shouldn't be here John, you don't want to be caught up in this, you're a man of God. It was out of respect for you and for your safety that we never spoke of these matters to you and fill you with obligations. You should go and stay with your sister, for a few days. Mary and young Tansey will mind the church."

The younger Tansey came bounding onto the group from his lookout on high ground, half a mile away. He stammered his message on seeing the priest, Hen hadn't been to church in many weeks, so busy

371

learning his trade in Killane with the giant, Kelly, who, in the youngster's eyes, was a hero in his heroic mind, a saint whose sanctity was a simple kind of rebelliousness. "They....they're over west at Boolavogue, I could see smoke, they're burning."

From the opposite direction, his brother, the priest's lieutenant, on Tom Donovan's cob horse, pulled the animal up. "They fired the church Father, the church is blazing. Mary and I have managed to save the vestments."

John Murphy was on his knees between the two corpses, his arms spread in benediction.

"You really should go, John, it's not safe for you to be here, we're going to take to the hills now, these curs keep to the roads as a rule."

Murphy pulled an old blanket over the haunted faces of the dead. "I'll stay a while, if that is alright with you, seeing as you're the one in charge." There was a touch of ice in the priest's voice, he had found Tom's silence over a thousand breakfasts as a bit of betrayal. Donovan had no apology in his reply. "There's danger in information these days, John. Father Francis Stapleton was hanged last week in Kildare, for not divulging the contents of a United man's confession. There are as many as fifty priests in jail as we speak and they'll swing, for sure."

Women from nearby cabins brought milk and boxty bread and looked aghast at their priest in the middle of the throng.

"Off the road now," called Donovan, make sure you're not seen. Four stay with the cart." To his surprise and annoyance, the priest pulled his horse into a copse a few yards away.

The four remained with the cart as a dozen military rounded the corner. As always, tolerance within the ranks overheated at the sight of prey, the goading and tormenting abating only where they saw a sufficiency of moping dispiritedness and suitable dejection. Their Corporal had, undoubtedly been drinking and thinking he might find something other than two bloodied corpses, he steadied his saturated eyes, called on three of his men and they pulled the dead Crotty and Carty from their bier, onto the road, rummaging in the blankets and straw for just anything untoward. The four peasants stood in silence as the Yeos moved away and young Tansey, in the cover of the field bushes and the fading light, bristled with anger, his temper rising, mainly because, all about him, big men and Tom Donovan were keeping theirs. John Kelly wouldn't let that happen, Mr. Donovan," he whispered.

"Starve your anger young fella." Donovan put a hand on Hen's shoulder "Starving it will make it fat."

As The Harrow swam between night and day and the moon was

brightening over Blackstairs, Wexford's first army of sixty men, their imperfections, chronically evident, stood in the middle of things. The priest was still with them.

At ten o'clock, a crescent of little houses burned in the fading light, a quarter mile ahead. The cries of women and children could be heard in the stillness. Homes burned where the men of the family couldn't be accounted for. Murphy could hear the riotous Yeos hooting and yelling their approval and within minutes came face to face with, as they perceived, an armed group of rebels, a priest mounted in their midst.

Lieutenant Bookey urged his horse forward, mesmerized at the sight of Father Murphy."You're an officer of His Majesty's Government, Lieutenant Bookey, pity you are unable to keep your men in some kind of check, "Murphy called. Then somebody shouted and a volley went up and Father John Murphy gave his first command. "Take cover in the ditch."

The motley group had a few rifles between them and the first to fire, was Tom Donovan, blowing a Private backward over heels. Then a second fell as the bewildered and half drunk militia tried to focus and take cognisance. With the fires to his back, the priest looked like some eerie manifestation, a reverent, come to smite them. Another soldier fell and suddenly rocks and missiles began to be pelted at the Redcoats. Bookey went for his sword, but Paudge Smith, revelling in his moment of revenge, rammed a pike through his windpipe, a second stab opened his midriff. The first commissioned officer to die in County Wexford fell to the ground. His horse sped about and headed through the darkening for Camolin. Two more Yeos fell while the rest scampered.

"There's no going back now John", panted Donovan. "We're here for the duration. One of those curs was my cousin, and no love lost between us, and nobody need tell them who you are."

In this place, North West Wexford, the land of The Mac Murroughs, the ancient kings of Leinster, will testify to a bloody heritage in early centuries. Wexford, a land with more rivers and streams than any other of Ireland's thirty two counties. " Loch Garemain", her ancient name, with its rich flattish landscape, mountains to the North, sloping valleys to the south West, is crisscrossed with the silver brimming opulence, brook voices making water songs, singing them among the heathers and little stone bridges and weirs.

Now, in the balmy innocence of The Harrow Road, that joined Boolavogue with the town of Ferns, on the 26th. of May in the year 1798, at 10.15 in the tired sticky night time, John Murphy would have hardly believed that a small imprudence, helped by some insignificant accident, was to chose the frame and weave the pattern of his destiny.

The great Irish rebellion had exploded on the land. It had, of its own volition, found its leader, a simple middle aged curate.

Again, the words of Father Philip Roche became painfully vivid in his mind, as John gathered his rebel army of sixty men and a handful of women, about him. He prayed over the dead, knowing the military would soon be at the scene. His men, still shaking after their first encounter, watched the transformation of Father Murphy, manifest itself on a lonely road, near The Harrow, before a burning crest of cabins. They watched, in silence, the death of the order of things.

Murphy unbuckled the scabbard from around Bookey's bloodied belly, clasped it around his own and, reverently, like he would a sacred vestment, replaced in it, the fallen sword.

At a date when Napoleon Bonaparte's gargantuan ambition for the world; to follow in the footsteps of his heroes, Alexander The Great and Julius Caesar, to conquer the world, Father John Murphy, with a rabble army of a few dozen, set out to clean his tiny country of an unmitigated evil. Within two weeks, the priest of Boolavogue would raise an army to equal that of Alexander and twice the size of Bonaparte's army for the invasion of Egypt. The man who left his church earlier, was not the Father Murphy as said Mass of the dead, only two days before, the man as pontificated the evils of violence, Sunday after Sunday. This man had a new face.

"How do you spread the word, we can't save Ireland with a few dozen men."The priest looked at Donovan, without any look of strain or tension in his face, his calmness almost brutal.

"Last year, when we were waiting for the French, we had built thirteen pyres on hills around Kilcormack, to welcome them to Wexford. They're still there, just need to be replenished with a few tufts of hay or heather." said Donovan. "Each location has a stringer man like myself."

"And each, as you call them, stringer man?" Murphy raised his eyebrows in enquiry.

"Each one has, like me, a hundred men to call on", said Tom, sizing up the priest for his next question. His answer was not short of a bit of pride

"Go to," Murphy chided, "all the while you fellows have perhaps fifteen hundred men at arms, and you allow those Red bellies torment you and kill you." He shook his head as if to a schoolchild, a half smile creasing his good face. "An army, broken into thirteen sections and located in several little cells, is useless, but together, Tom Donovan," he clenched his fist in a victory salute, now that's a different story altogether." He put a hand on Henry Tansy's shoulder. "I heard what you said earlier, Henry, now go find your friend Kelly and tell him to watch for the fires."

Hen, his chest heaving with pride, went to say something, the word stuck in his gullet, then he ran into the descending darkness.

Turning to Donovan, the priest said," tell your firelighters we'll assemble at Oulart Hill in the morning and invite the king of England to come and join us, then send someone to Conor Devereaux and get him to ask Sir George Palmer to move Old Cantankerous."

Chapter 50

Theobold Wolf Tone's aspirations, unimportant in the light of things while Napoleon Bonaparte sacrificed truth and sagacity to his vanity and the Irishman swam in a morass of bureaucracy like a fly in a saucer of honey.

The Treaty of Campo Forino had won, for France, the Austrian Netherlands, The Cisalpine Republic, The Ionian Islands, which closed off the Adriatic Sea, the Rhine Frontier and The Capital Fortress of Mainz. The Austrians were content with Venice and Venetia.

The little General had now in his sights, as the biggest armada since the Crusades sped through The Mediterranean, the invasion of Egypt, like Caesar and Alexander had done three and four thousand years before and rid the country of the Mameluke Oligarchy, which he maintained, was draining the region. He would establish friendship and the gratitude of The Ottoman Empire and appoint the French Directory's Tullyrand, as Ambassador to Constantinople. Bonaparte had respect of The Director, but since the dislodging of Carnot from power, Tullyrand had ambitions beyond his station, threatening his own ambition and a foreign posting would keep a possible opponent out of the way. Access to India by the British would be cut off and French possessions in the sub continent would be regained. A French Institute in Cairo manifested itself further, not withstanding all that, the wealth of treasure in The East was limitless. The archives and museums of Paris would be the envy of the world. As ever, Bonaparte, making God Himself his own accomplice, his hypocrisy was becoming a fashionable vice. He proposed a mission of mercy to take Syria and return the rambling Jewish race of the world to their native Palestine. Here again, their great wealth would reward him handsomely, their gratitude, boundless.

Compare this with the census taken in many of the counties in Ireland, in February of 1798. Take County Mayo on the west of the country, where it was once said that God Himself used it as stepping stones on His way to heaven, there were so many islands in Clew Bay and beyond. Mayo in the year of '98 boasted one thousand tables and one thousand and seven hundred chairs or rough stools and six hundred so called beds or cots. Cooking utensils consisted of swill pots, after the pig was fed and old kettles and old tin containers. So much for the peasantry of the west of Ireland.

"What would the great Napoleon want with Ireland, what miserable pygmies we, the unfortunate Irish are," Tone admitted to Lewins, his great friend, the friend with a price on his head back in "the old country." Tone was now, thirty five years old and despairing of ever succeeding in his endeavours.

"Don't dream, that way you will never despair, my friend", chided Lewins.

Tone had relinquished his post on the Rhine and a great void had pushed itself into his life at the loss of Lazare Hoche. He spent nearly all of his time now with his family at Nanterre and was almost happy. He had begun to find solace in the possibility that the task he had set himself had become an impossible one and in his false sense of security and collateral, Ireland was becoming as a distant and mystic analogue in another time.

However, a rare letter had reached him from James Attridge in County Wexford with news of the Death of Lord Edward Fitzgerald, the continuing struggles in Wicklow and Kildare and the arrest of Emmet, Bond and Mac Nevin and many of the leaders of the United Irishmen. James had been to see Thomas Russell in jail and had managed to enclose a hurried note from the Corkman urging him to continue his efforts on behalf of Ireland.

Not reluctantly, but to Matilda's chagrin and disappointment, Wolfe Tone renewed his undertaking and began, once again to bombard the authorities in Paris. He looked again to Holland, but the massive defeat by the English at Camperdown, two years before, forced him to knock on other doors.

The French Authority was now a vacillating establishment, ridden with intrigue and corruption and the purge that ousted Carnot left the door open for Napoleon Bonaparte to sweep it aside as soon as he returned from the Eastern campaign.

In April 1798, Wolfe Tone was posted as Adjutant General to the staff of Armee d'Angleterre in Ruen, just a few weeks before the break out of the Irish rebellion. In a short few years, Tone had managed to endear himself to the leaders of the French establishment, to, among others, Charles de Tullyrand, the ex bishop of Autun and now the forty four year old French Foreign Minister, and to General Kilmaine, who had taken over from Bonaparte at home. E. J. Lewins, the exiled Irishman with a price on his head, continued with renewed integrity in his quest for a second expedition and now, while Father Murphy embraced an acute metamorphosis on the roads and ditches of north Wexford, Lewins and Tone rekindled their efforts in the palaces and power corridors of Paris. Tone would have forgotten the quietly spoken cleric which he met at that fine house, the name of which he had forgotten, though the old gent who was the master, he could recall, especially the marvellous house without the stigma of British protocol. Edward Lewins, of course, would never have heard of Father John Murphy.

General Grouchy, who, undoubtedly was responsible for the failed Bantry expedition in '96, together with the elderly General Kilmaine, met the two Irishmen for lunch at the restaurant of the Tulleries Palace. Tone was wary of Grouchy. As the saying goes, her was like a Turkish infidel, the French officer consistently hesitated between two mosques. Hesitation and indecision was to be his hallmark in the army of France, eventually bringing him into disgrace at Waterloo, seventeen years later.

However, the senior Kilmaine surprised Tone when he revealed that General Bonaparte had actually reconsidered his stance of Ireland, after their latest confrontation. Consumptive Kilmaine laughed at the memory. "He called you a scrapping little Celt with the persistence of a gadfly on the scab of a heifer." He continued affably, "behind it all, Bonaparte respects you greatly, your honest bravery. Before he sailed for the East, he and I made a tour of the west coast. If the facilities were there, he would have considered invading England, on your suggestion, but not at the expense of the Eastern campaign. He abandoned that idea when he saw how bad the conditions were in the western ports."

Both French officers went to great pains to assure the Irishmen that the Directory remained committed to the cause of Ireland, but right now, the Navy was in a state of total disorganisation.

"It is bankrupt," sighed Grouchy.

To Tone's disgruntlement, the loyal generals omitted to mention the fact that Napoleon's preparations for his trip to Egypt had brought about the sorry state of, not just the Navy, but the whole nation. His insatiable avidity for conquest and his incontinent impulses left no quarter for temperance.

Sipping his wine, Kilmaine looked searchingly at Tone. "It has to be said, my friend, that the arrival, last month of your Mr. Napper Tandy in Paris with a few of his auxiliaries , to instigate an intrigue against you, is not helping your cause. Bonaparte refused to grant him an interview".

It had become to all, that the senior United Irishman had become jealous of Wolfe Tone's acceptance by the French and the fact that he had been decorated an Adjutant General, was a matter of great complexity in the man with "the hanging down look." Napper Tandy saw himself as Ireland's first Prime Minister, while fellow republicans saw him as bewildered, but harmless.

While varying offenses plagued him, small blessings came the way of the Irishman. His brother, William received yet another promotion in Poona, India, while through his influence, brother Matthew had obtained a commission in the French Navy and was now living in Paris.. Also, Tone had secured a place for their youngest brother, Arthur, in the Dutch Navy, at the age of sixteen.

Matilda cherished their dinner parties together when they would meet as often as possible at Nanterre, where oldest sibling would decry the fact that they were a crowd of vagrants, in every kind of uniform but an Irish one.

In the first week in May, the Directory decided to postpone a second invasion to Ireland, until a more favourable occasion presented itself.

**

On the 26th. Of May, 1798, about the time, father John Murphy buckled on Lieutenant Bookey's sword, near the Harrow, Wolfe Tone had hot and severe words with General Grouchy at a small dinner party in the cafe of the Palais Royale. The General's constant refusal to act immediately on an Irish expedition, until the return of Bonaparte, irked him and spurred him beyond tolerance.

"I have said it to the General, personally, to the Directory and to you, now, Sir, that Bonaparte will not succeed in Egypt. It will not be a happy adventure for him or for France. He continues to turn his back on his arch enemy, who is now preparing to follow him into the Mediterranean. Until the General stands up and confronts England in the Atlantic, he will have no success."

Tone slumped in his chair and apologised for his tantrum, saying, "but, my friend, my country is dying by the day for want of an ally."

Chapter 51

Through the early night of May 26th., the military, incensed by the death of a commissioned officer, set out from Camolin, Ferns and Carnew and within an hour, peasant homes burned all over north Wexford. Keeping to the fields and bogs around The Harrow, the new army for Ireland retaliated and any house that did not have a thatched roof was set alight for a change, very proper families were turfed out to shelter in with their livestock, for the peasant, the luscious fruit of revenge had, at last ripened. Their horses and drays became a precious commodity, work horses, hunters, chasers, my lady's pet, within a week all would be war horses.

Bookey's body was hardly cold, when Duhallow was to witness a scene that was for Mrs. Laffan, beyond rationality. The blacksmith had bounded up the sweep of the driveway on a sweating horse, something she had not seen in over twenty years. Conor always used the narrow lane way to the rear of the house, unseen and unhurried when he came to do his business in the forge, or that place that nobody ever spoke about. She looked through the kitchen window as he and Luther, moved the bull, old Cantankerous, moody and sluggish in his half sleep, a great moving mass in the light of the oil lamps. He would sleep in his meadow tonight.

Conor had received news of the Harrow by a panting stuttering youth, that the rising was up, and he was to "move Cantankerous", And Mr. Tom Donovan sends his respects." The lad had no idea that the name of a seething bull and the word respects would be of such consequence to the big blacksmith as to stir him almost to panic, by the agreed code words for the armoury of Duhallow. The innocence of the youngster saw nothing beyond the fires that the skies now displayed from the tops of thirteen hills displaying the sky's ethereal splendours, with an outpouring of hope and a rallying command from Heaven itself.

When he arrived at Duhallow, his surprise was evident. Two dozen men waited for him in agitation and expectancy and again the sweep to the house was suddenly filled with the scraping of gravel against hooves and crunching sounds of cart wheels, and a hundred willing hands woke the rebel refinements of war and carefully filled four carts.

Conor Devereaux heard a voice, vaguely familiar, but for a second dispensed with the idea, until it sounded again, this time, intense, yet the blacksmith could find no psychological design in his head that it should be the voice of John Murphy.

"The first dray will be armed, use the primed rifles, for you will come across hunting parties who will not be expecting you. Come up close and make every shot tell. We are up now, there's no going back."

A lanky intense man, never showing any kind of emotion, stood in the doorway. Stupefaction turned to almost stupidity as Devereaux saw the priest, still mounted, issuing orders and directions like his mind was already on the strategy of the fight to come. With barely a by your leave, but a side glance recognition of the blacksmith, Murphy turned his horse and led the column round the eastern gable of the house and onto the driveway, passing Duhallow's front portico. Kate and Mrs. Laffan stood under the columns where the twin plaques the masturbating Sheilas cast their venereal shadows, and Sir George, from his cosy window, watched the ghostly figure before the train, disappeared down onto the road.

Laffan, confused and with a haunted look at her new mistress, said, "was it the priest, I saw, Mrs. Attridge, or is it something up out of the grave, and should we wake Sir George?"

"It's not a bad dream you're having", said Kate, her heart skipping, "and I have a feeling that Sir George knows." She went to the cosy where James and Palmer were seated in the window, Palmer nodded and she could see his lack of surprise. She came and stood behind her husband, her hands resting on the back of his chair. "I'm glad and relieved all that steel is gone", whispered Palmer, and I suppose it's time it was put to good use."

He gave her a look that shone from, what she thought was a small private zone of acceptance. "You'll have much to write about now James Attridge Devereaux. Mr. Saoirse will be a busy man." Looking at Kate, his old eyes popping, "did you see the fine sword on him, Kate."

**

"Get up! Get up" shouted the messengers as they ran through the fields and bogs, "'tis the rising, we're up, we're up, the fires are on." It was an easy task for three quarters of the peasants, who hadn't slept in their cabins for three weeks, so much was the fear that haunted them. "Oulart, Oulart Hill." they shouted, and as Jimmy Sheehan reported to James Attridge, days later, "'twas like the ditches were coming alive, so many people slept in their shelter."

"He who has never learnt to obey, cannot expect that virtue in others," Attridge had heard Father Murphy say, once from his pulpit, but the benevolent attraction that the people had for their priest, from the outset, was strong enough and all encompassing to have carried the whole nation. His ability to marshal them like sheep, to lead and point the way, to an inglorious common mass of matter was too soon, confound the British, often leaving them aghast and ashamed in his shadow.

With a whispered apology to his friend, Lord Mountnorris, he attacked Camolin Park, where only hours before, he was coming on bended knees, for yet another favour, this time for himself. Camolin Park had been appointed one of the surrendering stations for arms over the past few weeks, so the mountain of guns, pikes and other accoutrements of war were loaded into two of His Lordship's fine drays and his two fine horses awakened from their sleep to be hitched on.

Mountnorris was away in Dublin, but in restraining his followers, Father Murphy was adamant the mansion be left standing. Ten horses were taken from their stables and the terrified night staff were shunted or given the option to join the rebels. It was to be the first of the priest's observations on the inefficiency of the English, that a virtual armoury of hundreds of weapons were left, attended by a few parlour maids.

The burden of self reproach and mild mortification at Murphy's decision to grasp the thorn of revolt, soon left him at the gates of Lieutenant Bookey's residence of Rockspring. The temple of tyranny and royal prostitution was stripped of its huge armoury and set alight, along with half a dozen solid houses in it's environs. Bookey's servants, all offered resistance and were the first to die, in the service of an English landlord.

As the priest mounted the grand stairway of Rockspring, to seek the surrender of five peasants, in the redcoats of King George, Paudge Smith, who saw himself now, as some sort of lieutenant, was blown to pieces, half a foot ahead of the priest, and John Murphy killed his first opponent; a twenty year old strapping boy, his big blue eyes, wide in surprise at the cut of the blade in his gut. The death of an unfortunate innocent traitor, the clay of his father's potato patch, still under his nails, held no glory for the sad cleric. The boy from Enniscorthy never had a bond to betray, it never gave him reason, not like the King of England, who gave him a shilling.

Tom Donovan had hastily scribbled the names of senior loyal United Irishmen and Murphy set up a corps of horsemen who rode through the night with dispatches to Wexford Town and Beauchamp Harvey, to the brothers, Colclough at Ballytigue, to William Hutton of Clonard, to John Grogan of Healthfield, to Edward Fitzgerald – not The Lord – of Garrylough, to the one armed veteran, Esmond Kyan of Mounthoward, to Michael Furlong of Templescoby and many others, none of whom the simple priest of Boolavogue, had the pleasure of ever having met, all but two: known Protestants.

To all points inbetween, went the word of the rebellion and the call to arms and men crawled from the corner of ditches, from cow sheds and from the sheltering hills to follow the cry for freedom. Whole families marched through the dark hours of May 26th., 1798, the thatch of their cabins pulled aside for the hidden pikes and, with a prayer on their lips for forgiveness, the graves of their loved ones were disturbed in the churchyards to grasp the weapons lying, waiting beneath the flowers, from chimney shafts, the weapons suddenly appeared, torn from old mattresses and from fetid purification of dung heaps and farm manure.

Early on Whit Sunday morning, the ever increasing party arrived at the sprawling village of Oulart, five miles south of The Harrow. Father John entered Mc Cauley's Hotel where women fussed over a breakfast for him and Donovan. Five hundred men waited outside in the chill, being fed by the women of the town. All were well armed, thanks to the raid on Camolin and Rockspring and later, the garrisoned home of the elderly Protestant rector of Kilmuckridge, where the old man, who had been overseeing the surrender of arms for the past two months, was piked and his garrison, slain.

By now, over a fine plate of cured ham and eggs and freshly baked bread, Murphy would have realized the severity of his decision and the difficulty facing him in trying to keep his men in control. It was a fit of madness on the part of the marauding peasants that killed the rector of The Glebe, a deed that would lie heavily on John's head in the eyes of the ascendancy. He would now be an outcast, responsible for the death of an innocent but powerful clergyman.

"Any clergyman who makes a garrison of his home, has to face up to the fact that he will be marked for retribution," said Donovan, seeing the priest's concern.

"And where does that leave me, Tom ?", Murphy asked.

"It leaves you and all of us, with no alternative, for all rationality has broken down, and nobody knows that better than you." He looked through the window onto the square, crowds still pouring out of the countryside, "and better than them".

**

The authorities moved slowly on the first day, to Murphy's surprise. Their objective seemed to be a campaign of retribution for the death of Lieutenant Bookey, so that they were mainly content to plunder and demolish mostly empty cabins of the peasantry. They had little apprehension of serious disturbance, as County Wexford, as far as they knew, was completely unarmed and had been non destructive on the whole. As a result, only a few hundred of the regular army was stationed in the entire county, along with most recently assembled corps of untrained Yeomanry.

Above the town of Oulart, the huge fire, lit during the night, was being maintained and was having its own adventure with the rising sun. On the steps of the hotel, the priest stood in wonderment. The crowd had doubled in one half hour. Groups of people flowed, ran into the square, raising green flags and various instruments of arms and shouting their support, only to fall back in disbelief at recognising their commander with a sabre strapped to him; the genial priest of Boolavogue, with a supreme sword strapped to his virtuous middle.

At the back of the crowd, two heavy drays had stalled, the horses sweating and spooked at the shouting and rattling of metals. Young Henry Tansey had busily uncovered the armoury from Duhallow and a dozen men were distributing the pikes among the ravenous crowd. Up on the driver seat, Conor O'Connor Devereaux and Big John Kelly of Killane looked, frozen in stupefaction and bewilderment, on the other cart, Jack Keohane sat motionless as the moment of recognition left him without words. The blacksmith , thinking what he had seen at Duhallow, had been an illusion or the result of impure shadows in the lamplight remained loose jawed, his resolve for war, now heightened by surprise. James Attridge, who had ridden behind the flotilla, watched the metamorphosis of John Murphy, as he stood alone on the steps. Tom Donovan and two or three others remained a few steps behind in a respect that bordered on reverence.

By 11 a.m. the rebels were assembled on the Hill of Oulart, where a Mass Rock was prepared and Father Murphy donned the vestments that Mary Donovan had rescued before the burning of his church. His sword , a fine specimen of craftsmanship, well afforded by the extravagant Bookey, peeped from under his vestments as he raised his hands in blessing. Two thousand peasant men and their families knelt in supplication as the priest recited the blessings of Whitsun. The women had brought bread, broken into pieces and blessed for the receiving of Communion.

The hill became a fortress with a view of the surrounding district. Entire families had committed to Father Murphy's rebellion, many of whom would never return to their simple homes, or what might be left of them. From his vantage point, he watched anxiously as the trails of people, armed and unarmed, on foot and in variety of transports, some bringing their livestock, streamed in endless ribbons of shouting masses on the roads, their eagerness and impetuosity filling him with dread and foreboding and sensing his own worthlessness at their rising expectations. He prayed that his dispatches had reached their destinations, feeling very alone, almost desolate and the huge crowd gathering at his command, seemed almost abstract, like a picture gallery of strangers, an optical deception, planted outside the realm of normality. He saw them as depressed luminaries, confident in his ability, to change the great wrongs in their lives. Body and soul, he was on his knees that Heaven might be ready and yet they came.

This throng made no distinction between Protestant and Catholic. What was needed now was an army for all depressed people of Ireland. Murphy's heart lightened as Donovan introduced him to the newcomers; Edward Roche of Garrylough, in full Yeoman regalia of sergeant in Le Hunt's Yeoman Cavalry of Shelmaleer, together with 150 of his corps. Then, more Yeomen, a hundred more, under George Sparks of Blackwater. Then came Jeremiah Cavanaugh, the veteran of George Washington's army with dozens of his warriors. Murphy knew Roche, no relative of his friend Father Philip Roche, whom he hadn't seen for some time and hoped he would be coming from whatever hideout he might be inhabiting, to join him. All the other leaders were strangers to him.

In their hurried parley, as matters were beginning to move rapidly, Murphy told them, "remove your fine tunics, Gentlemen or we will soon be killing one another."

By three in the afternoon, the hill had been transformed into a working commune. Fires and open kitchens had been set up. Every child had a chore to carry out and the women who were to prove themselves the stalwart patrons and the vigorous backbone of the entire campaign, had food in abundance at the ready, thanks to the Mountnorris farming stock and the generosity of Rockspring and The Glebe. Sheep and chickens were slaughtered, the curing sheds of the rich had been well stocked of pig meat.

Kavanagh and Sparks brought the priest up to date on events in the county within the last sixteen hours. Hawtrey white, with his North Cork Orangemen were evicting and burning in the South West, while Captain Boyd and Hunter Gowan were terrorizing all along the Eastern regions. Enniscorthy and surrounds was at the march of Archibold Jacob and Roger Owen. Pitchcapping, flogging and half hanging had become rampant where gender or age was no consideration. It was reported that between two and three hundred were murdered in retaliation for Bookey's and Burrow's deaths.

Edward Roche looked sullen as he reported the arrest of his friend

Anthony Parry of Perrymount, near Inch. A lieutenant in the Yeoman Cavalry, one held in high esteem by his superiors, but who resigned because of the wanton savagery they were committing against the peasantry and joined the United Irishmen. "They have arrested Perry," explained Kavanagh, "these two days hence, and dragged him to Gorey. I'm told he was subjected to savage torture until he eventually revealed the names of the leaders of our society, which led to the arrest of Beauchamp Bagnal Harvey of Bargey Castle, a very influential man, who we thought he would be our leader when the time came."

He looked at Murphy, the wonderment of the initial realization of the priest's position, still fresh in his eyes, "but now we have you, Father Murphy, whoever would have thought."

"Tell Mr. Harvey he can have my place any time he thinks fit, Mr. Kavanagh," said Murphy, looking again over the ever increasing army all about.

"With respect to Bagnal Harvey, Sir and anybody else that might have taken on the mantle of commander, nobody but nobody could rally a crowd like this in just two days. Recruitment would have had to take place in many districts, surely the women would have had to stay at home, war is a man's game, but I see their uses, so to speak." Disbelief creased his features as the huge kitchen spewed it's aroma of plenty.

The priest raised a finger in caution "A woman can do anything that those of us who love her, would have her do." He warned further, "remember, Sir, her desire for revenge outlasts all her other emotions, so King George, be careful, I say." He was sullen now. "Where are they being held: Perry and Harvey?"

"Wexford jail," replied Kavanagh, "I have been told they also have Edward Fitzgerald, he was arrested at his home at Newpark. He would be a great asset to us."

"Then we must go to Wexford soon, Mr. Kavanagh."

Still, no sign of a regular army of the authorities to be seen. But it had become open season for the likes of Captain Boyd, the man who had a confrontation with Wolf Tone in Wexford, four years earlier, and for the Rev. Francis Turner, the rector and magistrate, who up to two days ago was accepting arms with Captain Carnock at Ferns and who stood by while mayhem was rife in the town. They were now burning cottages and cabins on the outskirts of Oulart, in an effort to get the insurgents to come out, but the hovels were empty, their inhabitants already on Oulart Hill.

As the parley continued, which was now joined by Conor Devereaux and Attridge, John Murphy broke into a fit of accusatory laughter. "There's a wonderful Chinese proverb, Gentlemen, which says, when a finger points at the moon, the imbecile looks at the finger. Their heads are made of wax, they should never walk in the sun. The King's army in Ireland contents itself with the burning of empty houses and making examples of young boys, while I have an army waiting for them. O! The slender intellect of the Englishman."

It caused a levity all around, but the priest returned to the matter at hand. "And where are your Mr. Wolf Tone now, James Attridge, and your Mr. Monro and your Mr. Henry Joy Mac Cracken, Conor Devereaux, and His Excellency Lord Fitzgerald." He consulted Tom Donovan's list of leaders, so called: "the Shears Brothers, and this Doctor Drennan and a Mr. Grogan and all the others, whose names meen nothing to me."

"The brothers are in jail," Donovan said, sheepishly, "Lord Edward is dead, or near to it, he was severely injured at a Dublin meeting and was taken."

"Meetings, meetings," said Murphy, impatiently, I have been reading between the lines in The Journal and Mr. Attridge here has kept me informed that something was going to happen. In his eloquence, he writes for foreign newspapers and indeed any homespun source that will accept his accounts, that the seed of rebellion is being sewn in Ireland. Well let me tell you, Gentlemen, that seed has been shut up in its pod for too long, only the game fish swims up stream."

A new force was emerging, as they sat in disbelief at this man who was, suddenly all of one piece. There was no hesitation in his attitude as he crossed a threshold of emotion.

"For the first time in two hundred years," he continued, "the army of England turned and fled from the Irish peasant. At The Harrow, two days ago, eleven of King George's military ran from us like frightened chickens, only eleven, but their running footsteps will echo through eternity."

Devereaux quietly admonished Father John. "We, all of us have been doing our bit, John Murphy, but we were afraid to put the burden of knowledge on you. Only a week ago, you were decrying people like me and Donovan from your pulpit."

Murphy smiled, "there's a war waiting for us, Conor, and I have seen the great contribution you and your fellow blacksmiths have made in the cause, who I hope will be here soon. As for myself, well all I have to say in that regard, is that half the failures in life arise from pulling your horse before he starts to leap the fence." He hesitated for a minute, then smiled at the thought. "My young friend, Georgie Tansey, God love him, whose mother once made a britches or shirt or

387

something for the King of England, is an avid reader of The Times. He read for me the other day, that a General Lake has been named Commander-in-Chief of the Government forces, replacing Abercrombie, who, despite his loyalties, was not a bad sort. It's a case of tyranny now let loose in the country, without restraint. Lake's reputation speaks for itself, a devil incarnate. "Perhaps, if I was to point to any reason for my change of heart, it would be because of that man."

He turned to Attridge. "You will have great stories to write about, James, but I want you to report on matters from a safe distance. If anything should happen to you, I would have your new wife and Sir George to contend with, so also, who will tell the world that the croppies are in revolt. My young friend Tansey has been a disciple of yours, take care of him, in time, Boolavogue will need another priest".

"They'll have one when you return, Father," said Attridge and the priest gave him a side glance, a knowing look that told everything.

There was little time to a assess developments as in mid afternoon, a large force of Redcoat cavalry appeared, north of Oulart Hill, coming the Gorey Road. They cantered within sight, at their head, the accursed Hawtrey White himself. It was evident to John Murphy, by the leisurely attitude of the riders, that they regarded the exercise as a joust in the afternoon sun, a trapped game to be teased out and dealt with. About 250 in all, the column was superbly equipped and armed, a menacing sight to weaken reserve of the poorly turned out peasantry, where reaping hooks, scythes and hay forks made up over half the armoury, a maggoty army of men, women and children. John Murphy, untrained in any kind of warfare, saw the advantage of their location, taking cognisance of the small fields, the strong hedges and furze-clustered hillocks; an infantryman's paradise.

He felt the raw fear all around him and roared at them, mounting the long low ditch and running along it, his sword drawn. Accusingly, he eyeballed them one after the other, his voice a cannon roar.

"Now listen to me, all you're afraid of is the colour, that colour that has haunted you all of your lives, your unspeakable lives, drawn from all the death and misery that colour has wrought." He pulled a youth up beside him, put a hand on the young shoulder and pointed into the distance. "Look at it, the devil stalks the land in a red tunic, that colour speaks all languages. But look carefully now, in the tunic is a lesser man than you, because he is only precariously civilized and you have the propensity to send him back to his first nature. He bleeds like you and me, fears like you and me. Adversity is the test of a strong man and I want you to remember all the hardships that colour has brought to you and yours; the hangings, the accursed pitchcappings, think of Trasna, of

Dunlavin, think of the ball alley massacre."

He left the message sink in until the crowd erupted in a great shout of acceptance and James looked at Conor again in wonder.

"You've never been in a war, well let me tell you, neither have they. The King's real soldiers are trying to fight Mr. Napoleon Bonaparte. What you're looking at now is the dregs of English low culture, wrapped up in a red jacket." He raised his voice further above theirs as they repeated his calls in chorus.

"Now, when the order comes, I want you to cry out, loud and strong. I want to see the beauty of your souls shine out. Don't hesitate, for 'tis speed will take them."

For the second time in as many days, the British turned and ran, two hundred abd fifty of them, astonished to see almost a thousand men, wild and tempered, bearing down on them, while Edward Roche, whom Murphy had christened The General, with selected armed peasants, sought to outflank and surprise the cavalry. Roche had spent two hours instructing a hundred women in the art of reloading rifles and muskets with powder and ball in as short a time as would matter in the death of a man.

Conor Devereaux's pike, with the sharp billhook half way up the blade, was to prove a superb piece of weaponry. The running peasant was able to slip the hook inside the saddle strap or spancil and tear the leather asunder, unseating the rider, or hook the white cross straps over the rider's tunic, to yank him, unceremoniously from the horse.

Twenty Yeomen perished, while the red tide scampered, where perfect courage and rank cowardice were two extremes on this first day of battle. At four in the afternoon, a bigger threat was seen coming from Wexford direction. Word had eventually reached the authorities that something other than a skirmish had taken place on Oulart Hill. General Roche's scouts were able to report that there were four corps of North Cork Militia in Wexford town, as well as the garrison troops and Yeomen cavalry. As the dust cloud drew near, it was evident that a sizable detachment had been assembled.

Murphy took a vantage point again. Wrathful and projecting confidence and vitality of the challenge ahead, he instilled in his ever increasing army, an arousal of fury and endeavour. In a tide of energy, he blazoned the atrocities committed by the Redcoats, "the daemons of your youth."

By 4.30 in the warm afternoon the red army was within a mile of the camp, a blanket of smoke in its wake, where they had destroyed houses and cabins on the march.

"Don't be afraid of their accursed drums, they're meant to torment you, but remember, the man with the drum is unarmed and therefore more afraid than you are, so I want you to march to his beat, pretend it is for your benefit, but use it in double time, your two steps for each slap of that drum. You fight a blessed war, God will not punish a man who makes return for injury. You can now see their rifles, they have to reload themselves, you have your women to do that, she will carry and reload your second rifle and a rifle is no match for a pike, once it's discharged.

It was then he thought of the children.

The Yeos had stopped and were now, fully in sight. They were already in the trap. Ditches, high and low were on either side of them, and clumps of heavy gorse and rock presented cover for perfect guerrilla war. Edward Roche recognised his own commander, Captain Le Hunt of the Shelmalier Cavalry, the man entrenched in the Roche family estate of Garrylough and he relished a possible opportunity of a confrontation.

Murphy had directed The General and Sparks to place their best gunmen behind the ditches to the right of the main body. Having collected three dozen young people and borrowed a hundred hats and placed them behind the ditches to the left of the oncoming column. At a signal, the children would, while lying very low on their backs inside the ditch, suddenly raise the hats on their sticks above the rim of the stones, distracting the soldiers for a split second, causing many of them to fire.

"If you can't kill the two drummers, then kill the accursed drums, a drum cannot play with a hole in it".

Again he impressed on them the element of surprise, with loud shouting and hooting, not just from the fighters, but from the entire camp, the children with their shrill young piercing voices, the impertinence of their innocence, unstoppable, disorientating horse and rider.

The drums started up again, but died just as quickly, George Sparks, himself a perfect shot, had three loaded rifles by him and immediately picked off the two drummers, when the sudden silence further disturbed the Redcoats. Then at thirty five perches, the militia saw the hats above the ditches and two hundred rifles went off. Reloading feverishly began as the priest roared for action and the explosion of the shouting from two thousand throats and in the climax, many a Redcoat saw the image of his death. Like a horde of marauding Huns, the pikemen tore at the enemy, completely routing them. The Roche riflemen were still to the good and picked off the red targets, a second rifle at the ready by another or by a woman, many of them had quickly mastered the art of reloading. The pikemen ran along the diches on all sides, outflanking the North Corks, hooking them from their mounts. A pike could kill a running man from eight feet away. Murphy's gunmen used breach and barrel and the army's bayonets were no match for the Devereaux pike.

**

The cheering crowd sang the praises of their commander and already, sonnets were being composed in his honour. They found him bent over the seven dead rebels, which were laid out on the fresh grass of Oulart Hill. He had now entered into a labyrinth from which he would never escape. His friend and breakfast companion for ten years lay at his feet. Tom Donovan had a ball lodged in his skull, his lifeless eyes with a fixed glare in them, like colourless glass, as the sun sought out the death grimace in their severe contemplation.

One hundred and eighty Redcoats perished. They were stripped of their arms and Murphy's men were handsomely rewarded with their superb muskets and sabres. Twenty fine horses had now a new home.

Seven rebels died on Oulart on the first major confrontation, one: the gentle United Irishman of Boolavogue, Tom Donovan, another: little Agnes Murtagh of Oulart Town, cradled now in her mother's arms. "Agnes of Holy God, will you bless her, Father John."

Over the priest's shoulder, G. whispered, "Mary.... I'll tell her Father." Murphy looked at him, his eyes, full. "And stay with her, Georgie." Then, very seriously, "stay away from the fight, you and James, I saw him in the fight, with a rifle. You're both needed elsewhere."

Seven rebels were buried in Oulart cemetery later in the day. Even now, the three leaders couldn't believe the gross inefficiency and rank cowardice of the King's army. Hawtrey White, a man who for years had wielded terror in the hearts of the peasantry and his corps of Redcoats, the pick of the Gorey, Camolin and Castletown riflemen were busy retreating north, while the insurgents demolished Le Hunt's column to the south.

It had to be said, however, that they were stunned by John Murphy's power of leadership, it had to be a factor in their inability to come to terms, but Edward Roche and James Attridge, who still remained with the camp, knew that it was the mortifying infirmity of rank cowardice that lost them the day.

"Cowards die many times before their deaths, the valiant never taste of death but once." Attridge wrote the proverb as an introduction to his firsthand account of the battle of Oulart on May 27th. 1798.

Fiddlers and fife music stormed the hill as the last of the Orange banners faded into the distance. The two huge Lambe drums lay torn and silent in the stones, a drummer stretched, the offensive rods still in his lifeless hands.

Big fish were landed. Roche pointed out the trophies of the fight, most of whom Father Murphy would not have known, indeed he could hardly read the insignia of their ranks, but by their dress, looked very important indeed. Stretched near the broken drum; the Hon. Captain de Courcey, brother of The Earl of Kinsale, Lieutenants Barry, Williams, Crabtree, Worth, Captain Warren and others.

Chapter 52

Word spread about this priest at the head of a great rebel army of men, boys, women and children and already, he was being committed to folklore, that a great light, a sacred aureole followed him, seated on a mounted glowing horse. The fact that Father Murphy was, at times, terrified, he was always resolute and all the time, in anxiety whether or not the French were coming and if so, when and where. As for his horse, the faithful mare was tired and he rode her as little as possible, keeping her well away from the fray. Murphy's preferred place was at the front of his column with his pikemen.

The unrest of his spirit marked his time and the high heathered mounds and hills of north Wexford became his sanctuary. John moved his ragged multitude north of Ferns to Carrigrew Hill, a central point for more recruits as they continued to answer his call. From the hill, he could see how the military were active in their endeavours, his scouts continually reporting. The telltale pyres of burning cottages and even now, the cornfields, not fully ripened, were being set alight.

Exhaustion overcame the fighting men and women after thirty six hours of continual manoeuvres and they slept mercifully while new fresh recruits kept watch and scouts reported back on the enemy's activities. Grain from last year's harvest was still in the storehouses, grain kept for the king's horses was now plentiful and milk was in abundance, the cows had not been milked for more than a day. Loyalist livestock provided meat a plenty. Father Murphy's scouts were jubilant. The Town of Camolin was deserted before them. The military, the Yeos, the Hessians had fled in the night and were now assembling at Gorey. All that remained in the straggling town were a few peasants and their dogs.

Richard Monaghan, known as "The Monk", from the working area of John Street in Wexford Town requested permission to burn the town, but Murphy refused. "We were thinking, Father, that there would now be a fine house for yourself to live in, the grand house of the Rev. Owen, seeing that he has scampered," said the big jovial Wexfordman. A cheer went up in support. "I'll never live in a grand house, Mr. Monaghan, not in this life anyway," replied the priest. The comment, though said flippantly, carried a fraction of undeniable sadness in its timbre and for a minute, the crowd around fell silent.

The Monk broke the silence. "But then we thought, Father John, after full consideration, 'twasn't fit enough for yourself, that you would have to perform one of them exorcisms or whatever the good Lord would have you do to get rid of all the devils inside it."

"The devils we seek are over there, my friend," smiled Murphy, pointing to the town of Enniscorthy to the west. God doesn't need to point them out to us, so let you and I go and do all the exorcisms we can, God is busy enough."

The Monk raised his strong arms, a muscular fieldman, ready for any event, looking for any event. " Then let us be doing that then, Captain and make God all the busier."

Before the march to Enniscorthy, a treck of five miles, Monaghan returned. "I heard you saying, Father Murphy, that colours come in many languages."

The men had pinned the black Chasuble to a frame as a banner and draped it with green ribbons. "I'm told you wear it when you say your Mass for the dead. I'm Protestant, so I wouldn't know. The big man knelt before the priest, "then let it be for them, Father, when we carry it into the fight."

John put his hands on the proud head in a blessing for the man from John Street.

Eight thousand rebels crowded through the streets of Camolin and John Murphy entered, for the second time, the grounds of Lord Charles Mountnorris. The Loyalist priest, Father John Redmond, once a friend, who dined with him on many an occasion here in Camolin Park and at Duhallow with George Palmer, stood at the doorway and bravely remonstrated before the mob. Redmond had become notorious recently for his refusal of absolution to known United Irishmen and Defenders. Hostility was always a natural fundamental condition in the man. Murphy hastily pushed him beyond the doorway into the sumptuous hallway. Mountnorris was still in Dublin and one or two parlour maids ran about the house like cackling hens, terrified and pleading.

"There are men and women out there, would kill you," Murphy hissed. "Whether we torch this house or not is entirely in my hands. The only difference between you and a Redcoat, is the colour of your cloth and for now it will protect you."

"Our Brothers in Christ are unanimous with our bishops in condemning a fellow priest who would commit murder," Redmond fumed. "You, along with the rest of us, decried the violence of the United Irishmen, as a crowd of tyrants as recently as last week. In God's name, John, what has come over you?" He hunted for words, straining to retain composure.

"Go back to your Brothers in Christ, Father, and to your bishops and ask them what they are doing to stop the slaughter of the innocence. The peasants of Wexford gave up their arms when you and I asked them to do so, only to be cut down for having any in the first place." Murphy remained calm, keeping his voice low, so that the crowd outside, waiting for an outcome, saw only the two clerics in whispered conflict. "I have seen that there is no pleasing the authorities, who daily and nightly impose savage and barbaric vengeance on a faceless people. Last week, somebody said to me that the King of England wishes to wipe the Irish race from the face of the Earth." He eyeballed the other. "You ask me what has got into me, well John Redmond, that is what has got into me, the realization that that might happen."

Suddenly Murphy felt the need to restrain himself and stepped back. "While my Brothers in Christ and my Bishop in Christ, cower behind their self importance, the Orangemen are burning homes with women and children still inside them. Is a six year old girl a United Irishman, is a seventy year old man a danger to the king. They're dying because they're Catholic and what you and your kind are doing, is creating a holy war. Our children are growing up, if they're lucky, who picture their devil, not just a Redcoat, but a Protestant. Half of my army is Protestant. This English army is the vice of our time, destroying the delicate magic of life, when a child's body is no longer a sanctuary of God."

"You speak of armies", shouted Redmond, without fear, what do you call that mob outside?"

"Blessed are those who fight in a just cause, in a just war, for them it is an easy entry to Heaven," quoted Murphy, "and as for the children, they are safer here with me than at home in their straw beds, waiting for the military to come."

"You're no better than the hairy hoards entering the city of Rome, with Attila","shouted Redmond.

"Rome was a cauldron of vice and corruption, like your king's army, so go now and tell them that truth will win out, tell them in Dublin castle, that den of all iniquity, that my men have nothing to lose but their anger and they will buy revenge with their very souls."

Murphy stood on the steps with his fellow priest and demanded safe passage for him. He spared the old mansion, though it was contrary of his true feeling, so he sent a detachment to the equally grand house of Roger Owen, a house he had made many a belittling excursion to, to be derided and humiliated, to rake and burn it. It was obvious the bold Roger, his Missus and Henrietta had fled the coup.

Jack Keohane, with the strutting young Hen Tansey led the fire detail. The spirit of Raefil Keane hovered over the crippled loyalist zodiac, fanning the flames with great billowing cheeks under rogues eyes. Hen's chest swelled with pride, that Mr. Keohane had chosen him to help set the fireball.

Keohane and Monk Monaghan wanted to fire the whole town. In them, the passion for destruction was becoming almost a creativity. The impulse to burn was endemic in Kate Keohane's uncle. But Murphy had no desire to wreak his revenge on simple houses, he needed to move on to Enniscorthy, finding it was becoming more and more difficult to restrain the insurgents.

From high ground to the east of the episcopal city of Ferns, the rebel army rested. The sprawling urban garrison looked quiet, almost sleepy in the late morning of May 28th. Shadowless and majestic the hills of County Wicklow emerged from the mist to the north and the great spinal cord of sandstone and granite that was the Blackstairs to the west, encompassed the sunny county of Wexford in a protective sierra from Kildare, south to New Ross.

The army had also fled Ferns, the old town open and unprotected to the rebels. "What a crowd of cowards, they are," Murphy thought, "their cowardice is incorrigible, that even their love of power is unable to overcome." Despite his efforts at restraint, Keohane and his team of arsonists insisted on burning known Orange and loyalist housing.

The velvet mantle of the dying morning, before the sun reached its splendour, spread over the landscape. The scene from Carrigrew Hill was almost pastoral, where the dew had not completely evaporated. Cows were grazing, hens rooting and scratching the earth in a human and personal scene, but in it's great beauty, John Murphy could only see the hidden sadness of his surroundings. It ripped up his emotions that this heavenly tranquillity would soon host a terrible war.

Enniscorthy waited.

But first he had to practice a little patience and to humour the continued acclimations being heaped on him by the ever growing multitude.

Asked to wait and mounted on his horse in the shadow of the medieval Norman castle, they tore branches from the trees and in great pantomimic loops and trips, proceeded to sweep the dust before the mare's hooves, leading her, all the time through the ornate gateway of Bishop Cleaver's palace. The English Prelate had fled and from inside the mansion, the happy mob dragged his throne onto the steps and made the priest dismount and sit in the chair.

The Monk came before him once again in a great awkward gesture of courtesy, then sobered in a severe observance of the Catholic cleric who captured, in two days, the minds, hearts and souls of thousands and for now at least, the terror of England.

"You see this place, Father Murphy," Monaghan spread his great arms before the edifice, "no Catholic was ever inside these gates in two hundred years until today. Little children would be made to walk on the other side of the road, when passing by, not allowed to look, eyes to the ground when passing and with a quickened step, by God. Let Keohane burn it , Sir and let it stand a dark and terrible ruin for all time."

"We won't burn it Mr. Monaghan, nor any more fine houses of Wexford. They were built with the sweat and blood of your ancestors, their bodies lie in the foundations, but you will peruse the house and take anything that you think might be of use to us in the days ahead. Murphy sprang to his feet, "enough of your fun for now, let us be moving, there's a battle to be won, we have a six mile treck to Enniscorthy." He raised his voice to a tumultuous applause. "We move on now, not to keep the King of England waiting."

An avalanche of humanity left Camolin and Carrigrew Hill. The amount of heavy transports was becoming more plentiful as chose houses and farms of known loyalists were stripped of their contents. Monk Monaghan had secured for himself, a find dray and pair, among the artefacts, the gilded chair of His Lordship Bishop Eusabio Cleaver, three urchins spread on its sacred velvets.

Already the women were making their mark in John Murphy's army. When it came to entertaining the opposite sex, John Murphy's ideas were fragile and timid. In the company of women he found his powerful warden upon chastity and found women in bulk more chastening than the lone individual.

He found the very being of a woman a great secret, like poetry, beautiful and unexplaining, to love them, a lovely and fearful thing. To keep a lovely unassuming woman at arm's length, was not so much as to refuse the sweets of life or the suppression of lust, as to feed the ego of his cloistered virtue and to leave them to weave their devastating power on a more responsive victim. But this supreme self denial, gave him a kind of innocence that made him ashamed of nothing.

Looking at the strong pent up line now before the next confrontation, their faces, good and full of purpose and proud, he called on that unexplainable power that was inherent in the Irish woman, whose very life was a cauldron of kinetic strength, built around the working out of the process of multiple creations, to love their children twenty four hours a day and still have room for ploughing, turfing, crop saving and suckling. All their strength was built out of sheer necessity. Their bodies, shaped in the supple roundness, designed for the omniscience of childbearing, was a total phenomena that he could do little about.

The Blacksmith of Annamore in County Wicklow, Phelim Toole

and friend of Conor Devereaux, brought his daughter Suzy Toole with a transport of pikes and blades. Suzy was an expert at making gun powder, as was another, Madge Dixon, who, with her husband performed in the fight, as strong as any man. Nowhere in the world, had a soldier of any king or thick-voiced militarist, with his fine stock of accessories, ever come face to face with a woman in war mood. In the bristle of the bayonets, surprise and stupefaction at the sight of women warriors and priests at arms led to a moment's hesitation in a goodly Redcoat, who, as a consequence, never saw tomorrow's sunrise. Mary Doyle of Castleboro commandeered one hundred women, naming her elite corps, "The Moving Magazine." Their effort for the rebellion soon became notorious, running among the fallen militia, cutting off the cross belts together with the cartouche boxes, securing ball cartridge and ammunition. Refuelling with ball and powder became an art with them, following the riflemen into the heart of the battle, first becoming evident at Oulart, but perfected at Enniscorthy and all the battles to come.

Murphy's determination and morale pressed a step further with the report that pockets of rebels, endeavouring to join him were intercepted in a number of locations. Massacres took place at locations as far away as Naas and Clane and at Rathangan, short distances from Dublin, but the insurgents were victorious at Prosperous. It was at Prosperous that the United Irishman, Anthony Perry was arrested and tortured until he was forced to name his leaders. Forty rebels, having been shot in Dunlavin and the defeat of the rebels at Tara marked the end of the rebellion in County Meath. Government troops sacked Ballintore, but all the while, Father Murphy's army increased in size. That determination spurred further with the arrival of his friend, Father Michael at Ballyorril Hill. The younger cleric, from Ballycanew, near Gorey an ardent campaigner for the United Irishmen and for it, censured by the authorities and his bishop, presented a sorry sight, as his men were the object of savage reprisals when their village was attacked and over two hundred, slaughtered. He had three hundred men with him, poorly armed, but at the sight of the huge army before them, found a new courage, borrowed from the mob. Arms were found for them, but while Michael accepted the authority of his fellow priest as commander of what to his great surprise was an immense army, reasonably well disciplined, he did so, with a certain reservation which was to torment him for the duration of his short but illustrious contribution to the struggle. Father Michael found it ironic that the breach in the line of authority caused by the imprisonment of the leading United men in Wexford, like Bagnal Harvey and Fitzgerald was now being filled by a priest, unknown but for his pulpit thumping objections to the very cause that now brought him to this, and United men of all ranks were accepting John Murphy as such and without question.

The Commander had now lieutenants and he felt the comfort in the knowledge. Within an hour, he was to welcome yet another; a young man that would prove a superb general, considering his young age of eighteen summers. He brought with him a band of well armed insurgents and having introduced himself as Myles Byrne of Monaseed, he brought before the leaders, some of his company and introduced them with pride; John Doyle, Ned Fennell of Ballyellis, Nick Murphy, Michael Redmond and many others. Like many in the past two days, the young rebel tried, without much success to hide his surprise at the gait and apparel of his new commander.

After formalities, the young newcomer made himself very clear on one subject. "I make no apologies to any man for the truth, that Mr. Anthony Perry, who is accused in many quarters as the traitor who betrayed our cause and stands responsible for the incarceration of many of our leaders, is a man of great character and is a friend of mine."

"We bear Mr. Perry no ill will, Sir," said John, "for a man to for whatever purpose, betrays his country, there must have been a moral bond first, and none of us, yet know the circumstances of that betrayal."

Byrne replied, "I thank you for your compassion, Sir, but I am told he was subjected to atrocious agonies and now he stands in worse case of woe."

The confidence and brashness of the handsome Byrne impressed the priest and the youth was to impress further as the days progressed, while regarding the courageous and simple cleric with unconditional and uncritical affection.

An hour before the march to Enniscorthy, another priest, Father Mogue Kearns arrived with his two brothers and two hundred United men of Kiltealy, the picturesque landscape at the foot of the Scullogue Gap, where Mount Leinster separates from the Blackstairs Mountains. Big strapping men, stout and rustic as the land that spawned them and often adversaries of Father Murphy's hurling men of Kilcormack, standing now, in awe of him, hanging on his every word. Kearns himself, outlawed and boisterous as ever and excitable, who the loyalists tried to hang in Paris a few years before for his part in their revolution, but his size and bulk collapsed the gallows, embraced now, his old hunting partner before joining him and Father Michael in a prayer for victory.

"My destiny and yours, begins here, my friends in Ireland," John addressed them. "Gentlemen, I say to you to accept the quirk of fate that brought me here. Fate has a terrible power, it leads the willing but drags along the reluctant and the necessity to accept it is often harsh." He looked at Myles Byrne. "Though I have never met your friend Anthony Perry, he bears that responsibility, for indeed it seems that Beauchamp Bagnal Harvey of Wexford Town, whom I have also never met, should be standing here instead of me. I pledge you, and all the croppies, that, if we are successful at Enniscorthy, we will go to Wexford Town and secure the release of those worthy men, you have my word on it."

A scout reported the scene at Enniscorthy. With anxiety, the leaders listened, forming in their own minds, the action to follow. The garrison consisted of North Cork Militia of Enniscorthy and the Scarawalsh Yeomanry – about five hundred men, under Captain Snow. The entrance to the town from the west at the Duffry Gate was powerfully defended by Captain Joshua Pounden and the notorious Captain Wrenne, with a corps of about two hundred and fifty riflemen and three six pounder artillery units.

The town, from the west, has The River Slaney running along one side, with houses on the other. Father Murphy sent three hundred firearms, the faithful "moving magazines", in close attention, and flanked by his own pikemen along the sloped western approach toward the gate. The so called Gate had been constructed two centuries before and had only the pillars remaining.

"They're afraid of you, they're half the man you are, you can't miss, see their red tunics stand out like ripe berries, remember Carnew, remember us at Oulart." The priest's voice rang out in the afternoon sunshine. The Duffry Gate was intensely protected and the Yeos fired from all angles, even from the upper floors of the houses into the thickening crowd and rebels died in prompt succession. Captain Carnock rode out with the Scarawalsh, only to be beaten back by the pikemen and the rifles, now commanded by Roche at one side and Myles Byrne at the other, but the pikemen were committing suicide if it had been allowed to continue.

Murphy called for a retreat to high ground. It was four in the afternoon.

Five thousand pressed around him to attack again. The priest sat, stone faced, looking down on the town. It was an impenetrable fortress, the red berries lined along the wall to each side of the only entrance. Should he retreat as far back as Bunclody, he could re-route toward Ballycarney and through the byroad, eastward to Ferns and back onto the Gorey Road and attack by way of Island Road, with Slaney on his left flank now. But it was John Murphy's next bout of Inspiration that won for them another day and constituted the greatest victory of the insurrection. If he were to come at the enemy from the east, the sun would be to his disadvantage, as he fought into its fiery ball.

"Holy Mother of God, I can't send them into that" he whispered to Father Michael.

Michael's restlessness had him toing and froing before his men.

"Surely 'tis what we're here for," he bellowed, " 'tis they're the cowards, they'll run again, go to it man."

This wasn't the time for personal conflict. John Murphy was well aware of his friend's resentment at the superior position he found himself in, that it was trust upon him was, for the moment, beside the point. Father Michael was already keen to make his own mark. A mild jealousy shone out on his youthful ardent face, apprehension that he was equally loved by all. Michael had no need for such sentiments, John Murphy was always well aware of the younger man's courage, overzealous, quick to temper, but courage before adversity, before his bishop, before the authorities was always in abundance.

Conor Devereaux who had been in close earshot, confronted the younger cleric with steel in his eyes, threatening, "He's done very well up to now, Sir."

Another hour went by and the red berries below began to look complacent as they began to bake in their hot outfits. Murphy called his leaders and proposed his plan that had been fermenting in his mind for an hour.

"We'll call on Nature herself and she'll serve us well, but we'll wait another half hour, when she dances her sun on the rim of the Blackstairs." He smiled broadly at his little council of war. They shot suspicious glances at him, full of concern, but nowhere was there mistrust. He was again, authoritive and assuring, his eyes as if to say, "I have it, we'll blind them with our science." In the same breath, he called to The Monk. "Mr. Monaghan, how many cattle have we with us?"

The Wexford man looked at him, wild-eyed and stammered, "b.b.bout sixty or seventy round about the hill, Sir."

"Bulls, Mr. Monaghan?"

"Bulls, Father?"

"Have we bulls?"

"We left them below, Father, sure they're troublesome beasts."

"Find half a dozen drovers and bring three of them onto the front, and hurry, Mr. Monaghan, no time to be lost."

401

The garrison of Enniscorthy strained to locate the source of the thunder burst rushing toward them out of the blinding sun. Shading his eyes, Captain Pounden caught form of a massive golden dust cloud coming headlong at the Gate. The croppies roared, women screamed and jabbed at the terrified animals. Guns were fired off to keep them in line.

The soldiers, blind and confused, let off wasted shot, had no time to refuel as the stampede, led by three marauding and massive bulls, roared through Duffry, like an impassioned pageant, down into the centre of the town, overturning, man, cart, artillery pieces alike. Many a Hessian and many a Yeo had had an inglorious death as they rolled like rag dolls under the hooves of a frenzied milker, stolen earlier from the estate of Rev. Roger Owen, of Camolin.

Three thousand pikemen screamed into the town behind the frothing herd and General Roche, with prepared pitch torches, set his men about burning the houses in Guttle Street, while the military trapped inside tried frantically to reload their heavy muskets and blunderbusses.

The rebels torched Irish Street and Drumgoold and eventually took the bridge. The North Corks were completely routed, as captain Snow ordered the retreat. Pikes, scythes, hayforks and great cudgels followed the running Redcoats into St. John's Wood, where the outrage of the past few days and the tyranny of centuries, fed the peasant hunger for revenge.

Father Murphy had tried to impress on the rebels, that a Protestant was not the enemy, but anything in a uniform was. However the loyalist houses burned, many with their residents inside them, as the croppies, so eager in their endeavours, had little compunction about killing a defender of the town. But the rebel army was not without its martyrs. A hundred died, men and women of Shelmalier, Monaseed, Kiltealy, Boolavogue, Trasna, Ferns, Camolin and all places in between, victims of the rebellion with the name of John Murphy and Ireland on their lips. Joshua Pounden, the keeper of The Gate had been trampled to death. Lieutenant Le Hunt lay dead in the square, about him, well known loyalists, privates, corporals, sergeants. Those running now from the fight; Captain Snowe, Hamilton Jacob, Solomon Richards of Solsboro, who it has to be said was in favour of the Catholics right of emancipation, were all recipients of the lands of Ireland, confiscated by their ancestors under Oliver Cromwell, a hundred and fifty years before. As was Captain Isaac Carnock, who lay in the square mortally wounded. He had been a part of the defence of The Gate with his Yeomanry Column. A magistrate, he was regarded as fair minded and was a friend of Father Murphy, when they rode together, sat at the tables of Mountnorris and Sir George Palmer together.

There were five priests at the battle for Enniscorthy and John Murphy asked that they would walk among the dead and dying to administer last rights, if asked to do so. John Murphy knelt by his hunting partner and the Captain asked for a blessing.

**

Young Myles Byrne, a veritable horseman from the town land of Ballyhack on the inner harbour of Waterford, a young man with a bravery expected in a veteran, was himself, awestruck at the pious priest, fighting under a black banner, a shortened pike in one hand, a sword in the other, tearing at the enemy, where the animals and the elements answer to his call.

The youngster sat with John, outside the burning town, their backs to a warm stone, as the detail for burial set about its task. Grieving and ecstatic women saw to the necessities of feeding and nursing the wounded, as new recruits flocked from the surrounding districts, to swell the rebel army.

"They might service the battles," sighed Murphy, "but will they survive the hunger, how do you feed thousands on a hillside."

"Didn't God Himself feed the thousands, Father, on a hillside like this, and He didn't have lambs and chickens and hogs to do so, as we have."

A young girl genuflected before the two, a lump of bread and some meat for the priest's dinner. Nervously, she handed over the meal. "Child, will you stop bobbing at me now, there's a good girl." She smiled through the scruffiness of her tangles and her innocent beauty, bobbed again and ran off. He watched her shyly look at him again from the safety of her mother's skirts in the hillside kitchen.

"What is your name, lovely girl," he called to her.

"She's Teresa, Father John", said the mother, with not a little pride, and 'tis yourself will be giving her first holy communion, this time next year. She's called after Saint Teresa, The Little Flower."

He whispered to Byrne, "the trustful innocence of a child who sees nothing beyond its mother's eyes, and God created woman because of the inefficiency of man. Good God, does she know that next year is a thousand years away."

Then, coming out of his little trance, he said loudly, "Mr. Byrne, the difference between God on the mount and here, is that The Almighty didn't have the English to face in the fight."

Myles Byrne laughed heartily, then sobered. "You must stand back

Father, the others want you safe. Edward wants you to leave the front line to him, or to Sparks. There are men here who fought in France, in America, experienced soldiers who could lead from the front."

Murphy argued, "these lads are all able to do what they do best, on the fringes. The riflemen, with the women are more valuable on the flanks, the likes of Roche, Sparks, Fennelly, Doyle, Jeramiah Prendergast, are all seasoned and can train the newcomers. Father Michael and Kearns and myself are just rousers and shouters and unskilled, it won't matter if we go down."

"You know, that is not a fact, Sir, without you, this army would disintegrate, you owe it to us to stay safe," said Byrne, sternly.

Murphy smiled wearily. "He who would have the fruit must climb the tree, young man, my place is with the pikes, I can't fire a gun very well. This life has taught me to reap satisfaction and sustenance from the effort, whatever that might be at the time, but I always leave the outcome to God." He slugged at a mug of milky tea. "If we get to Wexford and free the real leaders, then one of them will take command. Until then, we will need an artillery expert, see if you can find one."

"But we have no artillery," said Byrne, "the stampede destroyed the units at the Gate."

The priest winked at the youth. "No, but God might think fit to provide and when he does, we must be ready."

The rebels crossed The Slaney and flowed through Templeshannon and Shannon Quay and through the rough lanes to Vinegar Hill. More than a hill, less than a mountain. The cone shaped mass was an excellent vantage point and central to the main towns and villages of north Wexford. It was to be fortified as a permanent camp

The officers convened a council and John Murphy was brought up to date with developments in the county. Because of the evacuation of the towns and the threat of the rebels, a state of chaos existed, not just in the county, but in the capital also. The meeting sat in the night glare of the inferno that was Enniscorthy. A garrison was left below in the streets and the square where loyalists and deserting military were being hounded from haylofts, cellars, copses and riverbanks. Fiddles and pipes played before a hundred campfires, while ale from the cellars of Rudds Inn was passed around in abundance. Expensive wines from the grand houses of Enniscorthy and Ferns was being swigged from rude cups and from the necks of bottles, without due reverence to their vintage or exclusive origin.

James Attridge was to report to his network in Europe and in America, an ever growing audience, he was always careful that truth did not suffer a radical distortion .He wrote;

"A mister Thomas Barker was appointed keeper of Enniscorthy, where his specific orders were to try to restore some kind of order. This reporter must say that I was sickened at the sight of the carnage, as I made my way through the smoke, the smell of pitch and gunpowder and burning buildings, the rancid odour of burning flesh as corpses in red tunics were fed to the flame. As I passed by the junction of Main Street and Castle Street, I saw a dozen militia being lined against the gable wall of the ruined townhouse of Mr. Ivor Barrington for execution. About twenty men in green cockades, some of them wearing the hurling sashes of Shelmalier and Kilcormack and Killeen, were now playing a different game, as they waited the order to fire. Unknown to the commander priest, the town had become a bable, as the mob became more and more incensed and the dragon teeth of exactness ground its way through the carnage, as the peasantry regarded it their right to return evil for evil, that the day's victory would be somewhat flawed without it."

"Saoirse"

The priest had ordered that nobody was to emulate the loyalist North Corks, Hessians or the Orangemen by the mutilation and desecration of bodies. Death itself was to be dignified and not prolonged. All enemy corpses were to be cremated as soon as possible, as dogs were beginning to savage the remains. All insurrection casualties were to receive burial. The burning houses became the stinking crematorium that took four hundred of the enemy to hell.

John Murphy had two visitations on the afternoon of 29th. May. James Attridge and his new wife arrived in one of Duhallow's fine coaches. Foxy Paddy was hardly recognisable in a fine jacket and britches and Mr. And Mrs. Attridge O'Connor Devereaux, alighted from the carriage, dressed for a more auspicious occasion than a tramp camp on Vinegar Hill. Furtive glances were thrown at the couple as Father John came to meet them, but levity prevailed as Attridge asked for assistance to relieve the carriage of over one hundred short handled pikes, concealed in the false floor and fifty rifles from behind the plush velvet seat backs. These particular weapons were masterpieces of Conor Devereaux's fertile mind. A coupling at the centre of the shaft, allowed it to be broken and assembled at will, depending on the closeness of the conflict; broken, it became two weapons.

Father Murphy cautioned the couple for their recklessness on a blind chance that the military should allow them passage, or worse still, to find the weapons in their possession.

"Dressed like this, Father", Attridge assured him, "you must admit, we look very ascendancy." He laughed nervously under the scrutiny of the cleric.

"You're taking a great chance, both of you, I insist you stay at Duhallow."

"I'll take Kate back now, Father, that the armoury is empty, but I'll be around you, I'm a journalist, it is what I do."

The priest was insistent. "You have responsibilities now, James, to your wife, but to Duhallow and the people of the estate, to Trasna and to Boolavogue. When all this is over, they will need a landlord they can trust. If anything happens to you, the estate will be annexed, people like Mountnorris, Owen, Cope, will take it."

Conor Devereaux was suddenly by his side. "John Murphy is right, lad, if you die, Duhallow will be lost. Looking severely at Kate, he said, "take him home and keep him there, and bring The Master Dunne to Duhallow, they'll burn him out for sure."

Kate cut him off. "The Master is dead, Conor." Her eyes filled, "they burned him out on Sunday night, we buried him on the hill of the Priest Leap, Norah Scully is at Duhallow, but she says she won't stay long, as soon as it's the Month's Mind, she will be going." The words caught in her throat. "They burned your church Father John."

Murphy grasped her shoulders, assuringly. "Ah, child," he said assuringly, where liberty is concerned, there's bound to be some irreverence. Go now, you have a duty beyond any one of us here, build the church again in time, let you, that way you will wipe out all the badness of today."

Attridge noticed the blacksmith looking darkly at him, a show of feeling that was full and deep and cherishing, then the blacksmith turned and walked into the crowd.

James took the priest aside. "I've had communications from Mr. Wolfe Tone in Paris. He assures me there will be no French invasion, at least for several months. General Bonaparte has taken every available ship on his mission to Egypt and left the country pauperised."

"When then?" said Murphy.

"It would be September, Father."

"Or not at all, James." A wry smile like " I told you so," crossed the priest's tired face.

 "Or not at all, Father".

"There's something else," James continued, "good news." Counties Antrim and Down are ready for rebellion. My contact in Belfast, however, informs me, as we speak, General Lake is awaiting the arrival of ten thousand more troops from England".

"Why doesn't the good general then, turn his attention to France, with nobody there to confront him and leave us alone," sighed Murphy.

"Is there any chance you could join forces with Antrim and Down, Father, what an army it would make. I've met Monro and Mc. Cracken."

"We will, hopefully," said Murphy, putting a strong hand on the younger man's shoulder, "but first, we must take Wexford town, then this army will have a new commander and maybe I can go home." His look was a question mark with its own inevitability.

Kate knelt before him for his blessing on Vinegar Hill Road, where patriotism had now become a new religion. The backdrop of the black banner, was suddenly the embodiment of their lives. The vestment of Good Friday and of the stern sentence of burial services now had a meaning and a message that was appallingly out of place, perhaps blasphemous.

Trying to shut out the scenes in the town, Kate stifled a sob. "The Master always said that the devil makes more room in hell, in times of war."

Chapter 53

The rock outcrop of Vinegar Hill awoke to great activity in a glorious burst of sunshine. Sixteen thousand rebels occupied the mount and the town and yet more and more came.

William Barker, the keeper of Enniscorthy, a brewer and a veteran of the French army, big John Kelly of Killane with his stalwart mountain men, marched in perfect formation up the slopes to the ruined Mill on the summit. Thomas Cloney of Moneyhore, with his personal army of three hundred from the Barony of Bantry, to the west, Michael Furlong of Templescoby, Garret Byrne of Ballymanus all were to swell the ranks of the croppy army and many distinguish themselves in the days to come.

Among the day's arrivals was Mr. John Hay of Newcastle. A veteran of the Irish Brigade of France, who had vast experience of warfare on the Continent, having been honoured by the French on many occasions for distinction in the field. He was to accept John Murphy's leadership with great but respectful scepticism and it was soon obvious that he would take sides with Father Michael in a consorted attempt to replace the Boolavogue man, who once had trenchantly opposed armed revolt.

At a late breakfast council meeting on 29th. May, Hay outlined his reservations for their success, given the fragile nature of their military situation, the lack of weapons and trained personnel. There were others in the camp who would have been sitting, waiting to take one side or the other, where private wars of revenge could break up the rebel army into small guerrilla bands. Conor Devereaux tried to remain calm, his temper, always an edged tool. In a controlled voice, his anger in his eyes, he said, "you gentlemen wouldn't know much about it, but John Murphy did very well up to now".

He was about to continue and Murphy could see the beginning of a Devereaux onslaught. The priest intervened, with a look of appreciation to the blacksmith. "We must be careful, Gentlemen not to belittle the iron will and the bravery of the croppies." He was again, ready to make enemies among the fresh arrivals, full of new and untested ideas for victory.

"I have one question for the council. Mr. Napoleon Bonaparte, according to my friend James Attridge, a man of writing and reading, and may I say, a man who has met Mr. Bonaparte, quotes him as saying that nothing is more difficult and, therefore more precious, than to be able to decide. I want you to decide now, but before you do, answer this." He looked at them with half contemptuous respect.

"Where were you all before last Sunday?"

The question found it's mark."Between saying and doing, Gentlemen, many a fine pair of boots are worn out". He left the snub sink in, allowing a significant pause, many eyes were downcast. He took special notice of his friend Father Michael's discomfort, then continued. "We will fortify this hill, send scouts on ahead, then this army will take the town of Wexford, the very hub of our discontent, after which we will march on Dublin, Join Monro and Mac Cracken and, with two hundred thousand men, we will take the city, and the country."

He smiled at a few raised eyebrows. "Now, I know that the whole Society of the United Irishmen have been talking about this, talking and meeting, and meeting and talking, conferences and committees, for a very long time. I thought of it yesterday, Gentlemen. Somebody said one time that a committee is a group that keeps the minutes, but loses the hours."

He pointed a cautionary finger at Hay. "If, at Wexford, with the release of Bagnal Harvey, who, from all accounts is a mighty man, and if they haven't already hanged him and if my resignation is sought, then I will gladly move aside."

Silence fell like a cold draught on the council. Those who had been with him since Sunday, suppressed the urge to punch the air. Hay stood and shook the priest's hand. "My people and I pledge our support Sir, I think only of victory."

Father Michael gazed eastward to the rising sun and remained noncommittal.

The tension was diffused with the second arrival of the early day, of Edward Fitzgerald of Newpark, the twenty eight year old popular founder member of the United Irishmen and affectionately known as Lord Edward by his adoring followers, who called to him and ran after his horse, all the way through the town and the lanes of Vinegar, in waves of welcome. Fitzgerald would have added another two thousand men to the army, but he had come directly from Wexford with his companion, Mr. John Henry Colclough of Ballytigue castle, another powerful Protestant landlord, and like many more of his ilk, a campaigner for Catholic relief. Once again, their surprise was evident when they were brought before the curate of Boolavogue.

Fitzgerald asked for a council meeting at which he outlined his mission. "Yesterday, Colclough and I were released from jail in Wexford, as was the brave Mr. Anthony Perry. It is true that, under inhuman torture, Perry released our names and that of our leader,

Beauchamp Bagnal Harvey. Mr. Perry is free at the moment, wandering about the roads, out of his mind in his torment. He was pitchcapped and flogged within an inch of his life, until he cried out our names. Harvey is still in prison."

Fitzgerald looked at the steely face of the priest, and he wondered, after all, if this middle aged, middle sized paragon of divinity, was the gentle seraph, spoken about in whispers and reverent phrases, the length and breadth of the country, or a veritable war machine in altar linens. "We were released on bail of a sizable sum of money to the coffers of Captain James Boyd, on condition we would approach the rebels, as envoys on behalf of the crown garrison and wishes to advise the insurgent army that he is prepared to accept their surrender of all arms held in their possession, in return for which, the crown will allow all those who have taken up arms against the king to return safely to their homes."

Murphy asked for refreshments for the travellers and said, very simply that a victorious army does not sue for terms, but dictate them. "We march on Wexford today, Mr. Fitzgerald and the people of Wexford will know of our arrival."

Colclough was sent back to Wexford, while Fitzgerald agreed to join the ranks of the revolutionaries.

Preparations were made to mobilize on the county Seat. Emissaries were sent in all directions to catholic and protestant alike to come to Vinegar Hill, the symbol of their defence and point of assembly.

By early afternoon, eighteen thousand souls turned south west for the picturesque capital, hope and fear, their only waking dream. Their instructions were to make for The Three Rocks, a shoulder of Forth Mountain, less than two miles from Wexford town and in sight of the garrison. The vantage point offered a panoramic view of the Sun County, even to her coasts to the south and east. More and more flocked to the black banner as the villages of Tagmon, Camross, Adamstown, Foulksmills, Tullycanna and Wexford itself disgorged themselves of their able bodied men and women to swell Murphy's ranks. From Shelmalier, Ballaghkeen, Bantry, Scarawalsh, Little Limerick, they came, dragging their families before them and their livestock after them, the sight of the strolling shouting ribbons of humanity, a greater concern to the commander than the enemy itself. They came out of Wexford town in their hundreds, their courage heightening at the size of the mob, courage, now, their salvation.

Never resting, John Murphy circled in and out of the hillocks and crevices of The Three Rocks as the feeding fires lit up the hillside. His voice could be heard on the calm air urging them to sleep soundly, that down there, below were those responsible for the suffering of the nation. Around his own camp fire, he wondered again at the infirmity of the English and their inability to use common sense. " Common sense is the most fairly distributed thing in the world, yet, surely the British were behind the door when the good Lord dispensed his bounty," he said to the leaders. "Surely they have scouts, though our scouts say they saw none, for they could have set upon us as we came south on so many occasions, with high ground in abundance. At Oulart I tried to find their weakness, but by God, 'tis everywhere, their biological weakness is the condition of their human culture, it is why they have to appear so grandiose."

The cooking fires burned in the night like a great glow-worm circling the base of the mountain and John Murphy's private tenebrae matched the darkness beyond the fires.

At daybreak of May 30th., on an outrock the priests celebrated Mass. It was a hurried celebration, as scouts reported enemy reinforcements and cavalry, coming from Duncannon Fort on the shores of Waterford Harbour and now streaming through the village of Tagmon, just a few miles away, on its way to Wexford. The two priests sat on a vantage point, their breakfast spread on a flat stone. Father Michael, despite his reservations in terms of his friend's ability to continue as the army grew out of all expected proportions, could not but feel with awe, at his ability to draw people to him, his ability to marshal by simple sympathetic attractions. If the younger priest were to be honest with himself, the mild jealousy he was feeling, was nothing more than being deprived, nothing more. From the high knoll of the friendly mountain, the two wondered again at the stupidity and the bumptious apathy of the King's troupes.

Two hundred men, no outriders, no scouts, approaching a rebel camp of thousands, sauntered their way toward them, like the procession of a royal funeral, unhurried and full of pomposity and pride. "A royal funeral it is then," John whispered, then called to Myles Byrne, who came strutting up the heather. The handsome youth, his sprouting moustache, black curly locks, making him looking older than his eighteen years, saluted, a smile of expectation creasing his good looks.

"There now, Mr. Byrne, said the Boolavogueman, God's artillery, delivered to your door, through the courtesy of the King of England. Go down now and inform Mr. Tom Cloney and Mr. Thomas Barker and let you and them make a list together, and take delivery."

Byrne took the order with pride. "See you wait until they come under the Three Rocks and we'll be looking down on you."

411

Thomas Cloney, of Moneyhore, took charge of the attack, with a detachment of five hundred men of The Blackstairs, Templescoby and Kilcormack. Cloney, with Michael Furlong and Byrne positioned them above the road and waited.

Captain Adams, with his men of the Meath Militia, gunners of the Royal Artillery Regiment, with four six pounders and two Howitzer cannon, were completely unprepared for the frenzied onslaught that contained little military skill, but rather the rampant vigorousness of an impetuous hurling team. A few guns managed to be fired off, but nothing could cope with the massive pikes that ripped the tired column asunder, with the first plunge. It was over in less than half an hour and the noonday sun rose above the Forth Mountain, to light on the polished buttons of one hundred dead militia, along with half a dozen officers. Father Murphy's orders were to keep the gunners alive and Myles Byrne smiled, remembering the priest's promise.

By noon, five pieces of artillery were trained on the road to Wexford, two of them the powerful Howitzers, two gunners tethered to each gun with a pike in their ears, should they fire askew. At the Three Rocks, the king's soldiers would fire on the king's soldiers. Word had reached Wexford of a massive offensive on the Forth Mountain and the town went into a panic. The Officers had been waiting for the arrival of the artillery from Duncannon Fort which was now trained on them. "Let them come to us as before, we can dictate the outcome, if we pick the spot." Murphy called out, and they came.

Edward Fitzgerald was able to name the officers of the town, not that Father Murphy was interested in name or rank. Fitzgerald tried to assure Murphy of his loyalty, while many in the camp were sceptical of that loyalty, after all he was an emissary of the enemy and only a week ago, was accepting weapons from frightened peasants, to his mansion at Newpark, but then so was Father Murphy, who only a week ago was demanding the surrender of all weaponry.

The young Fitzgerald tried to impress on the commander, his allegiance, by naming the officers inside Wexford Town; the senior officer, Col. Jonas Watson was in charge of the barricades, Col. Maxwell was commanding the Donegal Militia and The North Corks. Generals Adams and Fawcett, had, it seems decided to wait for the Duncannon armoury to arrive before deciding strategy. Inside were the Heathfield Yeos under Captain John Grogan, Fawcett himself commanded the 13th. Reg. Meath Militia while Captain Fox commanded the Tagmon Cavalry.

"The names and the ranks mean nothing to us, Mr. Fitzgerald", said Murphy, sternly, " take it from me, all we see is a uniform, not the ribbons and bows. If these officers were any good, they wouldn't be here, but off fighting Napoleon Bonaparte, and not herding a poor nation of defenceless peasantry." The priest, looking at the younger man under his eyes, gested, "tell me now, Mr. Fitzgerald, all those colonels, captains and generals, are there any soldiers in there at all, at all?"

Impatiently, Watson rode out with three hundred men, to check the district and find news of the Duncannon Militia, only to be fired on by the massive cannon and Howitzer bombardment in which the elderly Colonel was killed. The army once again scampered before the rebels, pounding back over their dead comrades of the previous encounter.

With the frailty of the king's troops now being demolished by their own cannon, Father John thought of following them into the town, but for some reason he decided not to. It was a decision he was to regret later.

The reports coming back to Wexford of an army of thousands, camped on their doorstep, fuelled massive confusion, tumult and even panic and the timidity displayed by the rampant Orangemen, Yeomen and Militarists alike resembled a prologue to a stage play of cowardly courtesies and perfect chicken heartedness. They portrayed themselves of little capacity and little or no intelligence, running about the town trying to find safe quarters. Many commandeered boats in the harbour to flee to Wales, more dressing as women in their efforts at concealment. Among the runners were the notorious Magistrates Boyd and Jacob, the latter fleeing to England out of Waterford. Captain Boyd was seen running the length of the quayside, eventually persuading a terrified skipper of a small boat at the point of a pistol. Boyd was not to get far. To fan the flame of panic among the loyalists, word was about, that the French had landed.

There wasn't a royal troop to stand guard in Wexford. Epaulets and insignia were torn from uniforms to hide rank as they made their escape. A telltale white mass of wispy vapour shot through with gold and tinged with colours of a Summer afternoon, began to spread from beyond the town, westward toward Taghmon and Folksmills and Slaney. The smoke cloud soon thickened like a pallium over the countryside as the retreating militia burned cabins and yet, unripened saplings of corn and wheat in the supple moist fields. Horses and carriers were driven through potato patches and vegetable gardens, their revenge to be a punctual paymaster.

John Murphy pondered heavily on the maximum opportunity that had been lost and Father Michael was the first to decry that decision not to attack the town while the enemy was in sight. This cowardly army was now loose on the people, to do as much damage as possible and would be available another day. A thousand militia had vacated the town without firing a shot.

Conor Devereaux rode with the priest as the rebels poured into Wexford Town. The peasantry had come out to greet them and Murphy was well aware of the possibility that many of them would have their loyalties elsewhere, but for now and for them, they would measure their loyalty by the strength on their doorstep. The devil you know is better than the devil you don't.

Conor looked younger and stronger in his new resolve, having fought his first battle at Three Rocks. "I'm wondering," said Murphy, with not a little edge of sarcasm, "if you and I have not been committed by God to chase King George all over the kingdom for the rest of our days."

The blacksmith replied with an equal share of wit. "Sure, John Murphy, God knows that, even the savage has a bit of dignity and pride, but that sentiment never sat easily with that crowd, so I have two things to say to you. I'm longer in this world than you are, and I have lived with this king for longer than you have, but your showing of this etiquette, courtesy and even respect, and not levelling this town, with all these tyrants inside it, was a mistake, and the other matter, I say Vinegar Hill is a bad decision for your camp. Your guerrilla type has paid you well, Vinegar is open to the elements and to the enemy. Scrub, ditches, copses, bog lands have been your success, Vinegar is bald as Mountnorris is under his wigs."

Murphy spoke above the din of the crowd, coming out of their houses, crowding to see the priest that the whole world was talking about. "They keep talking to me about this Bagnal Harvey fellow, Conor, this important man and I say again, where has he been all along.? The military would have hanged him, surely, if we had struck. He seems to me to be too important to the rebellion. If truth be known, I was hoping the cowards might parley."

"Take it from me, John Murphy, Beauchamp Bagnal Harvey is far from your opinion of him, and from their opinion of him." He beckoned darkly at the likes of Fitzgerald and the few leaders who still held the priest in a limbo of acceptance.

"You know him, Conor?" asked Murphy.

"I know him."

A small scouting party rode up to the pair. General Fawcett who had come out from Duncannon Fort to meet the fleeing Orange army was burning and killing in droves in the areas of Moyglass, and south west toward the towns of Newbawn, Camross and Taghmon.

"Well now, John Murphy." The blacksmith's craggy face was stern as old leather. "We know this other cheek now, I always have, for I always looked for it. You have no choice but to continue, for there's small choice in rotten apples".

As the multitude poured through St. John's Gate in triumph and consumed the narrow streets, the Bullring, The Cornmarket, where Tone had spoken over five years before, John Murphy now became the central object of the approbation and rapture and adulation of the townspeople, hooting and shouting inn waves of welcome. Houses were quickly festooned with flags and boughs.

The priest's black mare pricked her ears at the deafening acclimation from respectable houses, a line of proud pikemen walked at her flanks, while women, draped in green distributed cockades to all and sundry. Orangemen who were obliged to stay behind in the town with their families had discarded the obnoxious colours of their order were now the most vociferous of the throng. Known Yeomen and loyalists greeted the mob, nervous in their mendacity, that retribution might follow in the wake of the euphoria.

All prisoners were released from the Stonebridge jailhouse, leaving a garrison in vulnerable places, while dancing, singing and welcome rivalry into the night.

Beauchamp Bagnal Harvey was nowhere to be found within the walls of the dark depressing building which was the Stonebridge Jailhouse. They were about to torch it, when Jack Keohane found him, standing inside the huge Inglenook of the swill hall, three quarters of his heavy body, up the chimney, petrified in dread of his enemies.

An ultimatum had been issued to all insurgents and croppies that there was to be no retribution foisted on a town that was open to them and in surrender, that all women were to be respected and protected and no abuse was to be tolerated. The priest was now well aware of the underlying ferocity for past violence on the part of the loyalists, many of them still resided in Wexford and were locked up in their houses.

**

The townhouse of Bagnal Harvey, within a few hours of his release, was vibrating with merriment. The windows, upper and lower, looked out onto Selkar Street and as night fell were superbly lit up for his homecoming celebration. Word had been sent out to the priest commander to join the celebrations, but Murphy declined right away, preferring to police the town with a chosen corps, as he omitted to do in Enniscorthy, where Protestants and loyalists died needlessly, two days before. He called to Byrne and Roche to have a consignment ready on Cullimore Quay within the hour. They would walk through the night in the wake of the retreating loyalist army and engage them as soon as possible. Then he asked the blacksmith and Father Michael to accompany him to the home of Bagnal Harvey. He assured Conor, who was reluctant, that it was purely out of courtesy.

The United chiefs, most of whom, Murphy had never met, were seated at the sumptuous table and a cheer went up on Murphy's entrance. Beauchamp Bagnal Harvey, a Protestant lawyer, landlord and businessman of Bargey Castle and a man of liberal principles, supporting the ideals of government reform and catholic emancipation, sat at the head of the table, being paid the deference due to his rank as Commander-in-Chief of the United Irishmen in Wexford. It was immediately obvious the thirty six year old was well used to the applause and the approval of people.

The chief was full of good cheer, already well soused, spreading his arms in welcome, urging the trio to join them. Hero of The Three Rocks, Thomas Cloney was present, as was Henry Prendergast, John Hay and Henry Colclough, who had been, just yesterday an emissary of the loyalists, and many local insurgents who had already been promoted to exalted rank. Others were introduced; Burghers of the Baronies of Forth and Bargy, Hughes and Furlong, all well inebriated, their overzealous hand shaking, some obviously concealing their feelings of scepticism behind a facade of exaggerated approval. To his surprise, Father Michael, a seasoned United Man, recognised, among the revellers, known loyalists and proven antagonists, whose green cockades and scarves, now worn with aplomb, in other circumstances would be a different colour.

John Murphy tried not to see meanings beyond the obvious, but with a brutal look around the huge table, he reported in calm, unhurried and respectful voice. "I have four columns of men drawn up on the quayside, Sir, under John Kelly, Conor Devereaux, here with me and Father Michael, also here, and down below waiting to mobilise is General Edward Roche. Four thousand men and five hundred women are waiting for the off. The enemy is camped at Taghmon, under Colonel Watson on its way to Duncannon Fort, where he will be substantially reinforced by General Loftus and the Fifth Dragoon Guards, the Dunbartonshire Hyland Regiment and the Ross and Wexford Yeomanry. I suggest we move now this night against Watson and cut their army in two. It's just a few miles away."

Harvey stood for the first time. He was a man of strong physique, though going into flesh and dressed, even now in red Yeoman livery.

"And who is this General, you speak of?" Harvey frowned

"Edward Roche of Garrylough, Sir, already distinguished himself at Oulart and Enniscorthy," replied Murphy.

"But you're the hero of the rising, Sir", demanded Harvey, "this Roche fellow, I know him. A simple tenant, you say a General?"

"A term of endearment, Mr. Harvey, at the time he was the only experienced soldier in the whole army, we didn't have time to hand out insignia of rank, nor does the army desire it."

"If there was to be a General, Father Murphy, it should be you," insisted Harvey.

"I'm just a simple priest, Sir. I wish to simply return to my church or what's left of it and leave matters in capable hands."

For the first time, Father Michael spoke, a voice that mixed pity with contempt, "something I'm afraid is not to be found in this room."

Harvey, with malice, replied to the younger belligerent priest, "there is only one General in the army of the United Irishman, and I have been proclaimed as such, Sir, and he doesn't go about in a Roman collar and a frock coat."

"Then," cut in John Murphy, "I'm asking the General if I might be allowed to engage our enemy as they slink away, before they regroup and torment us another day."

Cordiality returned. The Commander-in-Chief came to where the three were standing

"Our men are tired, Gentlemen, 'tis night time, let them rest, we've decided to meet tomorrow morning on Windmill Hill to discuss tactics."

John Murphy was losing patience, as the carafes were being passed about the table. "My men on the quayside have been kept under discipline since we arrive, "tomorrow will be too late."

Conor Devereaux raised his voice half a decibel, looking down on the new commander, there were no courtesies, no titles. "The only reason why you are still alive, is because the authorities wished to use you to their own benefit and purpose and it seems to me, they have succeeded."

Bagnal Harvey ignored the snub, one could fear this big man who seems to be held in good esteem by Murphy. "Bed, Father Murphy, let the men go to bed, we have had a great victory, the army must rest. Steadying himself, Harvey put a hand on the priest's shoulder, seeing, for the first time, up close the tenacity and dogged commitment of this strange cleric.

"I see no reason to wrap ourselves in victory garlands, Mr. Harvey," said John Murphy. "We have had only a moral victory. It neither suits the vanquished or the victor. You were stuck up a chimney a couple of hours ago, in dread of the authorities, this evening you have been handed a glorious bounty and if it is a burden to you, then say so now, for twenty thousand rebels, who have fought to secure that gift will weigh how it is acknowledged and if you do so with open hand and open heart, then I am relieved at the prospect."

"Tomorrow we strike, Father Murphy and you'll rebuild your church. A good general has to adhere to strategy, otherwise, chaos will devour him. God builds His Temples on the ruins of churches and in the hearts of men." General Bagnal Harvey held out his hand in a condescending gesture and John Murphy took it. It was weak and cold. The three again refused refreshments and left the room to a nervous group. Michael and Conor refused the courtesy.

Chapter 54

The spirit of the great march of events of the past two days, though Father Murphy wasn't to know it yet, was about to be decimated by three events. His hesitancy to bombard Wexford Town, while the enemy still occupied it, the succession of Beauchamp Bagnal Harvey as Commander – in – Chief and the recent appointment of General Gerrard Lake of The Buckinghamshire town of Aylesbury in England, famous for its ducks and it's lace making, as Supreme Military Commander in Ireland.

If it should be known, on the first day of June, 1798, Gerrard Lake would have preferred to be with his home hunt, scouting the fertile pastures of his native Chiltern Hills, than pouring over accounts in his Dublin Castle office, of degrading defeats of his army at the hands of the Irish peasants. Indeed, if truth be known, he would have liked even more, to be in India, where the subjugation of the pending Marathas rebellion against his king, would be a much easier proposition than the struggle against the lunatic and unexpected impetuosity of a rebel band in the spell of some popish priest.

A thick throat militant of fifty four years, the veteran of Seven Year War, the War of American Independence and Commander of the Brigade of Guards at Flanders and at Lancelets in '93, was now afforded full powers of The Indemnity Bill and The Insurrection Act, without recourse to any magistrate or court of law, to see his strategy for the disenfranchisement of the natives, Catholic, Protestant and Presbyterian alike, and helotism, villeinage and murder were the weapons he sought to use for his purpose. This heavy-jowled tyrant with a thick line of bushy shag across the top of his eyes, the fanatic warlord saw himself as the hammer of God. Lake was a marauder who portrayed the ethos and the idiosyncrasy of Orangism. Within a day of the uprising on the Harrow Road, he commissioned a special unit of Military and civil servants to set up recruiting stations in the more subdued counties, outside of Antrim, Down, Wicklow, Kildare and Wexford. The purpose had been endorsed by Prime Minister Pitt. At crossroads, in village squares in Cork, Kerry, Limerick, Galway, Mayo, Donegal and central counties, boys and young men were offered The King's Shilling to join The British army. Villains from jailhouses in Limerick and Galway joined the wide eyed imbeciles from asylums of Longford, Tipperary and Kerry to swell the ranks of what had become known as The Regent Corps.

It had been reported that the fleeing army had left Wexford bereft of every item of armoury and , again, John Murphy regretted his hesitancy on an immediate offensive, the previous morning. Five hours delay at the Three Rocks allowed ample time for the evacuation, now only strengthened his objection to any kind of parley on Windmill Hill, which he did not attend, preferring to stay with his troops and the mob in the town.

He did, however authorise a volunteer group to seek out the two tyrant magistrates, James Boyd and Hamilton Jacob. Boyd was found hiding in the house of his brother on George's Street and he and seven more activists of the Orange Order were hanged on Wexford Bridge, the notorious gibbet, where over the years, hundreds of rebels and antagonists had met their ends. The bridge had become synonymous with the guillotine on Paris's Place Louis XIV.

They brought Father Michael before the Boyd residence and then to the handsome pile that was the home of Lord Kingsborough, the head of The North Cork Militia, which was near the Cornmarket.

Father Michael stood before the house, an Orange banner had been trampled on at the grand entrance. Looking up at the handsome fascias, the turret chimneys, a glorified autobiography, written by some pompous architect and he said to nobody in particular, "is he in there?"

Jack Keohane, his obsession for revenge now a revolving wheel in his head, laughed into the priest's ear. "You know he's not, Father, like all the other cowards, he scampered at the sight of us." Keohane continued to sow seeds of his personal propaganda, putting his trust in the right words. " They say that half a dozen of us are buried in the foundations of that thing, Father, buried where they fel.". He pushed on with verve. "There's a room in there where Kingsborough signed his death warrants and arranged his night raids on the people. There's another room, Father, where young women were dragged before him, for his pleasure and personal entertainment. I bet it was here he gave the order to burn your church."

Michael thought deeply, aware that Father John was nearby and would not tolerate any further burning of empty buildings, but the full flavour of Keohane's argument, though his words came softly, almost in a whisper, was a sweet persuasion to his ears.

"Burn the building, Mr. Keohane, a pity he's not in it, and the same for Boyd's den, fire that too."

"With the satisfaction of a dung fly on his heap, Keohane smiled, "surely will Father Michael."

**

420

He found the big priest sitting on a low wall in a corner of The Cornmarket. Philip Roche, his frock coat, almost white with the dust of the Wexford Summer, rose to meet him, a wry smile on a face that hadn't seen a razor in days.

"I'm trying to believe something that cannot be true", said Father Roche, looking about him at a town choked to capacity with hell raising rebels, many of them armed and ready for something. "I'm trying to believe 'tis John Murphy is responsible for all this."

" Spare yourself the ordeal, my friend, for 'tis a nightmare from which I have been trying to wake from, these past few days, and where have you been, when I needed you?"

Roche grasped the outstretched hand, with a mixture of wonder and worship. "Well forgive me, Father Murphy, but were I to know that yourself was about to cause a rebellion on the King of England, I would have been the first to tell you you're a crazy old cleric."

"Sometimes accidents happen in life, Philip, from which we have need of a little madness to extricate ourselves successfully." Murphy looked severely at the big man. "I have work for you, that you might not like."

"So has Bagnal Harvey", said Roche, I'm to meet him this afternoon."

"How well do you know him," asked Murphy.

"He's a United Irishman, as I am, John, and don't look so surprised, you've known all along of my affiliations."

"Then we'll both meet him, he has sent for me."

John Murphy felt the unease of a complication about to present itself. In the afternoon, Bagnal Harvey set up the parlour of his town house, where he interviewed members of the central committee and the leaders of the rebellion. From the waiting corridor, a wig wearing red coated young man called for Father Murphy to attend what was a sort of screening of personnel before the new commander in chief, who allowed the night and morning to devour precious time while the enemy regrouped.

John was obliged, under an embarrassment, indeed more embarrassing for Roche and his fine ego, than for Murphy, to relate details of his movements since May 26th and his reasons for mobilising in the way he did.

Did Father Murphy not know that many loyal United Irishmen who were in the Society these past ten years, at the side of Wolfe Tone, had related to him, their displeasure that the insurrection was perpetrated by, in their minds, a loyalist priest, who was responsible for the denuding of his flock of their weaponry of defence against forces of the crown. Did the priest of Boolavogue not consider letting such an important move to one of those who had been agitating and drilling for over six years, liberal Protestants like Edward Fitzgerald, Grogan, Hatton and others.

Murphy had come too far now, and to confront the commander would be to cause unrest, even a rift in the ranks. Roche tried to hold his peace at the outlandish snub. He knew that Murphy could have walked out of Wexford and over forty thousand would follow him.

Beauchamp Bagnal Harvey was a pompous, but very influential man and he did, from the beginning, champion the Catholic cause, so, conscious of his own prestige, Harvey felt, that all bells should echo his own thoughts.

"I was alone, General", said John, trying to remain respectful. He was standing, motionless, looking into the crowded street and tightened his fists in his hard shell of discomfort. He sent Roche a warning frown to keep his mouth shut. "Circumstances can be so different within the turn of a coin and I found no joy in these circumstances. I am pleased to hand over command and I await your orders."

Here was a man who had never learned to obey, and to give way was a foreign language. He dismissed them, in a haze of alcoholic aftermath and Father Roche wanted to kill him there and then.

The four priests ate a late lunch on a rough table on the quayside with about a hundred pikemen in the Bullring while the council of war met on Windmill Hill. Croppies, hearing of his arrival among them, flocked to the square, simply to be in his presence and fiddlers and fifes played lively tunes for his amusement. For an hour, sonnets were made for the hero of two great battles and the fight that was yet to come. Women fussed about Father Murphy's dinner, that he should have enough to eat. Then they were summoned to Windmill Hill.

The four priest walked before their horses to the large canvas tent, bedecked with flags and bunting, the British Standard in centre position. Father Mogue Kearns muttered his discontent. "The man bedecks his war tent with the standard of the enemy, who is this so called commander, John?"

Each of the council, about twenty in all, greeted Murphy personally and while their enthusiasm and congratulatory verve was genuine, he felt an asterisk of condescension about it, a mild prejudice. Few of them knew him, fewer still had never heard of him until now, a priest who had never embraced the purpose of the United Irishmen.He apologised for missing the council meeting, but explained that discipline was essential in the town.

There was the beginning of applause, instigated by the youth, Myles

Byrne, standing upright from his seat, followed by Edward Roche and Bagnal Harvey himself. Grogan, Keogh, Grey, Hughes shouted " here, here", as the stilted band made a mild contribution.

"It is the decision", said Harvey, putting on his commander face, though it was obvious his face and all the rest of him was feeling the after effects of the night before, to divide this fine army of brave fighting men and women, between your good self, Father Murphy and myself, that I maintain the position of Commander-in-Chief and I will take my troops westward to New Ross, with father Roche as my second in command."

Roche raised his eyebrows in surprise, sending daggers to his fellow priests. He looked pleadingly at John Murphy

"We will take Ross," continued the commander and then push on to Waterford, at my head; Mr. John Kelly, Dr. John Colclough, The Furlong Brothers, and Mr. Henry Hughes." He looked with authority at John Murphy."You, Sir, will take the second division north to take Gorey and Arklow, to join the Wicklow insurgents, under Mr. Michael Dwyer and from there, you will advance to take Dublin. At your head will be your so called"general" Edward Roche, Mr. John Hay and your friend this Father Michael. Also, as a part of your division will be yet another friend of yours, and a veteran of the French struggle, I am told, who will sever connections at Enniscorthy and, with a column of 2,000, push through the lowlands of The Blackstairs and take Bunclody. At his head will be, Mr. Myles Byrne and Captain Matthew Keogh of Wexford Town, a former British army officer, who will be installed as Military Governor of the entire area.

Father Murphy moved closer to the assembly table. It was obvious to Myles Byrne and Edward Roche that the priest strove to keep tolerance in his voice in which there was not a little disappointment.

"My informant is a personal friend of Mr. Theobold Wolfe Tone, who still maintains his every effort to secure the help of France. We believe Mr. Napper Tandy, who is a member of the Irish Parliament, is also in Paris on the same endeavour." He softened a little. "Mr. Benjamin Franklin of America has said that whoever lives in hope, will die fasting. Let me advise now gentlemen, there will be no French invasion, at least not for another year or more and even then it is very uncertain. Napoleon Bonaparte is seeking glory in the East, so France has no resources to commit to our cause at this time I have not told my.....the insurgent army, I suggest we let them fight and die in hope and not in expectation. I pray God's blessing on your efforts, for with that, we don't need the French." He hesitated before continuing. "This army is made of a mob, it fights like a mob, tribal and brave. I suggest,

Sir, you do not divide them, their strength is in each other. Take us, en masse to New Ross, we can take it in a day, then head north."

Bagnal Harvey had an edge to his smile. "I have made a decision and the council is in agreement, Father Murphy, and may I say, again, how grateful we are for your immense contribution so far." It was a blatent diswmissal.

**

Five rebel priests co-celebrated Mass in The Cornmarket before the army assembled to move out. Officers and croppies made their objections be known at the idea of the army being dissected. Murphy assured them that, after New Ross, they would assemble again and march on Dublin. The priest had a dreadful premonition of disaster for those being sent to New Ross How you lie the loudest when you lie to yourself.

Among the crowd of the packed square, was the ageing Cornelious Grogan of Johnstown Castle. The seventy year old Protestant landlord looked red eyed and agitated. He had been on Windmill Hill but had been subdued and confused at the deliberations. Bagnal Harvey, in his opinion, is capable of undoing all the victories of the past week. An armchair commander, he will be worthless in the fray.

"I would wish to go with you, Father Murphy," he said, wearily, but I would be of no use to you. I promised my people I would find an army for them, when I heard of Oulart, so I brought three hundred of my tenants with me, and now we march back the way we came with Harvey." His voice faltered, full and rich like an old relic. "They came out of this town, yesterday, The North Corks, and their Orange plumage, the Dunbartonshires, scampering before you like whipped dogs, ravenous for revenge. My people at Whiterock, Moorfield and Rathaspeck and all the way west to Taghmont, innocent women and children were slaughtered in a marauding rage. In a village, not far from Foulksmills, a certain Captain Cowthorpe ordered the execution of the entire hamlet of thirty eight souls, on finding an old man wearing a green cockade and who shouted your name before he died."

What will you do, Sir?" asked Murphy.

"A savage horde is let loose in Ireland, Sir, "he replied, and it must be stopped, it has no standards and is turned away from God" He looked severely at the priests, from one to the other "Bagnal Harvey is well known to me. He is a social climber and has divided interests and likes to keep his powder dry." Tired and despondent, the old man spurred his horse forward and about three hundred men sifted from the throng to follow him. Not all were armed. Women and children ran to keep up.

Myles Byrne found him. Wherever they send me, Father, I would want to be at your head."

"We must do as we are told, Mr. Byrne," said Murphy, disconcertedly.

"Father, there's someone here who needs your acquaintance, he's in a looted house off The Bullring."

Murphy followed the young rebel through the market, cooking pots over reddened coals, in every corner, hands stretched out to meet him, his name, high on the warm atmosphere.

"God, Son, how an army is such a great walking stomach." Father John acknowledged the falicitations all around.

The man was seated in a dark corner of a half demolished house, once owned by Captain Boyd. Two young men tended him and a frightened wide eyed horse pranced on the hard floor, nearby. The man was swathed in head bandages, that hung loosely about his head and shoulders. He was, obviously in great pain and a kind of greasy unguent seeped from his pitchcapped head, down his scarred face from which much of the skin had been dragged away, with most of his scalp. One shoulder had been bared of his silk shirt, where the pitch had solidified and became embedded in the tissue in great black pods.

Murphy saw again, the awful result of the efficiency of British totalitarianism as the man looked through the dressings with agonised eyes. He hissed through the pain. "I'm Anthony Perry of Inch, Sir, I have something to say." He dismissed the two youths and indicated to Byrne to stay. "I'm the one who ratted to James Boyd, the names of the leaders, It was I put them to prison." There was silence for a minute or two. "He did this to me in this very house, until I could take no more." He shook involuntarily in the warm dark room. "I wish to fight with you. I have, with me, over five hundred men of my home place at Inch, I'll lead them for you and maybe I will be forgiven in time."

Murphy looked at Myles Byrne for a minute. "Are your people here in Wexford, Mr. Perry?"

"I'm told they arrived earlier, assembled near the drilling yard."

"Then you'll ride with us, and welcome," said Murphy.

Byrne said, relief showing on his handsome face, "many of your people have been enquiring about you, Mr. Perry, they think you're dead."

"Not yet, Myles Byrne," Perry's face cracked into a smile. "Not yet. They tell me Boyd is dead, then I feel better already."

"Can you ride now," asked the priest.

The man from Inch caressed the grey horse's head and pulled a broad rimmed red hat from the saddlebag.. "They'll know my horse, they'll know my hat." He summoned the two youths and suddenly all the pain seemed to leave him by some great profusion of courage and resolve. The boys managed to tidy the dressings up under his hat, and bringing the grey outside, helped him to mount. "Let's go and tell them you're not dead," said Byrne as he and Murphy led the grey horse through the waiting crowd where he was immediately recognised.

"To your colours", he shouted more in a screech of pain and sheer euphoria. "Inch, Kilmurray, Big Rock, Castletown Bridge, Hydepark......."

His name reverberated like a great gush of wind about the market and the quays, and his clan shouted like a prayer to Heaven. "'Tis Perry, 'tis Mr. Perry, as they flocked to him, his appalling condition, a spur to their resolve.

The army of Father John Murphy began mobilising onto the great wooden bridge which spanned the inner harbour. About forty red coated bodies hung like trussed dogs on the wide parapets, a further dozen lay in the harbour's slushy banks far below.

"Fishermen, Father, revenge of the fishermen of Wexford." said Byrne loudly, indicating the corpses, swaying like outed red lanterns.

Murphy looked at the youth. "I'd say now, Mr. Byrne that you could make a little lie go a long way".

Women and children of the hanged looked up at the priest as he rode by, their dark eyes, accusatory and bitter.

Chapter 55

At Carrigrew Hill, 23 miles north of Wexford and just north east of Ferns, the weary army set up their camp, and within an hour, more and more came to join the rebellion. The provisions detachment, now with its own quartermasters corps, had food in abundance and again beacons lit up the night skies of North Wexford. Dozens of cooking fires comforted the crannies and ditches of the mountain like a gigantic hearth and fearful loyalist camps and fortresses in the distant Clahamon and Clogh and Ballycarney closed shops and their Yeomanry rode through the night to safer ground, while further rebel reinforcements answered John Murphy's call and with any weapon available to them, steered toward the summoning tower of Carrigrew, many of them passing the retreating Redcoats on the road.

A dispatch came in the night, Gorey was empty of troops and stood open to the rebels, with just now, Arklow between them and Dublin.

"Dear God," Murphy prayed, thirty thousand of King George's lackeys and I can't find them."

His title glowed for an hour and died, without even leaving a signature. On Thursday 31st. May as the big Father Mogue Kearns, with his two brothers and Myles Byrne were leaving, with 2,000 men to take Bunclody, some ten miles north of Ferns, a menacing piece of news was dispatched to John Murphy, by Father Philip, who was still in Wexford Town and the flaw in the Southern army was already becoming evident.

Blind with good will and camaraderie, and euphoric at the sparing of his life, The Commander-In-Chief, Beauchamp Bagnal Harvey, became a paragon of importance in his own town. Instead of pressing on westward, the general found himself in filtered awe of his office and returned to his house from Windmill Hill, to entertain friends and foe alike. To Roche's disgust, a prominent guest on George Street's dinner table was none other than the Rev. Cope of Carnew, the musket wielding Protestant Orangemen whose initial outrage at the handball alley helped to light the first spark of the rebellion. While a diner with the half witted Wexford Commander of the United Irishmen, the now, hard of hearing rector of Carnew, was biding his time, to report to the authorities and take back the town.

The finest and most experienced men of the insurrection, like Father Philip Roche, Cloney, John Kelly, Sweetman, the Devereaux Brothers, The Furlong brothers, Hughes and others, waited, with all the captured artillery and at the ready, while all the time, Harvey allowed the enemy to regroup and strengthen, so that, in the thirty six hours since Father Murphy left Wexford, New Ross had become a fortress.

A whole new corps had joined John and Father Michael, at Carrigrew, choosing to join the priests than to go westward with Bagnal Harvey. The new Faythe corps consisted of volunteers from the fishing fraternity and the John Street Corps, whose leader, the street fighter, Richard The Monk Monaghan, was already with the rebels.

A whole new phenomenon now manifested itself that was to spread in a wave of hope and fear and newfound loyalty across the county. Yeomen were deserting by the hundreds and joining the croppies, many of them, prisoners of fate, having shunned the dark confidences and the power that preyed upon their nation and pitched them against family and friend alike.

"Defeat is a thing of incoherence, and to dwell on it is futile," said John Murphy to his two depleted fellow clerics, when failure began to infiltrate the ranks.

On June 2nd., Father Michael, still anxious for his own command, with a column of 1,000 men, pike and rifle, were cut to pieces at Ballyminaun. Two hundred and seventy rebels died in the dust, all horses and ammunition, lost. On June 3rd., Myles Byrne was to report to his commander, a further catastrophe. Father Mogue Kearns had a superb victory at Bunclody, and within an hour, 600 regular infantry and Yeoman cavalry were routed, and retreating once again, on the Carlow Road, wading through the murky swamps of The Slaney and scurrying across the lowlands of The Blackstairs. But Myles was to report that Father Kearns, though a fierce and brave fighter, had no commanding skills, nor did he have ability to exercise any control over the insurgents.

"I urged him," cried Myles Byrne, in frustration, "to pursue the Redcoats and engage them on the Carlow Road and finish them off, as you continue to tell us. They were at our mercy, but he had no rallying points or re-grouping strategy and he let our army run amok in the town, burning and looting, while he knelt in prayer for the victory. The military re-grouped to the north of the town, which is the first time the English did anything positive." Byrne seethed at the memory. "They charged us, Father and cut us to piece."

The young man looked worn out. "Let me fight at your head, Father," he pleaded, "we lost half the column and most of them were drunk and merrymaking when they died."

Careful not to do anything to create antagonists among the leaders and not to apportion blame, though feeling desolate at the double defeat, Father Murphy sought to maintain confidence in the camp. He insisted on fires to burn more brightly and music to fill the night, while, all the time, inside himself, not to feel totally brutalised. His fellow clerics sensed the palpable pain and rejection all around, but John Murphy was even more frightened and anxious about what was happening with Bagnal Harvey and New Ross.

Half nauseous and remorseful, Father Mogue Kearns felt the sensation of failure knot his guts. The black mood quickened in the big priest and finding a secluded niche, high on the mountain, he blunted his anger and remorse on three bottles of Lynch Bages, brought up to him by young Jimmy Crowley of Little Limerick, the complements of the very exclusive cellar of the Bunclody barrister and loyalist, Mr. Henry Crofts, who died trying to save it.

Father Michael was more forthcoming and tried to justify his mishap before The General, John Hay and Father John, but eventually admitted that he should have installed more verve and commitment in his men, should have drilled them into alternative formation, running columns like the commander had used at Oulart, found some trick to outsmart the enemy. He admitted he was over confident, a thousand men to three hundred and he failed with such odds.

There is nothing more aggravating than a failure that was almost a success," said John Murphy, comforting his friend. At Enniscorthy we were done for and I was on the verge of going home, fearing a slaughter, but the elements turned in our favour." He laughed hoarsely. "Until then, I thought a humble cow was created for the sole purpose of producing milk, but the creature took on a whole new dimension that day, unknown to herself, she became a fighting machine.

He sent for Kearns and the small party of his war council partook of more of Mr. Croft's wine, but Michael continued his self discrimination. "But you looked for three miracles all about you, John, and to think I was among your critics. I ask for your forgiveness, and am humbled by my jealousy."

"It is not jealousy, Michael," assured John, "I was in a certain place at a certain time, and the frame of our destiny was designed at that time. Don't talk of jealousy, my friend ,for a touch of jealousy is only proof of love, where there is no jealousy, there is no love. Your followers would die for you."

"They already have, Sir," whispered Michael.

"Perhaps tomorrow, Gentlemen, perhaps, Arklow, we are still winning." Murphy looked at John Hay. "Perhaps you might check on lookouts, then a good night's sleep for all."

In the early morning of June 3rd., it was established that the king's forces had used their victories at Bunclody and Ballycanew to advantage and taken possession of Gorey, a shining gem, situated on the rising foothills of the Wicklow Mountains. The human and personal scenery, with it's air, thick and delicious with the odour of sweet grasses, was, again to be a cauldron, for it was on this day, that, once again, the inability of an immense trained army, supposedly, the finest in Europe, feared by the French, the Dutch, the Spaniards, the Indians, the Australians and ' till now, the bane of the Americans, to come to terms with a loose marauding multitude of redundant humanity, on an idyllic green sward of summer meadows, in a land, forgotten by all, but nature itself.

John Murphy stood with his old lieutenant, Georgie Tansey on a high place and looked north east along the handsome fairways, ripening now in the early summer, toward the sleeping town, the great hills of Wicklow, in ripples and swells of blue and purple and green and gold.

The priest's eyes misted over. "Jonathan Swift once said that vision is the art of seeing things, Georgie, of seeing things invisible. It's only at times like this that we come to appreciate the beauty all around us. We are blind to it, mostly, because we take the miracles of God for granted and then, every now and then, the novelty surprises us, and it has been there all the time."

James Attridge had come up from Trasna, with the young Deacon. He was down below in the camp, savagely recording accounts of the past few days.

Sir George had given a barn building which Tansey had converted to a kind of chapel, and the people left behind, had been coming for prayer. "It's very good, Father", assured G., Duhallow feeds them, so that body and soul are looked after. Kate.....Mrs. Attridge is a godsend, it's just that the essentials are missing, I cannot say Mass for them."

"No, you can't Georgie," said Murphy, but you can do everything else. Lead them through the Mass, you can baptise, and lead them in prayer."

He looked again at the tranquillity beyond. "Prey with me now, lad, then it's home for you."

The priest always had a tacit reprehension for those, constantly looking for cheap miracles, believing that man can create his own miracles, by using the courage and intelligence that God has given him; reach up for the ripe fruit.

There was plenty of cattle, could he use them again. Two of the bulls died at Enniscorthy, there were more about the place. However, this was an open plane, toward Gorey, with no narrowing entrance like at Enniscorthy. The stupid animals would gad all over the place. The sun, promising another hot day, was too high in the sky, to favour either side and it would be an early battle, as already his scouts were reporting military outriders from Gorey, full of business.

"Dear Lord, send me just a small disconformity, then help me to do the rest. So many depending."

The real war was about to begin.

Major General Loftus with 2,500 men of the Antrim and Tyrone Light Hessian and Welsh Regiments, with half a dozen artillery pieces were assembling to leave Bunclody, while General Walpole, with 1,800 men of the Garrisons of Camolin and Carnew, could be seen on the road, just outside Gorey.

Father Michael and John Hay were for dividing the rebel army in two and defending the hilly camp from both sides. Edward Fitzgerald was for that plan, while Edward Roche and Myles Byrne and Conor Devereaux sided with John Murphy to keep the rebels in one mass as before. On a day when the rebels were still reeling from two massive defeats, Father Murphy perfected his authority and after his calming stroking rhetoric of the night before, this morning, he was prepared to make enemies. He had spent the night agonising on his plan. Bunclody would have been a natural exit from Wexford into Carlow and the midlands. Arklow would open up the route into Wicklow and onwards to Dublin, while New Ross would pave the way into Kilkenny and towards Munster. After the defeats, Murphy had to reconsider the whole strategy. Running short on Earthly miracles, and God Himself, keeping His cards close to His Divine chest, he would put in place a tactic he had been devising for Arklow, but now, Gorey called.

On the idle day that was the day before, when they were locked together in indecision and self reproach, the man from Boolavogue summoned together, 200 of the stronger women and placed the two Irish amazons, Suzy Toole and Madge Dixon at their head and again perfected the idea of the Moving Magazines, along with 100 young boys, below the age of fifteen. Fifteen year olds were not allowed on the field of battle. He called together, 200 of his best riflemen, mostly Yeomen who had, the day before, deserted their king. All day long, the women and youths were drilled in the business of running, stooping, priming, loading of weapons, until it became a contest in their eagerness. Not alone this, but he found to his amazement, that a number of these handsome females had the talent of a marksman, without ever knowing it. Now, at almost noon, with Walpole in sight, word came that Loftus was about to leave Bunclody and John Murphy sent for The Monk Monaghan

"How long will it take Loftus to get here from Bunclody, Mr. Monaghan," he asked the Wexford street fighter.

"General Loftus is the greatest dilly-dallier in the whole world, Sir, and he's a terrible coward into the bargain," replied The Monk, "he'll have to troop the colours and prance up and down in his importance before making up his mind to move. A man with a crooked collar in the ranks, could delay him half an hour. It will take him well over two hours before you see him on the road."

"Then let's be off, Mr. Monaghan, for we have two hours to beat the life out of Lord Ancram's army and General Walpole and take back Gorey," Murphy said, and The Monk smiled his approval.

Shortly after noon on 3rd. June, Walpole was well in sight, complete with six heavy artillery pieces, cannon primed and ready. In his now characteristic style, a voice, strident and totally, it would seem, out of character, almost a cunning deceit to stir their confidence, Father Murphy called on the croppies to strike without hesitation, to shout and hoot and scream, with the purpose of upsetting the cavalry, more than the infantry.

Five thousand at the ready, the pikemen were flanked by the rifles and the women. "Thank God for the low ditches."

A dozen rebels raced towards Walpole, each with a brace of ready-made torches, dipped in tar pitch, a little bag of gunpowder attached to each shaft. Suzy Toole had devised the weapon, having learned the art in her father's forge in Wicklow.

Murphy could not believe his eyesight. Walpole, for some reason had his column with the cavalry up front. Four of the twelve Croppies died, but not before all missiles found their mark among the cavalry. The gunpowder caught the flame, cracking and hissing among the horses, fire spreading among their frantic hooves, sending the animals in all directions. The infantry, behind the cavalry had no targets and the rebel flanks, from inside the ditches, picked them off, while the marching, Running Magazines fed chambers like women possessed.

Momentarily caught off guard, the cavalry tried to make way for the infantry and the central body of the Wexfordmen raced toward the enemy, shouting and hooting and a new and disturbing sound raked the quiet day, unsettling rider and horse. For Walpole, confusion and chaos was invented. A thousand children, in petticoats and britches, out of range of danger, up among the heathers and scrub, off to the right and to the left, joined the noon chorus, an impertinent screeching crescendo that neither man or animal could close an ear to.

The king's rifles and cannon were silent for a precious minute while the frenzied militia tried to refuel. No man can be sure of his bravery until it is called upon, but in the Ireland of 1798, life was so often more terrible than death, and hatred and lust for revenge, superseded any thought of personal danger in the hearts of the rebels, so that in their unorthodox military custom, their valour rested somewhere between rashness and moral courage.

The pitchcapped leader, having been attended to by nursing females and one of three camp doctors, Anthony Perry, his red hat planted on his aching head, bandages flowing from underneath, looked like an old pirate king, as, screaming at the top of his voice, he urged his men forward, flailing his rampant sword at all sides.

From the right flank, Myles Byrne pulled his horse and took a minute to study Father John Murphy, and he was to write later in his report for the journalist, James Attridge: " Father John Murphy, a man with the simplicity of a child, was a lion in the fight. In short, he knew not or cared not for his own safety, from the moment he took to the field. He was seen in every critical situation, encouraging the rebels and exposing himself to the greatest danger, wherever he thought his presence could be useful. The riflemen on the flanks blazed at the thick red mass, while these handsome women reloaded each spare musket. I saw the cannon roar and two dozen croppies died. Then I saw a spectacle that will remain embedded in my memory 'till the day I die. I remember crying out with such an intensity and depth of feeling, that I thought my heart would burst, with my tears of joy and admiration. A huge man, a ploughman with the strength and the size of his horses, pushed his way to the priest's side at the head of the pikemen. He had a long scythe-like tool in one hand and a pike with a short handle in the other, and just before our second assault, I saw him standing to front, to back and all around the curate in a protective manner. The scene was immense, he was like Gabriel himself, and I swear I saw deadly fear in the faces of the Yeos, before the two, as they tried to back away. The cannon roared again and we stepped over the dead and I saw John Murphy run toward the open mouth of the cannon and draped his green scarf over the yawning menace. I saw his whole countenance change, as his pent up anger exploded in his cry – " NOW" The croppies echoed his cry and for the next fifteen minutes that ploughman swung right and left, clearing a protective pathway for Murphy, until the troops were completely routed."

And once again the Londonderry Militia, Armagh Militia, Tyrone Light Company. Ancient Britons and the Hessian Dragoons turned heel and ran.

Murphy cut his lines in two, sending a column of men under Roche, Perry and Byrne to cut off the retreating army, even before they took a yard backward and within ten minutes, their own cannon, one still wearing it's green garland, were turned on King George's forces and they died for him, their last image in this life, of frocked priests, women marksmen, 5,000 bogmen and off in the distance, screeching youngsters, picking up fallen weapons and carrying them back to Tubberneering Rock. But the image that took them to Heaven or Hell, was of a middle aged man in black, a black square banner at his back and a giant of a man hitting out right and left in his shadow on the sunny plains outside Gorey.

The bewildered General Walpole died, the only nephew of Sir Robert, the First Earl of Orford of the massively wealthy landowning family of Norfolk, a family of The Garter, which directed its policy to the one supreme object of advancing its own material prosperity and that of the British nation.

Robert, the younger was now pulled aside, unceremoniously, to be denuded of his fine sword of supreme British steel, ornate scabbard and his pistol which was not fired on the day, while the body of young Fergal Sinnot, an apprentice carpenter from Hollyforth, could be taken from under him and ceremoniously buried at Gorey Hill.

Still on time, the commander turned his army about at the entrance to Gorey, to face south and immediately regrouped in preparation for Loftus, whose customary pomp and ceremony in true British style, made him hopelessly late for his grand entrance. Expecting to meet the retreating rebels being driven south by Walpole, the general was greeted with the sickening sight of his compatriots strewn on the roadway and the ditches of Gorey Hill, among them, Walpole himself. A scout reported the advancing rebels were just two miles away, armed with the cannon of the fallen regiments. Deciding to fight another day, two thousand troops of The Fifth Dragoon Guards, Dunbartonshire Hyland Regiment and Yeoman Cavalry, turned and retreated, only to lose their way in the lower byways and slopes of Mount Leinster and paid a local peasant who said he was not in the mind for a fight, a sizable sum to lead them back through Bunclody, Ballon and onto the road to Tullow town.

The story was fastened into the folklore of the area, for the sight of Tamas Carey on his donkey and cart, leading the mighty army of King George of England out of the danger zone. General Walpole had wagered, in the town of Gorey, that morning, that he would annihilate the insurgents within twenty minutes. Wagers were made in fast succession. The king's troops not only lost their wagers.

On Wednesday, 6th. June, Gorey burned. The frenzied mob, elated at another victory, sought out the huge properties of Hunter Gowan, Hawtrey White, at Mount Nebo, the estates of The Ram Brothers at Ramsforth and Clonattin and lesser holdings of loyalists and

Orangemen and the calling card of the insurgents was again produced as the properties were fired. John Murphy, as time passed, realized only too well, that he was losing control, as new leaders in the persons of Anthony Perry and the fifty year old, one armed Esmond Kyan, a former British army artillery officer, and a wealthy Catholic.

Anti loyalist was becoming the new religion among the insurgents, all were regarded the enemy, those of significance and those of little significance and little feuds began to break out between Catholic and Protestant, in many cases, for no other reason but how one recited The Our Father, compared with the other.

However, Father Murphy was ecstatically welcomed into Gorey, where more and more volunteers assembled from as far north as Woodenbridge in county Wicklow, Shillelagh and Aughrim. The men of the Wicklow Mountains of Michael Dwyer's private rebel army, marched into the town, armed and ready, and brought with them that the town of Arklow was deserted. The whole garrison and all the loyalist personnel had fled to Dublin. The entire British army, constantly in retreat, were now trapped in the confines of the crowded city of Dublin, their backs to the sea.

He quoted Pittacus. "Know Thine Opportunity," to his war council, in an attempt to assert his authority. The door was now open and as the numbers of new recruits increased, he could see total victory ahead. The right of conquest beckoned. His army was twice the size of that taken to Egypt by Napoleon Bonaparte. Now with a victory at New Ross, two hundred thousand would march on Dublin within a week. But a type of democracy was creeping into the council, which was increasing as men of so called substance and self importance stamped their authority, especially among their own followers.

Captain Hay with Father Michael, once again sought to open that chasm between the two clerics. John Murphy was nearing exhaustion, but decided to move on Arklow immediately and open up the way to Dublin. The duo called for a day's respite, and spread the word about the camp.

The peasant army, were quick to accept the decision. Tired and ill from an orgy of extravagant binges of eating and drinking, a hunger they sought to satisfy without thinking of the consequences. A hungry stomach has no ears or eyes, and large intake of fresh and succulent meat and rich fortified wines was alien to a lifetime of restricted diets.

John awaited word from Bagnal Harvey in New Ross, and was prepared to move on Arklow within an hour or two, word or no word. But there was also, the running army of General Loftus, who was somewhere in the vicinity of The Harrow, and he had to be taken before the push to the north.

Arklow was now empty of loyalists, but John Murphy knew it wouldn't wait, it had to be fortified immediately. Also, Loftus had to be pursued and engaged and put out of the equation. Murphy was a broom, cleaning all before him, for he knew that, in this precarious world, every mistake and infirmity has to be paid for in full. After cleansing the county Wexford of the dreaded red tide of loyalism, he would press into the midlands, meet up with the men of Kildare and Meath, anxious to join him after suffering defeat in their skirmishes at Tara on 26th, May and further defeats of the insurgents in Kildare, Laois, Tipperary and Offaly in April. However, the blunders that were to happen in the next few days, were nothing short of criminal, bungling that was to produce nothing but mischief and death to thousands.

Confrontation to Father Murphy won out and the council of war opted to send 20,000 men to the garrison of Carnew, but as ever, the town was empty before them. "A scout or two would have made the journey," said Murphy, in disgust, as the insurgents marched through the town, drums, banners and fifes proclaiming a token victory. "What a waste of God given time." John Murphy called his disgust to the war party on their return to Gorey Hill.

By evening on the 7th. June, the very bastion of British imperialism in the midlands of Ireland was on its knees and the flames of liberty engulfed it in a massive proclamation of the rights of freedom for four million people. Before burning the castle and the home of The Rev. Cope; the butcher of Carnew, the rebels crowded into the ball alley, shouting and crying out the names of those who died in the massacre of two weeks before, some weeping openly against the wall where the splintered stone bore stark evidence of the atrocity.

The army returned to Gorey Hill. Fourteen miles round trip just to march through an empty town, a commission, Jack Keohane and what had become by now, his trusty lieutenant, Henry Tansy, would have been glad to complete, the burning of two great houses.

John Murphy convulsed with rage on hearing that the march to Carnew had now cost them the strategic town of Arklow. The military had returned and the loyalists were now in full control of the town. A campaign of violence and slaughter was embarked upon by the disgruntled Yeos and Father Michael began, without compunction, to gather together volunteers and with the catholic aristocrat, Garret Byrne and the young Myles Byrne, no relation, and with Dick the Monk Monaghan, prepared to march on Arklow, with 5,000 men and the minimum of preparations.

It was on this day that Anthony Perry, now close to his own territory of Inch and partly out of his mind with pain and fever, took a small company to scour the suburbs of Gorey for significant loyalist sympathisers on the run. Many of the small estates were familiar to him. Within an hour, he returned to camp with a dozen or more prisoners, among them, the racketeer clergyman Roger Owen and the two notorious Arklow Yeomen, James Wheatley and Frances Rogan of Castletown.

In a secluded place on the northern slopes, he engulfed the three, heating a furnace in his mind, so severe, he singed his himself further. Wheatley and Rogan were the two who had entered his cell in Wexford jail on the instructions of Captain Boyd, to extract his damning information. These were the faces he saw before the searing pain of the molten pitch dislodged his intellect and anaesthetised his brain for all time. Perry removed his hat and unwound his bandages, sucking in gulps of air in his pain and crawled closer to his prisoners, two dozen comrades urging him on. With dragon's teeth, they shouted for a last judgement.

Wheatley was sick at the sight while Rev. Owen tried, in his tethers, to turn away, calling to Perry to have a care for a man of the Church. Their cries for mercy were a sweet corridor of revenge, as an aid tended the fire on which the pitch was melting.

Father John scoured the camp, having heard of Perry's intentions. He had long since, sent dispatches to all leaders, including to Bagnal Harvey that he would not permit demonical acts to be committed while he still had command. Repulsed at the atrocities being committed, mirroring the past tyranny of the king's forces, Murphy pleaded that many of the enemy had found themselves in a uniform of necessity and are not the enemy of Ireland, and not to let the Orange sentiments of religious provocation, blind their instinct.

"Have you ever seen a man, still alive, Father Murphy", Perry sobbed, still ogling the prisoners, while Rev. Owen began shouting abuse at the priest, reminding him who he was. "A man, still alive," continued Perry, without arms or legs, the trunk of his body shaking and writhing, trying to die, half hanged and dragged through the stones by a rampant horse?"

Murphy ignored the savage looks of Owen, as if he were not there. "Well I've seen it Father," continued Perry. "Done to young men and old men and it would leave a thorn in your brain forever."

Then, with a cry of anguish, swiftly, in one continuous movement, designed almost to reach its conclusion before any other impulse could stop him, he grabbed the nearest pike, he skewered the two in lightening succession. Murphy jumped him before he reached Roger

Owen.

On the morning of June 7th., a dozen prisoners were found running about the camp of Gorey Hill in near dementia. A vigilante group had pitchcapped them during the night, Rev. Owen among them. His beard and hair had been forcibly removed with lighted gunpowder.

Gentry, in their hundreds were evacuating through all ports, families of Anglican bishops and priests, military officers, Government officials and other ascendancy toffs, from a trickle, into a flood. Lady Camden, the wife of the Lord Lieutenant, was no exception. The ports of England and Wales had an overnight crisis on their hands, dealing with a new breed of VIP refugees.

"Arklow would be a grand landing place for Mr. Bonaparte, when he comes," said The Monk, trumpeting the benefits that would await the French. The huge harbour, in history, the great Norman fortress of The Ormonds on the mouth of the Avoca River. "With room for a hundred ships, not like Bantry," said the street fighter.

But now, again, the town was glutted with Yeos and Hessian militia, their very presence destroying the beauty all around.

Some kind of euphoria crept, like a bad breath through the camp and the majority of the United leaders began to turn their loyalty and confidences toward father Michael and comrades like Esmond Khan and Captain Hay. Many saw the slow erosion of John Murphy's power and authority as a positive move by the council to relieve him of his duties for when the final victory would come. The leader, responsible for the destruction of the enemy garrisons of the whole of Wexford, was being edged out and the first call in that direction, was to send Father Michael to liberate Arklow. John felt the beginning of loneliness out on the fringes. After all, Father Michael had been a rebel and an agitator for four years, a leader in the cause of the United Irishmen, disobedience before his bishop, rebellion, a courageous virtue in the man, whereas, John Murphy, on the other hand, was unheard of before last week, except for his opposition to all things United, all things violent and his submission made slaves of his flock and of his own will and virtue.

The big ploughman would lose himself after battle, go home to Tomgarrow and wait for word of the next manoeuvre, or stay in the background and help with ammunitions preparations. He had been seen in the slaughter sheds, gutting sheep and chickens for the stew pots.

"Who are you?" John Murphy had asked him after his first encounter.

"I'm James Gallagher of Tomgarrow, Father." The big fellow cleaned his hands of entrails and went on one knee before the priest in a pious and childlike gesture.

"And what have you in my safety, James Gallagher, who fights with a sickle and short pike?" Murphy put his hands on the massive shoulders and beckoned him to stand.

"I'm no good with the musket, Father, 'twas your sister sent me," he said, rising and crossing himself. "To look out for you, she said."

Murphy managed a smile

"I remember the day they priested you, Father, my mother came to your house over in Tomahurra and asked you to look out for me, I was a wilder then."

"And are you married?"

"I am, that, with three sons to the good."

"And my sister asked you to leave your family to come and mind me?, and your wife, James, what does she say?"

"She waits my going back. My mother is with her, Father."

"I don't want you putting yourself in danger for me, James Gallagher. You're a big man and you stand out in the crowd."

The big face softened in a toothy smile. "I'll be in no danger at all, sure Father, when I'm with yourself."

John laughed heartily, not wishing to confront the paradoxical, every truth having a counterpart to contradict it. He shook the shovel like hand extended to him.

"How we increase the cares of life for our mothers and wives, James Gallagher, there is no such slave as they. What they sing to our cradles goes all the way down to our graves."

"I was coming through Castletown a while ago, Father," Gallagher said, "there's a woman asking after you in the village if you should be passing. She's dying, a priest is nowhere about."

Chapter 56

Three miles from Arklow, the army was making slow progress. It was coming toward mid afternoon and John rode to where Father Michael and Captain Hay led the column onto the open road. In order that no conflict should be seen by the rebels, John had urged the two to postpone their confrontation until to-morrow, to send for reinforcements to Michael Dwyer, who would be in Arklow within twenty four hours. The insurgents were tired, having spent much of their energy at Carnew and a camp with food and rest would insure a better team in the new day. He was going to Castletown and would join them in an hour. He pointed toward the town. "General Needham is in there. My scout reports he has 7,000 men and new artillery and reserves have landed in the harbour, sent from Wales." He spoke under his breath, out of ear of the mob, which waited, suspicion rising at the delay up front. "Needham is not Loftus, Michael, where are the women, the moving magazines, where are your flankers, he'll tear you asunder, your condemning your men to a slaughter"

"We have real soldiers now, John," Hay retorted, arrogant and commanding, we no longer need the services of women, putting them in danger, nor indeed screeching children, nor, God forbid, gadding milking cows."

Murphy fumed, this time raising his voice, this time for the benefit of those closer to the dispute. "I am putting it on record and I insist you stand down the army until I return. I have a strategy for Arklow and I demand you heed my instructions."

With his companion, James Gallagher, he turned the mare while those about pleaded with him to stay.

John Murphy never returned on that fatal day of June 7th. This battle by committee directive was about to be put to the grimmest test without it's commander.

**

The woman, raked with consumption, whispered to him as she held his hands in hers, the gaunt cadaverous eyes burned at him from sore empty sockets.. The ages of the children about the cabin, suggested she was no more than thirty years old.

"You blessed me once before, Father, you churched me and gave me sherry wine in Boolavogue."

John administered the blessed unction of the last rights. For a precious moment, the loveliest of lovely things surrounded him, when a dark hovel on the side of a ditch became the most beautiful order of things and a sorrowful pilgrim knew pain and sorrow no longer. As she slipped into unconsciousness and fell like a fragile dewdrop from creation, the priest thought on the one certainty of life, that all is ephemeral; for this sorrowful creature, for every one of the rebel army, for the enemy militia, for King George of England, for Pitt The Younger, for fame and the famous, for himself, John Murphy of Boolavogue.

The chair was big and comfortable and the old woman of the house had the tea ready. He read his office for the young mother's soul and two hours later the patient ploughman stepped into the cabin to enquire of the priest. The old woman put a finger to her lips and pulled aside the faded old blanket that hung as a divider of the one roomed bathan. Father Murphy was slumped sideways in his chair, his head resting, comfortably against a soft pillow.

"She died two hours ago, Sir," the woman whispered."We wouldn't wake her yet for she's in good company, nor wake himself either until he's good and ready, for he's worn out, he is." She wept into her apron. Six urchins sat outside, haunted innocents, victims of a never broken, never ending poverty that began for each of them on the first day of their lives. A group of neighbours had come to grieve, waiting respectfully for the priest to come out into the afternoon sunshine.

The pounding of the battle for Arklow had been all around them. Old people of Castletown stood at their hovels, crossing themselves at every explosion and the old woman asked Gallagher if she might wake the good Father, that he might be needed at the war.

The ploughman accepted a basin of buttermilk. "Let him sleep, woman, for 'tis the only peaceful sleep he's had in a week." Looking north toward the tumult where the skies over Arklow were stained with gun smoke and thick with grapeshot, he whispered, "let them see how they do without him."

John woke with a start. Thick sleep had partly paralyzed his body. Someone had covered the dead woman's face. Through a haze of stupor, he concentrated for a minute on the worn marbled hands. The pale limbs, drawn together in death like a variegated sculpture, veins standing out, proud of the flesh like sinewy rivulets of green ointment, were now interwoven with a garland of rosary beads. From the other half of the house, the monotone of a dark cheerless lament floated.

He raised his hand in blessing over the bowed heads and pondered again, the possibility of seeking terms of peace with the authorities. But the look on the suntanned face of the ploughman soon fragmented the

441

pious ideas in that direction. Two dispatch riders sat with Gallagher on the soft ditch across the road. Murphy was about to chastise him for allowing the time to run, when the ploughman relayed the troubled contents of the dispatches.

Arklow was lost, and there was turmoil in New Ross.

On the afternoon of June 7th., God, in His Heaven prepared Himself to confound all traits of distinction and all virtues and all vices to be summed up justly, where uniforms and trophies make no impression, and kings and beggars are called to account, as ten thousand joined the poor mother of six, to become souls about His universe; to His right hand, the transcendental, to His left hand, the proscribed.

"Dear God, you have a busy day."

To the assembly point at Gorey Hill, the straggling remnants of the rebel armies crowded south from Arklow and the beginnings of the retreat from New Ross in the south, began to appear out of Ferns and Camolin. Exhausted and spiritless, the rebels repeated over and over, that there was nobody able to take command at Arklow, nobody to dictate the directions, nobody to head them.

Myles Byrne released an uncharacteristic flood of aggression at the priest for not stamping his authority on the leaders as he had done in the past week. The youth, his eyes filling up in a mixture of remorse and frustration before the man he deified, slowly reported the events of the day. He praised the bravery of, especially, Garret Byrne and Father Michael and Kyan and Mr. Moynihan, who were bravery itself when the artillery was called into action.

"But we were totally in disarray, Father, and Captain Hay, for some reason, dispensed with the usual formation of leading with the riflemen, flanking the pikes, and keeping our artillery in reserve. There were no women at Arklow and loading and re-loading was a disaster. Myself and General Roche commanded the two sectors of the pikemen and at one stage, we had them on the run, but there was no central plan of battle, no regrouping, and eventually, somebody called for a retreat, losing the day."

"And Father Michael," asked John.

"Father Michael, Sir, mirrors yourself on two fronts, but only two, that's his bravery in battle and the identity of a noble name. However, your gift of leadership, surpasses in every way, any aspirations Michael might have had. He was like many of the other leaders, merely following out in front, they do not marshal us like you do. Father Michael had his band of Ballycanew, Courtown and Killena, march up to the mouth of the cannon. Unflinching, and short of ammunition, line after line of the croppies stood up to the terrible artillery pieces, taking the full force of the grapeshot, so the next line of pikemen could take advantage of the time spent in trying to reload."

The horseman hesitated, his words, forced and haltered. "Father Michael died with the call for freedom on his lips, not so, the stout experienced Captain Philip Hay, who supported him in the plan of attack and persuaded him to ignore your own instructions.. As soon as the hopelessness of the situation presented itself, I saw him absconding to safer ground. You were right, Needham is a good leader. He was ready for us, as we took time out to revel in Carnew, an empty town. Needham had his troops in perfect formation. We were unprotected, and where were the women, my men were destroyed, without time to reload?"

"Will you ask them to bring Michael to the Mass rock, please, Mr. Byrne."

As the night descended and the torches were lit and cooking fires dotted about the hillside, Father Murphy led thousands in prayer.

Later, after the rebellion, James Attridge was to report that having been interviewed in Dublin, General Needham said that in all his experience of warfare, at home and abroad, the daring advances made, time and time again, by the insurgents, despite the hopeless inefficiency of their leadership, brought before him at Arklow, a kind of bravery and ostentatious disregard for personal safety, he found in no other place and for no other cause.

James Attridge came into the camp early in the morning of June 10th. To find Father John saying Mass. Father Michael's body, draped in a green banner, over his vestments, lay before the Mass Rock. The banner hanging over him, which had been commissioned by the priest of Ballycanew himself, had the words emblazoned on it, "Liberty or Death." They took him away for burial at castle Ellis, with a cortege of 300 men.

James saw the result of the great rebellion was having on his friend. The graft of the dally demands of war and the intolerable depression of a succession of sleepless nights, leaving him drained, and now the loss of his friend.

"You should be at Duhallow, James", Murphy began, as he disrobed, two women waiting to accept his vestments. Murphy saw Georgie Tansy. "And you, Sir, should be minding the house."

"He insisted on coming with me, Father, he's a great comfort to the people left behind at Boolavogue and Trasna. You'll be glad to hear that Lord Mountnorris has signed a document of protection on Duhallow, having heard you spared Camolin Park, but he told me to tell you he thinks you have lost your mind," James said, with a tinge of passion, "he wishes you safety and a safe return home".

The priest sighed a laugh, a sigh of resignation. "I suppose he's right, the old man is not all that bad. Take it from me, he has too much respect for Sir George, and a touch of fear thrown in. We'll have a bit of breakfast now, and I want you to tell me of New Ross.

G. watched the cortage bearing the remains of the martyred priest. "What was his name, Father John; Father Michael? He had been making notes in this shorthand leaqrned from the new master of Duhallow.

"Michael Murphy, is his name, Georgie, same as myself, but no relation, common enough name."

"I was at New Ross, Sir," said James, "I've recorded an account for the American papers, most of my accounts are being either refused or condensed by the London papers, even the Journal is censured in whole or in part. I was going to send it to you, but it was done in a hurry and the writing is partly in short hand."

"Read it to me after breakfast then. One thing we have in abundance here is food." He put an arm about the young deacon. "Your young brother is in bad company. I expect he's with Jack Keohane somewhere. Keohane hasn't been here these past few days. He's not a bad man, just full of anger. Try your best to keep Henry away, especially from the fight.

"Hen wants to be a rebel, Father, he says he wants to be a rebel like you."

"John Kelly is dead, G.", said Attridge, "and so is Keohane, but Henry is not in New Ross, as far as I can make out."

James produced a sheaf of papers and Murphy called the leaders of the council, hanging on every word of the report.

Attridge began, smoothing the papers along his thighs and checking they were in numerical order.

"By the time General Beauchamp Bagnal Harvey had committed himself to the task of liberating Ireland, father John Murphy of the village of Boolavogue, had five campaigns under his belt and had routed corps after corps of enemy personnel, about four thousand of whom now enriched the already fertile soil of Wexford.

It was the 4th.of June, six days after the official inauguration as Commander-In-Chief of the rebel forces in Wexford, that Bagnal Harvey finally rested on Corbett Hill, within a mile of New Ross, where the idyllic twin Rivers of Nore and Barrow meet the inland harbour, a distance of thirty miles from Wexford Town.

Harvey had a scornful insular way of wasting time, and ceremony and proper decorum took precedence over other less primary matters, like proper food kitchens, with linens and all culinary etiquette, on the part of his officers, before fire and ball, and to give all courtesy to the enemy before engaging him. He grumbled about small difficulties and would make light of great problems, pretending they didn't exist."

Murphy smiled into his cup of cooling tea, remembering his one meeting with Harvey and the self importance of the man.

Attridge continued;

"General Harvey paid the loyalist keeper of Ross, General Johnson, the complement of inviting him outside the gates of the town, and surrender to the insurgent army. The complement, or rather, this insult to a senior officer of the crown, who was given the gift of four days to fortify Ross into an impenetrable fortress with an accumulated army of almost 10,000 well armed regulars and Yeomanry reserves, while this observer scrutinised proceedings from the margins, observed a gentleman named Mr. Roger Furlong being draped by Harvey himself, in a flag of truce and sent within range of the gate, where General Johnson, personally shot him. I believe it is an international sacrilege to shoot down a flag of truce, anywhere in the world, except in Ireland. It is, I believe, the ultimate insult."

James broke off and smiled at the priest, the fresh bread and boiled eggs tasted good in the morning air. "I watched Harvey, when Furlong's body was brought before him and could imagine his mind and the indecision of it. I tell you, Father, the man wasn't even vexed by the atrocity, while John Kelly and your friend Father Philip Roche, even Jack Keohane, ranted and called on him for action."

He smiled more broadly. "I could see him, wondering to himself as to what John Murphy would do if he were here." Murphy waved the complement aside. "Read on," his frown deepening.

"This reporter saw, once again, the lack of leadership, as happened in Arklow. It became obvious that some kind of madness or affliction blocked his sense of purpose, which I am loathe to call cowardice, but he seemed unable to face the present and at least, took refuge in evasion. Bagnal Harvey committed only a portion of his army of 25,000 to the battle of New Ross, while he insisted the majority remain camped with him on Corbett Hill.

The leaders beseeched him to commit, knowing the severity of the odds presented by Johnson, with a row of six pounders and Howitzers, and who was given plenty of time to place them in strategic locations.

Eventually, Commander Harvey sent the Killane giant, John Kelly against the fifth squadron of the Dragoon Guards and the rampant men from the mountains took the Three Bullet Gate and swarmed into the town, but Bagnal Harvey dithered again and there were no reserves to

445

Kelly's back. The man, built like a tower fell, but not before he had General Johnson in retreat, while the Clare Militia, under Major Vaudeleur maintained ground at the Irishtown suburb. Again there were no orders to press home advantage. The rebels had control of the town, for more than six hours, but the insurgents were so consumed with hatred for all things ascendancy, military or religious, that in a show of personal vendetta and insubordination, they sacked the town, burning all before them, irrespective of ownership and sought out, once again the cellars and the inns, instead of skirting the jurisdiction where they would have found Vaudeleur."

Attridge looked at Murphy. The priest had his head deep in his shoulders, studying the tufted grass at his feet. "Shall I go on, Sir?" Murphy's demeanour suggested he knew what was coming.

"And Bagnal Harvey?"

James continued. "All the while the commander-in-chief remained outside the fight and continued to horde the greater part of his army at Corbett Hill. Why he chose such a strategy, nobody knows, but the king's troops were allowed to regroup and eleven hours after the battle had commenced, 5,000 rebels lay dead and survivors retreated, many with Ganeral Harvey, back to Wexford Town."

James sighed heavily, knowing how the report was weighing heavily on his friend's shoulders.

"This reporter, on 7th. June 1798, is saddened to bring the reader a tale of unspeakable savagery committed on both sides at the battle of New Ross. Cicero said almost two thousand years ago that laws are silent in times of war, but I believe myself to be the huntsman for truth because the first duty of a newspaper reporter is to be accurate and fair. No prisoners were taken. General Johnson, a disciple of General Gerard Lake, the commander-in-chief of the British forces in Ireland, had rebel survivors shot by the hundred. Following Lake's policy of cleansing the countryside ethnically, men of all ages were marched before the walls of Ross, where genocide was committed without compunction. As a consequence, a nation's hatred, so long passive and held without expression, controlled involuntarily to the point of exasperation, now broke the limits of its restraint and burst into flame. All virtue gone, the peasants could take no more and matched crime for crime.

I followed the surviving insurgents back toward Corbett Hill and then through the lands of Mr. Francis King of Scullabogue, which skirt along the lowlands of Carrickburn Mountain. The landlord's barn, within sight of his mansion, had been commandeered and the huge building was used as a jailhouse, in which 200 prisoners, most of them, Protestants and residents of the area, were incarcerated. Under a heavy guard, I have to report that a number of children insisted on joining their parents inside the barn, as they felt it offered more protection than the town itself, where Johnson's men were rampant. His so-called Elite Corps was on patrols, combing south Wexford for the minutest reason to commit atrocities. It is the belief of this reporter that most of those locked into Mr. King's barn shed, were non political.

Fifty Catholics, of dubious loyalties were added to the throng until there was hardly breathing room in the building, already half full of dry hay. Among the retreating peasants was a gentleman who was known to me and who I am not at liberty to name. He had been fighting at the side of Father Philip Roche, the good priest who assumed command when Beauchamp Bagnal Harvey failed to assert. This gentleman, arrogant and desperate with fire constantly at boiling point, as he watched, as we did, the executions by Johnson's men in their hundreds, came upon the protected house and barn shed of Scullabogue and his dementia for revenge progressed further.

He and his men relieved the guard of their duties and Mr. King and his household watched in terror as lighted torches were thrown onto the thatched roof while more missiles were thrown through the two windows. I heard the cries of women and children as it dawned on the enslaved occupants, that they were about to be burned alive. Men tried, frantically to break out, some managed to squeeze through the splintered panelling, only to be shot or piked in the process. Fury was wild and unreasoning as the outer limits of madness took hold of what was now a mob and when the people of Mr. King's household ran out to intervene, over thirty of them were executed on the lawn. The screaming of the victims of the inferno rent the air and I could feel the force of the searing heat from the straw, the timber and soon, the bodies, as almost 200 innocent souls were slowly consumed by the flames. Young children were pushed through the flames with a final plea for mercy, only to be skewered on the pikes and hurled back into the inferno."

Signed by "Saoirse."

James put away the crumpled report . The silence had a climax as the image impaled itself on the council.

Eventually the priest said, "who was this gentleman known to you, James?"

"It was my uncle-in-law, Jack Keohane."

"Sure as God is in His heaven, that man was born into trouble, it's his affliction, he'll come to a bad end."

"He already has," said Attridge. Back in Wexford, Bagnal Harvey, possibly to court favour with the authorities and with Johnson, who has already taken back the town, offered a reward for the capture of the culprits of Scullabogue. While the remnants of the barn still smouldered, Jack Keohane and two dozen culprits were shot on the northern slopes of Corbett Hill."

Georgie looked searchingly at James. "There is no account of your brother, G. and I did not see him. But Johnson, thanks to Bagnal Harvey, is loose and hunting for revenge."

Chapter 57

Kate Attridge had brought tea to Sir George in his room and urged him to join herself and James later for dinner. Getting more and more frail by the day, the shock of Master O'Duinn's death turned him inwards and he was inclined to hug the privacy of his warm bedroom for long periods. The congestion in his lungs troubled him greatly and he began to look at life with sombre anticipation.

The Yeos had come in the night, and fired the schoolhouse, pulling unceremoniously, the two occupants onto the slab. There was nobody about, no shouting women to protest in defiance, like when Conor Devereaux was threatened. It was too much for the old man and his heart gave out, as Norah Scully, with the help of a Yeoman Private, pulled many of the old books to safety, a Yeoman soldier, who had learned his ABC's at the feet of The Master.

James had many dispatches delivered in the last few days, from his correspondents and he was busy, preparing his releases for publication. Nowadays, evil reports carried further than any applause." I cannot understand, nor could there be a reason to the complexities of this revolution," he wrote.

He sat in the warmth of the early evening sunshine, inside the expansive window of the parlour. Duhallow had become a crypt for the dispossessed of Trasna. Refugees came daily from the burnt out cabins, offering to work in the fields in return for protection, more reason in them to fear than to hope. There were few men among them and many of the outhouses and storage sheds were empty, awaiting the new harvest. The stout walls of Duhallow were a blessed protectorate, but nothing so, than the patronage of Sir George Palmer and the new mistress of the estate. Many had brought gifts, units of livestock, bastible bread and in the mornings, the steps of Duhallow would be strewn with humble generosity, gifts conferred with open palms, little portions of the giver; home crafted play things, squares of white crisp linen, a menagerie to hold a candle, wild flowers, knitted shawls, mittens.

The two men teased their dinner. Complex, where's the complexity," Palmer urged. "Oppressed people decided, once and for all, to rise up and break free of their bonds, there is no complexity in that, Son."

I mean, Sir, it's so fragmented, there's no system to it, no order"."

"They're poor peasants, James," argued the old man. "like the rest of us, they know nothing about making war."

449

"Sir George is right," said Kate, we saw them at Vinegar Hill." She had come join them and poured herself a cup of tea.

Palmer continued. "Thomas Jefferson of America said the tree of liberty must be refreshed from time to time with the blood of patriots and tyrants alike, it is the natural manure. Revolutions never have a pattern to them." He smiled at Kate as she replenished his glass. "Revolutions destroy everything, it is their nature not to go by military laws, but to make their own. This is where the revenge comes into it, each rebel has his own war to fight, his own retribution to seek out, like he was ever the only one violated."

"The American revolution, the French revolution," argued James, "they stood up to their oppressors and swept them away. There was already an army in place. Ireland doesn't have an army, a few thousand rough croppies, pigmen and farmers and a priest here and there." He sifted through his papers. "It isn't so long ago, I wrote about the lofty ideals of the United Irishmen."

Kate stood by the window and looked into the yellowness of the evening, as if looking outside the room for some psychological design to the madness that had befallen the whole glorious adventure and said a silent prayer for The Master and for Father Murphy. Her husband's voice was a distant monotone, as her eyes filled.

"What has become of the young eloquent orators and honoured chiefs, I was so impressed with in the early days of the decade; Butler, Tandy, Russell, Drennan, Bond, Keogh, Mc. Cormack, the wonderful aristocratic O'Connor, Addis Emmet, Mc. Nevin, Lawless.? All their marvellous ideals, now scuppered, all the great meetings with their Northern Presbyterian brothers, like Mc. Tier, Neilson, Mac Cracken, Munro, where are they now that Father Murphy needs them. Lord Edward Fitzgerald, run to ground like a dog, dead of his wounds, a martyr for Ireland without ever firing a shot, yet in America, he fired many a shot."

Attridge sipped his wine and moved his papers about. "I can only think it was endemic Scottish cautiousness that caused the Northerners to hesitate in coming into the insurrection. They should have done so in the final days of May." He looked pleadingly at the older man. "But this is what I mean, Sir, when I talk about complexities and discouraging circumstances."

He consulted his notes again. "Down and Antrim, chose to rise on the same day, June 5th, less than a week ago. on the same day Bagnal Harvey made a mess of New Ross and our friend John Kelly was killed, a man named Steel Dixon of the men of Down was arrested within an hour of his own private rebellion, while next door in Antrim, the

450

Antrim leader, his name escapes me, resigned on his first day. Some rebellion indeed."

He remonstrated, standing and walking about the room. "But that was already eight days too late. John Murphy had sent three thousand of the enemy to their maker by then. Then two men, I have had the pleasure of meeting took charge in those unhappy counties, Henry Joy Mac Cracken of County Antrim and Mr. Henry Munro of County Down. It took Mac Cracken two days further to prepare and with 3,500 men he marched on Antrim Town, but Colonal Lumney's garrison of Light dragoons, soon brought him to heel and the new leader of Antrim was taken."

Attridge continued. "Munro lasted a bit longer. His army dallied and came to life, some two weeks after John Murphy took his first strike. Munro had skirmishes with some success, but Ballinahinch was his downfall, with three generals, Nugent, Barker and Stapleton at his throat. No doubt these fine gentlemen will hang." James pleaded for Palmer to see his point. "Don't you see, Sir, if they had come south to join Murphy and swell his army and leadership, they could be at his side today."

Palmer sighed into his wine and nodded his agreement.

"Again, dare I say it and dare any newspaper print it within the realm. Antrim, 3,500 men, Down, 8,000 men, while Wexford County, which never boasted a substantial United stronghold, must have between Vinegar Hill, Gorey, Enniscorthy, Three Rocks, Camolin, New Ross and Wexford," he pointed to the scribbled figures on the margin of his notes......fifty thousand insurgents, a substantial portion of which have already died."

"So many," said the old man, wild-eyed, his voice full of feeling. "John Murphy will give his life for his part in all this."

James put a hand on the frail shoulder. "John Murphy is not concerned about his life, Sir George, what the good priest is worried about is whether he has given his soul for it."

"And Conor?" asked Palmer.

"I'm told he returned to Vinegar Hill," said James.

"Conor thinks he's still a boy," said Sir George. There was an undercurrent of anxiety in the glib remark, as cherished prisms of good memories made him feel old and sad.

The huge armoury shelter was empty now and old Cantankerous had been moved to more remote quarters. It was now a community complex for the many homeless of Trasna. The men had constructed a central furnace with a shaft through the roof, where they cooked and sat around for comfort and conversation.

451

In the evening, after dinner, Sir George linked her and Kate put a rug about his shoulders. They went through the kitchen in the direction of the music and the smell of cooking and willing hands fought to set a comfortable place of himself and Kate. Great applause greeted the benefactor and a child approached him with a little posy of wild flowers. The old shed, for many years, dark and foreboding, the repository for angry weapons of war and destruction had become a sentimental place, a warm corner, people in adversity in a single hope for a better day. Many of them were already, orphans and widows.

There were heated conversations and debate that Father Murphy was calling for a new army of 100,000, to swipe the English away forever.

**

The small horse dragged the cart, with its single occupant past the front portico of the house and around the back to the gravelled yard. James Attridge stood in the doorway looking into the motley collection. The youngsters had taken up the challenge and were dancing to the music, as old men beat time on the hard floor with heavy and unlaced boots on blackened unstockinged feet. James looked through the dusk at the visitor.

Norah Scully was dressed in her usual black, her hair, white and elegant, severely screwed back, ribboned and hanging in a sleek shining mane at her back. From behind, she looked like an eighteen year old girl, full of kinetic energy and purpose, the face, that of a woman of nearly sixty years, scrubbed and well worn and hard in features, unyielding as the life she had led.

"I'm away, James." She looked up into his face, the shoulders of her narrow frame, stiff and determined.

"But Norah, you must stay, Kate and I insist on it. Sir George is already arranging to have the house rebuilt, the minute the war is over. There is a home here for you, I've already told you that."

She put a cold finger to his lips. "God bless Sir George and Duhallow, 'tis a blessing of all that's good in the distemper all around us. But my place is out there somewhere, 'tis where I came from. There's no place here for a contrary old woman, now that himself is gone. I have to go out and find my soul again, westward, Cork maybe, Kerry maybe. I like Kerry, 'tis a peaceful place and safe."

There were always weighty reasons in Nora Scully's arguments, a cunning debater and a point scorer in all disputes. The power of Nora's arguments was always greater than the power of her sense.

"I have something for you." She uncovered three large boxes, brimful with The Master's priceless books. "He wanted you to have them, James."

"But the fire." Attridge was ecstatic, his eyes misting over.

"A sure, himself was always a step before the sheriff, he had them hidden away, long before the patrols came. The young soldier who helped me, thinks he's the saviour of the universe."

"I must pay you, you'll have to have money." Said James

"Himself left me well off enough to travel Ireland twice. Anyway, he left them to you, James, they are not mine to sell, not that I would, for they were yours since the first time he saw the pleasure of your reading them."

He piled the heavy boxes onto the gravel. She stood in the shadows, looking into the noisy covert, which looked almost comfortable, people sitting around the fire and some kind of merriment in old Cantankerous's domain.

"He was sad, The Master."

It was the only time she had referred to O'Duinn, other than "himself" or "the owl fella," "sad at hearing of the killings and the murder and the rape. I can't remember what he would say out of that old mouth of his, something about injustice on the land.

"Injustice, swift, erect and unconfined, sweeps the wide Earth and tramples oe'r mankind," James instructed.

"Like himself, you have a grand way with the words."

She was looking in at Kate, at her dark hair glistening in the light of the lamps.

"I'll call her," said James.

"No!" she put a hand on his arm. "Goodbyes stick in my craw. When we're short of good things in our lives, some things are twice as good. You mind that sweet girl, James Attridge." She shot a glance at him in mock reprimand. "And go out and bring that mad father of yours, home, he's foolish and strong headed enough to think he can save Ireland all on his own."

He helped her onto the cart. "Rebuild the old house, James, and put children in there for the learning and hunt out the old ghosts."

He walked along with the cart. "Kate will never forgive me, letting you go like that," whispered Attridge. "Kate is all forgiving, and well you know it, and if there's a God in the terrible heart of all this, let Him be by you and by her." She faded into the dusk.

Chapter 58

The revolt in Ulster was soon over. Mr. Henry Munro, it had been reported, was hanged outside his own home in Lisbourne. Retreating insurgents from New Ross flocked to Father Murphy's side. Father Philip Roche had taken over from Bagnal Harvey, unable to understand the unexplainable eccentricities of the commander and in his report to John Murphy, he referred to the Wexfordman as a paragon of importance. What recruits he could muster after the debacle of Ross, he brought with him to Wexford Town, knowing the loyalists would soon return, after their victory at Arklow and New Ross.

Murphy's war continued unabated, as the desperate unyielding knot tightened around the mass confusion that engulfed the county. There was no middle course now. Flags of truce were being unrecognised by the military, while the North Corks and their imported counterparts, the Ancient Britons, a handpicked uniformed society of despots, butchered without compunction, in the once safe areas of South Wicklow, North West Wexford and the region of Shillelagh, Kilcavan and Carrigroe.

The military were on the march again, but as so often before, irresolution; incorrigible in the majority of the king's generals, presented itself in the lowlands of the Wicklow Hills. Still without one victory to his credit, the senior General Loftus, from Tullow, joined his counterpart, Dundas from Hacketstown, their mortified minds, screaming out for one good strike.

Slaves to impatience and desperation, they prepared for a strike on this priest of magic and trickology, that pulverized the over fertile minds of the native Yeomanry, rendering them useless and impossible to control. It's one thing for custom built generals to demand in their men on the field of battle, that all things be done decently and in order and systematically, where disorder is the true enemy, but in all the good generals' national and international experience, nowhere did all decent realities elude them at the sight of a marauding army, flanked by women and children and at their head, priests in sacred finery.

The confrontation lasted less than fifteen minutes. The two columns of military; infantry and cavalry and regular Yeomen, simply turned heel after letting off first shot. In confusion at the screaming women and the surging raging phalanx of pikemen roaring toward them, from the high ground, north of Mountpleasant, the flanking riflemen of Myles Byrne and Edward Roche, and the now familiar war totems of the flying skirts of the supporting "moving magazines," caused the confused troops to fire randomly. All the while, this priest, front and centre, concentrated the vision and the minds of an awe-inflicted opposition. The commander in full black attire, with a tower of a man flailing right and left to either side of him, virtually stunned them, filling many with fear and weakening their judgement. His army faced toward the west, so his strike was early in the day, while the great daily drama hung over his left shoulder, and the Sun God, once again smiled and Loftus, once again found a reverse gear.

However, Murphy mourned the experience and acumen in not always taking the initiative to follow the retreating enemy. The eight hundred troops would be to the good tomorrow in another place, so the British army would continue to retreat, until their numbers would swell withthe reinforcements the new Lord Lieutenant Camden was importing from England on a daily basis. John Murphy found little cause to celebrate as his army collected the bounty left behind on the roads outside of Tinahely.

The bright gold of the day darkened to an evening purple and shades of colours without any names, when the heat had cooled and the cooking fires were lit. The tranquilized fiery growth was all around as the priest rode out alone into the thick delicious air. Shrouded in beauty, mystery and tranquillity, the rounded towering peaks of the mountains swept downwards, folding into one another, like an unmade bed, enclosing the wooded slopes and lower fields in their deepening purple. Zephyrs, wafting into his face, the refreshing odours of the Wicklow Gap, the singing waterfall that never sleeps, and in the breeze, wisps of fragrances, tumbling, hurtling down, his head, stretching in search of each one.

In his corroding corrupt world, he had forgotten again, what beauty was. His soul had become too narrow to recognise that it was all around him, that rare thing that only a savage mind can blot out. He closed his eyes and reached his mind over the whole of time and grasped it, an asylum from his terrors. He opened his eyes again. The purple darkened to black silhouettes where the sinking sun shines upwards. Here was beauty, like nothing he had ever seen in Seville, here was a special place set aside for it.

"Dear Lord of Heaven, how you always lie ahead and are always there for the asking."

A pounding sound of hooves sent his thoughts scurrying. "Interruptus desideratum," he sighed. The mare pricked her ears. Conor O'Connor Devereaux reprimanded him for riding out alone toward the enemy and the night coming down, and did he intend taking on the enemy all by himself, but then, sure as God, the Loftus cur would only run again.

Still half consumed in the opium of heathers and fireweed and goosefoot, Murphy had no thoughts of General Loftus or anyone in a red jacket. He dismounted and ran a yard or two to where a rock, the height of a table stood proud of the hill. He stood like a statue of stone on the smooth surface.

The blacksmith looked furtively about. "We should be getting back to camp now, John Murphy," he cautioned

Ignoring the older man's concern, John said, "what direction am I facing now, Conor?"

"East."

He turned on the slab, "and now?"

"North," answered Conor, perplexed.

"And this way?"

"South."

"And again, this way?"

"What are you at, West, surely," said Conor in a half smile.

"So north to south and east to west, lie the borders of Leinster, just 8,000 square miles, the size of a good farm over there in America. So this is where the great Irish rebellion is taking place, lesser still, if we take out Dublin, for there's nobody fighting up there yet. "Liberty, Equality, Fraternity."

He hesitated, afraid of the obvious, the misgivings and the contempt that would choke him and betray his true feelings and his fears.

"Now beyond these borders, four times that and more, 40,000 square miles of our beautiful hills and plains and mountains and towns and houses and cities, and yes, people, four million of the beautiful people."

He was silent for a minute, his voice full of pain and rejection, his arms outstretched.

"Where are they, Conor Devereaux?"

He let his arms drop, came back onto the roadway and looked deep and hard into the mare's docile eyes. Big black pools of affection riveted on her master.

Conor said, tenderly, "I don't know, Sir."

"Your son reported the grand aspirations of Lord Edward fitzgerald. Mr. Wolfe Tone spoke to the people of Wexford and made promises and he told Mr. Bonaparte that a million, nay, two million would rise up and run the English out, once and for all. Promises, promises, Conor, we promise according to our hopes, vows made in storms are soon forgotten when it calms."

He said accusingly to the horse, "two million, he said two million, but in God's name where are they, all the so called active United

Irishmen. Lord Edward, dead, died at a meeting, another meeting, this country could sell stamps for meetings, and where is Wolf Tone?"

"It's getting dark, John Murphy, we could be sitting ducks out here," coaxed the blacksmith

The priest rose stiffly into his saddle. "This little country doesn't need the French. She has been fighting other nations' battles for centuries, it's time we fought our own." His voice lightened. " And don't you know, Conor, we're dead safe out here at night, sure the English are afraid of the dark, didn't you know that. Now I want you to go home, go back to Duhallow, James tells me Sir George is failing."

**

After the defeat of Mc. Cracken and Munro in the north, skirmishes broke out in many locations, like Kilcock in Kildare and Kilcavan in Wexford. On June 19th. Father Philip Roche and his lieutenant, Matthew Keogh were forced to retreat from Wexford Town and two days later, Government forces recapture Enniscorthy and Wexford Town and Roche was defeated at Goff's Bridge and at Folksmills, by Sir John Moore's forces. The military were slowly getting a grip on strategic locations, as the rebels forces were splintering. Thomas Dixon and his followers massacred almost one hundred loyalist prisoners on Wexford Town Bridge, while John Murphy's army continued on its victories at Goresbridge and Castlecomer in county Kilkenny, where he hoped the miners would join him. Having taken Hacketstown in county Carlow, his army was defeated at Kilcumney Hill in that county, on June 26th.

The campaign by general Gerard Lake, the fifty year old Middlesex man, was one built out of fear. " Fearing", he said, "the wrath of an embittered and exasperated people." This fear had become sharp sighted, robbing his mind of all its powers of acting with reason. As a consequence, he carried out his task with brutal efficiency.

"Cooking fires," he instructed his generals, "are lighted targets, it's where they gather to eat and tell their fairy stories. Whenever possible, let the fires be your first targets."

Sir John Moore offered his objection. "It's where the children gather also, Sir."

Lake, with a fixed glare, simply stared at Moore and made no reply, no reply was needed.

His campaign, by mid June, had subdued Ulster, by what had been referred to as a process of exhaustion. The great symbol of Ireland's outward and visible grace, Lord Edward Fitzgerald, had died of his wounds in prison.

"Gone is the comfort and the inspiration, his powerful person had offered his fellow United Irishmen, and with him, the influence of many leading members which now sank back into a respectable conformity." So wrote James attridge in his piece for the Times.

The Irish Directory however, had its own martyrs and dispossessed. Mr. Oliver Bond, in whose premises, Lord Edward Fitzgerald was shot, died of apoplexy. The two Shears brothers, along with six rebel priests, among them, fathers Quigley and Byrne, were hanged. Information and intelligence was extracted from many quarters and all prisoners harbouring affection for the Society were brought before the "Committee of Parliament" where leaders of the United Irishmen like Addis Emmet, Mc. Nevin and O'Connor, protested fearlessly of the despotic policy of the Irish Parliament, under a yoke, where the peasantry had no option but to rebel. However, fortune favoured these leaders. The dreaded Lord Camden had been exiled, reputed as a man who could cause a rebellion in heaven, and a new administration installed in Dublin Castle. Under Camden the remaining members of the Directory would certainly have hanged, but Lord Cornwallis, the new Lord Lieutenant, for whatever purpose, extended clemency and sentenced them to three years imprisonment to Fort George in the Scottish highlands, after which the majority of them were to be deported to "where their influence could never again bewilder the minds of the ignorant."

Father Murphy and his fellow leaders were now exposed to the wrath of General Lake. Vinegar Hill beckoned again. On 29th. June 1798, 25,000 peasants, unorganised, untrained and for most part, unarmed, swarmed onto the gentle slopes like homing locusts. Like a great and powerful pilgrimage place, Vinegar focused itself on a nation about to be obliterated in a mass exercise of genocide and swept to oblivion.

Cnoc Fiadh na gCaor, The Hill Of The Wood Of The Berries dominates the flatlands in the abode of The Mac Murrough-Kavanaghs, the ancient kings of Leinster, which for centuries, had testified to a bloody heritage. Vinegar Hill dominates the sweeping fertile landscape, a tapestry spreading in a breathtaking crisscross of a network of rivers and quiet streams toward the multicoloured heathers of Mount Leinster to the west and the seaboard of The Macamores Mountains in the east, where long golden beeches were ever ready to welcome a redeemer of any nationality under the sun England was the enemy of the whole world at the end of the century, any redeemer would do.

John Murphy looked down from a secluded perch near the ancient mill at the summit, on a pitiful sight that was Enniscorthy and bemoaned the devastation of war. The very seat of the nation's Christianity, the home of the 6th. Century Saint Senan, disciple of St. Patrick Himself, spread out before him, pitiful and condemnatory of sad events. Castle Hill with its turreted fortress was a dark ghost in the distance, where once the crawling, grovelling Lord Spenser was well compensated for his poem in praise of the beauty of the horse-faced Elizabeth I, "and will we ever be rid of them," pleaded Murphy to himself.

"England had never committed more than 20,000 men to battle, not even in her wars in the fight for American Independence. A supreme military machine with the most up to date equipment and armoury, she prided herself at being the world leader in warfare, the imperial conceit of her generals, often the aesthetic to dull the pain of their stupidity and often, their cowardice." And so wrote James attridge as he looked up at Vinegar and the preparation on both sides, reaching fever pitch.

"Her preparations to quell the insurrection in County Wexford, was vast," he wrote later. "In her recent history, England had never complemented an enemy so, by paying the half armed peasantry of a tiny county of a tiny country, the courtesy of fielding, the largest army in her modern history. But in Ireland, it wasn't pride that prompted such a movement. It was raw fear that the stubborn resistance of the Wexford men and women might arouse the rest of the country from their obvious and unaccountable apathy. Tired of retreating before the pikemen, it was obvious that the 25,000 rebels who assembled on vinegar Hill, would fight to the death. General Lake was more than willing to oblige, adamant that his generals would never again underestimate the courage of the Irish peasant."

On June 19th., regiments under orders from Lake, were on the march from all quarters, leaving camps and garrisons in the midlands and the western counties, unprotected and open to any retribution the peasants might try. No retribution was made. The devastation caused by the troops on the move, established, once and for all, a policy of complete indiscrimination, perpetuated by legitimate authority. General Lake's orders were the form on which the Orange text would be established, to promote the Prime Minister's cherished scheme of legislative union with England, on the death of the rebellion. Should there be any remnant of the rebel army remaining after the final battle, the countryside was to be laid waste and all peasant housing and dependence, destroyed. All houses, ripening crops and livestock was to be destroyed, or taken into custody in respect of livestock, with good conscience and young and old who dared to stand in the path, to be killed. The destruction by the armies on the way to Vinegar Hill became so savage that human laws had no longer any place in normal happenings The peasantry of old people were made to run before the moving prowling military, or remain to die in defence of their miserable homesteads.

The scouts had made their reports. John Murphy called for a leader council and with his watch as an indicator, brought them up to date of the enemy position. With Vinegar Hill, the cone shaped high rise as the central axis, he outlined the darkening inevitably of a massive defensive, with his fob watch as his graph.

At 12 o'clock on the dial, General Dundas approaching south from Tinahelly and Carnew. At 11 o'clock, General Loftus, from Tullow, through Bunclody. At 10 o'clock, General Duff, from Ballycarney. At 8 o'clock, General Johnson, up from New Ross, through Ballymackessy. At 7 o'clock, General Moore, through Bakllyhack and Folksmills, where it was reported, after a great struggle, he defeated Father Philip Roche and 3,000 insurgents. At 2 o'clock, General Needham was marching from Arklow, through Gorey and Arklow and Oulart. For good measure, there were five other generals awaiting their orders, at the arrival of General Lake. By tomorrow, every unit of the king's forces, including the two mercenary units; the Hopesch Cavalry and the dreaded Hessians would be assembled at the base of Vinegar, over 30,000 in all.

There had been great disagreement between the rebel leaders, at the choice of Vinegar Hill as a battle field as all their efforts would have been defensive. Among them, the youthful Myles Byrne, who for the past few days had been causing havoc in the area of Tinahely, making destructive stabs at military posts and firing known Orange houses, as far north as Hacketstown and Rathshanmore. He pleaded for a mass movement toward Rathdrum and cut off Lake's forces and take the offensive as always.

But by the afternoon of June 20th., the rebel army was committed. There was no trace of despondency on Vinegar Hill. In their hundreds, they were seen to dance and jibe at the ascendancy forces, as the Redcoats arrived in their thousands and prepared to circle the skirts of Vinegar and militia and what seemed, a thousand pieces of artillery, so John Murphy, looking down at the pageant, soon lost count.

When Father Philip would arrive from the south with his valuable Shelmalier riflemen, there would be more or less, the same amount on both sides, but the comparison ended there. The rebels had 3,000 firearms with a poor provision of powder and a few artillery pieces, with little to feed them. Old rifles would soon be turned about and used as bludgeons by the croppies. Those with the cherished pikes, now and forever, the symbol of Wexford's struggle, would once again prove the heroes. The military, on the other hand, had a train of ammunitions and stores, like they were prepared to stay as guests for the whole summer, among their armoury, the dreaded hissing bomb, that, having landed, would give the impression of being a dud, only to explode on a delayed trigger mechanism.

"Daily, they find new ways to kill us, Lord".

Watching the exclusiveness of the whole operation, Murphy realised this was now a very different opponent to what he had encountered at Harrow, Enniscorthy or Three Rocks. This was now a war machine of massive proportions and he wondered again, why it isn't located outside Paris, worrying Mr. Bonaparte, than to be here on the dirt roads of Enniscorthy John Murphy drew up strategies for organised retreat, to much dismay among the rebels who wanted no mention of such an event. Yet, retreat toward Wexford Town had to be an option.

A young man played a fiddle, his back to the old mill wall, at the summit. The building stood, silhouetted against the deep ochre sea of the setting sun, that lingered on the lofty towers of the Blackstairs. The priest found a corner to sit in, listening to the soulful drone of the instrument. The rough bogboy fingers caressed the strings, stroking them, finding the soul of the fiddle until another instrument further on, found the tune and when it was finished, there was a silence, intense and alien, until a lively lilt came from the other and the bogboy found it and a jig in tandem brought a smile to the face of the priest, tapping his feet against a stone.

Two youths came out of the glare of the fire. The brothers Tansey stood before him. " I had to come, Father," said Georgie. "I had to find Henry, he was in New Ross with father Philip."

"John Kelly is badly wounded, Father John," said Henry, "they took him away."

"I'm aware of that, Son, but you're too young to be in the fight."

Hen was ever arrogant, ready to defend. "I'm almost sixteen, and I was with John Kelly and Father Roche."

"And with Jack Keohane, too, Henry?"

The youth lowered his head, his brother answered for him. "He wasn't at the burning of Scullabogue, Father, he assures me of that."

Murphy looked at the two and the contrast in them; Georgie, affable and pliant, blended into groups of all kinds. The younger brother, even now, with a daily accusation against fate.

"Where is Father Philip, Hen?", Murphy frowned.

G. gave his brother a look, all encompassing, that was edged with a cautious reprimand.

"I think he's gone to Wexford Town, Sir," said the boy, more politely.

"I want you boys to go home, Mary Donovan will need you now more than ever and she'll be worried. You've taken certain responsibilities, Georgie and this is no place for either of you"

Henry knelt before him in a surprising burst of piety and the priest bestowed a blessing on the bowed head that hardly saw a drop of clean water in a fortnight. In the dancing light of their fires, one of the many priests who had joined the rebels in the past two days, Father Clinch from The Hook on the eastern shore of the Waterford estuary, led the croppy army in prayer, that what for thousands, would be their last.

A thousand voices rose in answer, "our Father who art in heaven...." and then a thousand more and ten thousand, as the words began in a sibilant whisper, then rising to a surging monologue, as though the mountain itself was on her knees. In the lap of the hill, the Tanseys had found a hollow that offered comfort for the night before returning home, just a few yards from a camp fire where they were offered food. "Hallowed be Thy name, Thy kingdom come...."

What Georgie thought to be the vibrating chords echoing against the summit and sweeping down to him, the rebel army in prayer, suddenly became like a babble of discordant sound and he realised the Lord's Prayer was coming at him from both directions. Down below, half the red army was on its knees......" Thy will be done on Earth as it is in heaven..."

From above...." lead us not into temptation but deliver from evil, amen."

From below... "but deliver us from evil, for Thine is the kingdom, the power and the glory, amen".

G. sat with his head against a soft tuft of grass and looked up at the darkening sky. "What a stupid chicken man is. With one single prayer, he's asking for the laws of the universe be annulled for one single petition. In his prayer he says, "Thy will be done," but he means his own."

"They're saying their prayers," said Hen, indignantly looking down through the descending dusk.

"It's their right, Hen, half of them are Irish, and at least, one time were Catholic. Whatever ill befalls a man, Father Murphy says, he never forgets the words of his prayers, even the wish to pray is a prayer in itself."

"Yes, well their prayers will never reach heaven, and that's for certain," complained the youngster.

"Heaven is a big place", said G., softly, and all the people down there and all the people up there, all think they have a right to it. Father John says the gate of heaven is small with a low overhang, and the only way in is on your knees."

The night was a prayerful preamble to a violent day and John Murphy felt the red flag of selfishness flutter in his belly, as like himself leading his flock into the saying of The Rosary, the many clergymen down below continued to pray over the heads of the king's army.

"Are their prayers heard above ours, Lord," Murphy thought. "Whatever attitude You find my body, remember my soul is on its knees."

Circling the summit and sensing the vibrancy, the palpable dynamic human dimension of the throng, a smile broke onto his tenseness. The segment of Vinegar Hill, facing southward, was still dark and unprotected. General Needham had not arrived from Gorey, so that, if the situation continued, the rebels would have a corridor of retreat. "Small mercies, Lord." However, Father Philip had not arrived and John tried not to worry just yet.

God save you King George and all belonging to you," came a strangled guttural eruption from the Dumbartonshires, but fell away again in the devotional ritual that spread back and forth across the faces of Vinegar. Half of King George's army was bowed in prayer, many on their knees and General Dundas, the most senior of the English warlords after Lake, turned to little things in his tent. Just after nightfall, cannon fire bursts were heard as one column saluted another and the priest looked toward the dawn with diminishing vigour. Later, the thunderous cannon fire and uncontrolled shouting of the army, echoed around the hillside. Welcome was unbridled for the commander-in-chief. General Gerrard Lake had made his entrance, after his long march from Dublin. Triumphalism was a studied insult to the rebels, as though the battle had already been won.

His tent prepared, food and wine at the ready, a huge soft down mattress had been brought from Bloomfield House for his comfort.

Tomorrow, he would direct proceedings and pile the final deceit against an entire nation on the conflagration now simmering. A superbly constructed fraud, once and for all, to enact out the final vows that helped to bind all evils together and make slaves of Orangemen for all time. The spirit of that oath; "To annihilate all Catholics from the Kingdom of Ireland", was, on the night of June 20th. 1798, enacted to it's very essence.

The rustle of importance, in starched and decorated finery, sat

463

around the general's table as he summoned his officers to his council of war. Leather faced and irreproachable, Lake rechristened their honourable calling, as that of a necessary part of cleansing of the land of all infidelity against the sacred person of His Majesty. Tomorrow was to be one of the great epochs of their lives, that after five hundred years, this thorn will be plucked and will no longer be a source of infinite adversity to the monarchy, that the real evil was now perched like a plague of locusts on Vinegar Hill and England will not surrender to it, her freedom in her own colonies. To ignore it would be senseless now, to punish it, divine.

No prisoners were to be taken. He looked at them, one to the other, his face cool and pitiless. The body opposing them on the hill, was neither man, woman or child, but an unsexed, uncultured and unimportant, and above all, their enemy in all its forms. After the battle, they were to be hunted down and despatched, all homesteads to be burnt so that no trace of them were to survive to blight the land further. This was to be achieved by the royal troops retracing their steps; Dundas toward Dublin, Loftus, north east to Carlow, Duff to the west through north Kilkenny, Johnson to the south west through Waterford, Needham, south toward Wexford Town and Lake himself would take the town of Wexford.

"I want a holocaust, that this country will remember into the third millennium." Scouts were sent out to bring up Genaral Needham.

The heavy jowled, horse lipped supreme military commander, was a fanatical warlord, a modern day Nero, who saw himself as a disciple of the Archangel, smiting all evils in his path, a marauder who portrayed the ethos and the idiosyncrasy of Orangism. Within twelve hours of the first signs of rebellion of this priest on the Harrow road, three ships were prepared at Portsmouth to carry the scum of British jails; madmen, murderers and despots and swarmed onto the Dublin quays, intolerable, thick-voiced blockheads, yesterday's caged criminals, seriously out of equilibrium with normality, to-day, a rude militia, with bristling bayonets, uniform and stock, their ears and dense minds, full of propaganda, that the Irish are a crowd of bandits who do not deserve to live, and no quarter given to man, woman or child, as perceived as their interpretation of the Orange oath.

At the same time, Lake commissioned a special unit of militia and civil servants to rake the lunatic asylums of the western counties to set up the so called Regent Corps, named for the Prince of Wales. The famous Captain Wharton, villain of the Tansey youths was a willing contributor to a simpleton army, consisting of mildly deranged and forgotten young men, shy, naive bourgeoisie, who, for the first time in their pathetic lives, were offered payment for a day's work. Six pennies, less one penny for the Buckingham tax, a fine red uniform with solid boots, even a gun to give them their first taste of respectability. To help the cause, two thousand plebeians and have-nots, were marched eastward to fight for king and country, the oath to His Majesty, printed on a slip of paper in a uniform pocket. Laughing and childish, in a disguise of fine clothes, always satisfied and happy, each one a fool, each one a potential king, the regiment of The Prince of Wales, was the enlisted gun fodder for General Lake's new campaign

The strategy for war dispensed with vigour, the dark shag across the tops of his eyes lifted and he looked through the flap of his tent at the darkness. The fires on Vinegar beckoned like a gigantic fly-wheel and he stood for a moment before going outside. His generals followed, hanging on his words.

"The fires are the stars, Gentlemen and when you look at the stars, there is nothing but blackness between one and the other, nothing but black space. Observe the blackness on this hill, Gentlemen, in between the fires. That blackness is the enemy, for where do people gather for eats and warmth but around the vicinity of the fires. Kill the fires and you kill the enemy."

General Lake was notorious for making a grand entrance to battle scenes, many of his episodes, contrary to international rules of war, he would stamp his authority, before a battle, regarding it as blooding his hounds. His generals in tow, he walked to where a six pounder was parked, it's great barrel shining in the light of the fire. A detail stood to attention on his arrival.

"What is your name, Corporal?", he demanded of Corporal Triggs, standing to attention by the beast.

"Corporal Ivor Triggs, Sir," the young soldier replied, perplexed and intimidated at being singled out by the Commander. The royal pageant of generals standing about, looked equally surprised.

"Well, Corporal Ivor Triggs, I want you to prime and load your beautiful gun."

"Sir?"

"Now, Mr. Triggs."

Triggs called for his assistants. It took just a minute or two to have the six pounder ready

"Now, Corporal, there's a fire, third up from the base of the hill, at one o'clock on your time piece. You can read a time piece, Corporal?"

"One o'clock it is, Sir." The corporal looked pleadingly at the officers. "Fire your gun, Corporal," Lake said with cold simplicity, throwing the unfortunate soldier the mad eye of the fourth personal singular.

The gun barked, sending the wheels of the carriage backwards and the blackness about fire number three exploded in fire and death.

"I have to object, General, this act is going against all convention of warfare, there were children and women." General Sir John Moore, the forty year old commander of the Government forces in Wexford Town, who, three days before had defeated Father Philip Roche at Goff's Bridge and Folksmills, was openly critical.

"My dear General, is it not true that women and children were instrumental in at least five defeats of our forces." He looked up at the chaos. "It takes care of, at least the next generation, Sir, and if you hadn't been so habitually indecisive at Wexford, you would have annihilated that accursed priest in quarter time, when he came very near to routing you."

Attending the dead and dying about fire number three, John Murphy looked out into the darkness at the enemy with no face, but the face of evil looked back at him, a hydra-headed monster, swollen to a horror.

Chapter 59

On the longest day of the year, John Murphy shivered himself awake in his modest tent and arose before the sun. In the shifting dull light the sky was striated in the east by radiant alternating bands of red and pink and pale yellow, fading away to dark purple and blue where the new day had not yet reached. He felt the comfortless dejection and inadequacy of the enormity of the task the day was preparing for him and it seeped through his emotions. To the west where the sky was still almost black and foreboding, his soul sailed on the edges of the fading night and he wished to go with it, over the glorious Kerry mountains and onward to where the sun would never have to shine on this day's evil doing.

The priest wondered if, in God's view, he had the right to conquest, if God approved of the stand he had taken, and in doing so, had, undoubtedly caused the deaths of thousands. As a true Christian and a man of God, should he have tried to conquer, not by arms, but by love and magnanimity. Yet, had he not tried that route.

"God, if it be Thy will............", nor would he ask for favours and would it be impudent to entertain some hope of victory, when General Lake, no doubt feels his entitlements equally strong. But in the name of their mutual God, what kind of savage barbarity would steer a man to murder children in the night, before they could me moved to safety in the morning, for here, surely was an evil to be fought.

He prayed for the women and children and the old, who had, against his wishes, flowed into the camp, the previous day; the floating jetsam of peasantry, the terrified farm animals on pieces of rope and paltry belongings, like they were resigned never to leave Vinegar. He looked up to the higher level above him to the ruin of the old mill, where two thousand women and children were housed, and where fires had been re-kindled for the rough breakfasts. He had spread the word that fires were not to be lit on the open slopes after General Lake's little game of roulette had taken the lives of twenty one souls, eight of them, children, but felt these inside the mill would be out of range, and in the event of a rout, women and children would be given quarter.

Before full light, the rebel leaders began naming the columns to their pre assigned posts, and was it too late to apply to Lake for terms of surrender?

In the night, two batteries of royal artillery had been drawn up from General Loftus's brigade, a good distance up the slopes of the north-east side of the hill, with only one purpose in mind; to seek out the first sighs of newly lit fires, where the rebels would throng for breakfast. "They're just one walking belly," scoffed Loftus, seated before his immaculate dish of cured pig bacon, eggs and sheep's liver, as he squinted through his field glass.

**

The two cannon pieces rent the morning and as Father Murphy gazed prayerfully to where the women and children were safely entrenched, the whole east wall of the mill disintegrated and before the awful reality struck him, the pieces were reloaded and committed the deed all over again. Three score innocents perished. The purpose to surprise was achieved. Frenzied croppies, half dressed, half asleep, ran shouting and gadding toward the mortars as two more shots of grape were released, blowing half a dozen of them to pieces, but the group kept running, tumbling down the grassy slope, hurtling themselves at Redcoats, before a further reloading could be achieved. Eighteen military commanders were cut to pieces, while the brigade looked up through their field glasses from the safety of the enemy camp.

The battle of Vinegar Hill had begun. In the early morning light, John could see the brigades of the cream of England's army spread out before him and the scene was both awesome and terrifying.

**

Barker and Mogue Kearns, the huge priest who they failed to hang in a Paris street, five years before, were engaging General Johnson outside of Enniscorthy on the New Ross road, while the military, skirting the hill and the rebel army prepared to face each other. Johnson lost 300 men in his fight to join his fellow generals at Vinegar, but to do so, he had to push through the town and cross the bridge that led to the battle.

Father Kearns had three hundred riflemen in the upper floors of the burnt out houses, who poured musket fire into the red army and though Johnson was driven back through the Duffry gate, the Redcoats regrouped and the rebels were forced backwards to the bridge. At the same time, the forces of the king were preparing for the assent of the hill, under cannon, grape, musket and canister, from east to north, and when the rebel artillery had silenced, having run out of powder, the calling of directions by Lake was nothing short of debauchery and a positive crime, dictated all the way from St. James's Palace, and the king of England.

Down below, Barker fought like a man possessed. He put a cannon on a cart, and for a while, he forced Johnson back into Market Square, while Kearns had pikemen on the river banks, seizing opportunity after opportunity to strike whenever the rifles fell silent.

**

The brothers, Henry and Georgie tansy stayed the night on Vinegar Hill and as day broke, they ate some boxty and a cantankerous Hen agreed, reluctantly, to return to Trasna with his brother. Henry had remained of small stature, a result of the asthma that had plagued him in early years. But his time spent in outdoor activities, on Mary Donovan's little farm and with his idol, John Kelly of Killane, had virtually cured him of the malady. He had become strong but enigmatic, after his mother's death but the time spent at Captain Wharton's madhouse, left him emotionally damaged, with a sort of a defective understanding, ready to oppose all opinions.

The field pieces began to create havoc, forcing the rebels back toward the summit of Vinegar, making the work of the cannon, easier. Behind a low ditch, the two brothers watched in awe at the spectacle of 50,000 consumed in a madness that was out of control. The pikemen would rush at the cannon, right up to the menacing maw, some with nothing but a hay fork to call a weapon. Lakes Howitzers spat death from a great distance, as the Redcoats moved slowly upwards behind the mayhem.

It was then, Georgie saw the imbeciles. Child faces, in total confusion, some crying, some laughing, like straw dolls blown about by the wind and the struggle upwards, over and across, back and forth, lost in the noise and the morass. Like sleigh dogs being whipped and pushed from behind, the infantry of the Loftus and Duff brigades prodded them forward as front liners to take the brunt of the rebel onslaught, a human shield of frightened and paralyzed youths in the king's uniform, the uniform without a face. They made no effort at defending themselves, their bayonets uncocked, but with a curious bewilderment breaking on their stupid faces, they took the ball and the pikehead full force, making way for the troops to step over them and progress further.

Hen pointed, the name sticking in his craw. "Wharton" whispered G., in a sudden burst of recognition.

Captain Wharton stood off from their line. Totally out of equilibrium, the wretched Regent Corps trudged upwards, Wharton's guttural in their ears, "up! Up! Up!," a dog call that became their mantra, some of the poor creatures were actually echoing the call of the despot.

From their seclusion, Hen rushed to where a Regent had fallen, wide eyed and dead. He pulled the youth nearer the ditch, tearing at the red jacket, with its shining buttons. The dead youth still had his bayonet clutched in his death grip. G. objected heatedly as his brother hastily tried to get into the coat from a half sitting position and before there could be any more controversy, Hen scampered toward the captain, doing his best to look as foolish and as lost as the rest. Then G saw Henry stumble and laugh and looked as though he were lost and tripped toward Wharton. The Yeo rushed to grab him and shouted, "Up,Up,Up, good soldier, good soldier," and Hen dribbled and repeated " good soldier," then, with surprising strength, he pulled the unsuspecting Wharton toward the ditch and rammed the bayonet into the heavy gut. Lying on stones, the captain of St. George's home for the bewildered, gasped, more in surprise and stupefaction than in pain. Hen dislodged the skewer and Wharton opened his mouth as the beginning of panic seized him

"My name is Henry Tansey," Hen hissed. The glazed bloodshot eyes showed no recognition. "You pulled me into your bed once and I puked all over you." He hesitated until the eyes began to focus. One side of the overfed face still showed the scars. "I'm the fella who spooked your lovely white horse, they said you needed new skin." The pain of five years ago came rushing back. As Wharton seemed to react, the bayonet went in again, where ribs cracked and arteries were severed.

"I'll go back with you now," he said to his brother, tearing the red jacket from his shoulders and throwing it on the warm jerking body.

**

The small fields half ways up the slopes on the north and east and south were crawling with redcoats, armed with rifles and light infantry. Where they had trouble, on the rough surface, with the lighter cannon, the pikemen tore at them, but the heavy Howitzers had the range to cover the hill all the way to the top and soon the rebels were committed to the defence of the camp and to their deaths. Below in Enniscorthy, Johnson had, eventually broken through to the bridge, General Aspill, hot on his heels.

Father Murphy saw Mogue Kearns fall along with sixty of his riflemen in the face of two six pounders. The Howitzers of the Dumbartonshires couldn't be silenced, the gun had huge range and was merciless in its destruction. Murphy was still in the line of fire and James Gallagher, as ever by his side and the brave William Barker fell wounded and still there was no sign of Father Philip Roche.

The priest from The Hook was blown from his white charger and the Hessian rifleman called out in triumph that he had killed the leader of the rebels, only to be piked by Gallagher and the last the mercenary saw in this world, was the face of John Murphy.

But there was no wisdom in staying. Savagry was all around and no quarter was given to the women and children. Murphy would end this war by losing it. The slopes of Vinegar, facing south east which were in darkness in the night, were still unoccupied, leaving open, the Drumgooled and Templeshannon sector, next to the east bank of the River Slaney and the road to Wexford Town. General Needham, for some wonderful reason had not arrived from Gorey

Though the retreat was made general, a number of the croppies chose to remain and act as rearguard, until they could fight no more.

"For many," Attridge wrote, "this war was their release. They had nowhere to go and knew they would be hunted down, so to die here on the symbol of Ireland's liberty, would be their release and their victory.

The cavalry now came into the fray, following the insurgents through Templeshannon. Sabres drawn, they sliced at the running mob, stooping low in their saddles to dispatch anyone in their path. On Vinegar Hill Lane, headless corpses of children were found near their dead mothers.

On the Wexford Road, Murphy turned his remnant army to engage the troops in hand to hand combat, and within fifteen minutes, devastated the cavalry. Replenished by William Baker's remaining divisions from Enniscorthy Bridge, the croppies sought out Darby's Gap. More cavalry were deployed and were gaining the upper hand and John Murphy feared the end, as Needham was sure to have garrisoned the gap. Needham had to be somewhere in the vicinity.

Where was Myles Byrne, Where was Monk Monaghan and Edward Roche? Murphy knew they did not fall at Vinegar, and surely some misfortune must have visited father Philip. There was some activity up ahead at The Gap and as the rebels approached, a shout went up as the croppies recognised salvation. Monaghan and Roche, with their men were in complete control of the outcrop, and Byrne had his troops, strategically planted in flanks on both sides of the Gap, with the last of his riflemen and the scrapings of ammunition. They had moved forward earlier, when Murphy had sounded retreat.

Necessity can turn any weapon to advantage and for weeks now, necessity was their creed, when nothing else in the world has more strength. The rebels opened attack on their pursuers and General Lake's army, used now to the unpredictable whimsicality of Father Murphy's croppies, were forced, once again to hold back, as the insurgents tore through Darby's, thanks to General Needham's irresolution.

Conor O'Connor Devereaux was one of the first to fall at Vinegar Hill. When the early assault by the Howitzer on the old mill began, he was tending one of the fires near where he had set up a forge, two days before. Many woke to the sound of the music of his hammer and anvil in the semi darkness and four other blacksmiths had joined him in the shaping of rough tools of war, any bit of metal strip that could be sharpened into a blade or a hook. When the bomb hit, he had been out of direct impact and his four comrades died, along with dozens inside the mill. Conor had been unconscious for the duration of the battle, until he came around to the commotion of the hand to hand fighting all around him, and the screams of women and the awful hissing sound of the anti-personnel mines, like sniffing ferrets, before exploding.

The whole area of the mill had been devastated. He could see through the gaping hole in the wall, the bodies of the women and their helpers, sprawled in ungainly postures across the scarred debris. Many had been upended into the flames. Great pots of half prepared food and limbs of slaughtered livestock had gone up with the explosions, so that mangled flesh of beast and human were mutually interchanged.

He was unable to move for a while, his chest and left arm ached and he knew his rib cage had been crushed. He could see the panicked evacuation of Enniscorthy and the huge exodus of the insurgent army was underway. He should have listened to Kate and gone back with her to Duhallow. The awful futility of it all pressed heavier than the big stone that crushed his chest. Small men should only succeed at small things. Simple mudlarks can never be hornbills. They should have left the quiet priest on his altar, but there was in the peasant, for a short space of time, an hour of glory, the indomitable urge to extend beyond life's narrow boundaries, and for that glorious hour, he embraced the enabled vanity of an exalted though impossible aim. In his wild ambition, the mudlark soared high, his reach exceeding his grasp.

Suddenly the Light brigade was swarming all around the summit, their red and white, screaming at the sun. The bombardment had now stopped, as enemy victory was in sight. A raucous crude set of obscenities were issued in prompt succession; "nobody to be left alive, but no mercy killing, sufficiently wounded, the enemy is to be left to die in his own time."

Before the arrival of the victors, cries of pain and desperation raked the plateau, as the injured and the dying cried out to the elements for an end to their pain. Now, in the presence of their enemies, a euphoria of silence and repose settled that was defiant in its tranquillity, and the

Hessian captain Wrenne cursed inwardly at their lack of acquiescence before him, as he shouted at them to plea for mercy.

Through shattered eyelids, Devereaux feigned death, covering his face, as the instigator of his immense suffering in Carnew, three years before, carried the red, white and blue Union Jack to where a rebel banner was embedded in a mound of stones, within a couple of feet of the blacksmith.

In a scoffing, clowning fit of horseplay, Wrenne tore the green standard from the mound, threw it aside and sank the Union flag in its place, claiming the hill. Conor Devereaux found his last ounce of strength that momentarily surprised him. The rebel flag fell across his prostate body. Just vengeance suddenly became the paymaster. The heavy pole, with its ornate pikehead, a creation of his own, was weightless as he sank it to the hilt in the squat offensive body. Wrenne jerked and thrashed and spun around, surprise and agony creasing his face.

"I believe you know me Sir," the blacksmith whispered, and he saw the dawn of recognition in the Hessian Captain. He died, face up, with the flag of Irish freedom buried in his belly. Conor had managed to stay on his feet long enough to feast on the spectacle, then he fell forward, as a young private cocked his pistol and the ball eased all the pain. The blacksmith of Trasna collided with the Union Jack, tearing it down. King George's colours folded around him in a shroud.

**

General Lake, a man constantly haunted by his own demons and filled with a compulsive neurosis, had his finest hour in the taking of Vinegar Hill and he was quick to take retribution for the damage and the embarrassment of the past month. Every peasant left alive in houses, in the streets, the roadways and the ditches were regarded as rebels and those who were found, died at his hand. Father Murphy had set up two field hospitals, one in the town and one at the base of Vinegar. Three hundred rebels were being treated by volunteer nurses when the command to retreat was established. Remembering the inferno of Scullabogue in New Ross, three days earlier, Lake issued a command from his own hell; both sanctuaries to be torched and all protesting medics shot.

Six thousand rebels died at Vinegar Hill on June 21st. And four thousand more, were butchered in the aftermath, despite any exercise in surrender.

Attridge had tried to persuade his wife to stay at home, but she would have none of it. Word had come that Vinegar Hill was lost and she would not rest until she had word of Conor and Father Murphy and her Uncle Jack.

With Georgie Tansey, they set out for Enniscorthy on the evening of the battle and were sickened at the devastation in the streets. The stink of burning, hissing flesh mingled with the smell of gun powder assaulted her senses. Rabid dogs were beginning to tear at human flesh and a pall of noxious fetidness fixed her in an intensity that was revolting and painful. Soldiers were still about the town, but paid the visitors no heed. A child soldier stared at her through lifeless blue eyes, the surprise of sudden death marked him in a half smile. The peasant youth stood for simple things, not the complex institutions of Government overthrow and the grandeur of patriotism, but for the freedom of coming and going, without compulsion, his simplicity written by his short life. Wild liberty is all he sought, the door of his dungeon was open for a minute and he dashed to the sunlight.

Georgie cried unashamedly at the carnage, as they climbed Vinegar. The Master had said, the day before he died, on hearing of the revolt and the atrocities already being committed by the Orangemen, that there were things a man must not do, even to save a nation.

Exhausted and in despair, James reached his father's body, lying in the crumpled folds of the Union flag. Kate held back her choking grief as Attridge cradled the long hard body in his arms, and wept for the lost days and years. The younger man prayed his deacon prayers. Kate, recognising the Hessian Captain wondered if destiny had brought the two here, to act out their final performance, as she read the tableau that had taken place, two hours before. James released the impaled captain Wrenne of the bolt, without much respect, untangled Conor of his unlikely wrappings, and replaced it with the green banner with its little gold harps and shamrocks on its adorned edges. The pike that held the flag had the blacksmith's initials hammered on the blade, C.O.C.D., as was his custom. Slowly they descended the hill with the body. Kate was out of sight at the far side of the mill, tripping among the dead. She tried not to look at the murdered innocence.

She caught up. "I'm looking for Father John, we can't leave him here if he's dead," she cried.

"They would have carried him away, Kate," said James, "either side. For the loyalists, a trophy, for the rebels, a hero."

However, they spent the next hour traipsing the hill.

Phantom images slouched out of the torn houses, the bogs, the ditches, the caves in the falling dusk and silently took away their dead.

Chapter 60

John Murphy remained busy as ever, which had become his distinguishing stamp. With Gallagher in his shadow, and the undying support of Myles Byrne and The Monk Monaghan, the priest collected what remained of his army and headed North West beyond the Blackstairs, into County Laois, to the coalmining district of Castlecomer, where one of the first insurrections broke out in early May. There the brawny miningmen of the Canal Coal Company would join him, and he woild rebuild his army and take the fight to Dublin.But first, he would join up with Michael Dwyer in the Wicklow Mountains, while the men of Carlow and Kilkenny were still to be rallied.

At Carrigbyrne, he came across the exhausted figure of Father Philip Roche and about three hundred of the defeated army of New Ross. Philip was totally demoralised at the defeat by Johnson, the incompetence of Bagnal Harvey, together with the savagery of the burning of the barn at Scullabogue, but above all, the unexpected reception he and his men received at the hands of the people of Wexford Town.

Delighted to see his friend, Murphy tried to comfort him and set up camp where food and refreshments were prepared.

Melancholy consumed the tall priest as he related the aftermath of New Ross. The entire demeanour of the town changed from the euphoria that greeted them a few days before when the triumphant insurgents, with Father John at their head, marched victoriously across the bridge. The high spirit was gone, the skittish effervescent abandon had slunk away into secluded corners, back into the sombre quarter life of before. But it was the underlying kinetic fear and the urgency to rid Wexford of the rebels that surprised Roche. "The people came onto the streets," he told Murphy, " in total disorder, to harangue us, to insult us that the whole town was in danger, because of our presence, with the fearful expectation of Generals Lake and Moore. Our Bishop Caulfield, actually led the protest, shouting that the blood of Wexford would be on our hand."

In the midst of the sorrowful dishevelled crowd, Father Mogue Kearns had been carried on a dray into the camp, his left arm, shattered and losing blood. Murphy was concerned and suggested a safe house for the big man. Kearns refused in his inimitable stubbornness.

Pale and labouring under a broken ankle, Roche asked for a council of war, where he beseeched the remaining leaders to go back to Wexford Town with him. General Sir John Moore had sent word ahead, that he would spare the town of Wexford, on condition that no rebels were found in arms or in gangs, otherwise, his superior, General Lake had warned that every man, woman and child would suffer, as they did at Vinegar. And he reminded the Governor, Matthew Keogh of the massacre perpetuated by his idol, Oliver Cromwell, one hundred and fifty years before.

Roche pleaded with them to accept Moore's terms of a truce, but Murphy, once again incited the men to his plan to revitalise the miners of Castlecomer and take the entire midlands. He let loose another impassioned outburst, his voice echoing through the boughs of Sleedagh Lake.

"I have a low mean suspicion of a man who will authorise the killing of innocent women and children, a man who seeks to take life that is already nearly extinct, and having killed, will commit sodomy and gross mutilations in the most foul way. Gerrard Lake has advocated the ancient brutal act of half hanging half drawing and then quartering of the body, and demands an audience of peasants be present. In this man, sent to destroy us by the King of England, is the total absence of standards, to which any appeal of clemency can be made. He and his generals, you have seen how they kill the bearer of the sacred flag of truce. Nowhere, not even among the savages of the Earth, do we kill the messenger. I strongly advise you to accept no quarters from England."

Father Philip was adamant in his resolve. The man presented himself as one, crucified in body and soul, a man of only half health. It was as if nobody else mattered and he had become his own exclusive object. Priest watched priest cross a threshold of emotion that Murphy never thought existed in the huge and once unstretchable character and he was suddenly concerned for his friend.

"We're all going to die, John," Roche whispered, "do you want to be a martyr?"

"Yes, of course we're going to die," Murphy cried, a tinge of annoyance edging his voice, "but we'll do it with resolution and not help our enemy in our own extinction. It's the cause and not the death that makes a martyr, Philip, and I have 3,000 men here who prefer living heroism, than self-inflicted martyrdom."

Mounted on his horse, Roche turned to his friend. "Where will I find you, in the event of a truce, for I believe terms can be negotiated with the English, that the war is over?"

"You won't be looking for me, Father." He raised his hand in blessing. "God go with you, friend."

The tall priest rode leisurely away. With a mixture of hope, fear and dignity, he turned his horse eastwards. Obstacles crushed him, indecision tormented him. Roche had lost direction in his ambition and he began to bend in the winds of dubiety.

The big figure in its black frock coat would be easily recognised, as any of the illustrious peers and noblemen that were showing themselves in public once again. He would seek out the other leaders, those that were still alive, and those, still incarcerated, and put together an arrangement for truce with the commander-In-chief of the king's forces, then invite the rebel army, still at large to help him usher in peace.

**

Coming off the huge bridge, he was suddenly surrounded by jibing, mocking Redcoats. He began to protest, saying he was here for the purpose of a council with General Lake on behalf of the insurrectionist army of Ireland. They laughed all the more, that the most powerful general in Ireland should entertain a popish priest. The horse was pulled from under him and at the end of a rope, he was dragged through the town of Wexford, to Windmill Hill and back to the jailhouse at Stonebridge until his body was a bloodied quivering mass. At a hastily convened court-martial, at which he could neither see or hear the proceedings, he was condemned

In the fading light of June 25th., Philip Roche was hanged on Wexford Bridge. He never met Lake. Because he couldn't see with the blood clots in his eyes, he wasn't to know that on the night, there were more than twenty more swinging from the sturdy beams, among them, the pitch-capped Anthony Perry, where some comedian had stuffed his red broad brimmed hat on his head, also, among the dead, was Matthew Keogh, who, until Lake's arrival, had held the exalted office of Governor of Wexford. Hanging like an old puppet, whose puppeteer had just left the scene, was the seventy five year old Cornelious Grogan, the liberal Lord of Johnstown Castle, who had watched in anger and disgust, as the retreating loyalist army flayed his innocent tenants to pieces after the battle of New Ross. His sin was to personally pound the doors of the town council in opposition to the savagery.

In the morning, the sacred English custom of beheading the dead was carried out and once again, the spikes of the railings of the jailhouse were festooned with the trophies of barbarism. Grotesque and obscene, the expressions on the rigid faces, caused them to be difficult to recognise, however, Perry's red hat stood out, as did Philip Roche. They had found his sacred stole, the long narrow shoulder sash, in his saddle bag and tied it about the severed head like a sweat band.

The diminutive Bishop Caulfield, with crosier and mitre, walked the bridge nightly, in his exalted effort at sending all the lost souls to heaven.

**

On June 22nd., in the glorious wild human country beyond the Scullogue Gap, Father John Murphy had sprouted, once again, as a great thorn in the guts of British Loyalist.

Standing out as a fester on the tranquil earth of greens and purples and alternating bands of sun and shade, was the garrisoned village of Kelledmond, it's red standards, shouting at the day, in a kind of blaspheme, but it fell to Murphy's modest army, as pikes outflanked and outmanoeuvred rifle, bayonet and sword. This victory was repeated at Goresbridge, a few miles from Kilkenny, and again at Castlecomer.

General Lake contemplated his nemesis; this priest that no one among his officers could honestly describe. A report said there were thirteen priests in his army, further reports said at least, fifty. This rank amateur had become the demon that haunted the commander, day and night. Hysteria was a caricature of his compulsive neurosis and he threatened hell and brimstone if this "popish pest" is not found. He called out, in his dementia, the words of King Henry 11, six hundred years before about another pest of a priest; will no one rid me of this turbulent priest."

There were, in fact a dozen priests in Murphy's army, but Myles Byrne, in one of his many dupes, to confuse the enemy, had fifty of his Monaseed stalwarts dress in all black, their women to cut a piece of starched white linen in the shape of a Roman collar. Each one carried the same identification as Father John Murphy. Byrne asked for fifty volunteers, 150 stood up to the mark. Father John had objected vociferously, but to no avail.

**

The millwheel of chance turned more slowly toward the end of June. On the day they hanged Father Philip, the rebels captured Hackettstown in County Carlow, but they were defeated at Kilcumney Hill.

The commander-in-chief (for a day). Beauchamp Bagnal Harvey, was captured and hanged on the gibbet of Wexford Bridge. The last of John Murphy's victories over The Ancient Britons, was to be at Ballyellis in County Wexford. His happy prospects of a miners' army, never materialized. He had lived for days now with great expectations,

479

but fewer and fewer new recruits came to his calling night fires, nor did his recruiting scouts have any success when doors closed against them. In the central counties they found little support as they had in Wexford where the commitment to the cause shut out all other aspirations, where the peasantry switched their allegiance from servile master, to the pursuit of liberty.

As happened in Wexford, earlier in the year, the patrols were mobilised to strike terror in the people, so that they were unable to think sanely about anything but their own safety, and accept any measure of austerity the authorities might impose, in return for total submission. All around the great ridge of the mountain range, the peasants were powerless in their fear. Murphy could feel the raw dread in the atmosphere in the streets in the country, in the earth.

The brewery at Cloneen Bridge was raided and for the first time in over a week, the rebels found respite and relief, wasting time, drinking to extreme, and though Murphy's endurance and ability to bear extremities was godlike in their eyes, and they had pushed themselves beyond their own limits, to please him, exhaustion was taking over.

They crossed the River Deen and entered Queen's County of Laois. At Fairy Mount, they rested and many complained inability to continue any further. Disillusion respects nothing only hope and in the dawn, that hope began to fade. Scouts returned to camp to report that the hillsides of Laois were empty of volunteers. Bonfires were lit to call them to assembly but nobody came. Ganeral Garrard Lake was doing his job very well. At the outskirts of Clonbrack, they had come across five hanged young men. A notice on the gibbet said they had broken the curfew, able bodied men, found out of their homes after eight in the evening. The midlands, in their fear, had decided to accept the yoke as the message went out to all colliers. Body parts had been found on remote roadways, where vain resource to sub human retribution served only as a substitute terror for the respect the authorities had no means of obtaining. The satanic medieval practice of half hanging, drawn and quartered had been dragged out of antiquity, an ignominious spectre that seemed to live with a kind of unspeakable life, drawn from all the murder it had wrought over centuries.

"Good Lord, Mr. Gallagher," whispered the priest, "isn't it enough to hang them, do they not know their bodies are temples, that only The Almighty can create."

Slowly, the colliers would slink away from the column in a poltroonish spiritlessness, disappearing in the night, or falling behind to fade into the mists of Mount Leinster's shroud. Trepidation and fear was all around and slowly the midlands became hostile, as had happened to Roche in Wexford Town. The rebels were being made isolated as intruders and with the threat of curfew exacting it's dues, the dream became destroyed. Local people now became the enemy, in the preservation of their own existence and would actually report back to the nearest garrisons of the whereabouts and the strength of the rebel column.

When they left Slatt Lower in the shade of the mountain and pushed to the safety of the Gap, the whole midland region breathed a great sigh of relief and nobody assembled to see them off. Father John Murphy had been supreme commander for just one month, with an army that exploded to 30,000, plus, that had no soldiers of experience, with just seven officers, thirteen priests and at least 500 women.

Now, grudgingly, the remainder maintained a steady march back into County Kilkenny, through the bog of Baunreagh, then south to the bogs of Annagar, through Duninga and back to Goresbridge. Many were missing, a number having died in the bogs and ditches.

All the while, General Asgill played a stalking game. Murphy's scouts had the Redcoats in their sights, through one county after another, as troops, cavalry and Yeos followed at a distance and surrounded the remnants, leaving fatigue and hunger, now take toll. They camped on Kilcumney Hill and by dawn, the guts of the rebels were gone, fearing for their families and knowing the futility of further encounters.

Myles Byrne cursed the deserters and wanted to pursue them back into Laois and put an end to their chicken livered nidgeting. Myles' youth, even in the sorrows of the inevitable failure still had a brilliancy of its own. He wanted to regroup and take Askill on.

Murphy put a comforting arm about the tense shoulders. "They came out of their houses for me, they preferred honour to life itself and thousands went to their maker, that honour, unsullied. They walked fearlessly into the path of the cannon and not a stipend for it.Their honour held them to an ideal, though it might have been inconvenient, unprofitable and damned dangerous. You can ask no more of any man."

" But, Wexford is still with us, Father", Byrne argued, we can rise again".

"Another day, another war, Mr. Byrne", consoled the priest. "Askill is all around us, stalking us, I will not send any more to their deaths, I've caused too many already, the colliers will not fight."

The young face quivered with emotion. "Where will you go, Father?". James Gallagher sat silently, studying the two. "Mr. Gallagher and I will go home and mind our business," he smiled.

Both men knew there was a fate awaiting them, a fate designed by others. Murphy had tried to persuade Gallagher to return home, but the big man had his own ideas, that when he got the priest safely to the rebels, still in the Wicklow Hills with Michael Dwyer, he would then leave. Both men knew their moment of reality had arrived.

" We will go to Wicklow and meet up with Michael Dwyer then, I'm told Dwyer is a good man. If we had met up earlier, who knows what could have been done."

**

Clouds of atmospheric moisture hung over the hills, uncertain in their destination and in contradiction of the weather pattern of an exceptionally hot summer. In its murky folds, the Redcoats moved to surround Kilcumney, shrouding their strength and numbers. Reports of 3,000 men came in, so the rebels would soon be sitting dogs as soon as the fog cleared. On John Murphy's Orders, the camp broke up, the remaining insurgents, now down to about 300, collected their wounded and meagre belongings and withdrew to the Blackstairs and the Scullogue Gap. In anger, hopeless frustration and vituperation, they came before him, sharing in the intimacy of their tragedy. He prayed over them then, in little groups they receded into the protection of the mist. Like whipped animals, they went, soon to be swallowed up by the gloom. In less than an hour, the fighting men and women of Wexford walked out of John Murphy's life forever.

" For the next two years," James Attridge was to write for The New York Evening Post and The Journal, "30,000 would be homeless, one third of them would die in the ditches, or be hunted down. Ireland was to become a nation of vagrants and beggars, exciting anger and recrimination from their own.

John's destitution increased with the realization that his faithful horse was no longer fit for the gruelling task ahead in a never ending traverse of the Wicklow mountain range, to live indefinitely, the life of an outcast. A local farmer presented the priest with a young strong beast, a valuable animal. Murphy wept into the warm shoulder of his faithful mare, her nose and proud head, responding to his touch and his breath. His benefactor assured him that the horse would be well looked after in her retirement.

The priest had last considerable weight and presented a sorrowful sight to a number of safe homes he and Gallagher had availed of in the coming days.

**

At Rossdillig, news came of a great massacre at the Scullogue Gap. His men had successfully made it through the mountains and the mist, back into county Wexford, with few fatalities, but General Sir George Askill, displeased with the success of their escape through the density of a heaven sent fog and getting himself lost in the rough terrain, exacted his revenge on the peasantry of the area of ten square miles. Three hundred and seventy innocents were slaughtered in a manner, wrote Attridge, beholding to a savagery of a long past age, when any excuse served a barbarian.

For Askill, the falsehood of his report to Dublin castle, lay deep in the necessity to counteract the depth of his past failures and those of his fellow officers, before the rebels. He reported to his superior that, at the Scullogue Gap, he had left 1,100 insurgents dead in the field, among them, their invulnerable commander, the popish priest, Murphy.

John Murphy, now in poor civilian garb, at the insistence of the bodyguard, read of his own demise in The Journal of June 30th, and felt the nearness of his mortality.

Tullow, forty miles north of Enniscorthy, in County Carlow, was the headquarters of General Sir James Duff, the officer credited with the massacre of three hundred unarmed and unprepared rebels at Dunlavin, after they had surrendered and handed over their weapons, in May. Tullow was infested with military of all kinds, three to every civilian. The regular army and the Yeos patrolled day and night.

**

John had met the genial Bishop Delaney of Kildare and Leighlin on just two or three occasions and was impressed by the prelate's genuine qualities of understanding and compassion. Delaney lived in Tullow and some sort of relentless logic drew the priest to the stately two storey mansion on the northern suburbs of the town. Whatever pattern of destiny had been woven for the man from Boolavogue, it sought out all the sorrows and dangers of his life and laid them out on the dusty streets of Tullow, one of the biggest garrisons outside of Dublin.

On the 1st. July, he was to say his last Mass in a safe house, make his last confession and suffer an ignominious death in the scenic town, that itself, had put up a gallant defence against the English forces of Oliver Cromwell in a previous century. Crawling now with military, loud with a rude dialect that crossed the hearts of the ever abject and pliant peasantry, John moved through the hot busy streets toward the bishop's residence. James Gallagher had found a safe place to wait with the horses, in a remote barn on the land of a Presbyterian tenant farmer.

In a soft cap and tattered jacket and britches and a gait, properly humble and acceptable to the bawdy feudatory of the town, crouched and cretin-like, the man to whom, six lords general of the English army, had shown respect, even fear, before their armies ran cowardly and amok, and under whose guidance, simple men of plain living and involuntary poverty, became giants and heroes, kept to the dark corners and shadows.

Bishop Delaney was a heavy bodied man of fifty years. A large Roman nose and high forehead gave him the look of a rabbi, though he was clean shaven. His shoulder length dark hair showed little signs of ageing. He sought to comfort his visitor and put him at his ease. However, his furtive movements and glances through the large window of his parlour, at the busy roadway, and his quiet reticence in the presence of his staff, showed he was evidently fearful that the commander of the revolution should be found in his house. General Duff wouldn't hesitate to hang both of them and the whole household, from the balustrades.

"So the leader of the revolution requests absolution." His tone was friendly.

The priest was subdued. He felt a moment of blind desolation in the sombre surroundings, with its ancient pictures of long dead predecessors and images of stately saints. An icon of The Virgin Mother, had pride of place over a bulky sideboard. From his gilded frame, Pope Pious VI looked down at him in a condemnatory gesture of discontent. Murphy avoided the dark staring Italian eyes.

"Is there guilt in your soul, my Son," the bishop poured some tea.

"There is responsibility, Lordship."

"Responsibility is a detachable burden Father, easily shifted to the shoulders of God, or to fate, or to fortune." The bishop frowned judgementally.

"We must assume responsibility for our world, Sir, no longer heap it on religion," said Murphy.

"And guilt, Father, they say many thousands died."

"If there is guilt in my endeavours to rid the land of a tyrant, to bestow some sort of worth and honour to a tortured people and to seek to praise God in the way He, Himself has fashioned, then I have no choice but to be guilty."

The bishop sighed. "I know you, John Murphy, more than you know. You were never rebellious, a sensitive man, 'tis easy to compel a sensitive man to be guilty."

The priest ate the chicken and bread ravenously and the bishop was painfully aware of how brutalized this quiet man had become, and he felt the pangs of compassion stab at him. He stood at his window and studied the wide sweep of his garden and the piece of road beyond the gate, his hands behind his back. "Injustice; swift and erect and unconfined, sweeps the wide Earth and tramples o'er mankind," he mused loudly, "even Homer sides with you."

"Homer was no rebel, Bishop," smiled the priest. "I doubt he would take out from their homes, a vast ignorant peasantry and ask them to confront a goliath."

"Homer's duty was to teach," said Delaney.

"And my duty was to administer, and perhaps that's where my sin lies. Duty, honour; we make these words say whatever we want."

"New occasions call for new duties," sighed the bishop again, looking onto the road.

"Will you give me absolution, Lordship?"

"Is there contrition in your heart, John Murphy."

"There is."

"Then do you repent?"

"I cannot have remorse, for I have done no evil. The call to stamp out injustice was as strong as my call to ordination. You cannot lay remorse upon the innocent, nor lift it from the hearts of the guilty."

Murphy stood and looked into the sad eyes of the Virgin Mother. "If I have remorse, then I decry to damnation, all those who fought with me, and the many who died."

Delaney frowned and came and sat in his chair, Murphy, respectfully returned to his. "Then you have no repentance, Father?" He gave the priest a regard that mixed pity with anxiety and seeing the prelate's troubled brow, Murphy continued.

"From my childhood, on my mother's knee, I have known that there is a God. When I was a boy, there was a god for young boys. When I was a priest, there was a god for priests. Everything under the sun tells me there is a god for everything under the sun. The tiniest worm that crawls tells me that. And now I find there is a god for kings, even bad kings, and a god for corrupt parliaments and for servile landlords, even for rampant madmen in red coats. He is a god of complexities, and He often disappoints."

Murphy paused, wearily collecting his thoughts. "I clung to the hope that a reconciliation might be made, especially when I saw a penchant in them to kill the children, to kill off our next generation. On three occasions, they shot the standard bearer of the sacred flag of truce. I believed that what I was doing was righteous, seeking humanitarianism for humanity, but it takes a long time for a trustful person to reconcile himself to the idea that God will not help. You and I, Lordship, were born under a foreign monarchy and made subject to the whims and desires of that administration. I wanted the right for myself and my people to obey ,God, which is freedom to worship Him, day and night."

He spat the words in a half cry, "and God did not help."

Murphy was on his feet, and seemed, suddenly agitated.

The bishop replied, gently. "There is always strife between God's ways and our ways, Father Murphy, you could be damned by me and absolved by God, or vice versa."

Murphy sat, hands clasped, knuckled white and straining."I saw great wrongs being committed by an authority with a passion for destruction, inventing ingenious and new ways to kill us, with good conscience." His eyes filled and the boy in him shone out in a cracked voice. "I called the people and they came in great number.".

Delaney put out a hand in comfort. "He that is common to the greatest number, has the least care bestowed upon himself. The Hindus say, the tree casts it's protective shade on all, even the wood cutter."

"I sought no glory, Bishop, it is a vain pursuit and leaves no fruit, I have only humility in the sacrifice and the blood of my followers."

Bishop Delaney embraced the country priest. "Kneel with me, my Son, that God will open heaven to all insurgents and authoritarians, no matter how adorned."

He prayed devoutly, coaxing Murphy to his side. "I am sensible, O my God, that I have in many ways, offended Thy Divine Majesty."

"My one and only sovereign," interjected Murphy.

".....my one and only sovereign," the bishop repeated, with a cautious look at the priest.

".......and provoked Thy wrath by my sins, and that, if I do not obtain pardon, I will be cast out of Thy sight forever."

Delaney continued now in the pleadings of desire for absolution. "I do not have the power, O Lord, to absolve this just man from his sins, but I commend my brother priest to Your mercy. Individually righteous, is the first of all his duties, but he would not permit the honour of a just people, be taken and he struck out. He walks, humbly in Your presence, and fearlessly in that of his enemies, as You did yourself, dear Lord. Let Thy mercy take the place of Thy justice."

Delaney stood before the bowed head, dishevelled and dirty, and laid on his hands, gently.

"Judicia me, Deus, et discerne causam meam de genta non sancta......" I absolve thee in the name of the Father, Son, and Holy Ghost."

John Murphy kissed the bishop's ring and stood.

"You are in grave danger, John Murphy, your path of duty may get you nowhere, history will tell that."

They embraced and Murphy went to find Gallagher, the remnants of the food in his pocket.

**

Inscrutable hostiles were everywhere in Tullow on a warm July afternoon. Delaney looked at the man, now sought as a fugitive all over the south east of the country. Despite reports from his officers that John Murphy was dead, General Lake had become obsessed with the idea that he was still at large, and demanded a special corps to comb the county until he was satisfied that the pest was caught and brought before him, and he was to be identified by none other than Rev. Cope of Carnew. Men in black were dragged to Carnew by the cart load, until the reverned flew into a rage of a murderous infernal pitch, sometimes being woken in the night to peruse the faces of unfortunate clerics.

At the gates of the bishop's mansion, Murphy seemed to disappear into the heat mist, like his life, eroding into automated oblivion.

In Wexford, an orgy of retribution and recompense, under Lake, continued and Needham, anxious to make amends for his shortcomings at Vinegar Hill, created havoc in the outskirts. Their dignity still blunted, they sought revenge in a cleansing process that washed blood for blood. The hangings on Wexford Bridge became the spectacle to equal the death carts of Madame Guillotine in far off Paris.

The North Corks, under their leader, Lord Kingsborough, together with the Hompesch Dragoons, became infamous for their savagery against the helpless and women were particularly targeted.

In the first ten days of July 1798, twice as many were killed in patrol raids as fell at Vinegar and it was now feared, not by just the Catholic clergy, but by the Liberals in the Irish Parliament itself, that the Orange test would be consummated to it's very last syllable.

The pikes of the railings outside the Stonehouse jail and the Custom House, became the spires of a satanic ritual, surrounded with ceremonies to an antagonistic power. The heads of hundreds of good men, stuck with gore to the rusted iron, nodded and swung in the breeze, like they were following you with their dead eyes, brazen eyes, still open in their final spasm, mouths like torn pockets, almost in a half smile.

The blonde head of John Kelly of Killane was taken down and thrown to the waiting baying troops who remembered his great size at New Ross. For almost an hour, boots became stained with cranium matter and bloody glands, as the Orangemen kicked it about the quayside in a frenzied delight.

Esmond Kyan, the one armed armoury expert of Father John's artillery, was hanged, despite a Certificate of pardon, signed by General Dundas, a week before.

**

In the town land of Castlemore, south west of the town of Tullow, the O'Toole family scratched out an existence on a tired piece of land. It was an early harvest, the weather being so exceptional and a few neighbours came to help with the work.

Julia O'Tool was standing to her two old horses when the Yeos came. They were commandeering horses for the army, when the tired and angry woman suggested she be left alone, her pair was old and why don't they go and see to the two fine horses above in her barn.

The barn was already warm in the early morning and John Murphy watched his friend James Gallagher as the big man slept on the hay bed. It was the priest's intention to send Gallagher home this day, though, to be truthful, he knew his bodyguard, because of his size, would be easily recognised, having been in the front line of many battles.

The sunshine streamed through the broken door and Murphy threw open one of the windows hoardings. It was then he saw the Redcoats, about twenty of them, climbing the sloping field toward them. He let go the wooden shutter and it swung back against the wall in a clanging code of distress. Through a hole in the gable, he could see more military coming from the seclusion of the ditches.

Gallagher, with a start and sensing trouble, reached for his pistol. "Put it up now James," the priest said, calmly, " put it up now."

Like a swarm, the Yeos crowded into the shed. The saddle bags were searched, while the two were held at gunpoint.

"He's a priest, a bloody popish priest on the run," roared the corporal, the satisfaction in his voice, wrathful and discordant. He held up the prayer stole, pyx and a small vial of oil. "And 'tisn't you, big fella, for you tried to kill me at Enniscorthy and again at Vinegar Hill."

"I remember that," scoffed Gallagher, "you showed me your back on all occasions."

The butt of the rifle caught him on the temple, as the Yeo let swing, drawing blood. "Yeah! Well I'm not running now, am I, bloody papist."

"How brave," hissed Gallagher.

" Yes, and before this day is out, you'll tell us, where this Father Murphy is hiding out."

Chapter 61

They were dragged, unceremoniously, through the streets of Tullow, where a hasty court-martial under Sir James Duff, known as the butcher of Dunlavin, passed the sentence of death, the execution to be carried out publicly in the market square, at the pleasure of the Yeomanry, under Major Hall.

The bigger of the two men seemed to be somewhat subservient to the other, protective and minding. The Redcoats were jubilant; a Catholic priest with the signs of battle on him. Gallagher insisted he was the priest, but Hall needed no convincing. Murphy's serenity and aristocratic disregard for the proceedings, his quiet challenge to their authority, showed his sophistication. That sophistication and genteelness convinced Duff that here was not the priest all Wexford was looking for.

The square at Tullow was crowded. Many of the military, were off duty and had come for the spectacle, drunk and obscene. Beggars and traders lined the market and Major Hall of the Yeomanry of Lord Roden, decided on a special event, an entertainment on a hot day for the tired veterans of a long, hard fought campaign, in the putting down of the rebellion. For Major Jonathan Hall, there was an accompanying joy, his brother Andrew had died at Vinegar Hill. Through a loud hailer, he reminded the mob, of the thousands of His Majesty's faithful that had died in the rebellion.

To expose their prey to public ridicule had become, for the militia, a prelude to their coition, Propriety had become in Ireland, the least of all British laws. The vulgarity of nakedness, offensive to the onlooker and degrading to the victim had become highly infectious to them and inspired perversity, in all its forms. The sight of a priest, naked and defenceless, slowly simmered their brains to boiling point in the cauldron of military depravity, which was fearsomely deranged.

The big man died horribly. Pressed again for rebel information, the whereabouts of the remaining leaders and the location of arms, and especially, the whereabouts of the leader, John Murphy, he was subjected to one hundred lashes, where the soldiers, who took turns to administer the strokes, lost count.Then his head was coated in gunpowder and set alight. He was then half hanged, then pulled from the jib and disembowelled. James Gallagher, friend and personal bodyguard to Commander In Chief, Father John Murphy of Boolavogue, was dragged and thrown against the wall of Paudy Mulcahy's house in Market Square, while still alive, part of his entrails, pouring onto his lap. No word of protest or cry of anguish passed his lips, but he kept looking through fevered eyes at the priest, like he were a beacon of comfort to him and all his pain seemed to dissipate when John signed him a blessing through the ranting Yeos.

John Himself became the final subject of Major Hall's tender mercies. The barrel of boiling pitch bubbled over a fire. After a whipping that lasted twenty minutes, they hoisted him onto the gibbet, while a group of frenzied viragoes tended the barrel, like hell hags. The petrified onlookers, even the loyalists of Tullow, the merchants and the ascendancy classes who had come to watch, fell into a refrigerated silence. Some, frowning deeply and visibly upset, were quick to disregard the savagery and stole away, their pride and ignorance as incestuous as an unyielding General Duff himself. The silence of the victims was the main factor that upset them and angered the soldiers even more. Women wept silently, afraid of compliance, but crossed themselves as the priest defiantly imparted a final blessing on the crowd. His back, torn to shreds, the garrotte was spun around his neck, but the Orangemen shouted for a public ritual of burning alive.

In the skirmish for gamesmanship, the major lost control of the mob and a free for all ensued. Among the junior viragoes was Major Hall's nephew, the son of his sister, protected by his uncle and tutored for prompt promotion in the ranks. The seventeen year old's face lighted with sultry expectations, as his uncle handed him the long bladed knife and indicated the fallen priest. The young cur had watched the disembowelling of Gallagher and progressed his apprenticeship a step further, and dug an aperture the size of his head in the priest's lower belly, and dug further until Murphy's staring eyes, stern and forbidding, caught his, as in a trance and the youth dropped the sabre. Then somebody pulled on the rope again, half hanging the priest, before he was torn down, and in the final minutes of his life, was decapitated.

Father Murphy was a couple of inches short of six feet, but had a broad frame. He wouldn't fit the barrel, so they hacked at the body, dumping the limbs into the boiling pitch and the square in Tullow filled with the smoke and stink of burning flesh and bone. A group of sympathisers stood to the back of the crowd, behind them Gallagher's ravaged body was propped up against the wall of Mulch's house. Father Murphy's body was being pushed further into the pitch. A sobbing woman whispered through her tears, "in God's name, when will they stop, or what more do they want?"

"His soul," another whispered. Behind them, James Gallagher moved under an old blanket that someone had thrown over him in respect. Catholics were dragged from their houses and made to walk around the burning bier in procession, to immerse themselves in "holy incense." As the crowd moved away, a Yeo shouted that Gallagher was still alive. It was a part of the ritual of public execution of known trouble mongers, that the victim's heart was left intact for as long as possible, the last muscle that adheres to life, God's best gift. The executioner knows the protection of the heart, extends the suffering. In his dementia, death is what James Gallagher wanted, here in Tullow where the anguish of living, he could hardly bear. He tried to prop himself into a sitting position, his entrails in his lap, and the youngster, who had pitchcapped him saw the blanket move. Major Hall's nephew, now blooded and seeking to impress his uncle further, a sadist in the making, pulled away the blanket and leaned further into the scarred face, looking for life, knife in hand.

Unprepared, nephew smiled, spittle on his boy lips, when Gallagher made his last and glorious move on this Earth. His huge right hand grabbed at the narrow neck, while with the left, he turned the knife, still in the girl-like hand. It would never be established which stroke killed Nephew, but John Murphy's bodyguard had the satisfaction of hearing the spinal crack of a young neck and the feel of the blade sinking into flesh. Peasants saw the drama and applauded in silence, then moved away in fear.

**

While half the king's troops searched the neighbouring counties for the papist leader of the rebellion, Father Murphy's head was displayed on a pike outside the Sessions House in Tullow, and for the next two months thinking their man was still at large, his capture became an obsession with every officer in the army, so great was the reward being offered. He was reported seen in dozens of places at once and General Gerrard Lake, who had been transferred to India, had seen the priest of Boolavogue in his dementia, at the head of a Marathas tribe, bounding toward him out of the Indian sun. The image remained with him in his waking and in his sleeping; a man of gargantuan size, swathed in black flowing garments, at the head of a million pikemen, in a halo of light, smiting the king's army.

Had General Duff not had such an aversion to all things popish, especially a priest's prayer book, which he condemned to the fire, along with the vial and the sacred stole, he would have found his rebel commander.

Written inside the back cover; a simple dedication, lovingly written in a childish uneducated hand; " To my Son, John Murphy of Tincurry, on the occasion of his priesting, and he going away to Spain, 10th. July, 1780. Pray for me. Johanna Murphy.

The Rev. Cope, tired and almost deaf, would have been delighted to identify his arch enemy, John Murphy, but refused to travel to Tullow on that day.

**

The merciful entrance of the new Viceroy, Lord Cornwallace, the defeated veteran of His Majesty's forces in America, had removed Lake from the scene. Cornwallice, no doubt, sat in Dublin Castle, licking his wounds, that he couldn't win for his mad king, the territories of the new United States of America, was being brought up to date on matters in Ireland, but was disturbed at the awful atrocities being committed in the name of the same king.

On July 3rd., the Dublin Gazette printed the general pardon to all those who had taken part in the insurrection, offering, "His Majesty's pardon to those who had been forced from their allegiance to His majesty, that they should surrender themselves and their arms, that they should desert their leaders that incited them to rebellion, that they should enter their names, acknowledge their guilt, promise good behaviour for the future and take a public oath of allegiance to King George."

Tens of thousands of homes were visited by the patrols, to deliver and explain the details of amnesty and drag the peasants to the nearest magistrate for submission, but three quarters of the homes were empty and the cabins were torched without compassion.

A veil of silence and abject melcholia hung like a caul of depression over town and countryside. The people were living in hillsides ditches and bogs in a kind of wild fearful liberty. It was fear that brought them to rebellion and was the instrument of their great sagacity, when for a sweet hour, liberty called. Now it stalked them again, weakening their judgement, rendering them incapable to think sanely. His Honour from England, Mr. Cornwallis, the man accused for the loss of America, at the battles of Guilfort Green and especially at Yorktown, disguised his despair as a kind of virtue, knowing that patience would achieve more than force. Leave the peasants in the wild, and like the wild animals, winter would drive them into the arms of the king.

Chapter 62

There were to be three more attempts to land a French contingency in Ireland. The genial General Humbert, whom Tone had met on only two occasions in Paris, landed in County Mayo in the West, with one thousand men and fortified his army with eight thousand peasants. It was to be General Lake's last campaign, but not before his red tail was seen, once again, high and running out of Castlebar, marauding peasants and bewildered Frenchmen in hot pursuit. In a carnival of euphoria and romanticism, a local Catholic gentleman, Mr. John Moore was appointed President of The Provence of Connaught, " the poorest province in all the world." Frenchmen danced jigs in the streets, Guinness porter running down their chins.

But, ill advised and isolated on the shores of the Atlantic Ocean, Humbert waited in vain for support, as once again, incompetence, non-coordination and lack of funds, delayed the promised departure of six thousand men from Brest, to the Irish cause.

On 8th. September, The French general surrendered at Ballinamuck, Lake having had the time to regroup. In the serene, heaven like land of the western seaboard, once again, a bitter and emphatic example was made in a spectacle of unprecedented slaughter, the likes Connaught had never seen in a thousand years. The French were taken as prisoners of war, the first time in the whole campaign that the British army adhered to any code of international etiquette, being aware a foreign eye was trained on proceedings. There was, however, no amnesty for the peasants. Hunted through the plains of Mayo and Ellistrin, through ditches, and across bog lands, they were slaughtered without mercy, and to no avail. Cabins and cottages were burned in a trail of devastation.

James Attridge was to write later; "It was a Culloden in many forms, when fifty years ago, the Duke of Cumberland massacred 7,000 of Charles Stuart's Highland Army, without mercy. But The Jacobite Rebellion was well armed and army faced army, and there were no children at Culloden. In Ballinamuck in 1798, at a time when it was said, the world was marching toward civilization, the forces of the king buried their abominations with their morals in the soft earth. Children were murdered in a Herodian orgy that will be forever, committed to folklore, and the peasantry sent back into monastic apartheid for another century."

The United Irishman and Northern Presbyterian Bartholomew Teeling and Mr. Mathew Tone, the brother of Wolfe tone, were captured and taken to the Provost's prison in Dublin. They were tried within a week and were hanged.

**

A man, always in doubt as to whether to expose himself to martyrdom or not, Mr. James Napper Tandy, the prominent radical and volunteer of the glorious marches of 1782, when, with Mr. Grattan he and others were going to liberate all the Catholics of Ireland, led the pathetic second French " invasion."

Obscure and unheeded and possibly unsound, and with the rank of Major General, to compete with Wolf Tone, the Dubliner sailed from Dunkirk on the last day of August, with just 270 French Grenadiers. With Hell's Hole, Banba's Crown and Wee House of Malin to port, Napper's warship sailed into Inishtrahull Sound on the very quiff of Ireland. The major general picked the most northern tip of the Donegal coast to issue his proclamation before the world. On a quiet day, as glorious and serene as the countryside, that once sheltered Bonny Prince Charlie, after Culloden, when the prince ran from his own five minute rebellion, the ship, Anacreon anchored off the tiny windswept island and expressed surprise and anger before his bewildered French comrades, that the expected 3o,ooo insurgents and rebels failed to appear. Napper Tandy, the man who was going to save Ireland, had never heard of Father John Murphy.

Pompous and affectatious, Tandy planted the green flag of Ireland on the barren ridge of Innisthrahull, declared a republic and sailed back to Europe. The man with "the hanging down look," lived out his life among the vinyards of Bordeaux.

**

James Attridge, in summarizing the pathetic efforts of another expedition, wondered by the great mistakes made by intelligent people. This included the naivety of his friend Wolfe Tone. "To think," he wrote, "three expeditions to reach Ireland at the same time, but in separate landings and neither knowing what the other was about, or where he was. One can only wonder at the stupidity, even of the French, in all of this, especially, Humbert, to leave France, hoping others would follow."

"Is there no end to my frustration," Theobold Wolf Tone wrote to Attridge, in late September. " Monro, Mc. Cracken, this Father Murphy, all dead, all fighting their own little wars. What a general your

John Murphy would have made, at the side of his French counterparts. General Humbert, should have found me and told me he was heading for Ireland, and Tandy, trying to raise an army of his own. We are as full of potentiality as we are of impotence. In Ireland, impotence has won out. In God's name why didn't they wait for me? When I think on your reports and the wonder of these brave men and all who followed them, I think with great disappointment on the fine expectations, but now to face up to their realization is a great ordeal."

**

Thoebold Wolfe Tone, unaware of his brother's execution, was, in fact oblivious to the fact that Matthew had found his way to fight with General Humbert in the west. Tone had joined the staff of General Jean Hardy at Brest where he cursed, once again, the influence of Napoleon Bonaparte in the significant delay that the armada for Egypt was causing his efforts for Ireland. The Irish barrister was at the far end of despair, when he heard that Humbert was engaging the enemy somewhere in County Mayo, depending desperately on Hardy's support. Instead, the cause for Ireland slowly starved to death as the good general sought out donations from local merchants, with the promise of trade and commerce with Ireland after she was liberated. The Frenchmen; soldiers and sailors were prepared to work for no wages, so the ammunition and stocks could be secured, but the armada out of Brest was to be a much smaller affair than the huge fleet that foundered in Bantry, two years before, the terrible failure, a rife and persistent haunting in the minds of those who had witnessed it.

It took three weeks to reach the northern coast. Again, several days of storms whipped sea and blood in one vigorous pulse, asserting their western circuits like a sea monarch gone mad. Then the wild eddies turned and the impassive faced tyrant blew from the North Atlantic, through Tory Sound between the twin heads of Fanad and Dunaff, into the jaws of the Lough, a great narrow wedge of water, the shape of a hound's tooth that bites inland for fifty miles to the tip of Letterkenny.

But not as in '96. This little armada was no secret. It had become common knowledge. Authorities in London were kept informed of the preparations at Brest, of the problems General Hardy was having, with the demands of Bonaparte in the Mediterranean and the lack of strength that was about to sail to Ireland. French newspapers carried the details, even on a matter that Adjunct colonel Theobold Wolfe Tone would sail abort the flagship, "Hoche."

On the morning of October 12th. An English fleet under Sir John

Warren, hove to in the lea of Dunaff Bay, where batteries had only recently been constructed on the bluff of the rock, jutting above the headland, like a huge crouching guard dog, watching the Lough.

A schooner came alongside "Hoche", to report an English fleet of eighteen ships was bearing down on the visitors in the heart of the storm. The French Admiral Bombard, together with his senior officers tried to persuade Wolfe Tone to go aboard the schooner and head for safety. They pleaded with him that the smaller ship could outmanoeuvre the British more easily than the cumbersome flagship. He would not be persuaded, he would not have his gallant French comrades fight a battle without him. He knew they would become prisoners of war, and that he would certainly hang.

The storm continued unabated and the ensuing battle lasted a week. Letterkenny hosted the prisoners, the officers allowed to dress in their respective insignia, Wolfe Tone, resplendent in the brilliant uniform of a French Adjutant general; a large cocked hat with broad gold braid, blue uniform coat with gold embroidered collar, gold epaulettes, blue pantaloons and short boots, bound with gold lacing.

He mingled unnoticed at a surprise reception held at the garrison for the staff of General Hardy. The British were even over hospitable in a strained atmosphere, where language served as a welcome protective mantle. Tone's French was excellent by now, but Hardy was concerned for the Irishman, among his most ardent enemies. A few were planted who had professed they would know Wolfe Tone, even among a thousand Frenchmen, their politeness a refined hypocrisy, easily recognised.

A heavily built man oiled his way among the officers, moving all the while toward his prey. He was dressed in a Yeoman uniform of the rank of Major. Like a royal pageant, the vaguely familiar slangancy of his vocals beat a code of alarm in the tired regions of Tone's brain. A voiced bellows, Sir George Hill enunciated his arrival at each cluster of officers, speaking now in English, now in a grotesque standard French and now in a pathetic combination of both, all the while, looking over shoulders for a profile and stance, he remembered well. His fellow student at Trinity College, whom he last hailed in a deluge of reminiscences and reprimand for a lack of political etiquette on the steps of Duhallow in Wexford, four years previously, now stood just a breath away.

Unable to contain himself any further, Hill stood before this Irish rebel in a resplendent French General's uniform. "I know you, Sir," he spat, his thick hands clasped behind his back, suddenly looking very famous.

There was no bonanza, material or spiritual awaiting the Irishman. Major Jonathan Sandys, a specialist in violent incarceration, a dragon of extravagant perversion, was the keeper of The Provosts Prison at Arbour Hill in Dublin. In the cold month of November, the orphan from the slums of Bristol prepared cell number 35 for its most distinguished guest.

To sandy's disappointment, it wasn't a broken man that was delivered to him. The defeat at Lough Swilly was far from total in the dogged and precocious officer. That strong current of life and respiration and the disregard for the authorities around him, unhinged Sandy's composure every time he stood in his prisoners dark dank cell. Tone would demand privileges befitting his rank, always demanding he was a prisoner of war, so that the Englishman felt almost powerless to refuse. There was a magnetism about this man that made the Provost want to rid himself of him as quickly as possible.

While Tone's future was discussed at court-martial with the talented Irish lawyer, John Philpott Curren, who tremendously argued that General Wolfe Tone was a French officer of war and should be treated as such. Tone quickly took advantage of such privileges, by demanding that he be allowed entertain his co-prisoners in cell number 35, many already under sentence of death, where he would share a bottle of wine and some rough prison food. Still in his uniform, he would enthral them with his endeavours on behalf of Ireland, his encounters with Napoleon Bonaparte and the expedition to Bantry in '96.

Lukie Sommers was the occupier of cell number 34 for over a year. In his mid sixties, Lukie was consumptive and frail, his white hair and beard, unkempt and perfunctory. Bloodshot, in wrinkled sockets, his eyes were lively and concentrated and he opted to be the very shadow of such an important neighbour, seeking to tend his needs, bring fresh water daily, tend the fire and he would sit and watch General Tone's efforts at self preservation in spite of limited facilities and instruments.

"I have a shaver, General." said Lukie, through his cavernous teeth, as he would watch Tone drag a rough blade across his face. The old man shuffled from the room, returning with a small bundle. He unwrapped the soiled piece of velvet material and a sensation of heat exploded around the soldier's heart, as he recognised the mother-of-pearl razor and brush with the little butterfly motif.

Sommers saw, with anxiety the impetus of the moment hit a nerve in the new prisoner. The old eyes focussed. His hands shook with delight, thinking Tone's expression, one of gratitude.

"Gave to me by the man they took out of here, Sir, three weeks ago. He frowned, trying to remember when. Days mean nothing in here, Sir, they let me walk around the place, sure I'm no threat to anyone."

"Do you remember his name, Mr. Sommers?" Tone was on fire.

Lukie looked through the tiny barred window, at the dark courtyard, two floors below. Two sets of gallows stood out in stark detail against the darkening evening, supreme and gaunt, the hemlock of the Eternal Footman.

"They took him down there, and he smiled up at me before they hanged him. They hanged the two of them together and then they went and had their breakfast, the buggars."

He focused on Tone. "He only ever gave me his first name." He went to the stone built fireplace, and pointed to a scrawled signature on a corner stone. "His name was Matthew, he said to call him Captain Matthew. I saw his name on the hanging list , Captain Matthew," the old man wheezed, "He gave me the razor and myself not having a shave since I was a boy. He told me to mind it, it was a special present from his brother, all the way from France. There was a tobacco knife, but his brother kept that, Captain Matthew said he didn't smoke."

Through Tone's memory, hazy as a dream, laden down with baggage, shone a light beam character of a youth on the quayside in Wexford Town and he ran his fingers over the childish inscription; M T. 1798. "He refused to give them his name, Sir and they hanged him without knowing who he was." The stark lonely statement, hewn with a knife or a spoon handle, in it, he felt his brother's desperate control, as he tore at the stone, Matthew's heavy spirit crying out now from the tiny shrine.

"Captain Matthew told us all how they ran the British out of Castlebar, they ran all the way back to Tuam and the big Frenchman running after them, a man with a name I don't know."

"Humbert, General Humbert, Mr. Sommers," whispered Tone, his fingers caressing the initials.

"Did you know Captain Matthew, General?"

"Yes, Mr. Sommers, I knew him."

"The races of Castlebar, they called it, General, but then there was Ballinamuck, where were slaughtered without mercy," Lukie looked at the dead fire. "The young fella was taken there, but not before he ran a dozen of the bastards through."

He began to stoke the fire. "I could make us a cup of tae, General and get the fire going."

The old man soon had the flames rising around the kettle, hanging from the crane.The intimacy of the dark sombre building seized him, as, eyes smarting, Tone looked down at the heavy crude gibbet and stroked the pearl handle of the razor. The scaffold was hardly visible now. Little strands of mezzotint would, now and then break the blackness like little shots of lightening stabbing at the killing machine, the six steps upwards, the acute angle of the crossbar, the heavy beam buttressing the contraption.

**

It was 11th. November before James Attridge's application to visit cell number 35, the dark room with the number of Theobold Wolfe Tone's years on its door, and which had housed his condemned brother, a month before.

The room was heavy with the sensation of death. There was a sentry posted at the door. An old man sat near the bed, but scampered at James's appearance. "He tried to commit suicide, Sir, the young soldier said, respectfully, in a distinct Dublin accent, tried to cut his throat with his razor, Sir, the doctor said Mr. Tone missed the jugular, but cut his windpipe and suffered a stroke." He said it, matter-of-factly, like he had been rehearsing the piece for some time.

James made his way to the corner cot. The fire had been well reddened and the flames danced in great shadows along the granite walls, covering the bed and it's occupant in a haunting and gaunt embodiment that came and went as the firelight dictated. James called for a second lamp and the young jailor took a candle cluster from over the fireplace.

"Leave us," said Attridge

The soldier hesitated, recognised a tone of authority, then left the room, pulling the door to.

Wolfe Tone was half sitting, half lying on the mattress with a mound of soiled pillows at his back. Bandages bound his neck in a heavy bloodied swath, and it was evident the stroke left him disabled. His left arm lay across the blanket like a broken wing, his face, ashen and distorted.

Resentment welled up in the visitor and he shook his head in a fit of despair, at the terrible waste, the crushing sadness of it all. The sunken face, with all its lights and friendly geniality dissipated, the brazenness and vitality wasted away in one angry and demented act. Attridge struggled for control as he watched the eyelids flutter in recognition. Suddenly the scourged eyes were open, focusing and fevered.

Attridge grasped the dead hand "It's James, Sir, James Attridge."

A feeble smile played about the stubbled mouth. "Perhaps you have found more dignity this way, only you can rest with this. I have been told they were to hang you."

Attridge pulled his chair closer. The eyelids closed again and Tone moved his right hand, gripping James's. His handgrip was strong and assuring. "Do not despair, Theobold". It was the first time in six years that James had used his Christian name. "You would have been proud of the heroes gone before you. A hundred thousand rose up in your shadow, and your name was shouted, along with that of Father Murphy and Lord Edward, from the hillsides and valleys of Enniscorthy, Gorey, Carnew, Wexford, New Ross and Vinegar Hill and in places all over the north. Reports of your exploits with Napoleon Bonaparte have been published in any newspaper that would accept them, especially in America."

The hand pressure increased at the mention of Bonaparte. "Your name became a battle cry, and your counsel in court, named you as a great Irish patriot, along with the rebel, Hugh O'Donnell, Cucuchallen and Brian Boru. Mr. Philpott Curran placed himself in ridicule, even danger before a hostile court, but his words will be remembered for centuries to come."

Attridge leaned closer still. "When I found my father, Conor Devereaux on Vinegar Hill, he was wrapped in the Union Jack, like he had fallen into it, while the green flag of Ireland had its pike buried in the body of a Hessian Officer, I found this in Conor's pocked before we buried him." James wept openly as he took a small green pennant from inside his coat. "It's a little green flag, Theobold, with a gold harp as it's emblem. Somewhere, sometime, my father had had inscribed on it, in a gold thread, "Ireland and Wolfe Tone.""

The dying eyes remained tightly closed, and tears squeezed through. Tone sighed heavily, then he seemed to sleep. The room was filled with the stench of laudanum and stale urine, a brutal inelegance to an elegant man.

James called the young soldier from the corridor. "Empty those swill pots," he hissed, "the pots, the pots," he spat, then went and stoked the fire and wept again, as smoke drifted through the sad room, thankfully a more welcome pungency.

"I'll get you something to drink, Sir," the young man whispered, while a man, bent in servitude, took away the foul smelling pots. Attridge shook his head wearily and placed a hand on the soldier's arm. "Just leave us, Son."

He sat for a further spell until the day was gone, his mind in turmoil. Later, he spent a little while with Lukie Sommers. The old man had a mug of cheap wine for him, and a soiled rag, wrapped around the pearl handled razor and brush. Attridge started, feeling Tone's agony. "You seem to be a friend, Sir, the General would want you to have it." He saw the other's hesitancy. "General Tone didn't use it to kill himself, Sir, they said he did.......it, when he heard he was to be hanged. Take a look at his chin, Sir, I was with him, the last time he shaved himself, a week ago, then he gave me the shaver, said he wouldn't be using it again."

The old eyes pleaded with the visitor. "You didn't see the wound, Sir, 'tis a big gaping hole, done by someone with a bayonet or a big kitchen knife."

**

How the American papers welcomed his reports. The editor of the New York Times wrote to him, " Mr. Attridge, your reports in the name of Saoirse, are so informative. In publishing, I fear legalities, even at this distance, but we will continue and be damned. Surely, there is a great book in your pages. When the time comes, you will, I'm sure, allow us to publish, exclusively"

**

Theobold Wolfe Tone died on November 19th, 1798. Mr. John Philpott Curran, the fifty year old liberal Protestant solicitor, and known affectionately as the Monk of Screw, after the social organisation he helped to establish, devoted to good wine and corkscrews, fought tirelessly to have the case against Wolfe Tone, transferred from a military court to The Court of Kings, arguing that General Wolfe Tone had no commission under His Majesty and he should be tried as a prisoner of war. The well known lawyer, who had in the past, represented many United Irishmen and who was a native Irish speaker, called for the court to uphold the law and move for a Habeas Corpus. The court considered his demands and word was received from the prison that Major Sandy's, the keeper of the Provost's Prison refused the order and would carry out the order of Lord Cornwallis. The demand was repeated by the court, that the prisoner should be handed over to the Sheriff, only to be told that, in the night, Mr. Tone had attempted to cut his own throat and was near death.

" This reporter, as well as many more, who chose to think so, that Theobold Wolfe Tone did not commit suicide, but merely as choosing the method of his own death and not to hang as a common felon. For those close to him, possibly found some tranquil comfort in this belief, however, those who knew his undaunting spirit and zest for life, would express otherwise and would look with great suspicion on the keepers of the prison at Arbour Hill, as in his last few days, General Tone believed hopefully about the possibilities of justice would happen in his favour, had the prison at Arbour Hill bowed to the first demands for Habeas Corpus"

"Saoirse."

Attridge was obliged to read his reports to Sir George Palmer, whose health was failing daily. The old man would have fits of depression that the beacon of his life, the majestic Duhallow and its lands had suffered so. Over two hundred of the peasantry were living in the armoury shed and the outhouses, while twice that amount tried to exist in the burnt out shells of the cabins and cottages of Trasna and Boolavogue. People who were, a short time ago, household names at Duhallow were dead or missing and three quarters of the crops of the past summer were destroyed or taken by the marauding armies, returning from Vinegar Hill and New Ross. Twenty thousand acres were a black lifeless morass, where nothing of nature was seen to survive.

"What a world to bring little children into," he grieved, as Kate came into the parlour. She sat by him before the fire and poured his tea. She saw his pain as he studied her, her beauty, if anything, enhanced in the bloom of her pregnancy. He had insisted, long ago that they call him simply " Palmer".

She put a pillow to his back and pulled her seat nearer. "You gave away all you had, Palmer, to strangers. The destruction to the land, no matter how violent, is only the beginning of a new creation, like the child within my body. The burning of the soil will only strengthen new growth. Only today, near Trasna, I saw new young shoots and the woods are beginning to come alive. In every corner and in all forgotten nooks, nature is pouring life back into dead things. Droleen says that God has only hidden His nature from evil, that they can't extinguish it with a torch. It will all come in the spring with our baby."

Palmer took her hand. "Your little sister is more clever than we think." He asked James to continue, knowing that much of the manuscripts were those bequeathed by The Master Dunn.

These were lists that were both ambitious and prohibitive in the importance of the subject of, as he had called them; trespassers. The old pages were filled with the thoughts of ever reversing the curse of the most cruelly punitive expedition ever made on a small country, in the reigns of Elizabeth I and of Oliver Cromwell, who were, between them, responsible for the deaths or dispossession of over two million souls. Attridge quoted, for their benefit, from references and markings and punctuations in the easily readable notations.

" Marquesses of Waterford, Hertford,, Earls of Shannon, Londonderry, Fingal, Lucan, Darnley, Lords Coledon, Glentworth, Gosford, Abercorn, Kenmare, Longueville, Yelverton, Cavandish, Devonshire, Erne, Ely,, Mountnorris, Tottenham......, the list is endless", James quoted the Master, " landowners, by tyranny, with no natural ties to Ireland, yet who represents the peasantry without mandate in the Houses of Parliament, for centuries."

James turned page after page. "Then The Master has here, further compilations of lower, as he called them, trespassers and squatters, more minor players in the plantation of the country, and their lesser holdings, marked and named, even in many of the counties east of The Shannon, where Mr. Cromwell drove the peasants beyond the great river into barren Connaught, or to hell.

**

James Attridge wrote tirelessly of Tone. After the death of the patriot, Attridge was to write in a subsequent article for the Journal, of the man who held the fate of Europe within his grasp, but for the complacency of Napoleon Bonaparte, his personal ambitions and his possible dislike for Wolf Tone, though, James was aware, on seeing them together, that the Corsican might have had a hidden polite recognition for the Irishman's resemblance to himself.

Attridge's article castigated the commander of the armada to Bantry in 1796, General Grouchy, who, in the absence of General Hoche, showed wavering indecision, even cowardice, in refusing to land, even a thousand men. The final snub to Wolfe Tone, was the appointment of the ageing and sickly General Kilmaine, as head of the army in Bonaparte's absence. There would be no further effort on the part of the French Directory to any substantial expeditions to Ireland.

Attridge wrote passionately of Tone's despair at the lack of action and commitment by the people of Ulster, to the insurrection of Father John Murphy. Their passive submission to Loyalism and Orangism contrasted grotesquely with the zeal and passion and energy displayed five years earlier. When called to act, the patriots of Ulster were scarce men, as scarce as the men of twenty other counties of Ireland.

Attridge quoted the Duke of Wellington, " a most extraordinary man in the time of curious history – with a hundred guineas in his pocket, unknown and unrecommended, the Irish barrister went to Paris in order

503

to overturn the British Government in Ireland. Had Napoleon listened to his counsel, the Empire would surely have fallen. Had the storms of 1796 not been a Protestant phenomenon and a friend to England, as sung in a lay, composed by the loyalist Lord Shannon of Cork, Ireland would be liberated for the new century."

"And all through these troubled times," wrote Saoirse "a dozen generals oversaw the destruction of over 30,000 peasants in the name of the king, Britain languished in the madness of the monarch."

Chapter 63

It was cold in Paris. The northerly winds, like the cold ridges of a serrated knife-edge swept down from the frozen fjords and held the city in a freezing blight. Hoary ghosts lurked in every corner and doorway, impassive-faced tyrants with runny eyes and noses. It was how the traveller perceived it and wanted urgently to vacate it for warmer climates.

In defeat, Paris awaited his return anxiously, but at least, for now, he would rest in Versailles, away from the sham and insincerity of the authorities who were eager to scrutinize his misfortunes and be unsparing in their criticism. These civil servants, who knew nothing of warfare in savage climates, apt at censuring others, would find fault with perfection itself.

How, onetime he hated the extravagance and utter waste that was Versailles, where for its grandeur, a king and his kingdom were brought down, now it was his to languor in, yet right now, there was nothing in his life so disenchanting as it's attainment. Napoleon felt no great comfort in the stark images before him. His little trip to Egypt was a total disaster, the effects of which would be enjoyed by his enemies, for years to come.. He wanted to be alone with his guilt feelings and with his inadequacies for a while. There would be recriminations, even conspiracies and instant autocracy and bureaucracy, which would seek to denounce him and throw light upon his shortcomings and mad extravagance. He needed time to think and meet them head on.

General Bonaparte had aged in the year and a half since he left Toulon with a gargantuan fleet to conquer Africa. He had put on weight and his intelligent temples and forehead were ever more evident with a considerable loss of hair.

Though he hated Versailles and all it stood for, the tranquillity of its royal quarters was soothing and he had carried with him, a small company of servants and valets, about thirty five of an entourage.

He had written to Josephine from Corsica, that he would be home in a week, telling her not to wash. He hated the artificial smells that women kept in little bottles and pretty boxes, often quoting Pluto that a woman smells well when she smells of nothing.

He would send for his Josephine tomorrow. After absence of eighteen months, tender embraces could wait another night, the cross purpose of desire would not be diluted by his self-denial, his favourite mistress would eke out the night with him. A woman, full of implication where sex and all other human activities were inextricably entwined, she would show him the sheer anarchy of where in their climax, pain would become extract, revulsion, become allurement with animal sexuality.

Madame de Georges, procured for him and tutored for him, by Josephine herself, sat across from him now. A tall woman, considerably taller than he, Gabrielle de Georges had a body that pleased him greatly. She was handsome, by the sheer force of her features; not pretty like his Josephine, but long legged and angular faced, with full breasts that bounced with a slow oscillatory motion. He would have her walk about the salon, naked, for hours, without a word being passed between them, but inspire love in "her general", was her greatest ambition.

Some letters were spread on the table, recent letters and despatches he had collected when the accounts from Kilmaine on the state of the army and navy, or rather, what was left of them, were depressing reading. Tullyrand's open dismay and condemnation of the unsuccessful expedition to Egypt, was less welcome. He had, however, read the account of the Irish rebellion and the death of Mr. Wolfe Tone. He found himself reading it now again, like he were drawn to it, like the will to set it aside could not be quenched.

A letter from the Irishman had been waiting for him at Toulon in May, last year, which, due to pressure of business he had not received, until reaching Malta, two weeks later. The document contained an apology for Tone's outburst and general behaviour, that previous month and while wishing the general God's speed and the prayers of an Irish rebel, he had warned him again of the dangers of the east, the barbaric attitudes of Egypt, a country with no natural resources, where plaque and sickness was rampant. He advised the general of the vagaries of the nomadic tribes of the desert, the Ottoman Empire, built on savagery and intrigue, as unpredictable and shifting as the sands that spawned it. "But above all, my dear General, beware of Britain, and remember, I have given you an excellent base from which to defeat them, to sandwich them between France and Ireland, when I will place half a million men at your disposal. England is the greatest maritime nation in the world, Sir, and she just might take the notion to follow you into the Med. In the mean time, Ireland will await your favours."

"Did you know, Madame, this Wolfe Tone," Napoleon mused, without looking at her.

"I know, only my general", she purred exquisitely. She had put a warm robe over her nakedness, the palace at Versailles was empty and cold, despite a blazing fire. The General's colour was rising with the temperature of the room and he had already consumed a goodly amount of wine. To celebrate his victories in the Italian campaign, four years before, the Charente district gathered its finest distilled from its finest oak and introduced a new Cognac, blended and flavoured to perfection, in his honour. In its superb Italian carafe, it danced tantalizingly in crystal transparency, an oracle to be savoured and caressed. He poured the golden liquid from one hand crafted masterpiece to another, holding the heavy drinking balloon, it's stem nestling between his cupped fingers.

"His letter is like a prophes,", he said to the swirling liquid. She had been trying to chase his emotions all evening, seeking out his desires in her lust to please him, but even in all her glory, her tireless preparations against his arrival, in her own mind, a dish for the gods, the little general was unappreciative and hasty. If he were to drink further, she would lose him for the night and to be ahead of Josephine de Beauharnais into his bed, after so long a campaign, would be a divine trophy indeed.

Whose letter, My General?"

Bonaparte frowned impatiently. "Mr. Tone", he said, roughly. He reached across the table from his sedan. "There it is."

The little gold harp was ever present, on the left hand corner of the velum. Drowsiness was crowding in on him and he felt tired and alone, for now, not relishing the criticisms and the wrath of the directory. They would be snapping at his heels, but to hell with them. Tullyrand, Marat and Sieyes is still on his side, as is Kilmaine, what's left of the directory is not worth worrying about. A coup would overthrow them in a day. Self deliberation lightened his spirits for a moment and he looked across at Madame, curled up in her enormous chair. Like a mating signal, she stroked her sultry mien, heated and tempered before the firelight and she quickly allowed the robe to fall open, exposing a generous breast, while a bare knee, then thigh, jutted out at him, provocatively, and Bonaparte mentioned him again.

"He was just a slight man, not a fighting man like me, but brave," he slurred, very brave, wasn't afraid of me." He slugged at the cognac. "He was right about Nelson."

"Nelson, My General?" She focussed. "Which is the Irish one, Cherrie General, this Nelson?"

He looked at her, dismissively and stomping from her chair, she poured a cognac for herself. Bonaparte looked at her total nakedness with diminishing vigour, the raw animal heat he would have witnessed at another time, dispelled, in a climate of imminent changes of crisis waiting around the corner. Tonight, her dwelling place would be in the dreams of the impotent.

Like there was nobody else in the huge red and gold salon, with its velvet drapes and exquisite furnishings, the general digressed again into articulated soliloquy, apostrophizing on events.

"We took Malta, you know, in half a day. The Knights of Saint John of Jerusalem handed over treasure beyond description. They now lie in the sands of the desert of Suez." He broke off to reflect, staring at the flames. "We were superb in Egypt, made Alexandria, the throne room of the Pharaohs, the boudoir of Cleopatra and Caesar, was ours. We brought the Ottoman and the Mameluke to heel and, in the shadow of the pyramids, we taxed the Egyptians to their eyeballs. We struck at the very heart of British colonialism, Madame," he slurred, "and would have taken Palestine but some shameless cretin by the name of Smith, Mr. Sydney Smith, if you please, we weren't expecting and he stopped us at Acre. Is it an appropriate name for an Englishman, I ask you Madame, who thinks everything wrong that is not English, who is afraid to express his emotions and even open his mouth too wide when speaking. His jaw is hinged, precisely in the public school fashion."

A woman of few words, de Georges was totally lost now to his drunken convolutions and lost to his bed.

"Smith," she shouted, "how can a Smith beat Bonaparte, never....never."

His eyes smarted with indignation. "Now, a Nelson might."

The woman raised an eyebrow at the name again and in reluctant surrender, Madame poured her reluctant lover another brandy. "My General," she whispered, in one final effort.

"And Nelson DID",he said, "Now Madame, that's a good name for fighting man, Horatio Nelson, like Napoleon Bonaparte." He raised his voice in emphasis, and his glass in salute, "strong and descriptive and daring."

The letter with the little gold harp lay on his lap. "And Wolf Tone – Theobold Wolfe Tone, that's a good name, Madame. Great names abase instead of elevating those who do not know how to bear them. His name is a part of his vocabulary, a second skin, but Smith, ba-h-h-h."

His crystal exploded against the back wall of the huge fireplace, the patent spirit, lighting up the room in an angry blue and gold flamed explosion and Madame de Georges shrieked in pantomimic fear. The flames died again, a halo of multi-colours, surrounding the fire mound like a crepe suzette on a pan. She hurried to find him another balloon, then came and sat at his feet. He ran his fingers through her raven hair. She purred inwardly, then knelt before him. He stroked her shoulders gently, all animosity gone.She began undoing his tunic, caressing each button stretched over the relaxed paunch.

"Mr. Tone was right. He warned me that East was barbaric, without natural resources, everything happened as he said they might. Damned Nelson, with his one arm and his one eye, took my fleet at Aboukir. The Sultan made peace with England and the Austrians took MY Italy, when I was not looking. All my victories, gone for nothing. France is bankrupt, Madame. Smallpox, Bubonic Plague, Vomiting, Swelling of bodies, dying Frenchmen everywhere, he said it all."

Suddenly he felt older and pushed the woman's probing hands away. "Leave me Madame."

De Georges returned to her chair and sat back in a private sulk. Napoleon read again the account of the Irish rebellion, sent to him by general Kilmaine and documented by someone named, Attridge. He felt a curious weakening excitement as the great adventure unfolded again from the written pages and an admiration and wonderment at the raw courage of the Irish peasantry. The place names where the battles took place meant nothing to him, but names like Carnew, Arklow, Enniscorthy, Wexford, like lights glowing on the sea waves, remained with him. Images broke before him, men and women, even children in battle, against fierce and insurmountable odds, their deep seated refusal to accept tyranny shone out of the pages and humbled him. If he had courage like that in his ranks, he would conquer the world. But the French soldier must be pampered, must be paid or he won't do battle, and yet, the small fleet that took Mr. Tone to Ireland, did so, without payment. And this priest, Murphy, Tone never mentioned this warlord, what he could do with a man like that by him.

Madame noticed the letters shaking involuntarily in his hands and tried to comfort him. "You will meet this Nelson again, my General, he is not worth your tears."

Bonaparte sighed heavily and after a long pause, he said, very quietly. "I'm not grieved by Nelson, you stupid woman, I am crying for the Irishman."

Chapter 64

The new century stormed in over the English Channel, bringing with it, the remorseless workings, the treachery and dishonesty of a British institution, built on corruption and tyranny, even more dire than before. Mr. Pitt, the British Prime Minister, said that a formal coordination of commerce and defence was necessary between Great Britain and Ireland.

Lord Cornwallis, the Viceroy, trying to deal with the Parliamentarians and the civil servants, complained to Pitt, that he was obliged to negotiate with the most corrupt people under heaven in order to bring about the greatest single disaster ever perpetrated on a small nation, to establish the union with Britain. An orgy of Parliamentary corruption was to set the stage for untold poverty and misery for millions of peasants, began with the stroke of a pen. The population was to escalate to eight million, only to be reduced to half that amount within a few dozen years.

**

It was to be another memorable day for Attridge. Just three years since the Union with Britain, and Dublin was, already a slum. In the afternoon, he found himself in Thomas Street, where a crowd had gathered. He felt himself being carried along with the mob and having time to spare, he went, unprotesting. A gallows had been erected in the centre of the thoroughfare, where it widened to accommodate a number of laneways and little streets; a centre artery of the inner city. Eager and impetuous, the crowd seemed vaguely hostile, without subtlety.

Wolfe Tone had told him once, of the feeling of foreboding he had felt, standing with the masses on Plase Louis XV, when the hostility of the mob would be without compassion and uncivilised. The chomping sound of the guillotine would release a great "hurrah" in the mass mind of the herd, rising and falling according to its passions.

James felt it now, in the heart of Dublin, an Irish mob that seemed to direct its venom, not against the hundreds of military all about, sullen faced and unpredictable, but toward some other force that seemed to be the subject of its ire, not yet in focus.

A great roar went up, a shout of triumph, to his amazement, and suddenly, a tall young man stood handcuffed before them on the platform, under the hanging noose. James squinted against the autumn sun, shading his eyes, and it wasn't until the young man turned profile that Attridge recognised the aristocratic trust of the square chin. He turned again, outward and the handsome dark Emmet features blazoned on him.

"I know that man." It was a depressing cry, more than a statement.

"All Dublin knows him." An elderly gentleman stood with his shoulder pressed against James's in the frenzied crush. "Young Robert Emmet, a student with boy followers and boy soldiers to be at his back. Thought they'd break the might of England, God help us. He marched through the city with his little army, his little rebellion lasted a few hours."

"But he's still a boy," protested Attridge, and a few sullied faces turned in his direction.

"Big enough to rebel, big enough to defy, big enough to hang," someone shouted.

Emmet's clear blue eyes looked out over the jeering crowd, and Attridge thought how many of the youth's adversaries had to be natives, even college peers and fellow gregarians of the Dublin social scene, come to gloat. A number, however, toward the front, near the gibbet were pleading on his behalf, mainly students and young radicals, who felt safe and comfortable in their numbers and inexperience. Others hissed and jibed and punched the air in a show of solidarity with the authorities, ignorant, blind and bewildered, a crowd of frightened people, seeking assurance in collective action, by the nose, their imagination easily led. Many others simply stood in silence, in the quiet preamble to violence.

Ireland had been dragged into the new century, shackled to Britain by the Union, that thousands had fought and died to prevent. She was now accustomed to public persecutions and executions and great manifestations of so called justice.

Attridge was to write later, "justice, the custodian of the British Isles, where justice itself has become the criminal."

Women prayed, their knuckles, white and stretched in terror. There were people in the upper floors of the tenement houses, calling and shouting above the din. Many were crying for the lost youth. There was a skirmish at the bottom of the steps to the gibbet and James recognised the young poet, whom he had met at Addis Emmet's house in Rathfarnham. The short figure of Thomas Moore tried to mount the steps, but was pushed back into the crowd. A young girl cried out to Emmet, in a pathetic pleading. "That's young Sarah Curran, daughter of the barrister, Philpott Curran, the man who pleaded for the life of Wolfe Tone explained the gentleman, I suppose you've heard of Wolfe Tone, Sir."

The man took his hat off as a show of respect, as they put the noose about the groomed proud head. Emmet's courage seemed to mount with the occasion and he refused the blindfold. Not yet having a clear sense of life's pains and pleasures, he steeled his eyes to heaven and died quickly. He was taken down and beheaded before the students took him away.

James put a hand on the young shoulder as the crowd dispersed. "You remember me, Mr. Moore, my name is James Attridge."

Thomas Moore looked shaken and in great distress. "I do, Sir, we.... Robert and I met you at the home of Mr. Addis Emmet."

"And I remember, Mr. Moore, you're his poet friend." They shook hands, the younger man seemed lost, looking about him at the incredulous scene. "We've taken him away, Mr. Attridge, before they desecrate his body any further. He's to be buried in secret, it was his last wish, he spoke of it from the dock. Lord Norbury wanted him hanged and drawn and quartered, but our student society appealed to Lord Cornwallis."

"My God, Mr. Moore, have they not been barbarians long enough, I believe the British are actually afraid of civilization."

The young poet took a sheaf of papers from his inside pocket. "I made copies of Robert's speech, I would like you to have, it's a hurried job, my old printing machine is in a poor state, but I hope you will write well of him, Sir." He moved after the student body and disappeared in the crowd.

James moved closer the scaffold and looked up at the crude structure, a dark cloud like a satanic halo at its back. His heart pined for the loss of his many friends, and now for the young comet like patriot, who reached for his hour of glory and paid the price. The gibbet scowled down at him, the monster created by a judge and a carpenter, the instrument of death, with its own life, drawn from all the death it had wrought. A jailor threw a bucket of water on the platform, where they severed his head from his body, like a butcher would clean up after slaughter.

In a tavern later, Attridge found a quiet corner and over a bottle of wine, he mourned for the total domination of a nation and its people. The courage that brought them through five hundred years of hardship by a neighbour and a tempest of a revolution, was gone, beaten like their dead into the ground, with nobody to blow life back into it. The Irish were now left naked, without hope, without courage. Slavery had returned.

Through a haze of frustration, he glanced at the pages of Thomas Moore's transcription of Emmet's speech to the court. It must have been three thousand words in duration, and he noticed that here and there, Moore had written the words, "Interrupted by the court."

It was the last paragraph that bore into his tiredness. Emmet's style shone out, leapt from the page without effort and he remembered his voice and his gestures in making a point, a style intrinsic in him, partly a matter of inheritance, James remembered the brother Addis, partly of cultivation;

"Be yet patient, My Lords, I have but a few words more to say. I am going to my cold and silent grave; my lamp of life is nearly extinguished; my race is run; the grave opens to receive me, and I sink into its bosom. I have but one request to ask of my departure from this world – it is the charity of its silence. Let no man write my epitaph; for as no man who knows my motives dare no vindicate them. Let them and me repose in obscurity and peace, and my tomb remain uninscribed, until other times and other men, can do justice to my character. When my country takes its place among the nations of the Earth, then, and not 'till then, let my epitaph be written. I have done."

The final resting place of Robert Emmet , like that of Father John Murphy would be an unknown entity.

**

His wrath was that of a tiger, when Attridge read accounts of the London Parliament, in October. In a year that the government of England became, in the eyes of the Irish peasantry, a supernatural source of evil, Mr. Pitt said in The House of commons;

" Let us do justice to ourselves. We have been enabled to stand forth, the saviour of mankind. We have presented a phenomenon in the character of nations."

At a time when women and children, seeking the protection of government, huddled together in Kildare, Kilmacthomas, Dunlavin, Carnew and a dozen other places, were slaughtered in great numbers, when thousands of Catholics and Presbyterians were made homeless and pauperism became the new phenomenon in the Irish psyche, that Mr. Pitt spoke about, he wrote to the Viceroy Of Ireland; "France, under the Directorate is a system of tyranny, the most galling, the most horrible, the most undisguised in all its parts and attributes, that has stained the pages of history, or disgraced the annals of the world."

In a year when, without the consent of eight tenths of the Irish people, Britain annexed her to her Union, sent thousands into slavery, in the Archipelago of Hispaniola, filled coffin ships to Van Diemen's Land, a year when new advances on the part of King George were ravaging the sub continent, Pitt The Younger said, in The House;

"If France is really desirous of peace and friendship with England, she must now show herself disposed to renounce her views of aggression and aggrandisement, and to confine herself within her own territory, without insulting other governments, without disturbing their tranquillity, without violating their rights"

In the warmth of the parlour fire, James slapped down , with frustration, reports and accounts , sent to him by his agents, in the north and I n Dublin.

"My God", he said to Kate, "the English are never so themselves as when they are being scornful and self-righteous, and downright hypocritical. Their absurd nature allows them to consecrate their massacres and atrocities with prayer and Te Deums and benedictions for their crimes. What a sub tribe they are, and to think I was nearly one of them. Somebody said that when it comes to the Englishman in love with himself, he'll encounter few rivals."

He moved the papers around in frustration. "Andrews reports from Belfast, and do you know what the king said," he hesitated to smile at her, "and by the way, do you know what he calls his wife, the queen, calls her Mrs. King, well he said to the Prime Minister recently, "bloodshot is not what I delight in, Mr. Pitt, but it seems to be the only way of restoring obedience to our royal person."

Chapter 65

Georgetown, District of Columbia, two miles north of the State of Washington, stands on the Pontomac, with its confluence with Rock Creek. A residential area, with tree lined avenues and idyllic surroundings, it serviced the University of Georgetown, the first Roman Catholic College to be built in the United States of America. Opened in 1789, as a school for diplomatic careers, Attridge thought, how appropriate; a retiring home for the wife of the greatest diplomat, the past century had known, and possibly, the new century besides.

The seat of government, by an act of congress in 1790, is attractively hilly and undulating with lush fertile valleys, watered by the Pontomac, and it's eastern contributory, The Annacostia.

It was in this exquisite location that James passed a few days at the Avenue Hotel, as guest of The New York times, having, eventually agreed a contract with them for the publication of his book. On the day before he had arranged to visit Mrs. Matilda Tone, he had an early lunch and brought a copy of the book to the little park skirting the river and found a seat among the Sycamores and Chestnuts where the laden branches arched the flow.

Attridge was pleased with the quality of the publication, and had not yet read it through, critically. The pages fluttered through his fingers and opened at the end of the chapter depicting the death of young Robert Emmet. His retentive memory soared back to the day, a hazy dream and it's heavy spirits of the time. He turned the page and a smile broke as he caressed the paper and the words of the poem flowed with the song of the river; "Oh better than the minting of a gold crowned king – is the safe-kept memory of a lovely thing."

It was the day after they hanged young Robert Emmet and it soon became known that his body had been spirited away to an unknown, unmarked grave as were his final wishes. James had heard so much about the Workhouse at James's Street from Georgie Tansey, accounts of his early days there with his mother and Hen, though the younger brother was never forthcoming about their experiences, as though it were a disrespect to his mother to talk of that dark period in their lives. Remembering G's account of their efforts, almost eight years before, at trying to gain entry and the crowd outside the gates, it would seem to him now, that nothing had changed, except, perhaps, with the increasing poverty of the capitol, the crowd would have doubled in size.

**

On the day he had stood among the rabble outside the Workhouse, a few days after they had killed Robert Emmet, James had asked the guard for an audience with Captain Bundy, and if he might mention the name of Mrs. Rose Tansey as a reference.

He was shown into Bundy's quarters, remembering G.'s vivid description of the huge grey building, the dark corridors and the well appointed quarters. He was left alone for a minute, when the door busted open and a heavyset man was suddenly framed in the doorway, a look on his face that bristled with expectation.

"You are, Sir?" he said, slightly breathless.

Attridge extended a friendly hand, and Bundy took it, cautiously. James introduced himself and quickly referred to George Tansey, as his colleague and his young brother Henry.

The heavy face softened. "And their mother, Sir?"

"I have never had the pleasure of knowing Mrs. Tansey, Captain Bundy, the lady died before I met the boys."

The Master of St. James's, was suddenly agreeable looking at the implication of the words, and James felt the bond that G. had often spoken of and understood now, how there was no need for references, or trawling through records, the Tanseys, still a beacon in the memory of the ageing Bundy.

"The boys speak very highly of you, Captain, your kindness to them and their mother, indeed they still maintain you were their saviour, I promised them I would come to see you, while in Dublin, and give you their respects."

" You're very kind Sir, said Bundy, " I have often wondered what became of the little family. I was able to be in contact with them when they were in Killane, but suddenly, my correspondence was returned."

"The boys have had a traumatic few years, Captain, we have been taking care of them since," said James.

Suddenly, Bundy stared pensively at the visitor. "May I ask you, Sir, the name of the mother of that little family?"

Attridge smiled. "I realize you must be careful of what might seem an intruder, Captain, that what goes on here in this establishment, is of the utmost integrity on your part and confidences exist at all quarters. The lady's name was, Bridget Rose."

Bundy shook his hand again, this time with more warmth and commitment. "You'll have a glass of wine with me Sir, for should you be still in communication with young Georgie Tansey and his brother, there is a matter I would ask you to discuss with them."

They sat at Captain Bundy's polished table before a carafe of port wine and biscuits. "There is a matter of a considerable sum of money, which it has been my duty to supervise over, on behalf of the late Mrs. Tansey, and which has caused me some distress that I was not able to communicate to her over the past few years. Mrs. Tansey and I had," he hesitated, reaching for a suitable explanation, "we had a business arrangement to do with her supreme skills at embroidery, and, .."

Attridge interrupted. "Young Georgie has told me of your business, together with his mother, Captain, however, I don't think he knows of any outstanding amounts, nor is he, I believe, familiar with the commerce attached to it. I am simply here to extend to you, his regards, as he wasn't sure if you were still here, and his desire to come to Dublin sometime, with the hope of calling to you."

"Splendid, Sir," beamed Bundy. "I shall look forward to it, when we will go the Bank of Ireland, at Mary's Abbey, hopefully you will come with him. At the time we lost contact, I had written to Mrs Tansey in Wexford to advise that I had opened an account in her name, as any monies accumulating to her in Dublin from her franchise arrangement with Mr. Goldberg's shop in Grafton Street, not to mention her private accounts with some very important people, not just in Dublin, but in London, needed to be properly supervised and taken care of."

"You're an honourable man, Captain Bundy," said James.

"I was associating with a very honourable lady, Mr. Attridge."

**

Sitting on the banks of the Annacostia, his book open on his lap, he stayed with the good memories, for a while further. Georgie had gone to Dublin with him, his first time returning to the city since leaving, after nine years. Bundy was more than courteous. It was obvious their friendship had had a certain parallelism in their lives, a single soul in two bodies, as they reminisced, and the older man's eyes moistened at the constant mention of the "most gracious lady." He insisted they return to where he first introduced the "little family" to the grandeurs of Dublin and sought a table in the window of the Shelbourne Hotel, for afternoon tea, before going, on appointment to the Bank of Ireland at Mary's Abbey, just off Caple Street, where G. was to find that he and his brother were suddenly richer by almost two hundred pounds, the pile had been accumulating, thanks to the accruing of interest over the years, though deposits had ceased when Bridie's stocks had run out. "How light gains make heavy purses," James remembered Bundy saying, as Georgie signed for the transition of the account to him and his brother. The bank manager was courtesy itself, giving G.

instructions as to the bank's agent in Wexford town, with whom he could transact. Georgie, excused himself and asked if there was a toilet, where he wept in final mourning and gratitude.

The new church at Boolavogue was rebuilt in 1810. Restrictions on the Catholic community dictated the size and quality of the structure, so that the building was no better than the old church of Father Murphy, but a church, nevertheless. Sir George Palmer, commissioned the structure before he died, in honour of his friend, John Murphy and on Father Georgie Tansey's return from Seville, the ageing Bishop Delaney performed the consecration ceremony.

James turned the pages of his book and found the paragraph, one of many paragraphs that he found a joy to remember and put to paper.

"A week before the consecration, I found the new priest, as I thought, tending the little garden to the rear of the new church. My wife, Kate, had insisted it be kept in condition over the years since Father Murphy died, though the site had been cleared of debris, after the Yeos burned the church, in '98. Father G., as we called him, had clay on his boots, and I found, to my surprise, that he was opening a hole in the soil, the size of a table, disturbing the flowers and shrubs. Then he asked me to help him pull something into the light. I heard the chink of metal against metal from inside a sheet of heavy canvas and G. spread it open to reveal the instruments of Mass that shone out in the afternoon sun, bright and pristine as the day Father John buried them for safety. Father Tansy fell to his knees and prayed over the trove. "God has returned to us, James, God be praised."

James closed the book with a sigh. It was time for the visit.

**

Matilda Tone opened the door to him and the frail timid figure sparked in him, the lost memories of Kildare. Mrs. Theobold Wolfe Tone had yielded sadly to age; the years, a burden to her. Her eyes were still vital, even if nestled in alabaster wrinkles, mirrors to the hurt and the loneliness of her existence, of which, even now, he had yet to learn it's severity.

It was August 1829 and she remarked that she thought her visitor had worn his years very well. As he had pre- warned her of his visit, after the Convention of International Journalists in Washington, she had a little table set out for tea, with linen napkins and superb china. A Negro woman hovered in the back of the house and Mrs. Tone introduced her as Meggie.

As he sat across from her in her small parlour, he had to prompt himself that this elderly lady, full of grace and wrinkles, was only half a dozen years older than his darling Kate, who still rode and carted on the estate at Duhallow, her raven beauty still intact, her passions, only gently relaxed.

"He was terribly fond of you, Mr. Attridge," she said, studying the good features. "He thought you were very clever and an excellent journalist."

"And I, of him, Madam, and as for cleverness, I was, as all of us were, in his shadow."

"Was it that cleverness that brought him to disaster, to martyrdom?"

" History will show that his martyrdom will have been more costly to humanity than to himself, Mrs. Tone."

"To die a martyr does not create a martyr," she said sharply. "He must wish his own execution. His final expedition was nothing more than a death wish, a handful of men a few broken ships, in the ice cold waters of Lough Swilly," she scoffed, her voice on a tremor. "That's where he was taken, you know, but of course you do, Mr. Attridge, you wrote of it."

She composed herself, though her dainty cup played a tiny tattoo on the saucer. "Did you know that the Irish name of Lough Swilly, is The Lake of Shadows?, how appropriate."

"Mr. Tone is already being hailed as the father of nationalism in Ireland," he hurried on.

"Every nation thinks it's own madness as normal, Sir, normal and requisite. Too many have died in the name of nationalism, it can become a form of incest, an idolatry, even an insanity, and I have wondered, over the years, if it was all worthwhile. Ireland is more than ever in chains, is she not?"

"She is," he sighed heavily. The union with Britain of 1800 is a foul and deceitful thing and should have no part in normality. The atrocities being committed in the name of the King of England and Ireland is something you cannot balance on a scales. All the wonderful passions are quelled and the consequence for Ireland will be worse than her previous misfortunes. It's a tragic age and now, famine is a regular happening., the fields are dying in need of fertilization, as most of the landlords have left with the government and the land is controlled by gombeenmen. Almost a million people died just two years ago, as the union creates a nation of paupers."

" And Dublin, Mr. Attridge?"

"The city has changed, since the Parliament was shifted to London. The fine houses in the inner city, once the town mansions of the nobility and the welltodo, are now slums. The people have come to town from the countryside and where once lived nobility and privileged, now these houses are homes to families living in one roomed apartments, as many as ten to a pair of rooms. There is nothing for them in the country, hope exists in the cities only, where the bread winner can find work."

He accepted a refill from the ornate silver teapot and, delicately, she pinched two lumps of sugar with a little tweezers and dropped them into his tea cup.

"I believe, Mrs. Tone, for what it is worth, that France treated Wolfe Tone badly. Grouchy should have landed in '96. Napoleon Bonaparte admitted publicly, that he should have listened to your husband's counsel and not gone to the east, when he did, and Kilmaine and Hardy reneged to accompany him on his final mission. It is my considered opinion that Mr. Bonaparte contrived against him. I believe General Bonaparte had General Hoche deliberately taken off course on the Bantry expedition."

"I loved my husband, Mr. Attridge." There was a stern edge to Matilda Tone's voice. "He was a fool, sometimes, a dreamer, and dreaming men are often, haunted men. They say that dreams are often faithful interpreters of our inclinations, but there is art required to understand and sort them. Theobold was like that, he dreamed the impossible."

"You must not torture yourself so," James said urgently.

The Negro woman came with fresh tea and he waited until she had left the room. "These dreams and endeavours came so close to changing the course of history, not just for Ireland, but for the whole European Continent." He continued earnestly. "Mrs. Tone, it was Theobold's unfaltering wish to establish liberty in Ireland, through peaceful means and through the brothership of all her people, irrespective of creed or persuasion. Tyranny and bigotry at home and poor management abroad robbed him of that achievement, but I believe he wrote the most glorious page of our history and gave us a precious inheritance for the future, and it is only future generations will come to appreciate that."

Her small features softened. "I have read your many features in The Times, many, I fear, glorify him beyond humanity. He would be pleased, because, like all heroes, my husband was easily touched by praise." She looked beyond him at some distant sublime notion. "Yes, it was a pity he didn't succeed, he would have made a good statesman."

"A great Prime Minister, Madam," cautioned the visitor.

She gave him a narrow smile. "He so much appreciated your letters in Paris, and the time you spent with us there. I am also aware of your involvement to have him incarcerated in Bodenstown, how he loved

Kildare." She brightened further, "and I remember you inherited a vast estate in Wexford, and you married."

"Indeed, yes, I married a local lady, a better inheritance than any property. We have four children.I have three grandchildren. I don't mind saying that Duhallow is one of the few good estates, both for owner and tenant alike.

"You sound happy, Mr. Attridge."

"Blissfully Madam, thank you," he replied.

Again the quietness of the small house struck him; the unlived-in look of the room and the clinical neatness all around. "And your family, I remember you had....."

She put her cup away and stood to look out the window. Attridge rose, respectfully, then she returned to where a number of small etchings lined the mantle over the fireplace. "I believe you must have heard of Mr. Thomas Wilson, of Dullatur in Scotland. He was a great friend and benefactor, while Theobold was away. We came here to America and married in 1816. He was a good kind man and took care of my son, William and me."

A stocky bespectacled man looked out at them, from a small frame. "He died in 1824."

"I'm sorry," James said. Looking at the other frames. "Your children, I remember there were three or four, in Kildare, you kept them pretty well out of the way."

She smiled; a hueless pallid simper. "My father-in-law was, let me say, selective as to when they should be heard or seen, but really, because of Thobold's commitments, the old gentleman, it was my opinion, was simply concerned for their safety."

"And now, your family," Attridge enquired, conscious again of the silence all around.

"They're all dead, Sir."

She looked at her visitor with a curious glazed look. "My dear Mr. Attridge, they're all dead. My beautiful Maria died shortly after her father, of consumption. Francis died at only sixteen in 1806, of the same malady. Then my friend, benefactor and husband, Thomas Wilson, died of stroke in 1824, and finally, my son William Theobold, just last year. William had been living here with me in Georgetown."

Matilda ignored the sheer palpable look on his face. Crushed under the barrage of the gentle onslaught, James stood before the fireplace in a morass of agitation and despair for her and for his dead friend, for providence and for injustice. He grieved openly for the injustice that has a terrible way of lingering restlessly on some men's doorstep, like a question that has no answer, the bitch that is bad luck brings her

521

knitting. He sighed heavily, moist eyed and helpless. Her voice came in from the distance and refocused.

"They're all gone now, Mr. Attridge, Thomas Russell, my husband's partner in erranty; hanged. Young Robert Emmet; hanged, that extraordinary priest in Wexford and they say some 30,000 of his sympathisers, all of them and what a waste, how they would have served Ireland if......" She sat in silence for a minute, while James remained standing. "I've upset you, I can see. Perhaps it's because I've lived with tragedy almost all of my life, that God strengthens me in this way. I've become the expert in psychic adjustment, just waiting for one sequence after another." She smiled up at him. " Matthew Tone is gone and God knows what he was doing fighting with the French in County Mayo. William, I believe, died in Poona, where he excelled in the military, fighting for the king of England, while the king of England was killing his brothers. Arthur, Theobold's youngest brother has been unheard of, since joining the Dutch army in 1797. There isn't a member of the Tone family left in the world. Like all proletarians, Mr. Attridge, I have nothing left to lose, just like three quarters of the people of Ireland."

She poured him a brandy from the neat sideboard and he accepted it gratefully.

"I do not begrudge them their martyrdom," she continued, pouring a thimbleful for herself, out of courtesy. "Their efforts and their ambitions were noble enough to have succeeded, but people will forget. History has a habit of sliding away. You have written well of them, I have read as much as I could get my hands on. Mr. James Monroe, four years ago, while still President of the United States of America, called here to my house and had great things to say. Poor Meggie nearly had a stroke with the fuss. He had worked hard with Theobold in France to persuade the Directory to sail to Ireland, and my husband always said that, one day, he would be President."

She looked about her narrow surroundings, and for the first time, her voice faltered. "Imagine, the President of America in my home, Theobold would have been pleased."

"Attridge excused himself for a moment and went out to his carriage and returned with a leather bound book.

"Before I go, Madam, may I be so bold as to ask you a very personal question," he said, cautiously.

"You were his good friend," she replied.

"Then, do you believe your husband took his own life in the Arbour Hill prison?"

She hardly hesitated, to his surprise, nor was she at all upset at the intrusion, like she had tried to find an answer to such a question on other occasions.

"Aristotle wrote in the fourth century before Christ, to run away from trouble is a form of cowardice, and while it is true that the suicide braves death, he does it, not for some noble object, but to escape some ill."

Then she looked at him intensely. "I have read your report over and over, and I believe that if the Provost at that prison had obeyed his orders of Habeas Corpus on the first occasion of he being instructed to do so, Theobold would have been re-tried as a prisoner of war. I don't believe my husband died at his own hand."

Attridge handed her the manuscript. "I am launching my latest book in New York before I return to Ireland," he said. "I wish you to have the first copy off the presses."

This time she allowed the tears to show. It was a large heavy register. She opened the leather bound cover. "It's about Theobold Wolfe Tone and his influence on the history of Ireland."

She ran her small hand over the title; "The Croppy Boy, The story Of An Irish Hero", By James Devereaux Attridge."

Matilda Tone turned the many pages to the postscript, and in a faltering voice, read aloud, the words of a great priest and Irishman;

"The Irish heart is of too generous a nature to bow down before the idol of power, just because success has crowned it, or to forsake a just cause because it has proved not triumphant. The Irish people know that the charter of their country's liberty was written by the hand of God, and that the hand of man can never efface the sublime record."

As his carriage moved away from the picket fence, Attridge, immersed in grim lamentation, saw a tiny hand pull back a corner of the lace curtain.

Matilda Tone's delicate face was framed there, like an alabaster carving, a face, minted on his mind forever.

END

Poet's Corner

Moloney is the poet of "Wexford". He secured for himself, a dark corner of Mr. People's whisky house on Trasna Bridge, where he wrote his tracts; the very best of words in the very best of order.

"Moloney dosen't write for immortality," said Peoples to James, on the Englishman's first visit. "He has no objection to the present day's praise, and he'll paint the power of the wind for you in return for a pint or two of Mr. Guinness's porter."

At Boolavogue as the sun was setting
Oe'r the bright May meadows of Shelmalier,
A rebel hand set the heather blazing,
And brought the neighbours from far and near.
Then, Father Murphy from old Kilcormack,
Spurred up the rocks with a warning cry.
" Arm! Arm!" he cried, " for I come to lead you,
For Ireland's freedom we'll fight or die

He led us on 'gainst the coming soldiers,
And the cowardly Yeommen he put to flight,
'Twas at The Harrow the boys of Wexford
Showed Bookey's regiment how men could fight.
Look out for hirelings, King George of England,
Search every kingdom where breaths a slave
For Father Murphy of County Wexford,
Sweeps o'er the land like a mighty wave.

We took Camolin and Enniscorthy,
And Wexford storming, drove out our foes,
'Twas at Sleibh Coillte our pike were reeking,
With the crimson stream of the beaten Yeos.
At Tubberneering and Ballyellis,
Full many a Hessian lay in his gore.
Ah! Father Murphy had aid come over,
The green flag floated from shore to shore!

At Vinegar Hill, o'er the pleasant Slaney,
Our heroes vainly stood back to back,

And the Yeos at Tullow took father Murphy,
And burnt his body upon the rack.
God grant you glory brave Father Murphy,
And open Heaven to all your men
The cause that called you may call tomorrow,
In another fight for the green again.

Mc Call.

**

THE WEXFORD PIKE

O' Rourke, the blacksmith honed the pike, no better ever made,
Eight feet long, the ashen handle, four feet long, the blade.
Brave Father Murphy blessed it, one night on Slaney's side,
And Brian Bawn caressed it, as a lover would, his bride.

Through the night he carried it, to the Three Rocks battleground
And the Yeoman's blood had sullied it, to the victory cries all 'round.
And when the Croppy finally fell, his body brutally slain,
Another Croppy picked it up and fought the fight again.

At Enniscorthy and Wexford Town, New Ross and at Carnew,
It drove the tyrant English dog and the tyrant dog it slew.
The croppy honed the hook and bill, and handled it with care,
Then climbed the slopes of Vinegar Hill, with the men of Shelmaleer.

By Father Murphy's side it stood, from early day 'till night
Thrust and cut of blade and wood, the force of England's might.
So when they buried it with him, in Ireland's great amen,
The Croppy laid his tired head down and caressed it once again.

(The first verse of The Wexford Pike, was writted by Father F. F.
Kavanagh, the remainder by the author "Moloney")

**

THE KING OF ENGLAND

The king of England said to me
"I think we'll play today.

We'll go to Ireland 'cross the sea.
And blow them all away".
"But King", said I, "it would be wrong,
To make a genocide.
To hunt and kill the Irish throng.
With no place safe to hide".
"Then I'll tell you what we'll do", he said.
"After all I am a god.
We'll take their stock, their land, their bread.
And make them eat the sod.
And then we'll sit and watch them die,
While the spuds, they stink and rot.
Two million will be blown away,
And we needn't fire a shot".

Moloney.

**

NEVER A DANCE

"But never a dance", said I "was here
"O yes, there was" he said.
"But that was many a yesteryear,
The dance, a long time dead".

"But never a song was here", said I.
"My friend, there was", he said
"'Twas sung in God's sweet bye and bye,
No song has since been read".

"But never a piper played", I'd say.
"The piper played", said he.
The hills resounded to his lay,
But the lay, no more will be."

"but death lies heavy upon the air,
My friend, I pray you tell".
"The dance, the song, the piper's lay,
King George sent all to hell".

**

THE Staff Of Life

Bread, the staff of life is heaven given,
But in the strife of life, is tyrant taken.
And Christ looks down, a new dawn to awaken,
But in His busy day, had us, forsaken.

So what will you do now, Lord, that all is fraught?,
A busy day to segregate the good from evil.
But in Thy clemency, remember those who fought,
For dignity, the foundation of Thy will.

Maloney.

**

The Croppy Boy

The youth has knelt to tell his sins.
"In Nominae Deo", the youth begins.
At " Mea Culpa", he beats his breast,
And in broken murmurs, he speaks the rest.

"I've cursed three times since last easter day,
At Mass time once, I went to play.
I passed the churchyard one day in haste,
And forgot to pray for my mother's rest.

I bear no hate against living things,
But I love my country above my king.
So bless me, father and let me go,
To die, if God has ordained it so".

Maloney

**

The Penny George

Taxes rose and tithes increased across the ravaged land
Despite the fact the people lived each day to mouth from hand.
But one more levy was imposed, by England's House of Lords,

Upon the Irish peasantry, 'twas called the" Penny George."

For every day in every life, the pennies, they would wing
Toward the palace they were buying , to house our gracious king.
St. James's Palace was too small, to house his ample horde,
So that an offer soon was made to Buckingham, the lord.

"Thirty thousand pounds I want", said Buckingham, "what offers?"
Said William Pitt, "the war with France has bankrupt all our coffers".
So he looked to Ireland for the tax; three million pence a day
Would clear the debt in thirty months. "My word, I'll have my say".

So Buckingham became the place, where King George The Third
resided,
And no one ever had to know, and in nobody confided.
And in the year of ninty-eight, Bucking Palace burst,
Upon the scene of London Town, While Ireland all,
Came tumbling
Down...
**

Old Moloney, the poet, finished his lilting near the cold fireplace at
Lousyheads, and a pint of Guinness Porter was passed across to him,
through the dark interior of the inn.
    James Attridge tried to remember the words, the rhyme, the
message, and thought the toothless bard might lilt it again. It would be
worth a second pint. Old Fergus laughed again; a gummy cackle, as he
slugged the fine dark liquid. "Ha, Ha, Ha!, me boys, here's to Farmer
George".

**

Outside of Father Murphy's church, Driscoll took the oath,
Then passed the holy book to Swann, O'Donovan and Roche.
And twenty others made the pledge, as people stood to stare,
To join the United Irishmen and arm themselves right there.

A pike or two was all they had, not a single gun was there
A cutter's scythe, a fork, a rake, an ashen cudgel pair
In and out of step they strode, past Boolavogue and Kill
And at the pub of Trasna Bridge, they sat and drank their fill.

528

Then in the early afternoon, they armed themselves again,
But drink had taken a heavy toll, now there were only ten.
Undaunted by the summer's heat, they struck for Gorey Town
To find the British tyrant foe, and slay and cut them down.

Lieutenant Bookey came their way, with a company of Dragoons,
aAnd saw the drunken army sway, with the gait of wild baboons.
O' Driscoll danced before the troop and swung his sythe in jest,
And the soldiers laughed to spur him on, ignoring all the rest.

And when they had their fill of him, they dragged him all the way,
To Camolin Court and Roger Owen and Driscoll heard him say.
"For disturbance of a quiet day and bringing peace all down,
I'm sending you for punishment, this day to Wexford Town.

But first, they raked him with the scythe, in front and in the back.
Then Captain Boyd of Wexford Town, he hanged him on the rack.
Unlikely hero, draped in green and gold, his death surprising.
But it rang the knell and lit the hell of the ninety-eight uprising.

Maloney.

**

The road that turns inward to my heart,
Was once an artery to my outward pride.
With stiffened back, my sights were forward looking,
Grasping the rose from stinging briar, did I part.

And on that outward road, you measured my every stepping
With your own stout and comforting prance.
Your music filled my soul, I thought, forever.
I never knew there would be need for weeping.

But that inward road has bent the stiffened back
With burdens, though I'm not very old.
You fall behind, your sweetness flagged, not yielding.
Your scorched and haunted land upon the rack.

But I will mourn you at my lonesome hearth
'Till the tyrant from across the sea is laid to waste.

The scavenger who devours the infant at your breast,
And returns to eat the afterbirth.

When will I hold you, once again within my pride,
And from the mountain, proclaim, "this land is mine".
We'll stop at every crossroad pattern and we'll dance,
And call to God once more with us abide.

Moloney.

That's all folks

CPSIA information can be obtained at www.ICGtesting.com
Printed in the USA
LVOW08s1428250214

375114LV00006B/917/P